JADE
LEGACY

BY FONDA LEE

THE GREEN BONE SAGA

Jade City

Jade War

Jade Legacy

THE EXO NOVELS

Exo

Cross Fire

Zeroboxer

JADE LEGACY

THE GREEN BONE SAGA:
BOOK THREE

FONDA LEE

orbitbooks.net

Copyright © 2021 by Fonda Lee

Cover design by Lisa Marie Pompilio
Cover art © Alamy, Arcangel, and Shutterstock
Cover copyright © 2021 by Hachette Book Group, Inc.
Maps by Tim Paul

Orbit
Hachette Book Group
1290 Avenue of the Americas
New York, NY 10104
orbitbooks.net

First Edition: November 2021
Simultaneously published in Great Britain by Orbit

Orbit is an imprint of Hachette Book Group.
The Orbit name and logo are trademarks of Little, Brown Book Group Limited.

The publisher is not responsible for websites (or their content) that are not owned by the publisher.

The Hachette Speakers Bureau provides a wide range of authors for speaking events. To find out more, go to www.hachettespeakersbureau.com or call (866) 376-6591.

Library of Congress Cataloging-in-Publication Data

Names: Lee, Fonda, author.
Title: Jade legacy / Fonda Lee.
Description: First edition. | New York, NY : Orbit, 2021. | Series: The Green
    Bone saga ; book 3
Identifiers: LCCN 2021007934 | ISBN 9780316440974 (hardcover) |
    ISBN 9780316440950 (ebook)
Subjects: GSAFD: Fantasy fiction.
Classification: LCC PS3612.E34285 J37 2021 | DDC 813/.6—dc23
LC record available at https://lccn.loc.gov/

ISBNs: 9780316440974 (hardcover), 9780316440950 (ebook)

Printed in the United States of America

LSC-H

Printing 2, 2021

For Lahna and Aaron.
With love and pride for my small clan.

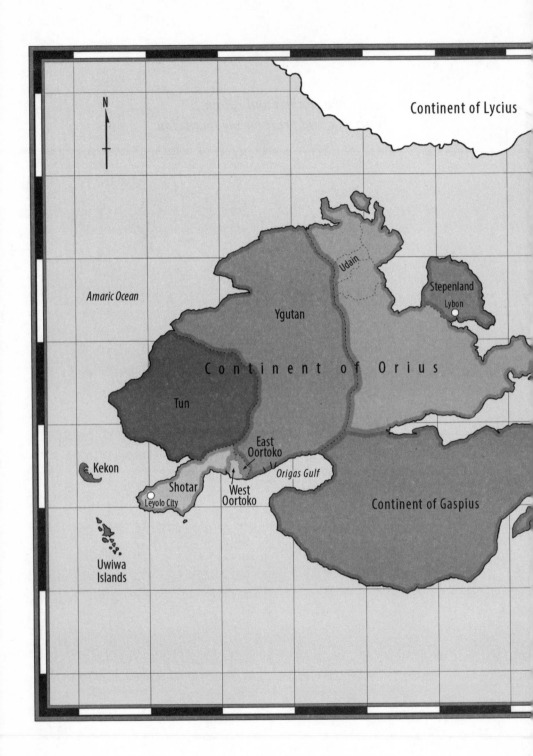

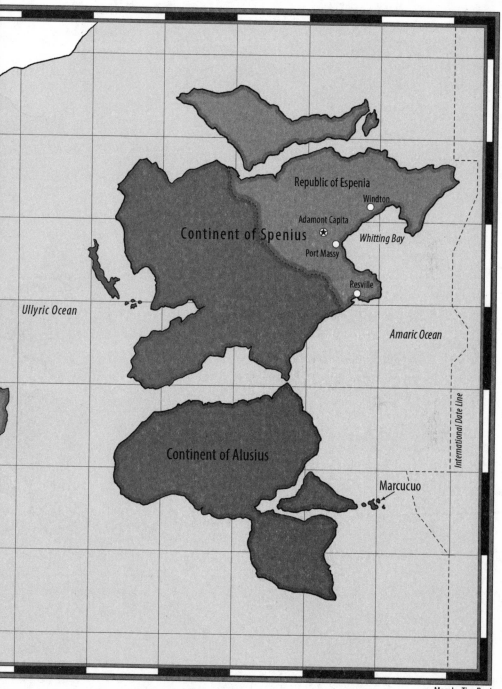

Republic of Espenia

Windton

Adamont Capita ⍟

Continent of Spenius

Whitting Bay

Port Massy

Resville

Ullyric Ocean

Amaric Ocean

International Date Line

Continent of Alusius

Marcucuo

Map by Tim Paul

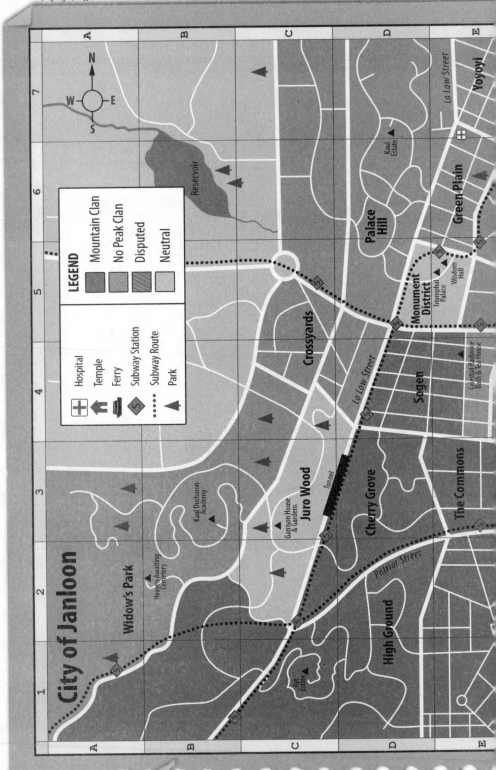

City of Janloon

Map by Tim Paul

LEGEND

- Mountain Clan
- No Peak Clan
- Disputed
- Neutral

- Hospital
- Temple
- Ferry
- Subway Station
- Subway Route
- Park

Reservoir

Widow's Park

Heaven Awaiting Cemetery

Kaul Dushuron Academy

Garrison House & Gardens

Juro Wood

Tunnel

Crossyards

Palace Hill

Kaul Estate

Monument District

Triumphal Palace

Wisdom Hall

Green Plain

Yoyoyi

Lo Low Street

Sogen

Celestial Radiance Bath & Tea House

Cherry Grove

The Commons

Patriot Street

High Ground

Ayt Estate

The Stump

Fishtown

North Sotto

Way Away Bridge

KI-1 Freeway

Coinwash

The Docks

Sotto Village

Paw-Paw

The Forge

Keton Jade Alliance

S U M M E R   H A R B O R

General's Ride

Old Town

Temple District

Janloon General Hospital

Janloon Temple of Divine Return

Financial District

No Peak office tower

Ship St.

Twice Lucky Restaurant

To Euman

Little Hammer

The Armpit

Junko

Pai Station

To Little Button

The Wallows

Dog's Head

Little Persimmon Lounge

Poor Man's Rd

Spearpoint

KI-1 Freeway

Summer Park

Typhoon Shelter

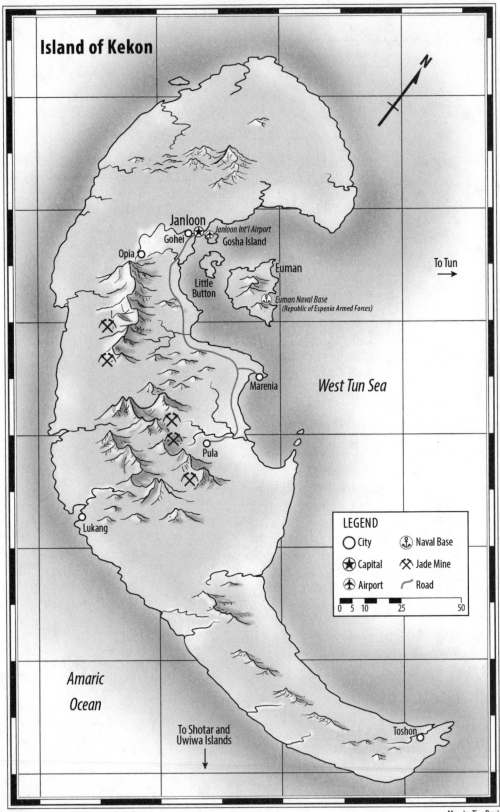

Island of Kekon

N

Janloon
Gohei
Janloon Int'l Airport
Gosha Island

Opia

Euman

Little
Button

⚓ *Euman Naval Base*
(Republic of Espenia Armed Forces)

To Tun →

⛏

⛏

Marenia

West Tun Sea

⛏

Pula

⛏

Lukang

LEGEND
◯ City   ⚓ Naval Base
★ Capital   ⛏ Jade Mine
✈ Airport   ⌒ Road

0 5 10   25   50

Amaric

Ocean

To Shotar and
Uwiwa Islands
↓

Toshon

Map by Tim Paul

The Green Bone Clans

Along with Their Associates and Enemies

The No Peak Clan
KAUL HILOSHUDON, Pillar
KAUL SHAELINSAN, Weather Man
EMERY ANDEN, a Kaul by adoption
KAUL MAIK WENRUXIAN, wife of Kaul Hilo, a stone-eye
KAUL LANSHINWAN, former Pillar of the clan, elder brother to Hilo and Shae; deceased

KAUL NIKOYAN, son of Kaul Lan, adoptive son of Hilo and Wen
KAUL RULINSHIN, son of Hilo and Wen, a stone-eye
KAUL JAYALUN, daughter of Hilo and Wen

JUEN NURENDO, Horn
JUEN IMRIEJIN, wife of the Horn
JUEN RITTO, JUEN DIN, twin sons of the Horn

MAIK TARMINGU, Pillarman
MAIK KEHNUGO, former Horn; deceased
MAIK SHO LINALIN, Kehn's widow
MAIK CAMIKO, son of Kehn and Lina

LOTT JINRHU, a Fist of the clan

WOON PAPIDONWA, Weather Man's Shadow
WOON RO KIYALIN, wife of Woon Papi

HAMI TUMASHON, Rainmaker
HAMI YASUTU, son of Hami Tuma

TERUN BINTONO, a Luckbringer
LUTO TAGUNIN, a Luckbringer

KAUL SENINGTUN, the Torch of Kekon, patriarch of the family; deceased
KAUL DUSHURON, son of Kaul Sen, father of Lan, Hilo, and Shae; deceased
KAUL WAN RIAMASAN, widow of Kaul Du, mother of Lan, Hilo, and Shae

YUN DORUPON, former Weather Man, a traitor; deceased
HARU EYNISHUN, ex-wife of Kaul Lan; deceased

KYANLA, housekeeper of the Kaul estate
SULIMA, housekeeper of the Kaul estate

Other Fists and Fingers
VUAY YUDIJO, First Fist to Juen Nu
IYN ROLUAN, a first-rank Fist
VIN SOLUNU, a first-rank Fist talented in Perception
DUDO, TAKO, personal bodyguards of Kaul Maik Wen
HEJO, TON, SUYO, TOYI, Fists of the clan
KITU, KENJO, SIM, Fingers of the clan

Future Green Bones
MAL GING, student at Kaul Du Academy, classmate of Jaya
NOYU HANATA, student at Kaul Du Academy, classmate of Jaya
NOYU KAINCAU, elder brother of Noyu Hana
EITEN ASHASAN, daughter of a former Fist, heiress to the Cursed Beauty distillery
TEIJE INNO, a distant cousin of the Kaul family

Notable Lantern Men
MR. UNE, proprietor of the Twice Lucky restaurant
MRS. SUGO, proprietor of the Lilac Divine Gentleman's Club
FUYIN, TINO, EHO, retail industry Lantern Men

The Mountain Clan
AYT MADASHI, Pillar
IWE KALUNDO, Weather Man
NAU SUENZEN, Horn

AYT (KOBEN) ATOSHO, nephew of Ayt Mada
KOBEN YIROVU, head of the Koben family
KOBEN TIN BETTANA, wife of Koben Yiro
KOBEN ASHITIN, a Fist, son of Yiro and Bett

KOBEN OPONYO, a Lantern Man, uncle of Ayt Ato
SANDO KINTANIN, a Fist, cousin of Ayt Ato

ABEN SOROGUN, a first-rank Fist
NIRU VONONU, a junior Fist

GONT ASCHENTU, former Horn of the clan; deceased
VEN SANDOLAN, a former Lantern Man of the clan; deceased

AYT YUGONTIN, the Spear of Kekon, adoptive father to Mada, Im, and Eodo; deceased
AYT IMMINSHO, adopted elder son of Ayt Yu; deceased
AYT EODOYATU, adopted second son of Ayt Yu; deceased

TANKU USHIJAN, former Horn under Ayt Yugontin; deceased
TANKU DINGUMIN, a Fist, son of Tanku Ushijan; deceased

Minor Clans
JIO WASUJO, Pillar of the Six Hands Unity clan
JIO SOMUSEN, Horn of the Six Hands Unity clan
TYNE RETUBIN, Weather Man of the Six Hands Unity clan

SANGUN YENTU, Pillar of the Jo Sun clan
ICHO DANJIN, brother-in-law to Sangun Yen
ICHO TENNSUNO, a Fist from the Jo Sun clan

DURN SOSHUNURO, Pillar of the Black Tail clan

The Clanless Future Movement
BERO, a criminal
GURIHO, founding member of the CFM
OTONYO, founding member of the CFM
TADINO, member of the CFM, bar runner at the Little Persimmon Lounge
EMA, a new member of the CFM
VASTIK EYA MOLOVNI, a nekolva agent from Ygutan

Others in Kekon
JIM SUNTO, a former Navy Angel of the Republic of Espenia

GUIM ENMENO, chancellor of the Royal Council of Kekon, a Mountain loyalist

GENERAL RONU YASUGON, senior military advisor to the Royal Council
CANTO PAN, chairman of the Kekon Jade Alliance
SON TOMARHO, former chancellor of the Royal Council; deceased

REN JIRHUYA, an artist
SIAN KUGO, film producer and co-owner of Cinema Shore
TOH KITARU, news anchor for Kekon National Broadcasting

DANO, a student at Jan Royal University

LULA, a courtesan

DR. TIMO, DR. YON, Green Bone physicians
MASTER AIDO, private trainer in the jade disciplines
GRANDMASTER LE, head instructor at Kaul Dushuron Academy

Representatives of the Espenian Government
GALO, an agent in the ROE Military Intelligence Service
BERGLUND, an agent in the ROE Military Intelligence Service

ARA LONARD, Republic of Espenia ambassador to Kekon
COLONEL JORGEN BASSO, commanding officer at Euman Naval Base

In Espenia

The Kekonese-Espenians
DAUK LOSUNYIN, Pillar of Southtrap
DAUK SANASAN, wife of Dauk Losun, his "Weather Man"
DAUK CORUJON, "Cory," son of Losun and Sana, a lawyer
DAUK KELISHON, "Kelly," Cory's sister, deputy secretary of the Industry Department

SAMMY, KUNO, TOD, Green Bones in Port Massy

REMI JONJUNIN (JON REMI), a Green Bone leader in Resville
MIGU SUNJIKI, a Green Bone leader in Adamont Capita
HASHO BAKUTA, a Green Bone leader in Evenfield
MR. AND MRS. HIAN, former host family to Emery Anden
ROHN TOROGON, the former "Horn" of Southtrap; deceased

DANNY SINJO, an athlete and actor

The Crews
WILLUM "SKINNY" REAMS, Boss of the Southside Crew
JOREN "JO BOY" GASSON, Boss of the Baker Street Crew
RICKART "SHARP RICKY" SLATTER, Boss of the Wormingwood Crew; in prison
BLAISE "THE BULL" KROMNER, former Boss of the Southside Crew; in prison

Others in Espenia
DR. ELAN MARTGEN, senior researcher at Demphey Medical Research Center
RIGLY HOLLIN, partner and vice president of WBH Focus
WALFORD, BERNETT, additional partners of WBH Focus

ART WYLES, CEO of Anorco Global Resources

ASSEMBLYMAN BLAKE SONNEN, chairman of the National Panel on Health
DR. GILSPAR, secretary of the Espenian Physicians Society

Elsewhere
IYILO, jade smuggler, leader of Ti Pasuiga; Uwiwa Islands

GUTTANO, executive at Diamond Light Motion Pictures; Shotar
CHOYULO, a leader of the Faltas barukan gang; Shotar
BATIYO, a member of the Faltas barukan gang; Shotar

SEL LUCANITO, entertainment tycoon, owner of Spectacle One; Marcucuo

FALSTON, an Espenian soldier
HICKS, an Espenian soldier

JADE
LEGACY

CHAPTER

1

Clanless

The Double Double hotel and casino was an unlikely place to incite revolution. It was merely a convenient target because Bero worked there and knew how to get past security. While the city of Janloon shivered at the sudden onset of the coldest, wettest winter in decades, the bright lights and clamor of the gambling floor continued unabated at all hours, pouring money from high rollers and foreign tourists into the coffers of the No Peak clan. That would not be the case today.

At ten minutes to noon, Bero pushed a luggage cart with three suitcases across the casino floor and into an elevator. Three business-men in the elevator were carrying on a heated conversation. "The Mountain is offering me a tribute rate that's fifteen percent lower. The Kauls can't match that," grumbled a bald man in a blue suit. "Yet they're still expecting me to compete with the foreign chain stores that are popping up like weeds because of the trade deals they've pushed on the country."

His colleague grimaced. "Would you rather pay tribute to Ayt Mada, though?"

"Ayt's a power-hungry murderer, but so what? They all are. She did what she had to do, to keep the Mountain clan in line," said the tanned third businessman. "At least she puts Kekonese interests first, and now that she's finally named an heir, I think—"

The elevator door, which had begun to close, opened again and two foreigners stepped inside, taking up the remaining space next to Bero's luggage cart. They were in plainclothes, but they didn't seem like tourists. The three businessmen stopped talking and eyed the strangers with polite suspicion. Janloon was crawling with foreign corporate and government agents these days.

The elevator descended to the parking level and opened with a quiet ping. When all the other occupants had exited, Bero rolled the luggage cart and its contents into the parking lot and looked at his watch. Green Bones of the No Peak clan kept a close eye on the lucrative betting houses of Poor Man's Road, but there were only so many of them patrolling the district. Eiten, the former Fist who'd given Bero his job at the Double Double, was not in today. After weeks of timing the security shifts, Bero knew that at precisely noon, none of the clan's other jade warriors would be on the premises either. Of course, once the commotion started, they would arrive in short order, so speed was vital.

A van pulled into the parking space next to Bero. Tadino jumped out of the driver's seat; Otonyo and Guriho got out of the rear. Bero did not particularly like the three Oortokons, with their foreign accents and ugly Ygutanian clothes, especially Tadino, who had the sharp bark and narrow face of a rat terrier. Nevertheless, they were the only people Bero had met who hated the Green Bone clans as much as he did, who wanted to see them come crashing down.

"Didn't get stopped or questioned at all," Tadino crowed. Even if they had been, there were no weapons or other suspicious items in the van. Bero pulled the suitcases off the luggage cart and threw them open on the ground. Guriho, Otonyo, and Tadino pulled out the contents: gas masks, spray paint, crowbars, handguns, and tear gas grenades.

When they were fully equipped, Bero used his employee key to get them into the stairwell next to the elevators. At the top of the stairs, he unlocked the upper set of doors, letting them out into the carpeted hallway behind the casino's kitchen.

Tadino grinned and pulled the gas mask over his face. Guriho and Otonyo clapped each other on the back and did the same, Guriho struggling for a moment to stuff his long beard under the seal of the mask. They didn't glance back at Bero as they rushed down the hall. Otonyo rolled one of the tear gas canisters into the kitchen and Tadino hurled another one onto the casino floor, where it began to hiss and spew its contents. Bero flattened himself out of sight against the door of the stairwell as the shouting began, followed by sounds of coughing, gagging, and stampeding feet. A gunshot went off, and noise erupted in earnest—cries of alarm above the toppling of dishes and furniture, the breaking of glass, the metallic banging of emergency exits, and the rapid whap of the casino's revolving doors as the patrons of the Double Double fled choking from the premises, spilling in a panicked rush from the dim warm comfort of their games tables onto the main strip of Poor Man's Road.

Bero wrapped a bandana over his nose and mouth and peered around the corner of the stairwell. He could still hear an awful lot of noise, but it was hard to see anything through the smoke. Part of him wished he was out there causing chaos with the others—firing into the air, swinging a crowbar into the glass bar tops, defacing the walls and furniture. The damage would be repaired, but it would cost No Peak. It would humiliate them and make a statement that couldn't be ignored. Bero scowled. He was more daring and thick-blooded than any of the others. He'd done things that would make those Oorto-kon mongrels piss themselves.

He pulled his head back into the stairwell and shut the door. He had nothing to prove by going out there. If the Green Bones showed up, they would smash the legs of the fools they caught. Enough close calls had made Bero value his limbs. At one time, he'd possessed jade of his own and enough shine to keep him flush with money, but that wasn't the case anymore. He hated the clans, but he needed this job.

The door banged open and the three men staggered into the stairwell, their eyes wild and bright, hair sweaty and chests heaving for breath. Bero hurried with them back down to the parking level. He went out first, ducking behind a corner as the nearby elevator opened and disgorged half a dozen escaping floor and kitchen staff members. When they were gone, Bero hit the emergency stop button in the elevator to prevent it from going back up, then he let the men out of the stairwell. They tore off their masks and threw their gear into the suitcases. "Lie low for two weeks and meet back at the Little Persimmon," Guriho reminded them as they got back into the van. The vehicle peeled out of the parking lot, leaving Bero alone.

Bero wheeled the suitcases and their damning contents to the garbage chute and dumped them. He made sure his employee uniform was straight and unstained, then he walked out of the parking lot and went on his regular lunch break. When he returned thirty minutes later, there were two police cars and a fire truck parked outside of the Double Double, as well as three No Peak Green Bones walking around, angrily surveying the damage. Stranded hotel guests shivered on the sidewalk, waiting to be let back into their rooms. Bero stuffed his hands into his pockets and waited with them, hiding his smile at the red message spray-painted across the interior width of the casino's front glass doors: THE FUTURE IS CLANLESS.

CHAPTER

2

Betrayal

the sixth year, first month

Kaul Hiloshudon studied the six businessmen dining with him and hoped he would not have to kill any of them. They were gathered in the largest private room in the Twice Lucky restaurant and there was still plenty of food on the table, but he had little appetite. Taking the lives of enemies was something Hilo could do without hesitation, but these were men of his own clan, who he knew and had been friendly with to some extent in the past. No Peak needed every loyal member.

"How's your wife's health, Kaul-jen?" asked the Lantern Man Fuyin Kan, bringing the rest of the casual conversation around the table to an awkward pause.

Hilo didn't lose his smile, but the warmth left his eyes as he met the man's gaze across the table. "Recovery takes time, but she's doing better. Thank you for asking."

Fuyin said, "That's good to hear. There's nothing more important than the health and safety of our families, after all. May the gods shine favor on No Peak." He raised a glass of hoji in Hilo's direction and the other businessmen echoed him and followed suit.

Fuyin was not a typical jadeless Lantern Man. He wore two jade rings, jade studs in his ears, and an elaborate jade buckle on his belt. A former Fist, he'd left the military side of No Peak fifteen years ago to run his family's retail business. Despite the man's words of polite concern, Hilo could Perceive Fuyin's jade aura as a thick roiling cloud, bristling with unmistakable resentment and suspicion.

Hilo pushed aside his plate and sat back as waiters removed empty dishes and refilled cups of tea. He didn't look at Shae sitting next to him, but he could sense the tautness in her aura. She didn't appear to have eaten much either. There was no more putting off the conversation.

"I've invited you all here because my Weather Man tells me you have concerns that need to be brought up and answered directly by me as Pillar," Hilo said. "You're all respected and valued Lantern Men in the clan, so of course, I want to talk things through and solve problems before they become serious misunderstandings."

It was not Fuyin, but the bald man next to him, Mr. Tino, who spoke up first. He was an old-timer in the clan, a friend of Hilo's late grandfather. "Kaul-jen," Tino said, "given the economy today and the competition we face not only from rivals in the Mountain clan but also foreign companies, we've repeatedly asked the Weather Man's office for lower tribute rates. As I'm sure you remember, No Peak raised tribute to fight the clan war, but hasn't substantially lowered it for six years."

"We're still fighting the clan war, even if it's not out in the open," Hilo reminded him. "The Mountain intends to conquer us sooner or later. We've kept tribute at a reasonable level for everyone and used the money to strengthen the clan as the Weather Man sees fit."

Shae sat forward at his mention and said, "We have to grow No

Peak's capabilities if we hope to prevail against our enemies. We've been upgrading technology systems, expanding Kaul Dushuron Academy to be able to train more Green Bones, and building up our overseas offices and businesses." The Weather Man's chief of staff, Woon Papidonwa, immediately handed her a file folder. Shae opened it and began to extract a sheaf of papers. "I can show you the clan's budget for the coming year and exactly where the tribute income is being—"

Another Lantern Man, the darkly tanned Mr. Eho, waved down the gesture impatiently. "I don't doubt you're spending the money. The problem is *how* you're spending it. No Peak continues chasing business in Espenia, which will surely harm our country in the long run." He avoided looking at the Weather Man, who he'd disapproved of on previous occasions. "Young people are too influenced by foreign ways. That's why you see more crime and social problems these days. What happened last week at the Double Double casino, for example. Disgraceful. And the hooligans responsible weren't caught."

Hilo's eyes narrowed at Eho's lecturing tone. "If you want to blame someone for crime, think about how many barukan gang members the Mountain clan has brought into the country to pad their ranks. But that's beside the point. I know the Mountain is undercutting us, offering you lower tribute rates, and suddenly you feel it's unfair to pay your usual amount when it seems you could do better." The uncomfortable silence that answered him was ample confirmation. Several of the Lantern Men were studiously avoiding his stare.

Fuyin Kan, however, did not look away.

"Switching allegiance would be a drastic and difficult decision," Fuyin said. It would not only affect a Lantern Man's finances, but where he chose to live, which martial school his children could attend, his social connections, and who his friends and enemies would be. "We don't want to go that far, which is why we've come as a group hoping for accommodation."

The rest of the Lantern Men sat forward in agreement. Fuyin had let others speak first, but it was apparent that he was the leader among them, as Hilo had suspected. *This is going to end badly.* Hilo felt certain of this, but nevertheless, he said, "We can't lower tribute right away. I can give you my word as Pillar that as our overseas businesses grow, we'll share that benefit with the whole clan. The Weather Man's office will adjust your tribute downward in stages, over the next five years." He had no idea if that made financial sense, but it sounded reasonable. Since Shae's aura didn't begin to surge with ire toward him, he assumed she could get it done.

Fuyin shook his head. "That's hardly any compromise at all. We've all agreed that it would be only fair for No Peak to match the Mountain's offer. And we believe strongly that there needs to be a change in the direction of the clan. An end to growing business overseas and focusing instead on defending our interests at home."

Shae's jade aura rippled with consternation, but she spoke firmly. "If we lower tribute payments while also giving up on our fastest growing source of revenue, the clan would lose money on both ends. We'd be setting ourselves up to be destroyed."

Some of the Lantern Men muttered at this, but Fuyin spread his hands. "The Mountain is doing fine. Are you saying the No Peak clan can't do the same? If so, can you blame us if we decide to act together for the sake of our futures?"

It did not sound like a threat, but it was. Fuyin had gathered together half a dozen disaffected Lantern Men and now he was saying that if No Peak refused to meet their collective demands, they would defect en masse to the Mountain clan. Even Shae had no immediate reply to such daring extortion.

An anger weighty with disappointment settled over Hilo. "Fuyin-jen," he said, fixing all his attention on the former Fist and ignoring the other men in the room, "why would you come here to ask me for anything, when you've already turned to the Mountain? Is it on Ayt Mada's orders that you're trying to drag these other people down with you?"

Fuyin's expression became a blank wall. "What are you talking about?"

"You've been paying tribute to the Mountain clan for months. I can show everyone the proof that Maik Tar dug up—or you can admit it rather than lie to my face." Hilo's words were spoken calmly but with unmistakable cold portent. "You're not just a Lantern Man like these others. You're a Green Bone who's betrayed his clan oaths."

Complete silence fell across the table. The oblivious burble of noise from the rest of the Twice Lucky beyond the sliding doors seemed cacophonous. The other Lantern Men edged back in their seats, the color draining from their faces, as Fuyin slowly stood. "You accuse me of betraying the clan? I was a first-rank Fist when you were still an insolent boy in the Academy. You're the one, Kaul Hiloshudon, who's betrayed all of us."

The bitterness Hilo had sensed in Fuyin's aura swelled into a storm, and the careful veneer of politeness he'd maintained until now fell away. "My father built a thriving business out of nothing but his sweat and grit and the patronage of the clan. Thank the gods he's no longer alive to see his company pushed out of the market, all because you've opened up our country to foreigners like a whore opening her legs." Fuyin's voice thickened and trembled. "My son admired you so much and wanted to be just like you. He was only twenty years old, barely a Finger for six months, when he was killed for *nothing*, in a clan war that would never have happened under your brother or grandfather. You have the arrogance to expect my allegiance? No, Kaul-jen, you're a pup of a Pillar, and your sister licks Espenian boots. I owe nothing to you."

Hilo did not speak for an uncharacteristically long moment. He could Perceive the thudding heartbeats and held breaths all around him, especially Shae's, but they seemed distant compared to the sensation of building pressure in his hands and head. At last he said, "Fuyin-jen, I can see that the hardships you've suffered have made you hate me, but you were wrong to let yourself be used by Ayt Mada." He stood to face the man. "You could've come to talk to me at any point if you were so unhappy. Whether it's business trouble that's making you feel like giving up on life, or if you can't forgive me for the death of your son, you could've asked to leave honorably, maybe even to form your own small clan in another part of the country. Because of your family's good standing and past sacrifice, I would've allowed that. You shouldn't have defected to the Mountain, and you shouldn't have swept others along with you by trying to damage No Peak with this fucking charade."

Fuyin straightened to his full height. He was taller than the Pillar, in his forties but still in excellent physical shape, known for training with much younger Green Bones. "You suggest I should've begged to leave the city I was born in, to live like a worthless outcast? Do you expect me to cut off my ear now to grovel for my own life? *Never.*" The man's face hardened with terrible resolve. "Kaul Hiloshudon, Pillar of No Peak, I offer you a clean blade."

A murmur of stunned apprehension traveled through the room. No one had challenged Kaul Hilo to a duel in years. Fuyin said, "Name the place and wea—"

"I refuse." Hilo's words stopped the air in the room. The Pillar's famous temper came into his face. "You're a traitor. You don't deserve a duel. I'm sorry for your son and your misfortune in business, but many of us suffer terrible tragedy in our lives yet we don't break our brotherly oaths."

Fuyin was nonplussed for a moment. Even Shae and Woon stared at Hilo in surprise. To anyone's knowledge, Kaul Hiloshudon had never turned down a personal challenge. Fuyin rocked back on his heels in disbelief. "You're a coward," he spat.

"I'm the Pillar of the clan," Hilo said. "I'd be foolish not to assume you're still a capable fighter, Fuyin-jen. Maybe you have nothing to live for anymore, but I can't afford to risk any injuries that might make me take time away from my family and responsibilities." Hilo frowned at his own words, aware that he was explaining his refusal to himself more than Fuyin. "If you want to keep your life, you can give what you own to the clan and accept exile from Kekon. Otherwise, I can grant you a death of consequence, with a blade in your hand. That's all."

As Hilo spoke, the door to the room slid open and Juen Nu, the Horn of No Peak, came in with Maik Tar and Iyn Ro. The three Green Bones had been waiting downstairs on Hilo's orders, prepared to enter if they Perceived any threat from the men at the table. Mr. Tino and Mr. Eho edged away from Fuyin with wide eyes, as if he'd become a ticking explosive. Fuyin's eyes darted and his hands twitched as he stood alone. Juen, Maik, and Iyn began to walk around the large round table toward him from either side. None of the Lantern Men they passed dared to leave their seats.

Shae began to stand, her aura crackling with alarm. The Weather Man had called together these Lantern Men for what was supposed to be a conciliatory business lunch that was about to turn into an execution. "Hilo," she hissed, loudly enough to be heard. "It's not right to do it here like this. Let—"

No one heard the rest of her suggestion because Fuyin yanked a compact pistol from a concealed waistband holster and began firing.

Tar reacted at once, raising a Deflection in front of the Pillar that sent the small-caliber rounds straight up into the dining room's ceiling, knocking out two of the hanging lights. Woon seized Shae by the arm and pulled her behind him. Juen and Iyn pushed the other Lantern Men to the ground. Fuyin Kan dropped his gun and hurled himself Light, clearing the span of the dining table in one snarling bound, his drawn talon knife seeking Hilo's throat.

Hilo met the attack, hopping Light onto the table and catching Fuyin's elbow, jamming his momentum and the trajectory of his weapon. Shoving back hard into his opponent's center of gravity, he unbalanced Fuyin as soon as the man's grip on Lightness faltered and his feet touched the table. The former Fist stumbled, but threw a lethal Channeling strike that narrowly glanced off Hilo's Steel as the Pillar twisted his torso, pivoting sharply and dragging the other man forward with his rotation. Fuyin's foot caught a bowl half-full of cooling soup as he went staggering headlong toward the edge of the table. Plates, glasses, and food went flying from under their feet.

Many years ago, when he was a teenager in the Academy, Hilo had done balance and Lightness drills by sparring opponents on thin ledges and wobbly platforms. At the time, he thought the exercises silly. Fights happened on asphalt and concrete, not on logs over waterfalls like one might see in movies. On the dais of the dining table, he entertained a fractional second remembrance of his instructors lecturing him that no Green Bone, no matter how well prepared, is assured of choosing ideal conditions. Tangled close, with both of them tipping forward, Hilo's left hand darted up and encircled Fuyin's head from behind as if it were a relayball he were preparing to pass. The talon knife that appeared in his right hand came up in a flash and sank into Fuyin's throat. Gripping the man's hair, he pushed Fuyin's face onto the table and his neck further onto the blade as he landed on his knees with a crash of broken plates. Hilo tore the knife upward with all his Strength, severing the windpipe.

Fuyin thrashed for a second, scattering more objects off the table before he lay still, the pool of blood under his chin spreading in a dark stain across the red tablecloth and mingling with the spilled soup broth and chunks of strewn food. Hilo got down off the dining table. It had all happened in less than a minute, and his hearing was still muffled from the gunshots in the enclosed space. When he spoke to the remaining five Lantern Men, who were picking themselves up off the ground, he couldn't be sure if he was yelling or talking normally. "Is there anyone else who has a personal grievance, or is so dissatisfied that he wants to take up Fuyin's demands?"

The Lantern Men climbed to their feet meekly. Mr. Eho looked at Fuyin's body and swallowed noisily before touching his clasped hands to his forehead and bending in a deep salute to the Pillar. "Kaul-jen, I'm embarrassed to say I went along with Fuyin out of financial selfishness. I knew nothing of his shocking and abhorrent treachery to the clan. I'm grateful and perfectly happy with your suggested compromise on tribute rates."

"Same with me, Kaul-jen," said Mr. Tino quickly, brushing off his pants. "Forgive my foolishness. I thought Fuyin was standing up for all of us, but now I see that I was wrong to trust him. We're fortunate you saw through him right away." The other Lantern Men nodded shamefacedly, reiterating their steadfast allegiance to the clan.

Hilo stifled a desire to have each of them soundly beaten before demanding they cut off their ears in front of him to retain their patronage. But he didn't think the businessmen had thick enough blood to handle that, and with Fuyin's body still on the table, he'd already made his point. There would be little to gain in cowing them further, besides the satisfaction. Hilo turned away in disgust. "Get them out of here," he said to his Fists.

Iyn Ro escorted the chastised Lantern Men out of the building. They were only too eager to leave, casting brief, nervous glances backward as they departed. A few of them might indeed be repentant or worried enough to come back with their ears in boxes, but Hilo didn't care. In his opinion, jadeless Lantern Men could never be counted on. Protected by aisho and motivated by money, they expected strength and protection from a patron clan but would switch allegiance for their own benefit and survival. Ayt couldn't be blamed for trying her best to steal them.

Juen said, "I'd better go talk to Mr. Une and calm everything down." The sounds of gunshots and violence had surely disrupted the Twice Lucky's lunch hour and agitated the old restaurateur. After the Horn had left, Tar threw his arm over Hilo's shoulders and said with mock petulance, "You took him down too quickly, Hilo-jen. I'm your Pillarman, couldn't you have let me earn even a bit of his green?"

Hilo scowled over sourly at Fuyin's sprawled body without returning his brother-in-law's grin. "Take his jade for the clan," he said. "I don't feel like wearing it, not when I know his son died for No Peak while I was Horn." He started for the door.

Shae blocked his path, her jade aura rasping against his with displeasure. "You're going to walk out of here without saying anything else?" she demanded.

Hilo's nostrils flared at the tone of her voice. "What else do you want me to say? You told me we had to have this meeting to sort things out with those grumbling Lantern Men. They're not grumbling anymore, are they?"

"Don't you think we should've talked beforehand if you were planning to execute Fuyin in front of everyone? Why didn't you tell me you had proof that he turned to the Mountain?"

"Because I didn't," he snapped. "I had a feeling. When I saw his reaction, then I knew for sure. He already had a grudge, so it's no wonder Ayt got to him. He was determined to die and bring me to the grave with him." Despite knowing this, Hilo could not help but take the treason of a former Fist personally. Fuyin's accusations rattled in his head and he wanted to get out of the room, away from the man's body.

He began to push past Shae, but she moved into his path again. "This isn't good, Hilo," she insisted. "Executing a traitor might keep people in line for a while, but it doesn't solve the problems that made those Lantern Men turn against us in the first place. We haven't been talking about the issues the way a Pillar and Weather Man ought to."

Hilo bared his teeth as he leaned over his sister. "You want to talk to me as Weather Man? Then do the Weather Man's *job*. Tell me how the fuck the Mountain is outspending us and stealing our businesses with tribute rates that we know are unsustainable. Tell me how we stop them and *win*. If you can't tell me that, then spare me your godsdamned lectures."

Shae opened her mouth to retort, then shut it again so hard he heard the snap of her back teeth coming together. She glowered at him, face flushed with aggravation. Woon, who'd been hovering nearby, put a hand on the Weather Man's shoulder and drew her back as Hilo finally barged out of the room.

Juen was still in conversation with an anxious Mr. Une, so Hilo was spared any of the aging restaurateur's hand-wringing or brow mopping. Some of the usual lunch crowd at the Twice Lucky had cleared out during the brief spate of violence, perhaps worried it might spill out into the rest of the restaurant, or spooked by last week's attack by anarchists at the Double Double casino. Others, however, were loitering nearby. At Hilo's appearance, they muttered respectfully, touching their foreheads and trying to get a glimpse past him into the room with the body, craning their necks with the sort of morbid curiosity afforded to spectacular automobile crashes and burning buildings. By evening, word would be out all over Janloon that Fuyin Kan was dead, a traitor to his clan.

Hilo went out the front doors and got into the driver's seat of the Duchesse Signa. He had his own parking spot at the Twice Lucky, guarded every time he dined there. Tar followed him out and tapped the passenger-side window, leaning his arms through when Hilo rolled down the glass. "Where are you going?" the Pillarman asked, with a grumpiness that might've been protective concern or merely displeasure at being left behind.

"I'm going to take a drive, to clear my head," Hilo said, putting the key in the ignition. "Just help Juen and Iyn clean things up here." There were times Hilo would hesitate to leave Maik Tar and Iyn Ro together in handling clan matters, on account of their wildly hot and cold relationship, but they were getting along right now. "And get ready for your trip to Port Massy. It's going to be cold over there; bring warm clothes. You got everything else you need? Tickets, passport, and everything?"

"Yeah, sure," his brother-in-law said.

"I'll be back home in a couple hours." He left Tar in the parking lot, looking vaguely forlorn in the rearview mirror as he watched the Duchesse drive away.

———

Hilo drove for half an hour in no particular direction, blasting the heater in defiance of the icy air pressing down on the city like a cold towel against the skin. The streets were uncommonly subdued, Janloon's bright colors washed out by a gray and sunless sky. People were excited that snow was falling in the mountains.

He found himself, without any real thought, driving into the Docks and pulling up in front of the Lilac Divine Gentleman's Club. A lot of things had changed in Janloon over the years, but the Lilac Divine was not one of them. It was, Hilo mused wryly, a reliable business unthreatened by modern times or foreign competition. A valet took his car, and as soon as he stepped through the door, Mrs. Sugo, the Lantern Man proprietor, greeted him with a smile that struck Hilo as patently false. She never showed him any discourtesy of course, and she always made certain his visits were exactly as he asked for, but she was decidedly unenthusiastic about the Pillar's irregular and unannounced appearances.

"Kaul-jen," said Mrs. Sugo, saluting him and showing him into a plush, rose-scented room with a sofa. "How good to see you again. Would you like me to send for Sumi? Or Vina?"

Hilo shook his head. "Someone else."

Mrs. Sugo's painted smile wavered but remained gamely in place. "If I might ask, Kaul-jen, in the interest of serving you better, is there anything objectionable about any of the women you've spent time with here?"

"They're whores," said Hilo, not with any kind of meanness, merely fatigue. He tossed his jacket over the back of the sofa and poured himself a glass of citrus-infused water from the jug on the table. "Just don't send me any of the ones my brother used. I don't like the idea of that."

Mrs. Sugo pressed her lips together, hiding her discontent with a bow of acquiescence as she retreated from the room and closed the door behind her. Hilo flopped down onto the sofa and closed his eyes, rubbing the corners of them with his thumbs. He'd never understood why Lan used to come to this place and thought his brother must've been desperately lonely. Now he felt rather sorry for himself, to be in the same situation. He'd been Pillar of the clan for six years. Longer than Lan. He and his brother had not been much alike, but perhaps the position of Pillar did the same thing to every man—isolated him and wore him down before killing him, either quickly or slowly.

He couldn't help but wonder if Ayt Mada, who'd murdered many people in her own clan, ever felt deeply disappointed or hurt the way he did, or if she was naturally coldhearted and able to act without feeling. He'd tried unsuccessfully to have Ayt assassinated by the Ven family in the Mountain, so it ought to be no surprise that his enemy would likewise try to exploit any discontent or weakness in No Peak. Still, Shae was right, as much as Hilo hated to admit it. Fuyin's betrayal was not an isolated grievance, and his death would not solve the bigger, glaring problem: After having failed on multiple occasions to have Hilo killed, the Mountain was now waging a persistent campaign to destroy No Peak economically.

A gentle knock came. Hilo got off the sofa and opened the door to find a lovely woman, darker skinned and curvier than the one who'd attended him on his last visit some two or three months ago. She was carrying an ebony tray with a bottle of hoji, some date cakes arranged on a delicate clay plate, and two cups. "Kaul-jen," she said solicitously, but with a tight undercurrent to her voice that suggested Mrs. Sugo and the other charm girls had prepared her for what to expect. "May I come in?"

Hilo held the door open for her. She placed the tray on the low table in front of the sofa, knelt next to it, and folded the draping hem of her sleeve back fastidiously as she opened the bottle of hoji and poured two servings into the small cups. The hoji was well aged, with a robust and complex scent.

Hilo drank it down, then said, "Get on the bed."

"Kaul-jen," the woman said, in a suggestive and soothing tone, "we're in no rush at all. You can stay all night. Why not relax for a while and let me treat you to a more enjoyable experience? Surely you could use some time away from the demands of being the Pillar. Let's have another drink and you can tell me about your day."

Hilo lips quirked wryly. "I have a wife and children at home. I don't need conversation." He stood. "I won't take long if you cooperate."

The charm girl stared at him. She opened her mouth as if to try again to persuade him, before apparently coming to the indignant decision to not bother. Without any further attempt at pretense, she tipped back her shot of hoji in one quick gulp, then stood and unfastened the sash around her silk robe, letting it fall to the ground in a heap. She lay down naked on the bed, with a scowl of resignation that Hilo decided was more attractive than her practiced smile, on account of being genuine. She was smooth-skinned and had a mole on the flat of her stomach, near her navel.

Hilo undressed. The charm girl's eyes widened at the bloodstains on his shirt cuffs as he unbuttoned them, and the talon knife he unbuckled and laid on the table next to the tray. They widened further at the sight of his bare torso—collarbone, chest, and nipples studded with glinting pieces of jade. "Don't touch any of it, and it won't do anything to you," he said, reading the anxiety in her eyes. He took one of the complimentary condoms from the nightstand. "Turn around and get on your hands and knees."

After he was done fucking her and she had gotten up to go to the bathroom, Hilo dressed, gathered his jacket and knife, and ate two of the date cakes on the tray. He left a generous tip on the bedside table. Charm girls made their real money from long-term clients, who often bought them gifts and paid extra for exclusive access. Since he didn't expect to see the woman again, he thought it only right that he leave extra compensation for her wasted time.

Downstairs, Mrs. Sugo wished him good night with a stiff smile. He could understand her annoyance. The Lilac Divine was a high-class establishment, with charm girls who could play music and recite poetry and accompany clients to black-tie galas. He was using it like a cheap brothel. The Duchesse was waiting for him at the front of the building. The valet had not bothered to park his car elsewhere, knowing from prior visits that he was unlikely to be long in the club. Hilo walked all around his prized vehicle and bent down to peer underneath it. Ever since Maik Kehn, his brother-in-law and former Horn, had been killed by a car bomb, Hilo was exceedingly careful with the family's cars and drivers, watchful for threats that could not be Perceived with jade senses. "Has it been out of your sight at all, even for a second?" he demanded. The valet promised on his life that it had not. Satisfied that his car had not been tampered with, Hilo got in, turned the key, and headed for home.

———

He walked into the house before dinner. His mother and Kyanla, the housekeeper, were talking in the kitchen, and he could smell frying vegetables. Niko, a precocious reader, looked up from his spot on the sofa only long enough to say, "Hi, Uncle," before turning back to his comic book, but Ru and Jaya ran to greet him, both of them jabbering over each other to get his attention and tell him things. Hilo kissed his son on the head and let his daughter climb onto his back, carrying her up the stairs.

"Da, show me your new jade!" Ru said, skipping close behind his father.

Hilo turned at the top of the staircase and looked down at the boy. "What new jade are you talking about?"

"The new jade you won," Ru demanded, standing up on his toes and grabbing Hilo around the waist. "Uncle Tar said you killed someone today, a man who was in the clan but who turned bad. Where's your new jade?"

Hilo made a low, disapproving noise in his throat. His brother-in-law must've arrived home earlier and already filled the children's ears with a simplified account of the day's events. Tar was always honest with his nephews and niece about the realities of being a Green Bone and felt it was only right that they understand their father was not just their father, but also the leader of a large and powerful clan, which was why he was often busy and not at home. He had enemies who wanted to kill him, and sometimes he would have to kill them first, so that he could return home each evening to tuck them into bed.

It wasn't that Hilo disagreed with Tar, but he didn't want Ru's head filled with Green Bone stories. They would only make him dwell on what he lacked, instead of confident in who he was. Ru was a stone-eye; he could never wear jade or hold any significant rank in No Peak. It saddened Hilo that his son could not become a jade warrior, but it was somewhat of a relief as well, to know that one of his children might have a simpler, safer life.

Hilo said sternly, "I don't have any new jade. I wear enough and we should save the green we take for the future, since we're already very fortunate. And stop listening to everything your uncle Tar tells you." Hilo bent and set Jaya down, giving both of their heads an affectionate rub. "Go back downstairs and get ready for dinner."

After the children ran off, Hilo stood back up and pushed open the bedroom door. Wen was resting, propped up in bed with pillows supporting her back against the headboard. She looked weary, as she always did after her physiotherapy appointments. Relearning how to do simple things, like walk smoothly, pass a cup from one hand into another, or stand without need for support, required a tremendous effort that left her physically and emotionally drained.

Hilo stood in the doorway for a few seconds, then walked over and sat down next to her on the edge of the bed. He placed a hand on her outstretched leg. "How was it today?"

"Not terrible," Wen said. "I can... t-touch my toes and... stand up again without falling down." She smiled wanly. "Quite a v-victory."

It broke Hilo's heart every day to see Wen so feeble and incompetent, to hear her speak with such ponderous difficulty. He'd had to leave the room at times, unable to bear seeing her driven to helpless tears of frustration by her inability to do something as simple as complete a sentence that was perfectly formed in her mind but would not come out correctly. At least she was much improved from a year ago, when she couldn't move one side of her body at all and could barely speak coherently. Back then, when he wasn't even certain if her mind and personality had survived intact, he was ashamed to say there had been a few awful periods of despair when he'd wondered if it would've been less cruel to both of them if Anden had not succeeded in reviving her from death.

Wen had always been graceful and well-spoken, confident in a gentle way, with a perceptive and determined will. He'd loved her more than anything in the world. Now he did not know how he felt. Sometimes when he looked at his wife he felt a surge of the feverish, all-consuming desire to hold her and make love to her and protect her at all costs. More often, however, he felt a numb aching anger, a cold disbelief and unforgiving rage. She had disobeyed him, kept so many of her activities secret from him, put herself in harm's way, nearly leaving him a widower and their children motherless. He'd done all he could to keep her safe and give her everything she could want, to be good to her, and she had brought all this pain on them.

"Is Shae . . . coming over . . . this evening?" Wen asked.

"No," he said.

"You should. . . . in-in-in—" He could see her grasping for the word, trying to push it out of her throat like a bit of stuck food. "*Ask* her . . . to come over more often."

Hilo stood up to go without answering. Wen reached out to him, but he stepped away from her. He saw the hurt in her eyes. She must be used to this by now—the indecision of his affection. At times, he hated himself for it, but another part of him wanted to punish her, to hurt her as she had so badly hurt him.

"Dinner's ready," Hilo said over his shoulder as he left the room. "If you don't feel like coming down, I'll have Kyanla bring a plate up to the room."

CHAPTER

3

Unreadable Clouds

After her brother left the room, Shae sat down hard in one of the chairs farthest away from Fuyin Kan's body, and rested her forehead in her hands. It wasn't her fault the lunch meeting had ended with drawn knives and bloodshed. She told herself this, but the shallow self-reassurance was not convincing.

She was the Weather Man; it was her job to be one step ahead of everyone. *The Weather Man reads the clouds*, so the saying went. Today, Hilo's instincts had been sharper than her judgment. The fact stung badly. And it was true that she'd pursued trade with Espenia in ways that benefited No Peak but opened up Kekonese industries to more foreign competition. She'd contributed to Fuyin's troubles and couldn't blame the man for his hatred. It was her responsibility to maintain the loyalty of No Peak's Lantern Men so that her brother did not have to execute them.

Woon crouched down next to her seat and put a hand on her knee.

Thank the gods he hadn't been injured in the mayhem. Her chief of staff rarely acted without thinking, but the moment Fuyin had drawn the gun, he'd instinctively tried to shield her even though she wore more jade than he did. She wasn't sure whether to thank or admonish him.

"Shae-jen, you did the right thing, trying to broker a compromise," the Weather Man's Shadow said quietly. "Fuyin was the one who provoked violence, probably for a considerable reward."

"It's the sort of trap Ayt Mada would set," Shae agreed glumly. If No Peak gave in to the Lantern Men's demands, it would invite financial ruin. If it let businesses leave without consequence, it would fail even faster. Shae lifted her head. At least now, with Fuyin dead and his treachery revealed, they had other options. "We can still get something out of this mess if we move quickly to make sure Fuyin's assets stay within the clan."

Her chief of staff nodded at once. "Fortunately, the Pillar didn't agree to a duel." The victor of a clean-bladed duel could claim his opponent's jade but couldn't touch his family or assets. "We can buy out Fuyin's heirs and sell his company piecemeal at a discount to our other Lantern Men in the retail sector who've been asking for relief. That should more than mollify them. I'll go to the most important ones and speak to them in person this week." That would ensure the message was clear and delivered straight from the Weather Man's office: The traitor was dead and everything his family had built would go to those who were loyal.

"Thank you, Papi-jen." Shae put her hand on top of his. "I don't know what I'd do without you." A little of the strain in her shoulders loosened, although Hilo's harsh words were still a weight on her chest. She was no stranger to her brother's opprobrium, but the last time they'd been on such bad terms, she'd been able to escape to another country for two years. Now, she had to work with Hilo to manage the clan while putting up with his avoidance and recrimination. She couldn't even claim it was undeserved. She'd kept secrets from the Pillar, disobeyed him, sent Anden and Wen to carry out an assassination plan in Port Massy that had nearly gotten them killed.

And Hilo was right about something else: She did not know how Ayt was winning, or how to stop her.

The restaurant staff had closed off the area around the dining room. Tar and Iyn carried Fuyin's body out the back of the building without disturbing the other diners, and Mr. Une came in with Juen to inspect the damage to the light fixtures and walls, which the clan would compensate him for. Waiters efficiently cleared away the bloodstained tablecloth and cleaned up the spilled food.

"We should get back to the office." Shae forced herself to stand. "Hami is probably waiting for us."

———

Hami Tumashon was different from how Shae remembered him. After three and a half years abroad, he'd put on some weight and adopted a few Espenian affectations; he was wearing an athletic shirt under his suit jacket and drinking from an oversized travel mug full of nutmeg spiced coffee when he came into the Weather Man's office. Most noticeably to Shae, he had not yet put his jade back on, and the absence of his usual sturdy jade aura made him seem like a split-reality version of himself.

Shae had taken off her jade as well, years ago, then reclaimed all of it, then violently lost much of it again. She wondered if, at each of those traumatic turning points in her life, reality had indeed fractured. Perhaps in some alternate timeline, a different Shae had continued on in another way, and the woman that remained had seemed to other people to be a disconcertingly altered replacement.

While she and Woon had been in the Twice Lucky, lunch had been catered into the main conference room so the office could celebrate Hami's triumphant return to Janloon. The former Master Luckbringer had grown the clan's branch operations in Port Massy to a staff of twenty and recently moved it into a larger downtown office. Revenue out of Espenian holdings had expanded to an impressive eight percent of the clan's total, even before taking into account the uplift to No Peak's tributary businesses in Kekon as a result of the clan facilitating import and export activities. For a man to have been executed today over the backlash to this one bright spot in No Peak's fortunes was a sour irony.

"Terun Bin works like an ox and has a mind as sharp as a talon knife. He'll do fine over there," Hami declared, settling across from Shae in the sitting area of her office. Terun Bin would be Hami's successor. He was already a highly regarded senior Luckbringer at the age of twenty-eight, but unfortunately, his jade aptitude was poor, perhaps because he was one-quarter Abukei, although he did not appear to be of mixed blood at all and the fact was not common knowledge. He'd been educated at a competitive academic school instead of a martial academy, earning only a single jade stone through private training. At Woon's suggestion, Shae had promoted Terun and sent him to Port Massy, where his lack of green would not drag down his reputation, and Hami had spent the past two months transitioning him into the top role there.

"You've accomplished even more than I expected," Shae said. "Terun will have a large shadow to fill." She motioned for her secretary to bring tea into the room. Her nerves were still frayed, and she was glad that without his jade, Hami could not Perceive the lingering jitteriness in her aura. Woon probably could, but he would never let on.

One thing that had not changed about Hami was his candor. "The problem we have in Espenia is that jade is still illegal in that country. That's something Terun can't solve, no matter how smart and hardworking he is. As long as that remains the case, everything we've built there is at risk and could drag the clan down in the long run."

Woon was sitting between them in the armchair to Shae's right. "We've kept our businesses in Espenia completely separate from any activity involving jade on the Horn's side of the clan, and taken precautions to insulate them legally."

"All of that is extra effort and cost to the clan," Hami pointed out. "I've hired Luckbringers from Janloon into the Port Massy branch over the years, but several turned down the opportunity because they or their family members were Green Bones unwilling to take off their jade to move to Espenia. And the problem extends beyond the Weather Man's office. Many of our tributary Kekonese companies would like to grow internationally, but it's too difficult for their staff to travel to and from Espenia when every Green Bone has to go through the trouble of securing a visa with extra paperwork documenting their jade upon entry and exit, and even so, they're only allowed to stay for twenty days out of the year."

Shae sighed. She knew it was a problem. "We're hiring more lawyers to handle the work, and looking for ways to streamline the process."

Hami plowed on. "How many of the clan-sponsored students who've gone to study overseas are Green Bones? I'm guessing not many. What family wants to send their son or daughter to Kaul Dushuron Academy for eight years to become proficient in the jade disciplines, only to have them move away to a place where wearing jade is a crime? Yet it's Green Bones we would most like to sponsor. They're the ones who're most loyal to the clan, who would return and use a foreign education for No Peak's benefit." Hami blew out a loud breath. "This pointless and ignorant law in Espenia is creating far too much costly business friction for us."

Shae cupped her hands around the warm teacup her secretary set down in front of her. She was disheartened but not surprised by all that Hami had said so far. The former Master Luckbringer was not done, however; he took a noisy sip of his coffee and said, "It might get even worse, Kaul-jen. There are rumblings that the law could change again and there will be heavy penalties placed on Espenian companies who do business with whatever the Espenian government deems as 'criminal organizations.' Since civilian ownership of jade is illegal, and the Green Bone clans hold and distribute jade, they could declare No Peak a 'criminal organization' and not only prevent other companies from working with us, but in the worst-case scenario, bar us from operating in that country altogether if they wanted to."

Woon drew his head back in disbelief. "The Espenian government itself purchases jade from Kekon for military use. If they can declare us to be criminals for something that has been in our culture for thousands of years, wouldn't they have to also declare their own government to be illegal?"

Hami threw his hands up. "It's Espenia," he exclaimed. "They do what they like and why should hypocrisy stand in their way? They use money and tricky laws like we use the jade disciplines—as a kind of fighting science. While I was there, I heard a story of a landlord in their country hundreds of years ago who outlawed taking water from a certain river so he could hang the leaders of an entire town. Maybe it's just a myth, but I would believe it."

There was a knock on Shae's door. Woon's secretary opened the door partway and put her head inside, bobbing it apologetically. "I'm sorry to interrupt, but, Woon-jen, your wife is on the phone. I told her you were in a meeting with the Weather Man, but she insisted I find you."

Woon's face tightened with embarrassment and uncharacteristic irritation. "Unless it's an emergency, tell her I'll call her back," he said. When his secretary backed away in chagrin and closed the door, Woon said to Shae and Hami, "I apologize."

"There's no need to do so." Shae glanced at her aide in concern. The brief perturbation in Woon's expression was gone and he seemed fine again, but she was so familiar with his jade aura that she could Perceive the faint static hum of disquiet that had come into it.

"We were close to finishing anyways," she said, and turned back to Hami. "You're right to bring this issue up. I agree it's a long-term problem that we need to address, though one that's too big for us to solve today. For now, do you feel like you have what you need to get settled back into Janloon and started in your new position, Hami-jen?" Out of habit, she addressed him with the respectful Green Bone suffix even though he was not wearing jade, and realizing her error, she amended, a bit awkwardly, "It's your decision, of course, whether to put your jade back on." She understood more than anyone that it was a personal choice, one that might be more difficult than other people realized.

Hami pursed his lips thoughtfully. "I think I will, but not right away. I need some time to deal with family things and get back into a routine before I'm ready to carry jade again." Hami's family had moved into a new house and Hami's eldest son would soon be entering Kaul Dushuron Academy as a year-one student. "Also, I expect I'll continue traveling to and from Port Massy regularly, so to prevent all the legal hassle we've discussed, the less green I am, the better, from a practical standpoint."

Starting today, Hami would be the clan's Rainmaker—a new and necessary position Shae had created, one that her former Belforte Business School classmates might've called a director of international business development. Hami and a few subordinates would be responsible for improving communication and coordination between the Janloon office and the clan's Port Massy branch, as well as seeking out additional growth opportunities overseas, something that seemed even more important now.

"You were right, Kaul-jen," Hami admitted. "Away from home, one gets used to being jadeless, and it's a strange feeling to come back. In some ways, it's easier to not be green. As soon as I wear my jade again, I'll have to return to being a certain type of person." He snorted and gestured with wry self-deprecation at the extra padding around his middle. "It'll take me months to get back into shape and regain my jade abilities after such an absence."

"You're invaluable to the clan either way, Hami-jen," Shae said, using the suffix deliberately this time. "It's good to have you back home."

After Hami departed, Woon said, "Do you need anything else from me right now, Shae-jen? Otherwise, I'll start dealing with Fuyin's assets like we talked about."

"Don't forget to phone your wife, first," Shae reminded him as he stood, but the teasing comment failed to elicit even a small smile. She asked, "Papi-jen...is everything all right? You haven't been quite yourself this week." She hadn't intended to bring it up, but the Weather Man's Shadow had seemed unusually tired, and his normally clean-shaven jaw was darkened with faint stubble.

Woon grimaced and rubbed a hand self-consciously over the side of his face. A throb of unhappiness clouded his aura. "I'm sorry, Shae-jen. I know I've been distracted. I'll try to do better."

"I didn't mean it as a criticism." If Woon's performance had slipped, she hadn't noticed at all, and she'd worked with him every day for more than six years. "I'm only asking as a friend. If you don't want to talk about it, that's fine." Shae was suddenly worried that she'd spoken clumsily—sounded uncaring, or inappropriately caring, too defensive, or too apologetic.

Woon hesitated. Then he admitted quietly, "Kiya had another miscarriage." He averted his eyes, as if ashamed to be sharing such a personal misfortune. "I think it's been very hard on her. On both of us."

Shae searched inadequately for what to say. "I'm sorry. Is there anything I can do to help? Do you need some time off?"

The chief of staff shook his head. "We've been through this before, and I know there's nothing I can say or do to make her feel better. At work, I can be useful to you and the clan. But Kiya's been calling me at the office several times a day, sometimes angrily. She doesn't understand that—" He cut himself off with a grimace.

Shae gripped the empty teacup in her hands, then put it down before she could unintentionally break it. Woon worked relentlessly on her behalf. She depended on him more than anyone, not only to advance her agenda across the entire business side of the clan, but to privately challenge and advise her at all times. But she knew it could not be easy for Woon's wife to see so little of him and receive less attention than she deserved because her husband was constantly at the side of another woman, even if that woman was the Weather Man of the clan.

Shae wished she could say something sincere and encouraging, but it would be awkward to talk about Kiya. She suspected the woman disliked her. She reached out and squeezed her friend's arm in what she hoped he would accept as a gesture of understanding.

Woon's arm tensed under her hand. He lowered himself back down into the seat he'd vacated and sat forward with his elbows on his knees, studying the floor for a moment before reluctantly raising his eyes to hers. When he was concerned or deep in thought, a dimple appeared on the right side of Woon's forehead, one that Shae was often tempted to reach over and flatten out with her thumb.

"Shae-jen...This job...it's not very good for family life. The Weather Man is always thinking of the clan, and the Shadow's first priority is always the Weather Man." His steadfast jade aura gave a soft, cheerless pulse. "This isn't the way I wanted to bring it up, but it won't get any easier if I put it off. I think it might be time for me to think about moving into another role."

Shae managed to nod. "Of course, I can understand that." The words felt stilted as they left her mouth. She couldn't pretend to be happy about Woon asking to leave his post. "I'm sorry for not realizing that you needed a change. You asked for one years ago and ended up staying on far longer than I had any right to expect of you."

Woon's face colored. "That was...under different circumstances. And it's not that I want to leave. I'm thinking of what's best for my marriage. If I were thinking only of myself, this wouldn't be an issue."

With effort, she gave him a supportive smile. "Let's both think about what the best next role is for you. I'll support you in it, whatever it is. I only hope you can be patient for a little longer, until we identify someone to replace you as Weather Man's Shadow."

"Of course I wouldn't leave until then." Woon's posture relaxed in relief at Shae's quick acquiescence, though a troubled look remained in his eyes. "Thank you for understanding, Shae-jen." He stood back up and paused, seeming for a moment as if he wanted to say something else. Instead, he gave Shae a wan smile and exited her office, leaving her to listen to the clatter from the nearby halls and cubicles and wonder how it was possible to be surrounded by hundreds of people and yet feel entirely alone.

4

The Pillarman Abroad

Maik Tar liked to have things to do that kept him busy, even if that meant being sent halfway around the world and finding himself on a boat in Whitting Bay in the middle of an Espenian winter. Having specific tasks to focus on—securing a fake passport and paperwork, collecting information, talking to the right people, planning, getting the boat and equipment—kept him from drinking too much and falling into terrible moods. And then, at the end of all the preparation: the surge of anticipation and adrenaline, the sharp tang of violent satisfaction. Hilo-jen trusted him above anyone else, gave him work that was difficult and brutal because no one else would be as tenacious, effective, and discreet. This knowledge was a light for Tar even in the darkest of moments.

Tar had been told that during the busy summer months in Port Massy, tour boats and private watercraft crowded the harbor and went up and down the Camres River, but this late in the evening in the off-season, there were no other vessels on the water. Tar stamped his feet and blew into his cupped hands, cursing the ridiculous cold as he watched the dim outline of the pier recede into the distance. When he could barely see the shore, Tar shouted out to Sammy in the cockpit. "We're far enough out now. Cut the engine."

The motorboat bobbed gently in the dark. Tar went below deck, ducking his head and holding on to the handrail. The cabin was lit with two orange overhead lights and the floor covered with black plastic sheeting and drop cloths. In the center of the room, a man was tied into an aluminum deck chair. The first time Tar had laid eyes on Willum "Skinny" Reams, he'd been wearing a charcoal-gray suit and brimmed felt hat, sitting next to Boss Kromner in Thorick Mansion. Now he was shirtless, goosepimples raising the fine dark hairs of his chest, his face bruised where he'd been knocked about and gagged during transit. His shoes and socks had been removed and his bare toes were curled against the cold.

"How's it going down here?" Tar asked.

Kuno was kneeling next to a large metal washtub, stirring quick-dry concrete mix with a small shovel. He sat back on his haunches and wiped a gloved hand over his brow. "This stuff will take longer to dry with it being so cold out," he said.

"There's a space heater in the closet over there. We can plug it in." Tar went himself to take it out and set it up. The night would go faster with more hands to help, but he'd brought only Sammy and Kuno with him. The fewer people the better, as he didn't know or trust these Kekonese-Espenian Green Bones as much as his own men in Janloon. He would've preferred to have Doun or Tyin with him, but it had been troublesome enough to set up one false identity, and for the sake of minimizing risk and maintaining good relations with Dauk Losunyin, the local Pillar, Kaul Hilo had not wanted it to appear as if No Peak was overextending its authority in Port Massy.

Reams looked around the boat room with cold rage and a complete lack of surprise. "You keck bastards."

Tar stood in front of the man and looked down at him. "Why you end up here? Do you know?" he asked in Espenian. Tar did not speak the language well, but this was not his first trip to the country. He'd accompanied the Pillar on his initial visit here, over three years ago. Since then, he'd returned a few times on behalf of No Peak, to train the local Green Bones and do some work for the clan. He'd learned enough to get by. He didn't need to talk much.

Skinny Reams opened his hands, which were bound at the wrists to the arms of the chair. "I've put my share of men in the river," he admitted somberly. "God knows there's no shortage of people who'd say I deserve to end up there myself." He regarded Tar with disgust. "Didn't think you kecks would be the ones to do it, though. You're sore about Rohn Toro, but you couldn't have pulled this off yourself."

"Rohn Toro is a reason, yes," Tar said. Sammy and Kuno had been among Rohn's friends and protégés in the Keko-Espenian Green Bone community; they'd witnessed years of brutal harassment by the Crews against the Kekonese neighborhood in Southtrap, and had been the first to arrive on the scene of Rohn's murder. That was why they were here, with Dauk Losun's approval, to exact justice. However, Reams was correct: As the new Boss of the Southside Crew, he was too careful and too well guarded for anyone, even Green Bones, to have snatched him unawares without inside help. "You spennies, though, you are all the same," Tar said. "Can't be trusted, not even by each other."

Kuno turned around from where he was still stirring concrete. He pointed the tip of the hand shovel at the prisoner. "Your fellow Bosses, they're not too sad to see you go, Skinny," he said in fluent Espenian. "Jo Boy Gasson and the Slatters all figure you helped put Kromner in prison in the first place, and after the police heat you brought down on everyone from murdering Rohn and nearly killing two Kekonese nationals, they would just as soon be rid of you and make peace with us."

"Shortsighted fuckers. Turning on a fellow crewboy like that, when it's you ungodly kecks and your poisonous rocks that need to be wiped off the face of the earth." He spat on the floor of the boat. The toes of his bare feet were white with cold. "Get on with it then."

Tar shook his head. "You killed Rohn Toro. And made enemies of your own people. But that is not all. Not why *I* am here." Tar took off his coat and set it aside. It was getting warmer in the boat now. He rolled up his sleeves and drew the talon knife from the sheath at his waist. "You strangled my sister nearly to death. Now she can't walk or talk right. You don't know who she is, or who I am, do you? Doesn't matter. All you should know is this is personal from the No Peak clan."

Skinny Reams had been a crewboy all his adult life and was considered by everyone in the Port Massy underworld to be as tough as they got, but Tar could Perceive the animal fear swelling in him as his eyes traveled up from the edge of the hooked blade to the Green Bone's face, to the stamp of madness there.

"Kuno, go up to the deck with Sammy," Tar said, speaking in Kekonese now. "I'll call you back down when I need you."

The younger Green Bone hesitated. "Maik-jen," he said uncertainly, licking his dry lips. "Dauk Losun said we should be quick and careful, the way Rohn-jen always…"

Tar turned his head with a sharp jerk, and the wild light in his dilated pupils along with the knife in his hand convinced the other man to obey without objection. Kuno laid the shovel down, took off his work gloves, and threw a wet drop cloth over the metal tub to prevent the concrete from drying. He took the steps up to the deck of the boat quickly, with only one apprehensive glance backward.

Tar turned back to the man in the chair. He was no longer Willum Reams, he was no longer anybody, just another enemy of the clan, one snaking head of a many-headed beast. The clan had numerous enemies and sometimes they blurred together in Tar's mind, because in the end they all had one terrible thing in common, and so in a way they were all the same. They should not be able to hurt and kill powerful Green Bones. Men who were better than them, men like Maik Kehn. But they did, and they had, and they might again. They were responsible for the hollowness that followed Tar everywhere now that he knew he would never see or speak to his brother again. So when the man in the chair began to scream, Tar felt as if he were hearing his own cries, drawing out his own feelings.

CHAPTER

5

Keeping Up Appearances

the sixth year, fourth month

During New Year's week, the Kaul family's schedule was jammed with festive obligations, the most important being the banquet and party for the upper echelon of the clan. The entire leadership of No Peak would be in attendance, along with the most senior Fists and Luckbringers, prominent Lantern Men, and clan-affiliated government officials and public figures. Wen was busy for weeks ahead of time, drawing up the guest list and making arrangements for food, music, decorations, and security. Hilo told her to delegate the work to estate staff and hire more help so as not to overtax herself, but she was determined to maintain oversight of the event. She was afraid of something going wrong at a time when the clan could not afford any further appearance of weakness.

On the evening of the party, her sister-in-law Lina came over to the house to help her dress, pin up her hair, and apply makeup. After Kehn's death, Lina had vacated the Horn's house for Juen Nu, moving off the Kaul property and closer to her own large family, but she and Wen remained close friends. "You look beautiful in lucky green," Lina said brightly as she did up the buttons on the back of Wen's dress, perhaps noticing the tightness in her shoulders and neck, the stiff anxiety in her set mouth. Wen could hear the rising noise from the courtyard as it began to fill with arriving guests. When she looked out the upstairs window, she could see expensive cars pulling up in the roundabout, one after the other, bringing men in suits and women in gowns.

Hilo came into the room, dressed in a tuxedo. "You're sure you want to go?" he asked. They had barely spoken in the busy past few weeks. She was often already asleep when he got home. At other times, he went to bed without touching her and was gone when she woke up. Now he looked at her steadily for what felt to Wen like the first time in months. His expression softened. "You don't have to. It's fine."

Wen smiled weakly. "You know it's...not fine." It was often difficult for her to put her trapped thoughts into words or to make those words come out smoothly and correctly, but she was perfectly capable of listening to the news and hearing the talk in the clan. The treason and public execution of a Green Bone Lantern Man was uncommon and much discussed, and the recent attack on the Double Double casino had prompted concern of additional stunts by fringe anti-clan extremists during the holidays. Both incidents had made No Peak appear to be on the defensive, scrambling to protect its holdings. It was not a good image at a time when fears were running high that Kekon could become the next hotspot in the global conflict between Espenia and Ygutan. Meanwhile, the Mountain clan seemed flush with cash and its members were pleased that Ayt Mada had positioned her teenage nephew as her heir. Their enemies were spending lavishly on their own New Year's celebrations.

She walked toward Hilo and he offered her his arm. She held on to it, steadying herself and feeling shorter than usual next to him without high heels, which were impossible for her now. "Don't...let me f-fall," she said. Tonight was about appearances. The Kaul family needed to put on its strongest and most unified face. As the wife of the Pillar, Wen was expected to be the hostess tonight. Her absence would only be seen as proof of her infirmity. Hilo said nothing, but walked patiently with her as they went down the stairs, positioning her stronger left side by the railing so she could step down with her weaker leg first, one step at a time.

"Today's...our wedding anniversary. Remember?" she asked him, slowing down the enunciation of her words to avoid slurring them. They had been married on New Year's Eve, the day before Hilo had gone to save the clan by facing a death of consequence.

"Sure," he said, not unkindly, but the casual curtness of the single-word answer made Wen bite her lip. Her husband's moments of outright cruelty were infrequent and brief—a cold look, a cutting remark, a flash of hurt or anger in response to any reminder of her past dishonesty and how she'd nearly been killed because of it. Each one felt corrosive on her soul, but far worse was the deliberate distance he'd placed between them. Having lived so long in the uncompromising sunlight of Hilo's love, the absence of his affection was a lifeless and unending winter.

Wen had assumed this would happen eventually—he would find out how deeply and for how long she'd been getting involved in clan affairs behind his back and against his wishes, using her deficiency as a stone-eye to move jade, putting her own life at risk. Of course he would be angry, but she'd counted on being able to explain herself, to talk to Hilo in the way she'd always been able, to reassure and calm him so that he would come to understand, as she was certain he eventually would.

She had not gotten that chance. At the time she most needed to communicate, she'd been barely able to express herself, struggling to even string a few words together coherently. And Hilo—if only he'd been able to rage at her, to give free rein to his hurt and sense of betrayal, he might've burned away some of the force of his feeling.

But the shock of her near death and her need for care meant he hadn't been able to do that.

At the bottom of the stairs, Wen paused to take a deep breath and ready herself. Hilo put his hand on the small of her back and she rested briefly against the gentle pressure. They went together out into the courtyard to face the clan.

A wave of clasped hands rising to foreheads in salute and shouts of "Kaul-jen! Our blood for the Pillar!" greeted them as soon as they stepped outside. Wen swallowed and forced a welcoming smile toward the sea of faces—important people from every part of the clan seeing her by the Pillar's side for the first time in more than a year and a half. She began to tighten her grip on Hilo's arm, but restrained herself, not wanting to appear as if she were clinging to him for balance.

Hilo raised his voice and his free arm high in acknowledgment, calling out to the crowd, "Brothers and sisters, my order as Pillar tonight is that you'd better eat all this food and finish those casks of hoji!" Laughter, followed by someone, probably a Fist who'd already had too much to drink, yelling cheerfully, "I am ready to die for the clan!" Wen caught a glimpse of Shae, in a conservative but flattering black dress, rolling her eyes and taking a drink from her glass of wine.

Ordinarily, they would walk around the festively decorated court-yard, greeting clan members and accepting their respect-paying, but tonight Hilo led Wen to the main table and helped her into her chair. He took his seat next to her and remained there as guests came by in small groups to speak to him. He seemed to everyone to be in a good mood, attentive, smiling in his usual relaxed way.

Wen returned well wishes, nodding and smiling more than speak-ing. Every time she opened her mouth she feared she would make a mistake. She used to possess a nearly perfect memory for faces and names, a skill that had served her well in every social situation, but she had lost that as well. *Just get through this*, she told herself.

The cold spell had lifted, but it was still uncommonly chilly for what was supposed to be the start of spring. Women pulled shawls over bare shoulders, and evenly spaced gas lanterns cast warmth and flickering firelight shadows against the erected red canopies sheltering the tables. The children were brought out by their grandmother right before dinner was served—Niko and Ru in little suits and ties, Jaya in a yellow dress and white tights that she'd somehow already managed to stain at the knees. She ran ahead of her brothers and tried to climb into Wen's lap and onto the table. "Jaya-se, sit down properly," Wen scolded, struggling to wrangle her youngest and breathing a sigh of relief when Lina took the toddler to play on the swing set on the garden lawn with her little cousin Cam.

"You're looking well, Mrs. Kaul," said Woon's wife, coming over to sit next to Wen while her husband was engaged in conversation with a handful of senior Luckbringers. "I pray the gods favor you with good health this year."

"Thank you . . . Kiya," Wen said, relieved she remembered the woman's name. Her words came out slow but otherwise normal. "I hope . . . the same for you."

The woman's smile faltered for a moment but she pulled it back into place and nodded over at Hilo, who was walking around with Niko and Ru, proudly letting people exclaim over them and indulging Ru's talkativeness. He gave each boy a bag of candy coins and sent them off with the mission to hand them out to all the other youngsters. "You have beautiful children," Kiya said to Wen with a wistful smile. "You must be very proud about the future of the clan."

Wen wondered how much Woon Papi told his wife when it came to clan affairs, whether she knew how much financial strain No Peak was under. "The future of . . . the clan," she reminded Kiya, nodding to the huge party, "is bigger than that."

Anyone observing the large and well-dressed crowd tonight, the overflowing food and hoji, the gleam of jade on hundreds of wrists and necks, would think the No Peak clan was invincible. That was by design. There was an art to shaping people's impressions—a small room could be made to seem big, flaws in a house could be transformed into assets. On this night, she'd made No Peak seem too wealthy and powerful to fall. Reality was more complicated. Wen had seen newspaper photographs of the graffitied proclamation on the glass doors of the Double Double. Although she knew no one would dare attack such a large gathering of Green Bones, especially on the eve of a holiday, her eyes searched out the figures of the guards standing watch by the estate's brick walls and iron gates. No one was guaranteed anything—not them, not their enemies.

Shae came over to take her spot at the head table as the waiters began to bring out the main courses. Kiya stood briskly. "I'd better collect my husband and get back to our own seats," she announced, and pulled insistently on Woon Papi's arm, leading him away. Juen Nu and his wife claimed their places next to Hilo. Tar, who'd recently returned from a trip to Espenia, arrived with his lover, Iyn Ro. Both of them seemed to be several glasses of hoji into the party and were hanging on to each other, laughing loudly. Anden quietly took the seat next to Wen, letting out a relieved breath and giving her a small smile. "I'm glad I'm sitting next to you, sister Wen."

Wen was glad to be sitting next to Anden as well. He alone understood what she'd been through on that horrible night in Port Massy. He'd confided that he too sometimes woke thrashing from nightmares in which he couldn't breathe. She owed Anden her life, but he was still the unassuming young man she'd always known. When her words stuck or slurred, he never looked at her with pity or impatience. All the strain she felt while trying to talk to the other guests vanished, and ironically, when she was relaxed, she had barely any trouble. "How's medical school?"

"It's a lot of work," he said ruefully, but didn't offer further complaint.

Wen tried to encourage him. "I've heard the first year is the hardest."

Anden nodded. "There's so much material in the first year, and you have to learn to think of jade abilities in a completely different way. I hope this next year will be a little easier." He saw Wen hesitating to pick up the soup ladle and reached for it himself, spooning the seafood soup into a bowl for her. "Sometimes, I wonder if it's worth it," he admitted, "but if I fail at this, there's nothing else I can do that'll be of any use."

"Anden," Wen said sternly, "you sh-shouldn't say that. Think about what you did even while living with . . . with . . . without jade in a foreign country. Growing up, everyone made you think your worth was about jade ability, when it's . . . it's obviously because of who you are as a person. Your cousins know that by now, even if you were to drop out of medical school tomorrow." She was so adamant about making her point that she barely noticed the triumph of speaking several sentences together with so few stumbles.

Anden flushed and seemed suddenly engrossed in pushing the shrimp on his plate around in a puddle of garlic sauce. "Thank you for saying so," he said after a moment. "I hope you're right."

"Of course I'm right." Wen could understand why the young man might be feeling uncertain tonight. Anden's place at the head table confirmed to everyone that the Pillar had brought his previously disgraced cousin back into the family, but that didn't mean the heavily jaded warriors and wealthy businessmen of the clan weren't eyeing him with pity and skepticism. As much pity and skepticism as they likely felt toward her, Wen thought. So much bad luck near the top, they would murmur.

Hilo's joking orders notwithstanding, it seemed food continued to arrive at a rate faster than it could be consumed. The tables were laden with roast suckling pig, steamed fish in ginger broth, pea shoots with garlic, fried octopus. A band of hired drummers escorted the previous year out with thunderous energy, and two adjacent tables of Fists challenged each other to a drinking game. Niko, Ru, and Jaya came over to hug their parents good night before Hilo's mother took them inside and put them to bed. A veil of exhaustion was descending over Wen's vision, turning everything gauzy, seeping into each muscle and gumming up her thoughts.

She noticed that Juen and his wife had left the table some time ago, but now the Horn appeared behind Wen's chair and leaned over to speak to Hilo. "Kaul-jen. My wife went back to our house to put the kids to bed, but she rushed back to tell me the news that's on the radio." He spoke near the Pillar's ear, but had to raise his voice enough over the sound of popping firecrackers that Wen could still hear him. "An Ygutanian spy plane was shot down by Espenian fighter craft over Euman Island two hours ago. It crashed near the naval base. The pilot survived the landing but killed himself before he could be captured. The Ygutanian and Espenian governments are throwing accusations at each other over the incident and threatening war in the Amaric."

As Juen spoke, Hilo's expression did not change much outwardly, but Wen saw the light in his eyes shift from relaxed good humor to disbelief to anger in a few seconds, like a flame turning from red to orange to blue. "Of *all* the *fucking* times," he breathed through his teeth.

"The Royal Council is meeting in an emergency session tomorrow." Juen looked at the exuberant party in progress. The drummers had begun a countdown to midnight and another cask of hoji was opened. Even Shae seemed to be having a good time. "Should we tell people?" the Horn asked.

The muscles of Hilo's jaw flexed under the skin. "No," he said. "They'll find out soon enough. Let everyone start the New Year in a good mood." He muttered darkly, "It might be the only chance we have to call down good luck, and we're going to fucking need it."

"I'll speak quietly only to the senior Fists, then," Juen suggested. "So they're ready to keep order in our territories if people start panicking about an invasion."

When the Horn departed, Wen reached for her husband's arm. She intended to say, "You need to talk to Shae tonight, too. The Weather Man's office should align with our loyalists in the Royal Council before anyone makes a statement." Instead, her elbow knocked over a full cup of tea, spilling it across both their laps. When she opened her mouth, nothing came out—she felt as if the words had been shoved back down into her chest. She could only look up at Hilo helplessly.

Hilo used a napkin to blot up the tea soaking into their clothes. "You're tired." He stood and drew Wen to her feet. She leaned against him as they made their way back to the house. For the moment, no one was paying attention to them. Nearly all the guests had migrated to the lawn to wait for the display of fireworks that would soon go off over the city. Once inside, Hilo helped her up the stairs and into bed. His hands were gentle but empty of affection or lust as he unbuttoned her elaborate gown and removed it before tucking her under the blankets.

Tears of regret and humiliation stung the back of Wen's eyes. Years ago, when they were young lovers, she used to spend the entire day in feverish anticipation of Hilo's arrival. He would come to her at last, a young Fist burning bright with the high of new jade taken in some skirmish or duel. She would make him recount his victories as she undressed him, pressing her mouth to the gems freshly studded into his body. They would have mind-blowing sex, over and over again. How exhilarating it had been, the erotic power she'd possessed over him.

Hilo never brought up the fact that he now occasionally used charm girls, but he made no effort to hide it either. She'd smelled perfume on his clothes a few times, had found matchbooks and mint wrappers from the Lilac Divine Gentleman's Club in his pockets. She could accept that he paid to have his needs met elsewhere during her long recuperation, but it was too painful to imagine, as she did now, that they'd lost the ability to find solace in each other. On the occasions they attempted lovemaking, Hilo was not himself, either handling her with extreme care, as if afraid of damaging her, or else copulating brusquely, as if engaged in an angry chore.

Hilo turned off the bedside lamp and sat down on the edge of the mattress, staring out the window at the city skyline as the first fireworks exploded high over the roofline of Wisdom Hall and the tiered conical tower of the Triumphal Palace. The flashes of light briefly illuminated his darkened profile, sharpened the pensive lines that did not fit on the face she'd fallen in love with. Outside, the drums boomed and the people at the party cheered the arrival of the New Year.

When Wen was seventeen years old, she'd sharpened a kitchen knife and slashed the tires on her brother's bicycle. She never told Kehn, who gave one of the neighbor boys a beating over it. After that, Kaul Hilo came around their house in his car every day to pick up

Kehn and Tar when the three of them went around town together, junior Fingers fresh out of the Academy, hungry to win jade and earn their reputations. Every day, Wen walked out to the Duchesse to bid her brothers goodbye and to welcome them home. Hilo once laughed as he pulled up to see her standing in the rain. He said she was the kindest and most devoted sister he'd ever met, that his own sister would never do such a thing.

Wen had to admit with some chagrin that she had been a lovesick teenage girl, but she hadn't simply pined uselessly. A small thing like a ruined bicycle could change fate, just as a stone-eye could tip the scales in a clan war. She searched now for the one thing she could say that would make Hilo turn toward her, the way he used to when he rolled down the window and leaned across the seat with a grin. But she was too weary.

"I have to go back out there," Hilo said. Wen turned onto her side. She felt the pressure of him lift off the mattress, and when the next burst of light from the fireworks struck the room, it lit empty space.

CHAPTER

6

Shifting Winds

A special shareholder meeting of the Kekon Jade Alliance was convened six days later. After much political outrage and tense military posturing on all sides, the diplomatic crisis between Espenia and Ygutan had not escalated into all-out war, but in Janloon and other cities across Kekon, there had been panicked runs on groceries and basic supplies at a time that would normally be a period of rest and celebration. The Green Bone clans had been out in force preventing crime and looting in their own districts, but that was a short-term concern. The Kekonese people were contemplating the possibility of foreign invasion for the first time since the Many Nations War. Even clan leaders that hated each other knew they needed to meet.

Shae went over to the main house early that morning and found the children watching cartoons while Kyanla cleaned up after breakfast. "Auntie Shae, we're watching *Beast Taming Warriors*," Ru informed her, pulling her toward the sofa. An animated show about

Green Bone royal guards of a fictitious pseudo Three Crowns–era dynasty, who not only had fantastically overpowered jade abilities but who could summon and ride enormous magical beasts into battle. A number of action figures of the show's characters were scattered on the carpet in front of the television.

Shae sat down on the sofa to appease her nephew. "Where's your da?"

Ru shrugged, but Niko said, with sudden worry, "Do you think he'll divorce Ma?"

Shae was taken aback by the six-year-old's question, coming seemingly out of nowhere, but before she could think of how to respond, Ru jumped on his brother and began hitting him in the shoulders and stomach. "Stop saying that! They're not getting divorced, you stupid dogface!" Jaya toddled over, giggling curiously.

Niko shoved his little brother aside impatiently without hitting back, and Shae separated the boys to opposite sides of the sofa. "Ru, you shouldn't use words like dogface," she told him. Hilo came down the stairs, glanced briefly at the sullen scene, and said, "Turn off the TV, you should be getting dressed for school." He strode for the door. Shae followed him.

A trusted driver took them downtown in the Duchesse. Hilo lit a cigarette and rolled down the back seat window.

Shae forced herself to break the thick silence that now seemed to descend every time she was alone with her brother. "The boys are worried about you and Wen."

Hilo said, "Niko worries too much. Who's ever met a kid like that?"

"It's because he pays attention," Shae said. The boy often seemed inattentive, lost in his own thoughts, but then he would say something that made it clear he overheard a great deal of what the adults discussed. "He knows you treat Wen differently now."

"I treat her just fine," Hilo snapped. "I've always taken care of her."

Shae wanted to smack her brother. She and Hilo had hurt each other enough in their lives that she was well fortified against his anger, but that was not the case for her sister-in-law, who was one of the strongest-minded women she knew but who lived on Hilo's love like oxygen. "If you have to keep blaming *me*, go ahead. But hasn't Wen been through enough already? Everything she did, she did for you and the clan. Can't you even bring yourself to tell her that you understand that?"

Hilo snorted as he ground his cigarette out violently in the car's ashtray. "You're the last person on earth qualified to give relationship advice, Shae. What about you and Woon?"

The sudden reversal caught Shae off guard as completely as the swift parry and reversal of a blade attack. "What *about* me and Woon?" she demanded, inwardly cringing at the defensiveness in her voice. "We're colleagues and good friends."

Hilo's laugh was cruel. "And you think *I'm* the one not saying what needs to be said? Woon's smart in other ways, but I don't know why he tortures himself working for you. You should've told him how you really feel, or fired him already."

Shae's face grew hot. She forgot that she'd begun this conversation about Wen. "Not all of us spew our feelings out like shrapnel, Hilo," she exclaimed. "Woon and I are professionals, and besides, he's moving into another role next week."

"And why do you think he needed to ask for that?" Hilo said. Before Shae could reply, the Duchesse pulled up at their destination. "Forget it. Just concentrate on not letting Ayt Mada and every other Pillar in the room see what a mess we are." Hilo pushed open the door and got out of the car, leaving her fuming that he'd managed to get the last word. She forced out a noisy breath, then stepped out after him.

The Kekon Jade Alliance was headquartered in a three-story concrete block of an office building in the Financial District, within walking distance of the clan's office tower on Ship Street to the east and the Temple of Divine Return two blocks to the west. Its blunt, heavy appearance radiated government bureaucracy and never failed to remind Shae that for all the cultural, economic, and spiritual significance of jade, its production and distribution required thousands of people doing mundane work in cubicles. At the security desk, she and Hilo surrendered their talon knives to two Green Bone guards wearing the flat cap and sash of the Haedo Shield clan. They took the elevator up to the top floor in silence. Shae could Perceive the hum of her brother's aura deepening like a growl. He disliked KJA meetings under even the best of circumstances.

When they entered the boardroom, Ayt Madashi was already seated and talking to the Pillar of Six Hands Unity, the Mountain's largest tributary clan. Ayt did not glance over at the arrival of her longtime enemies, but her distinctive dense jade aura swelled momentarily as Hilo and Shae walked to their usual seats. The boardroom's massive circular table had assigned places and name plaques for each representative of the fifteen Green Bone clans that currently comprised the shareholder body of Kekon's national jade cartel. The arrangement suggested that every Green Bone clan was equal in this room, that they all shared responsibility for safeguarding and managing the country's jade supply. Nevertheless, the Mountain and No Peak, by far the two largest clans in the country, were positioned directly across from each other, with representatives of the minor clans seated closer or farther to one side or the other depending on their respective loyalties. Whoever had optimistically designed the room to promote a sense of egalitarian cooperation, Shae mused wryly, had underestimated the Kekonese propensity to signal status and allegiance at every opportunity. Four Deitist penitents in traditional long green robes stood silently against the walls, ensuring communication with Heaven and ensuring good behavior between the clans even in this most officious of conflict zones.

Hilo nodded in greeting to the leaders of the tributary Stone Cup and Jo Sun clans, who saluted him as he dropped into his seat. Shae lowered herself into the chair next to him and tried to look elsewhere, busying herself by taking out unnecessary papers, but her gaze was nevertheless drawn unwillingly across the table, to the disfigurement of Ayt Mada's partially missing left ear. The old scar across Shae's abdomen prickled. The Pillar of the Mountain glanced in Shae's direction. Their eyes met for one wintry second. Then Ayt turned back to her conversation.

Ordinarily, the seat to Ayt's left would be occupied by Iwe Kalundo, the Weather Man of the Mountain, but sitting in Iwe's place today was a barrel-chested man with graying bushy hair combed back from a ruddy complexion. He wore jade around his left wrist and in his right ear, and his expansive jade aura felt thick and syrupy to Shae's Perception. He seemed vaguely familiar; who was he? Why was he here instead of Iwe? If Ayt had replaced her Weather Man, she would've heard of it.

"He's one of the Kobens," Hilo said in an undertone, apparently noticing her confusion. "The kid's uncle on his ma's side." He meant the uncle of Koben Ato, the fourteen-year-old ward and presumed heir to Ayt Mada. The boy had recently changed his name back to Ayt Ato, no doubt so his family could cement that presumption. Shae recalled now that she'd seen a recent magazine profile of the Koben family, but she was surprised Hilo would recognize them. Then she remembered that a few years ago, Hilo had stoked infighting within the Mountain clan by ordering one of the Kobens secretly assassinated, so of course he'd studied them.

Was Koben's presence further evidence of Ayt elevating her nephew and his family? Perhaps, after years of being dogged by the question of succession, she wished to publicly signal that she was indeed planning for her clan's future.

Hilo and Shae were among the last to arrive. In minutes, the seats were full and the heavy doors were shut. Floor-to-ceiling windows on one side of the room faced south, letting in ample sunlight, but the air in the room felt clogged with jade energy. KJA meetings were held every quarter, but most clan Pillars attended only the annual vote that determined the KJA budget and set quotas for jade production, export, and allocation. They left the other meetings to their Weather Men. It was only under unusual circumstances that all the clan leaders had gathered on such short notice.

Not everyone present at the table was a Green Bone. Although the clans were controlling stakeholders, the cartel was state run and managed, so there were always other directors and government officials in attendance, along with their aides. One of the jadeless officials, the chief operating officer of the KJA and current chair of the board, Canto Pan, stood up and spoke. "Thank you, everyone, for interrupting your holiday week to be here. May the gods shine favor on each of your clans." That was patently impossible, Shae thought, since any divine favor shown to the Mountain would be disaster for No Peak and vice versa, but she kept the thought to herself.

"As you all know by now, the Royal Council has issued a statement that has been publicly supported by every Green Bone clan in the country," Canto said.

The Kekonese government had strongly condemned Ygutan for sending spy planes over Euman Island, which it unequivocally reiterated was Kekonese territory despite the long-standing presence of foreign military "guests." It urged a reduction in conflict between the two powers through diplomatic channels, but also promised that any attempt by either side to invade or control Kekon would be met with swift and overwhelming resistance. "While Kekon wishes for peace, we remain a nation of warriors unlike any other in the world," Chancellor Guim, a Mountain clan loyalist, had declared on the floor of Wisdom Hall. "Throughout our long and proud history, we've shed rivers of blood for our independence. We are more than capable of doing so again."

The Espenian government had not been pleased by the harsh tone of an official speech that was, as Hilo put it, "A long-winded, pretty way of saying *fuck both of you.*"

Chairman Canto said, "We all stand behind the chancellor's words, but the fearful public reaction we've seen in the past few days proves that we have to do more than voice support. With that in mind, I turn the floor over to General Ronu Yasugon, senior military advisor to the Royal Council, who has asked to speak to you directly."

Ronu stood and touched his clasped hands to his forehead in salute to all the Green Bone leaders. He wore gold general's stripes on the sleeve of his uniform and jade stones in the steel band of his wristwatch. Shae had met the general before and thought he must be an honorable man with a difficult job, having long ago traded his status in the Mountain clan for a career in the small and underappreciated Kekonese army.

"The Kekonese people were forced to confront reality this week— a reality that military commanders have been pointing out for years." Ronu stood stiffly as he spoke, hands at his sides. "We are a small country caught between two tigers. For all of Chancellor Guim's outward confidence that we can resist foreign aggression, the truth is that our modest defense forces would be swiftly and easily overrun. Espenia and Ygutan escalate their military spending every year, but we continue to treat our own armed services as a low priority. Yesterday, I stood in front of the Royal Council and urged them to pass an emergency funding bill that would provide much-needed equipment, training, and personnel to rapidly improve our military readiness."

"We can't outspend countries that are so much larger than ours," pointed out Sangun Yen, the elderly but sharp-minded Pillar of the Jo Sun clan. "Our national security has always depended on a general citizenry populated with trained jade warriors who are ready to fight. The Green Bone clans see to that."

"Nearly a century ago, that ancient wisdom failed against the might of overwhelming force, resulting in decades of Shotarian occupation," Ronu pointed out.

"We had a meek and cowardly king at that time, and too many small, uncoordinated clans," Sangun countered. "It was a dark period in our history, yet nevertheless, we overthrew the invaders. Despite all their sword rattling, would any country today, even a large and powerful one like Ygutan, be so foolhardy as to risk an invasion of Kekon? They had difficulty enough in Oortoko, a place with only weak people. We shouldn't let this fuss over the spy plane turn into alarmism."

Sangun's son, the Weather Man of their clan, nodded in agreement, as did several other Green Bones. Shae had read the opinions of numerous political and military analysts, nearly all of them agreeing that while Kekon was vital to Espenian interests in the Amaric, and thus a logical target for Ygutanian aggression, the cost of invading and holding the historically impregnable island was simply too high to be worth it.

General Ronu said, "The clans may have grown larger and

stronger, but we're facing a far different world than our grand-parents did. We're no longer the only nation with jade warriors. The Republic of Espenia equips its own elite soldiers with jade that we sell to them under the auspices of the KJA. Jade on the black market reaches Ygutan and its vassal states. An improved formulation of SN1 that carries less severe health risks has been in development for some time. The Espenians are calling it SN2, and it will no doubt find its way into the wider world as well."

Shae noticed that on the other side of the table, the man from the Koben family was nodding vigorously and looked as if he wanted to jump out of his seat to agree.

Ronu's jade aura sharpened, thickening at the edges as he spoke with urgent conviction. "Oortoko was only the first of the proxy con-flicts between the Espenosphere and the Ygut coalition. Kekon can-not escape being caught up in the Slow War. Unlike any other time in history, we have to prepare for the possibility of facing foreign sol-diers who can use jade as well as we do."

The general's grim pronouncements elicited vexed murmurs from around the table. Despite accepting the revenue from KJA-controlled jade exports without much complaint, at heart, the Kekonese disdain the idea of other races using jade. They console themselves with the knowledge that they remain better at it than anyone else, and that foreigners who wear jade must use addictive drugs and risk an early death.

Ronu could see that he'd struck a nerve. He raised a hand and plowed onward. "The Royal Council can commit to an increase in money and equipment, but only the Green Bone clans can pro-vide jade and warriors. I ask you, as the shareholders of the KJA and the Pillars of your clans, to make a bold show of support for the Kekonese military. We currently receive less than four percent of annual jade production. Announce a special allocation to increase that to six and a half percent, effective this year. And lift the long-standing barriers to recruitment by allowing graduates of martial schools to enlist in the military immediately after graduation."

A wave of muted muttering accompanied the prickly swelling of dozens of jade auras. It was a bold request, thus far unheard of. Granting it would elevate Kekon's tiny military to a status approaching that of the Green Bone clans. "Six and a half percent of the nation's jade is more than most clans at this table receive, and more than the allocation given to major institutions in healthcare and education," protested the Pillar of the Stone Cup clan. "Who do you propose we take from to give to the army?"

"I'm more concerned about this recruitment plan," said Durn Soshu, the Pillar of the Black Tail clan. "It's always been traditional for graduates to swear oaths to their clan. A year or two spent as a Finger is the best thing for all young people." This time, there were many nods of agreement, although Shae knew the argument was not really about tradition or the well-being of youth. It was by design that the clans took all the jade talent straight out of schools for their own ranks, with exceptions made only for the noble professions of medicine, teaching, and religious penitence.

General Ronu stood with his shoulders back and his expression firm, having clearly anticipated the skepticism he would face. "Unfortunately, that tradition is part of the problem, Durn-jen," he said. "Green Bones in the national military arrive as recruits with different amounts of jade—granted at graduation, passed down from families, or earned in the clan. They've been steeped in clan culture and carry those allegiances into their units. They expect to be able to wear jade however they like and to win more by challenging their fellow soldiers. It's hard to train them to prioritize corps above clan, to value squad cohesion over individual prowess. I'm speaking as someone who once had to go through that transition myself. To be frank, Green Bones raised and trained in a major clan make excellent fighters, but poor soldiers.

"When I enlisted twenty years ago, I was met with disbelief and disapproval from my family and fellow Green Bones," Ronu went on. "As a mid-rank Fist, I was told by everyone that I was taking a step backward. That attitude has barely shifted in over two decades. I'm asking you to help me change that. By permitting graduates of the martial schools to enlist in the military before becoming set in clan ways, you would send the needed message that it's as respectable and honorable to serve the country in uniform as it is to swear oaths of brotherhood to a clan."

Shae scrawled rapidly on her notepad. *We need to run the numbers on impact to both sides of the clan. Suggest delaying vote until next quarterly meeting.* She pushed the note in front of Hilo. He glanced down at it, but the Pillar of the Six Hands Unity clan spoke up first. "General Ronu is proposing a consequential change that we need time to fully consider. We ought to let each clan discuss the issue among its leaders and with its allies, and we can reconvene in a month or so."

Chairman Canto began to stand back up. "That sounds reasona—"

"Surely, if there was ever a time to act decisively to reassure the public of our national unity, it would be now." Ayt Mada's voice interrupted the chairman mid-sentence and mid-motion. Every pair of eyes in the room pivoted toward her. "I agree completely with General Ronu that the Kekonese military ought to be accorded more jade, more people, and more respect."

Up until now, neither Ayt Mada nor Kaul Hilo had said anything. As the Pillars of the two largest clans, their opinions mattered the most and all decisions made in this room would ultimately come down to them. It was typical for experts, officials, and the leaders of the minor clans to speak first if they had anything to say or wished to exert any influence on Ayt or Kaul. It would not have been any surprise if the meeting had adjourned with neither of them yet declaring a position. No one had expected Ayt Madashi to weigh in so quickly.

"Since my Weather Man is out of the country on important clan business and could not be here today, I've brought Koben Yiro with me," Ayt said. "Koben-jen is a successful businessman who owns a number of radio stations and also has relatives in the military, so he has a better understanding than most of us when it comes to the concerns of ordinary civilians and soldiers at this anxious time."

With his Pillar's permission, Koben jumped into the conversation like a horse given its head. "I'm honored to offer any insight I can to my Pillar and to the KJA," he proclaimed in a deep, resonant voice.

"The Koben family is a large, proud, middle-class family with many Green Bones and jadeless relatives. Like all hardworking and patriotic Kekonese, we care most for the safety of our families, our livelihoods, and our cultural traditions. What happened on New Year's Eve has stirred hate for Ygutan, but the ROE presence that has loomed over the country for so long can't be trusted either. In the end, we can rely only on ourselves." Koben grew impassioned and jabbed a finger in the air. "That's why people are looking to the Green Bone clans they trust, hoping for a swift and strong message of resolve."

Ayt made a small motion with her hand, quieting the animated Koben, who looked as if he could go on, but checked himself and settled back in his seat at once. "We should set an example for the Royal Council by acting unhesitatingly," Ayt declared with crisp authority. "As Pillar of the Mountain, I support increasing the allocation of jade to the armed forces so long as the redistribution is done fairly, and I agree that national military service should be among the choices Green Bones have directly upon graduation." She paused, then added, almost as an afterthought, "That is, if my fellow Pillars agree. This is such a substantial change that we shouldn't enact it unless we're all of the same mind."

No one answered her. Even General Ronu seemed to be stunned to have Ayt Madashi's immediate and unequivocal support. Every head in the room now swung toward Hilo, sitting partly slouched directly across from his rival. Shae scribbled urgently on the notepad between them: *STALL.*

"No." Hilo's answer landed with the weight of a boulder dropped into the middle of a stream. "I'm okay with Ronu getting the jade he's asked for. We can take most of it out of what we've been giving to the temples—how much jade do the penitents really need to talk to the gods anyway?—and the rest from the national treasury. But I won't change the way the graduates of Kaul Dushuron Academy take their oaths. If you want to do things differently at Wie Lon Temple School, that's your decision."

Ayt Mada didn't miss a beat. "Surely, Kaul-jen, we should act in a unified and selfless way at this time," she said with calculating righteousness. "It's only right that the two clans with the most jade and people should give some of what we have."

"The military is one arm of the country. The clans are the spine." Hilo's eyes narrowed as he fixed his gaze across the table. "And not every clan has resources to spare after glutting itself with barukan recruits and black market profits."

The dense blanket of jade auras shifted apprehensively as attention swung between the two Pillars.

"Baseless accusations will not stop your Lantern Men from choosing a wiser allegiance, nor will it obscure the fact that you're standing in the way of the country's needs, Kaul-jen." Ayt's aura radiated smug heat as she turned regretfully to General Ronu but spoke to the room at large. "Unfortunately, not every Pillar is capable of putting the nation first. It seems the KJA is not able to support your commendable efforts at military reform, General. Not unless No Peak is willing to reconsider."

Shae understood now why Ayt had agreed to Ronu's request so quickly and with no apparent doubt. The Mountain could afford to lose some Fingers to the military. No Peak could not. Any loss of warriors meant it would be less able to protect its properties from criminals and anti-clan agitators, or defend its territorial borders against the Mountain's recently increased numbers. No Peak was already falling behind financially, and any further loss of confidence on the part of its Lantern Men would accelerate its ruin.

Ayt knew that No Peak would have to veto Ronu's proposal, so the measure was certain to fail. She'd seized the opportunity to position herself and the supportive Koben family as leaders with Kekon's best interests at heart, while once again casting No Peak as self-serving and unpatriotic—by now, an old and reliable attack against them that she was not going to abandon.

Underneath the table, Shae bent the pen in her hand so hard it snapped into plastic shards. She was enraged by Ayt's unrelenting traps—and furious at Hilo. As he had in the Twice Lucky with Fuyin Kan, her brother had seen the danger even faster than she had—but diplomacy was not in his nature.

"Kaul-jen," General Ronu began, "what would change your—"

"You don't need a surge of graduates from the martial schools," Hilo said to him. "The foreigners have less jade and thinner-blooded recruits, but they manage to cook scraps into a meal. Don't tell me you can't use all the money and jade you've been given to do more with what you already have."

No one, not even Ayt Mada, could speak with Hilo's tone of commanding finality. General Ronu fell as stiffly silent as a junior Finger who'd been put in his place by a senior Fist.

"This has certainly been a robust discussion," said Chairman Canto Pan, bravely springing to his feet to defuse the tension and head off any further rejoinders. "One that I think should continue at the next quarterly meeting, after we've all had some time to examine the alternatives and consider how best to support General Ronu's priorities, which we all agree are worthy despite disagreements over how to achieve them." No one objected as Canto thanked Ronu and brought the meeting to a close. Hilo was out of his chair at once, striding from the room without another word.

Shae stuffed papers into her bag. She could hear Koben Yiro's deep voice chatting amicably with the Mountain clan's tributary allies as she got up and hurried out of the room. Catching up to Hilo alone in hallway, she grabbed his elbow, forcing him to stop and face her. "I *told* you not to refuse outright," she hissed. "You did so without giving us the time to come up with a counterproposal. The Mountain is going to spin this against us badly. They'll make sure we get killed in the press."

Hilo's face twisted into a glare. "I'd rather be killed by the press than *actually* killed when all of Ayt's schemes finally pay off." He glanced at the people coming out into the hallway behind them and leaned close to snarl a whisper near her ear. "You want to do this now, in front of our enemies? I'm fighting every fire they set, Shae, and you're fighting *me*. The Pillar's word is final—but you're not good at remembering that, are you?" Hilo pulled out of her grasp and headed for the stairwell, avoiding the possibility of elevator lobby conversation with anyone else. Shae's shoulders knotted with frustration as she once again watched him go.

"Kaul-jen," said a voice behind her. Shae turned to see a tall Green Bone with wire-rimmed glasses, whom she recognized as the Weather Man of the Six Hands Unity clan. He'd been sitting two seats to the left of Ayt Mada in the meeting.

Shae took a covert calming breath to smooth the agitation out of her jade aura as she nodded toward the man politely, searching her memory for his name. He pushed the down button for the elevator. "That was an unusually lively KJA meeting, wasn't it? Very different from the usual budget discussions," he said conversationally. "The country may be caught between two tigers, as General Ronu put it, but the Mountain and No Peak are the two tigers of Kekon. Whenever you roar, we smaller creatures run back and forth, trying to decide who's less likely to eat us."

The elevator arrived and the doors opened. The Weather Man of Six Hands Unity motioned considerately for Shae to enter first. She eyed him warily as she did so. She Perceived no hostile intent and had no reason to consider the man a personal enemy, but he was, after all, an ally of the Mountain.

The man entered after her and immediately hit the button to close the doors before anyone else exiting the KJA meeting could get onto the same elevator. Shae tensed. Alone in the close quarters of the elevator, her sense of Perception flared. The man's pulse had gone up. He was nervous, but it didn't show on his face as he stood beside her and calmly pressed the button for the ground floor.

"Where's your Pillar?" Shae asked. "Aren't you leaving together?"

"He'll be along shortly, after he's done with his conversations," said the Green Bone. "We're returning to Lukang tomorrow morning." Six Hands Unity was based in the second-largest city in Kekon, on the island's southern coast. A single drop of sweat made its way down the side of the man's forehead. "Have you been to Lukang before, Kaul-jen?"

"Yes, though not recently," Shae said.

"I think you'd be impressed by how it's grown. You should come visit, when you have the time." The man extracted a business card from his breast pocket and handed it to her. On one side of the white card was the man's name, Tyne Retubin, and his contact information. The other side bore the stamped red insignia of his clan, a mark that carried the authority of his Pillar.

"The Six Hands Unity clan would be honored to host you," Tyne said. "You can call me directly, as one Weather Man to another."

The elevator came to a stop. The doors opened and Tyne walked out without another glance or word. Shae hung back, so they would not be seen together. She understood that Tyne Retu had accomplished a dangerous task given to him by his Pillar.

Shae slipped the business card into her pocket, fingering the edge of it as if testing the sharpness of a blade. She kept her hand on it as she walked the five blocks to Ship Street with her mind racing. The rectangle of stiff paper might be another trap by the Mountain. Or it might be a reversal of fortune, an answer from the gods that could solve No Peak's most pressing problems and vault it ahead of its enemies. Six Hands Unity, the largest tributary clan of the Mountain, was interested in changing allegiance.

———————

Woon's going-away celebration was a casual affair held after work that evening in a private room at the Drunk Duck hoji bar. Many of the clan's Luckbringers came by to enjoy the food and drink and wish Woon well, but they didn't linger for long. Woon Papidonwa was respected in the office, but he didn't have many close personal friends on Ship Street. There was a price to be paid for being the Weather Man's deputy, a man answering daily to a younger woman, even if she was a Kaul.

Afterward, Woon said, "It was a nice party, Shae-jen. Thank you." He hesitated, then confessed, "I would drive you home as usual, but I've had a few drinks. I should wait awhile."

"I'll drive," Shae said. "You can clear your head in the car." Woon handed over his keys and Shae drove to the Kaul estate in his car. Splatters of intermittent rain turned into the season's first heavy downpour by the time they arrived. Shae waved to the guards as she drove through the gate and past the main house, parking Woon's car at the front of the Weather Man's residence. Woon got out with an umbrella and walked Shae to the door with it held over both their heads. She let them into the house and took off her coat while Woon shook out the umbrella.

"Wait until this rain lets up and you feel okay to drive," Shae told him.

She made a pot of tea and brought it over to the sofa, where they sat down together. Woon accepted the cup she poured for him. "I'll probably drive here after work next week without thinking," he said. "And I'll jerk awake at night in a panic that I forgot to remind you of something in your schedule."

"Don't do that," Shae laughed. Turning serious, "I'm glad you're moving on to a new challenge and will hopefully have more time to spend with Kiya."

Woon nodded and drank the tea. He hadn't said any more about his wife's miscarriage, or whether they were still trying for children. "How did things go this morning?"

After Shae told him what had happened, he leapt to his feet and paced around her living room. "Turning Six Hands Unity would be a huge coup," Woon said. "Their tribute payments alone would be a significant financial boost, not to mention the manpower we would gain in Lukang. That city is growing fast, and taking control of it would be a far bigger win than the Mountain turning Fuyin Kan or any number of our Lantern Men." Woon's brow creased, the dimple appearing on the right side of his forehead as his mind chewed through the same calculations Shae had made earlier in the day. "Could it be a setup? A way to lure us into disclosing information or letting down our guard in some other way?"

Shae said, "I've been wondering the same thing." Tyne had seemed sincere, though. He wouldn't have been so tense in the elevator if his clan's fate was not truly at stake.

Woon reversed the direction of his pacing. "We have to pursue this carefully and step by step to be sure it's genuine before we meet with their leaders or make any commitment. And of course, we'll have to keep it entirely secret. I'll start gathering all the information we have about Six Hands Unity, and making discreet calls to our own people in Lukang to learn more."

Shae nodded and began to agree out loud, then caught herself. "No," she said. When Woon stopped and turned toward her in bewilderment, she reminded him, "That's not your job anymore. You have other responsibilities now." She smiled, trying to soften her answer. "You'll have plenty of other things to deal with on behalf of the clan as soon as you start in your new position on Firstday. Leave this work to Luto."

Woon would be the clan's Sealgiver, a newly created role they'd decided was overdue and would free some of Shae's schedule from endless meetings. As No Peak's spokesperson and dedicated political liaison, he would be the primary point of contact with the Royal Council, foreign government representatives, tributary minor clans, and the press. It was a good job for Woon, who could be counted on to convey messages precisely, to understand and hew to the clan's priorities, to speak carefully to outsiders and never too much.

Her chief of staff had seemed pleased and grateful with the new assignment, but now he protested, almost angrily, "This is too big and important to leave to Luto."

"You helped to hire him, Papi-jen," Shae reminded him. "You said he was exceptionally clever and organized and you were confident I'd work well with him."

"Yes, but—" Woon struggled for a moment. "He's brand new to the job. I've been training him as much as I can, but it'll still take time for him to learn how to be your Shadow. Turning a tributary clan is risky and difficult—we can't afford any mistakes. At least let me stay involved and oversee Luto's work."

Shae laughed weakly. "Don't you remember why you asked to leave in the first place? You're supposed to be working less from now on, not more." She hadn't been able to forget what Hilo had said to her in the car that morning. *I don't know why he tortures himself working for you.* Woon was insisting on remaining her aide in some capacity because he believed she needed him—which she did. "All right," she relented, "but have Luto do as much of the work as possible, and don't let it take time away from your real job."

Woon nodded in relief and sat down beside her on the sofa. "No matter what my official title is, my real job is always helping you in whatever way I can, Shae-jen."

The walls of Shae's throat felt as if they were thickening. She moved closer to her friend and put her arms around him in an embrace. "You've already done enough," she said, resting her chin on his shoulder. "I've relied on you constantly for six years and given you so little in return. When we take our oaths as Green Bones, we say we're ready to die for the clan. But *living* for the clan, every day, the way you have, Papi-jen—I think that's even more of a sacrifice."

A pulse of emotion shivered through Woon's jade aura. He leaned into her and rested his hand on her arm where it lay against his chest. "I'm afraid that you think I'm leaving my post because I'm tired or unhappy being your Shadow. Or that I..." He hesitated. "Or that I expected something more from you. That's not true."

Pressure was building inside Shae's rib cage. She hated that Hilo was right about her not being able to say the things that needed to be said—but she had a chance to change that now, before it was too late. "I could never blame you for wanting your own life back when I'm the one who took advantage of you," she confessed, glad he couldn't see her face, but knowing he could Perceive the thudding of her heart. "After Lan was killed, I exploited your grief to pull you into working for me when we both knew you could've been Weather Man yourself if only things had been different. I couldn't have survived on Ship Street without you, but I'm sorry for what I did. And I'm sorry it took me so long to say so."

Her former aide was silent for so long that Shae began to fear she'd made an awful mistake by bringing up Lan's death. It was a sorrow they had in common, but that they held individually. She let her arms fall away from him, but Woon turned toward her and wrapped his large hands around hers, holding on to them so tightly that she could feel the throb of his pulse in his palms.

"I could never have been the Weather Man you are, Shae-jen," he said roughly, his face lowered. "I wasn't the Pillarman that Lan-jen needed. I did everything that he asked and kept his secrets without question. That was a mistake. I should've spoken up, I should've confronted him, I should've gone to Hilo-jen. But I didn't. I was happy to be promoted, and even though I knew Lan was injured and taking shine, I left him alone when he most needed me."

Woon raised his eyes. His normally steady gaze seemed as fragile as paper. "I deserved to die for that failure. I promised myself I would do everything for Lan's sister that I failed to do for him—I would support her in any way she required, but I would also challenge her, and I would never fail to say things that needed to be said, so she would be the Weather Man I couldn't be."

Woon lifted a hand to brush away the tear that had begun to make its way down the side of Shae's nose. "It wasn't long before being your Shadow wasn't a duty, but what I selfishly wanted to do. It hasn't ever been easy, and there were times I was afraid I'd fail you—but if I had to do it all over again, I wouldn't hesitate. The clan is my blood, but for me, the Weather Man is its master."

Shae could not find any words in reply. The rain had stopped and the sky outside was clear. Woon let go of her hands and turned aside to hide the embarrassment in his face. "I should go," he said, beginning to stand.

Shae grabbed his wrist and was on her feet before he could fully rise. "Don't."

A ripple of mutual intent surged through both of their jade auras like a static charge. "Shae..." Woon began, his voice strange. Then the space between them vanished. Woon's mouth was pressed over hers, or her mouth was on his—she had no idea who'd moved first. All she knew was that a flimsy wall they'd been holding up from opposite sides had collapsed between them. She was on her toes, arms wrapped around his neck. Woon's hands were buried in her hair, cupping the back of her head as their lips and tongues sought each other with a trembling, desperate abandon that lit every square inch of Shae's body.

She sank straight into desire like a stone into the center of a still pool. It had been a long time since she'd been with anyone, nearly four years, and that relationship had ended in unspeakable tragedy.

Yet kissing Woon now, there was no tentativeness, no self-conscious surrender or shock of strangeness, only solid familiarity and a tumbling release as natural as gravity. She felt arousal blaze through his aura like kerosene going up in flames, blinding her sense of Perception with raging heat.

Woon made a low, frantic noise. He kissed her harder and his hands pushed under her blouse, seeking the bare skin of her stomach and back. Their breaths became ragged. She tugged at his belt, unbuckling it and freeing his shirt.

With a jerk, Woon caught her hand and held it still, pulling his face back and staring at her with mingled lust and bewilderment, his chest rising and falling as he fought for control. His aura churned as she stared at him wide-eyed like a bird caught mid-flight.

"*Why?*" he managed to say. "Why now?" Shae couldn't tell if it was a question he expected her to answer. Woon turned his face away and shook his head as if he'd taken a blow to the skull and was trying to clear spots from his vision. "*Gods, why,* after all this time?"

Shae wanted to seize him, to kiss him again, to drag him back into heedless passion, but he was backing away, fastening his belt and tucking in his shirt, unable to meet her eyes. She was stunned by how wounded she felt. "You were my chief of staff," she said. "We had a professional relationship. And..." She thought back on Maro with a queasy stab of remorse. "And we were with other people."

"Are," Woon corrected her. "*Are* with other people. I'm married." He pressed the heel of his hand to his brow, rubbing out the dimple. Shae had seen him do the same thing when they were sitting in her office, discussing some thorny business issue, and the familiar gesture was suddenly disconcerting to see, here in her house, with both of their faces flushed and clothes askew. She was so accustomed to Woon being her stolid and unflappable aide that the past few minutes seemed as if they couldn't really have happened. But looking at his deep-set eyes and firm mouth, his broad chest and long arms, she felt an odd wonder that it hadn't happened earlier.

"I should go," he said, this time with conviction.

Numb fear swirled into a cold ball in the bottom of Shae's stomach.

She'd ruined their friendship, lost his respect and affection. She was terrible with men, she decided, truly the worst.

Wordlessly, she dug through the pocket of her jacket for his car keys and handed them over. When their fingers met, the ache of longing and confusion running through Woon's jade aura swept into her Perception, charging the momentary touch in a way that seemed wildly out of proportion considering the threshold they had crossed. "I'm sorry," she whispered miserably. "I shouldn't have—"

Woon cut her off with a violent shake of his head. "Don't," he said. He picked up the umbrella by the door without looking at her. His shoulders were bowed. "Good night, Shae-jen," he said, trying and failing to sound normal as he opened the door.

"Good night. Drive safely." She tried desperately to think of something to say to mend the situation before he was gone, but came up with nothing.

She stood by the window and watched the headlights of Woon's car come on. After they receded down the driveway and were lost to sight beyond the gates of the family estate, Shae dragged a blanket over her shoulders and sat in silence, drinking the rest of the tea, now bitterly oversteeped and cold.

CHAPTER

7

A New Friend

The Clanless Future Movement met twice a week in the Little Persimmon lounge. A year and a half ago, when Bero had first climbed the narrow staircase to the dim second-floor room, he'd found only three men playing cards. Tonight, roughly thirty people were clustered at the bar and around the small tables, drinking brandy and smoking, passing around pamphlets printed on thin gray newsprint paper.

Outside, the ever-present street noise of Janloon rose from a murmur to a torrent as people got off work and spilled eagerly into a warm spring evening, but the Little Persimmon's few windows remained purposefully closed. The hanging red lamps over the black bar and small dance floor shed a hazy and claustrophobic glow over cautious faces. The daring attack on the Double Double casino four months ago had attracted prospective revolutionaries, but it had also made it more dangerous to gather. The No Peak clan had not managed to find the perpetrators, but it had energetically shaken down every known criminal outfit in its territories and spread the word that it would reward anyone who led them to the culprits. The offer was great enough that Bero was tempted to turn in Guriho, Otonyo, and Tadino himself, but they would likely rat him out in return before they were killed.

Bero made his way to the cushioned red benches along the wall and sat down between Tadino and a young woman wearing a pink scarf. He placed the backpack he carried on the ground between his feet, careful not to let its contents clang against the floor. Tadino nudged him with a bony elbow and whispered, "You brought the stuff? We're gonna go out after this and fuck some shit up, right?"

Guriho and Otonyo weren't planning any new dramatic actions. They said everyone should lie low for a while and focus on growing the CFM's numbers. But Bero and Tadino still went out occasionally with spray paint and crowbars and did what they could to damage clan businesses, always moving around between neighborhoods and without any pattern. They were like fish biting a whale, but that was how it had always been for Bero. He was used to being on the bottom. Paint could be cleaned off and windows repaired, but it still cost the clans every time. More people would see that Green Bones could be defied, even by small fish.

Guriho stood up at the front of the room with a clipboard and began speaking into a microphone. Every time Bero saw the man, he thought of a goat in a sweater. The mixed-blood Oortokon had small eyes and a long, coarse beard. He breathed heavily and paced as he spoke, and he always seemed vaguely unkempt. But he was an energetic speaker. "Jade is said to be a gift from Heaven, but it's a curse from hell and its demons. All over the world, people use it for evil. Here in Kekon, everyone lives under the tyranny of the Green Bones. In Shotar, barukan gang members wear jade while committing extortion, murder, and rape. The Espenian military's jade-wearing soldiers turned Oortoko into a war-torn wasteland." Guriho shouted, "And who controls jade? Who sits at the top of this pyramid of violence and corruption? The Green Bone clans of Kekon."

The crowd muttered its angry agreement and people stomped the floor in applause. The woman next to Bero was sitting forward at the edge of the bench, listening intently. She was pretty. Very pretty. Too young and pretty for a crowd like this. She had short, sexy hair and milky skin and slightly parted full lips.

"Hey, what's your name?" Bero asked her.

She turned to him, her eyebrows rising with suspicion and curiosity. It was a reaction Bero was accustomed to receiving from women, on account of his youth and his crooked face, which made him ugly but also suggested there was something interesting about him, that he might've been deformed in a duel or battle.

The girl with the scarf hesitated. "Ema," she said.

Bero would like to believe she was flirting with him by giving him a diminutive personal name and not her family name, but he knew it was only because no one at these meetings wanted to identify themselves. The crowd was an unlikely assortment of people from disreputable backgrounds and those with radical agendas—"new green" who wore jade illegally, ex-barukan, shine addicts, students, and political extremists such as militant Abukei rights activists, anti-dueling proponents, and anarchists. There was even, Bero noticed with surprise, a foreigner sitting near the back of the room. Many of these people would hate each other if they didn't hate the clans more.

"I'm Bero," Bero said to the woman, even though she hadn't asked for his name in return. She'd gone back to listening to Guriho, so he nudged her and added, "I used to have jade myself, you know. A lot of it. I always had to be on the run from Green Bones. The bastards nearly killed me, more than once. They're the reason my face is like this. I'm lucky to be alive." He could tell from her brief, irritated glance that she didn't believe him. "It's true. Let's go for a drink later and I'll tell you."

Guriho glared in the direction of the whispering and Bero fell grudgingly silent. Guriho held up one of the pamphlets that were being passed around. "The Manifesto of the Clanless Future Movement," he declared, and cleared his throat before beginning to read in a solemn and self-important timbre. "In the eternal fight for a more just and equal society free from the predations of the power-ful against the weak, the goal of our noble struggle is the liberation of the world from the destructive influence of jade and the end of clannism."

"That sounds very good, philosophically," interrupted a gruff, accented voice, speaking above the rest, "but what can you actually do against the clans?" Everyone turned. It was the foreigner in the room who'd asked the question. He was a short, muscular man, with a large nose, hooded eyes beneath a heavy brow, and curly hair the color of rust. Despite being out of place in the gathering, he ema-nated a certain physicality and intensity of gaze that Kekonese people who are accustomed to Green Bones recognize as the sign of a formi-dable man, a man who can fight. The way he addressed Guriho was not aggressive, but there was challenge in his tone.

"If you listened before asking questions, you'd find out, ey?" Guriho said with a frown. "The clans might be powerful, but they can't exist without the support of the people. The politicians, the Lantern Men, every person who pauses to salute a Green Bone on the street—they all feed the system. We must disrupt the system! We'll start by creating a groundswell of support by opening people's eyes—"

"Yes, yes, you have a nice logo, newsletters, and meetings." The foreigner spoke Kekonese clearly enough, but the words were clipped both by his accent and his impatience. "But the Green Bone clans have jade, money, weapons, and people. It seems you don't have much of any of those things."

Tadino got to his feet. He worked at the Little Persimmon as a bar runner, and it was on account of his stepfather being friends with Guriho that the lounge was a safe place to hold these meetings. "I don't know how things work where you're from," he exclaimed heat-edly, "but here we don't rudely interrupt people, especially if we're strangers who haven't introduced ourselves."

The foreigner stood as well, causing those around him to lean away warily. Tadino tensed, but after a thoughtful moment, the curly-haired man merely spread his hands. "You are right," he admitted, more humbly. "I apologize if I offend anyone with my blunt questions. You can see I'm not from here. My name is Molovni and I came to Janloon because I heard about your worthy cause."

A murmur of suspicion and astonishment went through the Little Persimmon. Even Guriho blinked his small eyes and seemed unsure of what to say.

"He's Ygutanian," Ema whispered with excitement.

"You may not know this, but there are many outside your country who are sympathetic to the plight of the Kekonese people living under the boot of the clans. I came here to learn more about your struggle." Molovni sat back down, nodding to Guriho. "I spoke out of turn, but please, continue your speech. It is ambitious, no doubt, but even goals that seem out of reach can be accomplished with the help of the right friends."

CHAPTER

8

⌒

Speaking for the Family

Emery Anden tried not to be made nervous by the half dozen foreign doctors watching his midterm exam. *Pretend they're not here,* he told himself firmly, turning away as he rolled up his sleeves and fastened the physician's training band around his left wrist. It was a snug-fitting piece of leather, similar to the one he'd worn as a teenager at Kaul Dushuron Academy, but dyed bright yellow to indicate he was a student in the medical profession. There were five pieces of jade on Anden's band, far less than he'd handled in the past, but sufficient for what was required today.

Anden closed his eyes and took five long, even breaths, pacing himself through the familiar adjustment, then walked over to the sink to wash his hands. His body hummed with jade energy and nerves. Six years ago—a lifetime, it seemed—he'd sworn he would never wear green again. Now he was putting it on and taking it off so frequently it had become routine and indistinguishable from the other drudgeries and stresses of medical school. In his second year at the College of Bioenergetic Medicine, he was required to gain a certain number of hours of clinical experience, but when he'd walked into Janloon General Hospital for the first time to begin training, he'd briefly considered turning around and quitting his studies. He had bad memories of this place. Sitting in the corridor as a child listening to his mother's screams. Waking up feverish and jade parched after killing Gont Asch. It had taken weeks for his stomach to stop clenching when he walked through the hospital doors. Being put on the spot in front of watching strangers in an operating room caused the buried discomfort to sit up again.

Six Espenian doctors stood against the wall in loaned scrubs, holding clipboards and pens. One of them had a 35 mm camera in hand. They were visitors from the Demphey Medical Research Center at Watersguard University in Adamont Capita, here to study the use of jade in the healthcare field. The Espenians had decades ago seen the military usefulness of jade, but only recently had some of them become interested in how the Kekonese employed jade abilities in other areas. They watched Anden with such intensely expectant scrutiny that he was reminded of being under the glare of Kaul Du Academy masters during final Trials.

The patient—a fifty-seven-year-old man with a vascular tumor of the liver—had already been anesthetized and prepped for surgery. Anden's job was purely preoperative; the surgeon had not yet come into the room. Dr. Timo, Anden's supervising Green Bone physician, checked the man's vital signs, then nodded for Anden to proceed. "Take your time," he encouraged.

Anden studied the X-ray images once more, to remind himself of the shape and size of the tumor to be removed, then he stretched out his Perception and burrowed his awareness into the unconscious man's energy. The steady throb of the patient's blood and organs resolved into a map in Anden's mind. After a broad glance around the landscape of the body, he brought the focus of his Perception into the network of blood flow within the man's torso, navigating his way through what felt like layers of connected piping, of varying lengths and widths, all of them humming with the life they carried. Anden's eyes went unfocused, sliding halfway shut in concentration.

Being a Green Bone doctor required as much finesse in Perception as it did in Channeling. Anden had always been naturally talented at the latter, but honing the former required countless hours of study and practice. As a student at the Academy, being trained for a future as a Fist of the No Peak clan, he'd learned to think of Perception and Channeling as shield and spear, to be deployed with fast, deadly, and unsubtle force. Perceiving the murderous intent of an assassin and Channeling to stop a heart were entirely different from the delicate work he had to bend his jade abilities toward now. Standing next to the operating table, Anden brought a hand to hover over the upper right portion of the man's abdomen. He isolated the hepatic artery and Channeled into it with a light, steady touch, feeding in enough energy to form a clot cutting off blood flow to the malignant tumor. It took only a few minutes. Dr. Timo stood nearby, following the procedure with his own Perception and ready to take over if need be. When Anden stepped back and dropped his hand, the doctor nodded in approval, then quickly and expertly closed off a few of the smaller veins, completing the job and ensuring the entire tumor could now be surgically removed with minimal blood loss.

Ordinarily, the surgeon would now step in to perform the resection, but because of the observing foreign visitors, Anden stood around and waited for fifteen minutes while more X-rays were taken and developed, verifying with contrast dye that blood flow to the cancerous growth had been shut down. The Espenians gathered around the X-ray films, making notes on their clipboards and talking to each other. Anden was free to go. He maneuvered unobtrusively past the arriving surgeon and the operating room personnel, stepped out of the room into the hallway, and sat down on a nearby bench. He took off the training band and leaned his head back against the wall, closing his eyes and riding through the momentary disorienting nausea.

Most Green Bone medical professionals did not take off their green, but Anden was strict about only wearing jade when he was on the job, so to speak. Like penitents and teachers, doctors were technically beholden to no clan and it was considered a breach of aisho to harm them, but Anden's situation was unique. He was a member of the Kaul family, well known to be the man who'd killed Gont Asch, the former Horn of the Mountain clan. He'd also done work for his cousins in Espenia, participating in the assassination of the smuggler Zapunyo. Doctor or not, he was a Green Bone of No Peak, and he was not willing to take any chances, either with the possibility that he would be considered one of the clan's warriors or that he would become one, reacting with jade abilities in a lethal way. It would not take much for him to be pulled back onto the path he'd so adamantly rejected.

Anden opened his eyes to see a couple of the Espenian doctors standing in front of him with expressions of great interest. The taller of them, a man with a trim beard and a broad smile, said, "That was an impressive demonstration you gave us back there. Might I ask, where are you from? Are you... What are..." He gestured with open hands, obviously asking Anden about his ambiguous ethnicity.

The translator standing beside the doctors began to repeat the question in Kekonese, but Anden stopped him and replied in Espenian, stifling the urge to grimace at the foreigner's awkward inquiry. "My father was Espenian," he explained. "But I never knew him. I was born in Janloon."

"You speak Espenian quite well, though," said the doctor.

"I lived in Port Massy for nearly four years," Anden explained. "I earned a college degree and worked there before coming back to Janloon."

"Is that so?" The foreign doctor's smile grew. "Do you ever go back to visit Port Massy? Would you consider coming to Adamont Capita?" He fished a business card from his wallet and handed it to Anden. "My name's Dr. Elan Martgen. I'm one of the principal investigative team leaders at the Demphey Medical Research Center. After what I've seen during this trip, I'd like to invite some of the practitioners from Kekon to visit us and put on demonstrations of bioenergetic healing techniques to a larger audience of healthcare professionals at our annual medical conference this summer. Of course, we would pay for your travel and accommodations."

Anden stood up and accepted the card, although he was confused by the invitation. "I'm glad your trip has been useful, but you should invite someone else to your conference. I'm only a student and not qualified to practice yet." Anden was ahead of his class; the arterial flow blocking he'd done back in the room was not typically performed by students until their third year, but was nevertheless a fairly simple and routine task that an experienced Green Bone physician like Dr. Timo could probably do in his sleep.

Dr. Martgen exchanged glances with his colleague, a younger, shorter man with curly hair, then turned back to Anden and said, "We're hoping to invite a select group of jade healers, and we'd very much like you to be among them."

"Most of the people we've met here don't speak Espenian as well as you do," said the younger doctor. "And to be frank, many of our colleagues aren't convinced of the medical potential of bioenergetic jade. They don't consider it as valid as the physical sciences and believe there's little reason to study practices that have up until now been confined to a small, faraway island."

"You could help us change their minds," said Dr. Martgen.

Anden looked between the two men and understood now that he'd been approached because of his appearance and his part-Espenian ancestry. If the people at Demphey could see someone who looked Espenian and who spoke Espenian practicing what was viewed as an obscure and mysterious foreign healing art, it would go a long way toward advancing Dr. Martgen's cause with whatever peers, superiors, or stakeholders he needed to impress.

"I'm happy to stay in contact," Anden said in a noncommittal way.

"Please do think about it," said Dr. Martgen, shaking Anden's hand before rejoining the rest of his group as they were led away to whatever was next on their schedule. When they were gone, Anden studied the card for a moment before stowing it in his pocket.

Until now, he had not thought seriously about returning to visit Espenia and found the idea both unexpectedly appealing and vaguely uncomfortable. Upon returning to Janloon, Anden had come to the strange and sobering realization that he'd never lived in the city of his birth as an adult. In many ways, he'd spent the last year and a half reinventing himself. He was a medical student now, he had his own apartment in Old Town near the hospital, he was an uncle to three small children. Port Massy seemed far away, his years there almost like a dream, parts of it happy, others bittersweet, a few truly nightmarish. Sometimes he thought about the people he'd become close to there: his host family, Mr. and Mrs. Hian; Dauk Losun and his wife, Sana; his friends from relayball and the grudge hall. And Cory. He still thought about Cory, occasionally with active longing but more often with wistful curiosity, wondering what he was doing.

The Espenian doctors had extended an invitation to Anden not because of his nascent medical skills, but because of what he represented. It was the first time in his life that he could recall strangers viewing his mixed blood as an advantage, something desirable instead of unfortunate. At the clan party, Wen had told Anden his worth lay not in jade ability, but who he was as a person. He had not quite been able to internalize his sister-in-law's encouragement, but he had not forgotten it either.

Anden went to the Kaul house on Sixthday to speak to his cousins. The Pillar, the Weather Man, and the Horn were in a meeting behind closed doors, so Anden sat with his nephews on the living room sofa, reading picture books to them while he waited. Niko listened quietly, but Ru asked so many questions on every page that they barely got through a single story before Jaya woke from her nap in the other room, crying and grumpy. Anden loved the children, especially Niko, but couldn't help but feel grateful that he would never have to be a parent himself.

When the door to the study opened and Juen Nu came out, Anden knocked and went in. Hilo was at his desk with his head propped heavily on one hand. The papers spread in front of him contained charts and numbers with highlighted notes in Shae's handwriting.

Anden couldn't tell if the Pillar's decidedly sullen expression was on account of being forced to study the dense information, or in response to the messages they conveyed. He glanced up. "What is it, Andy?"

Anden knew from tense dinner table conversation that the Mountain was throwing around its weight and spending heavily to squeeze No Peak from every direction. When Lan had been Pillar, Ayt Mada had waged a campaign to weaken No Peak by encroaching on its territories. Now their enemies were relying on money and the press instead of spies and street criminals. This time, however, Anden wasn't a teenager waiting helplessly to join the war. He was an adult who'd been in the war already and had his own networks and influence.

"I want to take a trip back to Espenia," he told his cousins.

After he explained his request, Hilo lit a cigarette and rubbed his eyebrow with his thumb. "Some people in the clan want us to pull out of that country altogether, not get even more tangled up over there." Espenia was in the news all the time these days. The ROE was planning to expand its naval base on Euman Island to bolster its strength in the region against Ygutan. The decision had drawn considerable public opposition in Kekon.

"It's worth a try, Hilo-jen," Anden said.

Shae was sitting in one of the armchairs with her arms crossed, some distance from Hilo. The Pillar and the Weather Man were still on poor terms. She gave Anden a wry smile. "Do you remember how upset you were when we first sent you there? And now you're asking to return." She said to Hilo, "Anden should go. Revenue from our Espenian businesses is saving us right now, but it's an ongoing problem that the two countries don't trust or understand each other. If there's anything we can do to change that, even in a single field like healthcare, it may help us."

Hilo didn't look entirely convinced, but he said, "All right, cousin. You can go and speak for the family."

At that moment, Niko shouted, "No!" The boy was standing in the partly open doorway to the study, his small fists clenched by his side. "Espenia is the place where Ma got hurt. Uncle Anden shouldn't go there. You can't make him!" The adults stared at Niko in astonishment.

Anden went to the six-year-old and crouched down in front of him, placing his hands on his nephew's trembling shoulders. "Niko-se, I asked to go," he reassured him. "It'll be a short trip, and not for anything dangerous. Of course, there's always some risk, but families like ours can't afford to not take risks."

———————

The Weather Man made phone calls to the dean of the College of Bio-energetic Medicine, impressing upon him the No Peak clan's interest in the matter, so the trip was arranged with impressive alacrity. Two months later, Anden and three of the best physicians on the college's faculty, including Dr. Timo, arrived in Adamont Capita. AC was an old city, with narrow cobblestone streets and historic brick buildings. White marble monuments were tucked around every corner behind glass office towers, imposing government institutions, and foreign embassies. Anden had never been to the capital of the Republic of Espenia before, even though it was only three hours away by bus from Port Massy, where he had lived and worked for nearly four years. It hadn't occurred to Anden to explore other cities, not when Port Massy had already seemed huge and strange and overwhelming to him as a nineteen-year-old.

Now, however, he appreciated the opportunity to act like a tourist. Dr. Martgen and the staff at the Demphey Medical Research Center were welcoming hosts, housing Anden and the three visiting Green Bone doctors in a well-appointed hotel and touring them around the Watersguard University campus and the major city sights when they weren't busy meeting people and doing demonstrations for intrigued researchers. As a mere student, Anden didn't lead any of the meetings or presentations, but he assisted on several occasions and acted as the translator for the entire group. At the end of the five-day conference, he felt far wearier from thinking and speaking in two languages, and navigating the opposing customs of both the visiting and hosting parties, than from any exertion of jade abilities.

Dr. Timo and the other doctors flew straight out of Adamont

Capita back to Janloon the morning afterward. Anden stayed. He took a taxi from the hotel to the federal Industry Department, which was housed in a fortress-like rectangular building down the block and across the boulevard from the National Assembly. As he waited on a sofa in the elevator lobby, he gazed out at the seat of government—an enormous white structure rising in square tiers to an imposing pyramidal peak, its sides lit with floodlights that changed color at night. Its straight lines and perfect planes seemed stark and forbidding to Anden, closed and inscrutable.

A secretary came out to meet him. She apologized for the wait and escorted Anden to a corner office on the seventh floor. The nameplate on the door read: KELLY DAUK, DEPUTY SECRETARY. Anden went in.

Cory's eldest sister, Dauk Kelishon, bore resemblance to her father and her brother in the shape of her face and mouth, which was lifted in a polite smile as she stood to shake Anden's hand. She motioned him into a chair across from her desk. "Mr. Emery, I presume?" The deputy secretary was perhaps forty years old, dressed in a chalk-gray skirt suit, black blouse, and pearl necklace. An immaculate chin-length bob framed her face. In her bright but stiff professional manner, she was wholly unlike her gregarious younger brother.

Anden said, in Kekonese, "Ms. Dauk, thank you for agreeing to see me."

The woman swiveled her chair sideways, leaning one arm on the desk and crossing her legs as she studied Anden, her polite smile unchanged. "I agreed to this meeting as a favor to my parents. My mother can be extremely insistent," she said, replying to him in Espenian. "According to them, you're a representative of one of the Kekonese clans. I'm afraid I'm unclear as to what that has to do with me and the Industry Department."

She was not being rude exactly, but Anden was a little surprised by the aloof tone and the switch back into Espenian. He reluctantly followed her into his second language, speaking more deliberately out of necessity. "I'm visiting Adamont Capita for other reasons, and while I'm here, I'm hoping to make some friendly connections in the Industry Department, on behalf of the Kaul family of No Peak."

"Is that the name of the clan you work for?"

Anden hesitated, unsure if she was being serious, or feigning ignorance in order to test him for some reason. "The No Peak clan is
one of the two major clans in Kekon," he said slowly. "We control
nearly half of the capital city, as well as jade mining, and businesses
in many industries across the country. Roughly half of the seats in
the Kekonese Royal Council are occupied by legislators who are
loyal to us. The Pillar of No Peak is my cousin. My other cousin runs
the business side as Weather Man. They've asked me to speak for
the family."

The deputy secretary replied, "Mr. Emery, my job here in the
Industry Department is to work alongside Secretary Hughart on
issues of domestic economic policy. Bioenergetic jade falls outside of
our purview."

"I understand," Anden said, "but jade isn't the clan's only concern.
We want to do business in Espenia and to build partnerships here,
but there are barriers to us being able to do so. We would like to advo-
cate our position with policymakers in the Espenian government. Of
course, my family converses with the Espenian ambassador and the
International Affairs Department, as well as the ROE military on
Euman Island, but we also need friends here in Adamont Capita who
have influence with the premier and the National Assembly."

Anden paused. Perhaps it was Kelly Dauk's persistently neutral
expression, or the fact that he did not normally speak in Espenian
at such length and in such complexity, but Anden felt as if the words
were coming slower and with increasing difficulty. He wondered if
he was muddling them, not making himself properly understood.
"I greatly respect your family, and I consider your parents and your
brother to be good personal friends."

Cory's sister regarded Anden for a long moment. "My parents," she
said at last, "are from an older generation of Kekonese immigrants
who still uphold traditional honor culture values revering clans and
jade. I'm sure that even in their old age, they're still bossing around
the neighbors in their little patch of Southtrap. They placed expectations on my brother ever since he was a little boy, to train to wear

jade, to be 'green,' as they say." Her polite smile grew but held no warmth. "I can see why they've taken such a liking to you, a young man from the old country."

Anden searched for a response, but before he could find one, Kelly Dauk laced her hands and said, "My parents and their friends complain endlessly about the government. They think it's the height of tyranny and racial prejudice that civilian ownership of jade is banned. Your clan associates in Kekon want to make money selling bioenergetic jade in this country, and wish to see that prohibition relaxed or overturned altogether. Am I understanding things correctly?"

Anden was taken aback and without thinking, he reverted back to speaking in Kekonese. "It's not about selling jade," he said. "Don't you want to see such an unreasonable law, one that targets and harms Kekonese people, removed? Especially when you come from a Green Bone family yourself?"

"I don't make the laws, Mr. Emery," Ms. Dauk responded, still speaking in Espenian. "But unlike some people, I do abide by them."

Anden protested, "My family would never expect or ask you to do anything difficult or inappropriate that might harm your own position. My only hope in coming here today was that you might be willing to speak to my cousins, to introduce them to Secretary Hughart and other top officials in your department, and maybe give us some valuable advice on how to go about lobbying the right people in government, since you have so much experience with how things work here in Adamont Capita. I would ask you for this favor, as a friend of your family, and as one Kekonese to another."

"I'm Espenian, Mr. Emery," said Kelly Dauk. "And an officeholder in the federal government." She rose from her desk in polite but firm dismissal, and her secretary opened the door to show Anden out. "If you want to push your clan's agenda, you'll have to go through other channels."

———

Anden took the three-hour express bus from Adamont Capita to Port Massy the following afternoon. He stared out the window at the familiar skyline of the metropolis, nursing a sense of profound and uneasy nostalgia as the bus crossed the Iron Eye Bridge and passed under the shadow of the famous Mast Building. Mr. Hian met Anden at the bus station in Quince and welcomed him as if he were a returning son, embracing him and remarking that he was looking healthy.

They went straight to the Dauks' home, where Mrs. Hian and Dauk Sana were preparing an enormous welcome dinner of broiled pepper fish, braised greens, five mushroom soup, and fried short noodles. Dauk Losun sat Anden at the head of the dinner table, and throughout the evening, Anden was plied with food and conversation. Old friends and acquaintances came by: Derek, who now owned and ran an auto repair shop; Sammy and two other Green Bones named Rick and Kuno; Tod, now a Navy Angels corporal, home on leave; Tami, who was working in a dental office and doing freelance photography. All of them were friendly but a little reserved, speaking to Anden less casually than they used to when he'd lived in the Southtrap neighborhood, as if he'd aged ten years during the past two, and was now older instead of younger than they were. Anden felt conscious that he was being treated so well not simply because people remembered him fondly from when he was a student boarding with the Hians, but because he was a representative of the No Peak clan, an important visitor from Janloon sent by the Kaul family.

Perhaps they'd also come out of curiosity, because they'd heard stories: He'd planned the assassination of an international jade smuggler; he'd nearly been executed by the Crews along with Rohn Toro; he was secretly a powerful Green Bone who'd put on jade to bring a woman back to life.

Cory arrived after dinner, claiming that he'd had to work late at the office. As usual, his entrance caused a minor stir of friendly shouting, backslapping, and laughter. He said hello to half a dozen people and came over to shake Anden's hand, smiling as if they were old but distant friends. He had a petite Espenian woman with him, whom he introduced as "Daria, a friend of mine from law school." Anden felt his mouth go uncomfortably dry. He had a hard time keeping up his end of the conversation when Cory asked him how he was doing, how he liked being back in Janloon, how his studies were going.

"I never pegged you as a doctor, Anden, though I'm sure you'll be toppers at it," Cory said with a laugh that was only slightly forced. "Goes to show what I know, right?" He used Anden's name and did not once call him *islander* in the affectionate, teasing way that he used to. Anden wondered painfully how Cory did it—how was he able to forgive and move on and act so normal?—but then again, his sunny disposition and easygoing nature were things Anden had admired about him and found endearing. Cory didn't stay at the house long, departing with his friend after less than an hour and leaving Anden sad and relieved.

At the end of the evening, as Mrs. Hian and Dauk Sana cleared dishes and tidied the kitchen, Dauk Losun stretched and said to Anden, "I'd like to go for a walk around the block to work off some of that meal. Will you join me?"

It was a warm summer evening, with enough humidity hanging in the air to threaten a thunderstorm later in the night. As Dauk and Anden strolled through Southtrap, people touched their foreheads in greeting, dipping into shallow salutes toward the man they called the Pillar. Anden slowed his stride to match Dauk's leisurely pace.

"I'm sorry, Anden, for the way my daughter treated you," Dauk said. "In truth, I'm ashamed."

"There's no need to apologize, Dauk-jen," Anden said.

"Kelishon is very independent, very driven," Dauk explained, shaking his head. "She's always chased achievement, and she wants nothing to do with what she sees as the old Kekonese ways, her parents' ways. So she lives by the rules of Espenia. Now that she's reached a high position in government, I hoped she would remember where she came from and be willing to help her own people, but it seems she's even more rigid and aloof and set on distancing herself from us."

"Some people turn out differently from the rest of their family, regardless of blood or upbringing," Anden pointed out. "It's no one's fault." He wasn't going to embarrass Dauk by showing any of his own disappointment, though he couldn't help but wonder how it was that in Espenia someone who was faithless to their family could still rise to such a high position in society.

"Maybe I should've tried harder to train my daughters to be Green Bones," Dauk said with a sigh. "When I was young it simply wasn't done, unless they were lay healers like Sana, or maybe penitents. Now you tell me there are women Green Bones in Kekon, including your own cousin, and even a woman Pillar. The world changes so quickly, and I'm an old man."

"You're not old yet, Dauk-jen," Anden said. Dauk was sixty-four and still possessed a hearty appetite and energetic laugh, although in the two years since the death of his good friend Rohn Toro, the Pillar of Southtrap seemed to have indeed aged quickly. There were heavy lines around his mouth now, his hairline had receded even farther, and Anden had seen him swallow pills with his meal.

"You know the old saying: 'Jade warriors are young, and then they are ancient.' I know which side I'm nearer to," Dauk said wryly, clasping his hands behind his back as they walked. "I'm sorry I couldn't be of more help, but even compared to those thugs in the Crews, we Kekonese have little clout in national politics in this country."

"My cousins appreciate every effort you've made on our behalf, Dauk-jen," Anden said. "The truth is that things aren't going so well in Kekon. The Slow War has worsened relations with the ROE and our enemies are using that against us, even as they attack us in many other ways. We need our businesses here in Espenia, so my cousins are looking for any leverage to improve our position, even long shots."

Dauk pursed his lips. "I would also like nothing more than to see the ban on jade lifted, but I'm not sure that's possible. The No Peak clan is powerful, but it can't change the attitudes and laws of an entire country of people who don't understand us."

After being so rudely rebuffed the previous day, Anden was inclined to agree with Dauk, but he said, "Only five years ago, we thought there was nothing we could do against the Crews except take their abuse, but look at how things have changed. Who's to say what could happen in the future?"

"Spoken with the optimism of a young man." Dauk snorted, but he smiled in the dark.

Anden asked, "Have you had any more trouble with the Crews lately?" Crewboys and Green Bones in Port Massy maintained a violent hatred for each other. The local Crews believed the Kekonese had deliberately sold them bad jade and were to blame for the ruin of Boss Kromner's Southside Crew and the resulting bloody and sensational Crew wars and police crackdown. The Kekonese would never forgive the brutal execution of Rohn Toro.

Dauk Losun's expression sobered. "The Crews are wounded, but wounded animals are still dangerous. We have more jade and more trained Green Bones than we used to, so the Crews have reason to respect and fear us. We have No Peak to thank for that, but it's possible to go too far, to expose ourselves to danger by acting too openly and forcefully." They'd arrived back at the Dauks' house. Anden could hear the Hians' and Sana's voices, but the Pillar didn't go inside yet. He paused on the walkway up to the door and rubbed a hand over the back of his neck before turning to face Anden, his brow furrowed as he chose his words.

"Your cousin, Kaul Hilo, sent his own Pillarman to help us punish the Southside Crew. They found and executed the men who murdered my good friend Rohn Toro and who nearly killed you and your sister-in-law."

Anden did not reply. He'd known Maik Tar had made trips to Espenia on Hilo's orders, and the purpose was of no surprise. However, Dauk's expression held no satisfaction; his face was unsettled. "Willum Reams's body was never found, but the two Green Bones who were with Maik that night, they told me what happened. Anden, it was too terrible. Maik went too far; there was no need for it."

On New Year's, as the fireworks were going off, Tar had drunkenly thrown an arm over Anden's shoulders. "I want you to know, I sent those spenny bastards to the afterlife screaming the whole way. For you, kid." He'd clinked Anden's glass of hoji with his own, then wheeled off into the party.

Dauk blew out a troubled breath. "It's only natural to take

vengeance for our friends and to punish our enemies, but if we're connected to horrible crimes, we'll only be seen as killers, and jade will always be covered in blood. You come here to tell me that No Peak wants to grow its businesses and build its influence. Acting in ways that make us seem even worse than the Crews—that goes against what you're hoping for."

Anden said quietly, "Dauk-jen, you're right to bring this up."

"You've lived here, Anden; you understand that in Espenia, we Green Bones have to tread much more carefully than in Janloon. As the Crews have gotten weaker, the police have turned their attention on us. They look for any excuse to arrest people in Kekonese neighborhoods and search them for jade, even if no other crime has been committed." Dauk grumbled, "It does keep Coru busy—he's had no shortage of defense counsel work. But it hurts our community. Young people these days, why would they want to train in the jade disciplines if it means facing persecution and living like outsiders? They choose instead to abandon their heritage to fit in like proper Espenians. Anden, my greatest fear is that in twenty years, there will not be any real Green Bones left in this country."

A strong breeze stirred the humid summer night. Somewhere in the distance, a siren rose and fell. Tomorrow, Anden would be on a plane headed home, with no tangible victories to report to his cousins, nothing that would materially help No Peak. The foreboding in Dauk's voice deepened his feelings of futility. He respected Dauk Losun and trusted his judgment, though he resented the man as well, for forcing him to give up Cory. "Dauk-jen, I hope you're wrong," Anden said.

Dauk reached under the collar of his shirt, closing a hand around the circular jade pendant he wore on a silver chain around his neck. "I hope so too. I worry about the future, but I can only do what I've always done, which is to talk to people reasonably, for the good of the community, while I still can." The Pillar of Southtrap clapped a reassuring hand to Anden's shoulder and led them back into the house to join the others. "It's good to see you, Anden. You were always too green for this city, but I'm glad you visit."

CHAPTER
9

The Seventh Discipline

the sixth year, ninth month

Of the numerous Green Bone training facilities in Janloon, the Seventh Discipline gym had a reputation for being the most welcoming to outsiders. Located in the Yoyoyi district, it was a No Peak property, but the owner, a retired clan Fist, charged only a modest additional fee to visiting practitioners, including Green Bones from tributary and neutral clans, travelers from as far away as Espenia, independent coaches who used the space to work with their clients, and even a few barukan immigrants with no sworn allegiance but who were trusted to behave themselves.

The training space was large and well-equipped, reputedly second only to the Mountain-controlled Factory in Spearpoint. A framed motivational quote over the entrance read, *Perfection of character is the seventh discipline of the jade warrior.* When Hilo walked inside the building on a Firstday afternoon, there were only a few of the clan's Fingers on the main training floor, sparring with dulled moon blades and practicing Lightness with weight vests. When they noticed the Pillar's entrance, they paused and saluted him, calling out, "Kaul-jen!" Hilo waved in acknowledgment but did not stop to chat.

On the mats at the back of the building, Master Aido was working on talon knife drills with a man whose unusual reputation had traveled up the clan's grapevine all the way to the Pillar. The stranger was shorter than Hilo had expected, fit and strongly built, with close-cropped dark hair and a shadow of facial stubble. His jade aura hummed with the strain of exertion but revealed little else—the psychic equivalent of a resting poker face. Hilo could see at once that the man possessed the confident physicality of a skilled fighter, but he moved differently from anyone else in the gym. He did not employ the usual techniques or classic combinations. As he defended and countered each of Master Aido's attacks, he seemed to rely surprisingly little on his jade abilities, slipping in Strength and Steel and sometimes a short Deflection in a fast and stealthy manner, as if trying to hide them behind movements that were simple and obvious. Green Bones often awed rivals and onlookers with raw jade ability—powerful Deflections, leaps of Lightness—especially in public duels where the outcome was not intentionally fatal. This man's constrained actions were entirely efficient and practical. Jade was a slim weapon, a final resort, drawn quickly to neutralize the enemy, but that was all. It was a modern soldier's approach to jade combat. IBJCS—the Integrated Bioenergetic Jade Combat System.

"Master Aido," Hilo said, stepping onto the mat. "Introduce me to this student of yours."

The old trainer seemed surprised to see the Pillar here. The Kaul estate had its own training hall and courtyard where Hilo normally met his private coaches. Aido wiped his brow and said, "Kaul-jen, this is Jim Sunto." To the other man, "Jim, this is Kaul Hiloshudon, the Pillar of the No Peak clan."

Sunto looked between Hilo and Master Aido. Hilo's eyes fell upon the man's jade: two green dog tags worn on a chain around his neck. They hung next to a second, shorter chain with a triangular gold pendant: the Truthbearers symbol of Mount Icana. Sunto appeared to be in his late twenties. Younger than Hilo. At thirty-four, it surprised Hilo to find so many people were now younger than him.

Sunto nodded warily but did not salute. "I know who Kaul Hilo is."

Hilo said to Master Aido, "I trust I didn't interrupt your session."

"We were just finishing," said the trainer, taking the hint. "Jim, I'll see you this time next week. Kaul-jen." He saluted the Pillar and tactfully withdrew, leaving the two men standing on the mat alone.

Sunto walked to a nearby towel rack. He wiped the sweat off his face and slung the towel over the back of his neck. "Is there a problem with me training here?" he asked over his shoulder.

No Green Bone in Janloon, friend or enemy, would speak to the Pillar of the No Peak clan in such a curt and rude way, turning his back, not saluting or showing proper respect. "No problem," Hilo said. "It's only that I heard there was an Espenian Navy Angel living and training here in Janloon, and I had to come see for myself."

"Ex-Angel," Sunto corrected. "I left a couple years ago."

"Word has gotten out among my Fists that you're a serious sparring partner," the Pillar said, strolling a partial circle around Sunto with his hands in his pockets. "They say you broke Heike's nose."

"An accident he deserved." Sunto spoke Kekonese fluently but with an obvious Espenian accent. "He got carried away throwing Deflections and didn't keep his guard up."

"You've been teaching classes around here."

"A few seminars. IBJCS basics, small arms concealment, nonlethal submission, that sort of thing. People have asked, and it's extra money for me." Sunto remained standing in place casually, but the suspicion was naked in his voice, and he kept glancing from side to side, as if expecting to see the clan's Fists closing in from all directions.

Hilo said, "Let's go somewhere to talk, Lieutenant."

"I'd rather talk right here, thanks."

"Suit yourself." Hilo dropped a hand onto the man's shoulder.

Sunto reacted at once, twisting away from the hold, seizing and locking Hilo's wrist. Hilo's other hand was already moving, Channeling into the man's right lung. The strike was far from the heart and would not do any permanent damage, but it would be terribly painful, collapse Sunto to the ground, and make it hard to breathe for minutes.

To Hilo's surprise, Sunto dropped the wristlock, Steeled, and cross-Channeled in one quick twist of his upper body, dispelling the attack and sending a muscle-cramping pain shooting into the socket of the Pillar's shoulder. The blast to Sunto's chest was still enough to double him up coughing, but despite having the air knocked out of him, the man did not hesitate; he brought a shin up into Hilo's groin.

Even Steeling didn't stop Hilo's eyes from watering in agony as he fell to one knee. Sunto dropped a knife-hand strike toward his carotid artery. Hilo drove himself sideways; the incapacitating blow glanced harmlessly off his shoulder as he hurled a precise horizontal Deflection that clotheslined Sunto at the waist and knocked him to the ground a few feet away. Regaining his footing, the Pillar sprang Light and landed with his full crushing Strength, not on top of Sunto's torso, but next to him, flattening the mat instead of the man's rib cage.

Sunto rolled to his feet in an instant, crouched defensively, but Hilo stood with a lopsided smile and walked up with his hands open, limping and bent forward slightly from the radiating pain in his abdomen. "I was wondering if your Espenian military training was real, or just a lot of big talk."

Sunto frowned in confusion. "So you're not here to kill me or beat the shit out of me."

"Did I say I was?" Hilo asked.

Sunto straightened slowly and skeptically, wincing and rubbing his chest. "The leader of one of the biggest Green Bone clans shows up unexpectedly to talk? You can't blame me for thinking I might not be walking out of here. A lot of people in this city don't like Espenian soldiers, even retired ones with Kekonese ancestry."

Every person in the Seventh Discipline gym had stopped to

stare at the extraordinary sight of No Peak's Pillar matching himself against an ex–Navy Angel. Someone was taking out a compact 35 mm camera. Hilo glanced over and snapped, "None of that, go back to whatever you were doing. I'm talking to a visitor here, can't you see that?" The chastised Fingers mumbled apologies and reluctantly drew away from the scene. Hilo turned back to Sunto. "If you were in trouble with me, you would know it for sure by now. I said I came to talk, didn't I? There's a restaurant across the street. I'll buy you a drink for that kick."

———

They had the Two Tigers Taproom to themselves, since the place was not technically open yet. Hilo had the manager bring two glasses of Espenian amber lager. Sunto refused the cigarette Hilo offered him, so the Pillar sat back and lit one for himself. The ex-Angel's jade aura was still bristly with suspicion, but he drank his beer and said, "What do you want to talk about?"

"Tell me how you became an Espenian soldier and military instructor." No Peak had already investigated Sunto's background, but Hilo believed you could always learn more about a man by hearing him talk about himself.

Sunto Jimonyon had been born in Janloon and raised by a single mother. When he was six years old, his mother remarried and his stepfather moved the family to Espenia. Sunto, who did not get along with his stepfather, left home at seventeen and joined the ROE military, where he was fast-tracked into IBJCS training and the Navy Angels. During his second tour of duty in Oortoko, he was injured by flying shrapnel and sent to Euman Naval Base to recover. While there, he took on duties training new cohorts of Angel cadets and became a well-regarded instructor. Facing reassignment at the end of the Oortokon War, Sunto resigned from the Angels, electing to stay in Kekon.

"I was tired of being ordered around," he explained with a shrug. "I wanted to spend more time living and training here, until I figure out what to do next."

"You were allowed to keep your jade," Hilo observed.

Sunto put a hand around his dog tags. "It's not my jade," he said. "It was issued to me by the Espenian government and I have it on indefinite loan because I'm still a contracted IBJCS instructor at Euman Naval Base. I live in officer's quarters when I'm over there, and I've got an apartment here in the city the rest of the time."

Hilo tilted his head curiously. "You don't want to duel for any green of your own?"

Sunto's eyes flicked down to the ample line of jade studs visible between the open buttons of Hilo's collar, then back up at the Pillar's face. "I was taught to carry only the jade I need," he said. "All of IBJCS is based on stripped-down methods—the most simple and effective reconnaissance and combat techniques that'll work for special forces soldiers equipped with the same standard issue of bioenergetic jade. Any more than that is an unnecessary risk." Sunto frowned as he turned his glass of beer, widening a circle of moisture on the table. "Some of the guys I was with in Oortoko, they aren't doing so well now. Mental illness, drug addiction, falling into unTruthful habits. I'm lucky to have Kekonese genetics on my side, but I don't need more jade just to show it off."

"That's true." Hilo's expression remained neutral as he stubbed out his cigarette. "You're a foreign serviceman, after all, not a Green Bone."

Sunto eyed the Pillar with caution and impatience. He pushed aside his beer and crossed his arms on the table. "Look, I know what a big deal your family is," he said, in a matter-of-fact tone that made it clear he was not stupid, that his lack of deference was not out of ignorance, but because he was an Espenian soldier who did not answer to any Green Bone clan leader. "I'm not in Janloon to challenge your men for jade or cause any trouble. My word on the Seer's Truth. I'm here to mind my own business and to make some decent money, that's all."

Unexpectedly, Hilo decided he liked Jim Sunto. Protected by his Espenian citizenship and military status, Sunto was an aberration in Janloon. He could wear and use jade, but he had no allegiance to any clan and took no shit either. A man who could kick the Pillar in the groin without fear of death was refreshing. It reminded Hilo of a much earlier time in his life, when he was not yet the Pillar or even the Horn, when anyone could challenge him and he had to earn respect daily with words or fists or knives. "I'm glad to hear that," he said, with a growing smile.

"Well then," Sunto said, finishing his beer and shifting his chair back to stand, "now that we've both had a chance to clear things up, I assume we're done here."

"Sit down, Lieutenant." Even though Sunto was no longer an enlisted officer, military rank seemed the most appropriate way to address him. "Do you think I'd go to the trouble of finding you in person just to growl at you like a big dog?" Hilo pointed the man back into his seat. "You said you're here to make money. I have a way for you to make a lot more. Do you want to hear about it or not?"

Sunto was not the first man to be startled by the Pillar's sudden change from relaxed good humor to pointed authority. He lowered himself warily back into his chair.

Hilo had the manager of the Two Tigers Taproom bring the man another beer. "What do you know about the Kekonese military?" the Pillar asked.

"When I was in the Angels, we did some training exercises with the Kekonese army. They're not shoddy, exactly, but underwhelming for a country with the most bioenergetic jade in the world."

"That's because the clans take all the jade and warriors, and some of them don't care about the country." Hilo's lips twisted sarcastically. "At least, that's what I've heard."

It infuriated Hilo that Ayt Mada had outmaneuvered him in the KJA meeting at the beginning of the year, in front of every other Green Bone leader in the country. Since then, the Mountain had predictably and relentlessly attacked No Peak in the battlefield of public opinion. Even though the KJA had recently voted unanimously to increase the allocation of jade to the armed forces, and No Peak loyalists in the Royal Council had helped to pass greater funding for national defense, if one were to believe Koben Yiro's zealous rants on the radio, Ygutan was on the verge of invading the country all because of No Peak's craven selfishness.

Koben taking enthusiastically to his new role as Ayt Mada's unfettered mouthpiece had certainly not hurt the Mountain's continued efforts to financially strangle their rivals. Shae's latest reports showed that so far this year, two-thirds of newly incorporated small businesses were seeking patronage from the Mountain over No Peak. Woon Papidonwa was working full time to manage the clan's public image and outside relationships, but as Shae had put it, *You can't sell thin air.* No Peak needed substantial political wins of its own.

"Let me get this straight," Jim Sunto said slowly, after Hilo explained his offer. "You want to hire me to help reform the Kekonese military?"

Hilo said, "You've been teaching IBJCS to Espenian Navy Angels and interested Green Bones on the side. The Kekonese military could use someone like you, to show them how to make the most of the jade they have. There's no denying that foreigners have done some things that even Green Bones can learn from."

Sunto sat back, arms crossed, chewing the inside of his cheek. "I'll admit that's not what I expected to hear from a clan Pillar. I know the ROE military brass also believes a stronger Kekonese army would be a deterrent against Ygutan." He fingered the triangular pendant around his neck, as if consulting his foreign God as well as his self-interest. "When would I meet this General Ronu?"

———

Wen prepared a dinner of crab soup, peppered sea bass, pea shoots with garlic, and stuffed buns. She had help from Kyanla, but was proud to have done most of the cooking herself, even though it had taken hours. She still suffered occasional numbness and weakness on the right side of her body, but her balance and motor control had greatly improved, and she'd gradually become adept at doing things one-handed.

When Hilo arrived home, he found her waiting in the dining room, wearing a soft blue dress and pearl necklace, the elaborate dinner for two laid out on the table.

"What's this about?" he said.

"I thought it would... be nice to have dinner together. Alone, for once."

Her husband took off his suit jacket and weapons, dropped his keys and wallet on the kitchen counter, then sat down at the table with an air of bemused suspicion. He glanced around the uncharacteristically quiet house. "Where are the kids?"

"I sent... Niko to sleep over at the Juens. Ru and Jaya are at your mother's house."

"Jaya's going to be furious." The three-and-a-half-year-old had strict ideas about how her bedtime routine was expected to proceed, beginning with an evening snack and ending with her father reading from a big book of children's stories about the hero Baijen. She was liable to throw a tantrum that could be Perceived, and possibly heard, from across the courtyard of the estate.

"She has to learn she... doesn't always get what she wants." Wen carefully ladled soup into two bowls, concentrating on keeping her arm steady. She worried about her children growing up spoiled or neglected, in some combination. They had relatives to care for them when she could not, but they still suffered from her inability to be a more attentive mother. She could not carry them, or run around with them, or even tie their shoelaces.

Hilo tasted the soup and said, "It's good," almost grudgingly. They ate in silence for a few minutes, but she could feel Hilo's eyes on her.

"That's the dress you wore when we were married," he said.

Wen smiled at his notice. "Does it still look good?" She was wearing support pantyhose and a padded bra under the silk. Birthing and nursing two children, and then loss of muscle function from traumatic brain damage, meant that the body inside the dress was not the one from six and a half years ago.

"Sure." A softness came into Hilo's eyes. "Maybe not quite as good as it looked the first time, only because I thought I'd die the next day. Everything's more beautiful when you don't think you'll see it again."

"Sometimes," Wen said as she took the lid off the fish plate, "it's more beautiful afterward, when you... realize you have a second ch-chance." She fumbled the spoon; nerves.

Hilo reached across the table and took the serving utensils from her. He placed some of the sea bass and pea shoots on her plate, but his movements grew sharp; he cut into the fish as if it were still alive and had to be killed. His voice had been kind, but now it held a pained edge. "There aren't any real second chances. Even when you live through the worst parts, life doesn't go back to what it was before." He sat back in his seat, scraping the legs noisily against the floor. "Just look at Tar. There are some things a person can't recover from."

Wen squeezed her hands together in her lap, reminding herself that this was what she'd wanted—an honest conversation with her husband. "Tar and Iyn Ro shouldn't get married," she said. "They're not good for each other."

"They've been hot and cold for years," Hilo grumbled. "Now they promise me they're finally serious enough to take oaths to each other, so why shouldn't I let them have their chance? Tar needs more people in his life, more things to do." Tar had been staying over at the main residence so often that he'd practically moved in with them, but after he and Iyn Ro had gotten engaged last month, he'd been spending most of his time with her in his apartment in Sogen.

Wen knew that Hilo had reduced his Pillarman's duties, had told him to take time off to relax, saying it was well earned after his travel to Espenia and accomplishing such difficult tasks there. That was true, but the real reason was that Anden had returned from his own trip to Port Massy and told the Pillar of his conversation with Dauk Losun.

"Hilo-jen," Wen had heard Anden say worriedly, the two of them standing in the Pillar's study, "Tar is green turning black."

Green turning black was an idiom for a jade warrior losing his sanity, usually from the Itches, possibly becoming a danger to himself and others. Someone like that might have to be confronted, might have to give up his jade or have it forcibly taken from him by intervening clan members. Wen was sure the problem with Tar had nothing to do with jade overexposure, however. Without Kehn, he was one wheel holding up a runaway rickshaw, his continued devotion to

Hilo a ballast against loneliness and bloodlust. The only thing that seemed to make him genuinely happy was spending time with the children, especially Kehn's son, Maik Cam, but he was so prone to filling their heads with violent stories that even Wen, who didn't believe in shielding children from reality, limited how much time the kids spent with their uncle Tar lest she have them coming into her bedroom at night wide-eyed with nightmares.

Tar's engagement to Iyn Ro last month had come as something of a surprise. "At least he's trying to change," Hilo pointed out. "Tar deserves to be happy."

"And the rest of us?" Wen asked cautiously. "What do we deserve?"

Hilo's chewing slowed. He eyed her from the side of his vision as he reached for the plate of warm stuffed buns. "What do you mean by that?"

Wen twisted the napkin in her lap, gathering her resolve. "We... can't st-stay apart and hurting like this, Hilo," she said. "The Pillar has to... keep the family strong. We're not strong now. We're stuck. You haven't..." She couldn't put her churning thoughts into the exact words she needed, and she saw her halting speech was arousing his pity and making him agitated. "What... do you... Do you want a divorce?"

Hilo pushed back in his chair. Wen had never feared her husband before; he had never hit her or even looked as if he would hit her, but the expression on his face now felt as if it would stop her heart. "Is that what *you* want?" he asked with soft rage. "After all this, you haven't betrayed me *enough*, now you're thinking to break up the family?"

She shook her head vigorously, but Hilo's voice rose, all his anger over the past gathering into a storm, the accusation in his eyes rendering her speechless. "*Why*, Wen? Haven't I always loved you and taken care of you, supported your career, done everything I could to keep you and our children safe? And you couldn't obey me, in only *one, simple way?*"

Wen had been determined to face her husband without tears, but now her vision blurred against her will. "There was too... much at stake. I knew you wouldn't let me out...of the safe box you put me in. So I convinced Shae. You made us...have to lie."

"*I* made you..." Hilo's mouth stayed open for a second. Then it snapped closed. He stood up, tossing his napkin down. "Sometimes I think liars are almost as bad as thieves," he said through a tight jaw. "They steal away trust, something that can't be returned." Before she could even rise from her chair, he left the house, his quick, sure movements and long strides easily outpacing hers.

———————

Hilo stormed out the door and got into the Duchesse, only to realize that in the heat of the moment, he'd left his car keys in the house along with his jacket, weapons, and wallet. He howled in frustration and banged the steering wheel, then rolled down the window and smoked three cigarettes in a row before he felt calm again.

He considered sleeping in the car tonight. Then he thought about walking over to the Weather Man's house and asking his sister to let him spend the night on her sofa. Both ideas struck him as so pathetic that he laughed out loud in the dark. Imagining the withering look that Shae would give him was amusing and sobering at the same time. Although—something had happened lately between her and Woon. She was distracted and unhappy, so perhaps they could get drunk together for the first time in their lives and both cry into their cups of hoji. Hilo chuckled again.

When he'd walked into the house that evening and seen Wen looking so beautiful, waiting for him with a meal she'd put such effort into preparing, he'd wanted nothing more than to give his heart back to her completely, to make amends for every harsh moment between them. It had once been an effortless thing to tell his wife he loved her—three simple words in a single breath. A goodbye at the end of a phone call, an invitation to make love, a whisper before sleep.

Now it seemed an impassable emotional mountain. Every time he longed to make things right with Wen, anger yanked him back, like a hand jerking away from flame or Steel rising against a blade. How often had he found fault with Shae for keeping people at a distance—for half the time not being honest with herself, and half the time not being honest with others? Now *he* was the one sealed off, nursing his invisible wounds alone, just as Lan had once done.

The thought filled Hilo with gloom and dread. He was not a naturally self-sufficient personality. He knew that about himself. Perhaps some men truly did not need others, but very few, and there was usually something wrong with them to make them that way. The brotherhood of the clan was a promise that its warriors were not alone. What was the point of Green Bone oaths, of all the sacrifices his family had made, of the relentless war against their enemies, if in the end, the promise couldn't even be kept for him and those he loved?

Still, he delayed. The hour grew late and he was out of cigarettes.

Hilo got out of the car and walked back to the house with heavy steps. A stalemate was no way to live in a marriage, that much he was forced to admit. The idea of divorce had nearly made his vision turn red and his head feel as if it were on fire. So that was not an option. He wasn't sure he could forgive his wife, or his sister—but Anden had once said that understanding was more important than forgiveness. His kid cousin could be canny, in his own way.

The lights in the house were out, but his eyes were already adjusted to the dark. Wen had put away the remains of the dinner and fallen asleep on the sofa in the living room, curled on her side under a throw blanket. Perhaps she'd been waiting for him, or perhaps the staircase had seemed too daunting. Hilo stood over her, watching the soft rise and fall of her pale shoulders in time with her breaths. She was the softest and most vulnerable creature; she was the strongest and most unyielding of his warriors.

He bent and gathered her easily in his arms. As he carried her up the stairs and into the bedroom, she woke and murmured, groggily, "Hilo? What time is it?"

"It's late," he answered. "But not too late." He laid her down on the bed and sat down on the mattress next to her. "I'm sorry about dinner. It was good, one of your best. But there'll be others, even better I'm sure. Or we'll go out next time."

She said quietly, "All right." She wiped her eyes with the backs of her hands.

"I shouldn't have lost my temper and left the house like that, but I didn't go anywhere—just out to the car." He leaned over and brushed away the strands of hair stuck to her cheeks. The gesture was gentle, but his voice was not. "I think maybe mistakes made out of love are the worst sort, and we've both made them. Don't ever talk about divorce again. I won't bring it up myself. Understand?" She nodded.

He undressed her, then took off his own clothes and got into bed next to her. Slowly, but firmly, he began to touch her stomach and breasts, her hips and buttocks. He reached between her thighs, drawing short strokes with his fingers as he brought his lips to her jaw.

Wen turned toward him and pressed her wet face to his chest and stomach. She slid under the covers and took him deep in her mouth. Before she could bring him past the point of control, Hilo pulled her up toward him and turned her over, working on Wen in turn until she was straining wetly against his attention. It had been a long time since they'd concentrated fully on each other's bodies; their movements were questioning but deliberate, like experienced lovers with new partners. They held their breaths in the shivering moment when he pushed inside her.

It was far from the most energetic or passionate sex they'd ever had, but it was the most determined. They jogged toward climax together, out of practice. Afterward, they didn't speak, but slept with their fingers laced together in the darkness.

CHAPTER

10

You Can't Win

the sixth year, tenth month

Shae opted to take the five-hour-long train ride to Lukang. The business-class train cars were more comfortable than Kekon Air's regional planes, and she could spend the time enjoying the passing countryside and getting work done.

She reviewed all that she'd learned about the Six Hands Unity clan with her new chief of staff, Luto Tagunin. Over the past six months, Luto had proven himself to be a fast learner, highly organized, and relentlessly energetic. He did not seem to need much sleep. The twenty-six-year-old worked late, went out carousing with friends, and seemed none the worse for it early the following morning. He was already adeptly navigating the complexity of the business side of the clan, and Shae had been impressed by his attention to detail.

The one thing that was likely to hold Luto back from advancement in the clan was the fact that he was not a Green Bone. That was not a strict barrier to most jobs on the business side of No Peak, but would be seen as a disadvantage at the upper levels of leadership and would shut him out of certain social circles. Overall, Shae was not in any specific way disappointed with Luto, except for the glaring and inescapable fact that he was not Woon Papidonwa.

Luto was not as thoughtful and experienced as Woon. He didn't have Woon's calm presence and he didn't anticipate her thoughts the way Woon seemed to. Luto couldn't Perceive when she needed him to appear in her office to discuss a difficult issue, he didn't know when and how to challenge her decisions or poke holes in her logic, he didn't wait to drive her home at the end of every workday.

Shae reminded herself that she was having difficulty adjusting because until recently, she'd had the same chief of staff since becoming Weather Man. It would take time to become accustomed to someone else in the role. It wasn't as if she didn't see Woon anymore. His new office was only one floor below hers, and they still spoke nearly every day. The clan's Sealgiver was busy handling the public announcement that No Peak was partnering with the Kekonese military and bringing in IBJCS experts to design a more robust and modern training program in the jade disciplines. Whenever Shae passed by the office of the Weather Man's Shadow down the hall from her own and felt a stab of disappointment to see it occupied by Luto instead of Woon, she would find some excuse to descend one floor simply to get close enough to Perceive his familiar aura.

After the kiss they'd shared in her house, Shae had mustered the courage to go to Woon's new office on Firstday morning. She was the Weather Man, after all, the higher-ranked Green Bone. She ought to resolve the situation. "Papi-jen," she said determinedly, walking in and shutting the door behind her. "About last week, I—"

Before she could get out another word, Woon stood up, nearly knocking over his own chair. "Don't say anything else, Shae-jen." He stared at her for only a few seconds before averting his eyes, as if she were standing in front of a floodlight and it was hard for him to look directly at her. He lowered his voice. "You know how I feel about you. If you apologize for what happened and tell me you didn't mean any of it, it'll be unbearable to me. If you tell me that you did mean it and you feel the same way, that would be even worse, because if I thought there was a chance..." The knob of his throat bobbed and his jade aura churned with conflicted feelings, a riot of textures that Shae couldn't parse. "I can't leave Kiya. It wouldn't be honorable of me. Not after everything we've been through. And I can't stand the idea of losing your respect and friendship either. Would it... would it be possible for us to keep working together and just... try not to let it get in the way?"

He raised his eyes fully to hers at last, and Shae almost wished he hadn't, because his soft, sincere expression tugged at her insides in painfully hungry ways. She stood in his office at a respectable distance in her business suit and thought of his lips on her neck, his large hands climbing up under her shirt. In that moment, she realized what a fool she was, to have finally fallen for her colleague and friend when it was too late.

She managed an answer. "Of course."

True to his word, Woon had overseen Luto's work as they carefully verified the sincerity of the overture from Six Hands Unity, thoroughly examined the smaller clan's finances and operations, and finally arranged for a secure and private meeting with its leaders. She'd spoken to him on the phone before she got on the train.

"Are you sure you have all the information you need, Shae-jen?" he asked her. They both knew how important this meeting would be. If Shae returned with the allegiance of Six Hands Unity, everything would change. They had been hypervigilant about secrecy. Only Hilo, Woon, and Juen even knew she was making the trip.

"Yes," Shae assured him. "Luto's done a good job compiling everything."

Woon hesitated on the other end of the line. He could've easily walked up one floor in the office tower to see her before she left, but he'd phoned instead. She'd half expected him to offer to make the trip to Lukang with her, as he normally would've as her Shadow, but he didn't do that either. She tried and abjectly failed not to be hurt by his entirely appropriate professional distance. It was better they didn't see each other in person. Her emotions would've been far too easy to Perceive.

Over the phone, it was easier to keep up their shields. "Have a good trip, Shae-jen, and good luck," Woon said, then hung up.

The train pulled into the station at Lukang late in the afternoon. While Janloon, the glamorous capital city, sits smoggy and sheltered by the warm waters and outlying islands of Kekon's curving eastern shore, Lukang, on the country's southern coast, is a windswept, sea-bleached city known for its sunny skies and unpretentious working-class character. Janlooners consider their southern countrymen to be less sophisticated, and make fun of their slow way of talking, but Lukang stands as a metropolis in its own right, fueled by the factories and telecom companies that have grown up around its bustling port.

A hired car and driver were waiting for Shae and her aide as soon as they got off the train. It drove them directly to the arranged meeting place deep inside Six Hands Unity territory. Lukang was a city controlled three ways. The Mountain and No Peak both had people and businesses here, but Six Hands Unity was the principal regional clan. For over a decade, it had maintained an arm's-length alliance with the Mountain, paying tribute in exchange for continued operational independence and access to the Mountain's greater resources and national reach. Shae hoped to change that.

At the entrance to the Unto & Sons Restaurant & Hoji Bar, they were met by Jio Wasujo, the Pillar of Six Hands Unity, along with two other men. "Kaul-jen," said Jio, saluting her respectfully. "I'm honored by your visit."

"I'm glad to make the trip, Jio-jen," Shae said, returning the salute. Jio Wasu was a physically formidable but aging Green Bone. He wore jade on a silver chain around his throat but a bald patch shone on the top of his head and he was a touch overweight. Shae had seen him sitting near Ayt Mada in the Kekon Jade Alliance meetings and noticed he was always one to watch and listen more than talk.

Jio motioned to the two men standing with him. "You know my

Weather Man, Tyne Retu." Shae nodded toward Tyne. They had been in discreet contact a number of times since their brief conversation in the elevator. Jio introduced the third, younger man as "my Horn and nephew, Jio Somu."

Shae and Luto were ushered politely but quickly into one of the bar's private rooms, where long shelves on the walls held display bottles of fine hoji of different distilleries and ages. The place was not yet open for the evening, and Shae's Perception told her no one else was in the building. The wooden shutters were closed, blocking what would've been an excellent view of the Amaric Ocean off the city's lengthy seawall.

"Stay out front and keep watch," Jio Wasu told his nephew. The Horn nodded and departed to do so. "I apologize for not welcoming you to Lukang in better style," Jio said, turning to Shae, "but I trust you understand the need to keep this conversation discreet."

"I understand completely, Jio-jen." Shae sat down at the table, which was set with a pot of tea and an assortment of snacking foods. Luto positioned his seat behind and to the left of her. Tyne Retu served the tea, pouring Shae's cup first. Shae ate some of the roasted nuts and pickled vegetables to be polite, but she was anxious to get on with the discussion and had little appetite.

Jio and Tyne seemed to feel the same way. After some small talk about the weather in the south versus the north, and mutual inquiries into the health of their respective families, the Pillar of Six Hands Unity shifted forward and said, in his slow, southern cadence, "Kaul-jen, I appreciate you taking the time to come to Lukang. We're not as big as Janloon, so sometimes people don't realize how much our city has to offer."

Shae said, "I would be a poor Weather Man if I didn't already know that Lukang is growing even faster than Janloon these days."

"The Six Hands Unity clan has had a partnership with the Mountain since Ayt Yugontin's time," Jio said, "but lately we've been faced with"—he exchanged glances with his Weather Man—"*issues* that have made me rethink what's best for my clan."

Shae hoped her Shadow was paying close attention. She was used to having Woon's reassuring jade aura right behind her and wished it wasn't absent in what might be a pivotal negotiation. She leaned forward to match Jio and said encouragingly, "What sort of issues are you facing, Jio-jen?"

Jio said, "Lukang is growing, but that also means big-city troubles. We're the nearest major port to the Uwiwa Islands, so we've always had problems with jade smuggling and illegal SN1, but it's gotten worse. Many of the refugees from Oortoko that came to Kekon over the past few years settled here, with the Mountain's sponsorship. Some of them are good citizens, but some are barukan who deal in shine and commit other crimes. Six Hands Unity is not a large clan. We don't have enough Green Bones to police the barukan. We've asked the Mountain to send more of their Fists and Fingers, but they prioritize their territories in Janloon."

Jio had begun speaking slowly, but now he picked up speed. "Ayt Mada has barukan working for her—members of the Matyos, the largest of the gangs in Shotar. They take delivery of jade that arrives in Lukang and transport it under guard to Janloon. So the Mountain is lenient on their other activities."

Shae was confused. "Jade arrives in Lukang?" she said. "From where? The mines?" To her knowledge, none of the KJA-controlled jade processing facilities were located in the area.

Again, Jio glanced at his Weather Man. Their jade auras seemed to tauten. Shae sensed that the leaders of Six Hands Unity had debated long and hard about whether to share this information with her. "We were surprised as well, at first," Jio said. "Usually, we're worried about jade going the other way, being smuggled out of the country. That's still happening, but the opposite is happening too—jade has been arriving by ship or plane from the Uwiwa Islands."

"Why would—" Shae began, then stopped before she could finish the question: Why would jade be brought *into* Kekon—the country it came from in the first place? The answer struck her in an instant.

Four years ago, after No Peak assassinated the Uwiwan smuggler Zapunyo, Ayt had struck an alliance with the Keko-Shotarian mercenaries who'd been employed as Zapunyo's bodyguards and enforcers.

A barukan man named Iyilo, originally from the Matyos gang and one of Zapunyo's longtime aides, had killed Zapunyo's sons and taken over his assets in the Uwiwa Islands to become the leader of Ti Pasuiga, the largest jade and shine smuggling ring in the region, which he now operated with as much ruthlessness as his predecessor. While the Green Bone clans had largely eradicated organized scrap picking from Kekon's mines, an inevitable amount of raw and cut jade was still ferreted away by enterprising criminals.

And according to Jio Wasu, the Mountain was buying it back.

To cement the alliance with Iyilo and the Matyos barukan, Ayt had whispered the name of the former Royal Council chancellor Son Tomarho, ensuring the passage of legislation allowing refugees from war-torn Oortoko—including jade-wearing barukan sponsored by the Mountain—to immigrate to Kekon, where Ayt had put them to work. Buying back raw jade from the Uwiwa Islands, bringing it into Lukang, and placing it in the Mountain's stores not only buttressed the clan's wealth against uncertainty in the financial markets, it constricted the supply and inflated the price of illegal jade. With jade prices high, the Mountain's unofficial sales to Ygutan, East Oortoko, and other countries would be far more profitable. Shae was also certain that Ayt was taking a cut of Ti Pasuiga's shine trade, as well as whatever black market rocks it didn't repatriate but instead allowed to reach other buyers.

Ayt Mada, who'd always believed in one clan controlling the global jade supply, had found a way to bring much of the black market jade trade under her purview, creating what amounted to a black market shadow of the KJA, with only one clan—the Mountain—in the cartel.

In the Twice Lucky, with Fuyin's body on the table, Hilo had demanded to know, *How the fuck is the Mountain outspending us and stealing our businesses with tribute rates that we know are unsustainable?* Now Shae knew the answer. The key to Ayt Mada's war chest was here in Lukang.

Her heart began to pound. She forced composure back into her body, not wanting the men to Perceive how important it was that she win them over. Ayt no doubt considered some disorder and crime in Lukang a small price to pay for ensuring that the barukan gangs remained her cooperative partners in controlling the illegal jade triangle that now existed between Kekon, the Uwiwa Islands, and Ygutan. If No Peak could ally with Six Hands Unity to seize incoming jade at the ports, she could deprive the Mountain of its stockpile and drive a wedge between Ayt and Iyilo. She said, calmly, "Jio-jen, I knew the Mountain was allied with the barukan, but I didn't realize until now that it was to such an extent as to cause harm to your city."

Jio blew out a troubled breath. "The Mountain is never going to care about the city of Lukang the way Six Hands Unity does. I want our local Lantern Men to be able to expand their businesses overseas. That's where the growth opportunities are now. And we need to attract foreign investment and international tourism to our city. My own son wants to go to graduate school in Espenia." The Pillar eyed Shae with a question in his eyes. "It's my understanding that the No Peak clan has advantages over the Mountain in those areas."

Shae gave a single nod, keeping her excitement in check. "You've understood correctly, Jio-jen. We have more assets and allies in Espenia than any other clan. If Six Hands Unity were to swear allegiance and tribute, No Peak would gladly offer our friendship and support to you in every way we can." Too late, she wished she hadn't been too proud to insist that Hilo come on the trip with her, to lend his natural persuasiveness. "As Weather Man of the clan, I speak on behalf of my brother the Pillar, who's known for keeping his promises."

A keyed-up sense of momentum was rising in the room. Jio knew full well that he was on the verge of taking an irrevocable step. By changing allegiances, he would make an enemy of Ayt Mada, something no sane person would want, in the hopes of bettering the prospects for his clan and his city. "The friendship of the No Peak clan is worth a great deal," he acknowledged. "We're a small clan in comparison, and don't have a great many Fists and Fingers, but the ones we do have are as green as they come. We have a strong regional presence and healthy businesses across several industries. Tyne-jen can provide every detail you need."

The Weather Man of Six Hands Unity acted promptly on this cue and opened a briefcase. He extracted a thick, unmarked manila envelope and placed it on the table in front of Shae. Inside would be details of the clan's operations: recent financial statements of its wholly owned and tributary businesses, a roster of the clan's leadership, an accounting of how many Green Bones it commanded and what their ranks were, and any other noteworthy assets the clan possessed, such as alliances with other minor clans or valuable political connections.

Of course, Woon and Luto had already dug up as much information as they could about Six Hands Unity from No Peak's own sources, so there would likely not be anything in Tyne's report to surprise her, but the disclosure step was a sign of intention and trust. She expected Jio and Tyne would not be one hundred percent honest—tributary entities might downplay their income in hopes of lower tribute rates, or conversely, pad their claims of wealth or warriors to make themselves more attractive to allies. She would have Luto corroborate the facts and examine the statements for any discrepancies, but the important thing was that the Pillar of Six Hands Unity had come prepared to switch his clan, and thus Lukang, to No Peak rule.

Shae accepted the envelope and placed it inside her bag. "I have no doubt of your word. You're taking a risk for your clan and city. Let me assure you that No Peak is loyal to its friends, and we're not without our own power in Lukang." She held a hand out to Luto, who immediately placed an unmarked envelope of their own into her outstretched palm. She set the envelope in front of Jio and Tyne. It contained a draft agreement of patronage, including how many warriors Juen Nu, the Horn of No Peak, had agreed to redeploy to Lukang to defend Six Hands Unity from potential retaliation by the Mountain (no tributary would switch allegiance unless it could count on protection) as well as an approximate tribute range, to be finalized pending closer inspection of the smaller clan's books.

"I've run the numbers based on last year's information, so these are only estimates. I can provide everyone with an updated proposal within the week," Luto assured them. "With the Weather Man's permission," he added hastily and with embarrassment. Shae had not technically given her chief of staff license to speak, but she forgave his enthusiasm. The young man was nearly vibrating. This was the sort of dramatic event Luto must've hoped he would witness when he became the Weather Man's Shadow. The alliance would not be official until the details had been agreed upon by both sides and Jio came up to Janloon to swear oaths to Kaul Hilo in person, but the clans had declared their intentions. It was a huge victory for No Peak. Things would have to be set into motion immediately.

Jio accepted the envelope and began to speak again, but before the words left his mouth, Shae's Perception caught a shift of energy outside of the building. Green Bone jade auras approaching, fast. Half a dozen of them at least. She jerked upright in her chair and shot a look at Jio Wasu. "Are those your people?" she demanded.

Luto, who was not green, and Tyne, who wore little jade and apparently had a poor sense of Perception, looked between the two Pillars in confusion. Jio stood up, alarm coursing through his aura and across his face. "No," he said. "Impossible. No one knows we're meeting here. Where's—"

The door to the room flung open. Jio Somu, the Horn of Six Hands Unity, stood in the entryway. Next to him was a tall, older man that Shae recognized at once as Nau Suenzen, Horn of the Mountain.

Shae's hand went for the talon knife strapped to the small of her back under her blazer, but Jio Wasu stood frozen, staring at his nephew in uncomprehending shock. The young man was sweating, but his face was resolved and his jade aura blazed with dark determination. "I'm sorry, Uncle," he said. "You left me no choice."

Nau Suen took a step into the room and four additional Mountain Green Bones came in after him, fanning out to either side. Shae could Perceive three others in the building, at the front and rear entrances. She edged away and pulled Luto with her by the arm, putting their backs against the wall. Her aide was wide-eyed and silent, his fear a sour tang in the periphery of her Perception. Shae's hand on the talon knife was steady but blood was roaring in her ears and her mind was racing. She cast about for some means of escape and found none.

The walls were made of thick wooden timbers and the windows were small—she wouldn't be able to crash through them with any amount of Strength and Steel.

Jio Wasu's eyes were still on his nephew. "You betrayed us," he whispered in disbelief.

"That's an ironic accusation coming from a clan Pillar who has just been caught breaking his tribute oaths and turning to No Peak," said Nau Suen, his cool, unblinking gaze scanning the room, settling on each occupant in turn. Shae's skin crawled as he nodded at her, almost cordially, before turning back to Jio Wasu. "You ought to know, Jio-jen, that your nephew told me of your treachery and provided the date and location of this meeting on the condition that you be spared from execution."

"The Mountain would've found out soon enough," Jio Somu said to his uncle, as if imploring him to understand. "And then we would've had to fight for our lives. What makes you think we'd be better off with No Peak? It's better for everyone this way. We don't want Lukang to turn into Janloon."

"What do you get out of this, Somu?" Jio Wasu asked numbly.

Nau answered for the young Horn. "Naturally, after you've been exiled, Jio Somu will become the Pillar of Six Hands Unity, which will continue to run the city of Lukang as a loyal tributary of the Mountain clan."

Tyne Retu made a noise of incoherent rage. "Somu, you worthless *dog*—" He launched himself at the younger Jio with a heedless shout, hands reaching for the traitor's throat. Two of Nau Suen's Green Bones seized the Weather Man of Six Hands Unity in an instant. A third put a moon blade through his chest. Shae saw the tip of white metal emerge from the left side of Tyne's back at the same instant that she Perceived the spasm of his punctured heart like a shriek in her mind.

Jio Wasu let out a roar of denial and tore a small handgun from a concealed shoulder holster under his jacket. Before he could even aim it, Nau Suen's men unloaded their weapons in unison. The room erupted in gunfire. Jio threw up a violent blast of Deflection and Steel that could not possibly save him in these tight quarters against so much flying ammunition; bullets swerved in every direction. Bottles of hoji shattered and crashed off the shelves, spraying glass across the room.

Shae hurled a tight vertical prow of Deflection into the narrow space between two of the Mountain Green Bones, knocking them staggering and driving a wedge into the Mountain's line. Desperate Strength and Lightness surged into Shae's limbs. With her grip still on Luto's arm, she leapt for the opening, plowing through the chaos—and stumbled as Luto's weight dragged her down. She turned in time to see him hit the ground, the side of his neck blown open.

Shae's mind recoiled, barely registering the sight before her right leg buckled under her and a searing pain tore through her thigh, radiating down her leg and up into her pelvis. She Steeled in a panic and tried to rise. Nau Suen threw a precise, forceful Deflection that hit Shae in the chest like a hard shove. She slammed unceremoniously into the back wall and crumpled.

The gunfire had stopped, but Shae could not hear a thing. She might as well have been underwater. Jio Wasu lay sprawled on the ground next to his Weather Man, his body riddled with bullets. Jio Somu, the disloyal nephew, stared at his uncle's corpse with a ghastly, contorted expression. Even though he hadn't personally pulled the trigger, from this moment on, he would be known as a man who'd murdered his own Pillar and kin.

The man's hands curled into fists by his sides. Shae saw his lips move, trembling. "You should've listened to me, old man." Two Mountain Green Bones tugged Jio Somu out of the room.

Shae looked over at Luto, her chief of staff for all of six months. Luto's lifeless eyes were wide open and he was staring at the ceiling, as if surprised.

Nau Suen stepped around the growing pools of blood and came over to her. "Kaul-jen."

"You promised the nephew you would let them live," Shae said through gritted teeth.

"They attacked first," Nau pointed out. "It's for the new Pillar's own good. His uncle might've come back for vengeance. Tell me, how does your own Pillar deal with those who've betrayed the clan?"

Shae could not see her talon knife anywhere. She must've dropped it at some point between being shot and thrown into a wall. She felt light-headed and Nau's words seemed muffled. Her hand was pressed tightly over the gunshot wound in her thigh and blood was pumping between her fingers, soaking the bottom of her skirt. The pain was excruciating. She was fascinated by how the narrow three-inch heel of her right leather pump was broken off, but except for the bullet hole, her pantyhose were intact. Behind Nau, two of the Mountain's Fists were bent over, removing the jade from Jio's and Tyne's bodies.

Nau crouched down next to her. Shae forced herself to focus, to meet the Horn's disconcertingly piercing gaze. "You realize, Nau-jen," she said, licking her dry lips, and managing a pained but venomous smile, "that there's no way to make my death here look like a heart attack."

The Horn looked at her with a curious, unsmiling expression. "If you die here, Kaul Hiloshudon will come down from the forest, and our clans will be at war in the streets by tomorrow morning. That's not what Ayt-jen sent me to accomplish in Lukang. I came here to punish a traitor, and to secure the city for the Mountain. Guns are messy, ridiculous weapons, though—flying metal and Deflections everywhere." His eyes traveled from her face down to her leg. "The bullet missed your femoral artery. You're lucky."

Shae turned her chin toward Luto's body. "You can't say the same for him."

"You brought a man with no jade into a meeting of Green Bone clans." Nau didn't even look at the body. "Carelessness. Like letting a child play in the middle of a busy street." A surge of remorse and hatred pounded in Shae's head. She wondered where her talon knife was, whether she could still get to Nau.

"You're welcome to try," said the Horn, as if she had spoken aloud. "I'm retiring next year. I stayed on as long as I did for Ayt-jen, but the Horn is a young man's job." Nau turned over his shoulder and gave quick orders to his men, instructing them to take Jio Somu away from the premises for his own protection and to return the jade-stripped bodies of Jio Wasu and Tyne Retu to their families. They left at once to do so.

Nau took three cloth napkins from the table and tied them together with strong knots. He wrapped the joined length of cloth around Shae's thigh above the wound and bound it with a firm yank that made her hiss in pain. He jammed a pair of chopsticks through two layers of the makeshift wrapping and twisted several times, cinching the tourniquet tight with the matter-of-fact efficiency of an army field medic. Nau must be nearly sixty. As a teenager, he'd been a resistance fighter during the Shotarian occupation, a comrade of Ayt Yu and her own grandfather. Despite his inhumanly high level of skill in Perception, he made no effort to use medical Channeling. Perhaps he'd only ever learned how to use his jade abilities to end lives, not preserve them.

"Tell your Pillar," Shae said, clenching her fists in the folds of her skirt to distract from the pain and the growing numbness in her leg, "that she hasn't won. I know what's she doing and I'm going to stop her."

Nau Suen stood and looked down at Shae lying propped against the wall, drawing ragged breaths. He spoke leisurely as he wiped the blood from his hands on a clean edge of the tablecloth. "When Ayt Yugontin—let the gods recognize him—was on his deathbed, his son, his Horn, and a number of his close advisors discussed dividing the Mountain clan. After the Spear of Kekon was gone, they said, the clan would lose its legendary warrior leader, its heart and soul. It would be best for everyone to go their separate ways, for each of the men who had the support of one faction of the clan to form their own, smaller clans, rather than vie for the difficult task of following in the great Pillar's shadow. I was there; I remember the conversation.

"Ayt Mada was Weather Man at the time. She rarely spoke of her birth family, but she said that she remembered her parents fighting. One evening her father stormed from the house, her sister and brother fled to their own friends, and she, an eight-year-old child, wandered down to the river. When the Shotarian bombs fell and the landslide engulfed their village, the rest of her family died apart and alone."

Nau ate two pieces of the untouched quartered plums and a handful of the roasted nuts remaining on the blood-spattered table. "Madajen told Ayt Yu's advisors that the strongest Green Bone among them should become Pillar after her father's passing. She offered to duel any of them for the leadership. They smiled and laughed at the idea. Women did not duel men. I had a better sense of Perception than anyone else, so I was the only one who knew better than to laugh. Ayt Mada killed all those men rather than let the Mountain be broken."

On his way out, the Horn of the Mountain took a moment to pick out one of the unbroken bottles of aged hoji left on the shelf. He turned over his shoulder, his penetrating gaze falling back onto Shae with a touch of cold sympathy. "I've known her for twenty-five years. You have no choice but to fight, of course. But you can't win."

Nau's boots crunched on glass as he left the room.

11

The Slow War

Shae dragged herself through the Unto & Sons Restaurant & Hoji Bar until she found a telephone behind the bar. She called the first number that came into her mind and reached Woon's office voicemail; the workday was over by now. She phoned his home number. After two rings, Woon's wife picked up the call.

"Is Papi there?" Shae asked. "I mean, Woon-jen—is he there?"

"Who is this?" Kiya asked, instantly suspicious.

"Kaul Shae, the Weather Man," Shae said, teeth clenched in pain, lying on the floor behind the bar. "I need to talk to your husband, is he—"

Before she could finish the sentence, there was a sound on the other end of the line as if the phone was being taken away, and then Woon's voice demanded, anxiously, "Shae-jen? What's happened?"

Ten minutes after she got off the phone with Woon, an ambulance arrived, followed within seconds by a car of No Peak Green Bones.

Shae recognized one of the Fists, a young man from Janloon with wavy hair named Lott, presumably in Lukang on assignment. "We'll follow you the entire way to the hospital, Kaul-jen," Lott said, jogging alongside the paramedics as they carried Shae out.

"The Pillar and Weather Man of Six Hands Unity are dead," she said, grabbing the Fist's arm before she was loaded into the ambulance. "Their Horn betrayed them to the Mountain. We need to secure our own territories before word gets out, and then take as much of Lukang as we can before the Mountain does."

At the hospital, Lott posted guards outside Shae's room. Woon chartered a small plane and was by her bedside two hours later. He arrived with Juen Nu and a dozen of the clan's Green Bone warriors. Sitting up in bed with her swollen leg wrapped and elevated, Shae explained the Mountain's scheme of moving black market jade through Lukang and gave the Horn the envelope in her bag containing the information about the people and assets of Six Hands Unity—all of them now under questionable ownership.

By nightfall, Six Hands Unity was in a state of civil war and Lukang was a battlefield. Shae slept restlessly for short periods at a time, Woon always in her room or on the phone in the hallway outside. Every few hours, Iyn Ro or Lott Jin would come back to the hospital to report on what was happening.

"That shameless kin killer Jio Somu has about two-thirds of Six Hands Unity behind him with the Mountain's support, but the other third and many of their top Lantern Men have come over to us, begging for help and vengeance," Iyn said, shortly after dawn. The Fist's short, spiky hair was disheveled and her aura was bright with adrenaline and new jade. Shae had heard rumors that Tar's fiancée was being considered for promotion to First Fist, which would make her the first woman to achieve such a high rank on the military side of the clan. "The bad news is that the Mountain moved into place before we even got here and they have the local barukan gangs on their side. So they were able to get ahead of us and are still holding on to control of most of Six Hands Unity's former territory."

"We can't win a street war for local businesses," Woon said, pacing near the foot of Shae's bed. "Based on what we know, the most important thing is that we take control of Lukang's port and go after the barukan who move jade for the Mountain."

"That's what we've been doing," Iyn replied with some surliness. Fists did not take well to being told what to do by suits on the business side. "The harbor district is where most of the fighting's concentrated. Juen-jen's ordered another fifteen Green Bones down from Janloon, but any more and we risk leaving our important territories up there undefended. We'll be lucky just to keep what we currently have in Lukang, unless there's something else the Weather Man's office can think of?" She arched an eyebrow at Shae and Woon before stalking out again.

———

Shae was discharged from the hospital after twenty-four hours and arrived back home in Janloon at one o'clock in the morning. Woon opened the front door of her house, then came back to the car and lifted her out carefully. The pain in Shae's leg had lessened, but she felt weak, and bleary from painkillers. She put her arms around Woon's neck and her head against his shoulder as he carried her inside. It was the closest she'd been to him in months, and the familiar, steadfast hum of his jade aura and the solidity of his body comforted her. When he settled her on the sofa in the living room, she let go of him reluctantly and felt cold as soon as she did so.

Woon brought pillows and a blanket down from her bedroom and placed them under her head and her wounded leg to make her more comfortable. Until she could climb stairs again, she would be better off sleeping on the main level, where she could more easily get to the kitchen and the bathroom. He sat down on the floor beside the sofa and laid his elbow and head down next to her on the cushions, exhausted after two days of little sleep. Shae reached out tentatively and placed a hand on his shoulder. "Thank you," she whispered. "Again."

Woon placed his hand over hers. With a sigh, he turned his head and brought her hand up to his cheek, pressing his face against her palm. Her fingers trembled against his skin. Despite all that had happened in the past thirty-six hours, an ache of want arose in her, so intense it seemed a physical thing, a hook through her navel. The tenor of Woon's jade aura deepened and he looked at her with a helpless question in his eyes. When she pulled him closer, he gave in with no resistance.

They kissed, and kept kissing. Shae's vision blurred; she forgot her injury and her fatigue. Woon's mouth moved with slow, deep neediness. Rising up on his knees, he leaned over her, supporting her under the head with one arm. His other hand touched her throat, then her chest. Shae arched toward him. Still kissing her, he undid the top buttons of her shirt. Almost fearfully it seemed, as if wading into certain danger, he began touching her breasts over her bra, closing his eyes as he brushed warm fingers over the hardened nipples straining against fabric.

With a groan, Woon drew his hands and mouth away and sank back down next to her, dropping his forehead to the sofa cushions. Shae hung on to him for a second, then let go.

"It's no use," he murmured, his voice muffled beside her. "I can't help that I'm in love with you."

Shae sagged against the sofa and reached for his hand. "I have no right to ask you for anything. I won't."

Hilo walked into the house. Shae and Woon had not been paying attention to anything besides each other and failed to Perceive the Pillar's approach before he was standing in the entrance of the living room with an impassive glare.

Woon got to his feet hastily and blinked a few times before bringing his hands up to his forehead in salute. "Kaul-jen." He cleared his throat.

"Go back to your home and your wife, Woon," Hilo ordered.

Woon flinched as if the Pillar had struck him. His face flushed more deeply than Shae had ever seen. For an extended moment, he seemed to struggle with the desire to explain himself; then, with a visible effort, he regained his usual composure. He nodded once, curtly, and walked past Hilo, out of the house to his car.

Shae's face burned as she turned away and did up the buttons of her shirt. She pushed herself angrily into a sitting position. "Why did you have to barge in like that and treat him so harshly?"

"Do you think what you're doing is kind to him?" Hilo replied without any remorse. "Are you planning to break his heart, or ruin his life?"

Shae mumbled, "Of course not."

Hilo's eyes narrowed as he came to stand over her. "What's wrong with you, Shae? Do you love him or not? If you do, you have to tell him to leave his wife. Otherwise, you have to fire him from the Weather Man's office, or transfer him out of Janloon. Didn't I tell you about this a long time ago, and you wait until now to do something about it?"

Shae opened her mouth; a dozen retorts rose to mind, the automatic responses she'd developed to Hilo over so many years. *Stay out of my life. You don't know anything. This is none of your business.* But of course, that was not true. Hilo was the Pillar and anything that affected the clan was his business, including a potentially ruinous affair between the Weather Man and its Sealgiver.

Shae closed her mouth, swallowing all the easy, childish things she wanted to say. Instead, she dropped her face and pressed her fingertips against her eyes. "Not yet, Hilo, please. I'm tired of losing people."

Her brother's jade aura shifted unexpectedly. A subtle withdrawal. He said nothing as she lifted her face out of her hands and pointed to the plastic container of pills on the nearby table. "Hand me those painkillers and a glass of water."

Hilo did as she asked. He sat down on the edge of the coffee table and took the empty glass from her when she was done. Shae could see their reflection in the windows. Outside it was a moonless night and the Kaul estate was quiet. It was difficult to believe that right now, the clan's warriors were waging fierce battle in another part of the country. "I was sorry to hear about your man, Luto," Hilo said, in a different voice. "Let the gods recognize him."

"Let the gods recognize him," Shae repeated. "He was young and smart, with the whole rest of his life ahead of him. He wasn't even a Green Bone; he shouldn't have died. It was a meaningless death."

Hilo regarded her with a stern sort of sympathy. "If a bullet had caught you in the neck, would you want me to say your death was meaningless? Luto wasn't green, but he gave his life for the clan, just like any Fist or Finger."

"Fists and Fingers wear jade and take oaths. They know they might have to do battle."

"Everything is a battle now," Hilo said grimly. "Every business, every town, every newspaper article or press conference or gods-damned vote in the Royal Council." The familiar ferocity in Hilo's voice was laced with deep resignation. "There used to be a way things were done, under the eyes of Old Uncle. We used to be able to count on certain things. Now there aren't any lines. Everyone in the clan is part of the fight."

Shae wondered if he was thinking of Wen. She was unsure of her ability to read him anymore. Over the past two years, he'd rarely spoken to her about anything outside of clan business. She remembered how much Hilo used to irritate her with his cheerfully aggressive openness, his physicality, the way he would throw his arms around her, goad and tease her. Looking at Hilo now, sitting on the table with his elbows on his knees, she found herself wishing for the grinning, arrogant brother she'd once had, the one who always seemed so sure of himself.

"We've been trying for *years* to break the Mountain and send Ayt Mada to the grave," Hilo said. "And here we still are—that bitch still on top of her clan, still coming after us. We won't win Lukang in the end. We'll take some of it, maybe a lot, but if that city is the key to her alliance with the barukan and control over the black market, she'll never let Six Hands Unity go to another clan."

Shae thought about what Nau had said to her, his complete certainty. "No, she won't," Shae agreed. "But I finally know what we have to do, to take Ayt's tools away. I figured it out with Woon in the hospital yesterday."

After she'd explained their plan, Hilo appeared impressed, but said, "Ayt and her Weather Man will find a way around that, sooner or later."

"Yes," Shae admitted, "but it'll slow them down badly and hamper them enough that they won't be able to keep up their efforts to buy out our Lantern Men."

"Juen is still going to have to take as much of Lukang as possible and send the barukan who work for the Mountain to prison or into graves, as many of them as we can."

Shae nodded as she placed another cushion under her injured thigh to relieve the throbbing ache. "We may have lost the chance to gain Six Hands Unity as a tributary—but it's possible we can still pull a victory out of this situation."

Hilo was quiet for a minute. "You're a good Weather Man, Shae." Grudging pride and a touch of bitterness sat in his voice.

She leaned her head back against the pillows and closed her eyes as exhaustion finally caught up with her. "You're a good wartime Pillar, Hilo," she murmured. "And we're fighting a war. Our own slow war."

She was nearly asleep as Hilo adjusted the blanket over her. "I told Andy to come over later today and take a look at that leg," he mentioned. "Who knows if the doctors in Lukang are any good?" She felt his lips plant a kiss on her brow, and a moment later, she heard the front door close behind him.

Shae hobbled into her office on crutches two days later. Although she noticed more of the clan's Fists and Fingers on the streets, tense and watchful, everything else in Janloon seemed normal. The weather was pleasant and red Autumn Festival lamps were everywhere, along with signs promoting seasonal retail sales. Hundreds of kilometers away, the violence in Lukang continued but Janlooners were treating the news as a regional issue in the south caused by a nasty internal schism in the minor Six Hands Unity clan. By unsaid mutual agreement, neither the Mountain nor No Peak were doing anything in Janloon to change that impression. The Mountain and its tributary forces still controlled most of Lukang, but No Peak and the breakaway faction of Six Hands Unity had successfully repelled barukan gangs to hang on to the valuable port districts.

The late Jio Wasu had worried, *Lukang is growing, but that also means big-city troubles.* Clan war was big-city troubles indeed. His traitor nephew, Jio Somu, had gone into hiding to escape his own relatives who wanted to kill him.

Shae passed Luto's office and stood outside of it for several remorseful minutes, leaning on her crutches. Only now that the young man was dead did the office feel like it should be his. She made the slow trek to her own office and told her secretary to begin gathering candidate resumes for a new chief of staff.

At noon, Shae turned on the television in her office to watch Woon Papi deliver No Peak's statement to the press calling for a trade embargo on the Uwiwa Islands.

"Yesterday, the Royal Council introduced strong and necessary legislation to reinforce national security and combat rising crime in our cities," the clan's Sealgiver announced in his reliably calm and factual manner. The reporters who were present took down his words politely, even though everyone was well aware the No Peak clan was behind the proposed embargo in the first place. Kaul Hilo and Woon Papi had gone to Wisdom Hall the morning after Shae had returned to Janloon and called a meeting of all the most senior No Peak–affiliated members of government. A bill had made it to the floor of the national legislature within twenty-four hours.

"The Uwiwa Islands is the first destination for jade smuggled out of Kekon, and one of the world's largest producers of illegal SN1," Woon said on-screen. He provided alarming statistics about jade trafficking, drug addiction, sex tourism, and street crime, then deftly connected the civil war in Six Hands Unity and the outbreak of street violence in Lukang to corrupting foreign influences. Woon was wearing a steel-gray suit and blue tie. Jade gleamed from his wrist. Shae thought he looked handsome on camera, in an understated and imperturbable way.

"The No Peak clan unreservedly backs the proposed trade embargo and the Pillar asks every loyal member of the clan and every concerned Kekonese citizen to do the same," the Sealgiver concluded. "We invite other Green Bone clans to join us in voicing their support, and we will of course lend any assistance that is within our ability to help the government enact and enforce these measures going forward."

When Shae had explained the strategy to Hilo, she'd said, "With an embargo in place, no goods, no money, and no jade will travel between Kekon and that country. Regardless of whether we win control of Lukang or not, if we block access to the Uwiwa Islands, we break the Mountain's connection to the black market. We do that, and we defund Ayt Mada's war chest." She was certain the Mountain was transferring funds from Iyilo's jade and shine sales through subsidiaries and shell companies, so the embargo would also outlaw any Kekonese company from doing business with any Uwiwan ones.

"The Mountain controls six more seats in the Royal Council than we do right now," Hilo had pointed out. She'd been surprised that he remembered this fact.

"So we'll need at least that many independents and councilmen from minor clans to side with us," Shae had said. "And they will."

She was correct. Within hours of Woon's statement on behalf of No Peak, Shae's people reported that the bill was meeting with favorable press coverage, strong public support, and even commitment from some Mountain-affiliated legislators. The country was hungry for policies and bold actions that safeguarded Kekon against the Slow War threats that seemed to surround it.

Shae allowed herself a smile as she propped her leg onto a chair and massaged the soreness that radiated down into her calf. Not even the Mountain could stop a train running on the momentum of the current zeitgeist. No Peak's loyalists in the government would push the bill into law in short order, along with Hilo's plan to reform the military. The clan had vastly improved its public standing, and Ayt Mada could hardly oppose them without appearing hypocritical and angering her own supporters.

Shae's improved mood lasted only until the final hour of the workday, when she received an unexpected visitor. The photo of Kiya that

Woon kept on his desk showed a young bride with a radiant smile, long hair trailing out from under a stylish wide-brimmed red hat. The woman who walked into Shae's office and sat down across from her wore a plain black turtleneck sweater and a balefully rigid expression that made apparent the shadows under her eyes and the paleness of her stiffly held lips.

"Kiya," Shae said, uncomfortably surprised. "What brings—"

"I'm leaving my husband," Kiya interrupted. "He's too much of a noble coward to ask for a divorce, so it's up to me to do it. I want you to know it was my decision. You didn't take him from me; I gave him up."

Shae had no answer for an entire minute. "That's not what I wanted," she said at last. Her voice came out flat, concealing waves of guilty relief and defensive remorse. "Believe me, I would never try to break up your marriage."

"Then you are even crueler than I thought," Kiya replied. "I could understand if you were choosing to take something from someone in a weaker position. I can accept losing to a better woman. But you're saying you never even thought of what you were doing, that it was all done carelessly."

Kiya's chin trembled for a second, but she lifted it and stared Shae in the face. "Everyone knows my husband spends nearly all his time with another woman, and not simply because he works for her. They all look the other way. When I was a little girl, my father and my brothers would never let anyone hurt me. They chased off one of my first boyfriends after he stood me up at the movie theater. Now I'm unhappy and humiliated, but they told me not to get on the bad side of the clan by confronting the Weather Man. They tried to talk me out of leaving, too, because Woon Papi is so high up in No Peak, and it's good for our family."

Angry tears were forming in Kiya's eyes. "My birthday was on Firstday this week. Papi left work early, and we were supposed to spend the evening together. The minute you phoned, he left without a word. He didn't tell me where he was going or when he would be back. He hardly even looked at me. Now he comes home to sleep and shower and leave again. He says only that it's clan business."

Shae's face was growing hot. "I'm sorry. It was an emergency. I rely on your husband to do important work for No Peak; there's no one more trustworthy or dependable. I needed him. I still do."

"I needed him more," Kiya shot back. "I'm not a Green Bone like you, yet I've been forced to give four years of my life for the clan, years that I'll never get back." She got to her feet and turned to leave.

"Kiya." Shae despised the sound of her own voice. "Is there anything you need? Anything I can do for you?"

Woon's wife paused and turned back around slowly, as if the question surprised her. "Kaul Shaelinsan, Weather Man of No Peak," she said, "you can fuck off and die."

CHAPTER

12

~

A New Job

Bero was arrested and thrown into jail. It was bad luck, of course; always bad luck. A newly installed security camera outside of a sporting goods store in Little Hammer captured an image of him the same week that the Janloon police happened to be out in force, maintaining order during a public rally protesting the planned expansion of the Espenian naval base. Bero was caught with cans of spray paint and a crowbar in his backpack. Tadino was sick with stomach flu, so Bero didn't even have anyone to take the fall with him when he was driven to the police station.

It was good luck, as well, though. He could've been caught by patrolling Green Bones instead and then he would likely be in a hospital instead of a jail cell. Bero had been through far worse situations than a few days in prison. He called in sick to his job at the Double Double casino and waited out the inconvenience of detention, speaking in monosyllables and shrugging contemptuously at the police sergeant who questioned him. After three days, his cell was unlocked and he was informed that he was being released with a fine for three thousand dien and an order to appear in court in two months' time to pay the fee, make formal apologies to the owner of the sporting goods store, and face possible further punishment depending on review of the damages caused.

Bero expected that would be the end of it, and was unpleasantly surprised when the police sergeant did not escort him out the front of the station, but led him to a back entrance where two men, one Kekonese and one foreigner, took custody of Bero and placed him, still handcuffed, in the back of a silver sport utility vehicle with tinted windows. They began driving away.

"Where the fuck are you taking me?" Bero demanded.

"Relax," said the Kekonese man, who must've been Kekonese by ancestry only, because he spoke with a foreign accent. "We just want to talk."

"Fuck you, whoever you are," Bero shouted, kicking the back of the driver's seat. "You've got no right to take me anywhere, you spenny pricks."

"Stop that," said the man. "If you want to be an asshole, we can drive you back to work, and you can explain to your boss what you've been up to in your spare time. The Double Double's a No Peak clan property, isn't it? And wasn't the Clanless Future Movement responsible for an incident there a little over a year ago?"

That shut Bero up. Whoever these foreigners were, they knew a lot more about him than the police did. The man put a cloth bag over Bero's head and said, "This is for your own protection. Just sit quietly with your mouth shut."

After perhaps twenty minutes, the car came to a stop. The door opened, and Bero was guided, still hooded and blindfolded, out of the back seat and into a building. He was escorted by the elbow down a hall, through a door, and maneuvered into a chair before the hood was taken off, and then the handcuffs. Bero rubbed his wrists and scowled at the two men who'd brought him here. The one who'd spoken to him in the car was clean-shaven with a strange-smelling cologne, the other one was pale-eyed and had a short haircut. They were in a plain, windowless, unfrightening room with a table and chairs. It appeared to be a small but ordinary meeting room in an office.

"Here, have something to drink," said the Kekonese-looking man, putting a bottle of watermelon soda on the table and opening another one himself. Despite his vexation, Bero was thirsty, so he snatched the bottle, still glaring.

"Now that we have some privacy, let's start with proper introductions." The man who spoke Kekonese was the one who did all the talking, but Bero suspected that the older foreigner, the one standing silent and off to the side with his arms crossed, was the boss. "My name is Galo, and this is Berglund. We work for the Republic of Espenia's Military Intelligence Service."

"No shit," sneered Bero. "I never would've guessed."

"We have a proposal for you," said Galo, unruffled by Bero's sarcasm. "Once you hear it, I think you'll see it's in your interest to accept." He placed a photograph on the table in front of Bero. "Do you recognize this man?"

The photograph was of the stocky, curly-haired foreigner who'd first shown up at the Little Persimmon lounge last year, the one who'd caused such a stir with his questions and his promise that there were other people ready to help the Clanless Future Movement. Afterward, he'd stayed behind to talk privately with Guriho and the others. Molovni, that was his name. Bero had seen the man several times since, sitting at the back of the meetings, seemingly on good terms with everyone now. Bero only showed up occasionally these days, hoping to get close to Ema, who hadn't yet agreed to go out for a drink with him, but who tolerated him just enough that Bero thought it was possible she would give in to him sooner or later.

"Yeah, so what?" Bero asked, curious despite himself.

Galo tapped the photo. "Vastik eya Molovni is one of the nekolva. It means 'child of the nation' in Ygut. Have you heard of them?"

"Nekolva?" Bero looked from Galo to the image of Molovni's face with skepticism. "They have jade abilities without wearing jade.

That's what people say. I've heard they're not real, that the Ygutanians made them up to scare people."

"They're real," said Galo, "but also exaggerated. The nekolva are the result of an Ygutanian military program that began after the Many Nations War. Over the past thirty years, hundreds of Abukei women have been trafficked to Ygutan or lured there with the promise of domestic work. When they arrive, they're forced to become surrogates for supposedly infertile couples. Beginning in childhood, the mixed-race offspring are dosed with low levels of SN1 and ground jade powder. Some of them suffer debilitating side effects or die as a result. The ones that show promise are given the country's best military training."

Bero exclaimed, "The Ygutanian soldiers *eat* jade?"

Galo glanced over at Berglund, who nodded for him to continue. "Ygutan doesn't have a reliable supply of high-quality bioenergetic jade. Lower-grade jade obtained on the black market and industrially ground into powder is more effective when ingested. The toll on the body dramatically cuts down their life expectancy, but without visible jade, the nekolva make excellent spies and operatives. They require regular doses of jade powder and SN1, so they're easier for handlers to control. They're Ygutan's answer to our Navy Angels or your country's Green Bone warriors. And they're here in Janloon."

No wonder Guriho and Otonyo and the other leaders of the Clanless Future Movement were eager to make friends with the Ygutanian, if he might be as powerful as a Green Bone. Bero pushed Molovni's photograph away. "I don't know him at all. It's not like we talk."

"If one of the nekolva is getting involved in subversive activities in Kekon, then the Ygutanian government is behind it. We want to find out what Molovni's up to. It could be of vital consequence to your country and ours." Galo had been standing, leaning over the table. Now he pulled out a chair and sat down across from Bero, lowering his voice in a serious and solicitously coaxing manner. "We know you take part in anti-clan gatherings and activities. We want you to increase your involvement in the CFM and report everything you observe to us: what goes on in the meetings, when Molovni shows up and what he says, who he talks to and spends time with."

Bero made an ugly face. "I'm not going to spy for you spennies."

A flash of irritation broke through Galo's professional demeanor. He opened his mouth to respond, but Berglund spoke up from where he was watching. Galo turned toward him and the two men had a brief conversation in their own language. When Galo faced Bero again, his expression was recomposed and he wore a small, coldly confident smile. "I should've mentioned earlier that we don't offer to make someone an informant for nothing. We identified and selected you, and we pulled strings with the Janloon police to bring you here. Of course, you can decline to work with us. We'll drive you back to the police station and pretend this conversation never happened. You'll go back to hiding from Green Bones and working your dead-end job. Probably best for you to leave before your employer finds out why you were arrested, but that'll make it tough to pay the hefty vandalism fine you've been saddled with. Or you can choose to receive a thousand Espenian thalirs in cash every month."

Bero nearly choked on a swallow of watermelon soda.

"We'll also take care of that unfortunate fine you owe," Galo said offhandedly, as if throwing a bonus item into a set of kitchen knives. "And think about this: Wouldn't it be helpful to have allies who want to keep you safe, who could even get you away from the Green Bone clans, if things start going badly for your friends in the Clanless Future Movement?"

"They're not my friends," Bero grumbled, but not really arguing. *A thousand thalirs a month!* How much was that in dien? Seven thousand? Eight thousand? A lot.

"That's why you're perfect for the job," said Galo. "I don't doubt that you have your own reasons for opposing the clans, or else you wouldn't have joined the CFM to begin with. But I can see you're no ideologue. I could try to convince you that we're on the same side, and cooperating with us would be doing a service to your country...but that doesn't matter to you, does it? You have no real loyalties. You do what you have to—you look out for yourself." Galo said all this with matter-of-fact equanimity and did not lose his small smile. "So what do you say?"

Bero finished the soda in the bottle. "I'll do it," he said.

CHAPTER
13

No Secrets

the seventh year, sixth month

One afternoon, Niko came into the house in tears. He and his siblings had been playing with their cousin Maik Cam and the Juen boys at the Horn's house. Juen Nu and his wife had four children, including twin boys who were ten months older than Niko, and Lina often brought Cam over to play with his cousins, so there were always small children running around the courtyard and grounds of the Kaul estate, going from house to house, leaving their toys and belongings everywhere.

Niko ran to Wen and complained that the Juen twins had been making fun of him. While Cam, Ru, and Jaya were building with toy blocks, the three older boys had stolen a pack of cigarettes and a lighter from a drawer and been playing with them. Juen's wife saw what they were up to and confiscated the items, admonishing them sternly that they might've burned the house to the ground. Niko, sobered by this reprimand, blamed his friends for coming up with the disobedient idea in the first place. Fires could kill people, he reminded them officiously. His own birth mother had died in a house fire; that was why he lived with his aunt and uncle.

The Juen twins laughed at him. "Who told you that?" they asked. His aunt Shae had explained it to him when he was little. Juen Ritto said, mockingly, "Do you really believe that? You're the Pillar's son, how can you be such a baby?" Niko balled his fists and demanded angrily to know what they meant, but they ran off.

Wen reassured Niko that his friends were only trying to goad him. That evening, after the children were in bed, she told her husband what had happened.

Hilo was annoyed at the Juen boys for being so tactless, but it wasn't their fault, nor the fault of their father. They were only kids who overheard what adults said and passed it around without thinking. Besides, he'd known he would have to face this moment eventually. Niko was eight years old, a mature boy for his age, certainly old enough to understand many adult concepts. He was bound to learn the truth sooner or later, and it was important that he get the complete story from Hilo himself and not someone else. Nevertheless, it was not a task Hilo looked forward to.

"I'll talk to him," he promised Wen.

Seeing his resigned expression, Wen finished the physiotherapy exercises she was doing in the living room and came over to sit next to him on the sofa. She reached for his hand, and when he didn't draw away, she tightened her grip and leaned against him. Nine months after that emotional crisis over dinner, they were still unsure around each other, and both of them suffered from days when sadness and resentment outweighed any chance of affection. As Wen regained strength and ability, however, it was getting easier to be relaxed and normal together, to have conversations the way they used to. "No more secrets," she reminded him.

"No more secrets," he agreed. So many problems between people, even those who loved each other, came from a lack of communication and honesty.

So on Sixthday morning, Hilo woke his nephew, who he thought of as his oldest son, and said that they were going out to breakfast together, just the two of them. No one else in the family was awake yet. The only people they passed on the way to the garage were the gardeners bringing in dozens of containers of red and yellow peonies, symbolizing marital happiness, for Shae and Woon's wedding next weekend.

As soon as the ink was dry on Woon's divorce, Hilo had confronted Woon, and Wen had talked to Shae, and a date was set. Hilo had walked into the hotel room where Shae's former chief of staff was temporarily living, and said, without preamble, "Woon-jen, I get upset even thinking about the problems my sister's poor dating record has caused me over the years. You were Lan's best friend, and now you're doing a good job as the clan's Sealgiver, so you'd better not become yet another bad situation. You can either move to the other side of the country—we could use more people in Lukang right now—or you can marry Shae, but decide soon because I'm sick of this drawn-out bullshit. I can't trust my sister to come to me properly about these things, so if you know your own heart at least, this is your chance."

Woon's expression had been extremely apprehensive—one would've thought the man expected to be executed—and now it transformed into one of cautious joy. "Kaul-jen," he said slowly, "may I have your permission to ask Shae-jen—"

"Yes, for fuck's sake, you have my blessing as Pillar." Hilo sighed.

He didn't know how the conversation went between Wen and Shae, but he was glad his wife handled that part, as Shae might refuse what she most wanted for no other reason than to deprive him of the position of having been right. When he asked Wen about it, she smiled confidently and said, "Don't worry, your sister simply needs to have another woman to talk to about this decision, you'll see."

The marriage of Kaul Shaelinsan, Weather Man of No Peak and granddaughter of the Torch of Kekon, ought to have been an enormous clan pageant held in the Temple of Divine Return and celebrated with a grand banquet in the General Star Hotel. Instead, it was going to be a relatively modest family affair held on the Kaul estate. Both bride and groom had agreed to marry quickly and with restraint, out of respect for Kiya's family, who were only of moderate status in the clan, but nevertheless deserved not to have their humiliation publicized.

Children were easier to have difficult conversations with. Niko loved fried bread, so Hilo took him to the Hot Hut chain's new location in the Docks, even though he knew Wen would say it wasn't a healthy breakfast for a child. They sat on a bench looking out across the water and eating the piping hot sticks fresh from the fryer. Niko threw crumbs into the water for the birds. The morning sun was burning away some of the pervasive moisture hanging in the air. Food, souvenir, and tour package vendors were setting up to take advantage of the guests soon to disembark the commercial cruise ships that had arrived and moored overnight.

None of the vessels had arrived via the Uwiwa Islands; the trade embargo made certain of that.

The clan was in a better position than it had been last year. The Mountain had retreated from its efforts to turn No Peak's Lantern Men, whose confidence had been renewed by the Kauls' successes. The conflict in Lukang was not resolved, but the situation had stabilized enough that Juen had pulled several of his senior Fists such as Iyn and Lott back to Janloon, leaving enough warriors to support the breakaway faction of Six Hands Unity. For the time being, the clans had battled each other to another draw—but Hilo was not as enraged by this as he once would've been. He'd long hoped to destroy the Mountain with some swift and fatal blow, even if it cost him his own life, but now he accepted that victory would take much longer to achieve. He needed to stay alive and outlast his enemies.

To wash down the fried bread, Hilo bought two cups of hot sweetened milk from one of the nearby stands and blew on one of them, cooling it down for Niko before giving it to him. Although he was excited by the special treatment and Hilo's undivided attention, the boy knew there must be some reason for it, and he was even quieter than usual, eating with concentration and glancing at his uncle frequently.

"Are you looking forward to Boat Day?" Hilo asked.

"I guess so," Niko said. He was a strange child, in Hilo's opinion—not easily upset, but rarely eager or expressive, either. Watchful and intelligent, ahead of his class in school, but with too much of Lan's melancholy, Hilo thought.

"On Boat Day, we'll come back here and watch the ship sinking. We'll get the sweet roasted nuts you like, and watermelon soda, and you can stay up as late as you want."

Niko brightened at this. "Can Uncle Anden come too?"

"Of course, if he's not busy." Without changing his easy and affectionate tone, Hilo said, "Niko-se, I heard the Juen boys were saying some things the other day that made you upset. Do you want to tell me about what happened?"

Niko's smile faded and he scuffed the ground beneath the bench with the tips of his shoes. Hilo continued speaking gently. "You might hear other kids talk about our family. They might even say things that seem mean or untrue. That's only to be expected because of our position in the clan. When you hear anything that you're not sure of, you shouldn't assume things or react right away. Just come to me or your ma. Your aunt Shae and your uncle Anden might try to protect your feelings, only because they love you, and your uncle Tar, he likes to tell big stories, sometimes too big. But I'll always tell you the truth."

Niko blurted, "They thought I was stupid for saying my ma—not Ma, but the first mother I used to have—died in a fire."

"You're not stupid," Hilo reassured him. "It's only that people are always quick to talk about someone else's tragedy behind their back. We didn't tell you much about what happened to your mother because you were too little to understand and it might've frightened or upset you. But you're old enough now and should hear it."

Hilo took a moment to finish his piece of fried bread and gather his thoughts. "Your da, my older brother, he was a good person, a powerful Green Bone, but too softhearted sometimes. I didn't use to understand it, but now that I'm older, I think I understand it more. After he became Pillar, his wife left him for another man, a foreigner, and they ran away together to another country far away."

Niko gazed at him expectantly with the same frowning look of concentration Hilo had seen on the boy's face when he was drawing or building or engrossed in a book, but Hilo could Perceive the boy's little heart thumping. Hilo patted his pockets, but let his hands drop. He tried not to smoke too much in front of the kids.

"Normally when someone betrays the Pillar and the clan, they have to be punished, they have to be killed, no matter who they are, even if they used to be a friend or someone you loved," Hilo explained. "Your aunt Shae had to kill the old Weather Man because he went against your father. And remember your uncle Tar told you the story about the time when we had to kill a man named Fuyin who used to be one of our own Fists, because he turned to the Mountain clan. I didn't want to execute him, but if I didn't, then I'd be failing my duty as the Pillar, and it would mean anyone could betray us."

"My da had to kill my own ma?" Niko asked, horrified.

"No, Niko, your da was softhearted like I said, and he let them go. Even though it was the wrong decision to make as a Pillar, it turned out to be a lucky thing, because she was pregnant with you at the time, and so you were born in Stepenland. You already know about the clan war with the Mountain and how your da was killed when you were a baby. He didn't know you'd been born. We didn't find out until almost two years later."

Hilo watched his nephew carefully as he went on. "When I found out about you, I went to Stepenland with your uncle Tar to talk to Eyni. For your sake, I forgave her for her betrayal and told her she could return to Janloon and live here with the family so you wouldn't have to grow up in a foreign place, far away from all of us who love you very much. She and her boyfriend agreed at first, but they lied and tried to steal you away again. They couldn't be reasoned with. It was bad enough that they had shamed your father, but now they wanted to keep you away from your country and your family. So you see that I couldn't let that happen."

Niko's lips trembled and his eyes welled with tears. "Was she really so bad that you had to kill her?" he asked plaintively, angry and ashamed that his own mother was among the lowest of people, a clan traitor.

"Niko-se, first of all, I did it very quick, so she didn't have any time to be scared and it didn't hurt at all. And it's not always that people are bad in their hearts so much as bad in their decisions. A good person can go through something in their life, or be around the wrong sorts of people, and have their mind twisted. Unfortunately, Eyni was one of those people, and if she'd taken you away, you would've never known me or your ma, or your uncles or aunts, or your brother or sister or cousins. You would never even know who your real father was. You'd never go to the Academy or become a Green Bone. Would you have wanted that?"

Niko shook his head with wretched vehemence. Hilo put his arms around the boy and pulled him into a tight hug. Niko was too big for Hilo to hold on his lap the way he used to, and he wondered at and regretted how quickly his children were growing, how rapidly time seemed to be passing.

Niko rubbed his teary face against the shoulder of Hilo's shirt. "Am I going to be a bad person too, if my mother was a traitor who had to be killed?"

"Don't ever think that," Hilo said sharply, drawing back and looking the boy seriously in the face. "No one is destined to become like their parents. In fact, we can learn from their mistakes and be less likely to repeat them. Your real ma is the one who raised you. She, and your uncle Tar, and your uncle Kehn—who was killed when you were young so you might not remember him as much—their own father was executed and their family was disgraced. They turned that around, and now the name Maik is at the top of the clan and spoken in the same breath as ours. You're your own person, Niko. You have many people who love you and are proud of you. And everyone says you take after your father, you look just like him. So never think that the bad way your mother died has anything to do with you. Understand?"

Niko sniffed and nodded, and Hilo drew him back into an embrace and kissed the top of his head. "Now you see why we didn't tell you this when you were younger," he said. "You wouldn't have understood, and you might've been scared or confused." There was probably still some fear and confusion, Hilo granted that much, but that was unavoidable and could only be alleviated with love and reassurance. "If you ever feel like you want to talk about this more, you should come straightaway to me or your ma."

"Do you ever feel bad for having to kill people, Uncle?" Niko asked quietly. "I don't think I could kill one of my own friends, like Ritto or Din, no matter what they did, even if they burned down the house."

"I don't feel bad about killing our enemies, anyone who would want to hurt our family. But sometimes, it's much harder, when it's someone you knew and maybe trusted. I feel a lot worse in those cases, but I still have to do it."

They sat together in silence for several minutes, Hilo stroking his nephew's hair and letting Niko lean against him as the boy absorbed everything his uncle had said. Hilo was relieved that it was done. He could only hope he'd done an adequate job of explaining such a painful topic to a child. Being a Kaul, a Green Bone, and the Pillar of the clan defined Hilo at all times, but even more important, he felt now, was being an honest and loving father to his children. Niko was the first son of the family. If he was to be Pillar someday, he needed to be raised well, supported but never coddled. "I love you, Niko, never forget that."

"I love you too, Uncle," Niko said, drying his eyes.

Hilo kissed Niko on the forehead and set him down. As they walked back to the car, he added, with a wink, "Don't tell Ru and Jaya that we went to Hot Hut, it'll make them whine with jealousy."

CHAPTER

14

Green Turning Black

Hilo was awoken by an unexpected phone call in the middle of the night. At first, he didn't recognize Tar's voice. His brother-in-law was incoherent, babbling and crying in panic. Hilo managed to figure out that he was at a pay phone outside his apartment building in Sogen. "Stay where you are," he ordered. "Are you listening to me? Stay exactly where you are until I get there." He hung up and got dressed. Wen was awake, sitting up in bed and staring at him with a mute and frightened question on her face. "Something's happened," Hilo said. "I'll find him and bring him back here as soon as I can."

He roused Juen and three Fists—Lott, Vin, and Ton—and they made it to Tar's location in fifteen minutes. Tar was no longer at the phone booth. They followed a trail of blood on the sidewalk. The

Pillarman had run for three blocks and collapsed behind a building. He was semi-lucid and his clothes were soaked red. He had knife wounds on his torso and arms. When he saw Hilo, his face collapsed into a baffling expression of relief, pleading, and fear. "Hilo-jen, help me," he begged, nearly choking. "I've done something awful."

Hilo could not believe his eyes. The sight of his most loyal and fearsome lieutenant lying crying and shivering, covered in blood in an alleyway, was not something that seemed as if it could be real. Juen and Lott knelt over Tar and Channeled into him enough to control the bleeding before lifting him into the back seat of one of the two cars. "Take him back to the house," Hilo instructed Lott and Ton. "Call Anden to come over and help patch him up. Don't let him leave, don't let him make any phone calls, don't let anyone else see him—not my wife, not my kids."

Hilo went with Juen and Vin back to the apartment building. Tar's unit was on the top floor, a spacious penthouse facing south over the city. The door was unlocked. Hilo walked inside to a terrible sight. The place was wrecked. Blood soaked into the beige carpet had gone tacky and the splatters on the wall were darkening to brown. Furniture and doors were splintered and broken, items scattered. Iyn Ro's body was sprawled partly across the sofa in the living room, the fatal wound in her throat a gaping red meaty opening that was difficult for even a seasoned knife fighter like Hilo to look at.

"Fuck the gods in Heaven," Juen whispered in horror.

The warmth was draining from Hilo's limbs. It was one thing to see a Green Bone slain by an enemy or killed in a fair duel. It was another entirely to look upon a scene of carnage inside a relative's home. His mind struggled against denial, not wanting to accept what his own eyes told him. Maik Tar, his Pillarman and brother-in-law, whom he'd loved and trusted since they were teens at the Academy, had murdered a fellow Green Bone of the clan, a woman he'd planned to marry next month. Iyn's jade earrings and bracelets were still on her body. The sight was obscene, as if she were an animal slaughtered for no reason at all, meat left to rot in the sun.

Hilo stayed long enough to ensure that arrangements were made for the body, then he left Juen and Vin with the tasks of seeing that they were carried out and informing Iyn's family. He drove back to the Kaul house alone in a numbed state, the streetlights passing over the white hood of the Duchesse with the monotonous pulse of a heartbeat in his ears.

Iyn Ro was not some victim of little account. She'd been a senior Fist of No Peak, one of the few women to ever reach such a high rank. She was known by everyone and looked up to by other women on the greener side of the clan. Hilo had taken notice of Iyn long ago when he'd been Horn, for being especially hardworking, and she'd been Juen's leading candidate to become First Fist when Vuay retired. Few men could match her intensity, or would want to, which was why she kept coming back to Maik Tar. And she had not died easily—the destroyed apartment and Tar's multiple wounds made that apparent.

It was the worst crime within No Peak that Hilo could remember. It would send shock waves through the clan. Iyn's relatives would demand justice.

When he arrived at the house, Anden and Lott were waiting on the front steps. They were standing together but not talking, both of them grave. Seeing them side by side, Hilo remembered that the two men were of the same age. They'd been classmates in the Academy, friends even, but they had turned out so differently.

Lott said, "We put him in the study, Hilo-jen. He hasn't tried to leave."

Under the orange glow of the house's front lights, Anden's face was pale. He was wearing his physician's jade and his aura was thin and weary; he'd been expending his energy. "His injuries won't kill him," he said in answer to Hilo's silent question. "One of them punctured his spleen, but I shut down the bleeding and got some fluids into him. I wasn't sure whether to do much more, since..." He trailed off unnecessarily. Hilo put a hand on his cousin's shoulder in thanks, then went into the house.

Lott had posted a total of three Fists around Tar—two in the room with him and one outside the door. It was a wise precaution; even injured, Maik Tar was one of the clan's best fighters and if he was out of his mind, there was no telling what he was capable of. When Hilo came into the room, however, he found his brother-in-law sitting quietly on the sofa, elbows on knees, his hands laced over the back of his lowered head, as if he were folding himself into the brace position for an airplane crash. His wounds had been bandaged and he was in fresh clothes brought down from Hilo's own closet.

Hilo motioned for the guards to leave the room and close the door behind them. Tar raised his head and looked up with the most wretched and pitiful expression Hilo had ever seen. "She's dead, isn't she?" When Hilo nodded, Tar began to sob—long, hard, soul-wracking sounds that Hilo had only heard from him once before, when he'd learned that Kehn had been killed.

He went to the man he thought of as a brother and sat down beside him, putting an arm around his shoulder and giving him some comfort as he wept. "I don't know what happened," Tar managed to choke out. "It started like any other fight, but it got so much worse. She was going to leave me, Hilo-jen. She said hurtful things..." Tar's jade aura was like broken glass, all shattered edges. More words pushed themselves out in the spaces between sobs. "I didn't mean to hurt her, I swear to the gods. I love her. I was going to fucking marry her. Sure, we can both get emotional sometimes. We fought too much in the past, but we were *done* with all that, we were finally going to make it work. But tonight after we got home, she said she was calling off the wedding and leaving me for good. She was sleeping with someone else, I know she was, she said as much. She was drunk, and I'd had a few drinks too...I don't know how we ended up drawing talon knives, I don't remember that part at all."

Hilo let Tar talk and cry himself out. None of what he said really mattered. There was no excuse for what he'd done, no explanation that could change the fact that a Fist of the clan was dead by his hand. But if Tar needed to say these things, to get them out, then the least Hilo could do was listen. When at last Tar fell silent, Hilo pulled out a packet of cigarettes. He offered his Pillarman a smoke and lit it for him, then lit one for himself; he needed to calm his nerves. He was not sure he could face what had to come next.

He saw now that he was responsible for the night's tragedy. He'd sent his Pillarman to do the clan's darkest work, had given him all the jobs that were the most difficult, the most sensitive, the most brutal and violent. During the clan war, he'd remade the Pillarman's role to take advantage of Maik Tar's nature: completely loyal, ferocious, dependable, and discreet. A man doing that kind of work needed an anchor, a counterpoint, some other force to maintain him as a human being and not simply a pointed instrument. Kehn had been that anchor, but Kehn had been gone for years, and Hilo and Wen had been sunk into their own rift, not paying close enough attention. Clinging to someone as fiery as Iyn Ro had been a mistake; she was bound to move on from him and Tar could not handle more abandonment.

Wen knew, Hilo thought miserably. But he had been optimistic. He'd cut back on Tar's duties believing it would be enough to curb his instincts. He'd blessed the marriage with the certainty that determined love would make Tar better and happier. So in the end it was all his fault, Hilo felt, for turning Tar into a monster.

"Tar," Hilo said gently. "You weren't yourself. You lost your mind tonight and you did something terrible that I know you would never have done if you'd been thinking at all clearly." Hilo wondered now, too late for it to be of any use, if perhaps there was a medical reason as well, if a sudden undetected onset of the Itches was to blame. Tar would be the sort to dismiss or ignore jade overexposure symptoms, convincing himself that they were some other temporary malady, something that did not threaten his sense of greenness. "What you've done can't be undone. You murdered one of our own, a Fist, a fellow Green Bone. It's a crime that can't be forgiven, you know that." It was hard for Hilo to even say the words, and it was harder for Tar to hear them. His hands began to tremble and he pressed them into stillness between his knees, his shoulders hunched. He looked as if he might be sick. Hilo could barely believe that this wretched man had been for so long one of the clan's most feared warriors.

"We need to go for a walk, Tar," Hilo said. The words came out of him against his will. "Do you think you can do it, or do you need some help?"

Tar looked up at the Pillar with misery but also understanding and resignation. He said, with some of his usual dependable courage, "I can walk."

"Can I trust you with your jade?" He had not given the order for Tar to be jade-stripped and did not want to humiliate him further in this moment if he could possibly avoid it.

"I won't be any trouble, Hilo-jen."

Hilo put a hand on his Pillarman's back and guided him out of the room and toward the door of the house. The Fists in the hallway stepped aside and gave them ample space to pass.

Tar said, "Can I see the kids? Just for a minute."

Hilo said, "I don't think that's a good idea. They're asleep."

Tar nodded, and they walked out of the house and onto the grounds together. Lott and Anden watched them go with grim faces, not knowing what to say and saying nothing.

The Kaul estate sprawled over five acres, with the compound of residences and main courtyard in the center. The gardens, pond, lawn, training hall, and small swath of woodland covered the remaining areas and separated the family's residences from its neighbors and the surrounding city. Hilo guided Tar onto one of the walking paths that wound through the property. They walked around the back of the Horn's house, down a small slope where the Juen children were always making forts and holding mock battles. Hilo walked alongside his Pillarman, who could not move quickly on account of his injuries. When he swayed or stumbled a little, Hilo put a hand under his elbow to steady him. It was three or four o'clock in the morning, as quiet as it ever got in Janloon. A holding place between the day that had gone and the one to come.

When they were well away from the houses, and completely alone so that Hilo could only distantly Perceive the auras of the other Green Bones on the property, he stopped and faced his Pillarman. Tar took a step back and lowered himself to his knees. "Hilo-jen," he said coarsely. "I'm sorry I let you down. Ever since we were kids in the Academy, I only ever wanted to follow you and be your best warrior. We've been through a lot together." His voice broke, and he took a second to recompose himself so that when he spoke again, his words were steady. "The clan is my blood, and the Pillar is its master." He touched his forehead to the ground and straightened up again with calm, apologetic expectancy—the opposite of whatever awful madness had brought him to this place tonight.

Hilo said, "Close your eyes." Tar obeyed. Hilo drew his talon knife and walked behind him. Tar's jade aura throbbed with grief and fear, his heartbeat thundering in the center of Hilo's Perception, but he did not move at all, not even when Hilo placed a hand on the top of his head. It had to be done: one swift stroke, left to right, across the throat. Hilo had killed men with the knife before; it would be an easy motion, over in less time than it took to gasp.

A second passed. Another. Then another. Hilo began to shake. He was clutching the talon knife so tightly he could feel the hilt starting to strain under his involuntary Strength. His other hand curled in Tar's hair, gripping the back of his brother-in-law's skull. The woods seemed to close in and blot out the edges of his vision.

Hilo's fingers spasmed open and the talon knife slipped from his grasp and fell into the gravel at his side. He spun away from Tar like a puppet jerked on strings. "*Godsdamnit,*" he whispered. "Fuck. *Fuck.*" He leaned a hand heavily on the nearest tree, head bowed, and put his other hand over his eyes.

"I'll do it, Hilo-jen," Tar said from behind him. He picked up Hilo's fallen talon knife and got unsteadily to his feet, brushing at the dirt on his knees. "Walk away and I'll handle it." This simple statement, delivered so easily, so matter-of-factly, snapped the last of Hilo's resolve. It was exactly what Tar had been doing for him for years—handling things. The worst, most vicious sorts of things, quietly, reliably, efficiently, and without complaint—so that Hilo could walk away.

Hilo turned around. "Give me back the knife, Tar." His Pillarman handed it to him and Hilo stowed it in its sheath. He pressed the heels of his palms to his eyes, his mind churning. "Here's what will happen." He lowered his hands and said, "You'll be stripped of your jade and exiled from Kekon. You can't come back, ever. If you try, your life will be forfeit and anyone can take it with my approval. The clan will want your blood, and I'll have to convince everyone that the Itches are to blame and you should be allowed to keep your life, so long as you never wear green again. I'm sending you away, Tar, to somewhere you'll have to start over, without jade and without clan."

Tar shook his head, his expression deeply confused, as if he wasn't sure whether to thank or blame Hilo for sparing him. "I'm nothing without jade and clan, Hilo-jen," he exclaimed. "Have someone else execute me, if you don't want to. It would be easier on everyone, and it's the right thing to do."

"Maybe," Hilo said quietly, "but I can't lose another brother. I've lost too many already." He put his hands on Tar's shoulders, and pulled him close. He dropped his forehead against Tar's. "I could always count on you. That's why I've always asked for too much. I'm asking you for one more thing now, the last thing I need from you. I'm asking you to live."

When Hilo came back into the house two hours later, he found Wen sitting on the floor in a corner of their bedroom, knees pulled up to her chest, the side of her head leaning against the wall. Her eyes were red and swollen. She barely raised them as he entered.

"Is it done?" she asked in a dull voice. "Is my brother dead?"

Hilo hung his jacket on the bedpost and sat down heavily on one corner of the mattress. "No," he said. "Stripped and exiled. He'll be gone by the time the sun comes up." He let out a breath full of emotional exhaustion, and pulled a handful of jade pieces—rings, studs, bell, watch—from his pocket and placed them on the bedside table. Tar's jade. Hilo had promised him it would go to Maik Cam someday. "There will be a lot of people in the clan who'll say he should've paid with his life. And they'll be right to be angry. Iyn and her family deserve better. So I'll have to deal with that. But I couldn't do it. I couldn't kill my brother. What kind of a person could do that?"

Wen was staring at him, her mouth slightly open as if she meant to speak but had lost the words. Hilo unbuttoned his shirt. The sky was beginning to lighten over the house and he desperately needed a couple hours of sleep before the certain storm of the day to come. "I'm going to make some changes," he said slowly. "Tar's people, his Nails, they'll go back under Juen. The whole greener side of the clan should answer to the Horn again. The Pillarman used to be something different under Grandda and Lan. Because of the clan war and who Tar is, I changed it. Whatever I sent him to do, he said yes. We needed that. But I don't want it to be that way anymore."

He glanced over as he took off his watch and talon knife and dropped them on the dresser. "The Pillarman used to be a person who didn't answer to the half of the clan with jade or the half with money," he said. "Someone who was always at the Pillar's side, someone who gave him advice he needed to hear, who made everything run smoother. Who helped the Pillar to be the Pillar."

Hilo got up and went over to Wen. He held out a hand and raised her to her feet. "You're that person," he said quietly. "I couldn't be Pillar without you, and I still can't. We've both hurt each other because we were too stubborn about what we expected, and we paid badly for that. But what's the point of life if we give up on the people we love?" He enfolded her into his arms and stroked her smooth hair. He kissed her on the forehead and cheeks and mouth. "Wen, will you be my Pillarman?"

Wen cupped her trembling hand against his jaw. "The clan is my blood," she whispered, her voice thick with emotion, but perfectly steady. She bowed her head and pressed her mouth to the hollow of his throat. "And the Pillar is its master."

The Long Judgment

The last king of Kekon, Eon II, presided over the darkest period of his nation's history and died as an ignominious failure. Kekon had been relatively peaceful and prosperous for three hundred years following the unification of the nation under the royal family of Jan, but by the time Eon II ascended to the throne at the age of nineteen, the country was facing political upheaval. Foreign entities had established a presence on Kekon. The merchant Bramsko Explorers Guild from Stepenland, the Tun Empire, which controlled the port city of Toshon in Kekon's southern peninsula, and the Shotarian navy that ruled the East Amaric Ocean were increasingly in conflict with each other and with the local population.

In the wake of several violent incidents and allegations of foreign bribes paid to the royal family, the country's numerous Green Bone clan families began to take sides against one another, with some remaining loyal to the beleaguered monarchy and others supporting its overthrow. When the Empire of Shotar invaded Kekon with the full might of its modern military, it faced a defending force of jade warriors who possessed exceptional abilities but no comparable organization or unity.

Despite this, the fighting was so fierce and casualties so high that documents later revealed Shotarian military commanders were prepared to burn the city of Janloon to the ground, arguing that otherwise every last Green Bone on the island would die fighting, each taking hundreds of enemy soldiers down with him. King Eon II was advised by his counselors to flee the country and continue the war in exile. Instead, the monarch commanded the clans to retreat. He surrendered to Shotar and abdicated the throne. The Shotarian government kept the former king in comfortable captivity, making his eventual death by poison at the hands of foreign overseers appear to be from natural causes.

The Kekonese so widely reviled King Eon II as a coward and a weakling that when the monarchy was symbolically if not functionally reestablished fifty years later, Eon's grandnephew Ioan III reigned under the title of prince to distance himself from his hated relative. More recent historical scholarship has been kinder to Eon II. His seemingly premature capitulation is estimated to have saved millions of lives and enabled the country's remaining Green Bone warriors to regroup and form the One Mountain Society—the indomitable national resistance network that would end Shotarian rule and be the precursor to today's modern clans. During his captivity, the former monarch urged peace and citizen cooperation with the foreign governors, but was later discovered to have sold off most of the royal family's possessions and secretly funneled the money to Green Bone guerillas via Lantern Men intermediaries. A Shotarian bodyguard who wrote a memoir about Eon II described him as private, bookish, and especially softhearted toward animals—the antithesis of the fierce and brutish Kekonese stereotype widely depicted by Shotarian propaganda.

On his deathbed, the disgraced king is said to have lamented, "I'll be remembered not for who I was, but for what I wasn't. Perhaps it's for the best. Let the gods judge me for what I did not do."

CHAPTER
15

Skeptics

the thirteenth year, sixth month

As the most junior physician on staff in the Paw-Paw district medical clinic, Anden was stuck with the least desirable working hours—late nights, early mornings, holidays. Out of the eighteen doctors, only three were Green Bones. Anden often worked even longer than his assigned shifts, or was called in outside of them. His reputation as a jade prodigy and his status as a member of the Kaul family meant that Fists and Fingers of the clan sought him out specifically, so he was always in demand. Also, Paw-Paw was a poor and violent neighborhood; there were often urgent cases to deal with. One evening, he was summoned to treat a patient with a collapsed lung and internal bleeding. He was surprised to see that the man on the bed was Lott Jin, his former classmate from Kaul Du Academy, now the No Peak clan's First Fist of Janloon.

"Lott-jen," Anden exclaimed, "how did this happen to you?" Lott's injuries were the result of blunt trauma. Remarkably, none of his bones were broken and the multiple knife wounds were shallow—clearly, Lott's Steel was excellent, but blood vessels and soft organs were difficult to protect even with good jade abilities.

"Barukan," Lott answered grimly, as if that was the only explanation required. Later, the two Fingers anxiously waiting in the reception area to hear of their captain's condition would explain that Lott had been ambushed by men with pipes, crowbars, and cleavers during a stakeout of a barukan gang hideout. The First Fist had killed four attackers before falling off a third-story fire escape. Some barukan gang members possessed enough self-taught jade ability to make them dangerous even against Green Bones, especially when they had an advantage of numbers. Most of them were originally from the Matyos gang in Shotar and claimed vague allegiance to the Mountain clan, which denounced and punished their illegal activities but also used them to do low-level work and to attack No Peak without getting directly involved themselves. Keeping the criminal class under heel while manipulating it against their rivals was a long-standing tradition of the clans.

Surgery would normally be called for to stop Lott's bleeding, but Anden was able to find the injury and seal the blood vessels with a few focused pulses of Channeling. He couldn't help but feel strange treating the classmate he used to have feelings for as a teenager, and he couldn't stop himself from noticing that even pale and injured—wavy hair damp with exertion, long-lashed eyes closed, sulky lips pressed together in pain—Lott was still attractive. He was also now one of the clan's top Green Bones.

"You're going to need to stay overnight, on an oxygen machine," Anden told him, Channeling slowly and diffusely to raise the man's circulation and speed healing. "You're sure to recover fully, Lott-jen, but it's going to take a few weeks."

Lott nodded, eyes still closed. Anden got up to wash his hands at the sink. "It could've been you, Emery." Lott spoke from behind him. "You were the best of our class at the Academy. I would've expected you to become First Fist, not me."

Anden turned around. Lott had opened his eyes and was look-ing at Anden with the corners of his full mouth raised in a sarcastic smile. He gestured at his own situation, his bandaged body. "Are you sure you made the right choice? No regrets?"

Anden frowned as he dried his hands. "Who knows what rank I would've reached. Maybe I'd already be dead, by the Mountain or by the Itches. Fate makes assignments in the clan as much as merit does. Probably more." That was true for Lott as well. Iyn Ro had been the one pegged for promotion to First Fist, until she'd been murdered by Tar. Thinking about that night made Anden shudder.

He could feel Lott's eyes on him, the slow swirling of the man's jade aura. Anden said, "I don't think anyone can ever know if they made the right choices, but I don't regret mine, so long as I'm still alive to be useful in other ways." He sat down in the chair next to Lott's bed, trying not to pay any attention to the man's dark eyes or the shadow of stubble on his jaw. "What about you, Lott-jen?" he asked. "When we were in the Academy, you never wanted to take oaths to the clan as a jade warrior. Why did you?"

Lott's expression hardened and his aura drew in. Anden assumed he wouldn't answer, but then he said, "Everyone said my da was a top Fist, as green as they come. When I was young, I didn't want to have anything in common with that bastard—let the gods rec-ognize him." Lott tried to take too deep of a breath and folded for-ward in discomfort. He leaned back against the raised head of the bed. "But after he died, it was the clan that was there, that took care of my ma and my siblings. Now, my sister's graduated from college. My ma started a catering business. They never would've dreamed of doing that before. Why shouldn't I rise to the highest rank I can? It's the best thing I can do for them." His eyes flashed defiantly, as if he expected Anden to argue with him. When he didn't, Lott's voice lost its defensive edge. "The Pillar was the first person in the clan who spoke to me like a man," he admitted. "He expected me to be my own person, not just a poor copy of my da. He made me think it might be possible to be green without being cruel and angry."

Anden said quietly, "I never thought of you as a copy of anyone.

It seemed to me you were always your own person." Impulsively, he reached a hand out toward Lott's, but the other man pulled his arm away, not sharply or quickly, but obviously enough. Anden withdrew his reach, stung, his face hot with embarrassment.

"I'm glad to see you're happy with your decisions," Lott said, not unkindly, but looking away to pretend he didn't see Anden's discomfort. "Thanks for patching me up, keke. Now that I'm the First Fist, life's more dangerous and I have further to fall if I'm unlucky. I can't afford to be careless or to make any mistakes."

A voice message in Espenian was waiting for Anden on the answering machine when he returned to the small office he shared with two other doctors, both of them gone for the day. Anden checked the clock and did a quick time zone calculation. It would be morning in Adamont Capita. To avoid expensive long-distance charges showing up on the clinic's phone bill, he used a calling card to reach Dr. Martgen, who answered on the second ring. "Thank the Seer I reached you," said the Espenian doctor. "We've run up against a wall, I'm afraid."

For the past six years, Dr. Martgen and a small number of passionate advocates in the Republic of Espenia, with discreet but considerable support from the No Peak clan, had been advocating for the legalization of bioenergetic jade in medical treatments based on Kekonese healing. A bill was now being debated in the National Assembly, but was being blocked by the Espenian Physicians Society. Martgen explained, "Not only is the EPS intent on killing the bill, they're proposing stiffer criminal penalties on anyone who, in their words, uses bioenergetic jade to perform 'unproven and potentially harmful medical procedures.'"

Anden pressed his knuckles into his desk. He wasn't surprised that most Espenian doctors misunderstood jade and saw it as an unacceptable threat to their established practices, but if the countermeasure passed, Green Bone healers like Dauk Sana, who'd been quietly helping people in the Keko-Espenian community for decades, could be arrested and face years of imprisonment. "Is there anything we can do?"

"There is some good news," Dr. Martgen said. "Yesterday we convinced Assemblyman Sonnen, the chairman of the National Panel on Health, to delay voting for three weeks and allow lawmakers to witness a public demonstration of bioenergetic medicine before making their decision." A brief pause on the line. "I realize this is extremely short notice, but is there any way..."

Anden sank into his chair. The legalization of jade in Espenia, even if it were limited to the medical field, was something No Peak had been wanting for years. "I'll get on a flight as soon as I can," he said. "I need to sort out some things at work and with my family, and I'll try to bring others with me. I'll call you back."

After hanging up, Anden let out a long breath and scrubbed his hands over his face. Then he got on the phone again. He called in favors from his coworkers, pleading with them to cover his shifts for the next three weeks, then left a message for the clinic's secretary to reschedule his less urgent appointments. That done, he called the Kaul house. Hilo was not home, but Anden explained the situation to Wen, who told him to arrange the trip to Espenia and act with the clan's full authority. It still startled Anden sometimes, to hear his sister-in-law say things such as, "I'll pass everything you said on to the Pillar," speaking of Hilo the way a Pillarman would, as if she didn't share a bed with him every night.

Having secured the clan's approval, Anden phoned Dr. Timo and Dr. Yon, two senior physicians who'd traveled with Anden to Espenia on professional visits to the Demphey Medical Research Center. Ordinarily, he would never think to be so presumptuous as to contact them personally at such an inconvenient time and ask them to upend their schedules. When he reached each of them, he apologized for bothering them at home and said, "My cousin, the Pillar of No Peak, has asked me to act for the clan," which made it clear he was making this request not as a junior colleague but as a representative of the Kaul family. He assured the men they could expect to be rewarded for their trouble and have their travel expenses taken care of.

After both physicians had agreed to make the trip, Anden made one final call to Kaul Dushuron Academy and dialed the extension for the boys' dormitory, followed by a two-digit room number. A couple of years ago, personal phones had been installed in each of the students' rooms, a luxury that Anden had never had when he was there. He told Niko he was sorry he wouldn't be able to take him to see the Janloon Spirits relayball game next weekend, but if the fourteen-year-old would go to Anden's apartment twice a week to collect his mail and water his houseplants, there would be a hundred dien in it for him.

"No problem, Uncle Anden," Niko said. "I hear there're a lot of thieves in Espenia. When you're over there, do you wear one of those money belts under your clothes to stop pickpockets?" Niko was an unusually cautious teenager, prone to imagining worst-case scenarios. After Anden explained that the area he was visiting in Adamont Capita was perfectly safe, his nephew asked, "Can you bring me back a bag of those sour sweets, like you did last time?" Anden promised to do so.

After a frustratingly long wait on hold with Kekon Air, Anden managed to book himself onto a direct flight to AC the following afternoon. The only seats left available in the main cabin were middle seats near the back of the aircraft. At the airport check-in counter, Anden spent a doubtful minute debating the issue with himself before upgrading to business class. Even when given full authority by his cousins, he was always hesitant to spend the clan's money, as he held no official rank in No Peak, and felt that he was in some sort of perpetual debt on account of how the Kaul family had raised him and paid for a Green Bone's education at Kaul Dushuron Academy, followed by an Espenian associate's degree, and then medical school at the College of Bioenergetic Medicine—all for what?

He was doing well enough for himself as a physician, his relationships with the Kekonese-Espenians in Port Massy had benefited the clan on both sides of the Amaric Ocean, and for years he'd been acting as the liaison between Martgen's research team and the Green Bone doctors in Janloon. But his adoptive grandfather, the late Kaul Seningtun, let the gods recognize him, had brought an orphan boy into his home expecting to add a prodigious jade warrior to the family, one that could help his own grandchildren lead the clan. Anden knew his cousins would not evaluate his worth in such a mercenary way, but he imagined other people did. Lott Jin had outright said as much when he'd suggested Anden could've been First Fist in his place. Anden often told himself that at the age of thirty-one, he was done caring about what others thought of him, but nevertheless, he couldn't help but feel he still had something to prove.

Once he was on the plane, Anden had no regrets about his decision. After a twelve-and-a-half-hour red-eye flight, he would have to arrive in the capital city of Espenia prepared to put his jade abilities on public display while facing skeptical and hostile foreign policymakers. It was more important that he be well rested and not fail his clan, his vocation, or his country than save a couple thousand dien.

When Anden arrived at the Capita View Hotel, he was met by Dr. Martgen and Rigly Hollin, who sat down with him in the hotel restaurant. Dr. Martgen was obviously under a great deal of stress; he had dark hollows under his pale eyes, and his normally trim beard looked coarse and unkempt. He wore the brave but fearful expression of a man facing the firing squad. Martgen's research into and championing of bioenergetic medicine had made him a pariah among many of his peers in the medical community, and if the legalization bill before the National Assembly failed, it would likely mean the end of his career.

Rigly Hollin, in contrast, was as excited and intensely focused as an athlete before competition. At times, Anden had to ask him to slow down or repeat himself simply to understand what he was saying. "This is great news for us, really great," he declared. "Assemblyman Sonnen gave us exactly what we need, a public demonstration. Anyone can dismiss or discredit data in a report. They can't argue against what people see with their own eyes. The ball is on our box line and it's our rucket now."

The sports reference was lost on Anden, who'd never developed an understanding or appreciation for the game of ruckets, but he was encouraged by the man's optimism. Rigly Hollin was the vice president of the advertising and public relations firm WBH Focus. He was married to a Kekonese woman. During a trip to Janloon five years ago, she had encouraged her husband to seek out bioenergetic medical treatment for a sports injury that had plagued him for more than a decade. Amazed by the improvement he experienced, Hollin was disappointed to discover that the practice was not legally available in Espenia, except in conjunction with a few medical research programs. That was how he'd come in contact with Dr. Elan Martgen. Since then, Hollin's company had partnered with Martgen and his colleagues to run a major campaign to raise awareness of bioenergetic medicine and push for its legalization. WBH Focus shot and ran a thirty-minute documentary on major television networks, publicized the results of Martgen's research in national newspapers, and collected hundreds of thousands of signatures petitioning lawmakers.

All the funding for the effort came indirectly from the No Peak clan. Demphey Medical Research Center was a nonprofit institution dependent on government grants; it could never afford to pay for film shoots and ads in major newspapers. Every year, the Weather Man's office issued a generous annual donation to the College of Bioenergetic Medicine, earmarked for cultural exchange and academic partnerships. The money, Kaul Shae had made abundantly clear, was meant for one purpose: promoting jade medicine in Espenia.

Martgen and Hollin explained to Anden that the demonstration would take place in a local private clinic that had agreed to a short-term lease on available space. Imaging equipment would be available on-site. The Espenian Physicians Society would send observers, and Hollin had arranged for news reporters and cameramen to be present. Anden and the two other Kekonese doctors, who were due to arrive tomorrow, would see anyone who requested treatment. The patient list so far included a large number of interested legislators and journalists.

"I realize we're asking a lot from you and your colleagues," Dr. Martgen said worriedly. "I wish this wasn't such a battle, but the

Espenian Physicians Society is a powerful and conservative entity. It doesn't change easily, especially when it comes to accepting influences from other countries and cultures."

According to conversations Anden heard around the Kaul family dinner table, the Mountain clan was now bypassing the embargo on the Uwiwa Islands via subsidiary operations in East Oortoko run by their barukan allies. There were also signs it was trying to enter Espenia, which for many years had been No Peak's greatest advantage. "As much as Ayt plays the anti-foreigner card in public, she knows the ROE is too big and important to leave to us," Hilo had said. "It's only a matter of time before the Mountain makes a move."

Anden's anxiety was rising, but he managed a smile. "I should get some sleep," he said to Martgen and Hollin. "It sounds like I'm going to be busy."

―――――――――

Anden would later recall the two weeks he spent at the clinic in Adamont Capita as one of the most exhausting and professionally challenging periods of his career. He saw over two hundred patients personally. Dr. Timo and Dr. Yon saw even more than that, so in total roughly eight hundred people were treated. The ailments Anden encountered varied considerably. Some people had chronic pain, nagging injuries, ulcers, or wounds that he treated by increasing blood flow to the affected areas and stimulating healing. Others needed kidney stones or arterial plaque broken up with precise Channeling. Anden cut blood supply to a number of tumors and fibroids, preventing them from growing any larger. On several occasions, the work was purely diagnostic—unexplained illness or pain that required him to strain his Perception and search out some abnormality in the body that might then have to be more finely imaged using MRI or CT scans or treated with physical medicine.

Most of the people who showed up seemed willing to try anything that might help them, and happy to receive free healthcare, but Anden worked in the shadow of several Espenian doctors who came in and watched him suspiciously, making notes and scowling, sometimes interrogating the patients to make sure they were real and not planted actors. Anden fielded questions from reporters and tried to keep up a commentary for the video cameras in the room. He explained to observers that the Kekonese martial discipline of Channeling was the basis for all bioenergetic medicine, but in the medical field, the word was rarely used, as it encompassed several distinct branches of treatment, categorized depending on whether the purpose was to increase, decrease, or redirect energy, the speed and force at which this was done, and the body system that was being manipulated—vascular, neurological, and so on.

Anden had never used his jade abilities at such a sustained rate, day after day, except during the final Trials at Kaul Dushuron Academy, and even that had not felt as difficult. Each day he would arrive at the clinic before the sun was up, work all day, then return to his hotel room in the dark and collapse in exhaustion, only to rise in the morning and repeat the process. Several legislators and journalists who were treated by the Kekonese physicians, or who had friends or family members who'd come to the clinic, were so impressed that they were now public supporters of the legalization bill, which had become widely reported upon in the news. Word of the visiting Green Bone doctors had spread, and hundreds more people showed up at the clinic, hoping to get in, some of them standing outside on the sidewalk for hours. Most, unfortunately, had to be turned away, causing a convenient public outcry. "I came to Adamont Capita hoping to influence legislation, not work as a charity nurse," Dr. Yon grumbled at one point, seeing the long line snaking outside the waiting room of the small clinic.

By the end of the two weeks, Anden felt as if his sense of Perception was so burned-out that the energy around him had smeared into a dim and indistinguishable blur in his mind, and he doubted he could muster the strength to Channel enough to stun a mouse. Dr. Timo and Dr. Yon were also worn-out, and although they were both passionate supporters of spreading jade medicine to the world, they intimated to Anden on more than one occasion that all this work had better be worth it. Perhaps, they mused aloud, the Weather Man of No Peak would be pleased enough by this effort that she would talk to the dean of the College of Bioenergetic Medicine about giving raises to certain members of the faculty.

Martgen and Hollin were ecstatic. "The vote on legalization will happen by the end of the week," Hollin told Anden. The Espenian Physicians Society had made an effort to have it further delayed pending "additional research," but Assemblyman Sonnen had denied the request. "We're in the end rucket," Hollin declared. "The will of the people can't be denied."

The ad executive's optimism was premature. Forty-eight hours before the scheduled vote, two lawyers knocked on Anden's hotel room door. The Espenian Physicians Society had successfully argued that the practitioner leading the demonstration ought to be questioned by legislators about his background and his ties to the No Peak clan. Anden was summoned to appear in front of a special hearing by the National Panel on Health the following morning.

This must be what it's like to be on trial, Anden thought. He was seated alone at a small table with a microphone, facing a long, raised semicircular bench with a dozen Espenian lawmakers staring down at him. They had perfunctorily queried him about his academic and professional credentials, all in a tone of polite interest, and now it seemed they were finally ready to get to the heart of the matter.

"Dr. Emery," said one of the panel members, Dr. Gilspar, who was also the current secretary of the Espenian Physicians Society. "Is it true that you were adopted and raised by Seningtun Kaul, the leader and patriarch of the No Peak clan, one of the two largest clans in Kekon that controls bioenergetic jade?"

"Yes," Anden answered. "That's true."

"And for eight years, the Kaul family sent you to one of Kekon's jade combat training schools, where students graduate into being street soldiers of the so-called Green Bone clans, is that also true?"

Anden scanned the long row of Espenians watching him. He was not wearing his jade, so he could not Perceive which of the panelists were sympathetic toward him and which ones were opposed; he could only try to guess based on their expressions and body language. Most of them, however, remained stone-faced as they regarded him. Anden said, "I graduated from Kaul Dushuron Academy, one of the best martial academies in the country. Many, but not all, graduates go on to join the No Peak clan. Others, such as myself, go into other professions, including medicine."

Another panel member said, "But you are a still a member of the No Peak clan, correct?"

"Most people who live in Janloon are affiliated with the Green Bone clans in some way," Anden explained. "They're vital institutions in our country, like the Trade Societies here in Espenia."

"For the people in this room who are not familiar with these Green Bone clans," said Gilspar, looking around at his fellow panelists importantly, "they effectively control the mining, processing, and distribution of Kekonese bioenergetic jade, nationally and internationally, legally and illegally. Their power in that small country is such that you could even describe them as a shadow government. And they're not above using whatever means they deem necessary to achieve their aims, including violence."

"Sounds like a Trade Society, all right," quipped a reporter, to some laughter.

Assemblyman Sonnen said, "What is the purpose of this line of questioning, Dr. Gilspar?"

Dr. Gilspar raised his voice defensively; it echoed in the officiously high-ceilinged chamber. "Mr. Chairman, I'm trying to ascertain whether Dr. Emery and his cohorts have motives contrary to the best interests of Espenian patients." He turned back to Anden. "Since you were raised in the ruling family, you're not an ordinary member of No Peak, are you, Dr. Emery? Is it accurate to say that you are, in fact, a leader in the clan?"

Anden leaned forward to speak more clearly into the microphone. "I'm personally close to the Kaul family, but I hold no title or rank in the No Peak clan. As a physician, I'm not beholden to any clan. My duty is to use jade abilities to heal those in need of care."

"However, you admit you've used your abilities to commit violence in the past?"

Anden felt as if he were walking on a narrow plank and this unpleasant Espenian man was trying to push and prod him in every direction to tip him off. "When I was young, I was trained to use jade in combat, and my home city of Janloon has been through times of conflict when I had to defend myself. Also, dueling is common practice in my country and nearly every man fights at some point."

"Sir, that is not an answer to the question," Gilspar countered.

Assemblyman Sonnen broke in impatiently. "What *is* the question you're dancing around, Dr. Gilspar? We're here to decide whether to approve the legal use of bioenergetic jade for medical purposes, not investigate every aspect of Dr. Emery's upbringing and personal character." Mumbles of agreement traveled through the room, and for the first time, Anden saw politicians nodding their heads.

Anden felt a surge of appreciation toward Sonnen. He'd been starting to wonder if anyone was going to point out the EPS representative's increasingly biased and irrelevant lines of inquiry. Gilspar, however, was not done. Feeling the tide turn against him, he placed his fists on the table and half rose from his seat, speaking with even greater vehemence. "Mr. Chairman, it's obvious what's going on here. The Kekonese make millions of thalirs selling jade through military contracts to the ROE. The clans ruling that island are ruthless, barbaric organizations, and now they want to take over our healthcare market as well. Are we going to let them do that? Are we really going to give a bunch of kecks legal license to practice their unTruthful methods on people in this country?"

The room broke into exclamations and heated discussion. The back of Anden's neck burned hot, and the shirt he wore under his dark suit was sticking to the small of his back with sweat, but he remained silent in his seat, showing none of his anger as voices rose around him and journalists snapped photographs. When he was younger, Anden had believed the people of Espenia to be like his own biological father—shallow, arrogant, faithless. Since then, he'd met enough Espenians to know that was simply a stereotype like any other, but this man who'd spoken so forcefully and rudely, this Gilspar—he was the sort of Espenian that made his people hated in the world. He spoke confident part-truths on things he knew nothing about, he had the conceit to judge others on the basis of his own hypocritical standards and motives, and he dared to show contempt for a stranger's family.

Assemblyman Sonnen banged a gavel and called for a thirty-minute recess. "Dr. Emery, please wait in the visitor's lounge until we decide whether we've any need to ask you further questions."

Anden was all too eager to escape. The visitor's lounge was merely an ordinary room with a few armchairs, a phone, and oil portraits of Espenian premiers. Martgen and Hollin met Anden there. They had only been allowed to watch the session from the panel room's balcony. Martgen was pale and wiping his brow, looking as if he'd been the one interrogated. Hollin clapped Anden on the back and said he'd handled everything perfectly and been the picture of credible professional calm compared to Gilspar.

Anden used the phone in the room to dial the front desk of the Capita View Hotel and ask if he'd received any messages. He'd explained the situation to Shae yesterday evening as soon as he learned what he would be facing, and he wanted to know if his cousins had any further instructions for him. The receptionist at the hotel told him that he had indeed received a message; she patched him through to the voicemail system. To Anden's surprise, Hilo's voice said, "Andy, call me at the house when you get this message. Call the family line. Use a pay phone. Don't worry if it's late over here, call anyway."

There were pay phones inside the building, but Anden was not sure they would count as secure enough. He made an excuse to go outside, saying he needed a smoke to calm his nerves, which was not entirely untrue. There was a phone booth a block down the street. Anden called collect to a number that went straight to the Pillar's study. He looked at his wristwatch; it was nearly midnight back in Janloon. Hilo picked up on the third ring.

"How're things going over there, cousin?" Hilo asked. Anden gave the Pillar a succinct report of what had happened. Hilo said, "Shae has people digging into this man, Gilspar. He takes a lot of money from the pharmaceutical companies. Also, he has at least two mistresses. If we have to shut him up, we can do it, but you've been doing a good job, so let's wait and see what happens."

Anden couldn't help venting a little. "Hilo-jen, I'm ashamed to have any Espenian blood."

"Don't say that, Andy," Hilo scolded. "You're going to let the words of some water-blooded spenny bureaucrat make you feel bad about yourself? Haven't I always said that in your case, some foreign blood made you better? Hasn't it been good for us that you can go around in that country looking like one of them?" Hilo paused and Anden heard the phone go muffled for a moment, perhaps held against Hilo's shoulder as he said, with mock severity, "Hey, you're not too old to hug your da good night, are you?"—no doubt speaking to Ru, the only one of his children still living at the Kaul house since Jaya had gone off to the Academy this year. Seconds later, Hilo came back onto the line. "Anyway, you've done everything you can there. I need you to go to Resville. Tomorrow, if possible."

"Resville?" A city in the far south of Espenia, a three-hour flight away. "Why?"

"That's where the Mountain is trying to get its hooks into Espenia," Hilo said. "We knew they'd make a move, and Resville is where they're doing it. They know we've got too much strength in Port Massy, so they've gone somewhere else, hoping we won't notice. We've got to wipe them out. I need you to meet with someone, to set it up for us."

Anden looked at his watch again. Thirty minutes had gone by and he was supposed to be inside, waiting to hear if he would be called back in front of the panel for further questioning. He'd already been in Adamont Capita for sixteen days. As a jade-wearing Kekonese citizen, he was only allowed to remain in the ROE for twenty days at a time, and he'd hoped to use his last few allowable days in the country to visit Port Massy and see Mr. Hian, who was in his eighties now. With Mrs. Hian gone—let the gods recognize her—who knew how much longer Mr. Hian had to live? Resville was nowhere near Port Massy.

"I have to go back inside, Hilo-jen, I'm late," Anden said. "I might still be stuck here for a while, I don't know yet. Of course, if we have a chance to destroy the Mountain in Resville before they get a foothold in this country, we should take it, but I can't leave without any warning, it'll be suspicious. I'll call you again tonight, first thing in the morning your time."

After he hung up the phone, Anden hurried back into the building, arriving ten minutes late and out of breath, apologizing to an anxious Dr. Martgen and saying he'd gone to the wrong entrance and gotten lost in the corridors. As it turned out, he needn't have rushed; it was another forty-five minutes before he was called back into the room before the panel.

Gilspar appeared flushed and deeply sullen. He did not speak or get a chance to ask any further questions. Assemblyman Sonnen cleared his throat and said to the room, "A majority of this panel has moved that the proposed legislation to legalize the use of bioenergetic jade for medical purposes proceed to a vote in the National Assembly tomorrow morning. We've heard enough from both sides of this debate, and despite some fiercely dissenting opinions, the evidence gathered is incontrovertible."

Several observers in the room began to applaud, but Sonnen held up a hand. "Dr. Emery, before I declare you free to go, I want to thank you for your hard work, patience, and advocacy. It's inspiring to see an accomplished biracial individual such as yourself showcasing the best of your heritage. The number of patients you've helped in the last two weeks is a testament to your dedication as a physician, and to the extent you've faced insensitive or prejudiced comments, I hope they pale in comparison to the many people who are eager to embrace what other cultures have to offer."

Anden thanked Assemblyman Sonnen and left the room amid appreciative applause. He stayed just long enough to accept relieved handshakes from Dr. Martgen and several members of his research group, and pleased backslaps from Rigly Hollin and his team. Anden returned to his hotel room and packed his bags. The following morning, after two hours of debate, the National Assembly voted, by a slim majority, to legalize the medical use of bioenergetic jade. By then, Anden was on a flight to Resville, on the orders of the Pillar, to see to the destruction of the clan's enemies.

CHAPTER

16

All Business

The address provided by his cousins led Anden into an industrial part of Resville, to a converted warehouse with no sign above the door. It was much warmer here than it had been in Adamont Capita. The stucco walls were sun-bleached and the surrounding concrete gleamed almost white in the dry heat. The inside of the building was dim in comparison to the stark midday sun outside and smelled strongly of stale sweat. Anden had expected something like the grudge hall he'd known in Port Massy—a secret training hall for Green Bones, converted into a social gathering spot in the evening—but the space he stepped into now bore little resemblance to the basement of the Kekonese community center in Southtrap. Most of the warehouse floor was taken up by what appeared to be a fighting ring with battered blue mats covering the concrete floor, cordoned off with thick floor-to-ceiling mesh barriers. The ring was not empty; scattered throughout the space were stacked wooden crates, metal oil drums, and cement blocks. Ropes dangled from the girders, and horizontal steel beams hung from above, suspended at either end by thick chains.

Inside the enclosed space, two Green Bones were sparring in dramatic fashion—leaping Light off the obstacles, hurling Deflections that sent ropes swinging and metal drums tumbling and rolling, clashing Strength against Strength, and Steeling against blows that sent them careening into splintered wooden crates. The men were not trying to truly hurt each other, but it was impressive to watch such a thrilling display of jade abilities—and in Espenia, of all places, where Green Bones had to practice in secret. Kaul Du Academy had some large, elaborate training fields and on certain occasions such as Heroes Day, the school would open its doors to the public and senior students would put on showy public demonstrations. This struck Anden as a low-budget version of that display, in an illicit, somewhat sordid environment.

A man was standing outside of the mesh barrier, watching the fighters and shouting at them. Most of his exclamations were expletives of encouragement or disappointment, like a spectator standing in front of a televised sporting match. "Fuck, yeah!" he bellowed, then, "Seer's balls, you're gonna let him do that to you? Move, goddamnit!" Anden walked up beside the man, who noticed him and gave him a brief, unwelcoming glance, but didn't turn his attention away from the action. The man was young, Anden noticed, in his midtwenties, and handsome in a brutish way, with sharp shoulders and elbows, dark lips and a strong brow. He wore faded jeans and an untucked black T-shirt. Elaborate tattoos wound up both his forearms. Anden could not see any jade on him—the Kekonese in Espenia did not wear jade openly—but Anden knew this man was a Green Bone, not only because he'd been told beforehand, but because even without his own jade, standing near the stranger, Anden could sense the edges of his aura, bright and cutting.

A loud bell went off, presumably to end the match. Breathing heavily and wiping their brows, the two fighters inside the ring stopped their contest and met in the center of the floor to slap hands and digress into their own conversation. Anden spoke to the man next to him. "Are you Jon Remi?"

"Who's asking?" said the man, eyeing Anden.

Anden turned and touched his head in abbreviated salute. "I'm Emery Anden of the No Peak clan," he said in Kekonese. "My cousins send their regards from Janloon. As does Dauk Losunyin in Port Massy."

Remi Jonjunin, better known as Jon Remi, did not entirely lose his standoffish manner, but he gave Anden his full attention now and said, in a more amicable voice, "So you're the man sent by the Kauls. I've heard about you. You were friends with Rohn Toro, back in the day."

"Let the gods recognize him," Anden added.

"I didn't know him," Remi said with a shrug, switching back to speaking in Espenian. "I was only a kid, and Port Massy is fucking far away from Resville. Just heard about him, like he was some kind of an urban legend. Greenest man in the country, they said. Went out in a bad way, though. Fucking Crews."

Anden said, "It's true that he was the greenest man in the country."

"And how's old man Dauk doing these days?" Remi asked. "Still cheating the grave, that one?"

Even though Dauk Losun was not truly a clan Pillar, Anden was not accustomed to hearing anyone speak of the aging Green Bone leader, the most influential in Port Massy and indeed all of Espenia, with such flippancy. Jon Remi, Anden had been told, was an ally of the Dauks and the man to speak to in Resville about all Green Bone matters. Espenians were more casual, and Remi had been born in this country, so perhaps there was no disrespect intended. Still, Anden answered guardedly now, following Remi back into Espenian, as that seemed to be what the man preferred. "I haven't had a chance to see Dauk-jen in person during this trip, but I hear he's doing well and has a fifth grandchild now, a boy."

"Good for him, good for him," said Remi, somewhat distractedly. The two Green Bones in the prop-strewn ring were stepping out through a pulled-back flap in the mesh barrier. "You see that man, the one with the longer hair?" Remi said, changing the subject as he pointed across the floor at the fighters. "Danny," he hollered, "you're a fucking jade animal, you're gonna kill everyone in the auditions, crumb." The other Green Bone waved in thanks, and Remi said with pride, "That's Danny Sinjo, he's been fighting in the shows in Marcucuo for two years, already got an 8–1 record and now he's been scouted for a role in a gangster flick by a Shotarian movie studio. Just remember, when you see him on the big screen in a few years, you can say you met him in Resville before he got famous, right here in Jon Remi's club."

Anden was not familiar with half of what Remi had said, but he took a long look at Sinjo and even from a distance agreed that he could be movie star material, at least when it came to physical appeal. Although, Anden admitted to himself glumly, his standards for attractiveness might be growing more generous. He winced inwardly, thinking of Lott Jin. What had he been expecting, reaching for a shallow teenage infatuation?

Rejection wouldn't sting so badly if he had other options, but it had been a long time since he'd had anything he might describe as romantic prospects. Part of the difficulty was that he'd spent his twenties in medical school and starting his career as a physician, but the larger problem was that he had no real idea how to meet suitable partners in Janloon. He had no interest in going to some of the places where men typically went to meet each other for casual encounters. He was too well known as a member of the Kaul family and didn't want to be seen in places and situations that would reflect poorly on him.

"I didn't think a Shotarian movie studio would hire a Kekonese Green Bone," he said to Remi.

"Sure they would. Danny's going for the role of the main villain, the barukan gang boss who kills the cop's wife and kids. They're popular, you know, the Shotarian crime dramas. All over the world. Big money in movies." Remi led the way across the floor of the warehouse, around the perimeter of the fighting ring, to an area with a pool table and several cracked leather sectional sofas. He flopped down on one of them and gestured grandly. "So, what do you think? As good as the gyms in Janloon?"

Anden did not want to say no, but he suspected Remi was asking the question merely to goad him into polite lying, which would be embarrassingly apparent to someone who could Perceive it. Instead he said, "I didn't expect there to be a place like this in Espenia. Aren't you worried about the police?"

Remi showed his teeth in a smile, as if he'd been expecting Anden to ask the question. "Resville is a Crew town, crumb. We're less than a third the size of Port Massy, but we've got at least six Crews jostling for a piece of the action. And on top of that, the drug cartels from Tomascio. The police, they don't pay attention to a few kecks with jade." There was scorn, even resentment, in Remi's voice. "Resville's different from the rest of the country. Let's just say rules here are more...relaxed."

No wonder, then, that this was where the Mountain had chosen to make a major entry into the country. Located only fifty kilometers from the border with Tomascio, Resville possessed year-round good weather, warm beaches, and copious entertainments that made it one of the country's top tourist locations. Anden sat down on the sofa across from Remi and said, "So you own this place?"

"My uncle owns it," Remi said. "I run it for him. It does all right. We hold matches here every month, and we fill the space about half the time. We're not nearly as big as the jadesports events at Marcucuo, but it's more intimate here. Some of what they do is fake, choreographed. The only thing you can't do here is lethal Channeling. Otherwise, we're no-holds-barred. So this is one of the few places on the continent guys can come to train and get amateur experience before trying to go big time in Marcucuo."

Anden felt he knew less than he should about the seedy world of jade combat for sport and profit. In Kekon, jade was not permitted in professional athletics of any kind. Green Bones were expected to adhere to aisho and serve their clans, or else use their abilities in noble professions such as medicine, teaching, or religion. Anden was sure that Hilo would curl his lip at the idea of a jade warrior stepping into a ring in front of a howling audience to win attention and money for himself. There were, however, obviously people who did it anyway, in places where such things were legal or at least overlooked. Anden couldn't help but think of Jon Remi as a lower type of Green Bone, not at all respectable.

Nevertheless, No Peak had bargained and associated with disreputable people before when necessary—from motorcycle gangs in Janloon, to the Crews, and the Espenian government itself. Anden had long ago learned not to hold Keko-Espenians and their ways to the same standards as Kekonese. According to No Peak's sources, Jon Remi was the top Green Bone in the city of Resville. He possessed a loyal group of followers, and he kept the Crews and the police out of Kekonese neighborhoods and businesses. He managed fighting dens, whorehouses, even shine dealers—unsavory activities—but a man who did not follow the rules was the sort of ally they needed in Resville at the moment. Anden said mildly, "I obviously have a lot to learn about this part of the country."

"We've never had close ties to the guys in Port Massy. Sure, we respect Dauk, and we follow the rules about keeping jade to ourselves. We've hosted visiting Fists from Janloon, and some of our people have gone to train in the old country and brought back some useful skills. I'm all for keeping up connections." Jon Remi crossed his arms. The tattoo of a black skull with snakes coming out of its eyes grinned at Anden from across the distance between them. "But we've always run things separate from Port Massy *and* from Janloon. So tell me: Why's the No Peak clan suddenly interested in Resville?"

"We go where our enemies are," Anden replied.

Remi said, "You mean the Mountain clan."

"They're buying their way into new construction here. They have a controlling stake in the Sands of Illusion casino over on the east side, and they're establishing a foothold in retail, restaurants, and sports betting." All areas where the Mountain had traditionally been strong in Janloon. "Whatever profits they make here, they'll send back to Kekon to use against No Peak. So you can see why this is a concern to us."

"And your cousins sent you here to talk to me about it." Remi smiled.

"We don't have many people in this city ourselves," Anden said. "We need a local partner. I was told that you were the person to talk to. It would be worthwhile for you, more profitable than this club."

"You're not the only one who's looking for a partner, you know." Remi leaned forward, his eyes fixed on Anden. "The Mountain has less here than you do. How do you imagine they plan to protect their investment from so far away, especially against the Crews, and against their mortal enemies, the Kauls?"

At Remi's words and the abruptly low, shrewd tone of his voice, Anden understood at once that he and his cousins had been preempted. The Mountain had already approached Jon Remi for an alliance. Anden half expected to be attacked and killed in that moment. He had to resist the urge to look around wildly for enemies. Yet no one emerged from some unseen position to slit his throat, and Remi remained seated exactly where he was, smiling, knowing full well that Anden's thoughts were racing with calculation and unease.

Anden sat still and kept his eyes on the other man's face. If Jon Remi was already working for Ayt Mada, he wouldn't have given Anden any chance. He must still be in play.

Anden said, calmly, "What did the Mountain offer you?"

"Exactly what you'd expect," Remi said. "Money, manpower, and jade, in exchange for protecting the Mountain's properties and business interests in Resville from crewboys and the No Peak clan."

Anden nodded. "And what did you tell them?"

"I said I'd think about it." Remi's thick lips curved. "I wanted to hear the competing offer."

"You have far better reasons to side with No Peak than the Mountain."

"I'm keen to hear them, crumb, but not now. You're a guest from Janloon, so let me show you a good time. I wouldn't want anyone to say that a representative of the No Peak clan left Resville without enjoying what the city has to offer." Remi stood. "Meet me at the Blue Olive tonight. Say you're with me, and they'll let you upstairs. That way I can buy you a drink, before you try to buy my loyalty."

———————

"This man, Remi," Anden said to Hilo over the phone. "He seems green enough on the outside, but he was born in Espenia and I don't have a good feeling about him. As far as I can tell, he doesn't respect anything and doesn't answer to anyone. I wouldn't want him working for the Mountain as our enemy, but even as an ally, I wouldn't say we can trust him."

"Can he do what we want him to?" Hilo asked. "That's as far as we need to trust him."

"How much are we willing to give him, Hilo-jen?" Anden looked at the clock on the hotel room table. "It has to be better than whatever the Mountain is offering. Would you grant him the same status as a tributary like the Jo Sun clan?" Anden made a face that the Pillar could not see. It seemed ludicrous to give a young Keko-Espenian gang leader like Jon Remi the same consideration as the Pillar of a minor Green Bone clan, but then again, Resville was a bigger city than anything the Jo Sun clan controlled.

There was also the possibility that if Remi decided to side with the Mountain, or had already done so and was deceiving Anden with this meeting, he might not walk out of the Blue Olive nightclub at all.

"Andy," Hilo said, "I can't say exactly without having met this man in person. I'd be there myself if I could be, but then the Mountain would know right away what we're doing. Figure out what he wants and give him no more than that. Don't let him get above his place or show disrespect, but make this happen for us. It's important. You've talked to Shae so you already know the numbers. I trust you, Andy."

———————

Anden did not have anything appropriate to wear to the Blue Olive; he'd packed for a work trip and not a Resville nightclub. He bought an overpriced resort-wear T-shirt from the hotel gift shop and wore it with black jeans and his suit jacket and formal shoes. He wouldn't be allowed to carry any weapons into the club, but for a long moment, he sat on the edge of the hotel bed and fingered the band of jade stones he wore only when treating patients. If something went wrong, if Remi was luring him into a trap on behalf of the Mountain, having his jade abilities might mean the difference between life and death.

Anden shut his jade into the room's safe. His instincts told him that if Jon Remi meant to harm him, he would already have done so. And if he started carrying his jade whenever he felt there might be danger, he might as well abandon his one ironclad personal rule and start wearing jade constantly. In no time at all, he would be back to being a Green Bone warrior of the clan, forced to kill or be killed.

He arrived at the Blue Olive to discover that he had overdressed, or rather, dressed incorrectly for the venue. A crush of half-naked bodies filled the dance floor, which throbbed with a mix of Espenian and Tomascian club music and red strobe lights. Two dancers of indeterminate gender gyrated in raised cages in the center of the crowd. Black vinyl stools surrounded the mirrored bar. As Anden passed, searching for the staircase, an older man in a fishnet top grabbed his ass. At first, Anden was too surprised to react. Then he did so without thinking, seizing the man's wrist, twisting it into a painful lock and slamming it against the bar top. The man screamed a curse over the loud music, but Anden was already regretting causing a scene. He let go and pushed past the people nearby, losing himself in the club's dark confines before the injured man or anyone else could pursue him. The staircase upstairs was barred with a velvet rope and two bouncers, who let Anden through when he said he was there to see Jon Remi.

He found Remi in the company of two trans women in identical red miniskirts who were both laughing at some joke he'd made. Two surly Kekonese men, who Anden assumed to be Remi's subordinates or bodyguards, loitered nearby, appearing bored. They looked Anden over as he approached, but at a word from their boss they let him pass. Remi smacked the women on their rears and told them to leave, as he had business to discuss. They did so with pouty faces, giving Anden coy looks as they left. Anden sat down across from Remi, who sat up and turned serious and solicitous.

"What'll you have to drink?" he asked. His pupils were dilated, his face slightly flushed.

"I don't suppose they serve hoji here," Anden said, thinking he could really use one.

"Nah, they should, though. It's getting more popular, you know."

"A beer, then," Anden said. "Whatever you recommend."

Remi flagged down a server, who brought Anden a lager and Remi a glass of some clear hard liquor. Anden's host pulled the purple curtain across the booth shut and said, "So you like this place? You check out the dance floor? Resville's a beautiful playground, it's got everything you could wish for, crumb. You're on vacation, so just tell me what you want and I'll hook you up. Do you like older men? Younger?"

For a second, Anden was astonished. Then he was intrigued and reluctantly tempted. He was far away from Janloon. No one could possibly recognize him as a member of the Kaul family. He could have liaisons with as many strangers as he liked over here and never have to see them again. But on the phone, he'd told Hilo that he wouldn't fully trust Jon Remi even as an ally; letting the man procure sex for him struck Anden as unwise. He suspected Remi had brought him here to unbalance him, to gain some sort of personal leverage. "I'm not on vacation," he corrected.

A brief flash of irritation, possibly anger, crossed Remi's face. "All business, huh? You're all *clan*, from the old country, too good for this scene?" When Anden didn't answer the rhetorical question, Remi snorted as if it had all been a joke and leaned forward intently, his face close enough that his brittle jade aura once again scratched at the edge of Anden's Perception. "All right, then, since you want to get straight to it. The Mountain will pay me a hundred and fifty thousand thalirs a month, plus a kilo of cut jade. They're allies with the barukan, so I'll get some muscle from the Shoto-Espenian gangs on my side here in Resville. Also, I'll be able to buy shine at a discount straight from the Uwiwa Islands, and the barukan say they can bring tourists from Shotar to the fighting dens and strip clubs." Remi sat back. "I can't think of many reasons to say no."

Anden took a swallow of his drink while he gathered his thoughts.

"You'd be breaking your alliance with Dauk Losun, who's a friend of the No Peak clan. You'd have no more jade or support from Port Massy. The Mountain's offer is lucrative, but it only makes you a paid enforcer, not a proper tributary. You won't get a cut of their profits and you won't be able to count on them if you run into any trouble. No Peak has more influence and more legitimate business interests and lawyers in this country."

Remi shrugged. "I'll take cold, hard cash over tributary status any day. What does that get me anyway? What do I care about clan prestige in Kekon? Or lawyers in Port Massy, for that matter?"

Anden could see that he was playing this incorrectly and tried to adjust. "We can match the money and jade," he said. "We can't sell you shine or bring you Shotarian tourists, but we can do something better. No Peak has an entire business office with dozens of people in Port Massy. If we had the local support to open a satellite office here in Resville, it would mean jobs and investment and an influx of people to the Kekonese population. That's more people and money directly to your businesses but also you would get a percentage of our profits here. So the better we do, the better you would do as well." As he spoke, additional things occurred to him and he said, "We already have a system in place of sending Green Bones between Kekon and Espenia for teaching and training opportunities. The fighters at your club, the up-and-coming ones who'll be the next Danny Sinjo, could take advantage of that. And jade is legal for medical use now, because of the No Peak clan. You could have a foot in the door in that area."

Remi listened to all of this with a thoughtful, calculating expression. "You're putting me in a tough spot, crumb," he said. He curled his bottom lip over his teeth and moved his jaw back and forth in a snidely indecisive manner. "Which clan should I pimp myself to? I know you old country islanders wouldn't normally waste your spit on a kespie punk like me, but suddenly both of the big clans are eager to woo the locals so you can stick it to each other, as if you haven't had enough opportunities to do so back home." Remi shrugged with exaggerated indifference. "No Peak does have something in its favor, though. Iwe Kalundo from the Mountain clan is a bald, ugly fuck, and you're not."

Remi unzipped his fly and pulled out his cock. It lay flaccid in the wedge of his open pants. A thin chain of jade stones sat bared across his pale, jutting hips. "Tell you what. You suck me off, on behalf of the No Peak clan, and we have a deal." He locked eyes with Anden. "You want to do it anyway. And then I'll do what your cousins ask. I'll take your side in Resville."

A prickly heat spread up Anden's neck. Outside the curtained booth, the muffled bass from the dance floor downstairs throbbed. Anden could feel it through the soles of his shoes, reverberating all the way up his spine to his head. Slowly, he shifted closer, until he was next to Remi on the bench. The man licked his lips, watching Anden's every move with anticipation.

Anden said, in a low voice that he did not entirely recognize as his own, "My cousin, the Pillar, told me to figure out what you want and to give it to you." He brushed Remi's hands aside and cupped the man's balls. Remi's cock began to stiffen. "It took me a bit of time to understand what that is.

"You want your own power. You want to live by your own rules, not as a tool of others, not according to the terms set by people who look down on you from both Kekon and Espenia. You're only a Resville kespie thug, so you have no choice but to choose between the big Kekonese clans at your door—but you want do it with a member of the Kaul family sucking your dick."

Anden's grip tightened on Remi's testicles. The man's eyes widened and his jade aura swelled, its sharp edges grating across Anden's Perception like steel filings.

"Forget everything I've said so far." Anden had never been on the military side of the clan, but he'd been raised as a Kaul and been around Fists all his life. So he knew instinctively how to speak in the calm, decisive way that commanded attention, that suggested violence. In that moment, he thought of his cousin Lan and tried to speak exactly as the former Pillar would have. "Here is the real offer. You get nothing, except this: a promise that No Peak will stay out of Resville, so long as the Mountain is gone from the city as well. Whatever you take from our enemies, you keep for yourself. If you need money, people, jade, or anything else to accomplish that, we can help with those things. Otherwise, we'll confine our activities to Port Massy and other parts of the country. As long as you maintain respect for Dauk's authority and other Green Bones, Resville will be yours. You have my word, on behalf of the Kaul family of No Peak.

"If you decide instead to side with the Mountain, we will send our own people from Janloon and Port Massy and go to war over this town. We've done it before in Kekon and we can do it overseas, even if it costs us. One of the clans will prevail, or maybe the Crews will take advantage of the situation and drive us both out, but whoever wins, it won't be you. You'll be in the middle, just street muscle, even lower than the barukan."

Anden pushed the man's cock back into his pants and fastened the zipper with a yank. He stood up and looked down at Remi sprawled on the sofa. "My flight to Janloon leaves tomorrow evening. My cousins will be expecting to hear from me before then. If you want to be a hireling of the Mountain, there's no need to do anything. If you want something else, call me before noon."

Anden walked out of the booth. He half expected Remi's two bodyguards to stop him, but they did not move to do so. He went down the staircase and out of the Blue Olive. Only when he was inside a taxi, out of range of the other man's Perception, did his heart begin to race as adrenaline emptied into his veins, as if his body had held back any reaction until it was sure he was safe, so that in the important moment, not even a Green Bone could've sensed his fear and rage.

CHAPTER
17

Enemies

Juen Nu was summoned to a Seventhday brunch meeting at the Twice Lucky. It was not one of his preferred places to eat; he personally thought the restaurant was overrated, riding on its long reputation and a few admittedly excellent signature dishes. Newer, more interesting dining options existed in the city. But the Twice Lucky was a Kaul family favorite, and it was impossible to be the Horn of No Peak without essentially becoming an associate member of the Kaul family, so Juen had no choice but to eat there more than he would out of personal inclination.

At least, thank the gods, there was now air-conditioning throughout the old building, so the dining room was a welcome refuge from the oppressive summer heat. When he arrived, the Pillar and his wife, the Weather Man and her husband, and their cousin Anden were at their usual table near the back and already partway through their meal. Whenever the Kaul family ate at the Twice Lucky, the proprietor, Mr. Une, ensured the tables nearby remained empty, and a painted folding screen cordoned them from sight of the rest of the dining room, so they could talk freely.

"Kaul-jens," Juen said, saluting informally before joining them.

"Juen-jen, there's still steamed egg and nut pastries but only two crispy squid balls left," said Wen, filling his teacup. "We can order some more food if you're feeling hungry."

"This is more than enough," Juen assured her. With the Pillar's permission, he preferred to have an early breakfast with his wife and children and spend the morning with them, arriving late to the Twice Lucky and eating only lightly before clan discussion began. Even though he was the Horn and his family lived on the Kaul estate (a decision his wife had supported for the sake of convenience and security), Juen did his best to maintain some personal boundaries. He had no desire to follow the fate of the tragic Maiks and see his own family subsumed into the Kauls. Despite all their strength, the Kauls were unlucky—with not one, but two stone-eyes, as well as an adopted cousin who was mixed race and queer. Juen liked the Kauls well enough, even the unlucky ones, and he would follow Hilo-jen no matter what, but he very much hoped to preserve the luck of his own family, beat the odds of occupying his dangerous position, and live to see retirement and grandchildren.

Taking Juen's arrival as a cue that the leaders were about to begin discussing clan issues, Anden put down his napkin and pushed back from the table to leave. Hilo said, "Do you have anywhere else you need to be, Andy? If not, stay." The suggestion was made casually, but Anden and everyone else at the table understood it to be an order. Anden hesitated, glancing around the table uncertainly, then sat back down.

Juen sighed inwardly. The Pillar had already made his unlucky wife his Pillarman, and now he was bringing his unlucky cousin, who held no official rank in the clan, into the inner circle of the leadership, no doubt because the doctor had recently accomplished so much in Espenia on the clan's behalf. Juen was not going to question the Pillar's decisions in areas beyond the Horn's purview, but he couldn't help but wonder if so much ill fortune concentrated near the top was a handicap on the entire clan that made his job as Horn more fraught in some invisible way.

Hilo turned to Juen. "How was your trip?"

"About what I expected." Juen had recently returned to Janloon after three days in Lukang. The stalemate there had persisted for years and was unlikely to change so long as Jio Somu remained the Pillar of Six Hands Unity. No Peak continued to support Jio's opponents, who would not rest in their goal to avenge the old Pillar and Weather Man and take back rightful control of the clan. "They want to send that kin killer to feed the worms, and weren't happy that I wouldn't commit more help to making that happen."

Juen was a pragmatic man and thought the odds of whispering Jio's name were low. The traitor kept guards around himself at all times and was so paranoid about assassination attempts that he rarely left his fortified residence. As far as Juen was concerned, killing Jio was not a high priority for No Peak. It was more important to consolidate and defend their existing holdings, and to tamp down the worrisome rise in activity from barukan gangs and anti-clan anarchists in Janloon.

When he said this, Hilo agreed. "We've been supporting our allies in Lukang for long enough. Give them three months to decide whether they want to form their own minor tributary clan, or take oaths to No Peak."

Juen gave a nod and helped himself to a nut pastry. "As for the anarchists, there's still confusion over whether Green Bones or the police should be in charge of dealing with them."

Anti-clan extremism was a low-level but persistent and spreading concern, like a stubborn fungal infection. Some misdeeds by the so-called clanless were disorderly, such as distributing pamphlets of their manifesto and spray-painting graffiti on public property, but some were more serious. Recently, a jade setter's shop had been set on fire, and although the shop was saved and the arsonists caught and punished, Juen pointed out the larger problem: "These extremists aren't anything like a clan, or even a street gang. They're opportunistic and loosely organized, and their goal isn't to control territory or businesses, or to steal jade or money. They just want to drum up discontent and create ugly attention so they can spread their poisonous ideas."

Anden said, with a confused frown, "There are always fanatics on the fringes of society. Why do there seem to be more of them now, and why are they so much bolder?"

Woon answered him. "Because now they can look to outsiders for sympathy and money. The Slow War has put Kekon on the map and jade on everyone's mind. There are foreign governments and organizations that encourage the anti-clan views."

Hilo said to Juen, "I'll come to the next meeting you have with the chief of police. You're right that we need to coordinate better with the cops to find these lunatics and cut them down." He ate the last crispy squid ball and wiped his mouth with a napkin. "But first, we've got a bigger problem to deal with."

The Pillar glanced at his Weather Man, who passed a file folder across the table to Juen. It contained a stack of enlarged photographs. They appeared to be aerial images, taken from a helicopter, capturing sections of rocky shoreline and surrounding ocean. A shape that appeared to be a ship was circled with black marker. Additional photographs, taken with telephoto lenses, showed the ship in greater detail—an industrial vessel with an orange hull, its deck crammed with heavy equipment.

"What is this?" Juen asked.

"A prototype mining ship," Hilo said. "Built by an Espenian company to dredge the ocean floor around Kekon for jade."

Juen exclaimed, in incredulous outrage, "They can do that? In Kekonese waters?"

Shae said, "It's currently located twenty-five kilometers off the coast of Euman Island. We were alerted to it by leaders of the Abukei tribes who fish in the area. The Espenian Navy controls those waters—in fact, given the number of battleships they have patrolling the Amaric, they control most of the waters around Kekon."

Anden spoke up. "If the Espenian military is allowing this, shouldn't it be an issue for the Royal Council to bring up with the ROE government?"

"They already have," Woon replied. "It's a diplomatic sore point. Relations have already been strained for years over the expansion of Euman Naval Base. Since the ROE wouldn't budge on the issue, the KJA reduced jade exports to Espenia. It seems the ROE response to *that* is a typically Espenian one: search for someone else to buy from."

"An Espenian company willing to dig through the ocean floor around Kekon," Juen finished for him. "Will it work? Is there actually any jade to find down there?"

Wen answered slowly, but clearly. "I spoke to several geologists at Jan Royal University who think so. Rivers have been eroding the mountains of Kekon and carrying jade into the surrounding ocean for millions of years. And there's also runoff from the mines being washed out to sea. The only question is whether it's possible for anyone to profitably sift through all that water and gravel for enough tiny pebbles of green."

"Art Wyles, the CEO of Anorco Global Resources, obviously thinks so," Shae said. "The Espenian tycoon has invested hundreds of millions of thalirs into developing undersea mining technology. This ship is the first real test. Wyles is also supposedly high up in the powerful Munitions Society and has a lot of political connections."

Woon Papi, who seemed to be more outspoken since marrying into the leadership of the Kaul family, grumbled, "If there's any time when the cost of such a foolish and arrogant venture might pay off, it would be now, with the price of jade so high. There are reports that Ygutan has jade soldiers of their own, and the Espenians are desperate to stay ahead of their enemies. They'd like nothing more than to bypass the KJA altogether and have a reliable Espenian company mining jade for them."

Juen put the photographs back into the folder. He'd noticed that the Pillar had not said anything further, allowing the rest of the family to explain. Up until now, the issue had been a political one. Now that the Horn was involved, it was a military one.

"Hilo-jen," Juen said, smiling with the excitement and trepidation of being handled a truly unusual challenge, "this is not going to be easy."

"I wouldn't ask you if it was," Hilo said. "I want that fucking ship destroyed."

———————

A common misperception, even within the clan, Juen thought, was that jade ability and martial prowess were the most important traits of a good Horn. Juen was without question an accomplished fighter, but he hardly considered it to be the most important qualification for his job. Certainly not in this day and age, when as Horn, he had to manage thousands of jade warriors deployed in different cities and even in different countries. The clans had become too big to attack each other directly without mutual catastrophe, so they waged proxy wars via tributaries and allies, criminal gangs, spies, politicians, and journalists, which further complicated Juen's responsibilities.

After Vuay had retired from the clan to take on a teaching position at the Academy, Juen had split the role of First Fist into three equal positions, all reporting directly to him—one to oversee Janloon, one for the rest of Kekon, and one dedicated to the management of White Rats. He'd folded Maik Tar's former Nails into this latter branch, and focused on modernizing its operations and planting informers among the barukan in Kekon and Shotar and the Uwiwa Islands with the goal of gathering more intelligence on the Mountain's activities. Juen had to constantly manage difficult people and limited resources and keep a thousand details organized in his mind. And now, he also had to deal with this foreign mining ship.

He made a phone call to his enemy: Aben Sorogun, the Horn of the Mountain. Aben had become Horn after the retirement of Nau Suenzen four years ago. Juen had only seen the man in person a few times at public events, although he possessed a great deal more information gathered by No Peak spies. "Aben-jen," Juen said when he reached the other Horn, "I assume you know about that Espenian company's ship off Euman Island that's an affront to all Green Bones. My Pillar wants it gone, and I suspect yours does as well. My name isn't Kaul, and yours isn't Ayt, so personally, I don't see why we shouldn't work together on this, even if nothing else changes between our clans."

Aben agreed, which was good news because Juen's plan was rather expensive, and might've raised attention from the Mountain unless they were involved. Six weeks after meeting with the Kauls in the Twice Lucky, Juen was standing on a beach in the middle of the night with two rigid inflatable boats, sourced from navy surplus thanks to No Peak's connections in the national military. Eight Green Bones—four from No Peak, four from the Mountain—were outfitted in diving gear. There were plenty of strong swimmers among the clan's Fists and Fingers, but not many with actual diving experience. Standing in one of the boats, Aben Soro commented wryly, "I don't know about Kaul Du Academy, but marine sabotage wasn't taught at Wie Lon Temple School. Maybe I should talk to the grandmaster."

In person, Aben was surprisingly amicable, not anything like the grizzled veteran Nau Suen or the calmly brutal Gont Asch. Perhaps Ayt Mada had decided the Mountain needed a younger, more likable face in the clan's leadership. Aben wore his jade as a heavy green chain around his neck and seemed like the sort of man who watched sports and owned large dogs, who could be friendly with everyone but exuded a down-to-earth toughness that was not to be fucked with. They were both acting pleasant and cooperating in this one manner, but Juen was not about to forget that elsewhere—in Lukang, and across the ocean in Resville—their respective forces were busy trying to destroy each other, and it was entirely possible that under different circumstances, one of them would kill the other.

Tonight, however, they shared an objective. Instead of launching from Euman Island, where they might be spotted by the Espenian military, they'd chosen the upper part of Kekon's main cove, a two-hour drive north from Janloon on a deserted stretch of shoreline. This far from the city, there was no light pollution and the clear sky was ink black and strewn with stars. The Green Bones in the two boats sped toward the foreign mining ship, bouncing rhythmically across gentle swells for ninety minutes before coming up on either side of the slow-moving vessel under cover of darkness.

Juen had found out everything he could about the ship beforehand. It was still being tested and not yet fully operational, so only a small crew was in place. Remote-controlled machines were sent to gather samples from the seafloor, which were evaluated for potential jade concentrations before an expensive, specialized crawler was deployed to dredge the area. The crawler was connected to the ship by an enormous hose that sucked up sediment and transported it to the equipment that extracted the gems. It was impressive, cutting-edge technology. Juen had to grudgingly admire the Espenians; when motivated by greed, they were truly ingenious.

They cut the engines. Divers from both sides went overboard with quiet splashes. Working with the sort of speed only Green Bones can muster, they magnetically attached limpet mines to the underside of the ship. In the silently bobbing boat, Juen kept his Perception trained above, but he didn't sense alertness or alarm from any approaching crew members. Every few minutes, he swung his Perception back toward Aben, more out of instinctive caution around an enemy Green Bone than any real fear of betrayal. They were out here together precisely so that neither side could take advantage.

Within thirty minutes, all the divers had returned to the boats and they were speeding back the way they had come. They would be long gone when the timed charges went off. The explosions would not be large enough to kill the people onboard—dead foreigners were best avoided—but they would destroy the rudder, propellor, and crawler hose, and tear holes into the ship's hull, hopefully damaging the equipment on board as well.

Ideally, that would be the end of the Anorco corporation's expensive foray into jade mining, but Juen thought it likely the ship would be repaired and they would have to destroy it again, perhaps several times before the venture was written off as too costly. The Espenians were sure to complain angrily to the Royal Council about the damage to private property, and the Kekonese government would smugly and rightfully deny any knowledge or involvement in the sabotage. Without another source of jade, and with Kekon still the linchpin of the ROE's regional defense strategy against Ygutan, complaining was all the foreigners could do.

When they returned to shore, Juen's face was stinging and his ears were sore from the hours of sea spray and wind. He jumped out of the boat and helped drag it onto shore, working quickly with his men to pile the boats and equipment onto a waiting trailer truck that would transport them into storage. It was still dark, but the sun would come up in a couple of hours, and they had to return to Janloon. Aben and his men worked efficiently alongside them. After the gear was loaded and the truck had driven away, the No Peak and Mountain Green Bones climbed into their separate vehicles, though not before checking for car bombs the other side might've planted.

"Juen-jen," Aben Soro said, touching his forehead.

"Aben-jen," Juen replied, returning the gesture. He got into the front of his Roewolfe G8 and sped with his Fists back to the city. When the sun rose, he and Aben Soro would be enemies as usual, and he had to get to work.

18

Catfish

Bero met his handlers every six to eight weeks, in different public places that he didn't usually frequent and where they wouldn't be overheard. Two days beforehand, he would get a note slipped under his apartment door with the date, place, and time of the meeting. He felt like a secret agent in a spy movie, except that it was not as glamorous as he'd hoped. He did not, for example, get a gun, or a secret phone, or a cyanide capsule with which to kill himself if he was ever caught by the Ygutanians. He did get a code name: Catfish. Bero disliked the name. Catfish were ugly bottom-feeders. He hadn't been given any choice in the matter, however. He always spoke only with Galo, the Keko-Espenian man, while Galo's partner, Berglund, kept watch by walking around nearby, disguised as a foreign tourist.

"Do you have any *specific details* about what they're planning?" Galo pressed him again today, as they walked around the nearly empty art museum. Bero had never been in an art museum before.

He pretended to study a display of indigenous Abukei pottery while speaking to Galo.

"They keep talking about doing something big, striking a blow, making a statement, vague shit like that," Bero said, frustrated more at Galo's incessant prodding than by his failure to garner detailed information about Vastik eya Molovni's involvement with the Clanless Future Movement.

The clanless had grown. That much, Bero could tell them for certain. There were more people at the meetings, more people daring to stand up to the clans. Guriho's speeches were getting so exuberant that sometimes Bero thought the man would begin frothing at the mouth or give himself an aneurysm. They had momentum now, Guriho said. The people were ready to defy the corrupt and oppressive forces of government, religion, and capitalism that had fettered them with the manacles of clannism. Or something like that. Bero couldn't remember all the man's flowery words.

"Guriho keeps saying that soon the moment will come for us to rise up in the streets and fight," Bero grumbled to his handler, "but it's not like he tells us exactly what that moment's going to look like or when it's going to be."

"Have you had any success getting closer to the leaders?" Galo demanded.

"I've *tried*, keke," Bero retorted, even though Galo was not a keke at all. "It's the four of them—Molovni, Guriho, Otonyo, and that girl, Ema. They don't bring anyone else in."

Galo moved away from the glass case of Abukei pottery toward a wall of Deitist religious iconography, expecting Bero to stay with him. In the corner of the room, Berglund stowed the museum brochure he'd been pretending to read and followed after them at a distance. "We know the background of the three men, but this woman, Ema, what's her story?" Galo asked. "She's not Ygutanian, or barukan, or anyone with a political motive, as far as you've told us. What makes her one of the group's leaders?"

Bero scowled, because he didn't understand it either. For some reason, the woman had been admitted into Molovni's inner circle, when

Bero had not. She must be letting them fuck her. It was the only explanation.

"I already told you what I know," Bero grumbled. "She works as a secretary somewhere downtown. She's spent time living in Tun. Her family has a business, or they used to. I think it went under. That's why she has a grudge against the clans, because they ruined her family, she says."

Shortly after he'd begun working for the Espenians, Bero had succeeded in convincing Ema to go to a bar and have a drink with him. They stayed out for a couple of hours. She was nice to look at, and she even laughed at some of his jokes. She seemed like a lonely person without friends. Bero told her the story of how he'd gotten his crooked face, from being caught and beaten by the Maik brothers when he was sixteen years old. Of course, he had even bigger stories to tell, but he thought he would save them for later, since she might not believe them. To Bero's disappointment, Ema was not as awed as he'd expected she would be. Worst of all, when he suggested they go back to his place, she said she had to work the next morning and gave him only a kiss on the cheek.

Since then, he'd managed to coax her out for drinks a few other times, and once, they went to see a late-night horror movie. He wasn't able to get any further on those occasions either, nor learn anything useful about her to satisfy the Espenians.

One evening, Bero waited in an alley outside of the Little Persimmon, hoping to catch her alone as she walked back to the subway, or follow her to where she lived. When twenty minutes passed and she still hadn't emerged, he went back up the stairs to the lounge. The room appeared to be empty but he could hear voices. When he walked behind the bar, he discovered a small room—perhaps an ample storage closet, or a space where musicians and performers could retreat between sets, or simply an eccentric secret area. Instead of a door, the entryway was covered by a hanging purple curtain, but it was not drawn all the way across, and through a gap, Bero could see Molovni, Guriho, Otonyo, and Ema talking in low voices, standing around large pieces of paper spread out on a table.

Perhaps the stories about the nekolva having jade abilities were true because Molovni turned around and flung the curtain open. Bero leapt backward at the man's ferocious glower. "What're you doing back here?" the Ygutanian demanded. "Meeting's over."

"I think I dropped my keys near the bar earlier," Bero lied quickly. "Anyone seen them?" He made a show of looking around the bar and the bench where he'd been sitting. Ema rolled up the papers on the table, but not before Bero glimpsed a map of Janloon and hand-drawn building blueprints. Guriho came over to help Bero look. Molovni's hooded eyes followed Bero with suspicion.

"None of us have seen your keys," Ema said. "We'll let you know if they turn up."

Bero pretended to be disappointed, then said, "So, what were you guys talking about? Whatever it is, I can help, you know. What's the plan?"

Molovni put a large hand on Bero's shoulder and guided him back toward the stairs. "We're still working on it, friend." The foreigner's grip was strong, as strong as a Green Bone. "If we need help, we'll surely ask you."

After that, Bero arrived early to the clanless meetings or stayed late, hoping to overhear more of what the ringleaders talked about, but he didn't have any more luck catching them in their discussions. It seemed Molovni and the others had moved their private meetings to some other time and location.

Bero couldn't figure out why they didn't trust him. Maybe they thought the clans were watching him, even though he'd quit his job at the Double Double casino a long time ago. Did they lump him in with that obnoxious tool Tadino? Perhaps they considered him a risk because he'd been picked up by the police for vandalism in the past. He'd been good about keeping his head down lately, though, hadn't he? It was possible they simply didn't like him.

For a while, Bero was stuck providing the Espenians with whatever information he could glean from the general meetings, such as how many people showed up each week, which ones Molovni talked to, how the clanless were recruiting and fundraising. Eventually, by dint of his regular attendance and persistent interest, he managed to become the secretary of the Clanless Future Movement, which meant that for the past year, he'd been responsible for recording attendance at the meetings, taking and keeping notes of the happenings, and maintaining all the secret membership lists. It was easy enough to make copies of all these documents and pass them along to Galo and Berglund on a regular basis. This steady stream of mundane but detailed information had been enough to keep the ROE military intelligence goons sated, and Bero's paychecks flowing, which was the most important thing.

Still, Galo and Berglund wanted more. They suspected the Ygutanians were supporting the aspiring Kekonese revolutionaries with money, guns, and other resources, and they wanted hard proof. They wanted a breakthrough.

From the other side of the exhibit room, Berglund caught his partner's eye and made a surreptitious gesture to finish up the conversation.

Galo turned back to Bero. "If this Ema woman has influence with Molovni, she could bring you in. Try to get close to her again."

Bero sneered at how easy Galo made it sound. "I'd like to, believe me."

Galo glanced at Bero with undisguised irritation. "You should try to become her friend, get to know her, not just get under her skirt. Where exactly does she work? Does she have ties to Ygutanian interests? *Details.* This is of national importance."

The Espenians had emphasized on several occasions that Ygutan wanted to encourage, manipulate, and take advantage of the nascent but growing anti-clan social movement in order to create political instability in Kekon. If the clans were thrown out of power, then jade would flood the market. Ygutan and its allies could acquire it more easily, instead of depending on illegal contracts and stingy black market middlemen. Civil unrest in Kekon might lead to a more pro-Ygutanian regime and a renegotiation of existing jade export contracts with the Republic of Espenia.

That was unacceptable, for Galo and Berglund and all their

superiors in Adamont Capita. They did not want anything to threaten their country's advantage in Kekon.

"Yeah, yeah, I hear you," Bero muttered. "I'm working on it."

Galo handed Bero the usual paper envelope of cash. Bero reached to take it, but the handler held on to it, giving Bero a long stare of almost paternal concern. "We've been investing in you for years, Catfish. We've paid you more than you could ever have made in your sorry life. Remember that this money runs out at the same time our patience does. The Espenian military protects our assets—but only the ones we consider valuable."

Galo let go of the envelope and left the gallery. Two minutes later, Berglund got up from the bench in the corner and followed, leaving Bero alone to curse everyone, himself included.

CHAPTER

19

~

Smiles and Words

the thirteenth year, eleventh month

Wen stood in front of the full-length mirror in the bedroom and examined herself. She'd chosen a forest-green designer dress, patterned with a subtle traditional print but cut in a flattering modern silhouette. She complemented it with dangling gold leaf-shaped earrings and dressy gold flats—any sort of heel made her too anxious about falling. She debated whether to wear her hair up or down before deciding to pull it away from her face in a fan-shaped clasp but to keep it down for a more informal appearance befitting a daytime event. She rehearsed her speech once more, taking the time to pause and carefully enunciate any words that she feared might trip her up and cause her to stammer when she was in front of a microphone. As a stone-eye and the wife of the Pillar, she'd long ago developed resilience against the negative opinions of others. She was accustomed to being judged for her physical appearance and her inherited deficiencies, so nothing anyone could say on those aspects worried her, but she was terrified of being regarded as a feeble Pillarman.

The Pillarman was not traditionally a visible role and did not ordinarily draw much interest from inside or outside the clan. However, Kaul Hilo appointing his stone-eye wife into the position formerly held by one of his closest and most feared warriors was unusual enough to have caused considerable comment. Some people viewed it as a shift in No Peak, a sign that the Pillar was stepping back from personal involvement in the military side of the clan by consolidating it back under the Horn and placing a non–Green Bone in the role of his closest aide. More callous remarks suggested Kaul Hilo simply needed a Maik at his side at all times and was down to his last one.

Six years had passed since Tar had been exiled. Wen grieved for her brother as if he were dead, which he might as well be, as he could never return or contact anyone in the clan again. Whenever she visited Kehn's gravesite in Widow's Park, she brought two baskets of flowers and fruit and asked the gods to recognize both of her brothers. She knew that Tar was in Port Massy, closely watched by clan allies who'd been instructed not to interfere with or harm him, but to kill him if he violated any of the rules laid upon him.

Every few months, she wrote letters to Tar, telling him news about the family and how his nephews and niece were doing. She did not hide this from Hilo, and he did not stop her, because Tar knew better than to ever write back. That was how Wen knew her lengthy messages were meaningful to him, a man who was a ghost; he never once risked losing them.

Wen put the cue cards containing her written speech into a sequined clutch and went down to the kitchen. Ru came downstairs in his school uniform. He threw the ball for Koko, then fed the yellow dog before sitting down and gobbling the breakfast of eggs and hot cereal that Wen set in front of him. "Can I go to my friend Tian's house after school today?" he asked.

"I won't be able to pick you up," Wen told him.

"I can walk to Uncle Anden's apartment and he can drive me home later."

"How far of a walk is it? Where does Tian live?"

"In the Commons." When Wen gave him a stern look, the twelve-year-old groaned dramatically. "Ma, his apartment is *two blocks* away from Old Town."

"It's still in Mountain territory."

"We're not at war with them," Ru protested.

"We're always at war with them, even when you don't see it."

"Ma!" When Ru was angry, color came into his face, and he looked even more like Hilo. "No one else in my class has parents who make a big deal out of walking two blocks in an 'enemy' district."

"No one else in your class is a Kaul." Wen was starting to feel exasperated herself. "It's not just the Mountain. There are plenty of other bad people out there. "

"In the *Commons?*" Ru exclaimed. "It's not like I'll be wandering alone at night in Dog's Head!"

"Still, our Fists and Fingers won't be nearby, and you can't walk into a store and expect there to be a No Peak Lantern Man who'll help you if you need help."

Hilo came in through the patio door. Ru wheeled on his father. "Da, can I go to Tian's house after school? It's *two blocks* into the Commons, and Ma is being paranoid about it. Please, Da!"

Hilo looked from his son to Wen. She sighed and shrugged in defeat. "Have your talon knife on you," Hilo said. "And phone your uncle's apartment before you leave, tell him when to expect you."

"I will, I promise," Ru exclaimed, instantly cheerful. He grabbed his school bag, bent to rub Koko's head, then ran out the front door toward the driveway, where Shae or Woon would pick him up and drive him to school on their way to the office. Koko ran out the door after his master, wagging his tail and whining at being left behind. Wen was not especially fond of the creature, who occasionally chewed her shoes or the furniture, but he'd been Hilo's gift to Ru when the boy was ten, on the day he would've begun training at Kaul Du Academy, if he hadn't been born a stone-eye.

Hilo sat down at the table. "He has to have some freedom, so he feels capable."

Wen said, "I know. But we don't know his friends or their families that well." Niko's and Jaya's classmates were from No Peak clan families; it was easy for Wen to pick up the phone and speak to their parents. Ru went to one of the best schools in the city, but it wasn't the Academy. Tian's father was a civil engineer and his mother stayed at home; they had no clan affiliation at all. They seemed like good people, and Wen's few interactions with them had been friendly, but it wasn't the same.

At times, when she missed Niko and Jaya, Wen was grateful that one of her children still lived at home, but at other times, his presence was a daily reminder of her own experience as a child, an outsider even in her own family.

As if sensing her concern, Hilo reminded her, "Things will be different for Ru than they were for you. People aren't as superstitious as they used to be, and besides, he has your example to look up to." He was looking at her the entire time as he stirred chives into a bowl of hot cereal. "Why are you so dressed up today?"

"I'm going to a charity luncheon," Wen said. "It's in support of the Kekon Parks & Nature Foundation."

A skeptical crease formed on Hilo's forehead. "What do you need to go to that for? Didn't you go to something similar a couple of weeks ago?"

"That was for the Janloon Small Business Council." Wen opened a black schedule book. "Going to all these events wouldn't be a good use of the Pillar's time. But someone from No Peak should go to them. Someone who can speak for the clan."

"We could send Woon."

Wen raised an eyebrow at him. "Woon might be the best person in the clan to give press conferences, but can you imagine him making small talk at a gala for the arts?" The Pillarman smiled and shook her head. "We shouldn't pass up these chances to show that No Peak stands for ordinary people and not just jade warriors. Especially now, with the extremists idealizing foreign ways and brainwashing people into thinking Kekon can do away with clans altogether."

Hilo gave her his lopsided smile. "I'll tell Juen that our new weapon against the clanless will be garden parties."

"Be serious," Wen said. "This is important."

Hilo finished his breakfast, then picked up the empty bowls on the table and put them into the sink, running the water to rinse them off. Kyanla was partly retired now, but she would come in later in the day to tidy up and make dinner. Wen could see Hilo considering what she'd said, frowning as he dried his hands on a towel. "You're probably right that going to these events and showing a good face to the public is worthwhile, but I still don't see why it should be you. That's not the Pillarman's job."

Wen got up and wrapped her arms around his waist from behind. "The Pillarman's job is whatever the Pillar says it is," she argued with sweet forcefulness. "And besides, I'm not only the Pillarman, I'm your wife. Let me get dressed up and meet people and enjoy my place a little. It might even be useful to us. Didn't you just say a person needs some freedom to feel capable?"

Hilo sighed and turned around, putting his arms around her and touching his lips to her forehead. She knew that even after making her his Pillarman, he struggled with his instinct to shield her. He wanted to trust her as he once did, but sometimes his questions were sharp and suspicious. Wen tried her best not to resent him for it, and to consciously shake the engrained habit of omitting information about her activities when they might meet with his disapproval. She could not win back his confidence all at once; trust that had been so dramatically spilled could only be refilled one drop at a time.

Wen propped the open schedule book against her husband's chest. She'd gone from a stealthy involvement in clan affairs to facing them daily as a complex, shifting arrangement of color-coded appointments and tasks. "Don't forget your meeting with General Ronu was moved to this afternoon. It's to review the report he'll be making to the Royal Council next week. Your sister phoned this morning and said she's not feeling well, so if she isn't able to be there, Woon will attend in her place."

Hilo's eyebrows rose. "Again? That's the third meeting she's missed this month. It's not like Shae to leave me alone in meetings when she thinks some random fact might come up that she knows more about than I do."

Wen fought hard against a smile. "Maybe you should ask her why she's feeling so unwell lately when no one else in the family's been sick."

"I suppose I should," Hilo said, so obliviously that Wen had to turn away and clap a hand over her mouth to stifle a laugh. Hilo's eyes narrowed with dawning realization. "No fucking way." When Wen smiled and shrugged as if she knew nothing, he burst into laughter. "Good for them. I didn't think Shae was the type, but it's just like her to wait too long and come around in the end."

"I didn't tell you anything," Wen declared. "Be nice to your sister and let her tell everyone herself when she's ready." She moved her finger down to the next note. "The Espenian ambassador called again about the destruction of the Anorco mining ship. I referred him back to Woon Papi."

Hilo snorted, then tugged the schedule book out of her hands. "Good. Woon can ignore him on the clan's behalf, that's his job as Sealgiver." He laid the book down on the kitchen counter. "Do you remember back when you used to lie in bed stretched out naked in the morning, tempting me away from clan business? Now clan business is all you want to talk about."

Wen tilted her chin as she looked up at her husband slyly. "Would you rather I neglected my duties as Pillarman?"

Hilo took her by the shoulders and turned her away from him. His lips moved near her ear from behind, warming the skin of her neck. "There are other ways to help your Pillar prepare for the day." He slid a hand down the front of her dress and squeezed her left breast. "I have half an hour in my schedule right now—it says so in your book. And you look so nice today, dressed up for other people and not even for me."

Wen braced against the kitchen table as he bent her over. Hilo lifted the dress over her hips and pulled down her panties. He nudged her legs apart with his knees before disappearing from view behind her. She felt him seize her inner thighs, spreading her wide open. Then the wet heat of his mouth. Wen shivered and rose onto her toes, lifting one leg to better accommodate him as he stood, unzipped his pants and plunged deeply into her with one smooth motion. She smiled as she bore down rhythmically on his thrusts. They were not young anymore, but Hilo was still impulsive by nature and there were undeniable advantages to having the house to themselves more frequently these days.

An hour later, her dress back in place and the inside of her thighs wiped down, Wen checked her makeup in a hand mirror. The driver opened the car door, and Wen stepped out of her Lumezza 6C convertible and walked through the entrance of Wie Lon Temple School.

She considered the hypocrisy of being concerned about her son visiting a friend two blocks inside a Mountain-controlled district while she strode straight into the heart of enemy territory. Wie Lon was the oldest martial school in the country, the Mountain's feeder school, the alma mater of Ayt Madashi and nearly every high-ranking Green Bone in that clan. Its spacious and imposing main training hall was also occasionally rented out for large private functions such as this one. Wen took in her surroundings with curiosity. Unlike Kaul Dushuron Academy, which was situated within Janloon, Wie Lon was a forty-five minute drive west of the city and had the feel of a secluded forest camp. A fitting place to put important patrons in the mood for supporting nature conservation.

Wen's personal bodyguards flanked her closely as she approached the entrance to the hall. Hilo no longer permitted her off the Kaul estate without security. Wen did not object. Dudo and Tako were both former Fists, good men, polite, unobtrusive enough unless obtrusiveness was called for. Wen had come to find their presence reassuring, a reminder that she was never helpless, that she had the weight of her husband and the clan he ruled behind her. She wasn't sure she would've had the confidence to step back into public life otherwise. And they were helpful to her in other ways. When she reached the front steps to the hall, Dudo handed Wen her cane, which she used to steady herself as she navigated the half dozen shallow steps to the door. She tried her best not to be seen hobbling, but falling would be even more painful and humiliating. When she reached the top step, she handed the cane back to Dudo, lifted her chin to gather her confidence again, and stepped through the main doors.

Soft natural sunlight bathed the hall from high windows. The wooden floor where Green Bone students trained was filled with round tables covered in green tablecloths and decorated with miniature rock garden centerpieces. Wen made her way to the head table at the front of the hall, stopping here and there to greet people—prominent Lantern Men of No Peak, the longtime KNB news anchor Toh Kita, a couple of sitting members of the Royal Council. She no longer possessed the nearly flawless memory she'd once been able to rely on. She had to make lists of names and use memory tricks to help her recollection in advance of situations like this.

When she reached the circular head table, she was greeted by the chairman of the Kekon Parks & Nature Foundation. "Mrs. Kaul," he said, "you honor us with your willingness to attend and say a few words on behalf of the clan. I know it'll make a big difference to our donors, to hear that the Pillar of No Peak supports the preservation of our country's natural spaces."

Wen doubted that Hilo had given much thought to the issue, if any at all, but she assured the chairman that it was her pleasure to be here to convey her husband's sentiments. Wen took her seat as the final two guests arrived at the head table. Wen recognized the middle-aged man at once. Koben Yiro, one of the most prominent and outspoken Green Bones in the Mountain clan, head of the sprawling Koben family and uncle to Ayt Ato. The heavyset woman with permed hair must be his wife.

"Mrs. Kaul," Koben Tin Bett exclaimed, smiling widely and seating herself next to Wen. She hung the oversized handbag she carried over the back of her chair. "What a delight to see you here. And looking so much healthier than I thought you would." She tugged on her husband's hand. "Sit down, Yiro-se, they're about to serve the food."

Koben Yiro unbuttoned his suit jacket and settled himself next to his wife, inclining his head toward Wen with a friendly but faintly condescending smile. "Mrs. Kaul." Wen had not met the Kobens in person before, but she'd heard Yiro's distinctive voice on the radio far more than she had any wish to, expounding on political and clan matters, usually with extreme bias toward the Mountain and scathing criticisms of No Peak. Ayt Mada seemed perfectly willing to let Koben shine in his own spotlight. Ayt was a polished orator and a fearsome Green Bone leader, but Koben Yiro was brash and relatable to ordinary Kekonese, making himself out to be everyone's opinionated but well-meaning uncle.

"Koben-jen," Wen said with a polite smile. "Mrs. Koben."

"Bett is fine," said the woman. She patted Wen's hand. "We wives needn't be standoffish with each other."

A photographer from the *Janloon Daily* asked to take a photograph of the head table, with Wen and the Kobens in the foreground. Wen smiled for the camera. She could already imagine the headline in the Notable People section: *Mountain and No Peak Clans Face Off Over Lunch in Support of Nature Conservation.*

"Are you here on your own?" Mrs. Koben asked Wen, plucked eyebrows arched in admiration and mild concern. "How courageous of you. Not that anyone would be low enough to tug their earlobes at a classy event like this, surely." She took out a hand-sanitizing wipe from her purse and cleaned her fingers before the meal, then put on reading glasses to study the luncheon's program while continuing to talk to Wen. "Of course, I can understand wanting to get away and enjoy yourself now that you've done your part for the clan and your children are a bit older. I hear your nephew—Niko, is it?—is doing quite well at the Academy. And you have a daughter who's normal and is there now as well, don't you?"

"Mrs. Koben, I'm embarrassed to admit you know more about my family than I do about yours." Wen gave the woman her sweetest smile. "Except for your nephew, of course, even though he doesn't have the Koben name anymore. Changing the boy's name to Ayt Ato was a clever way to elevate him."

"My nephew is twenty-one years old and a Fist, so hardly a boy anymore," Mrs. Koben reminded her.

"Twenty-one already? I thought he was younger. Perhaps that's because I heard he fought his first duel earlier this year. My husband and brothers were in their teens when they first started winning green for themselves, so I admit my benchmark is different." Wen shrugged and unfolded her napkin. When she was especially nervous or under stress, she was more likely to start stammering or losing the ability to find words, but she'd overcome far too much in life for someone like Mrs. Koben to intimidate her.

"Greenness has many aspects, of course," said Mrs. Koben with a maternally scolding tone. "A jadeless woman wouldn't be able to speak about it."

"Don't be so humble," Wen insisted. "Men need the help of their women. You're obviously a very involved wife and aunt and deserve as much credit as your husband for the Koben family's reputation."

The woman's eyes twitched, the look of an animal discovering it has bitten into a meal with spines. Fortunately, at that moment, the food arrived, and Koben Bett took the opportunity to turn back to her husband.

Jadeless women—we have so few weapons, Wen thought, with vicious self-satisfaction. *We duel each other with smiles and words the way our men duel with knives.*

She tried to enjoy the meal but couldn't bring herself to eat much. She was thinking of the speech she would soon have to give and imagining faltering and humiliating herself in front of everyone, including the smug Kobens. She turned to the guest seated on her other side and was surprised to see an Abukei man. He introduced himself with a Kekonese family name and an Abukei personal name, as Ren Jirhuya. He was young and handsome, in his early thirties, Wen guessed.

"What's your connection to the Parks & Nature Foundation, Mr. Ren?" she asked.

"I was named a cultural ambassador for the Yinao tribe." The man hesitated, then added, "And I'm an artist. I did all the artwork for the fundraising campaign and also the animation in the short film they're going to play after lunch. And please call me Jirhuya—it's what I'm more comfortable going by."

Wen admired the art on the posters and the programs, the designer in her appreciating the balance of color and the expressive modern style applied to indigenous motifs and themes. "Do you do much of this kind of work?"

"Whatever I can get," he admitted. "I work mostly in the film industry."

Wen noticed with fascination that Jirhuya was wearing a plain green gemstone ring on his right forefinger. Wearing bluffer's jade was considered gaudy and low-class in Kekon, a style associated with Keko-Shotarian gangsters. Jirhuya could not be barukan, and nothing else about him seemed cheap or careless. His pale blue linen suit was perfectly pressed and well tailored to his slight frame, a spot of color amid the indistinguishable dark outfits of the other men. His crinkly hair was short and well groomed, and his speech had none of the rolling lilt of an indigenous accent.

"I couldn't help but wonder about the ring you're wearing," Wen said. "Does it signify anything?"

Ren blushed a little. "It's an Abukei tradition. Adults wear a ring on the thumb if they're married or otherwise committed to someone, on the forefinger if they're single and open to a relationship, and on the little finger if they're not looking." It was Wen's turn to be embarrassed. She'd learned that fact at some point, perhaps from Kyanla, who wore a silver band around her right little finger, but she'd forgotten. She'd been curious because of the substance of the ring, not its position.

Jirhuya said, "Centuries ago, rings like this used to be made of jade, because of its sacred connection to the body of the First Mother goddess, Nimuma. That stopped a long time ago, for obvious reasons." Anyone who wore jade without being able to use jade abilities would be too easy a target for thieves. Certainly no Abukei or stone-eye would wear it unless they wished to court disaster or be accused of smuggling. Jirhuya turned the ring on his finger. "Wearing a green ring is a nod to ancient custom, and bluffer's jade is easier to obtain now that there's an overseas demand for it."

Servers cleared the plates away, a short film was played, and the chairman of the foundation stood up to thank all the guests and exhort them to give their financial and political backing to conservation efforts. He expressed particular thanks for the support of the country's Green Bone clans and invited Wen to make a few remarks.

Wen rose and walked to the podium, trying to make her gradual approach appear deliberate instead of physically cautious. Her hands were sweating. When she reached the microphone, she took a moment to look out across the gathered and attentive faces. Then she began speaking, as slowly as she had practiced, pretending that she was relating a family story to friends rather than delivering an address to strangers, so that her words would come out clearly and naturally, without stutters and lapses.

She began by telling an amusing anecdote about Hilo taking her into the mountains on a day trip many years ago and getting them hopelessly lost. At the time, he'd been the Horn of No Peak and knew the city of Janloon like a guard dog knows every rock and blade of grass in its yard, but he had less sense of direction in the wilderness. The audience laughed at the idea of the fearsome Kaul Hiloshudon trudging stubbornly through the forest in the wrong direction. Wen savored a warm rush of triumph. She imagined that Hilo would not appreciate her recounting the embarrassing event to a banquet of prominent Janloon society members, but he was not here to be annoyed. She alone was in the unique position to share the relatable, human side of the family, to show that the Kauls were powerful people, but still people.

"As our country's economy grows, as our cities expand and our factories multiply, we must balance our drive toward prosperity with prudence. Many would say that jade is Kekon's most valuable natural resource. Yet jade can only be used by a few people, while the natural beauty of our island belongs to us all, regardless of wealth, clan, blood, or ability. And so it's up to all of us to protect it as fiercely as we protect our families and our values." Wen returned to her seat at the table amid sustained applause, pleased and relieved to have gotten through it.

Jirhuya leaned in. "That was beautifully delivered, Mrs. Kaul," he said. "Would you be willing to speak at the Charitable Society for Jade Nonreactivity sometime? I volunteer for the organization and I know the members on the board. Having someone so prominent in the No Peak clan talk openly about being a stone-eye would go a long way toward destigmatizing nonreactivity. Would you consider it?"

"I would be pleased to do so, if my schedule allows," Wen told him.

Before they could continue the conversation, the chairman of the foundation returned to the podium and invited Koben Yiro to make a few remarks on behalf of the Mountain clan. Koben stood up, rebuttoned his suit across his broad chest, and made his way to the microphone. The audience fell silent and leaned forward.

"For much of its history, Kekon was a civilization at harmony with its natural surroundings," Koben began, in a dramatic, rumbling voice. "There's no better example of that than the great Wie Lon Temple School, where we gather today. Unfortunately, like so many other vital elements of Kekonese culture, those values are under attack."

Koben spoke about the long-term degradation of Kekon's wilderness caused by decades of grasping colonial interests: deforestation caused by jade mining for the purpose of fulfilling export contracts with the Republic of Espenia, pollution by foreign companies, and the loss of five square kilometers of natural habitat on Euman Island as a result of the expansion of the ROE naval base. "As I speak," Koben boomed, stabbing a finger in the air as his resonant voice vibrated with passion, "an Espenian company is dredging our coastal regions for jade. Brave patriots destroyed the first mining ship, but Espenian greed knows no bounds, and another was sent to steal jade from the ocean—and, in the process, ruin traditional indigenous fishing regions and destroy irreplaceable natural habitats.

"We can't solve environmental damage until we talk about their primary cause: *foreigners*," Koben proclaimed. "It's time we turn away from the destructive path we've been on for decades—time to stop bowing to foreign corporations, spending precious resources on refugees, and letting jade leave our shores." Some people in the audience tapped the table in polite applause; others stamped their feet and called out in vehement agreement. Koben, buoyed by the response, shook his fist in the air and concluded with conviction. "Together, we must root out foreign exploitation in all forms! Only then can we protect our beautiful island home."

Wen felt a flush rising up her neck. To her horror, her hands began to tremble. She set down the teacup she was holding before anyone could notice. She'd devoted careful time and energy into preparing for this evening. She'd sought to make a good impression, to represent her family in an inspiring and relatable manner.

She'd been a fool. Koben Yiro had delivered a rousing political diatribe, one that reinforced the Mountain's message that it was the clan more dedicated to preserving the country's resources and traditions. And he'd done so in a way that even Ayt Mada could not, further cementing the Koben family's popularity.

Koben Yiro stepped away from the podium amid resounding applause. Several Mountain clan members stood up at their tables to salute him. Press photographers snapped pictures.

"My husband is so silly," Koben Bett remarked, leaning toward Wen confidentially. "He was worried that the tone of the speech would be too heavy for this lunch crowd. Fortunately, I *insisted* that he stick with it. Well, now he'll have to admit he was right to listen to me." She settled back in her seat and sipped her tea with a placidly savage smile. "You're quite right, Mrs. Kaul. Men often do need our help. It's a shame our Pillars aren't here to see what we do for our clans."

CHAPTER

20

⌒

Progress

From the time he'd been the Horn of the clan, Hilo had hosted early morning drop-in training sessions for his top Fists on Seconddays and Fifthdays at the Kaul estate. He did so to ensure his highest-ranking warriors kept up their martial prowess, and also because he needed worthy sparring partners himself. When some responsibility as Pillar forced him to miss practice, Juen or Lott ran the sessions. It had become a mark of considerable status on the greener side of the No Peak clan, to be invited to train at the Pillar's home.

For the past three years, Hilo had invited Jim Sunto to join them. It had raised some eyebrows among the Fists, but Hilo had been interested in Sunto ever since their first encounter at the Seventh Discipline gym. He was intrigued by the idea of matching himself against an elite jade-endowed fighter trained by the Espenian system and seeing what he could learn.

On this morning, they faced each other as they first had seven years ago, only this time Hilo held a gun and Sunto had a knife. They were deliberately training their lesser proficiencies. Kaul Hilo's long-standing reputation as a talon knife fighter was unsurpassed, and Jim Sunto had extensive ability with firearms.

The sun was barely up and the gathered Green Bones blew into their cupped hands to warm them. The Pillar stood in the center of the lawn with his arms loose at his sides, a small, anticipatory smile tilting one side of his mouth. Sunto circled, casually—then moved in the space between one heartbeat and the next.

A capable Green Bone can cross ten meters of ground in far less time than it takes the average shooter to draw and aim a handgun. Hilo had used that fact to lethal advantage numerous times in his life. Anyone trying to draw a pistol on a Green Bone with a talon knife, especially in the close quarters of a Janloon city street, would likely fall to the knife before getting off a single shot.

Hilo needed to do the opposite of what he normally did in a fight—create distance instead of reducing it. Sunto had rushed in at an angle, so rather than try to escape backward or sideways, which he could not do in time, Hilo drew his gun as he dropped to the ground on his back. He fired upward.

The shot hit Sunto in the stomach. It was only a pellet gun, not enough to break Steel, but enough to sting. Hilo rolled away in the grass and fired again from a crouch. Now he'd created too much distance and his opponent Deflected the pellets with ease. To close the gap, however, Sunto had to charge through the danger zone where he was too close to effectively Deflect but still too far away to reach his target with the knife. Hilo shot the soldier again in the chest. It barely slowed him down. The talon knife flashed toward Hilo's face.

He caught Sunto's wrist, halting the blunted edge a fingertip's distance from his throat. Hilo grinned. "You could've finished me off if I hadn't seen the knife coming so easily," he said. "Draw my attention with your other hand, then switch grip and cut this way instead." He took the knife from Sunto and mimed a quick demonstration. The small cluster of watching Green Bones nodded.

Sunto made a noise of grudging appreciation. "Still didn't get in three shots, though," he said, rubbing at the bruise on his chest. The objective was to place three shots or a lethal cut. No disarms. With skilled fighters, it was a contest of who got there first. "Even if you're stuck here"—Sunto held the gun close to his own torso, as if trapped in a close quarters struggle, and shifting so the other Green Bones could see—"you can still fire, if you angle it like this, so the slide is clear of your own body. That's the third shot."

Hilo clapped the other man on the shoulder. Sunto wore too little green to equal Hilo or any of his first-rank Green Bones in a straight matchup of jade abilities. His proficiency with Lightness and Deflection—the two disciplines that required the greatest expulsion of jade energy—was below average. They were not emphasized in the Espenian military, as they broke unit formation and were of little use at long range against automatic weapons. But Sunto was fast and effective and practical, and he knew certain techniques that were not taught in the Academy curriculum or by any other private trainers as far as Hilo was aware of. Some of them were not of much use to Green Bones. Hilo doubted his Fists needed to know how to use ground-sweeping Deflection to set off pressure-sensitive or trip-wire bombs from a distance. Others were more valuable. At the Pillar's request, Sunto had taught a series of classes to the high-ranking Fists, as well as all the Green Bones in the Kaul family, on how to Steel to protect oneself against an improvised explosive device. Years after the tragedy, Hilo was still haunted by Kehn's death, the impersonal, dishonorable suddenness of it. If Sunto's methods had something to offer that might protect his family and other members of the clan from a car bombing, he would study them.

Hilo handed the gun to Lott while Sunto gave the knife to Vin, so they could take a turn. He watched his Fists spar until everyone had had a chance to practice. Observing those in their twenties, like Suyo and Toyi, made it clear to Hilo that he was no longer young. His jade abilities were as formidable as ever. His strength and stamina equaled that of much younger fighters, and experience was a powerful advantage he was glad to possess. But a life spent fighting took its toll. Since turning forty, Hilo had noticed small things: He was not as fast as he used to be, it took him longer to recover from minor injuries, and older, more serious ones that had not bothered him for years reminded him of past mistakes.

The sun was rising over the city, burning away the autumn chill. Hilo called an end to the training session. Sunto came up to him. "You mind if we talk for a minute?"

A couple of nearby Fists looked askance at the man for taking such a blunt and familiar tone with the Pillar, but Hilo was not offended. That was Sunto's natural way of speaking. In front of his own men, however, Hilo forced the soldier to be patient. "I have a few things to discuss with the Horn. They won't take long, then we can talk."

After he'd spoken with Juen, and the rest of the Green Bones had dispersed to attend to their own responsibilities, Hilo sat down with Sunto at the patio table. He propped his feet up on the seat of an empty chair. "How did General Ronu's report to the Royal Council go?"

"Well enough that they increased funding to the training program," Sunto said. "The chancellor commended us on how much progress we've made in seven years."

With the hired guidance of Sunto and other international experts, the Kekonese military had established the Special Warfare Command to oversee all special operations forces, most notably the Golden Spider Company—the army's growing cohort of jade-equipped soldiers, who had their own specialized training and participated in exercises with ROE Navy Angels. The Kekonese military was still tiny in comparison to most other countries, but now that it was seen as a further safeguard against possible Ygutanian aggression, the Espenians were highly supportive of its growth, other disagreements between the two countries notwithstanding.

"I hear enlistment went up after the requirements were changed," Hilo said. "Master Aido said he's had dozens of calls from new students. Even Grandmaster Le is thinking about using one of the Academy's training fields to run an evening or weekend program if enough instructors are willing to do it." He lit a cigarette. "I'm impressed, Sunto. You've actually made people want to join the army."

In the past, only recruits who graduated from a martial school and had at least one year of experience as a clan Finger could enlist with their jade, but Sunto had successfully argued that was unnecessary, even counterproductive. "If we're limited only to Fingers who leave the clan, we'll barely fill a room each year," he'd pointed out. All that was required now was a medical certificate attesting to sufficient jade tolerance and basic proficiency in the six jade disciplines—roughly the equivalent of a year-four education at the Academy. That one change opened the doors to those trained through after-school programs and private instructors.

The patio door slid open and the new housekeeper, Sulima, brought out tea, pastries, and sliced fruit for them. Sunto accepted a cup of tea, but didn't eat. "General Ronu could get even more recruits if we started accepting adults without prior jade training."

Hilo replied with impatience. "Don't bother going there again."

"ROE Angels don't start acclimating to jade at the age of ten. That's not needed when we have modern methods," Sunto said, stubbornly ignoring the Pillar's warning. "SN2 is safer than SN1 was ten or fifteen years ago. There are fewer long-term health effects and less risk of overdose. It's still not good for you, but neither is going to war."

"I've told you before," Hilo said. "You won't get any support for the idea of doping Kekonese soldiers. Shine's legal only when medically necessary." Even when it *was* necessary, Hilo thought sadly, the shame was too great. It had been for Lan.

Sunto snorted in defeat. "That's the same line I get from Ronu. The stigma of SN1 is so high in this country, the Kekonese military's not willing to consider even voluntary dosing."

"You're trying to improve the prestige of the armed forces, aren't you? No family would want their son to join an army of thin-blooded shine addicts."

Sunto's jade aura was ordinarily pale in Hilo's mind. Not weak or dim, but pale—like a color that didn't stand out or catch the eye. Now, however, he felt it swell and darken. "Thin-blooded shine addicts," the man repeated. "I suppose that's what you Green Bones think of all Espenian soldiers. In case you haven't noticed, we're out here protecting this island, this whole region of the world, and we're using jade to do it, risking our lives and our health. Not everyone is genetically gifted with jade tolerance, but that's what science is for. That's what progress is for."

Sunto's indignation made no sense to Hilo. The man was not Espenian by blood, he did not use shine himself, and he had voluntarily left the Navy Angels many years ago. But he spoke as if he were still an ROE soldier, so Hilo spoke to him as one. "Progress for us doesn't mean becoming like you. You should know that by now."

Sunto sat back. "I do know it," he said, no longer arguing but clearly dissatisfied. "This isn't how I wanted to come to the point, but it does help explain my decision. I've done all that I can with the training program. General Ronu has been a good partner and we've made a lot of improvements, but it's time for me to move on. I'm leaving at the end of the month. The Kekonese army has a strong foundation to work from, and Ronu will continue building on what we've accomplished so far, with someone else in charge."

Hilo was accustomed to Sunto's bluff manners, but he wasn't pleased to hear the former Navy Angel was leaving the job that No Peak had placed directly in his lap, and he disliked the way the man was delivering the news, as a thing that was already done. Sunto was not a Green Bone of the clan, and so was under no obligation to come to the Pillar for permission before making the decision, but they were hardly strangers either. Sunto's role with the military had raised his profile and wealth, he'd trained with Hilo and his men, he'd been a guest at the Kaul estate many times.

Hilo let a reproachful pause rest between them before he responded. "I'm disappointed to hear that, Lieutenant. I can see you've made your decision, though, so I won't try to convince you otherwise. You've done everything I hoped you would when we first met, and I've been glad to have you training with my Fists. So let's part as friends." He stood and extended his hand to Sunto, who stood as well and shook it.

They walked together toward the gates of the Kaul estate. When they reached Sunto's car, the man stopped before getting in. He brought a hand up absently to the gold icon of Mount Icana hanging around his neck next to his jade dog tags, then dropped his arm and turned to face the Pillar.

"There's something else," he said. "Working with the Kekonese military has been a valuable career experience, and I've learned a lot from training with the Green Bones in your clan. I appreciate you giving me those opportunities. I respect you as a leader, which is why I want you to hear this from me directly and not from anyone else later."

Sunto's pale jade aura shifted, as did his feet. "I'm starting my own company. It'll provide training, security services, and combat support to governments and organizations. I've been talking about it for some time with a couple of ex-Angel friends who're coming on as my partners."

When the Pillar's initial reply to this announcement was an immobile silence, Sunto explained, "It's the ideal way to combine all of my experiences as a Navy Angel, an IBJCS instructor, the additional training I've picked up in Janloon, and the work I've done reforming the Kekonese military. With all the conflicts the ROE military is engaged in around the world, there's a distinct and urgent need for contractors. My company will be the first with deep military experience and skilled operatives who have the ability to use bioenergetic jade."

"A company of jade soldiers," Hilo said. "Mercenaries."

Sunto frowned, but stood his ground against the increasingly dangerous look in Hilo's eyes. "I don't agree with that term. This wouldn't be a band of hired guns. I want to create a professional organization, one that adheres to high standards and Truthbearing ideals."

"Truthbearing ideals. *Foreign* ideals." Hilo's posture was subtly changing; his shoulders came forward, his fingers curled, his chin tilted down.

"I wouldn't expect the Pillar of a Green Bone clan to understand or approve."

"You're right about that at least," Hilo snarled. The flare of the Pillar's jade aura made the estate's guards look over in alarm. "Jade belongs on warriors who take oaths to their clan. Not on corporate soldiers."

Sunto bristled defensively, his posture subtly coiling. "Your antiquated attitudes aren't shared by everyone. I have contacts in the ROE War Department who're supportive. And the wealthy entrepreneur Art Wyles has signed on as our first major investor."

The guards came toward them, looking questioningly at Hilo for direction. The Pillar held them in place with a glance, but took a single step toward Sunto. "I handed you a career. I trained with you. I treated you as a friend." He spoke as if slowly drawing a weapon. "Think carefully about what you're doing, Lieutenant Sunto."

Sunto took a step back and opened the door to his car, not taking his eyes off Hilo. "I was afraid you'd react this way, but there's nothing personal going on here, Kaul. When we first met, I told you I was here to mind my own business and make some money. That hasn't changed." Sunto looked pointedly at the guards and the closed gates, knowing he was at the Pillar's mercy, but unafraid. "This may be hard for you to accept, but there's room in the world for more than one type of jade warrior. I'm not founding a rival Green Bone clan that's out to get you. The company will be headquartered in Espenia, with a secondary office on Euman Island, under Espenian military jurisdiction, with jade supplied by the Espenian government. You'll lead your clan according to your principles, and I'll run my company based on mine. There's no reason for us to be at odds."

"You're blindingly naive if you think that's true." With a sharp gesture, Hilo motioned for the gates to be opened. When Sunto got into the car, Hilo came over and put his hands on the door frame, leaning in and speaking through the open window. "This should be obvious, but I'm going to say it so that there's no doubt between us: Don't involve your military company and its foreign mercenaries here in Kekon. *Ever.*"

Sunto started the car. "The company's called Ganlu Solutions International," he said, calmly but with rare anger swirling through his jade aura like dark ink spreading through water. "The name comes from a prince of Kekon who left the island and was forgotten by his people, but who changed the world."

"Get off my property," Hilo said. "Before I kill you." He turned and stalked back to the house, not bothering to watch as Sunto's car rolled out of the gates of the Kaul estate.

CHAPTER

21

The Meaning of Green

the fourteenth year, second month

Shae's doctor had cleared her to fly, and she was comfortably seated in business class, but nevertheless, the eleven-and-a-half-hour flight to Port Massy was not enjoyable at the best of times and was even less so when one was pregnant. There was no avoiding it, however. In a few months, she wouldn't be able to make the transamaric flight at all, and she had matters to deal with before then. She kept hydrated and got up every hour to go to the bathroom and stretch her legs by walking around the plane. Thank the gods that at least she was past the nausea and exhaustion of the first trimester. She envied Hami Tumashon in the seat next to her. The clan's Rainmaker was accustomed to this flight and didn't seem to mind it at all. He spent the first two hours working productively, reading correspondence and writing memos, then perused the *Port Massy Post* before falling asleep easily for the rest of the trip.

When they arrived in Port Massy, Shae was amazed by the cold and the sight of dirty snow drifts lining every street. The white winter light stung her eyes as she and Hami exited the airport bundled in coats and scarves. Terun Bin, the clan's Master Luckbringer in Espenia, met them personally with a car and driver. He saluted them and exclaimed, "Kaul-jen, why didn't you bring some Janloon weather with you?"

Once they were in the car, Terun blasted the heater, and when the driver pulled aggressively into the exit lane in front of irate honking cab drivers, he yelled back out the window in Espenian with a casual vociferousness on par with that of a Port Massy native. Terun's highly animated but demanding personality seemed to serve him well in Espenia. He'd been growing the clan's business in the country capably for eight years but had decided that at age thirty-five, it was time to start searching for a wife and maybe have a family. So he'd asked to return to Kekon in the spring, and a hunt was on within the clan for his replacement. Shae was looking forward to having him back in Janloon, as Terun was one of the most keenly intelligent business minds she'd ever worked with, the sort of person who could absorb a remarkable amount of information and see solutions before others were done asking the question.

Terun turned over his shoulder and said, "Kaul-jen, I've made all the arrangements we discussed. The meeting is set for tomorrow afternoon. We have reservations for a group dinner tonight at a restaurant not far from your hotel. If you're feeling up for it, I know the staff here in Port Massy would be honored to spend time with the Weather Man."

Shae would've preferred to order in room service and go to bed early, but she accepted Terun's invitation. As Rainmaker, Hami made frequent trips between the clan's branch offices, admirably coordinating No Peak's international business efforts between Janloon, Port Massy, the smaller, secondary Espenian office in Adamont Capita, and now Khitak in Tun—but it was still important that the

Weather Man herself make an appearance, so that the Luckbringers (or associates, as they were referred to over here) saw that their work was personally valued by the Kaul family.

Shae went to the hotel and even though it was well past midnight back in Janloon, she called Woon to assure him she'd arrived safely, knowing he wouldn't sleep until she'd done so. He hadn't wanted her to make the trip at all even though Hami would be accompanying her and Anden had personally told him there was little health risk. Woon's first wife, Kiya, had miscarried several times, so he was fearful that something would go wrong. For many years, Shae had depended on her former Shadow's stoic, reasonable optimism. It was a strange role reversal for him to now be such a fretful husband. It was only because he could not give up his long habit of being her chief of staff that she was able to convince him to stay in Janloon and manage the clan's business affairs in her absence. Although two other people had held the role of Weather Man's Shadow since Luto's death, Woon was who she still trusted most to make important clan decisions on her behalf if the need arose.

At times, Shae still awoke next to her husband with a sense of bewilderment. They'd been colleagues for many years before they were married, and although they no longer worked within sight of each other every day, that history still occasionally caused odd moments of strain. Shae had once embarrassed Woon by saying, "You know you can kiss me without permission when we're not in the office, don't you?" More than once, he'd reminded her crossly, "You can't end discussion like that. I don't answer to you as Weather Man inside our own house." Woon claimed it didn't surprise or bother him that no one used Shae's married name and continued to call her "Kaul-jen," as they always had, but marrying into the Kaul family under scandalous circumstances couldn't have been easy even for someone as forbearing as Woon Papidonwa.

"There's a licensed Kekonese medicine clinic only four blocks away from the office on Jons Island," he reminded her over the phone. "The two doctors there are Janloon-trained. I called to make sure. Do you have the address and phone number?"

"Yes, Papi," Shae reassured him. "Anden told me already. Don't worry."

Her pregnancy had been exhausting but uncomplicated so far, but it was a comfort to know that she could legally obtain care from a qualified Green Bone doctor if necessary. She hadn't expected to conceive at the age of forty and, to be honest, was still surprised with herself. As much as she cared for her niece and nephews, Shae had never pegged herself as the maternal type. She wasn't sure she would've ever come around to the idea of having a child if it hadn't been for Woon, who was as happy as she'd ever seen him at the prospect of finally becoming a father.

"When Terun returns to Janloon, you could take some time off," he said.

"Let's talk about that later," she suggested. "How was the meeting with the Espenian ambassador?" She managed to distract her husband with talk of work, then got off the phone so he could get to bed. Sitting at the window and gazing out at the wintry skyline, she rubbed her gently swelling belly, hoping to feel one of the small fluttering sensations that she thought might be the baby's movement. She sometimes thought of her first, aborted pregnancy, and of Tau Maro, of how much he'd loved his little nieces and would never have any children of his own, with her or anyone else. Because she had executed him. In those moments, Shae would feel a cold, creeping fear that she didn't deserve this child, that something terrible would happen as just and fateful retribution.

Once, she shared her feelings of dread with her sister-in-law. Wen, who was not in the least superstitious, had scoffed, "Sister Shae, when is life ever like a story where the characters get exactly what they deserve, good or bad? You're not used to being afraid, but every new mother is afraid. What you're feeling is only natural."

Shae thought that was a touch unfair. She was no stranger to fear. Who else in the family regularly prayed to the gods? The most honest prayers were inspired by terror.

The dinner that evening was held at a Kekonese restaurant that was reputed to be the most authentic in Port Massy, with the exception of a few popular Espenicized dishes on the menu such as smoked pork on toast and fried shrimp salad. The food was surprisingly good, leagues better than anything Shae had had when she'd been a student in Windton fifteen years ago, and she was happy to talk to so many of the clan's expats and the local staff. Nevertheless, she begged off early to make sure she did indeed get enough sleep.

Late the following morning, she and Hami walked into the clan's Port Massy headquarters. The Kekon Trade Partnership Liaison Office, as it read on the stenciled brass plate on the door and on the black glass directory in the lobby of the building, had recently expanded to take over the entire twelfth floor in the towering Packer Avenue skyscraper. The location was smaller but almost as nice as the office tower on Ship Street in Janloon, and certainly a far cry from the squat, modest professional services building that had initially housed the clan's Espenian operations when Hami had first arrived in the country. As they walked onto a busy office floor filled with the sounds of ringing telephones, clacking keyboards, and conversations happening in Kekonese and Espenian, Shae saw the gruff satisfaction on Hami's face. No Peak's success overseas was his personal legacy in the clan.

That success was still deeply, troublingly vulnerable. When Rigly Hollin and the two other partners of the advertising agency WBH Focus arrived, Shae met them in the office's main conference room. She shook their hands, introduced Hami and Terun, and said, in Espenian, "I'm pleased to finally meet you in person, Mr. Hollin. My cousin, Dr. Emery, has told me about how effective you and your firm were at campaigning for the legalization of bioenergetic jade in the healthcare field. Your results speak for themselves."

"I've been looking forward to meeting you as well, Ms. Kaul-jen," Hollin said, impressing her by using the proper Green Bone suffix and touching his clasped hands to his forehead in a Kekonese salute. She was surprised, until she remembered that Hollin had a Kekonese wife. "WBH Focus is a global agency, and we're keen to serve international clients."

Shae gestured the advertising executives into chairs around the table. Hami and Terun, both of them accustomed to Espenian business customs, took seats next to her. Shae said, "I trust you've been briefed on why we're interested in hiring your firm."

Nodding avidly, Hollin opened his briefcase and began taking out documents. "Getting bioenergetic jade legalized for medical use moved it toward mainstream acceptance. But obviously you can't win the rucket unless you follow through on the toss off." Despite the victories Anden had secured, the Espenian Physicians Society remained opposed to jade medicine, and there was no movement toward a broader repeal of the civilian ban. Hollin handed out charts and tabulated survey responses. "Our preliminary market research reveals that among the general public, bioenergetic jade is still viewed as dangerous, even unnatural or unTruthful—a view that reinforces prejudice not only against Kekonese people, but also taints military veterans who find it difficult to reintegrate into civilian life without stigma."

Hollin laid several pages of photographs on the table. They depicted an open pit mine with scrawny men picking through piles of rocks, bombed-out buildings in war-torn Oortoko, and mug shots of barukan crime bosses. "These are the things people associate with jade right now." Hollin laid out a second set of images. "What if we could replace them with these ideas instead?" Shae saw ROE Navy Angels hoisting the Espenian flag, a Kekonese doctor with a jade medical bracelet talking to a mother and child, and a group of children training at the Academy. She wondered how Hollin had gotten a photograph from inside the Academy. Then she realized it was a publicity photo that the Academy itself used to promote its visiting student program to overseas Kekonese.

"We aren't selling soda or cars," Hami said skeptically. "Jade isn't something that ordinary people need, and they can't buy it for themselves. It'll be hard to change opinions when you're not offering any tangible benefit."

"That's what makes this such an exciting challenge," exclaimed one of Hollin's partners, a stout man with freckles who'd been introduced as Bernett. "A complex, prolonged marketing campaign to change widespread public perception of a product that can't be purchased? I'm not sure it's ever been done before, by any agency."

The third partner, a dark-skinned man named Walford, said, "We believe the key is to connect bioenergetic jade with positive social values, particularly ones that Espenians already admire about Kekonese culture, such as discipline, duty, honor, strength, and the warrior ethos of protecting the weak. People will be receptive to accepting jade if it feels as relevant to our country as yours."

Shae was surprised by the pang she felt at the foreigner's words. She picked up the photograph of the teenage Academy students, standing together attentively in their school training uniforms as an instructor and an assistant demonstrated a Deflection exercise. "Jade is a part of everything in Kekonese culture—our myths, our history, our way of life," she mused aloud. She touched the bracelet on her wrist. "Being green has greater significance than the abilities a person gains." Was it possible, she wondered, for anyone who was not Kekonese to understand that?

Hollin picked up a black permanent marker and began scrawling on the photo of the Navy Angels hoisting the flag and circling the words: warrior, honorable, green, patriot. "Bioenergetic jade has thousands of years of history in Kekon. That's not the case in Espenia. Which means we're in a position to define what jade means."

"We're not the largest agency you could hire," said Walford, "but with Rigly's experience and passion for the cause, you'd be assured of our full commitment."

One of the things that Shae appreciated about Espenians was how enthusiastically mercenary they were. Lured by the prospect of a unique professional challenge and a lucrative multiyear contract with a wealthy international client, one would think that the three foreigners were ready to kneel and swear oaths to the No Peak clan. Then again, she thought wryly, was that any different from how Lantern Men behaved?

Shae thanked the partners of WBH Focus for coming. She said she would review the additional materials they left for her and contact them again soon. When the Espenians were gone, she turned to her Rainmaker and Master Luckbringer.

"This could prove to be a massive waste of the clan's money," Terun admitted with a sigh, "but over the years, our attempts to gain greater influence in ROE politics haven't gotten us anywhere. Hami-jen was bringing up concerns about the ongoing costs and the enormous risk to the Espenian business even eight years ago when I first came here, and with Slow War frictions between the countries, our reasons to worry have only grown."

Hami nodded. "The bill on medical legalization succeeded only after the campaign went straight to the public. It could take a long time, but continuing that approach might blunt the effects of racial prejudice and create support for a complete repeal of the ban."

"Then we should pursue it," Shae said. "Terun, whoever succeeds you here will have to manage this additional priority. Hami-jen, as Rainmaker, it'll be important for you to be involved as well." Both men nodded.

Shae placed a hand over her belly. What kind of a world was her child being born into, where Espenian advertising executives might be defining the meaning of jade? Was that any sort of world, Shae wondered, in which to raise a Green Bone?

It's the world we have. At least she could ensure No Peak had a hand in it.

Terun said, "Kaul-jen, we should also talk about the news from Resville." The Master Luckbringer dropped a recent edition of the *Resville Gazette* onto the table. It had been opened and folded over to an article stating that the opening of the Sands of Illusion casino had been postponed for a second time, as a result of costly delays due to unexplained difficulties in hiring and retaining contractors.

Hami read the article and snorted. "The Mountain must be furious. It's a good thing this Jon Remi fellow is on our side." The Sands of Illusion casino was not the only Mountain-owned property in Resville that had been recently beset with problems. Several retail and gambling operations with Mountain backing had run into mysterious business trouble or were victims of robbery or arson. The Mountain was having a hard time defending its holdings and fighting back, as it possessed limited manpower on the ground in Espenia.

The Kekonese and Shotarian enforcers it brought in found it difficult to operate in a city like Resville, where the myriad of local gangsters knew and hated each other, but hated outsiders even more.

"Juen Nu has already sent Remi a secret shipment of jade, but the man is also asking No Peak for half a million thalirs to buy weapons and bribe local officials," Terun said. "The money would be delivered in cash by the Horn's side, but would first need to be moved into the country through No Peak shell companies."

"We can't have anything that happens in Resville connected to the business side of the clan," Hami said firmly. "Remi is a criminal, even if his crimes benefit us."

"There's a small risk, but we'll be careful to cover our tracks." Terun scribbled a few notes to himself on a legal pad. "But it'll be an expensive year for the clan."

Hami and Terun both looked to the Weather Man for the final say. In the same afternoon, she was authorizing a campaign to publicly promote the positive aspects of jade, and facilitating the transfer of secret funds to a Resville gangster. Trying to run a Green Bone clan in Espenia was a conundrum, fraught with contradictions. That was the cost of working in foreign territories and cultures, through intermediaries and allies. Of fighting proxy wars.

"Move the money," she said. "Quickly and quietly."

CHAPTER

22

~

Sons of the Clan

Kaul Rulinshin had been in Little Hammer before, on shopping trips and to school team relayball games, accompanied by an adult family member and at least two Green Bone bodyguards. Usually Aunt Lina, the mother of his cousin Maik Cam, or Aunt Imrie, the wife of the Horn, or occasionally Ru's uncle Anden, would take the children around town if the trip required leaving the city's neutral and No Peak–controlled districts. Ru's father and mother and his aunt Shae were too high in the clan to enter Mountain territory without important purpose and the permission or invitation of their adversaries. It was a matter of clan etiquette. Ru understood the rules; he was twelve years old, after all, and the son of the Pillar. So he knew that what he and his brother were doing now—sneaking unaccompanied into an enemy district to watch Ayt Atosho duel a challenger—was not technically forbidden by clan law but was also not something his parents would ever allow them to do.

It had taken threats to convince Niko to come along. Ru considered it necessary that his brother be part of the excursion so they would be in trouble together if their parents found out. Besides, Niko of all people should watch Ayt Ato fight so he could learn about the man he would one day have to contend with as a rival Pillar. It was for Niko's own good.

"I have exams coming up. I have to study." Niko was fifteen, a year-five at the Academy. "I'm sure our Fists will have spies with camcorders recording the whole thing. Even if they don't, there'll be plenty of informers selling footage afterward."

"Come on! Aren't you more cut than that?" Ru kept his voice down so Jaya wouldn't hear them. The whole family was home for Seventhday dinner, but the younger members had been sent outside after dinner so the adults could hold their usual conversations in the dining room. If Ru's sister knew what they were planning, she would demand to be included. She was only eleven, a whole fourteen months younger than him, entirely too young to participate, but that would not stop her from ratting them out to their parents if she did not get her way. "Hearing about something isn't nearly the same as being there in person," Ru insisted.

"Is that what you're going to say about the whipping you'll get from Da?" Niko asked with deadpan archness. The Pillar made Niko call him *uncle*, out of respect to his real father, but the boys spoke of their parents as siblings would.

Ru had long ago discovered that his brother was oddly impervious to goading. Not like Jaya. You could call Niko a coward, an idiot, an ugly dogface, and he would only respond with an unmoved, contemptuous stare. "Fine, then, I'll go by myself," Ru said, deploying his final weapon, which he knew was sure to succeed so long as he meant it, because in spite of all his apparent indifference, Niko would not allow his little stone-eye brother to get himself into deep shit.

The next day, a Firstday, they skipped school at the same time and met at the subway station on Lo Low Street, where they chained up their bikes and rode the train to their destination. They did not expect to be recognized, but Ru kept the hood of his sweatshirt pulled up over his head. Niko was wearing a billed cap and a zipped-up track jacket that covered his Kaul Dushuron Academy uniform shirt. They were careful not to talk about anything that might identify them as members of the Kaul family.

It was not, Ru reasoned, that they were in danger from enemy Green Bones. They were underage, and Ru was a stone-eye, so he was doubly protected by aisho. However, as Ru's mother frequently reminded him, opportunistic misfortune was always possible. Accidents and misunderstandings could be deadly. The wrong word or decision could have terrible consequences in another clan's territory. All the Kaul children had heard the story of their uncle Anden being abducted by Gont Asch as intimidation against No Peak when he was eighteen years old, as a result of unintentionally wandering into Summer Park.

When Ru and Niko emerged from the unfamiliar subway station in Little Hammer, they had to consult a map to find the plaza where the duel was supposed to take place. Once they were in the vicinity, it was easy to follow the crowd. Several Mountain Fists and Fingers were standing around, keeping a space clear for the combatants. The Kaul brothers maneuvered their way into an inconspicuous position among the spectators that still allowed them to clearly see all the action.

"That's him," Ru whispered. Ayt Atosho, twenty-two years old, a junior Fist of the Mountain, was dressed in loose black pants and a traditional leather vest, a thirty-three-inch moon blade slung over his shoulder. He was speaking to an older couple who were probably his aunt and uncle in the Koben family, but he paused to smile and pose with Mountain loyalists who approached him with cameras in hand. Having never seen Ayt Ato in person before, Ru had to unwillingly admit that the photographs did not lie. The young heir of the Mountain was tall and handsome, with smooth skin, spiky hair tinted red and fashionably mussed, and three jade stones pierced above each eyebrow. If he was nervous about the fight, it didn't show.

A short distance away, Ato's challenger paced back and forth. No one in No Peak knew much about Niru Von, other than he was a junior Fist from a poor family. He was probably of a similar age to his opponent, but his pockmarked face made him appear older. Rumor was that he and Ayt Ato had quarreled over the assignment of Fingers. Ato had made mocking comments about the other man's management style and southern accent. Niru offered a clean blade.

Rather than happening on the spot, as would be typical for most minor duels, the contest had been delayed for an entire week, for no apparent reason other than to allow the Koben family to spread the news to the entire city. Ayt Ato was a minor celebrity, after all, and his relatives were not about to waste an opportunity for publicity. Among the spectators crowding the plaza were photographers from several tabloid newspapers.

Ru craned his neck, hoping to catch sight of the Mountain clan's leaders. It gave him a nervous thrill to be so close to Green Bones he knew only by reputation as enemies of his family, men who would murder his father if given the chance. He felt as if he were squatting in a pit of snakes. The muscular man with the heavy chain-link necklace of jade must be Aben Soro, Horn of the Mountain. He was standing a short distance away, arms crossed, speaking to two of his other Fists. Ayt Madashi was nowhere in sight.

"What a circus," Niko grumbled.

At last the duel began, fifteen minutes late on account of Ayt Ato's extended conversations. The crowd quieted as the two men touched their moon blades to their foreheads in salute. Niru attacked first— a sudden rush combined with a classic sequence of rapid cuts. Ato deflected the barrage neatly, leaping back Light, moon blade flashing defensively as his opponent pressed him to the edge of the available space. At an expertly timed moment, Ato pivoted off the straight line and threw a tight Deflection that hit Niru between the shoulder blades from behind, sending the other Fist stumbling almost to his knees.

Ato made a move forward to seize the advantage, then hesitated. Ru wondered if he'd been coached not to end the fight too quickly. Instead, the young man let his opponent regain his balance and waited for him to attack again, this time with swift but predictable

whirling slashes. The white blades met and parted, striving, blocking, and countering. The two Mountain Fists fought back down the
length of the plaza, Ato now clearly on the offensive. Both men were
bleeding from cuts to their limbs where metal had made it past Steel
and skin, but the wounds seemed superficial, nothing that would end
the fight.

The tip of Niru's moon blade began to sag toward the paving
stones. He made a valiant rally, throwing a triple blast of Deflections
that Ato was hard-pressed to dispel, then lunging Light and bringing
all his Strength down in an overhead chop. Ato met the blow, directing its momentum past his shoulder and toward the ground with the
angle of his own blade. Niru tipped forward and threw his arms wide
to catch his balance. Ato swept the man's leading leg out from under
him, sending him to the ground.

Niru's moon blade clattered out of his hands as he broke his fall.
The man crawled to his knees tiredly and looked up the length of Ayt
Ato's extended blade. "I concede, Ayt-jen," he declared. He sounded
resigned and unsurprised, more defeated in spirit than in body. With
head bowed and eyes downcast, he removed his jade rings and lifted
a pendant of three stones from around his neck. He laid them on
the ground in surrender. "The clan is my blood, and the Pillar is its
master."

Invoking the Green Bone oath was an honorable gesture of submission and clan allegiance, but for nearly thirty years, Ayt Madashi
had been the only living person to be called "Ayt-jen." A prescient
hush fell over the spectators.

Ato wiped his moon blade along the inside of his sleeve and
sheathed it. "My blade is clean," he declared. "You fought well, Niru-
jen. I won only because my family and friends were here to give me
confidence." It was a polite note on which to claim victory, and the
tension broke. The crowd murmured appreciatively.

Ru's brother nudged him in the back. "There, we saw it," Niko
said. "Now let's get out of here."

Reluctantly, Ru followed as Niko weaved his way through the
slowly dispersing onlookers. Some people lingered to talk. One man

said to his friends, with disappointment, "Not nearly as exciting as Kaul Shaelinsan against Ayt Madashi twelve years ago. Now *that* was a real duel. Haven't seen a better one since." Ru smiled with pride for his aunt, and when he and Niko were away from the plaza, he told his brother what he'd overheard.

"That's a stupid comparison," Niko said. "Ayt Ato and Niru Von weren't fighting to kill. This was a show for the Mountain clan, and everyone else, too. That's why Niru put in a decent effort but didn't fight to his limit. I bet he took off some of his jade before the duel. If he won, he'd make enemies of the Koben family. Since he lost honorably and made Ayt Ato look good, I wouldn't be surprised if he has an envelope full of cash coming to him."

Rigged or not, Ru still thought the duel had been exciting. It had given them an excuse to skip school to sneak into Little Hammer and he still felt giddy with daring. He punched his brother in the arm. "Ayt Ato is pretty good, but you're better. You could beat him for sure."

Niko looked at his younger brother in surprise. Then he frowned, his left eye squinting. "I'm never going to fight Ayt Ato," he pointed out. "Unless both our clans have gone down in ashes and we're the last people standing, so you better hope it doesn't happen."

"The important thing is that you *could* beat him," Ru said. "He was, what, fifteenth in his class at Wie Lon? Not bad, but so far, you're in the top five, right?"

Niko stopped on the sidewalk and faced his brother. "How do you even know my school rank?"

Ru spread his hands. "What do you think, keke? I live at home and hear Ma and Da talk about stuff. And we're practically cousins with the Juen twins." Ritto and Din were in the class above Niko at the Academy.

Niko frowned and stuffed his hands into the pockets of his track jacket. He started walking again. Ru jogged past him, skipping backward in front of his brother. "Once you graduate, everyone will know you're a better Green Bone than that pretty boy, and smarter too. When *you* have your first big duel, I'll get everyone in my school to—" Ru glanced over his shoulder to check where he was going and spun to an abrupt stop. "What's *that*?"

Three people in black masks, two men and one woman, were plastering the brick wall outside of the subway station with posters. The largest one read, *Free Kekon from Jade and Tyrants!* It was followed by a long list of names. Ayt. Kaul. Maik. Koben. Juen. Iwe. And onward—thirty of the most prominent Green Bone families in the country. The rest of the wall was being covered with black-and-white newspaper photographs of the accused tyrants. The images were grainy from being enlarged and photocopied, but it took Ru only a second to find the faces of his father, his mother, his aunt Shae, uncle Papi, and the pictures of several other leaders in No Peak, parents of his cousins and friends.

A wave of disbelieving outrage swept over Ru. "What're you doing?" he shouted.

The three vandals stopped and glared at the intrusion, shoulders and legs tense, ready to run from the police or Green Bones. Seeing only two teenage boys, they relaxed and returned to their task. Ru glanced around furiously for any sign of a clan Finger on patrol, someone to whom he could report the crime—before remembering that he was in Mountain territory. Most, if not all, of the Mountain clan's Fingers and Fists in the vicinity had gone to the plaza to see the duel.

"*Stop that!* You don't know any of those people, how can you say that about them?" Ru had never yelled at adults, but these weren't people who deserved any respect. They were lowlifes who hid their identities like thieves. Ru had grown up with the knowledge that his family had enemies, but he'd always thought of the Mountain clan. Never had he imagined encountering random hatred from strangers.

Ru was a stone-eye boy, but he was from a Green Bone family and had been taught that offenses must always be answered. He drew his talon knife.

Niko seized him by the arm. "Don't be stupid," he said in a low voice.

Ru tugged against the grip, but his older brother was larger and

234 Fonda Lee

stronger. Ru pointed the tip of his talon knife at the hoodlums, who'd stopped at the sight of a weapon and were watching the boys with incredulous menace. "We can't let them keep doing that," Ru insisted.

Niko began to walk away, pulling Ru with him.

Ru planted his heels and refused to be dragged. He was tall for his age and good with the knife, and Niko was an Academy-trained future Green Bone. Why should they run? "We're not going to do anything about it?" he shouted at this brother. "What would Da think?"

"Da wouldn't want us to be here in the first place," Niko snapped.

People passing by on the street were pausing now. Most of them stared at the posters in disbelief and walked away, but the sight of Ru still brandishing his drawn talon knife was causing a stir, and murmurs of recognition began to rise.

One of the masked men jabbed an accusing finger at the Kaul brothers, then pointed at the wall of photographs. *You belong on there with your family.*

A black Roewolfe G8 pulled up to the curb and stopped with a squeal. The front doors flew open. Juen Nu and Lott Jin got out of the car. The Horn of No Peak strode onto the scene as if to kill everyone there. Ru had never seen the man so angry. The three masked vandals dropped everything and fled, pushing people out of the way as they sprinted away from the Green Bones in different directions. Juen took no notice of them. He seized Ru and Niko and shoved them toward the Roewolfe. "Get in the godsdamned car," he ordered.

A silver Victor GS pulled up in front of the Roewolfe. Three Green Bones of the Mountain—a Fist and two Fingers—got out. The Fist took in the scene—Juen and Lott, Niko and Ru, the bystanders now hurriedly backing away.

"Juen-jen," said the Fist warily. "You found what you were looking for."

"Tell your Horn that we're leaving and there's no trouble," Juen said calmly, although his grip tightened on the back of Ru's shirt. "We're all on the greener side here. We're used to handling small, foolish problems that don't require the attention of our Pillars, aren't we?"

A tense moment that felt like an eternity passed before the Mountain Fist moved his chin a few degrees to glance at the freshly plastered posters on the wall. "Did you see which way those clanless dogs fled?"

"There were three of them, and they split up." Lott Jin volunteered a description of the vandals and what they'd been wearing, then pointed out the directions they had escaped.

The Mountain Fist nodded cautiously and touched his forehead in salute. Lott opened the back door of the Roewolfe and Juen deposited Ru and Niko inside. The Horn and the First Fist got into the car. Lott pulled it into the street. Ru looked out the window to see the Mountain Green Bones watching them as they left.

Juen spun around. "What were the two of you *thinking*?" he demanded, so angrily that Ru shrank back into the seat. The Horn was the most fearsome position in any clan, but Ru had always viewed Juen as Ritto and Din's father, who lived in the house on the other side of the garden on the Kaul estate. He was stern and sharp-eyed but not frightening. Ru had heard other adults call Juen Nu a modern Horn, a manager Horn. It was said that he commanded the military side of No Peak not with the street charisma of Kaul Hilo or the stoic gravity of Maik Kehn, but with the organizational prowess of a man playing three games of circle chess at the same time. In that moment, however, Ru had no trouble believing that Juen Nu, like anyone who rises to a high level on the greener side of the clan, was a man capable of considerable violence. "Are you trying to cause a panic? Or a war?"

"We just wanted to see the duel," Ru explained. "We were coming straight back."

"Ayt Ato's duel? You thought it was worth skipping school and sneaking into Mountain territory for *that*?" The car crossed from Little Hammer into Old Town, back into No Peak territory. Juen pointed to the nearest pay phone and Lott swerved sharply and pulled over. The First Fist jumped out and ran into the booth to place a phone call. Juen leaned over the gear shift and turned off the engine.

"What's Lott-jen doing?" Ru asked.

"What did you think would happen when your school reported you missing?" Juen demanded. "There's an emergency phone chain for situations like this. Word goes out to hundreds of our Fists and Fingers in every part of the city. When the Academy couldn't find Niko, they pulled Jaya out of class and kept her under guard. She was furious. She also guessed where the two of you had gone. I had to send messengers running to Aben Soro to beg leave from our enemies to search inside their districts. It would've taken only one wrong rumor, one false witness, the suggestion that one of you had been taken or harmed, for something terrible to start. Lott is calling off the search now, before anything like that can happen." The Horn's voice rose in disbelief. "And when I find you, you're standing around pointing a talon knife like you're trying to start a street fight in the middle of Little Hammer."

"Did you see those people, what they were doing?" Ru protested.

"Clanless anarchists have pulled that stunt across the city," Juen spat. "They're trying to shock people, to get media coverage and foreign sympathy. Members of the Kaul family threatening them with talon knives is the sort of thing these lunatics *want*. We have to catch and punish these people, but that's for me to deal with as Horn in our districts, and for Aben Soro to deal with in Mountain territory. Not for *you*; you're a twelve-year-old boy."

Lott returned to the car and said, with relief, "Everything's okay. We're to take them back to the house."

Equal degrees of guilt and dread made Ru sink into his seat. "Please, Uncle Juen, don't tell our ma and da that we were in Little Hammer. Say you found us in the Armpit or somewhere else," Ru begged. "At least not Ma." Even when his father was furious, he was more forgiving of Ru's antics. Ru couldn't count on the same lenience from his mother.

"We can't deny we were in Little Hammer, not when the Mountain's people saw us there," Niko said, speaking for the first time since they'd gotten into the car. "Uncle Juen, we were at the duel because of me. We took the risk of going into Little Hammer so I could watch Ayt Ato fight and learn more about him and his family."

After a moment of stupefied silence, Ru blurted, "Hey, it was *my* idea!"

Niko quieted his younger brother with a flat and dangerous look that either came from being trained at the Academy as a Green Bone or occurred naturally to men of the Kaul family once they began nearing adulthood, because Ru had no idea how to summon it himself.

Juen studied them in the rearview mirror, eyes narrowed, perhaps trying to Perceive whether Niko was being sincere. Niko returned the Horn's gaze calmly. The children of Green Bones are adept at lying only by omission and never by being outright dishonest.

"Uncle Juen, we should take Ru back to his school," Niko said. "He has classes this afternoon and shouldn't miss them. I'm the older brother and we went to the duel for my benefit, so I'll go to the house and answer to our parents."

Ru clenched his fists and opened his mouth to argue again, but couldn't come up with anything else to say. Ru had always looked up to his older brother. Niko didn't tease him or act superior. Even when he was annoyed or exasperated, he didn't hit Ru. And Niko was smart, always seeming to know more than the other children in the family. But sometimes, Ru couldn't help but think it was unfair that Niko had taken his place as the eldest son in the family.

This was not because Ru felt sorry for himself as a stone-eye. He understood that he couldn't grow up to wear jade or lead the clan, but that didn't make him feel deficient or less loved. Of course, he felt excluded from the experiences of his siblings and cousins, but his father always reminded him that he also had things his brother and sister did not—his dog Koko, his own room at home with a video game console, more time for relayball.

Nevertheless, Ru felt that between him and Niko, *he* ought to be the one in charge. He was the one who talked more and came up with ideas for what they should do. Niko was quiet and went along with things—until he didn't. Only when it inexplicably suited him would he suddenly assume the mantle of firstborn son and clan heir.

Juen Nu took orders from no one but the Pillar. But Ru could tell, from the amused glance and shrug that Juen exchanged with Lott, that the men were impressed by the way Niko had made his point. Speaking reasonably, accepting responsibility, and most of all, taking a risk in order to gain knowledge and potential advantage over an enemy—all those things were a credit to his greenness.

"All right, Niko-se," Juen said, once again sounding like the good-natured uncle Ru knew. Ten minutes later, Ru was left standing on the front steps of his school, relieved and resentful, watching the Roewolfe turn out of the parking lot and drive toward home.

CHAPTER
23

Friends of Friends

the fourteenth year, sixth month

Wen attended the Janloon Film Festival as the guest of Ren Jirhuya, the artist she'd met seven months ago at a fundraiser luncheon. At his invitation, she'd given a speech at the annual conference of the Charitable Society for Jade Nonreactivity and done a short filmed interview, which was being used in television ads to raise awareness and combat superstition. Wen had taken a liking to the Abukei artist; he struck her as genuine, personable, and motivated. She was pleased when he landed a position as the assistant art director on a movie being produced by Cinema Shore, one of Kekon's few major film studios.

When Wen asked him to introduce her to people he knew in the industry, Jirhuya agreed but voiced reservations. "I'd like to help you, Mrs. Kaul, but I don't have any influence with the studio," he explained.

"I'm not seeking any sort of influence," Wen assured him. "I only want to learn about the business, and I prefer to meet people as friends of friends."

At the festival, Jirhuya introduced her to actors, directors, writers, and to Sian Kugo, producer and co-owner of Cinema Shore. "Mrs. Kaul," Sian exclaimed, glancing nervously at Wen's bodyguards. "I had no idea you'd be here." The Janloon Film Festival had been growing steadily over its six-year existence, but was not widely known. The country's movie industry was small compared to that of nearby Shotar.

"I enjoy getting out and attending cultural events whenever I can." It was easier for Wen to do so now that she was more confident in her body and needed to rely on the cane less often. She would never be completely healed, of course, but she'd become adept at hiding moments of weakness or imbalance. To most people, she appeared normal in speech and gait. "Mr. Sian, will you sit down with me at the bar? I'd like to ask you some questions about the business, if you'll indulge me."

The filmmaker was happy to talk. "Kekon is a small film market. It's hard to compete against the big-budget foreign films from Espenia and Shotar. And there's television, of course—everyone has a screen at home and people wait for movies to show up in video rental stores. I'm hoping the Janloon Film Festival will grow and attract more interest."

Wen took a sip from her cocktail glass. She was on her first drink; the effusive studio executive was on his third. "Why do you think the Shotarian films are so popular?"

Mr. Sian wrinkled his nose. "Because people have no taste!" Then he laughed and said, "I have to admit, they have a unique stylish, pulpy aesthetic. And their crime dramas are addictive. They're always about grumpy but heroic Shotarian policemen solving murders or conspiracies. The Shotarian studios probably employ more Kekonese actors than we do, just to portray barukan gangsters."

"So most of the time, when foreigners see Kekonese actors on-screen, they're watching them play criminals in Shotarian movies," Wen said. "Does that bother you, as a Kekonese filmmaker?"

Sian shrugged. "Sure, but that's capitalism. Shotar is a large market and if actors are able to make a living by taking these stock roles, what can you say?"

"When I was growing up, I remember my brothers were always reading comic books about Baijen, and there were movies set during the occupation with heroic Green Bones fighting the Shotarians."

"I grew up on those too, but war films aren't popular right now, and there's no international audience for Kekonese mythology," the producer opined. "I'm focusing Cinema Shore on medium-budget projects that have a better chance of getting overseas distribution. Action movies, spy thrillers, drama, horror."

Wen smiled and said, "Mr. Sian, I'm not a businesswoman and I don't know much about the film industry yet, but what I do have is the ear of the Pillar as well as the Weather Man." She paused. Even well on the way to his fourth drink, she could see she had Sian's full attention. "How would you go about growing the Kekonese film industry?"

Wen convinced her husband they should take a vacation, just the two of them. Niko and Jaya were at the Academy and could call their uncles or aunts if they needed anything. Ru could stay with his aunt Lina and cousin Cam for a few days, and besides, he was not allowed to go out with his friends for the rest of the month as punishment for the trouble he and his brother had caused. Hilo and Wen had no doubt whose idea that had been.

"Where do you want to go?" Hilo asked. "Marenia? Toshon?"

"I was thinking somewhere farther," Wen said. "Marcucuo."

"Marcucuo?" Hilo raised an eyebrow and asked slowly, "Why Marcucuo?"

"We hear about it all the time," Wen said. "Why not go and see for ourselves what it's like?" The tiny city-state island of Marcucuo, off the east coast of Alusius, possessed an official population of only eight hundred thousand people but five times that number of visitors, seasonal residents, and foreign workers.

Marcucuo was a tax haven for the rich and famous, a tropical tourist mecca with every form of entertainment and gambling. Green Bones spoke of Marcucuo in a tone of disdainful fascination, because it was the one place where jade was openly used for sport and entertainment, in one-on-one matches, staged stunts, and televised obstacle course challenges. Many of the competitors were of Kekonese ancestry—Keko-Shotarians and Keko-Espenians, primarily. Others were shine-using foreigners, self-taught or ex-military. And some, to the disgrace of proper Green Bones, were Kekonese—people who'd gotten their jade from families or schooling but had chosen not to take clan oaths, nor enter one of the noble professions.

Wen knew Hilo's opinion on the entire industry. "A waste to put jade on circus monkeys," he said. "Why give our money to that place?"

"Whatever we may think of it, people in other parts of the world are going to use jade differently than we do, and some Kekonese are going to be attracted to those foreign ways. We've fought the Mountain, and Ti Pasuiga, and the Matyos barukan, and the Espenian Crews—all of them have done things to corrupt the meaning of jade. But maybe we haven't thought enough about how we can shape that meaning ourselves and use modern-day culture to our own advantage."

Hilo gave her a long look. "This isn't really a vacation, is it?"

"Of course it's a vacation," Wen said, giving her husband a hurt look. "There are lots of things to see and do in Marcucuo, and the weather's nice. We can go to the beach, and I want to do some shopping, too. If we also happen to learn a few things or talk to a few people that could be useful to the clan, then so much the better."

She was pleasantly surprised when her husband agreed to the trip without pressing for more details. Hilo was a direct personality; Wen had heard him speak sharply to his men, demanding specifics if they made the mistake of giving him generalities or possibilities. But Wen held ideas close and quiet until they were nearer to reality. At times, she envied the apparent ease of Shae and Woon's working relationship, which she did not yet have with her own husband. Despite the relief of being able to talk openly about clan issues, she could tell Hilo chafed at how her role as Pillarman ate into their time together. It was easier to discuss things when they were contented as husband and wife first.

So it was only after they woke and made love and were lying spent and sweaty in bed on their second morning in the Golden Spire Hotel & Casino overlooking Grace Square in Marcucuo that Wen said, "We're going to a party tonight. It's at the mansion of Sel Lucanito. He's the Tomascian media and gaming tycoon who owns Spectacle One, the largest of the jadesports promotion companies."

Hilo rolled over and sat up. "All right," he said firmly. "You've been cagey for long enough about what we might gain from being here. Tell your Pillar why he should care about going to this party."

Wen looked up at him, noticing the way the tropical sunlight streaming in from the windows lit the jade on his body. "Do you remember I talked to you and Shae about No Peak investing in Cinema Shore and the Kekon film industry?"

"What about it?"

"The public relations campaign Shae's begun in Espenia has made me think about how there's a different kind of war going on these days. A war for people's thoughts and feelings. The Kobens already know it." She was still galled by how easily Koben Yiro had upstaged her with his zealous rhetoric. "So does the Clanless Future Movement, when they paint the clans and jade as outdated and evil. That's what some people are led to believe, when they see news about jade used in foreign wars, or watch movies with barukan villains." Wen got up and walked naked to the dresser, pinning up her hair. "We can change that."

Hilo lit a cigarette. She turned to give him a sour look—she was trying to encourage him to quit—but they were on vacation after all. "We're not getting into the jadesports business," Hilo said with finality.

"No," Wen agreed. "But we can take from it."

The phone on the desk rang. Wen picked it up. "I'm sorry to interrupt your vacation," said Juen's voice. "Is Hilo-jen there?" Wen handed the receiver to Hilo. She washed up and got dressed while her husband spoke to the Horn, smoking and pacing back and forth in the hotel room as far as the phone cord would allow. When he hung up, she gave him an anxious, questioning look.

"Five of our Green Bones were ambushed and killed in Lukang last night," he told her. "No one that you know," he added quickly, upon seeing her alarm. "They were former members of Six Hands Unity who decided to swear oaths to No Peak. The Mountain found out about it and whispered their names." He stubbed his cigarette out angrily, grinding it into the ashtray.

"Do we need to cut our trip short?" Wen asked worriedly.

Hilo shook his head. "Juen's got it under control."

Wen sat down on the end of the bed and watched her husband put on his clothes. Outside, Marcucuo's weather was balmy and cloudless. Birdsong and the fragrance of blooming flowers from the Golden Spire Hotel's lush gardens saturated the morning air beneath their hotel room balcony. No matter where they were in the world, however, they were never far from the feud, and the designs of their enemies.

Hilo finished buttoning up his shirt. He came over to her and cupped her jaw, then kissed the top of her head. "Ayt Mada's not going to ruin our vacation. I'll have things to deal with when we get home, but let's enjoy ourselves while we're here."

Eight hours later, they were welcomed into the foyer of a three-wing Alusian-style stucco mansion by Sel Lucanito. As the Pillar's wife and his Pillarman, Wen had met many wealthy and powerful people, but they were usually affiliated with No Peak and seeking audience with the Pillar. It was different to be walking into the home of a foreign stranger, with none of the clan's Fists or Fingers to be seen. She was not nervous—she was with Hilo, after all—but she did feel out of her element, reminded that as mighty as the No Peak clan had become, Kekon was still a small nation and there were people in the world with more money and influence than could be found on their island. A number of such people came to Marcucuo to entertain themselves in grand fashion and hobnob with fellow millionaires.

Sel Lucanito was a man who took up space not only with his height—he was a head taller than most of the other men in the room—but his expansive hyperenergetic presence. The multimillionaire owned residences in Tomascio, Espenia, and Marcucuo, spoke three languages, and owned several casinos, a network television company, and Spectacle One. Although he had never crossed paths with any of the Kauls in person, he knew who they were. It was impossible to be in a business with any connection to jade and not be aware of the Green Bone clans. Lucanito had gone to the trouble of learning "May the gods shine favor on you" in Kekonese, for the express purpose of greeting the Kauls on their arrival. With Tomascian chivalry, he bent into an impressively graceful bow given his height, then shook their hands with enthusiastic warmth and said, in Espenian, "I'm delighted you came. I have so much love and respect for the jade arts and your country's traditions. That's why I'm passionate about promoting a modern version of them to a global audience. I would love to see more Kekonese competitors involved in jadesports. There's nothing like the mystique of the traditional Green Bone warrior to draw viewers."

Hilo gave the entertainment tycoon the sort of smile that Wen knew he reserved for men he was treating nicely despite his personal opinion of them. She'd seen him use it on plenty of politicians, bureaucrats, and overly demanding Lantern Men. On the surface, it resembled his typical lopsided grin. Only someone who knew Hilo well could see when his eyes held none of the easy warmth of his true smile. She gave his hand a soft squeeze, reminding him to be polite, even to this foreigner whose true passion was making money off the jade abilities of others.

"You throw a great party," Hilo said in rough Espenian, nodding at the man's lavish house, the swarm of well-dressed guests, and the abundant spread of food and free-flowing alcohol. "My wife insisted we couldn't come to Marcucuo and pass it up."

Sel Lucanito beamed and threw his arm toward the revelry. "Please, enjoy yourselves! There's so much we could talk about, and I hope we do, but I won't monopolize your time. You're the first Green Bone clan leaders I've had the pleasure of hosting, and everyone is going to want to meet you."

Wen spoke up quickly, as if an exciting thought had occurred to her in that instant. "I heard that Danny Sinjo would be at this party. Is that true, Mr. Lucanito? I would love to meet him."

Lucanito was happy to confirm that, indeed, Sinjo was here, and he brought Hilo and Wen out to the poolside, where he introduced them to the Keko-Espenian jadesports star, his girlfriend, and his manager. Danny Sinjo was indeed movie-star handsome, with arresting eyes and a flawless jawline, but he had the build and posture of a real fighter. Like all Keko-Espenians, he wore his jade out of sight, but Wen could imagine him passing as a Fist on the streets of Janloon, if not for his jagged overlong haircut and a face that was a bit too pretty to appear credible.

Sinjo was caught off guard by the introduction. After setting down his drink and shaking their hands, he said, "Wow. This is sure something."

Wen said, "Congratulations on your big win." Sinjo had recently defeated a Shotarian fighter to retain his title as superchamp in Spectacle One's televised World Warrior event. Wen had first heard about Danny Sinjo from Anden, who'd described the underground jadesports training culture in Resville after his first trip to that Espenian city. Since then, she'd followed Sinjo's rise with interest. He might not be a proper Green Bone in Hilo's eyes, but there was no denying the man's jade abilities. He'd come from an expatriate Green Bone family. He'd been well trained and had made trips to Kekon to learn from the best private coaches there. Now he was an actor; he'd already appeared in a recent Shotarian film and was in talks about future roles.

"Do you speak Kekonese, Sinjo-jen?" Hilo asked.

The man blinked. Wen suspected that Sinjo, for all of his growing fame, had never been addressed with the respectful Green Bone suffix before. It surprised Wen as well, to hear Hilo use it, and to see her husband smiling, sincerely this time. Sinjo said, in Kekonese, "My Kekonese is okay, but not great."

"No problem," said Hilo. "You speak it well enough, and I know enough Espenian to get by. I'm glad to see another Kekonese face in this crowd. My cousin saw you years ago, in Resville. And now my own wife is a fan and insists I have to meet you."

Sinjo did not seem like a modest man. Wen had seen him posing and prancing for the audience on television. Now he glanced at the Kauls and seemed at a loss for words. "Seer's balls, I'm flattered."

Hilo said, "Have you ever thought about coming back to Kekon?"

"Honestly, no," Sinjo said. "No offense, but there's nothing for me there."

"There might be more than you think. No matter how many sport fights you win for Lucanito, or how many bad guys you play in the Shotarian movies, your face will always be Kekonese. No one will ever appreciate you as much as your own people." Hilo put a friendly hand on Sinjo's shoulder and handed him a drink from the tray of a passing waiter, taking one for himself as well. "It's crowded by the pool. Why don't we walk over there and have a quieter conversation? Bring your manager if you like."

Wen smiled encouragingly and struck up a conversation with Sinjo's girlfriend—a thin, pale-haired Espenian woman—so that the men could take a stroll and talk about serious matters. The party was getting increasingly crowded and noisy—a band had started playing, and several people had fallen drunkenly into the massive blue swimming pool—but Wen was relaxed now. She'd seen Sinjo's awestruck expression. For the most part, everyone who wore jade, no matter their upbringing, nationality, or bloodline, viewed the Green Bones of Kekon with a certain fearful reverence. The up-and-coming young movie star Danny Sinjo was not so far removed from his heritage that he could fail to appreciate the significance of receiving personal attention from the Pillar of the No Peak clan.

Wen had complete confidence in her husband's ability to compel any man he befriended. Tomorrow morning, she would call her sister-in-law in the Weather Man's office. By the end of the week, Sian Kugo would be a Lantern Man of No Peak, Cinema Shore would belong to the clan, and Danny Sinjo would star in its films.

CHAPTER
24

It's Finally Happening

Bero was surprised when he received a phone call one evening and heard Ema's voice on the other end. He'd never spoken to her on the phone before, even though he'd asked for her number many times. At Galo's urging, he'd tried to make friends with her, even taking her out for noodles and paying the bill, yet he still hadn't managed to get between her legs. Nor had Bero gotten closer to uncovering the details of Vastik eya Molovni's plans, much to the displeasure of his Espenian handlers. He was still considering forcing himself on Ema, but if she was fucking Molovni, that ugly Ygutanian bastard might kill him, or at least kick him out of the group, which would mean the end of his lucrative arrangement with the Espenians.

So when Ema told him, "I don't give out my number," he gave her his number instead. But she had never called. Until now.

"It's Ema," she said. "From the clanless meetings."

"Ah, hey," said Bero, frowning, but suddenly excited. "You called."

"Listen, I know that I haven't been all that nice to you. I...have a hard time letting other people get close to me. I know it must make me seem rude sometimes." She paused. "Anyway, I was wondering if you'd like to get together tonight."

Bero thought about saying no just to spite the standoffish bitch, but the impulse only lasted for half a second. "Sure," he said, trying to sound nonchalant. "I'm not doing anything right now. Where do you want to go?"

After a moment of silence, Ema said, "I don't feel like going out. Not tonight. I have a bottle of hoji here at my place. Do you want to come over?"

Bero went over. On the way, he stopped to buy a bag of hot fried bread from a fast food stand and a packet of condoms from the drugstore. Ema lived in an old, three-story apartment building behind an adult video rental shop in the Coinwash district. Bero climbed to the top floor and knocked on her apartment door. She opened it, smiled wordlessly, and held the door open for him to come in. She was wearing only a white bathrobe and no clothes underneath. The air in the apartment was damp and smelled of orange blossom; it seemed she'd just gotten out of a bath. She hadn't waited for him to arrive to open the bottle of hoji.

"Fried bread, thank the gods," she said, and took a stick of it from the bag.

Despite his eagerness to get started, Bero took a moment to walk around the one-bedroom apartment curiously. It was tiny, even smaller than his, but the things inside of it were expensive. Ema had an LCD television, and a stereo with a cassette tape deck. Her open closet was filled with brand-name clothes, handbags, and shoes, and the jewelry lying on her dresser was real gold. Bero couldn't think of why, if she had enough money to buy such nice things, she would be living in this neighborhood.

He sneered. All her belongings must be gifts from rich men.

Resentfully, he remembered that his Espenian handlers would want him to take this opportunity to gather information. There didn't seem to be many obvious clues about Ema's personal life besides a framed family photograph on top of her dresser. A man and woman with three boys and two girls, standing on the deck of a boat with the ocean in the background. Ema was a teenager in the photograph—the second-oldest child. She was standing beside her elder brother, a Green Bone.

"Come here," Ema said, patting the sofa cushion next to her. She poured him a glass of hoji. Bero took off his jacket and sat down next to her, accepting the drink.

"Why do you hate the clans so much if your brother is a Green Bone?" he asked.

Ema tipped back her drink, her throat bobbing as she swallowed. The soft skin of her neck and chest was flushed from the bath and the liquor. "My brother's dead," she said, putting the glass down and refilling it. "He was executed." She turned to Bero, eyes bright and glassy. "What about you? Do you have family?"

"No," Bero said.

"You don't have anyone you're close to?"

The hoji burned down Bero's throat and warmed him. He thought about the people he'd associated with over the years, especially the ones he might've said were something close to friends. Sampa. Cheeky. Mudt. All of them dead or gone. Bero's relationships did not last. "Something always got in the way," he said. "*Jade.* Jade always got in the way."

"I'm sorry for you." She didn't sound as if she were mocking him, just being honest. She moved closer to him. Her robe fell open and he saw her breasts and dark nipples. "Do you think the gods exist?" she asked unexpectedly. "Do you think they see and judge us, the way the penitents say they do?"

Bero's cock was pushing uncomfortably against his pants. He frowned at the question. It wasn't one he thought about deeply. He'd had enough close calls and strange swings of luck in his life that at times he thought surely some bigger force loomed over him, watching him, batting him around like a mouse.

At other times, he thought there was nothing out there, that desperate people were deluded and strived in vain, that they saw patterns and signs when there were none to see. In his own life, nothing he'd ever done truly added up to anything greater. There was no bigger picture; his runs of fortune and failure canceled each other out. Sometimes he skimmed above the water and sometimes he floundered below it, but still he was just a fish in the unknowable and merciless ocean.

"I don't think it matters if the gods exist," Bero said. "If they gave me this shitty lot in life, then I don't give a fuck what they think."

Ema gazed into his eyes with calm agreement. "Me neither."

She took his cock out of his pants and lowered her head into his lap. Her damp hair spilled over his stomach as she sucked him. When he was close to coming, he pushed her down and they fucked on the sofa. They moved to the single bed and fucked again. Ema fucked with her eyes closed, with relentless, mechanical, angry desperation. She didn't even make him put on a condom. After Bero was done, she kept riding him and rubbing herself urgently until she came. Bero was honestly bewildered. After years of rebuffing him, he would've liked it if she'd put on more of a show of her usual haughtiness, maybe resisted a little, made it more challenging. As it was, the sex was fine, very good, it was sex after all, but a bit anticlimactic considering how long he'd had to wait for it.

Afterward, he wanted to fall asleep, but she shook his shoulder and said, "You have to go." Bero rolled over and grumbled, but she shook him again and he raised his head in irritation. A couple of hours ago, Ema had been drunk and needy, but now she was standing up, wrapping herself in her robe, strangely sober and purposeful, with a vaguely vacant look in her eyes. "It's tomorrow," she told him. "It's happening tomorrow."

At first, he couldn't understand what she was talking about. Then he sat up. "What's happening tomorrow?" He was awake now. "It's what you and Molovni and the others have been planning, isn't it? The great strike of the clanless."

Ema wrote something down on a slip of paper and handed it to Bero. "Go to this address in the Docks at four o'clock tomorrow afternoon. That's where we're meeting after it's done. Vastik will be there with a boat nearby, ready to get us out of the country."

"Out of the *country*?" Bero repeated in confusion, scowling at the paper in his hand. "Why are you giving this to me? Molovni doesn't want anything to do with me. I was never brought into the plan."

Ema bent over him and placed a strangely chaste kiss on his cheek, the crooked one that had been damaged so many years ago. "You're in it now," she said, "because you're my friend. Vastik won't have a choice."

Bero said with a jealous sneer, "So you can get *Vastik* to do whatever you want?"

Ema gave a humorless laugh. "Molovni has to do what his masters in Dramsk tell him to do. Just because I hate the clans doesn't mean I have any love for the Ygutanians." She picked up Bero's discarded shirt and pants and handed them to him. As he dressed reluctantly, she rummaged in her purse and pulled out a wad of money. "Here," she said, handing it to him. "It's late. Take a taxi."

"That's more than I need for a taxi ride," he said, eyeing the cash but taking it anyway and stuffing it into his pocket. "Why won't you tell me what you're going to do? Maybe I could help, you know." He knew he sounded whiny. Angry.

Ema gave him a deflated smile and drew her robe more tightly around herself. "You have. I needed a good fuck tonight, and you gave me that." She went to the door and opened it for him. "Lie low tomorrow. Just be at that address on time."

———————

When Bero got back to his apartment, he called the special number he'd been given by the Espenians, the one he'd been told to use only for emergencies, if his position as an informer had been compromised, if he was in mortal danger, or if he had some vital or urgent information. It was past midnight. The phone picked up after the third ring. "Who is this?" demanded Galo's sleepy voice.

"Catfish." Bero winced; he still hated his code name. "It's tomorrow. Whatever Molovni is planning with the leaders of the clanless, it's going to go down tomorrow."

Galo was instantly alert. "How do you know this?"

"The girl. Ema. I finally got to her. I went to her apartment and everything."

"What exactly did she tell you?"

"She wouldn't tell me anything," Bero groused. "All I know is that it'll happen tomorrow, and Molovni has a plan to get them out of the country afterward."

"What's the girl's address?" Galo demanded.

Bero hesitated. He had a sudden vision of Espenian soldiers surrounding Ema's building in Coinwash and breaking down the door. He imagined her being dragged from her apartment and thrown into the back of an unmarked vehicle, to be taken to an Espenian military installation and never seen again.

He wasn't sure why the thought bothered him. He barely knew the girl. Just because he'd been wanting to bed her for a long time and finally succeeded didn't mean he owed her anything. She'd acted like an aloof bitch to him for years, and come to think of it, she'd been rude tonight, the way she'd kicked him out in the middle of the night. The Espenians, arrogant and demanding as they were, were paying Bero well. So he was confused by his own reluctance.

"What are you going to do to her?" he asked.

Galo was also surprised by Bero's question. "Why do you care?"

"I just want to know," Bero snapped. "She's just a girl, all right? A girl who got pulled into some shit by the barukan and that Ygutanian lout. If I tell you her address, what're you going to do to her?"

A long moment of silence from the other end of the line. Then Galo mumbled, "Catfish, you surprise me. Of all the times to grow a sliver of conscience, you have to do it now?" The Espenian went on in a slower, more soothing tone. "We're not going to hurt her. We're not going to tip our hand at all until we have to. Your girl is a line to Molovni, and Molovni is a line to the Ygutanian military and the nekolva training program. Tomorrow morning, we're going to watch her apartment, and we're going to follow her until she leads us to Molovni. I promise she won't be in danger from us." When Bero still failed to answer right away, Galo's voice turned sharp. "Give us the address, Catfish."

Bero gave them Ema's address. There was a strange, unfamiliar curl of worry in the pit of his stomach, and he disliked it. "What about me?" he asked. "What am I supposed to do? What if Molovni and the clanless find out that I ratted on them?"

"Don't do anything," Galo said. "Just stay out of the way. If it looks like you're in danger, we can pull you out. Keep this number handy, and don't say anything to anyone." He paused and Bero heard him speaking rapidly in Espenian to someone else before coming back onto the line. "Is there anything more you can tell us?"

Bero took out the slip of paper in his pocket and rubbed it between his fingers. If following Ema failed to lead the Espenians to Molovni and his coconspirators, this would be the surefire way to find all of them tomorrow, at four o'clock in the afternoon.

But a safe house with a getaway boat . . . That could be very useful to Bero. In case something went wrong. In case the Espenians hung him out to dry after all.

"No," he said. "Nothing else."

Galo said, "You've done a good thing, Catfish." He hung up.

CHAPTER
25

The Great Strike

the fourteenth year, seventh month

Hilo had never looked forward to KJA meetings, but he used to be able to avoid them. When it had been created forty years ago, the KJA's sole purpose was to manage the production and distribution of the nation's jade supply. The quarterly meetings were typically filled with discussion of budgeting, economic policy, export quotas, and domestic jade allocation. It was not uncommon for clan Pillars to let their Weather Men handle the meetings, sometimes arriving only at the end of the session to cast any necessary votes.

In recent years, however, the KJA had expanded well beyond its original purpose as a state cartel to become a wide-ranging policy group on all issues related to jade. Special sessions had been convened to discuss what the KJA's official position should be on military reform, non-Kekonese citizens studying at Kekonese martial schools, and jadesports in Marcucuo, among other issues. The Green Bone clans had used the KJA to take unified public stances opposing decriminalization of shine, anti-dueling laws, and political extremism. On one hand, the evolving function of the KJA did make for less boring discussions. On the other, Hilo was forced to spend far more time than he wanted sitting in a room with his enemies.

When he arrived with Woon, both he and the clan's Sealgiver were greeted with warm, respectful congratulations on the birth of a healthy child into the Kaul family. Woon, sleep-deprived and smiling constantly, was as happy as Hilo had ever seen the man. No doubt he would prefer to be with Shae and their newborn daughter at this moment, but he would be the acting Weather Man for the next several months, taking over Ship Street in Shae's absence, as he had at other times in the past.

Ayt Madashi arrived with Koben Yiro. Over the years, the Mountain had made changes to its organization as well. To Hilo's knowledge, Ayt had never had a Pillarman, but the insufferably grandstanding Koben Yiro appeared to have become her unofficial aide in addition to being her frequent mouthpiece. Hilo couldn't tell if Ayt kept Koben close to demonstrate unity with the popular Koben family, or to ensure they could not betray her.

The subject of discussion among the clan leaders today was what to do about the continued offshore jade mining by the Anorco corporation. After repeated sabotage of his ships, Art Wyles had installed security guards from Jim Sunto's private military company, Ganlu Solutions International. Now the vessel off the coast of Euman Island was protected day and night by jade-equipped ex-Espenian military personnel who could Perceive the approach of attackers and drop concussion grenades on them, and technicians who could remove attached mines.

"Invasion and theft!" Koben Yiro declared, pounding the table. "These arrogant foreigners have no respect for our country or the meaning of jade at all."

"No one disagrees with you on that, Koben-jen," said the Weather

Man of Six Hands Unity, with a touch of exasperation at the dramat-
ics. Hilo couldn't recall the man's name offhand, but the chair next
to him was empty. The kin killer Jio Somu never left the safety of his
own territory in Lukang, even with the assurance of penitents being
present. His Weather Man said, "But the CEO of Anorco, Wyles,
has plenty of money and political connections and it's clear he's not
going to be dissuaded. The company claims the ships are operating
in international waters."

"Lies," Koben pointed out. "They regularly encroach on Kekonese
territory."

"The legalities are ambiguous, but what are we supposed to do
when the Royal Council wants us to compromise?" asked the Pillar
of the Jo Sun clan.

It was no secret in this room that Green Bones from the Mountain
and No Peak clans had collaborated to damage the ships. The politicians in Wisdom Hall were extremely anxious about the escalating
situation. So far, no one had been killed, but dead Espenian citizens
or dead Green Bones from either clan could set off a disastrous diplomatic crisis. The government wanted to negotiate an agreement
whereby the clans agreed to stop attacking the foreign company's
property if the Espenians agreed to limit offshore jade mining to certain areas and amounts.

Koben declared, "Only thin-blooded cowards would negotiate
with thieves, begging them to steal only *some* of what belongs to us
instead of all of it!"

Ayt Mada did not rein in Koben for his outspokenness. Hilo was
reminded of shows and concerts where a lesser performer would
come on stage first to get the crowd excited before the main event.
Ayt allowed her vocal subordinate to rouse people up, so she could
then step in and appear all the more the poised commander.

She did so now, quieting Koben with a single look before saying, "We would not be in this situation were it not for the long-term
coddling of Espenian interests by certain clans in this room." She
fixed Hilo with a steady look of scorn that was deeply familiar to
him by now. "Perhaps Kaul Hilo could exert some influence over

the disgraceful private military company that guards the offending ships, since he's personal friends with the founder."

Hilo said, "Jim Sunto is no friend of mine. If you're all looking for someone to blame, remember we wouldn't have the Espenians breathing down our necks if certain *other* clan leaders hadn't made our country a haven for foreign criminals."

"Kaul-jen, Ayt-jen, please," interjected Chairman Canto Pan, with admirable bravery, or simply exasperation at how no meeting of the KJA passed without some reminder that after all these years, Kaul and Ayt still wanted each other dead. "No matter the circumstances that led us here, let's focus on the Royal Council's proposal. What strict limits on offshore mining might we accept?"

It was remarkable, Hilo thought, how you could get used to anything. He would never have believed he could learn to stomach regularly being in the same room with the person responsible for the death of his brother, his brother-in-law, and so many of his jade warriors— and be *bored*, even by their mutual persistent hatred. While they sat here, No Peak was hunting down and killing the leaders of the barukan street gang that did dirty work for the Mountain and had carried out the murders of the five Green Bones in Lukang.

What is it going to take to fucking win this thing? Hilo seethed quietly as the meeting continued. Could slow, simmering, scattered clan warfare continue forever, past his own life? The Pillar of the Mountain was in her *fifties*—with no husband and no children. How long could she hold on to power in a clan full of ambitious, younger Green Bones? *Why*, for the love of all the gods, couldn't the bitch tire and *give up*?

An office assistant that Hilo did not know came up behind him and said in a low, apologetic voice, "Kaul-jen, this envelope arrived for you at the front desk. The man who delivered it insisted that it was urgent and be delivered to you at once." Hilo examined the sealed envelope, but there were no identifying marks on the thick stationery. He tore it open.

Inside was a single piece of paper, with no salutation or signature, only one line of typed text. *Your life is in danger. Leave immediately.*

Hilo turned the paper over and looked inside the envelope, but there was nothing else besides the dire warning of the note. Wordlessly, Hilo handed the paper to Woon beside him. Woon was naturally adept at maintaining a calm, careful demeanor, but his eyes widened, and Hilo saw him glance surreptitiously from side to side, his jade aura sharpening in suspicion and alarm. He looked for the assistant who had delivered the envelope, but the young man had already left the room.

Hilo sent his eyes and Perception sweeping around the large meeting room. He sensed only the people who were supposed to be there: executives of the Kekon Jade Alliance, the Green Bone clan leaders and their respective Weather Men, four Deitist penitents standing in the corners, two secretaries refilling tea and carrying notes between the meeting participants. Hilo strained his Perception beyond the closed doors. The hallways directly outside of the room were empty. A bored security guard manned the desk in the elevator lobby. Beyond that, individual energies became hard to distinguish: The people moving around on the two lower levels of the building were a busy blur.

He brought his Perception back into the room and scanned the jade auras around him. He Perceived no immediate threat; no murderous intent emanated from any of the other Green Bones, not even Ayt Madashi. The Pillar of the Mountain was staring across the table at Hilo. She could tell that something had happened to put him on high alert. Years of mutual enmity had made both Pillars sensitive to any changes in the other's jade aura, and even without accounting for Perception, she could not fail to notice that his focus had left the discussion and that for several seconds, he had been sitting very still, gazing at nothing.

Hilo turned his head slightly toward Woon. "Take the note and leave the room. Quickly."

Woon paled. "I can't leave the Pillar," he insisted, with such urgent, fearful vehemence that Hilo remembered Woon had been Lan's best friend and Pillarman, and had already seen one Pillar killed under his watch. "I won't do it, Kaul-jen."

"Do as I say," Hilo ordered him. "Wait in the hallway. I'll be right behind you. Stop anyone who comes out ahead of me. I want you to go first so I know who in this room reacts to you leaving. Or if we're being played for fools." When Woon still did not move, Hilo snarled quietly, "*Now*, Woon-jen. Think of your daughter."

Woon swallowed, then snatched the mysterious paper and stood up, striding for the exit of the room. Hilo placed his hands on the circular table and stood up more slowly, causing the conversation to falter and come to a standstill. "I'm afraid there's been a family emergency," he said. Curious, concerned murmurs rose around the room. "Woon-jen and I have to leave. Continue the meeting without us."

Hilo walked purposefully but not too quickly toward the door that Woon had pushed through. The jadeless politicians and policymakers were merely confused, but a frisson of rising suspicion was traveling through the auras of the Green Bone leaders in the room. They could Perceive that Hilo was not being entirely truthful, that for some other unexplained reason his jade aura was humming at a high and violent pitch. Ayt Mada turned her head, eyes narrowed, to watch every step of Hilo's progress across the room. Hilo's Perception was so tightly strung that his hearing and vision blurred. The room seemed to be a dim and silent space filled with individual energies, each of which he held in his attention, expecting at least one of them to react with sudden malicious intent. *Show yourself.*

One of them did. In a room crowded full of Green Bone auras, it went unnoticed until the last second. Hilo spun around as he reached the doors; Ayt Mada had begun to rise from her seat. "You're lying. What are you really—" and from behind Ayt, the secretary who had begun to refill the Pillar's water glass dropped the jug, spilling water all over the table and Koben Yiro's papers, and in the same motion thrust a knife concealed under her sleeve into the side of Ayt Madashi's neck.

Ayt sensed the attack, but too late. Under ordinary circumstances, no one could imagine an assassin getting close enough to cut the throat of a Green Bone like Ayt Mada. It was only because the Mountain Pillar's attention was entirely focused on Kaul Hilo's suspicious behavior that the young woman succeeded. In the moment of collective silent shock that hit the room, everyone heard the secretary's words, a cry of high-pitched fear and triumph. "Look at me, Ayt Madashi, you butcher, you bitch. *Do you know who I am?* Ven Emashan, daughter of Ven Sando, sister of Ven Haku, the girl whose family—"

Ayt Mada's hand latched around the girl's throat in a grip of crushing Strength. With an almost inhuman cry, she spun and smashed the back of the young woman's head into the edge of the heavy table with so much force that the thick, polished black wood cracked along with the girl's skull. Blazing with explosive jade energy, Ayt hurled the limp body into the nearest window. It hit the glass with a sickening, meaty thud, creating a spiderweb's pattern of cracks before dropping like a heavy sack to the carpet.

From the corners of the room, the watching penitents raised their faces upward and chanted in unison, "Heaven has seen! Heaven has seen! Heaven has seen!" in a chilling chorus that made everyone in the room quail, tugging on earlobes with the horrible knowledge that Ven Ema had eternally damned her soul and the souls of her entire family for spilling blood in sight of the gods.

Ayt fell to her knees, her hands clamped around the wound in her neck, red streams pouring between her fingers around the protruding blade. Koben Yiro lurched to his feet in panic. "Ayt-jen!" He ran toward her, then stopped and spun around to face the stunned, staring faces of all the people in the room. "The Pillar's been wounded. Get help!"

The Weather Man of Six Hands Unity took half a dozen steps toward the hall before coming to a hesitant halt. Hilo was standing in front of the closed door. He had not moved; he was as shocked as anyone else by the sight of Ayt Mada on her knees, fatally wounded, her eyes wide with disbelief and pain. Ayt's mouth worked for air. Blood continued to seep out from under her tightly clamped hand, spreading a rich stain down her cream-colored cardigan. Hilo stared at her, then slowly raised his eyes to the others in the room, sweeping a coolly assessing gaze over the meeting's attendees. Without a word, he took two deliberate steps to block the exit.

A chilling realization fell across everyone assembled. If they did nothing, Ayt Mada would die. Hilo did not have to lift a finger to make it happen; he simply had to prevent anyone from leaving. Several of the people in the room did not wear jade. Among the other Green Bones present, none were as heavily jaded as Kaul Hilo or would individually be a match for him in martial ability. A few of them together could overcome him, but they were unlikely to be able to do so quickly. Woon was out in the hallway and could be at Hilo's side in an instant.

The Pillar of the Stone Cup clan sat back down in his chair and folded his arms, making it clear that he would not move against No Peak. The leaders of the Jo Sun clan and the Black Tail clan followed suit. The Mountain's tributary clan leaders looked to each uncertainly. They had all sworn oaths of allegiance to Ayt Mada, but with the woman bleeding out on the ground and Kaul Hilo standing in their way, was it worth risking their own lives to save her?

Koben Yiro took a threatening step toward Hilo, bellowing, "Someone do something, before it's too late!"

Hilo settled his predatory gaze on the man. "It's already too late, Koben-jen," he said in a dangerous whisper. "Out with the old, in with the new."

Koben Yiro swallowed. If Ayt Mada died, he would be personally saddled with the shame of having failed his Pillar. On the other hand, his nephew was the heir. His family would rise to lead the Mountain.

Three heartbeats of morbid stalemate blanketed the room. Ayt tried to speak, but although she opened her mouth, no words emerged. Hilo saw the realization dawning on her bloodless face. She was dying, surrounded by people, and none of them would help her, not even those allies who had pledged her their loyalty. Kaul Hiloshudon would stand in front of the door, triumphant, doing nothing, watching her die, and everyone else in the room would stand by quietly and do the same. She had been the strongest of them all, the most cunning, the most feared, but she was without true friends in this room. Hilo saw this horrible understanding in her eyes, and as eager as he was for Ayt to die, in that instant, he felt pity for her, too.

Rage and defiance lit Ayt Mada's jade aura, roiling it like magma. With a burst of superhuman effort, she pushed herself to her feet and ran—not for the door where Hilo stood in her way, but toward the window. She leapt Light over the body of Ven Ema and threw herself at the damaged glass, hitting it with her shoulder, shattering it with all her Strength.

With a snarl of disbelief, Hilo ran forward to see Ayt tumble three stories to the sidewalk below. Injured as she was, she managed to cling to her grip on Lightness and Steel. She crashed off the top of a parked van, denting the metal roof, rolled off, and landed on the concrete amid a shower of glass shards, eliciting shocked shouts and screams from people nearby. Ayt rose, staggered and fell, rose again, and began to run, stumbling, down the street.

"Fuck the gods," Hilo breathed in astonishment. He gathered himself to leap Lightly down after her—thinking only of giving chase and making sure she still died. Then his eyes landed on the van below. It was parked in a loading zone but there was no one inside. Ayt's Steeled body had warped the roof and caused one of the doors to buckle so it was cracked partway open.

Hilo remembered the note he'd received, the warning that he'd been trying to understand before the attack on Ayt had made him forget the immediacy of some other danger. He took several steps backward and then the van below the window detonated in an explosion that demolished the ground floor of the building and engulfed the side of the structure in an expanding fireball that traveled faster than the screams of the people it swallowed. Hilo had time only to register disbelief, to think of his wife and children, before the force of the blast reached him and the third-floor boardroom collapsed, bringing hundreds of kilograms of concrete rubble down on him.

CHAPTER

26

Nekolva

The address that Ema had given to Bero belonged to the end unit of an old rowhouse in the north part of the Docks not yet gentrified by waterfront condominium buildings, shops, and tourist attractions. Bero had grown up not far from here. When he was a child, the rows of industrial brown living quarters had been populated by dockhands and cannery workers. These days it seemed to be filled with Uwiwan and Oortokon immigrants who worked the city's low-wage factory and service sector jobs. Bero double-checked the slip of paper and approached the door cautiously, glancing up and down the street. The neighboring unit appeared to be unoccupied; the windows were still taped up against last year's typhoon season, and the yellow eviction notice on the door was so faded it was not legible. A tarp-covered eight-meter-long motorboat was moored in the water right across from the rowhouse.

Bero tried the door. It was locked. He jiggled the knob, trying to judge how hard it would be to break in, when the door jerked open. The shape of Vastik eya Molovni, with his thick arms and curly burnt-orange hair, stood in the dim entryway like a demon. Bero jumped back from the foreigner's terrifying glare.

"What the fuck are *you* doing here?" Molovni exclaimed.

"She told me to come here," Bero blurted. He hadn't expected to find Molovni here. It was only half past two in the afternoon. Wasn't the Ygutanian supposed to be carrying out his great plan? Weren't the Espenians supposed to be stopping him? "She told me," he repeated. "Ema. She said you'd get us out of town. She gave me this address."

Molovni's disbelieving stare and the twitch of his heavy jaw made Bero suspect that the man was debating whether to close the door on him or kill him. Deciding, apparently, that neither option—Bero free or Bero as a dead body—was an acceptable liability, he swore under his breath in Ygut, seized Bero by the front of his shirt, and pulled him into the narrow apartment, shutting the door behind them.

"Have you told anyone else?" Molovni demanded, pushing the slighter man against the wall with enough force that Bero lost any doubt the nekolva agent, though he wore no jade, possessed enough Strength to put Bero through the side of the building if he wished. "Anyone at all? Any of those other clanless fools?" The man spoke in a fast growl, his thick accent distorting the words so that Bero didn't immediately understand what he was saying. Molovni drew an Ankev pistol. *"Have you?"*

"No!" Bero sputtered. "I haven't told anyone."

Molovni's brutal face leaned in, close and menacing. Bero was still not sure if Molovni possessed any sense of Perception, but apparently satisfied that Bero was telling the truth, the Ygutanian released him and stowed the Ankev in his waistband. "You can't come," Molovni said, scowling at Bero as if he were a stray dog in the garbage. "No matter what the girl told you. There's no room for anyone else."

"That's bullshit," Bero exclaimed. "You've got a boat, don't you? You can't fit one extra person?"

"You are an idiot," said Molovni. "I'm not talking about the boat. Where do you think we're to go? There's a ship waiting on the other side of Gosha Island to take us to Ygutan under asylum. The men on that ship, they will only take the people I've told them to expect. You? They will shoot you." Somewhere in the distance, an ambulance siren started up. Another one followed. The Ygutanian locked and bolted the door behind Bero. "Find your own way out of the city, if you're trying to run from the clans. Or hide in the apartment next door, I don't care. But now that you're here, you can't leave. Not until I'm far away from this fucking island." He turned away from Bero and began to ascend the narrow stairs.

Bero stood stupefied for a minute. Then he followed after Molovni. The curtains on the second-floor windows were all drawn shut; only a few slivers of light filtered in between the cracks. The room was as spartan as a cell. Bero made out the shapes of a single bed, a dresser, a desk and chair. There was nothing on the walls, no visible personal belongings besides a few papers on the desk, and a radio.

Molovni was adjusting the antenna and fiddling with the dial of the radio. Classical music skipped to jiggy remix, then to static, then to the KNB news radio station.

Bero said, "Where's Ema?"

The Ygutanian didn't look up. "She's not coming."

"Not coming?" Bero exclaimed. "Where is she? Isn't she supposed to be meeting up with you?" If the Espenians had been watching Ema, where had she led them, if not to the nekolva agent and his plan?

Molovni held up a finger to silence Bero and turned up the volume on the radio. Kekon National Broadcasting news anchor Toh Kita was delivering a special report: A massive explosion had occurred in the Financial District of Janloon, collapsing the headquarters of the Kekon Jade Alliance during a board meeting. Dozens of government and clan representatives were suspected to be among the dead and injured. Police, emergency workers, and Green Bones of both the major clans were on-site. Toh Kita somberly promised listeners that he would share information as it became available.

"It's done." Molovni checked his watch. "If Guriho and Otonyo escape, they'll be here soon."

"You weren't even there?" Bero felt as if his understanding of the situation was coming apart. "The others did everything and you hid in here, doing nothing? What kind of Ygutanian spy are you?"

The foreigner wheeled on Bero with a glower of contempt. "I did *nothing*? I spent eight years in this fucking jade-infested city to make this happen. Who arranged *everything* for the clanless? Money, guns, information, explosives, political asylum—you think any of these are easy to get?" Molovni snorted. He began to pack items from his desk into a black satchel. "The revolution has to come from within, but it would've gotten *nowhere* if it weren't for me. If it weren't for nekolva."

Bero thought of his Espenian handlers and grumbled, "But why didn't they stop it?"

He realized his slip in an instant, but it was too late. Molovni turned back toward him slowly, placing the satchel down on the desk. His small eyes narrowed with suspicion. "Who are you talking about?"

Bero fumbled for a convincing lie, but Molovni was stalking toward him, his craggy face clouding with suspicion. If he did have a sense of Perception, then he could sense Bero's pulse racing. "What have you done, you useless creature?" he growled. "*Who are you working for?*"

Bero did not get a chance to answer. The windows shattered inward at the same time the door was smashed from its hinges. The small confines of the room erupted in a storm of splintering wood, flying glass, and violent movement. Bero's shock lasted for a whole second. Then he dove into a corner of the room as half a dozen masked men in military tactical gear burst into Molovni's apartment.

Molovni whirled with his Ankev drawn, firing at the nearest black-clad intruder. The bullet slammed into the man's body armor, throwing him against the wall. Molovni got off one more round before another masked man shot him in the back with twin needle-tipped electrical wires that stabbed through his clothes and into his skin. Molovni went as rigid as a wooden plank and toppled to the floor, jerking, making choked, guttural noises as electricity poured into his body. His eyes were furious and panicked, his mouth frozen open in rictus. Three men rushed in on the downed Ygutanian like wolves.

Even with his muscles spasming uncontrollably, Molovni managed to grasp for his jade abilities. He unleashed a powerful blast of Deflection that ripped through the apartment in a concentric wave. The intruders staggered back and blown shards of wood and glass debris pelted Bero's arms as he threw them over his head. The wires were yanked free of Molovni's back. The Ygutanian rolled to his feet in an instant and seized his fallen Ankev. Bero glimpsed the manic fear on the man's face as he turned the gun toward his own head.

A booted foot connected with Molovni's arm, sending the weapon flying out of his hand and skittering under the sofa.

Bero had known that Molovni was nekolva, and he'd heard of Espenian special operatives who wore jade, but he had never seen men who were not Green Bones move so quickly or brutally before. In a desperate final bid to escape through the shattered second-story window, Molovni flew Light across the length of his apartment. He nearly made it, but was seized out of the air and borne to the ground by the combined Strength of three soldiers. Molovni was pinned like a thrashing bull. He screamed profanities in Ygut, spittle flecking the corners of his mouth as his wrists were yanked behind his back and secured with tight plastic bindings. His ankles were zip-tied together as well, and a black canvas bag was pulled over his head. One of the masked men drew a syringe from a pocket on his tactical vest and jabbed it into Molovni's thigh, depressing the plunger. A few seconds later, the man's struggles grew uncoordinated and feeble, then ceased entirely. Two burly soldiers lifted the unconscious Ygutanian between them like a heavy carpet and carried him from the apartment and out of sight.

Bero hadn't moved from his spot in the corner of the room. The masked men in black ignored him as they began to tear apart Molovni's apartment. They pulled open drawers and dumped all the contents into yellow evidence sacks. They knocked on the walls and floor for hidden compartments, looked under and behind the furniture, and even took the garbage can. They paid special attention to the man's desk; Bero saw them place his satchel of papers, an answering machine, and a small stack of unopened mail in a special box. The bottles in the bathroom medicine cabinet were examined, photographed, and likewise gathered and carried out. The few words that the soldiers exchanged with each other were in Espenian.

Galo and Berglund walked into the room, dressed in dark civilian clothes, but armed and officious. Berglund looked around at the dismantled apartment with satisfaction and began to speak to one of the soldiers. The man who had been shot in the chest, who would be dead had he not been wearing an armored vest, managed to get to his feet with the combined support of two comrades and was helped from the scene. Bero didn't realize that the radio on the table was still playing until one of the Espenian operatives turned it off, unplugged it, and carried it away along with the rest of Vastik eya Molovni's belongings.

Galo walked over to Bero in the corner and shook his head with unsurprised disappointment. "You should've told us everything, Catfish. You didn't need to be in here." He offered Bero a hand up.

Bero stared at the hand without taking it. "You... *followed me* here?" he shouted.

Galo said, "Did you think we wouldn't have you under surveillance? It's a damned good thing we did. As undependable of an asset as you are, thanks to you, we have one of the nekolva in our custody, along with evidence that he was involved in inciting revolution on behalf of the Ygutanian government." Galo surveyed the nearly empty wrecked room with the pleased expression of a leopard licking clean bones. "We might finally crack open the secrets of the Ygutanian military program."

Bero got to his feet. "What about Ema? You were going to follow *her*. Where is she?"

Galo shook his head. "Sad to say, she was inside the KJA building when it collapsed."

"You fucking spennies, you didn't try to stop the great strike of the clanless at all. You just wanted Molovni. You knew she was going to be killed." Bero's hands were clenched and he was shouting again.

The Keko-Espenian man eyed Bero severely. "Right now, the ROE Navy is circling the waters around Gosha Island. With any luck, we'll find and capture the Ygutanian vessel waiting to help Molovni escape. The loss of life from the terrorist attack on the KJA building this afternoon was tragic. But if we'd intervened to prevent the bombing, it would've instantly tipped off Molovni and his superiors. The stakes were too high. The assets and information we've seized from our enemies today might save thousands or even millions of lives."

"Spenny lives," Bero spat.

"We tried to get word to our Kekonese allies before the bombing, but I'm afraid it wasn't successful." Galo squinted at Bero incredulously. "You joined the Clanless Future Movement to take down the clans. You worked for us to earn money on the side. You've accomplished both and come out alive. What are you upset about? That the girl sacrificed herself for a cause when you were finally getting pussy? Or finding out that you're not as clever as you think you are? You were manipulated, sure. But what did you expect?"

Ema had given him this address, not so he could escape with her, but to betray Molovni. *Just because I hate the clans doesn't mean I have any love for the Ygutanians.* Those had been her words. She'd wanted to bring down the clans, but would not hand the victory to the foreign agent and his masters. Ema must've suspected Bero was a spy, or she'd simply calculated that he would sell the information.

And now she was dead, dead for nothing, just like those dumb fucks Cheeky and Mudt and Soradiyo and so many others, and Bero was still alive. At one time, he would've been smug. He would've seen it as a sign that luck was on his side even when it toyed with him. Now he felt nothing.

"We're done here." Galo turned from Bero and began to walk away. "Let's go, Catfish."

Bero remained where he was. When Galo realized Bero was not following, he turned back around. "You don't want to stay here," the handler said. "We can get you out of Kekon, for your safety."

Bero said, "I don't want anything else from you spennies."

Galo's expression softened a fraction, approaching sympathy. "Look, we're not friends. You're an asset and I'm your handler. But this one time, I'm giving you advice that's for your own good." He gestured out the window. "The leaders of the major clans are dead. Janloon is going to be a fucking mess. There's an opportunity for the ROE to play a role in reshaping the political landscape, but it's also likely the whole country will descend into chaos. The Green Bones will come after anyone associated with the Clanless Future Movement. The Ygutanians or the clanless could find out you led us to Molovni. What reason do you have to stay here?"

Bero hated that he had no answer. Maybe he had nothing in Janloon, but Janloon had *him*. Even rats had a sewer to call home, and Janloon was *his* sewer.

"You've done valuable work for the ROE and earned the chance to start life again somewhere else," Galo said. "Maybe even be a different person."

The apartment had been stripped bare except for the furniture. Berglund and one of the remaining soldiers were standing by the door waiting for Galo. Outside, sirens continued to rise and fall in the distance. Bero thought he smelled smoke. He saw the masked Espenian soldier slide his hand down to the military sidearm he carried and glance at Berglund, questioning. Galo gave a tiny shake of his head and met his partner's impassive expression. A brief argument seemed to transpire silently between the Espenian agents.

Galo said to Bero, in an undertone, "I'm helping you out here, Catfish."

With a clarity he hadn't possessed until now, Bero wondered if the Espenians would subdue and abduct him, as they had with Molovni, or simply shoot him. He was a loose end, as expendable to them as everyone in the KJA building. With dull, resigned hatred, he said, "Where am I supposed to go?"

Galo turned toward the door. "Does it matter?"

"I guess not," Bero said numbly. He followed the handler out of the building, and the masked soldier fell in behind them.

CHAPTER

27

Heaven Has Seen

Shae had finished nursing her baby daughter and was settling her back to sleep when her mother let out a wail from the living room where she was watching television. Shae called out, "Ma, what's wrong?" When she received no answer, she put Tia down in the bassinet and hurried out to find Kaul Wan Ria with her hands clapped over her mouth, staring at the TV screen. KNB news was showing a scene that Shae did not at first understand. Only when she read the headline—EXPLOSION IN DOWNTOWN JANLOON—did she realize that she was looking at the smoking remains of the Kekon Jade Alliance headquarters.

It took her another two seconds to remember that there had been a KJA meeting this afternoon, that the Pillar and the acting Weather Man were in attendance. Her mother was unaware of this. "Horrible, horrible," Ria said, shaking her head and sitting down on the edge of the sofa in front of the television. "What kind of people would do such a thing? I hope that no one we know was inside at the time."

Shae's legs swayed. She put a hand out and braced herself against the back of the nearest chair. Perhaps she was having a feverish, post-partum nightmare. Perhaps she was mistaken about the date of the KJA meeting. Was it really Thirdday today, not Secondday?

The phone in the kitchen rang. She staggered toward it and picked it up. It was Juen Nu. "I can't reach the Pillar." The Horn's words, and the awful pause that followed them, shattered her denial. "Do you know if he was inside that building?"

Shae heard her own shallow breathing, and her voice, alarmingly weak. "I think so."

Silence from the other end of the line. Then the Horn said, "Stay where you are, Shae-jen. I'll send more Green Bones to the house, and all the rest I can spare to help the emergency workers. I'll call again as soon as I learn anything more." Another terrible, leaden pause. "Do you have anything you want to say to the clan, if you must?"

"Not yet," Shae said. "Not until we know who did this." She had no doubt that whoever was responsible for the explosion had meant to kill all the Green Bone clan leaders at once, but she wasn't ready to think that her brother and her husband were both dead, and that she was now the Pillar of the clan and a widowed single mother. "Some-one needs to tell Wen," she said. "And the children. Someone has to tell…" She trailed off, unable to finish the sentence because it had become hard to breathe. She pressed a hand to her chest. Her heart was thudding hard and irregularly.

"I'll send people to find Wen right away," Juen said. "And I'll have Fingers pick up Niko and Jaya at the Academy, and Ru from his school, and bring them all back to the house."

After Juen hung up, Shae said to her mother, "Ma," but couldn't manage to say anything else. Tia woke and began to fuss. Shae went into the bedroom. She picked up the baby and rocked her, pacing around the room, the sight of her two-week-old daughter's sweet, oblivious face blurring through a film of tears. "Why were you born into this family?" she whispered. "You're so perfect, and there's too much suffering here."

Her mother came into the room. "Shae-se, let me take her," Ria said, holding out her arms. "You should lie down and rest, the doctor said you shouldn't strain yourself." Shae's delivery had been uncomplicated, but afterward she'd suffered from shortness of breath and been diagnosed with mild peripartum cardiomyopathy. She was wearing a reduced amount of jade, and was supposed to refrain from exerting herself until she recovered, hopefully in three to six weeks.

She handed the baby to her mother. Woon was convinced that Tia resembled Shae, but Shae did not see it. She saw only Woon's complexion, and his ears. "I need to go out for a while, Ma," Shae said. She began dressing, putting on her old maternity pants and a sweater. "Can you look after Tia? There's a bottle of milk in the fridge, and baby formula in the cupboard, if I'm not back in a couple of hours."

Her mother pressed her lips together. She held her granddaughter close. "This is because of what happened downtown, that explosion," she said. "You have to go to work for the clan, even now." When Shae nodded without elaborating, her mother's face trembled. "Is it very bad for us?"

"I don't know yet." Shae tried to speak calmly, to not give anything away. "Just...wait here, and don't believe anything you hear, not until I find out for sure."

A deadened understanding came into her mother's eyes, an expression of powerlessness that would've broken Shae's heart if she was not already too full of dread. Kaul Wan Ria had been through this before. She had waited alone to hear of the death of her husband. Then her eldest son. And now her second son as well.

Shae knew she ought to do as Juen said, she ought to stay in the house where it was safe and wait for news, as her mother was resigned to do. She couldn't do that. She needed to go there, to see for herself, to know for certain. If she was truly the Pillar now, she had to be seen among the clan. She could not be a woman lying in her bedroom with an infant.

Shae ordered one of the estate's guards to drive her into the Financial District. Traffic was extremely slow all the way down the General's Ride. Several blocks away from the scene of disaster, they could go no farther. The roads were cordoned off and blocked by police

cars and fire trucks. Crowds of people were on the sidewalks, pointing and muttering, holding scarves and the hems of their shirts over
their noses to cut the pervasive stench of burning and the haze of ash
in the air. Green Bones of both the major clans and some minor ones
were everywhere, talking to each other, trying to calm concerned
Lantern Men and hurry people away from the disaster zone, their
rivalries forgotten for the time being.

Shae told the driver to stop the car and let her out. "Kaul-jen," the
driver protested, "are you sure that's a good idea?" He had enough
sense to know that he ought not to let her go alone into this disorderly scene, but Shae opened the door and stepped out before he
could think of how to stop her.

She pushed against the tide of people, weaving her way down the
street toward the remains of the Kekon Jade Alliance building. Chaos
flowed around her: movement, noise, smoke, jade energies—all of it
an assault against her senses. Her eyes and throat were stinging. She
moved too quickly for anyone to stop and recognize her. No one was
paying attention anyway. It took Shae twenty minutes to plow her
way to the center of the activity. She was sweating and gasping by
then, her hair and clothes covered in a fine layer of ash. Half of the
building was still standing, obscenely intact, hallways and rooms laid
open to the sky like an architect's model cut open to show the layout
of the interior. The southern half of the structure was a collapsed
pile of concrete and twisted metal around a crater of destruction. A
line of trees and two buildings on the other side of the street were
blackened, scorched from the blast. Suited firefighters were swarming
the site, and ambulances were pulling up, one after the other. Shae
saw a line of injured people—with bleeding head wounds, burns,
broken or sprained limbs—sitting or lying on the sidewalk, being
triaged and attended to by medics. She turned in a circle, dazed and
overwhelmed.

She followed her sense of Perception toward a familiar cluster of
jade auras and found Lott Jin, the clan's First Fist of Janloon, orga-
nizing a group of roughly fifty of No Peak's Green Bones. They were
all wearing work gloves, scarves wrapped around their faces, and red

plastic whistles around their necks. "Vin and Tato are leading the two search teams starting at opposite ends of the collapsed area and working toward each other," Lott shouted. "If you sense a survivor, don't spend your own Strength; we need you to focus all your efforts on Perception and keep moving. Send up long whistles at ten second intervals and stay at the site until firefighters or someone from one of the digging teams reaches you. Batto, Yan, and Toyi—you have the best Lightness here. You're going to carry water, medical supplies, and messages. Does everyone understand?" When the grimly assembled Fists and Fingers nodded, Lott said, "The Mountain is here too. Work with them, but remember: We search every square meter ourselves. If you Perceive Kaul-jen, or Woon-jen, send up three short whistle blasts in a row. For them and no one else."

Lott's men touched their clasped hands to their foreheads in salute and the group broke up into purposeful activity. "May the gods shine favor on No Peak," several of them murmured in prayer. Shae went up to Lott, causing him to spin in surprise.

"Kaul-jen," he exclaimed in angry surprise, forgetting his respect in the heat of the moment. "What are you doing here?"

"I wasn't learning a godsdamned thing sitting in the house watching the news." Shae wiped a hand across her brow, streaking it with dust. "What—" She put a hand to her chest and caught a tight, difficult breath. "What do you know about what happened? Who was responsible? Is there any..." She looked toward the destroyed building and the rescue crews swarming around it. "...Any sign of survivors, yet?"

Lott shook his head. "It's a confused mess right now," he said. "Juen-jen is talking to the police. We know the blast came from a truck full of high order explosives parked in a permit-only zone on the south side of the building, directly underneath where the KJA meeting was taking place. The bombers had inside knowledge. They knew the layout of the building, its security measures, and when the meeting was taking place. There are witnesses who say they saw two men in the truck this morning. And some people swear they saw Ayt Madashi fall from a window right before the explosion. The

Mountain's people are searching the area, but they don't have any more answers than we do."

Shae coughed and said, "What can I do to help?"

Lott looked at her in concern. "Kaul-jen," he said. "You don't look well."

"I'm fine," Shae said. Lott did not appear convinced. Shae imagined how she must appear to him—a forty-one-year-old woman, lacking most of her jade, weak from childbirth—and she suffered a surge of frustration and resentment, more toward herself than Lott. She felt foolish and helpless, not at all like a Green Bone or a Kaul or a Weather Man. What had she imagined she could accomplish here? "I need to be here. I need to know." She meant to sound declarative, but the words came out wretched. "My brother and my husband are in that pile of rubble."

Lott said, with conviction, "I promise on my jade that we'll find them." The First Fist put a hand on her elbow and walked with her to one of the clan's cars, parked alongside the line of emergency vehicles. "The clan needs you to preserve your strength. Only the gods know what's in store for us after this." He opened the passenger-side door for her and handed her a bottle of water from a flat of them sitting on the ground next to a pile of blankets. "It's not my place to ask you to leave, but at least sit down and rest."

Lott left her sitting in the car with the door open. Shae drained the bottle of water, then leaned her head back and put the heels of her dusty hands over her eyes. She felt dizzy and the tightness in her chest had progressed to outright pain. She was in no state to make decisions on behalf of No Peak, but she might soon have to. She watched the rescue efforts with sick fear in the pit of her stomach. Startled Fists and Fingers saluted when they passed her, but she was largely ignored. Injured people were seen to, others were driven away in ambulances. Whenever a whistle went up from the searchers, her heart leapt, but each time, it was a single long whistle, not the three short blasts she kept waiting for. More frequent than the survivors came the bodies, carried out of the rubble and placed in black body bags on the ground.

Shae got out of the car and walked numbly down the street. She couldn't bear to feel so useless, even though Lott was correct and she was in no shape to be exerting herself physically in the heavy wreckage and dust-choked air. No one noticed her leaving the scene. Maybe she should've stayed at home after all. Wen would've heard the news by now. Niko, Ru, and Jaya had been pulled out of school and she ought to be there to meet them when they got home. Her breasts were beginning to feel uncomfortably hard and swollen, and she realized she'd forgotten to tell her mother where the diapers were stored.

Shae's feet carried her through the eerily abandoned streets of the Financial District, and out of unthinking habit rather than any conscious decision, she found herself three blocks away, standing outside the Temple of Divine Return. The courtyard with its prayer trees was empty and silent. Even the wind seemed to have fallen still. Shae walked through the doors. The platform in front of the mural of Banishment and Return was empty. It seemed that in the immediate aftermath of such an unprecedented attack in the heart of Janloon, every nearby building had been evacuated, even the temple. The sight was disquieting. Over the years, she'd come to this place hundreds of times, sometimes early in the morning before work, sometimes late at night, but no matter the time of day, there had always been penitents sitting in dutiful meditation, eyes closed, hands resting on sacred orbs of jade, their auras a crooning hum of peaceful but vigilant energy filling the sanctum. Now that energy was absent, and she was alone.

That was not true. Shae's sense of Perception was foggy, not what it would normally be, but as she walked slowly down the aisle between the prayer cushions, she felt a tug on her senses, the flicker of an undeniably familiar aura. She turned around, slowly, disbelieving. Her eyes slid into the shadows at the back of the chamber and came to rest on a figure slumped against the back wall, unmoving.

Shae walked toward the hunched shape. The rough sound of her own breath and the tread of her shoes against the floor seemed intrusive, deafening. That dense red jade aura—she would recognize it anywhere. It was muted, thinning, the heat of a black coal evaporating in the cold. Ayt Mada lay with both hands pressed over the wound in her neck, her arms and shoulders caked with drying blood, her chest barely rising.

At Shae's approach, Ayt's eyes cracked open and gradually focused. A long surreal moment of mutual astonishment stretched between the two women. Then a slow, ironic smile lifted the corners of Ayt Mada's mouth and crawled across her glazed but glittering eyes. "Truly, the gods do have a sense of humor." Ayt's voice was barely audible. "Kaul Shae-jen. What a coincidence."

Shae lifted her face to the ceiling of the empty temple, where she and Ayt had met in years past, under the eyes of the gods in Heaven, to stake themselves irrevocably against each other. She brought her gaze back to the woman at her feet. "Perhaps not such a coincidence, Ayt-jen," she whispered.

Ayt rasped, "Your brother is dead. I wasn't even in the building, and the explosion threw me across the street." The matter-of-factness of Ayt's words chilled Shae to the soles of her feet. It was remarkable that the woman had survived her wounds, that she had managed, somehow, to stagger the distance to the temple, where perhaps she'd hoped to find aid and sanctuary. Shae took a few steps closer. Ayt's face was as pale as chalk, and her lips were turning blue. The stiffly curled fingers of her hands were white. Ayt had been Channeling into herself, a difficult feat for any Green Bone. She had clotted the grievous wound in her neck and slowed the bleeding by redirecting and spending her own life energy, drawing it from elsewhere in her body. It was an unsustainable tactic, like a starving man eating his own flesh. She would lose function elsewhere, go numb in her extremities and limbs, black out as her organs shut down.

"Who did it?" Shae was genuinely curious, almost bitterly admiring. Decades of murderous hatred between No Peak and the Mountain, and someone *else* had plunged a knife into Ayt's neck.

"I did," Ayt answered. She smiled again at Shae's uncomprehending silence. "I executed Ven Sando and his sons for treason ten years ago. But I let his wife and daughters live." Ayt's voice was a slurred, dry, acidic whisper. "It wasn't enough for Ven's daughter that I die in the bombing. She wanted me to know it was her. I made the error of underestimating another woman." The Pillar wetted her lips and fixed her eyes on Shae. "I've only done that one other time."

Shae looked down at her family's mortal enemy, the woman who was ultimately responsible for so much of the pain that had defined Shae's adult life. The murder of her brother Lan, the clan war, the loss of much of Shae's jade and her near death in a clean-bladed duel, the car bombing that had killed Maik Kehn, Tau Maro's treason and execution, the death of her short-lived chief of staff Luto. The list of everything that Ayt had inflicted upon No Peak went on and on, each one an ugly scar on Shae's soul.

She glanced at the empty platform at the front of the sanctum. Today, of all days, there were no penitents present to witness what happened in the temple and report the deeds to Heaven. Her hand moved to the small of her back, to the talon knife that she carried sheathed there. She drew it with the bone-deep certainty that the gods had turned their faces away on purpose, like sneaky relatives slipping a child a gift they should not be approving. The weapon settled in her hand, warm and solid with purpose. Her clan, her family, her life might be in ruins—but she had *this*. It was up to her now, to finish what her brothers could not, to finally end the war between the clans. Perhaps Lan was watching. Perhaps Hilo was as well.

Shae crouched warily. Ayt might be fatally wounded and close to death, but a tiger in a trap could use its dying breath to rip out one's throat. Ayt was wearing far more jade than Shae was, and might summon one last surge of vindictive willpower to take an enemy down with her.

Ayt shifted painfully. "I congratulate you, Kaul-jen. By tonight, you might be the only Pillar left standing in Kekon. I don't envy you." The scornful smile was gone from her face. She sounded weary and angry. "A word of advice: Don't ever make the mistake that I did. Don't show mercy."

Shae stilled. Ayt's words, filled with grim portent, seemed to add weight to the knife in her hand. *You might be the only Pillar left.*

The clans had fought each other for years. Yet it was a different enemy who had struck today, intent on destroying all the Green Bone clans at once. The extremists did not care about aisho, about killing hundreds of innocent people. They wanted to upend Kekonese society altogether, to sow chaos and destruction, to prove that even the country's most important institutions were vulnerable and even the strongest Green Bone leaders could be killed by people who had none of their powers.

She had seen the rubble left by the bombing, and as much as she wanted to deny it, she knew that what Ayt had said was likely true: The people in that building were dead. She saw clearly now what would happen. The minor clans would be thrown into crisis by the loss of their Pillars. Entire towns and industries would be cast into disarray. The country would look to the two major clans for direction. Ayt Mada's twenty-two-year-old nephew would become Pillar, and the Mountain clan would fall under the rule of the imprudent Koben family. The Kobens would blame immigrants and foreigners for the terrorist attack. They would whip people into a reactionary frenzy and wield all the Mountain's influence over the Royal Council to push for isolationist policies that would reverse the country's decades of growth, threaten No Peak's international operations, and provoke foreign aggression.

As for No Peak... Shae felt cold apprehension deep in the marrow of her bones. She was a new mother, likely a widow, physically unwell, and without most of her jade. She was in no condition to be Pillar. She did not want to be Pillar. The idea filled her with horror.

Was this how Hilo had felt, she wondered, on the night of Lan's death? She'd never truly spoken to him about it. It would be even worse for her, trying to lead No Peak, and perhaps the country itself, in the aftermath of a national disaster, with the other Green Bone clans in chaos and the people howling for retribution, while outside powers crouched, ready to sweep into the turmoil.

She tightened the grip on her talon knife. Ayt's eyes were lidded; her jade aura pulsed with feeble impatience, even as her breathing grew increasingly labored and shallow.

Shae made a noise under her breath and stowed her weapon. Without believing what she was doing, she moved to Ayt Mada's side and put a supporting arm under her back, sitting the other woman up. She put additional pressure on the seeping neck wound and began Channeling her precious energy, forcing warmth into Ayt's body.

Don't show mercy. "It would be a mercy to cut your throat, Ayt-jen," she hissed, "and spare you from being the Pillar at this awful time when you're most needed."

28

Make Your Choice

Anden had been through shocking events in his life, but not in his wildest imagination could he have envisioned his cousin Kaul Shae emerging from the back of the Temple of Divine Return with Ayt Mada's arm over her shoulder, both of them staggering, covered in Ayt's blood.

For several seconds, Anden stared in openmouthed horror and astonishment, unable to make sense of the impossible sight. Recovering himself, he got out of the car and went to help. When he reached them, he hesitated, drawing away from Ayt as if instinctively avoiding a viper. Then he put a hand under the injured woman's other arm and opened the rear door of the car, helping Shae to lay her down in the back.

Shae dropped into the front passenger seat. Anden got back into the driver's side. He turned to Shae with wide, questioning eyes. The Weather Man looked terrible. Ash coated her hair and darkened the film of sweat on her face so that she looked nearly as gray as a corpse herself.

"Shae-jen," Anden said slowly, "why exactly are we saving the life of Ayt Madashi?"

"We need her," Shae answered grimly. "The city needs her. This would be the worst time for the country's largest clan to fall into chaos, or to the Koben family, which might be nearly as bad." She read the stricken question in Anden's eyes, and said quietly, "I haven't gotten any news. Have you?"

Anden shook his head. "I've checked with all the hospitals." Shae had reached him at the clinic in Paw-Paw where he'd been working, dealing with the influx of injured people overwhelming Janloon's medical facilities. In between rushing around caring for patients, he'd been alternately phoning the main Kaul house, Shae's house, the Horn's house, the Weather Man's office—trying to find out if the rest of the family was safe. The phone lines were jammed; it was sheer luck that Shae had gotten through to him on a pay phone outside the temple after only three attempts. He was still in medical scrubs and wearing his jade, having rushed out immediately without telling anyone.

Anden glanced over his shoulder into the rear seat of his Ryuna 5T Wagon, an eminently practical vehicle that Hilo had teased him about, but whose nondescriptness he was now thankful for as it would be the last car anyone would think to scrutinize if they were searching for the Pillar of the Mountain. Ayt Mada was breathing, but not moving. "The bomb site is only a few blocks away and there are ambulances and Mountain clan Green Bones there," Anden said. "Or should we take her straight to Janloon General?"

"Neither," Ayt said, with enough vehemence that Anden flinched at the voice of his family's mortal enemy coming from directly behind his shoulder. "No one in the Mountain can see me like this. Do you understand?" Ayt took a rattling breath and tried to sit up. "I... I need to get back my strength first..."

"You need a doctor, Ayt-jen," Anden said. "You've lost too much blood."

"Enough that I might die of my injuries within an hour of being found. Get me away from everyone." The demand in Ayt's voice was laced with an emotion that Anden did not recognize at first: fear. It took him a moment to understand. There might be members of the Mountain clan, ardent supporters of the Koben family, or those who nursed a long grudge for the rivals Ayt had killed over the years, who would not be unhappy if the Pillar turned out to be simply another unfortunate casualty of today's heinous attacks. Even in a hospital under the care of her own Green Bones, in her weak and vulnerable state, Ayt could not be certain of her safety.

Cursing silently to himself, Anden wiped the grit from his glasses, then started the car and began to drive. Fortunately, the roads were empty—he'd managed to get through the security cordon around the disaster area only because he was a doctor—so it took less than fifteen minutes for him to reach the only place he could think of to go: his own apartment in Old Town. When they arrived, he pulled his car into the underground parking lot and parked next to the elevator, sending Shae ahead to make sure they wouldn't run into anyone in the hallway. Anden had a raincoat in his trunk, which he threw over Ayt's shoulders, pulling the hood over her head to hide her face. The Mountain Pillar was barely conscious; her aura was feeble, and she could not stand on her own. Anden lifted her easily in his arms and carried her into the elevator, then down the hall into his apartment. The Pillar's arms dangled, the multitude of gemstones on her body bright against pale skin, their energy creating a climbing pressure in Anden's head and chest. It was the most unreal thing he could've imagined: the formidable Ayt Madashi, laid so low, helpless in his arms.

Once inside, Anden laid Ayt down on the sofa and stood back, wiping his brow, which was covered with sweat from anxiety rather than exertion. Shae locked and deadbolted the door and drew the window blinds. For a second, the two of them stood in the darkened living room, breathing hard and staring at Ayt and each other in disbelief. Then Anden let out a tense breath. "Shae-jen, can you help me? I need the first aid kit from under the bathroom sink, and also, could you boil a pot of water?"

Shae nodded and went to do as he asked. Anden knelt next to the unconscious Ayt and ran his Perception through her body, making quick note of the worst injuries. Placing his hands over her torso, he began Channeling into her, slowly and steadily, so as not to overload her weakened system. The immediate problem was blood loss; he set to work shutting down the bleeding from the ugly stab wound as well as the invisible internal bleeding from physical trauma, likely sustained from falling out of the building or being thrown by the explosion. By the time Shae returned with the bandages and hot water, he'd gotten the worst of it under control, but that hardly meant Ayt would live. Blood pressure was still alarmingly low; circulation was extremely poor; dehydration and infection were distinct possibilities. He couldn't do any more until he got equipment and supplies from the clinic without rousing suspicion.

He gave his jade abilities a needed rest while he cleaned and stitched the knife wound. He'd already been exerting himself at the clinic and didn't have enough energy to keep Channeling without exhaustion. Shae hovered nearby, then went into the kitchen. Anden could hear her using the phone. After a few minutes, she came back into the living room. "I'm going back to the house for a while," she said. "The kids are there now, and Wen is on her way. And I need to feed Tia."

"Sit down for a few minutes, first, Shae-jen," Anden insisted. "You need to eat and drink something, and I'll check your heart and lungs before you go. You can't afford to cause any harm to yourself."

Shae glanced at Ayt on the sofa. "You have enough to deal with. Save your own energy."

"You think I care about Ayt Mada's life?" Anden demanded, more harshly than he'd intended. "I'll treat her on your orders, but I'm not going to put her life over yours."

Anden went into the kitchen and made two bowls of instant soup laden with as much protein as he could find in his cupboard and fridge—wheat noodles, boiled eggs, seaweed, and shredded dried fish—and made his cousin sit and eat with him. Shae turned on the television. Every news channel was reporting the breaking news that two men implicated in the bombing of the Kekon Jade Alliance building had been killed in a shootout with police. A tip from an unidentified source had unexpectedly led to the Docks, where Guriho and Otonyo—Oortokon-born ex-convicts and leaders of the Clanless Future Movement—were found attempting to escape the city by boat. Guriho had gone down in a furious exchange of gunfire, and Otonyo had shot himself before he could be apprehended.

The bombers were being hailed as heroes by violent supporters who'd incited a wave of smaller attacks in the wake of the bombing. Gunmen waving the black flag of the clanless and chanting, "The future is now! The future is clanless!" had attacked government institutions and prominent clan-owned properties in the city. Green Bones of the Haedo Shield clan were staunchly protecting the Kekon Treasury and Wisdom Hall, but there were reports of weapons fired, tear gas grenades and pipe bombs set off near the Factory, on Poor Man's Road, and in the Financial District. Shae sucked in a sharp breath at the sight of the lower floor of the No Peak tower on Ship Street wreathed in smoke.

The news returned to Toh Kita in the KNB studio, who reported that the current casualty toll from the KJA bombing rested at eighty-seven dead, a hundred and twenty-two wounded, and sixty-four missing, including the Pillars of both the No Peak and Mountain clans. Confirmed dead included the chairman of the KJA, the Pillars of the Jo Sun and Black Tail clans, and the well-known Mountain Green Bone Koben Yiro.

Toh Kita read a statement released by young Ayt Atosho on behalf of the Mountain clan. It expressed shock and grief, praised the work of the rescue workers, and declared that anyone, domestic or foreign, connected to the unconscionable acts of terrorism was a sworn enemy of the Mountain clan and the entire country. Aisho did not apply to those who dared to strike at the very fabric of Kekonese society. The Mountain would come down from the forest to destroy the Clanless Future Movement and anyone who aided it.

There had been no statement yet from the No Peak clan, Toh Kita told the viewers. Anden glanced at Shae worriedly. The Mountain's announcement was surprising not for its content but for its swiftness. Ayt Mada's body had not been found, but the Koben family was hurrying to ensure that the first official clan communication positioned Ayt Ato as the new Pillar—no doubt to dissuade other influential families in the Mountain who might consider challenging for the leadership. Now that the Mountain had spoken, however, it would not be long before No Peak was expected to do the same.

"I should go," she said. Anden suggested she phone the house and have bodyguards come pick her up. He didn't like the thought of his cousin going out alone given the threat of ongoing violence, nor the idea of her exerting herself further, but Shae argued that they couldn't risk any Green Bones in the clan Perceiving Ayt in his apartment. Anden still frowned with concern, but Shae's breathing and heartbeat were both normal enough that he called her a taxi and gave her a travel thermos of tea with a tincture to help her respiratory system.

Once the Weather Man had departed, Anden turned off the television. He could not bear to see the photographs of Kaul Hilo and Ayt Mada on-screen with the words MISSING underneath them, not when the one lying on his sofa, the one whose life he might be able to save, was not the right one. He watched Ayt's shallowly rising chest, her eyes twitching beneath her closed lids. He knew he ought to take a nap and regain his strength, but he didn't think he could sleep. He was too amped up with nerves and worry, and it seemed ludicrous to fall asleep in the same room with his family's worst enemy, no matter how little danger she seemed to pose. Anden sighed, and stretched out his jade abilities once again, sliding his own energy into Ayt's body, encouraging it to speed up production of plasma and red blood cells.

Ayt sensed him. Her eyes slitted partway open and settled on Anden. "Do you remember when we first met, Emery Anden?" the Pillar asked hoarsely. "Gont Asch brought you to see me. You were a frightened teenager, but you conducted yourself like a man. I knew then that you would become an asset to the Kauls." Ayt's bloodless lips lifted humorlessly. "At different times, I considered having you killed. Now I'm glad you never forced me to do so."

"You should save your strength, Ayt-jen," Anden said. "There's no need to talk."

———————

Shae was gone all evening. During that time, Anden hurriedly drove to the clinic where he worked and snuck out two bags of IV fluid along with a tube and stand, wound dressings, and antibiotics. He did so as quickly as possible and without talking to anyone. Even though Ayt was asleep, the thought of leaving the Pillar of the Mountain alone in his apartment was so strange that he didn't want to do it at all, but there was no choice. It didn't matter how much of his own energy he Channeled into Ayt to mitigate the effect of her injuries, none of it would matter if he didn't get fluids into her and stave off infection.

Ayt was still unconscious when he returned. Her skin was not as ashen as it had been, and she appeared to be breathing easier. Anden thought he ought to clean the blood off her, give her a new shirt to wear—but the thought of undressing Ayt made his mind recoil like a poked oyster. He set up the intravenous tube and said, "Ayt-jen, I need to start a drip, and also change your bandages." Ayt did not open her eyes, but her aura gave enough of a stir to suggest she'd heard him and understood. He didn't want to startle her awake and have her react to a needle jab in her arm by tearing his throat out. At the same time, he felt silly for still fearing her. She was a badly wounded middle-aged woman, not a demon.

Anden turned the television back on and watched the news while resting and regaining his strength in between bouts of Channeling. Footage continued of emergency workers and Green Bones digging through the rubble of the collapsed KJA building with headlamps and flashlights. Confirmed casualty figures were updated on the bottom of the television screen when they were received. A reporter managed to get in front of a grimy, sweaty Juen Nu and ask him if he still hoped to find his Pillar alive. The Horn of No Peak was normally a factual man, known for being clear-eyed and unsentimental, but he glared at the reporter and snapped that Green Bones didn't rely on hope so long as action remained to be taken, and everything would go faster if the media got out of the way and let them work.

Anden picked up the phone. He dialed the number for the main house but stopped at the last digit, his finger hovering over the button, the dial tone droning in his ear. He pictured the rest of the family together in the living room, or perhaps in the sparingly used prayer room, waiting for news. Wen, even in the grip of unbearable dread, would still be calmly telling the children that their father wouldn't want them to panic. Ru and Jaya would be scared and asking questions, but Niko would be quiet, holding his fear inside. Anden couldn't think of anything to say to them that would be of any reassurance. Calling would only tie up the phone line when it needed to be kept free. And how could he bear to lie to his family, to fabricate an excuse for why he wasn't at the house with them right now because he was secretly caring for Ayt Mada?

With a heavy heart, he set the receiver back into its cradle.

He would've thought that under the circumstances, he wouldn't be able to relax enough to fall asleep, but the sheer exhaustion from worry and expending jade energy turned out to be too great. He dozed off in the armchair still wearing his jade and was jolted awake by the sudden Perception of two Green Bones approaching his apartment door. One of the jade auras belonged to Shae. The other was unfamiliar to him—a cool, even energy like the stare of a hawk. Anden opened the door before Shae knocked. Standing behind the Weather Man was a tall, elderly man, thin and grizzled, nearly bald, but with piercingly clear eyes and jade carried on weathered leather bands around his left wrist.

"I'm sorry I took so long getting back," Shae said. "This is Nau Suen."

Anden had never met the former Horn of the Mountain in person. Most of Nau's time as the military leader of the enemy clan had occurred while Anden had been living abroad in Espenia, and then while he was ensconced in medical school. However, he knew of Nau's reputation as a devious assassin with a frightening level of Perception, well trusted by Ayt Mada whenever she whispered names. Even though the old man in the hallway had retired from his post years ago and was not physically formidable, Anden swallowed and touched his forehead warily as he held open the door. "Nau-jen," he said.

Nau stepped inside the apartment wordlessly and with barely a glance at Anden. He crouched down beside the sofa where Ayt Mada was now awake and weakly trying to push herself up into a sitting position. The former Horn put a gentle hand on Ayt Mada's forehead, as if she were a child with a fever.

"Hello, old friend," Ayt said with a rueful smile. "Come to bail me out again."

"Kaul Shae was the one who came to me," Nau admitted in a grumble. "Otherwise, I would've thought you were in that pile of rubble. That's what people have been saying, even the Kobens."

Ayt slid a look over her former Horn's shoulder, glancing at Shae with an expression that Anden thought was not gratitude, exactly, but bemused acknowledgment. "How disappointed some people are going to be," she said, implicitly including both clans in the statement.

Nau touched the thick bandages over Ayt's neck. "How did this happen?"

"Ven's daughter," Ayt explained bitterly. "Disguised as a secretary, and striking at the right moment."

Nau hissed a breath through his teeth. "Mada," he sighed. "Do you remember that I told you not to leave any of that family alive? We're both getting old, and our enemies are still young."

"At least you're retired, Suen-jen," Ayt said, with a wry lightness in her voice that Anden would never have imagined coming from her. Ayt pulled the IV tube from her arm and put her feet down on the ground, pushing herself off the sofa in an attempt to stand. She swayed alarmingly and nearly fell. Nau caught her around the shoulders and supported her weight. She leaned against him, sweat breaking out on her face. The old Horn lifted her in his arms, his lined face tensing for a moment, but his Strength was still more than enough to handle the burden. Ayt put her jade-adorned arms around Nau's neck and rested her head against his shoulder, breathing heavily. "Get me home," she muttered.

Anden and Shae stood to the side as Nau walked toward the door. Before he reached it, Anden came out of his stunned state and said, "Wait." He took a plastic grocery bag from the kitchen and filled it with the extra bandages and a pill bottle of antibiotics. The phone on the counter rang. Shae picked it up.

Anden handed the bag to Nau, who held it hanging awkwardly off one wrist as he carried Ayt. "Change the bandages every four hours, and take two pills each day." He met Nau's gaze. "Your Pillar needs a blood transfusion and should be in the hospital. At least have a Green Bone doctor treating and monitoring her."

Nau did not take his eyes off Anden's face. "May the gods shine favor on you for what you've done, Dr. Emery Anden," he said. "Even though I know you've never saved a life more unwillingly."

In that instant, Shae's jade aura pulsed with emotion strong enough that both men turned toward the Weather Man. The phone receiver slid from Shae's grasp, dangling on its cord as she steadied herself with both hands on the edge of the counter. Anden's heart seemed to stop in his chest. One second elongated into an eternity.

Shae looked up at him, eyes damp with relief. "They've been found," she breathed. "They're alive."

Anden's eyes flicked toward the television. It had been playing on mute, but the screen was no longer recycling the same clips. Now it was showing stretchers being carried into an ambulance. The camera was too far away for Anden to make out faces or details, but the line of text at the bottom of the screen read, NO PEAK CLAN PILLAR AND SEALGIVER FOUND ALIVE.

Anden went light-headed. His knees weakened and he put a hand on the back of the sofa. He'd never considered himself especially religious, but now he whispered devoutly, "Yatto, Father of All, Old Uncle Jenshu and all gods in Heaven, thank you."

Only because he was still wearing his jade did he notice the tension that charged the room in the instant that followed. Nau Suen's eyes were also on the television. His normally unreadable jade aura darkened and swelled in Anden's Perception.

As soon as Shae had uttered, *They're alive*, everything had changed.

For Kekon to lose the Pillars of both major clans in one blow was too great a national crisis. Shae had saved Ayt's life fearing that without her the entire country could be destabilized. However, if Kaul Hilo was alive, then he was still the Pillar of No Peak. There was no doubt of what he would expect Anden and Shae to do if they had Ayt Mada helpless and at their mercy. If Ayt were to die now, the Mountain would be thrown into turmoil, while No Peak remained intact. The Kauls would win.

Slowly, Nau shifted his unblinking gaze to Anden, who was standing between him and the door of the apartment. The former Horn of the Mountain had been a feared man, but even in his prime, he'd never been the most physically intimidating warrior. He defeated others with cunning and skill. Nau was an old man now, and Ayt was too weakened from her injuries to walk, much less fight. Shae and Anden were younger and stronger than the other two Green Bones. And Anden was wearing all his jade.

He could feel Nau's knife-like sense of Perception raking over him, gauging his intent, even as he sensed in Nau's jade aura a bitter readiness. The old man was prepared to fight, to die defending his Pillar and to take at least one of the Kauls with him. No one in the KJA building had been willing to do the same, not even the late Koben Yiro.

Anden remained where he was, standing in front of the woman who'd been his family's enemy for twenty years. He could do it. He was tired, but he had enough Strength to strike a deadly blow or Channel a lethal strike.

"Anden," Shae whispered, low and urgent. He didn't look at his cousin.

Nau shifted Ayt in his arms, preparing to set her down. Instead, the Pillar of the Mountain put her feet on the ground and stood under her own power, steadying herself on the shoulder of her former Horn, but straightening to her full height. She glanced at the news on the television and commented, with bitter humor, "I can't begin to tell you how many times I've wondered why Kaul Hilo isn't dead yet, and it seems I'm destined to keep wondering." Sweat stood out on her brow but her expression was iron in its calm as she looked at Anden. "Make your choice, Dr. Emery."

Anden could Perceive every heartbeat in the room, most of all his own. A pressure built in his chest, his jade energy compressed. He'd sworn to himself that he would never use jade to take lives again. But he could never have imagined this moment.

He would willingly sacrifice his medical career if it meant the Mountain couldn't harm anyone he cared about ever again. Would killing the woman he'd spent the last day working so hard to heal accomplish that? If he could end the war between the clans for good, how many more lives would that save in the future? Was it worth breaking his personal oath? Would it be what Lan wanted him to do?

Seconds passed, unnaturally long. Anden's hands curled into fists at his side. Without taking his eyes off Ayt and Nau, he stepped out of the way and opened the front door. Nau Suen's stare flickered and his face twitched. He shifted to support his Pillar, and the two of them walked through the door, down the hall and out of sight. Anden watched them go, standing in the doorway until he could no longer Perceive them.

"Did I choose wrong?" He whispered the question to himself.

Shae slumped against the wall. "I have no idea."

CHAPTER

29

Rude Awakenings

Kaul Hilo and Woon Papi were rushed to Janloon General Hospital, where they remained for over two weeks, with the clan's Fists guarding them continuously. Hilo suffered a concussion, a shattered scapula, ruptured spleen, burns, and contusions. Woon was bedridden with several broken ribs and a fractured pelvis, and he'd lost the hearing in one ear. By the time they'd been found and dug out of the rubble, both men were also badly dehydrated. That they had survived when many other people in the building had not, including other heavily jaded Green Bone leaders, was widely spoken of as a miracle and a sign of the gods' protection.

There was no miracle, Hilo explained, once he was lucid enough for conversation. Years ago, Hilo had asked the ex–Navy Angel Jim Sunto to teach him and all the top Green Bones of No Peak the Espenian IBJCS techniques against IEDs. Traditional Steeling techniques concentrated on the bones and the surface of the body, to ward against blows and blades. The most lethal effect of a nearby explosion, however, was the overpressurization of vital organs, particularly the lungs, intestines, eyes, and ears. The instant he'd realized what was happening, Hilo had Steeled for his life, concentrating all of his formidable jade energy inward, into his own head and torso, battening the pressure-sensitive parts of his body first, then pushing jade energy outward to protect against blunt trauma as he was thrown through the air, as he put it, "like a cat tossed into a fucking typhoon." Woon, too, had attended Sunto's IBJCS training sessions, and although his ability in Steeling was not as great as the Pillar's, he was already out in the hallway and thus farther away from the explosion; his injuries had been sustained by the building collapsing on top of them.

Shae took her baby daughter into her husband's hospital room. Woon was groggy with painkillers, but his eyes went soft with relief and happiness to see them. "While I was trapped in the dark, I kept thinking I might never see you or Tia again," he said to Shae. "I knew Hilo-jen was still alive, because I could Perceive him somewhere nearby, so I didn't lose all hope, but it was a terrible feeling."

Shae choked up at the sight of his injuries. "I feel as if everything bad that's ever happened to you is my fault." She wondered, not for the first time, if she was cursed to bring disaster to anyone who came too close to her.

Woon shook his head and reached for her hand. "I've been the Pillarman, and the Weather Man's Shadow, and the Sealgiver—so my place has always been standing behind someone else. In truth, that's where I've always felt most useful. I'm grateful the gods put me exactly where I needed to be. On any other day, it would've been you in that room."

Shae placed Tia in Woon's arms. The baby stirred but did not wake. So far, she was a calm infant, so much so that superstitious Green Bone families might be a little worried. "She's eating well and gaining weight," Shae said, "but she doesn't cry much."

"That's good," Woon said, cradling their daughter. "The Kaul family has enough thick-blooded warriors. I'll be glad if she takes some of my personality, since she already looks so much like you."

Shae sat beside Woon, feeling full of heavy, vaguely anxious gratitude, until he fell asleep. Then she nursed and changed Tia, and walked a short way down the hospital corridor to her brother's room.

Days after being dug out of the rubble, Hilo still looked terrible, with bandages covering much of his body, but he was sitting up in bed, eating a bowl of pureed fruit and saying cheerfully to Niko, Ru, and Jaya, "At least my face still looks good. You wouldn't want your da to look like a ghoul, right? Don't worry, I'll be home soon. Remember to help out your ma and don't give her any trouble while I'm in here."

The boys nodded solemnly, and Jaya threw her arms tightly around her father's neck. He winced at the impact and gently loosened her grip, then said, "All right, you've missed enough school for one week. Lott-jen will drive you back." His sons and daughter left with bodyguards surrounding them. Wen remained in the chair by Hilo's side. Juen Nu came in from the hallway and closed the door behind him.

With the children out of the room, Hilo's bright facade dropped and he glared up at Shae. "I still can't believe you saved Ayt." Word had spread that Ayt Mada had reappeared at her residence in High Ground and was shut away inside recovering, surrounded by her loyalists, including Nau Suen and her Weather Man, Iwe Kalundo. "I saw her with a *knife in her neck*," Hilo exclaimed, his voice rising. "You of all people, Shae. All you had to do was *walk the fuck away*."

Still cradling a sleeping Tia in her arms, Shae took the only other chair in the room, on the other side of the bed across from Wen. "I thought you were dead, Hilo," she said, unmoved by his ire. "Along with dozens of Green Bone leaders and government officials. Without Ayt as well, the country would've fallen into chaos."

"It's come close enough as it is," grumbled Juen. The Horn looked as if he hadn't showered or shaved in days. As soon as Hilo and Woon had been found, he'd turned his attention to dealing with the insurrectionist violence. In the immediate aftermath of the attack, with the clan leaders missing and so many Green Bones busy digging through the rubble for survivors, several loosely coordinated cells of armed extremists had heeded the Clanless Future Movement's call to rebellion and taken to the streets.

The Royal Council, fearing all the Green Bone Pillars to be dead and the clans in disarray, had called three thousand national military troops into Janloon, including the jade-equipped Golden Spider Company. Juen said, "I hate to admit it, but we're lucky that the government ordered soldiers into the city and bought us time to get our shit together. No one expected the CFM to be so well armed. We suspected they were relying on foreign support, but not to this extent."

"At least all the money and resources we gave to General Ronu turned out to be of some use." Hilo glowered and leaned his head back against the pillows for a moment, clearly fatigued even from being awake and doing simple things. "This is even worse than the time I was in here after getting the shit beaten out of me by Gont Asch. At least, that time, I woke up in the hospital to good news."

"Everyone suspects Ygutan was involved," Shae said. "Euman Naval Base is on high alert, which suggests the ROE thinks so too."

Hilo grimaced and closed his eyes. "A note was delivered to me during the KJA meeting, warning me to get out. There was no sign of who sent it, but now I'm guessing it came from the Espenians."

Wen squeezed her husband's hand. "Why didn't you listen?"

"As soon as I stood up, everyone in the room knew something was wrong. I sent Woon ahead of me, making an excuse about a family emergency. I thought the threat was from inside, that maybe Ayt had something to do with it." Hilo opened his eyes again. They glittered with fury. "If the Espenians sent that note, then they knew the bombing would happen. They could've saved everyone in the building, but they didn't."

Juen spat a curse. "Those two-faced foreign dogs likely *wanted* the anarchists to start a rebellion. It would've given them the perfect excuse to take control of Kekon by sending in their own troops to restore order."

Shae said, with a pensive frown, "I'm sure they were prepared to do so, but I don't think that was their goal. Considering the conflicts over the naval base, jade exports, and offshore mining, it's no surprise the Espenians have no love for the clans, especially the Mountain. But if they warned Hilo, then they hoped to keep him and No

Peak alive." She shifted Tia to her other arm, holding her sleeping daughter close. "Remember, the Espenians tackle problems with money before violence. Given a choice, they would prefer to control Kekon without risking their own soldiers. Placing the only surviving clan in their debt and dependent on their support, they could've pressured us into capitulating on the issues they want resolved in their favor."

Hilo's lips lifted in a snarl. "Besides me and Woon and the three of you, no one knows I got that godsdamned note. We don't owe the spennies a sack of shit." He picked at a bandage on his chest; some of his jade had been temporarily removed and his aura was uncharacteristically scratchy and uneven. He kept touching the bare spots where his jade was missing, like a man compulsively trying to locate an amputated limb.

Wen caught hold of his hand and stopped him from undoing the dressings. "We all wish Ayt had died," she said, "but the Weather Man has a good point. A country with two large clans is less likely to be controlled, manipulated, or destabilized right now."

"Fuck all those self-serving, scheming foreigners with sharp sticks," Hilo growled, "but not right now. We've got a mess to clean up first. The clanless fanatics wanted an uprising so badly, they let their movement get hijacked by outsiders. Now they've fucked themselves. The government, the press, the public—they'll all be baying for us to spill blood."

Juen nodded as he paced back and forth near the foot of the bed. "There were only two new attacks yesterday. Killing you and Ayt was the one thing the anarchists most needed, and finding out that you were both still alive was a terrible blow. Some of them are already giving up and trying to disappear. After we get the streets back under control, we'll need to act fast to wipe out as much of that organization as we can before it scurries underground again."

The Horn stopped his pacing and turned to the Pillar with grim shame and regret on his face. "We didn't treat the clanless as a serious enough threat before. No one did. I've been talking to Aben Soro about coordinating our actions against them from now on. I don't think he's Ayt's man in quite the same way Nau and Gont were. We can work with him."

"Pull in the minor clans as well, whichever ones are still able to function." Hilo took a minute to gather his breath and regain his energy. He pointed to the glass of water and package of painkillers on the bedside table, which Wen handed to him. "I can't believe I'm going to say this, but get some journalists in here too. The Kobens already put out a statement and I keep seeing Koben Yiro's weepy widow on TV, holding that old gasbag up as a martyr. The sooner people see proof that I'm not dead or in a coma, the better."

"What are you planning to say?" Shae asked, a bit apprehensively.

"Only what the Clanless Future Movement is going to find out soon enough." Hilo swallowed two pills with his water. "Anyone who thinks they can get rid of us so easily deserves what's coming to them. The clans are the spine of the country. We're not going fucking anywhere."

Vastik eya Molovni awoke in the crushing grip of jade and shine withdrawal, not in a concrete cell as he'd expected, but in a sterile room with lights so bright they assaulted his swollen eyes and pounding head. He was strapped to a gurney and two men were standing over him.

"Welcome back, Mr. Molovni," said one of them. A translator standing beyond his field of view repeated the words in Ygut. "Now that you're awake, we have some questions to ask you about the nekolva program."

"Get fucked, you Espenian pigs," Molovni said, his tongue dry and heavy in his mouth. He was in here because of that little worm, that man with the crooked face. If only he'd broken the rat's neck and then killed himself, as he'd been trained to do.

He'd also been trained to resist interrogation. "You won't get useful information from me," he growled. "My superiors would never tell me military secrets so important they would harm Ygutan even if I were to break under your torture." Despite his brave defiance, he erupted into a cold sweat and his heart rate rose precipitously.

"You have the wrong idea," said the other of his captors. "The ROE military has a policy against torture. It's barbaric and unreliable compared to the pharmaceutical tools at our disposal. Our labs created the SN1 that you depend on, after all." A needle slid into the nekolva agent's arm. "Your body will be perfectly fine, but with the right encouragement, your mind will split open like a ripe melon. You'll have lots to say. The process takes time, but we have plenty of that on our hands."

One Mountain

Wie Lon Temple School was founded, so the admissions office claims, over six hundred years ago, by three Green Bone masters, one of them a descendant of the legendary hero Baijen himself. At that time, there were no large clans such as the country has today, only many small, local family clans throughout the island that kept their own jade and fighting methods and protected their own communities. The visionary founding masters established Wie Lon to produce the island's most skilled and disciplined warriors while schooling them in arts, sciences, and the traditions of the Deitist faith. They built their institution in the interior mountainous region of Kekon, where students could train close to nature and the gods, far from the concerns of common people. Prospective pupils had to travel by foot for three days to reach its gates, but once there, the school accepted any student who could pass its entrance tests, regardless of what kingdom, clan, or family they hailed from.

Wie Lon brought together trainees from Green Bone families all over the island, as well as renowned masters who came to learn from their peers and refine their skills, to pass on to the next generation of practitioners. Over the following centuries, Green Bone warriors developed into an increasingly prominent and influential social class, its members bound by common training methods and connections that can largely be traced back to the original Wie Lon Temple School. Today, Kekon boasts over a dozen schools of martial study, and while the more recently established Kaul Dushuron Academy rivals Wie Lon in size and prestige, the historical mystique of the Wie Lon name remains second to none.

The school's current campus, located sixty-five kilometers west of Janloon, was established after the Many Nations War by merging three separate, secret training locations that operated during the foreign occupation of Kekon after the original Wie Lon Temple School was burned to the ground by Shotarian soldiers. During the destruction, nearly a hundred masters and novices who tried to defend the school were captured, stripped of jade, imprisoned, tortured, and executed.

Among those that escaped the purge was a sixteen-year-old trainee named Ayt Yugontin, who led a group of younger students away from the assault and into the forest where they hid from the enemy while their school and home burned all night, sending plumes of black smoke high into the air. In the morning, they fled into the wilderness ahead of Shotarian searchers, until they were found by scouts from the local resistance cell of the One Mountain Society. Ayt Yu, who would later become known as the Spear of Kekon, stood protectively in front of the crying, exhausted group of children and demanded to know the name and clan of the scouting party's leader.

"My name is Kaul Seningtun," answered the scout, "and the name of my clan doesn't matter anymore. All Green Bones in these mountains are brothers."

CHAPTER
30

The Bad Keck

the nineteenth year, third month

Dauk Losunyin passed away from heart failure at the age of seventy-six, leaving behind his wife, four grown children, six grandchildren, and the unofficial post as Pillar of Southtrap, which he'd held for so long. Anden and Hilo traveled to Port Massy for the funeral, to pay their respects as allies of the Dauk family and the Keko-Espenian Green Bone community. On the long flight over, Hilo watched a movie, then had a glass of hoji and fell asleep. Anden tried to follow his cousin's example, but he couldn't concentrate enough to read nor calm his mind enough to drift off. He found it hard to believe that Dauk was gone. It didn't seem that long ago that he sat in the man's dining room, eating Sana's home-cooked meals along with Cory and Rohn Toro.

Anden's sadness was compounded with worry. There were no clans in Espenia; people called Dauk the Pillar simply out of respect for his personal influence. With no formal organization or plan of succession, Dauk's death would not only change who held sway among Green Bones in Espenia, but possibly the very nature of the Keko-Espenian community, in ways that were certain to affect the No Peak clan.

The funeral services took place on an uncommonly bright winter morning. Brittle, frost-coated grass crunched under Anden's shoes, and his breath steamed in the sunlight. Over the view of Whitting Bay, the harsh black lines of the Iron Eye Bridge cut across a milk-white sky. In accordance with Dauk's wishes, the funeral was traditionally Kekonese, with certain modifications and additions of Espenian custom. There were no Deitist penitents in Port Massy senior enough to be ordained as Learned Ones, but three lay penitents from the local community temple, dressed in green hats and scarves, led the attendees in the proper recitations that would usher Dauk's spirit into the afterlife to await the Return. Afterward, Espenian mourning songs were sung and people gave speeches, many of them telling stories of the Pillar's character and how he'd assisted them in a time of need. Anden got up to deliver a bilingual address that began in a personal way, recounting how warmly and generously Dauk Losun had welcomed him into the community when he'd first arrived as a student, but ended on a more formal note, conveying the regards and condolences of the Kaul family.

"That was nicely said, Andy," Hilo told him afterward. Anden stood near his cousin and made introductions as funeral-goers came up to meet the Pillar of No Peak, saluting him or shaking his hand with nervous awe and curiosity before withdrawing to observe from a distance, as if he were a disguised media celebrity. Hilo accepted the respect-paying but maintained a somberness befitting the occasion, standing near the back of the gathering so as not to detract from the attention due to the grieving family. With his jade hidden beneath a black suit and tie and a long black wool coat, he could've passed as a visiting distant relative. The white envelope he placed in the collection plate by Dauk's casket was stamped with the insignia of the No Peak clan and was sure to cover all the funeral expenses.

After Dauk was laid to rest, a reception was held in the Kekonese community center, where for decades the Pillar of Southtrap had presided over the neighborhood grudge hall. Anden hadn't been inside the place in years, but he was struck by how essentially unchanged it was, despite being tastefully made up for the event. The walls were draped with white cloth and the tables that normally surrounded the cockfighting ring in the basement had been brought up and dressed with tablecloths and adorned with vases of white azaleas. The battered bookshelves and lumpy armchairs that ordinarily occupied the common area had been pushed into the corners and hidden from view behind painted folding screens. Lit incense candles and platters of fruit crowded the space in front of the small Deitist shrine.

"Ah, I miss this old neighborhood," lamented Mr. Hian, who now resided in the suburbs with his younger son. "Where I live now, there are no Kekonese newspapers in the library, and the grocery stores are too big." He sat Anden down and spent over an hour reminiscing, sometimes in an unfocused way, as his memory had begun to fail him in advanced age. Anden didn't mind; he knew it might be his last chance to spend time with the old man.

Cory Dauk came over to thank Anden for his speech. "It would've meant a lot to my da. You know how proud he always was to be a Green Bone from the old country."

"The only thing he was more proud of were his grandchildren, I think." Anden had never ceased to find interactions with his old boyfriend to be tinged with a certain nostalgia and awkwardness, but enough time had passed for both of them that their conversations were amicable. Cory was married now, with a cherubic two-year-old son and a baby daughter on the way. He'd put on some weight but was still in good shape from cycling on the weekends, and he cheerfully admitted to have grown his short beard so as to appear more intimidating when arguing in front of a judge. His wife was a second-generation Keko-Espenian social worker, six years younger than him. They'd met during one of his court cases. They seemed happy together.

Cory's sisters were there as well, of course. Although he hadn't forgotten how coldly she'd rebuffed his family's offer of friendship in the past, Anden greeted Kelly Dauk politely and introduced her to Hilo, who made no issue of her prior rudeness and said amiably, "Ms. Dauk, your mother tells me you recently started a new job." Cory's eldest sister had been plucked from the Industry Department to chair the federal Anti-Corruption Panel, whose purpose was to investigate and root out political graft and ties to organized crime.

"I'm not at liberty to discuss my work, Mr. Kaul," the woman replied. "Not even with my family and friends, much less to a Kekonese clan boss." She made a brisk social circuit around the gathering, then left the reception shortly thereafter.

Hilo did not seem offended, but Cory was apologetic for his sister's behavior. "Kelly works for the government, after all," he reminded them with a sigh. "She doesn't want to be seen associating with Green Bones."

There were, indeed, many Green Bones in attendance. The room was becoming so crowded that Anden could barely move. It seemed as if half the Kekonese population of the city was here. He recognized Tod and Sammy and several others, but there were many younger people from Southtrap that he didn't know, and some who'd come from other parts of the country.

An hour into the event, a silver limousine pulled up in front of the building. Jon Remi stepped out with three of his men, all of them wearing light-colored sport jackets, polished shoes, and big sunglasses like typical southern gangsters. Their entrance caused heads to turn. Anden felt a surge of distaste rise sour in the back of his throat. Remi's flippant crudeness, which Anden remembered all too well from that evening in the Blue Olive, seemed even more pronounced now that he dripped with wealth. His hair was slicked back from his tanned face, accentuating his strong brow and dark lips, parted with curious scorn.

The Crew Bosses and Tomascian drug lords in Resville called Jon Remi "the Bad Keck," a title he'd embraced. After using No Peak jade and money to run the Mountain out of the city, Remi had built his own small empire. He'd taken over his uncle's gym years ago and become a key figure in the gambling that accompanied that city's unsanctioned jadesports industry. In addition to dealing in shine and women, he'd expanded into other businesses normally controlled by the Crews, including loansharking and extortion. His men were notoriously vicious; Remi awarded them jade for carrying out assassinations against his rivals.

The opinion in Port Massy was that the Bad Keck was a volatile troublemaker and not a proper Green Bone at all. Even without his sense of Perception, Anden could feel the palpable unease ripple through the room as conversations died and people backed out of the path of the Resville men.

Remi strode up to Hilo, slowing and taking off his sunglasses as he neared. "So old man Dauk's finally left us for Heaven," he said in Espenian, "but the famous Kaul Hiloshudon has come to earth to visit us instead." Remi stopped, studying Hilo the way a dog watches a stranger approaching its door—tense, ready to bark. The Pillar returned the younger man's gaze with steady, motionless expectation.

Several seconds passed before Remi brought his clasped hands to his forehead and dipped into a shallow salute. "How does the saying in the old country go?" In accented Kekonese, "May the gods shine favor on you, Kaul-jen."

Anden went to the Pillar's side. "Hilo-jen, this is Remi Jonjunin, our friend from Resville. Forgive his poor Kekonese and awkward manners. I'm sure he's only nervous and means no disrespect."

The Bad Keck began to turn toward Anden, his expression darkening with insult. Anden hoped savagely that the man would do something stupid. He'd like to see Hilo put the gangster in his place, or better yet, break his jaw. But Hilo settled a hand on the man's shoulder as if they were old friends. "Remi-jen, I feel as if I know you already, having heard so much of your reputation. Go offer your condolences to the wife and children of Dauk Losun—let the gods recognize him—and we'll talk about business tomorrow, when it's more appropriate to do so."

Tod appeared next to them and said with forced conviviality, "I'll let Sana know you're here, Jon. What'll you have to drink?"

Remi seemed perplexed for a moment. Perhaps he'd built Kaul Hilo up in his mind over many years of being told he was one of the most dangerous men back in Kekon, and now he wasn't sure how to respond to a benign meeting. Remi snorted and said to Tod, with a shrug, "Hoji, even though I hate the stuff. In honor of the old man, right?"

He strode away without giving Hilo or Anden another glance. His men followed. As soon as they were out of earshot and normal conversation had started up again, Hilo turned to Anden with a stern look. "What's the matter with you, Andy?"

"He's a boor and a gangster, Hilo-jen," Anden replied with heat. "He was obviously trying to goad you, here at Dauk-jen's funeral in front of everyone. He has no respect for anything."

"Don't show off how much you hate a man until you're ready to be his enemy," Hilo admonished. "Remi's away from his own city where he's grown powerful, and he's the sort of man to act badly to prove his confidence. Even if he's not a good person, don't forget he's done everything we wanted against the Mountain."

Jon Remi and his gang, the Snakeheads, had indeed been invaluable to No Peak. After multiple setbacks, the Mountain's entry into Espenia never recovered. Iwe Kalundo, Ayt's Weather Man, had turned his clan's expansion priorities firmly on Shotar instead. Nearly twenty years after Anden had first come to Port Massy, No Peak remained the only Kekonese clan with substantial power in the Republic of Espenia.

Yet the clan had still not achieved the legal security it needed to preserve the business, and now, without Dauk Losun's influential friendship, accomplishing anything in the country would be much harder. Hilo watched the Resville Green Bones, their pale jackets easy to pick out at the bar. Anden felt the smooth edge of Hilo's jade aura swell momentarily. "Jon Remi is our ally until I say otherwise," the Pillar said in an undertone. "Whether it stays that way is up to him. We'll see how things go tomorrow."

Upon returning to their room in the Crestwood Hotel, Hilo said, "It's fucking cold in here." He took off his suit jacket and tie and shrugged into a sweater, then turned up the heat in the room. Anden had heard his cousin complain before that cold made his shoulder ache and sometimes his wrist as well. Years spent fighting took a heavy toll on the body, even before accounting for the injuries Hilo had sustained in the Janloon bombing. Surgery to stitch his spleen and repair his scapula had been followed by months of physiotherapy before he could train again. Five years later, the Pillar appeared fully recovered, as strong a Green Bone as ever, but Anden knew that even the best healers and trainers could only do so much. Those who were close to Hilo noticed the moments when he moved without his usual grace or winced at some lingering pain.

Anden said, "I'm going downstairs to the gift shop, to pick up some small things for coworkers at the clinic." It was a tiny lie, and if Hilo Perceived it, he didn't say.

Anden took the elevator down to the ground floor and used a calling card to place a long-distance phone call from one of the pay phones at the back of the lobby. When the call picked up, Anden said, "I'm glad I caught you before you went to work." It would be just past dawn in Janloon, and Jirhuya was an early riser.

"I'm not in a rush," Jirhu said. "I'm waiting for the director to get back to me on the budget anyway. So I'm enjoying breakfast and then going to the gym." Kekon's growing film industry, financed by the No Peak clan, had given the artist steady work for several years. Anden heard the sound of running water shut off in the background, then a pause. With sly suggestiveness, "Too bad you're not here with me."

"I wish I were," Anden said. "We need to stay a little longer to deal with some clan things. I'll be back on Fourthday." He couldn't hear Jirhu's reply because at that moment a large group of people passed through the hotel lobby, and Anden had to cover his other ear to block out their loud chatter. "Sorry, it's noisy here. What did you say?"

"Will you be okay?" It was the only thing Jirhuya ever asked when it came to Anden's activities on behalf of No Peak. Jirhu had no wish to have anything to do with the clans beyond day-to-day life in

Janloon. He knew Anden's world involved jade and money, politics and bloodshed, on a level even ordinary Kekonese did not understand, much less an Abukei artist. His only concern when it came to clan dealings was Anden's safety.

Wen had introduced them to each other ten months ago. "Anden," she'd said after dinner at the Kaul house one evening, taking his empty plate and drawing him into the kitchen, "are you free for lunch next Secondday? I'd like you to meet a friend of mine. He's a talented artist who works in the film industry. Also, he's handsome and single." She held up a hand before he could even think of what to say. "Just so you know, he's Abukei, but don't judge him until you meet him. I think the two of you would get along. I'll set it up so there's no pressure."

Anden had been rendered nearly speechless with embarrassment by the idea of Wen considering partners for him. Personally, he'd all but given up on meeting anyone suitable. His most recent relationship had lasted only a few dates, and his pool of prospects felt small. Lott Jin had gotten married to a woman Anden didn't know, then divorced three years later. He seemed uninterested in another relationship—not that Anden was holding out any hope on that front. On occasion, Anden had gone to social gatherings with the few queer friends he'd met in medical school and at work, but he was wary of creating professional complications. There were no other mixed-blood Green Bone physicians in all of Janloon. Anden could not hide who he was or where he was seen, even if he wanted to. And most men with the unlucky desire for other men did not want to risk the potential public scrutiny that came from associating with the Kaul family.

"How do you even know he would be interested?" Anden asked.

"Just come to lunch," Wen assured him.

Anden had been skeptical. He had no particular attraction to Abukei men and had never before contemplated dating one. So he was surprised at that first meeting, then faintly resentful of Wen's smugness. Jirhuya had sharp cheekbones, smooth bronze skin, and a slim, straight build that made all clothes look good on his body.

He used this fact to his advantage and was always well dressed, even when he was only going out for a short while. Although he didn't possess the physique of a fighter that Anden had always associated with male beauty, he'd grown up swimming and rock climbing and now kept up both activities in the gym. Jirhu possessed a ready smile and was easy to talk to because he was quick to open up about himself and genuinely curious about others. In that way, he reminded Anden of Cory, but Jirhu had a rich inner life—one awash with colors and ideas and feelings—that Anden didn't fully understand, and the man was more intensely devoted to his artistic vocation than Cory had been to anything. Anden was shocked, after their first few dates, to find himself the pursuer—calling Jirhu to invite him over, making dinner, renting movies.

A clicking on the line told Anden he was running out of time on his calling card. "We're just having a meeting tomorrow. There's nothing to worry about," Anden assured his boyfriend. That was not true; meetings could decide life or death, war or peace, but that was not what Jirhu was asking. They talked a little longer. After hanging up, Anden did indeed go into the hotel gift shop, where he bought some bags of sour candies and keychains shaped like the Mast Building. He could've saved himself the minor inconvenience by simply using the phone in the hotel room, but he hadn't yet mentioned his boyfriend to the Pillar. Even though Hilo probably already knew about the relationship, Anden wasn't sure how to properly bring up the subject. A hotel room in a foreign city after an already difficult day didn't seem like the right time or place.

The next day, Dauk Sana held a meeting in her home. Although they'd always lived modestly, the Dauks had invested in a number of Kekonese businesses that had grown successful with the assistance of the No Peak clan. Cory and his sisters were all financially secure, so the Dauks had become reasonably wealthy in their later years. Instead of downsizing, they'd built a much larger, nicer residence where they could host gatherings and have their children and grandchildren visit. They were not technically in Southtrap anymore, but they didn't need to be, as the neighborhood was increasingly being taken over by high-rent commercial space, and the Kekonese community had spread out over the years, with old K-Town remaining in Southtrap, but equally populous cultural pockets cropping up in Jons Island and Quince, among other places.

The meeting was held at a long mahogany table in the dining room. It was a far cry from the cozy space Anden remembered of the Dauks' old blue split-level house. Tea was poured and plates of snacks were passed around, which gave the gathering the incongruous feel of a family gathering, even though there were people in the room who'd never met one another and others who outright disliked each other. Dauk Sana, in a white sweater and face powder, sat at the head of the table with her son, Cory, the only Green Bone among her children, seated beside her.

Next to Cory was Etto Samishun, who Anden had known as Sammy when they were both young men. Now people called him Etto-jen and acknowledged him as the most capable Green Bone remaining in Southtrap. Sammy and a few other protégés of the late Rohn Toro were the leaders of a loose network of several dozen Green Bones that continued to protect the neighborhood and had remained loyal to Dauk Losun as Pillar until his passing.

Another familiar face at the table was Shun Todorho. Tod was an honorably discharged Navy Angels corporal and Oortokon war veteran who'd battled drug addiction and depression upon leaving the military, losing three jobs and a marriage before Dauk Losun stepped in and gave him work in the grudge hall on the condition that he attend rehab and therapy. Tod had since become a devout Deitist, remarried, and begun wearing his own jade again and teaching younger Green Bones. A close friend of the Dauks, he managed the newest grudge hall in the southern Port Massy suburb of Orslow, which was fast becoming a major city in its own right and boasted a growing population of newer, wealthier Kekonese immigrants.

The rest of the seats at the table were occupied by men that Anden didn't know well, although Sana had told him about some of them:

Migu Sun, an old friend of Rohn Toro who spoke for the Kekonese Green Bones in Adamont Capita; Hasho Baku, a representative from Evenfield, five hours away; and of course, Remi Jon. Each of them was accompanied by two or three of their own men, standing or sitting in extra chairs against the wall. In total there were close to twenty people in the dining room, all of them having traveled here for Dauk Losun's funeral and to find out how Green Bone affairs would be managed in the aftermath of his death.

Anden, too, was curious and apprehensive. Sana had always been her husband's partner and advisor, in truth his Weather Man, but she was an elderly woman now. Anden couldn't imagine the young men around the table accepting her authority. Cory was Dauk's son, but he was not like his father. Espenian-born and easygoing, his greatest use to the community was as a lawyer and someone who was outwardly legitimate and part of mainstream society in nearly all ways. The other men around the table who wore jade were acknowledged leaders in their own districts, but none of them had the national standing of Dauk Losun. This was not their failing; the Kekonese Green Bone population in Espenia was not the small, concentrated community in Southtrap that it had been when Dauk arrived in the country sixty years ago.

Everyone in the room was also well aware that the No Peak clan was sure to have a say. Kaul Hilo was not wearing the dark suit and tie and somber expression from yesterday. He sat slouched in his chair, one arm leaning on the table, taking up space in his usual casual way. Jade gleamed across the gap of his open collar—more jade than anyone else in the room, perhaps more than the entire rest of the room put together. He was not running the meeting, nor seated in any special place along the table, but he was also not hiding that he was the wealthiest and most powerful man in attendance. Anden sat on the Pillar's right-hand side.

Sana began by thanking everyone for their condolences over the past week. "I know my husband is in the afterlife looking down gladly at all the friends he has." Cory put a hand on his mother's arm in comfort and her wavering voice steadied. "I'm grateful to those of you who've traveled here from Evenfield and Adamont Capita and

Resville, and especially from Kekon." She turned toward Hilo and Anden. "Our whole community is honored that the Pillar of the No Peak clan himself would come from so far away to grieve with us, along with our dear friend Anden."

Hilo said, "I would never fail to pay my final respects to a friend and fellow Pillar."

Sana dabbed her eyes and nodded in mute gratitude before gathering herself and continuing. "Our Kekonese community and our Green Bone traditions were the most important things to Losun. All his life, he did his best to protect them. Now that he's gone, we have some decisions to make about the future."

Sana looked to her son, who sat forward as all eyes shifted to him. "No one can fill my father's shoes as Pillar," Cory said matter-of-factly, without any shame or criticism. "But my mother and I, along with Sammy and Tod, have been talking to as many Green Bones as we can in the Port Massy area. We want to bring all of you into the decision about what direction our community should take in the future."

Sana said, "Losun and I often talked about our hopes that we Kekonese could achieve the same things as anyone else who was born in this country, that our children and grandchildren could become business leaders or movie stars or assemblymen. Yet how will that happen so long as we're associated with jade, which is still misunderstood and has a bad reputation in Espenia?" The widow sighed deeply. "Should we give up our culture, our birthright for thousands of years, and become just like the weaker immigrants such as the Tuni or Shotarians? Or do we instead give up the chance to be accepted and have lawful influence? There's no good choice. We have to find another way. That's what our friends in No Peak have been trying to do."

She looked to Hilo. This was not Kekon, and these Green Bones had sworn no clan oaths, so when Hilo drew his gaze around the table and spoke, it was not with the quick, easy authority Anden was accustomed to, but mildly and persuasively. "Many of you know that No Peak has been trying to change the laws against jade in this country. My cousin Anden won us the first victory when he convinced Espenian doctors and politicians to legalize jade for medical use. Today, there are Kekonese doctors running clinics right here in Port Massy. Andy, tell us how many there are now."

Anden said, "There are sixty licensed jade medicine clinics and around two hundred recognized practitioners in Espenia. I was part of the panel of doctors from the College of Bioenergetic Medicine in Janloon that drafted the international standards of practice that these clinics are required to meet to be certified. The National Assembly has approved a special visa to allow Kekonese doctors to move to Espenia to practice medicine, and last year there were twelve Keko-Espenians admitted into the college in Janloon, the largest number of international students they've ever had."

Hilo said, "What Andy's done was a big step, but we're not there yet, not where we want to be. The clan has been working with a PR firm to change Espenian attitudes about jade. Maybe you've seen some of the ads. It seems the surest way to make anything happen in this country is to get on television." This garnered chuckles from around the table.

Rigly Hollin and his partners at WBH Focus, armed with research from focus groups and attitudinal studies, had taken out full-page magazine ads, billboards, and television spots that presented jade in a positive light. Anden had seen one in the Air Espenia in-flight magazine on their way over to Port Massy: a photograph of a group of Navy Angels holding up their jade dog tags with the exhortation to SUPPORT OUR JADE WARRIORS. It had made Hilo grimace with contempt, but no one could argue with Shae's strategy. The Espenians would never accept jade unless they believed they owned it as much as anyone in the world, even the Kekonese.

Sana said, "If jade was accepted by society, we could live openly as Green Bones without fear of the law. In our communities, there could be not only jade medicine clinics, but proper Deitist temples, and schools teaching the jade disciplines. Of course, it would never be the same as Kekon, but it would be much better than it is now." Sana's voice was still strong, but she was not used to being the center of attention. She looked around the table of Green Bone men before clutching her hands together and firming her lips. "Most importantly, we would no longer have to choose between being Kekonese or Espenians. We could be both. That is a dream I know Losun would want to see come true."

Cory nodded and straightened in his seat. "That's why we propose forming a national organization: the Kekonese Association of Espenia—to promote cultural understanding and to address issues that affect the entire Keko-Espenian community. We'll help new immigrants, promote Kekonese culture and transamaric business ties, and lobby the government to repeal the prohibition against jade." He turned toward Hilo and Anden. "It won't be a clan. There won't be a Pillar. But it'll be Green Bones working together to protect our community, so in that most important way, it'll be similar."

Dauk Losun must've been proud of his son in the end, Anden thought. Cory wasn't green in the soul in the traditional Kekonese sense, but he'd found his own way to be successful in his father's world. When he spoke, it was with a compelling confidence.

The lawyer grew more serious as he addressed the entire room again. "If we hope to accomplish our goals, however, we need to work together to shift certain cultural attitudes and change the way Kekonese-Espenians are viewed by the public. If we want the ban on jade repealed, then we need to demonstrate that Green Bones are law-abiding citizens in all other respects. Which means taking steps to pull out of illegal activities." An expectant silence fell over the dining table. "Take our grudge halls, for example. Before my da passed away we discussed implementing new rules: no more cockfighting or illegal gambling, and no more clean-bladed dueling. Nothing that will give the police an excuse to raid our properties."

A murmur of incredulity rose from the out-of-town Green Bones. "What's the point of even having the grudge halls without those things?" exclaimed Hasho Baku, the Green Bone leader from Evenfield. "People are going to duel no matter what you say. They'll just do it somewhere else and be even more likely to be caught."

"Fatal duels are the main problem," Cory said. "The law doesn't recognize clean blades, so if there are deaths or serious injuries, we expose ourselves to police scrutiny and criminal charges. We can find a way to allow people to settle issues of honor in a manner that's more legally acceptable. The grudge halls can continue to be centers of social life without violence."

Sammy spoke up. "On the whole, we've been successfully holding our own against the Crews. So successful, in fact, that there are areas of the country where we've pushed them out, but instead of making those neighborhoods safe for everyone, it's Kekonese gangsters who've taken over the drug dealing, prostitution, extortion, and racketeering." No one was looking directly at Jon Remi, but it was obvious who Sammy was referring to. "Every time a Kekonese man gets arrested or imprisoned for a serious crime while wearing jade, it reinforces negative stereotypes. As Green Bones, we need to enforce stricter standards about who we train and allow to be green, and what activities we shouldn't tolerate."

Jon Remi snorted. The sound was loud enough to be heard from the other end of the table. "And who's going to say what is or isn't allowed? You?" He turned his gaze on Hilo and Anden and crossed his tattooed arms. "Or will the great No Peak clan decide for us?"

"As a lawyer who's worked on dozens of these cases," Cory responded, "I can tell you that a person charged with jade possession, who isn't engaged in any other offense and has no prior criminal record, might be convicted of a minor offense that carries a one- or two-year sentence. We're almost always able to get prison time suspended in favor of a fine and community service. On the other hand, if someone is wearing jade when they're arrested for selling drugs, running a protection racket, or committing assault or murder, that's an aggravating factor and we're looking at felony crimes and life sentences."

Migu Sun, the older Green Bone who had come from Adamont Capita, cleared his throat and began to speak in a quiet, thoughtful voice. "I grew up in a Deitist family and was always taught that the gods left jade on earth as a test for us mortals. If they gave us back some of the power of Heaven, how would we use it? Would we wield that power over others and use it for evil? Or would we work for the common good, and protect the weak? I grew up hearing of legendary jade warrior heroes and cheering the resistance fighters of the One Mountain Society. But when jade was brought to these shores from the old country, it was corrupted by Espenian culture. Now young people see it as simply a way to get what they want. Many of them use shine and other drugs, and they don't train in the jade disciplines like they used to. Dauk Losun was a wise and influential man, and all his life he lived modestly and relied on the counsel of his wife and trusted friends. He only wanted us all to live better lives in this country."

Migu turned to Sana and Cory and said, "If we have to change the grudge halls, so be it. Let the Crews have the illegal businesses. If we don't stop our own people from getting into drugs and crime, Green Bones will end up in prison, and our jade in the hands of the government, and in the end, we'll be just like the barukan in Shotar, with no real prospects." Migu stood up, turned to Hilo and saluted him deeply. "Kaul-jen, your clan has already accomplished a great deal here. If you say you'll support us, surely anything is possible. May the gods shine favor on No Peak. For the sake of all Kekonese."

Remi barked a laugh as harsh as a gunshot. "You old fool. You think the No Peak clan is running ads and lobbying politicians for *our* sake?" He shook his head, smirking at Migu Sun. "The clans in Kekon don't give a shit about any of us. The Kauls only want to grow their business empire, and they want *us*—the kespies that they don't even think of as real Green Bones—to fall into line and behave ourselves so there's nothing to dirty the shiny image they show the Espenian government and the companies they work with. They expect us to take orders from them like their Fingers. Next, they'll suggest we give up our jade altogether."

"No one can ask that of anyone." Hilo's words cut the air as sharply as Remi's laugh. The attention in the room snapped toward him. "No Peak has many business interests in Espenia, it's true, and we want to grow and protect them. That's no surprise to anyone. We bring money and jobs and jade, so you benefit as much as we do." Hilo's steady gaze settled on Remi and the reminder hung between them. "Many years ago, I told Dauk Losun that if we worked together, we Kekonese would become more powerful in this country than the Crews. Now I'm telling all of you the same thing. The Dauks are right. The biggest threat to you isn't the Crews anymore. It's your lower status here that's a hardship. If you want to stop hiding your jade, then you have to stop doing things with it that need to be hidden."

"You expect me to swallow that hypocritical bullshit?" Remi pointed at Hilo. "The clans in Janloon collect tribute. Why shouldn't I do the same in Resville?"

"Tribute!" Sana exclaimed with indignation. "Do you think you're a Fist? Have you sworn oaths to a clan? Will you help a tributary business owner by accepting his son into a martial school, or extending him a loan to expand his store, or paying him if a typhoon hits his house? No, you think the way the Crews think—only taking and never giving. That's not how we'll ever succeed in this country."

Remi sat back in his chair and spread his arms arrogantly, indicating his expensive clothes and the trio of tough-looking young bodyguards standing behind him. "Then I guess we have different definitions of success."

Remi's men laughed. They clapped their boss on the shoulder and one of them stuck his tongue out at the room like a hyena, showing off his jade studs. Anden was astonished. Even in Espenia, he'd never seen Green Bones act so improperly in front of senior warriors, much less the Pillar. Sammy and Tod tensed as a warning murmur began to rise from the other men along the walls. Hilo remained motionless.

Cory stood up and spread his hands in a placating gesture to the room. "Take it easy, everyone. Nothing is going to change overnight. We all know the situation in Resville is different from Port Massy." He spoke amenably, a peacemaker seeking a middle ground. Anden stifled a grimace at the weakness of it, the un-Green-Bone-like retreat. "Look, Jon, if you have no interest in being involved in the association, that's fine," Cory said. "But we're asking you, for your own good as well as ours, to think ahead. Start taking steps to pull out of the riskiest businesses and activities. If you need any legal counsel about how to go legitimate—"

Remi rose from his seat, hands on the table. "I don't need your help, crumb. I don't answer to any *community association*, and I sure as *fuck* don't take orders from No Peak." He turned his head to the Pillar. There were not many men who could match Kaul Hilo's stare, but Jon Remi was one of them. "How many people have you killed or ordered to be killed, but you're telling *me* I've got to *behave*? Your clan's got office towers and vaults of money and a whole fucking island full of jade, but you've got the gall to tell me and my boys not to eat. You sponsor people to come here from Janloon, clan stooges who take up college spots and jobs and who send the money they make back to Kekon, but you want those of us who've clawed tooth and nail for our fair share in this country to walk away from our hard-won livelihoods and let the Crews come back in and snap it all up." Remi's nostrils flared, and his crudely handsome features darkened with dangerous resentment. "You agreed that I could have Resville. So long as I kept your enemies out, you'd leave me to run things my way. Well I've done what you asked, and now you're stepping on me? You old country kecks think you're better than the rest of us? No. You *owe* me, Kaul."

Anden was sitting close enough to Hilo to feel his cousin's jade aura ripple and sharpen like the end of a whip. The Pillar said, in a soft voice, "I owe you nothing. You're not a tributary clan, you're not a Lantern Man, you're not even a friend, because a friend wouldn't speak in such a way, even in disagreement. We had an arrangement. It made you a rich and powerful man. It's only out of respect for our past alliance that I'm not going to take offense at the things you've said. I came to pay my respects to Dauk Losun—let the gods recognize him—and to support his family and successors. I brought none of my Fists or Fingers with me. Look around the room. It's your fellow Green Bones that are asking you to change in a way that may be hard at first, but that everyone agrees will be better in the long run."

Remi stood to his full height. The tattoo of the black skull with the snakes coming out of its eye sockets seemed to stretch its deathly grin as he swung his pale sport jacket off the back of his chair and over his shoulder. "I don't give a shit about the tiny chance of jade being legalized, or No Peak's investments. I respected Dauk while he was alive, but we've got our own territories now and our own ways of handling things. I don't have a problem with anyone in this room so long as we mind our own businesses and leave each other to eat well. Do whatever you want in Port Massy, but I'll run Resville my own way."

The Bad Keck jerked his head to his men, and the Snakeheads walked out of the meeting. No one spoke or tried to stop them as they shouldered past the other Green Bones in the room, smirking beneath their sunglasses as they exited the house. An uncomfortable silence hung in their wake.

Reluctantly, Hasho Baku stood as well. "Jon spoke too bluntly and rudely," he said, "but I agree with him. I think the chances of repealing the laws against jade are too small to be worth the effort of creating this association, and the changes you propose will only create division between Green Bones." He saluted Dauk Sana and Kaul Hilo. "I respect your intentions and I won't stand in your way, but I think it would be best if we all return to our own cities and not try to dictate what other Green Bones do. That way, we can all remain friends." He nodded to everyone else around the table, then departed the house with his own men.

Cory expelled a loud breath. He scrubbed a hand through his hair and slumped back in his chair with a rueful frown. "Well, that could've gone better."

"We knew there would be holdouts," Tod said. "The rest of us are with you, Cory."

Migu Sun said, "I'll speak privately to Hasho later. I believe he'll come around if he starts to see that what we're hoping for can be accomplished. At least we know he won't oppose us or cause trouble, and his people in Evenfield can be counted on to be discreet with their jade. As for Remi..." The old Green Bone sighed. "I'll talk to some people that I know in Resville. Maybe they can bring him back to the table."

Anden had remained silent during the vociferous exchange, as Hilo would've expected him to, but he felt a little hot and sick, as he had after walking out of the Blue Olive nightclub. "Jon Remi can't be persuaded to give up any of his power."

"Andy's right," Hilo said. "It's too bad that Remi was born on this side of the ocean. A man like that, who stands up for himself and can command others—maybe if he'd been raised and trained as a proper Green Bone, he could've been a good Fist. But fate makes us who we are and can't be changed."

At the tone of finality in Hilo's voice, Dauk Sana sucked in a breath. She left her seat and lowered herself next to Hilo's chair. "Kaul-jen," she said anxiously, "there's no excuse for Remi's rudeness to you as a visitor, much less a Pillar! No one could blame you if you took offense and felt the need to respond. But for the sake of peace, and on account of the friendship you've shown to our family, please let those of us here in Espenia handle it, as it's our problem." She pressed Hilo's hand. "And if we can't, then we'll disavow all of those Green Bones in Resville, and work with the police to stop them."

Migu Sun nodded solemnly, but the younger Green Bones in the room looked a little stunned. It hadn't occurred to them as quickly as it had to Dauk Sana that Hilo might respond to Remi's insults with swift retaliation. The widow was begging the Pillar to stay his hand. If No Peak sent its Fists into Resville to kill Remi and go to war with his gang, it would surely attract more negative attention from the police and the public. For a powerful Janloon clan to murder Espenian citizens, even criminals like the Snakeheads, would undermine the influence of the Kekonese Association of Espenia in its crucial formative stages. Remi might even be expecting an attack now, Anden thought. He might be eager for a chance to go up against old country Green Bones and grow his own reputation.

Hilo was silent for a moment. Then he took Dauk Sana's hands and stood, smiling as he pulled her up with him. "No Peak has people and businesses in Espenia, but this isn't our country. As a guest, I wouldn't want to do anything that creates trouble for my friends or goes against the goals we share." Hilo spoke to everyone in the room. "No Peak will stay out of Resville, as we have so far. You have my word as Pillar."

Sana's shoulders came down in relief. "Thank you, Kaul-jen." She touched her clasped hands to her forehead. "I only wish Losun-se were here to thank you as well."

The meeting ended on that somber note. The other Green Bones broke apart to converse in small groups in the foyer and kitchen. Hilo and Anden offered their final condolences to Sana and Cory, accepted respectful salutes and well wishes for safe travel, and took their leave.

In the taxi on the way back to the Crestwood Hotel, Hilo sat back and tapped out a cigarette, the last one in the box. He rolled it between his fingers but didn't light it. "You were quiet back there, Andy. And you're being quiet now."

Anden said, "You told me yesterday not to make my opinions so obvious."

"You're bothered by Remi," Hilo inferred. "Was what happened today a surprise?"

"No, but just because it's an unsurprising problem doesn't mean it's not still a problem."

Hilo grinned and reached across the seat to shove his cousin's shoulder affectionately. "You would've been a great Fist, Andy. I know that's all in the past, so don't take it the wrong way, I'm only saying it as a compliment." He turned serious again. "Remi Jonjunin is like a Crew Boss with a Kekonese face. I thought there was a chance he would compromise to stay on good terms with the people in that room, but it's obvious he doesn't believe he needs us or anyone in Port Massy anymore. Why are you taking his insults so personally?"

"We *made* Remi," Anden exclaimed. "We gave him the money and jade that he used to become the Bad Keck of Resville. I was the one who spoke for the clan and gave him free rein in that city. So it's my fault that he's now a problem for us."

Hilo put the unlit cigarette into his mouth. "I trusted you to make the right decision at the time and you did. What was good for us then is bad for us now, but that's the way things happen sometimes. Your Port Massy friends are asking us to trust them to deal with the Bad Keck. That's just as well. We have to keep our attention at home, fighting the clanless."

Anden gave the Pillar a skeptical look. "Hilo-jen," he said. "Cory, Tod, Sammy—I like all of them. They're good people who care about their community and what it means to wear jade. I want their association to succeed. But they're not a clan. They're green in their own way, but not in the way that's needed to go up against someone with no morals like Jon Remi."

The taxi pulled up to the front of the Crestwood Hotel and they got out. Hilo drew his coat around his neck and paused outside the hotel's revolving doors. "Give it some time, Andy. Yesterday, I told you Remi was our ally until I said otherwise." He fingered his lighter, then reluctantly placed the lone cigarette back into its box. "Now I'm saying otherwise."

CHAPTER
31

Disappointment

Kaul Nikoyan lay on his back in the girl's apartment, watching the light from the silenced television screen flicker off the ceiling. The girl, Mera, was still gamely mouthing his cock, but they'd had sex already and his mind was elsewhere. The sun had gone down. He glanced at the clock on the bedside table. In an hour, he would be expected to report to Lott Jin, who would assign him to his duties for the night ahead.

Niko knew his uncle would disapprove of how he'd spent the afternoon. *No getting laid before work, not on the greener side of the clan,* Hilo would say, echoing commonly held jade warrior wisdom. Good Fists and Fingers did not go out into the street relaxed and unalert. They set out as sharp as wolves that had not yet eaten.

Niko didn't believe in old adages, and his uncle already found fault with him on a number of fronts, so why should one additional failing matter? Besides, although there might be an opportunity to exercise force tonight, perhaps even confiscate some illegally worn jade, he didn't expect to face anything too dangerous. There'd never been any question that Niko would become a Finger in the clan, but the Pillar had instructed Juen Nu not to coddle him. He was to be given the same amount of work, risk, and expectation of discipline as any new Green Bone. Juen Nu, however, would be retiring this year. The Pillar had already given his permission. Lott Jin was the leading candidate to become the next Horn, but until the promotion was official, Niko doubted the First Fist would risk his standing with the Kaul family by allowing the heir of the clan to come to any real harm under his supervision.

"Do you want to order in anything to eat?" Niko asked, as a way to get the girl to give up on trying to arouse him again. Mera pushed her hair back and flopped down next to him, her lipstick smeared. She was pretty, but other pretty girls had tried to capture Niko's attention before. He'd been sixteen years old when a girl had first offered herself to him in a dark corner of the garden on his family's estate during a clan New Year's party. He hadn't felt comfortable taking the opportunity that time, or the next, but his curiosity had finally gotten the better of him and he'd since been with a few girls, to varying degrees of satisfaction.

"We can order in if you want," Mera said, "but I'd rather go out, wouldn't you?"

"I'm not that hungry, and I can eat later. I just thought maybe you'd want something."

"The only thing I have an appetite for is *you*," Mera sighed, draping her arm across his chest and laying her head on his shoulder.

She sounded so dreamy that Niko suppressed a wince. At age twenty, he was already cynical about relationships. Mera was only the latest young hopeful vying to win the heart of the firstborn son of the Kaul family and marry into the leadership of the No Peak clan.

Niko blamed his parents. Everyone knew the romantic history of the young Kaul Hiloshudon falling in love with a stone-eye girl and elevating the formerly disgraced Maik family to the top of the clan. A few years ago, a cable network had tried to make a saccharine television movie out of the story, before the Weather Man's office had intervened and shut it down. Even the tragic fate of Niko's uncles, Kehn and Tar, had not significantly dimmed the tale, perhaps because Kaul Maik Wen played a far more visible role as the wife of the Pillar than any of her predecessors.

"I like spending time with you. You're a sweet girl," Niko said.

Mera stiffened at his patronizing kindness. "I'm not *sweet*. I'm the youngest of four and my parents couldn't afford to send a girl to the Academy, but that doesn't mean I'm a delicate flower. My brothers have dueled. My older sister's a Lantern Man. My family's middle class, but we're green."

"I never said anything against your family." Niko turned over and lay on his stomach; the pressure of the bed against his back was becoming uncomfortable against his itching, healing skin. Mera sat up and turned off the television. She drew her legs up and looked down at him with silent, intense frustration, as if having discovered the jigsaw puzzle she was working on was missing a piece. Girls were certain that underneath Niko's reserved demeanor there lurked a hot-blooded, passionate young Horn in the making, and were at a loss when they couldn't find that person.

Mera touched the tips of her fingers to the welts on his back and shoulders. "What happened?"

"I was whipped, what do you think?" he muttered into the pillow.

"Your father whipped you?" She sounded surprised, almost pleased, that the eldest son of the Pillar could be whipped for misbehaving, like any ordinary youth.

"He's my uncle, not my father," Niko corrected her. "And he whipped me for not behaving like a proper Green Bone."

Mera trailed her fingers up the back of his neck. "You seem like a proper Green Bone to me," she cooed, lightly touching the necklace resting against his skin. It was an intimate, daring gesture; there were Green Bone men who didn't even let their wives touch their jade. Niko's necklace had belonged to his father—his real father, Kaul Lan, a man he'd heard much about and never known. There were six jade beads on the chain. The others had been removed and safely stored away. They would be added back, his parents said, once he earned them.

Niko propped his chin onto his folded arms. "What *is* a proper Green Bone, anyway? Everyone seems to know what it *isn't*—yet, it's something we don't bother to explain. We take it for granted that we can recognize greenness when we see it. But can we, really? People take one look at my face, my name, and my jade and they think they know me." Niko chuckled absently and without much humor, then fell silent for some time. "You know what I think?" he mused out loud. "I think all they're seeing is a shell. A bright green empty shell."

Niko had been speaking mostly to himself and didn't expect the girl to respond, but after a couple of minutes, he noticed she'd gone quiet. Mera hadn't moved away from him on the bed, but her ardor had evaporated. She seemed closed off now, withdrawn.

Niko felt a crawl of irritation, then relief. He rolled away from her on the bed and got up. He began dressing—pulling on his pants, buttoning his shirt, strapping his talon knife to his belt and securing his pistol in a shoulder holster. Before he left the room, he sat down on the edge of the bed and placed a gentle kiss on Mera's cheek. She didn't move away, but she didn't tilt her face toward him with the expectation of anything more.

"I meant what I said. I enjoyed spending time with you," Niko said. "Sorry if I ended up being a disappointment." He stood and left the room.

———

The incident that had caused Niko's uncle to punish him so severely had started out innocuously enough the previous week, in the Pig & Pig pub, as a bet between Fingers over some unimportant thing, perhaps relayball. The loser of the bet, a young man named Kitu, took offense at something Niko said and offered to settle the disagreement with a physical contest. Niko, who'd been nursing a cold all week, declined more rudely than he'd intended, by saying he thought the other boy wasn't worth his time. Kitu offered a clean blade.

As far as duels went, this one was fairly typical, with no real personal grudges involved. No one expected either of the combatants would try to kill the other, although of course, because the winner would claim the loser's jade, the stakes were still serious. All the other people in the pub began clearing space between the tables for the contest to happen.

Niko remained seated. "Kitu, you don't want to duel me. You'll lose."

This was not in fact a foregone conclusion. Kitu's family was not well off, but he was of respectable account as a fighter, and the jade he wore as a second-rank Finger had been won, not inherited. Kaul Niko, in comparison, was naturally talented and his family employed a bevy of personal coaches, but within the clan, people quietly said he didn't put in the effort to be at the level one would expect from a Kaul.

Even if Kitu lost the duel, he would gain regard simply for having had the thick blood to challenge the first son of the Kaul family, and if he made an especially good showing, he would be taken more seriously and others might measure him to be worth a future contest. Kitu said, impatiently, "Are you going to get up or not?"

Niko said, "I fought a duel a month ago, keke." That duel had been closer than Niko would've liked to admit and had nearly broken his jaw. "I don't feel like it tonight."

The refusal surprised and disappointed everyone, Kitu most of all. Young Green Bones intending to advance on the military side of the clan looked for opportunities to duel, and it was poor form to refuse a clean blade so long as it was sincerely offered and there wasn't some extenuating circumstance. "If you're too drunk or lazy right now, I'll meet you tomorrow at noon," Kitu said, and waited for the other man to name the place and weapon of choice.

"Are you that eager to get your ass kicked and lose your jade?" Niko spoke indifferently, but he was filled with a sudden, ferocious resentment. It wasn't that he disdained Kitu's skill or was afraid to face him. He'd come to the Pig & Pig to relax and didn't see why he had to upend his evening simply because someone wanted the chance to make a name for himself. And he was galled by how quickly even his own friends had jumped up to move chairs and tables, expecting him to duel at the drop of a pin.

Niko took out the car keys from his jacket pocket and held them up. He was indeed slightly inebriated, but not so much that he wasn't able to think clearly or had a strong enough excuse not to accept the challenge. "Kitu, you know what you need more than a broken face? A new car. That piece of junk you drive has got to be twenty years old. Isn't it your ma's old two-door Tezzo?" Niko jangled the keys. "I'll tell you what," he said, "you can have a clean-bladed duel, or you can have my car. It's a Roewolfe SX Coupe, only two years old. My parents gave it to me when I graduated from the Academy. It's sitting out in the parking lot right now." He tossed the car keys onto the table. They skidded a little and came to rest between the two young men.

The entire pub had gone silent. Kitu looked from Niko to the keys and back again. "You're joking."

Niko shrugged and gestured at the keys. "Take them," he said. "We'll agree I've paid for insulting you, and you'll get a piece of Kaul property without any blood loss or broken bones."

One of Niko's friends said, uncomfortably, "Um, Niko-jen, are you sure you want to do this? I mean, it doesn't seem right. Why don't you wait until tomorrow and see if you're both ready to fight the duel then." Several others murmured agreement. No one was sure if what Niko was doing went against aisho per se, but it certainly was not in accordance with dueling custom of any sort.

Niko said, "What's your decision, Kitu?"

Kitu's face went through a series of contortions. His brows drew together, his nose wrinkled, his lips twitched and twisted. He picked up the car keys and stood there tense for several seconds, expecting Niko to laugh at him for taking the joke seriously and then demand his car keys back. When this didn't happen, he seemed unable to put the keys back down on the table.

It was true what Niko had said, that Kitu's mother's old car was on its last legs and he didn't have the money for a new one. And it was also true that the outcome of any duel was uncertain; he might be injured, or lose his jade, or even be killed. He'd been willing to take the risk, but now he was not so sure. He had a feeling that he was being toyed with, but he was not sure what to do about it.

Kitu backed away slowly, his eyes still on Niko and his jade aura taut with incredulity. He backed up all the way to the door of the pub and exited the building. A minute later, everyone in the unnaturally quiet room heard Niko's Roewolfe start up and drive away.

A fit of laughter broke out then—less in mirth or amusement than disbelief and discomfort. Everyone felt as if Niko had somehow beaten and humiliated Kitu even though he'd given him an expensive car. But it had reflected badly on Niko as well, had shown him to be cruel in a very strange way. It was as if a man had stopped beside a homeless person and offered him a thousand dien to bark like a dog, and the poor bastard had done it.

By the time Niko got home that night, his uncle had heard of what happened. Word must've reached one of the clan's Fists, who had told the Horn, who had called the Pillar.

"What on earth is wrong with you?" Hilo demanded. "That boy challenged you fairly. It was bad enough that you refused to duel, but you made him *and* yourself look like idiots." Perhaps he expected Niko to say something, to defend himself, to act contrite or defiant, but Niko only stood there silently. Hilo lost his temper entirely. "You're a Kaul. You're the Pillar's son! Your father and your grandfather are curled up with shame in their godsdamned graves right now. Your mother and I didn't raise you to act so disgracefully."

"I didn't feel like fighting tonight," Niko grumbled. "I have a cold."

"If you felt too sick to defend your own jade, maybe you shouldn't have gone out in the first place," Hilo shouted. They were shut in the Pillar's study, but everyone in the house, and possibly the entire estate, could hear him. "No one is going to blame you for putting off a duel for a few days if you're getting over some bug. Instead, everyone is talking about how you gave away your car to avoid a challenge. How can you even call yourself a Green Bone?"

Niko watched his uncle struggle to come up with what sort of punishment would be adequate for such a failure of good sense. In the end, he made Niko strip off his shirt and kneel to receive a dozen lashes with a wooden rod. From now on, Niko would be required to do two extra training sessions each week with private coaches and Hilo would be attending the lessons once a month to gauge his nephew's martial development for himself. Also, Niko was cut off from family funds until he earned some more jade for himself in a respectable way, and of course he would not be getting a new car.

Niko left the room wincing from the welts on his back and stewing under a bitterly dark cloud. Ru had been waiting outside of the room to ask his father something, but after listening to his brother being censured so grievously, he decided against entering the study and went to the fridge to get Niko some ice for his injuries. Jaya, who was home from the Academy over the spring blossom long weekend, looked up briefly from the video game she was playing to say, "So you really fucked up, huh?"

In Niko's opinion, what was fucked up was that no one thought what he'd done was preferable, or even acceptable. Kitu *did* need a new car. Niko had willingly given his away as compensation for not providing the other man with the duel he wanted at that moment. What exactly, Niko fumed, was the problem? What use was all of his family's power and wealth, if it didn't give him the freedom to do as he wished with his own time and property? Of all the people in the world who wore jade, only Green Bones were expected to abide by strict rules that didn't even make sense.

Kitu's father brought the Roewolfe SX Coupe back to the Kaul estate the next day, with his shamefaced son in tow. The Pillar assured them that their profuse apologies were unnecessary. Niko, he explained, had been drunk and taken a joke too far. He certainly hadn't meant to embarrass Kitu or his family. "Young men do stupid things sometimes," Hilo had sighed in commiseration with Kitu's father.

After leaving Mera's apartment, Niko reported to Lott Jin at the Plum Bun, a bakery in the Forge owned by a Lantern Man of the clan.

Between the time it closed to customers in the afternoon and when the bakers came to work in the early hours of the following morning, the bakery was a meeting location, one of dozens throughout the city where Fists could convene with their Fingers. Niko wished he'd eaten something at Mera's after all; the pervasive scent of bread and sweet cakes made his mouth water. Two of Lott's other Green Bones were already there when Niko arrived. Kenjo was dark and compact and an expert when it came to guns and cars. Like Niko, he was a first-rank Finger and would soon be up for promotion to Fist. Sim was two and a half months out of the Academy, with three stones of graduation jade and the twitchy, puffed-up energy of a gamecock at its first fight.

Niko expected the three of them would be assigned to patrol the Forge, where there'd been a recent spate of violence between Uwiwan and barukan youth street gangs. To his surprise, Lott Jin said, "I hope you're all hungry to wet your blades tonight. We're acting on a tip about a couple of arms smugglers who sold a hundred military-grade Ankev rifles to the Clanless Future Movement before the Janloon bombing. The information came from one of our White Rats, but it leads into the Stump, and there are outstanding arrest warrants. So, it's a three-ring."

They all groaned. A "three-ring" had become the colloquial term on the military side of the clan for a situation requiring the involvement of both the No Peak and Mountain clans as well as the Janloon police. In the relentless campaign to root out and destroy anti-clan elements, three-ring operations had become common. Green Bones hated them. The clans traditionally exercised control over their own districts and kept out of each other's territory. It was a time-honored tactic for criminals to escape across territorial borders to evade Green Bones, and an equally long-standing tradition for Fists and Fingers to exchange information and favors with counterparts in rival clans, even during war, even when their leaders were mortal enemies. An arsonist who set fire to a Mountain property would be caught by No Peak and handed over in exchange for a shine dealer who plied his trade in Coinwash but had escaped to Fishtown. The Janloon police handled everything that fell below clan notice—petty crime, the average murder or armed robbery, traffic infractions—and were grudgingly accustomed to working under the influence of both major clans as well as cleaning up after them. Everyone liked it that way, even the criminals.

After the Janloon bombing, however, the eradication of anti-clan extremism became the top national priority. The Clanless Future Movement's armed uprising had been dramatic and frightening, but swiftly crushed. The Royal Council promptly banned the terrorist group and urged the clans and the police to coordinate their efforts to a far greater extent than before. Niko's family would never see Ayt Mada as anything but the bitterest enemy, and on a national and international level, the contest for jade, business, and political power continued unabated between the Mountain and No Peak. But the streets of Janloon were the domain of the Horn. Juen Nu and Aben Soro were pragmatic men, loyal to their clans but not members of the Kaul and Ayt families. Decades of clan rivalry, while not set aside, were relegated below the need for day-to-day cooperation against the threat of clanless agitators.

The efforts were paying off. In recent years, thousands of CFM members and supporters had been arrested or killed. No one liked three-rings, but it seemed they were here to stay. Lott Jin passed around several black-and-white photographs of the two arms dealers walking down the street, entering or exiting buildings, talking to people. "Take a good look. Tonight they're making a sale out of a hideout on Banya Street. We're going in with three of the Mountain's people."

Niko was the last to study the photographs. One of the arms dealers was Kekonese, the other was an Uwiwan. Banya Street was in the middle of a crowded Uwiwan immigrant neighborhood in the Stump. As if reading Niko's thoughts, or merely Perceiving his unease, Lott cautioned them all, "It's on unfamiliar turf for us, and there'll be a lot of people around. If we fuck up, it means problems between Juen-jen and Aben-jen. That means problems for me, which means problems for you. If there's a mess, let the Mountain handle it; it's their territory."

Lott flicked open a lighter and burned the photographs. They would need to identify the targets from memory and ensure they were captured or killed. Simply handing the photos to the Mountain and trusting them to do the deed was out of the question. Information gleaned from the images—when and where they were taken, at what angle, from what distance—might compromise the identity of a valuable White Rat, one the Mountain would happily find and kill if they could, since the spy was no doubt also providing information to No Peak about the Mountain's activities.

They drove in Lott's savagely beautiful red Lumezza FT Scorpion and parked near the fish head—the oddly shaped intersection of Way Street and Magnolia Avenue that sat on the clan border between the poor neighborhoods of Coinwash and Fishtown. The men got out of the car and waited. The city had been damp with Northern Sweat all week, but earlier in the evening the clouds had dissolved and it didn't look as if it would rain further. Niko scratched at his itching back.

Sim came up to him. "Niko-jen, I was wondering…" He rubbed the side of his acne-scarred face nervously. "My little niece, the one who's been in the hospital… Her birthday is coming up. She's a huge Janloon Spirits relayball fan, and I know that the clan has stadium boxes. I was told that you have to be second-rank Fist or above to get on the waitlist, but do you think there's *any* chance, if it's no trouble…"

Niko shrugged. "I can ask my uncle. Maybe there's room to squeeze a couple more people into the box at the next game."

Sim's face split in a huge grin. "It would mean Heaven and earth to her. I'd be eternally grateful if the Pillar made an exception. Of course, I understand if it's not possible." He touched his forehead. "Thank you, Niko-jen."

It occurred to Niko minutes later that he should've asked Sim his niece's name, how old she was, how long she'd been a relayball fan. Get to know his fellow Fingers, the men he fought alongside, who might one day save his life, or rise to be his most dependable Fists when he became Pillar.

His uncle wouldn't have even had to think about it. It was Kaul

Hilo's great talent. He could have a single ordinary conversation with a man and make him loyal for life. Niko's mother would not only ask the name of Sim's niece, she would remember her birthday and send her a Janloon Spirits jersey the following year. Both Ru and Jaya would've easily come up with *something* more to say.

Such behavior did not come naturally to Niko. The tending of relationships and influence, the leading of men. Much of the time, he preferred to be alone, and he especially disliked being forced into the social spotlight. He didn't extend or accept trust easily. He had close friends such as the Juen twins and his cousin Maik Cam, and he didn't think of himself as unfriendly, but many of the classmates and fellow Fingers who'd tried to get close to him over the years had found the task difficult. Mera was only the latest example.

A few days after Niko had been punished for failing to duel Kitu, the Pillar had taken him out for breakfast, just the two of them. Hilo had cooled down by then and wanted to talk. "Niko-se," he sighed, "I'm hard on you only because I love you. When the time comes for you to lead the clan, I want you to be well prepared, much more than I was. Everything you do now, even as a Finger, is a bit of a picture you're filling in about yourself and the family."

Niko hadn't pointed out to his uncle that it seemed the picture was already very much filled in, and his job was to fit himself into it. Sometimes, to his shame, he even envied Ru for being a stone-eye and Jaya for being a girl—at least *they* had other options. He didn't dare to admit these feelings to his uncle.

Lott Jin checked his watch and scowled. Anyone who worked under Juen Nu was accustomed to timeliness. Niko studied the First Fist, trying selfishly to figure out what made him exceptional, what had enabled him to climb above hundreds of other warriors in the clan. Jade ability was only part of the equation. Lott was certainly a strong Green Bone, and his skill with throwing knives was legendary, but there were others of equal or greater martial prowess. Nor was Lott the most well-liked of the senior Fists. At times, he could be pessimistic and confrontational, scornful in his criticisms and spare with praise. Yet, something about him had attracted the Pillar's attention years ago. Niko tried to find the right word. *Resolved.* Lott Jin seemed to have shaped himself around being a Green Bone of the clan. Some people simply lived by following their natural inclinations. Others decided what they wished to be and then made themselves that way.

Three metallic green Torroyo RP800 motorcycles drove through the fish head intersection and pulled up around the Lumezza. The lead Mountain Fist got off his bike and strode toward Lott Jin. An unpleasant jolt of recognition stiffened Niko's spine as he straightened away from the car. It had been several years since he'd laid eyes on Ayt Atosho in person, although he'd seen him on television a few times. In recent years, the man's good looks had settled, like a clay sculpture after firing. Lines of small jade studs pierced over both eyebrows drew attention to his heavy-lidded eyes. He wore a traditional fitted leather vest over a bold red shirt with jade cuff links. Ayt Ato was a picture of urban Green Bone style.

Niko had heard it said jokingly that every woman in the Mountain clan was in love with Ayt Ato. Sadly for them, Ayt Mada had purportedly forbidden her twenty-seven-year-old nephew from dating until he completed his university degree, which he'd been working toward on a part-time basis for the past six years.

"Lott-jen," Ayt Ato called out as he strolled toward them. "I'm told you'll soon be the Horn of No Peak."

"That's for the Pillar to decide," the First Fist replied curtly. Lott's father had been murdered and beheaded by the Mountain many years ago. Necessity compelled Lott to work with Green Bones on the other side, but he was never friendly toward anyone in the Mountain clan.

Ayt Ato's gaze drifted past Lott and fell on Niko. "Kaul-jen." Ayt Ato's aura was at odds with his physical confidence—tight and wary, like a cloak worn over the shoulders.

"Ayt-jen," Niko said.

It was the first time the two of them had stood before each other and exchanged so much as a word. An odd hesitation stretched across the moment. Niko became acutely aware of the other jade auras around him, the pressure of them against his Perception. He thought he ought to do or say something subtle but powerful in that instant to show himself an equal to this rival he'd never met or asked for. Perhaps doing so would be easier if he could muster some personal hate for the man instead of merely a vague resentment toward his existence. Instead, all Niko could think of was how obvious it was that he was the younger, less heavily jaded Green Bone, not as well dressed, and merely a subordinate Finger, not a leader with his own warriors.

Ayt Ato broke the awkwardness by introducing the other Mountain Green Bones who'd come up behind him. "This is Koben Ashi," he said, indicating the taller one, son of the late Koben Yiro. "And Sando Kin." Another of his cousins, by marriage of his mother's sister.

Lott made perfunctory introductions on the No Peak side, then confirmed the details of the mission and officially asked for permission to enter Mountain territory. Ayt Ato granted it. He glanced at Niko. "Should we get going, then?"

The Mountain Green Bones got back onto their motorcycles and escorted the Lumezza into the Stump. Lott glanced over at Niko as he drove, perhaps sensing the agitation in his aura. "I didn't know it would be Ayt Ato and the Kobens," said the First Fist.

"It doesn't matter," Niko said, too quickly.

Lott frowned, though not without sympathy. "You're right; it doesn't. So don't let it get to you. We're all on the same side tonight."

Niko decided this was his uncle's fault. Not the encounter with Ayt Ato, but the fact that he was in this situation at all. The Pillar had ordered Juen and Lott to give him more opportunities to earn green and prove himself. Niko fingered his pistol and talon knife, then the jade beads around his throat. He hated surprises that forced him to react quickly. He liked to think about things by himself, sometimes for a long while, before making decisions.

The address on Banya Street belonged to a pool hall, sandwiched between a barbershop and an adult video store. The name Tialuhiya Nights blinked in red neon over darkened windows. "Get ready," Lott said.

Lott roared his sports car up to the front entrance while Ayt Ato and his cousins swerved their bikes into the narrow alley behind the rear doors. Immediately, two sentries posted on the sidewalk bolted into the pool hall like rabbits into a warren. The instant the No Peak men were out of the car, a volley of gunfire erupted from the front of the building, shattering the street-facing windows and sending bystanders screaming and running for cover.

Niko fell to a crouch and launched an instinctive rising Deflection. It overlapped with Kenjo's wave and the interference sent up a vertical blast of force that hurled bullets upward and tore clothes off the lines that stretched between balconies in the narrow confines of the avenue. A stray shot shattered one of the Lumezza's rear taillights.

"Sons of dogfucking *bitches*." Lott Jin unleashed a massive Deflection that swept through the broken front windows, sending glass flying back into the pool hall in a maelstrom. Both of the visible shooters inside were knocked staggering. The First Fist strode across the sidewalk, whipping throwing knives one after the other, half a dozen of them, until the sheath strapped to the small of his back was empty.

Niko and the other Fingers rushed through the ruined front entry on Lott's heels. One gunman was already dead, a knife protruding from his throat and another from his left eye socket. The other was lying on the ground, gurgling, hands clamped around the slim blade in his chest. Kenjo nudged his head over with a toe to get a closer look at his face, then put a bullet between his eyes. Neither of the men were the arms dealers from the photos.

A dozen people were huddled against the walls or under the pool tables, including the bartender and two staff members. Their thick, sour fear crowded Niko's sense of Perception and heightened his racing adrenaline, but no spikes of murderous intent shot through the thick haze. Sim shouted, "Everyone stay where you are! Don't get in the way and you won't be hurt."

Kenjo tilted his head. "In the back."

"Niko, take the lead," Lott ordered.

Niko swallowed as he drew his talon knife and moved quickly but cautiously toward the rear of the building. His shoes crunched on broken glass. Lott was right behind him, Kenjo and Sim on either side, but he still felt like a student from the back of the classroom suddenly called up to the blackboard to face a question alone. The gems embedded in the hilt of his talon knife streamed hot, tense jade energy into his body. He could feel its bright currents swirling in his gut, thrumming up and down his arms and legs, swimming through his head. He held the energy coiled, ready to Steel or Deflect, to spring into motion with Strength and Lightness. Perception was Niko's weakest discipline, but he strained it forward and picked out four men waiting behind the closed door, their energies burning an alarming, murderous crimson.

He tensed. This was it. *Move.*

A tremendous crashing noise exploded ahead of him. Niko launched himself forward and kicked the door open; it splintered under his Strength. At first all he could comprehend was a blur of fighting—gunfire, screaming, raging jade auras. A man with a gun ran wild-eyed toward him. Before Niko could react, an exiting bullet opened a hole in the man's forehead, pitching him toward the floor.

Lott shoved Niko aside with one arm—to protect him, or simply because he was in the way. The First Fist swept the room with the other arm extended, his Ankev pistol raised and jade aura blazing like a gasoline fire.

Then he lowered his weapon and stepped inside.

Niko pushed himself off the wall. The gunfire had fallen silent. The only sound that remained was an animal-like moaning from a man lying on the floor, clutching his stomach. Three other men were on the ground, two of them dead. Ayt Ato and his cousins were stalking through the room. Sando Kin was grimacing and clutching a bloodied arm, but his injury didn't seem serious. Through the rear door that the Kobens had torn from its hinges, a breeze from the alley outside flowed into the building and began to disperse the smell of gunpowder.

Koben Ashi walked around the grisly scene, shrugged, and tossed a smirk at the staring No Peak Green Bones. "Next time, we'll try to leave a few of them for you."

Sim retorted, "We took out the trash in the front, you smug ass," but it wasn't said with venom and both men laughed. Niko stood rooted in place, talon knife still in hand.

The room contained stacked plastic supply bins, a water cooler, a fax machine, and a table with an open briefcase and several stacks of cash, with more bills scattered across the floor by the violence. Three hard-sided metal cases sat on the ground. Lott pulled one of them onto the table and tore off the lock. Kenjo looked over Lott's shoulder and made a noise of appreciation. Cushioned inside the case were two Fullerton P1 carbines with spare magazines and ammunition.

Ayt Ato caught Niko's eye. "Kaul-jen," he said, gesturing at the prone men on the ground. "Would you be so good as to tell us which of these men we came here for?"

Lott's eyes narrowed at the tone of polite condescension in Ayt Ato's voice, but Niko ignored it. He took a close look, comparing the faces to the images he'd seen in the photographs. "Those two," he said. One of their targets was already dead. He'd been hard to recognize at first, on account of his shaved head and part of his jaw having been blown away. The other dealer, the Uwiwan, was the gut-shot one flopping on the floor, his dark face contorted in agony. "Die screaming, you miserable whoreson curs," he wheezed, trying to sit up. "Fuck every last one of you all the way to *hell*." He cursed them in Uwiwan and Kekonese, spitting every profanity he knew in both languages as blood saturated his shirt and pants.

Ayt Ato edged his shiny black shoes away from the expanding pool on the concrete and motioned to his cousin, Koben Ashi, who bent down and opened the man's throat from behind with a talon knife.

Ayt Ato turned to Niko. "It's not so hard for us to work together after all. Who says we have to follow the examples of our elders?" The man's arresting eyes were guileless, though a touch of wary curiosity turned up the corners of his shapely mouth.

Niko watched the man walk out of the building to meet the police, who'd arrived as instructed, right on time to avoid getting in the way during the fighting but swiftly enough to secure the area, clean up the scene, and arrest any surviving accomplices. Reporters in news trucks arrived seconds later. They pressed in around the Mountain Green Bones, taking photographs and video footage of the confiscated money and weapons being handed over to the police.

A few members of the media spotted the No Peak men exiting the pool hall and hurried toward them, eager to be the first to snap photographs of Kaul Niko and Ayt Ato in the same image. Lott Jin shot them a warning glare. "Not a chance," he snarled, "unless you want to take it up with the Pillar of No Peak." That made them back off. Kaul Hilo was well known for being intolerant of the press following anyone in the family, especially Wen and Ru, for security reasons, but more generally because he thought they were leeches and disdained the Kobens for pandering to them.

"Let's go," Lott ordered his Fingers. "We're done here."

Kenjo grumbled, "We found those crooks and the Mountain takes all the credit? I don't think Ayt Ato even drew his weapon. What do *we* get out of it?"

Lott turned on the Finger with a black glare. "We kept those foreign arms dealers from putting Fullerton machine guns into the hands of clanless scum, *that's* what we get. Have you forgotten that extremists nearly killed the Pillar and still want to destroy the country? We helped the Mountain in the Stump today, so Aben Soro will do the same for us in one of our territories in the future. Do you remember what it means to be a Green Bone, or do you think we're out here to get on television?"

Kenjo dropped his gaze, chastised. "Forgive me for thinking so selfishly, Lott-jen."

Lott spoke to Niko with blunt reassurance. "Don't worry about what happened back there. You'll have plenty of other chances, Niko."

Niko wished Lott hadn't said anything. But now he knew it was true, that it hadn't only been in his head. Everyone really *was* waiting for him to distinguish himself, to make as much of an impression as Ayt Ato. Tonight might've been that night, a moment to repair his reputation after the incident with Kitu, but it hadn't turned out that way.

Three other Mountain Green Bones had arrived to help the Kobens, who were rounding up half a dozen civilians. Four men and two women were kneeling on the glass-strewn sidewalk in front of the ruined Tialuhiya Nights pool hall. The bartender and two staff members were among them. Some of the people in the line were weeping or pleading with the Green Bones, others were quiet and resigned, heads bowed. Sando Kin, his wounded arm roughly bandaged, emerged from the neighboring barbershop and deposited the protesting barber on the ground next to the others.

Ayt Ato broke off talking to the press but glanced over his shoulder to make sure they kept watching him as he walked down the row of kneeling Uwiwans. Ato looked at each frightened face with concern and disappointment. At last, he stopped and declared in a loud, clear voice, "You all worked in the pool hall or in the neighboring shops. You knew the men we came for tonight were criminals and enemies of the clan. If you deny it, every Green Bone here will Perceive your lies."

An interpreter supplied by the police department translated the Fist's words into Uwiwan through a bullhorn, so all the nearby residents and bystanders could hear. "You could've gone to any Finger with this information, but you chose to shelter these clanless dogs in your neighborhood. You're not in the lawless Uwiwa Islands anymore, where there are no consequences to your actions."

Lott muttered under his breath, "Here we go with the drama." He walked back toward the Lumezza, examined the broken taillight, and spat on the ground in disgust. He got into the car. Sim and Kenjo followed.

"Extremist elements are like cancer cells in a body. They have to be identified and cut out, and those who feed the cancer have to be held to account." Ato must've received extensive speech training because he was nearly as good an orator as his aunt Mada. His smooth face was serious and determined. Every eye and camera followed him hungrily. Earlier in the evening, Niko had wished he could muster more personal dislike for the man. Now he found it easier to do so.

"If I committed an offense against my clan, I'd cut off my ear and carry that disgraceful scar with me for the rest of my life," Ato went on. "Anyone who supports anti-clan activities, through action or inaction, should face their neighbors every day with the shame of their wrongdoing, so they're always reminded of the need to better themselves."

Koben Ashi held a short steel pipe. As the police translator repeated Ayt Ato's words in Uwiwan, Koben started up a butane torch and held the end of the pipe in the flame until the metal glowed red. Sando Kin held down the wide-eyed, struggling owner of the barbershop as Koben pressed the end of the hot pipe to the man's cheek. The barber shrieked loud enough to waken the dead. The nauseating smell of scorched flesh hit Niko's nostrils. When Sando released the man, he dropped to the sidewalk, curled in pain, a perfect circle burned into the side of his face. Koben Ashi reheated the end of the pipe with the torch and moved on to the next person.

Niko opened the passenger side door and got into the Lumezza. Lott Jin's knuckles were white around the steering wheel and his face was a stiff mask. The First Fist was a fierce fighter but the sight of cruelty against helpless creatures could set him off. Niko had heard a rumor that Lott had once beaten a fellow Fist for kicking a dog. Lott started the car and threw it into gear, then cursed as he was forced to edge slowly around all the other vehicles parked in the street.

A few reporters from the news trucks jogged after the Lumezza. "Kaul-jen," one of them called out to Niko, "will your family follow the Mountain clan's lead and brand clanless sympathizers caught in No Peak territories?"

"Don't answer that," Lott ordered Niko, finally clearing the jam and turning off Banya Street. He hit the gas and they sped out of the Stump, back toward No Peak turf. "That goes for all of you. There are four people who can make public statements on behalf of the clan—the Pillar, the Weather Man, the Horn, and the Sealgiver. You're not any of them."

"Neither is Ayt Ato," Niko observed. He was angry, but the feeling was indistinct and shapeless, sitting in the pit of his stomach, inside that green shell of himself, now filled with black doubt.

Lott Jin snorted. "Ayt Ato wears the Ayt name like a crown, but he's the prince of the Koben family. Prince of a troop of monkeys."

Niko didn't say anything further, but he thought, in a jarring revelation, *Yes, that's it. Ayt Ato knows he's a prince.* Lott Jin and Ayt Ato had one important thing in common—they understood who they were supposed to be.

Niko didn't feel that way about himself. He had too many questions; he saw too many things that made him uncertain. He didn't see how he was qualified to be the future Pillar of No Peak for any reason other than bloodline, nor why he should feel compelled to accept that destiny, when anyone with an ounce of logic would know that heredity was not enough. He often wondered what he was missing, what he didn't know, what other possibilities lay behind doors that had been summarily closed for him when he was too young to know they existed.

Niko leaned his head against the window and watched the streets of Janloon pass by, filled with vague but intense curiosity and quiet, sullen despair.

CHAPTER

32

Passages

the nineteenth year, eighth month

The Temple of Divine Return was full of people, almost all of them Green Bones of the Mountain clan. All the cushions were already occupied; Shae slipped into the back row and knelt on the floor. She was wearing a broad summer hat and sunglasses so the lower-ranked clan members kneeling nearest to her at the back of the sanctum didn't recognize her, and there were so many jade auras in the building that she expected one more to go unnoticed. Even so, across all the rows of heads, she caught sight of Ayt Madashi at the very front. As her gaze landed on Ayt's back, the Pillar turned slowly over her shoulder to look into the crowd of faces behind her. Perhaps Shae only imagined that Ayt had Perceived her entrance, that with narrowed eyes she was trying to spot Shae in the shadowed corner of this room where they had faced each other so fatefully in times past. Ayt's face was dusted white and a white silk scarf was tied around her neck, hiding the ugly scar that Shae knew to be underneath.

Ayt Mada turned back toward the front and took up the chant of the penitents.

Shae whispered along with everyone else in the temple, reciting the Scripture of Return's promise that virtuous souls would one day ascend to godliness and reunite with their divine kin in Heaven.

Perhaps she should not be here. She was not a member of the Mountain or even a respectful outsider. She had not known or loved Nau Suenzen. She'd been his enemy and would've sent him to the afterlife herself if given the chance during his tenure as Horn. Nau Suen did not exemplify the four Divine Virtues of humility, compassion, courage, and goodness. He'd been the Ayt family's most loyal and cunning assassin for fifty years; he'd slit the throats of Shotarian generals, of Ayt Mada's brother Eodo, and all the men of the Ven family. And Shae was certain he'd murdered Chancellor Son Tomarho. After all that, he'd retired and succumbed not to the blade but to respiratory illness at the age of seventy, dying peacefully in his sleep despite all the lives he'd ended so violently.

Shae was not sure he deserved any prayers, but then again, she did not know who did. She prayed for the souls of men like her grandfather, and Yun Dorupon, and Maik Kehn, and surely if it were her or Hilo in the coffin there would be people who would judge them no more deserving of the gods' recognition than Nau Suen. Even though Nau had been her enemy, she could not forget the look in his aged eyes that afternoon in Anden's apartment as he held Ayt Mada in his thin arms. Shae had never before seen Ayt Mada bow in the temple, but now the Pillar of the Mountain touched her head to the ground, resting it there as the penitents raised their voices.

I hope you're in pain. It gave Shae a certain savage pleasure to think that Ayt could feel loss, that she could mourn the death of a friend. Otherwise, it wasn't fair; the scales could never be remotely balanced between them. "Let the gods recognize him," she echoed in a murmur. And why shouldn't they? On the day of the Return, the gods would never be able to sort the deserving from the undeserving without breaking apart families. They should recognize everyone, flawed as they were, imperfect in the Divine Virtues—or recognize no one at all.

Shae rose and shuffled out of the memorial service at the head of the exiting crowd. Dozens of cars filled the parking lot and every available spot along the streets. Private drivers and taxis were pulling up at the entrance. Shae walked away from the scene and stood on the street corner, watching. Nau Suen's death, although undramatic, was still newsworthy. Journalists and cameramen waited outside, fanning themselves in the cloying heat, trying to catch senior members of the Mountain clan as they left the temple.

A flurry of activity and conversation erupted as Ayt Ato exited the temple amid a small throng of his relatives. Clan members saluted him and approached to offer condolences even though the young man had no relationship to Nau Suenzen and had been a student at Wie Lon, not even a Finger yet, when Nau had retired. *He's so young*, Shae thought. Then she remembered with a start that she'd been the same age when she'd become Weather Man of No Peak.

A reporter asked Ato a question, and the accompanying cameraman focused upon the Fist's handsome face. "Nau Suenzen was a role model for me, almost like a second grandfather," Ato avowed. "He was full of energy and will, right up until the very end, as green in body and soul as Baijen himself."

Ayt Mada emerged from the temple. The Pillar of the Mountain was as straight and commanding as ever, but walking more slowly than she used to. Shae wondered if it was due to grief, or if the knife that Ven's daughter had plunged into her neck had done some irreparable physical harm that she would never make public. Shae pulled down the brim of her hat, not that it would make any difference to Ayt's ability to Perceive her, but the woman did not so much as glance in Shae's direction. She likewise ignored all the clan loyalists who pressed in to pay their respects and offer condolences. Instead, she laid a swift glance of contempt on the scene around Ayt Ato, then said something curt that was too quiet for Shae to hear.

The young man stiffened. Shae couldn't see the expression on his face as he turned away from the remaining reporters and followed his aunt obediently toward the waiting cars. Aben Soro jerked his head in signal to two of his Green Bones, who moved to politely but firmly disperse the media and prevent them from following. Ayt Mada got into the front of her silver Stravaconi Primus S6. Ayt Ato got into the back. In minutes, the lingering crowd in front of the temple was gone, leaving the ordinary bustle of a summer afternoon to fill the streets still littered with debris from last week's parade and fireworks. Heroes Day. Truly a fitting time for an old war veteran like Nau Suen to make his exit from the world.

Shae hailed a taxi and asked the driver to take her back to the Kaul estate. She wondered if Ayt Mada had put her nephew in his place because she considered his actions shallow and unbecoming of a future Pillar. Ayt knew how to use the media, feeding it information that elevated the Mountain and was damaging to her enemies, but she didn't pander to the press or offer vain sound bites.

The Kobens, on the other hand, showed no compunction about appearing on talk shows and engineering photo opportunities. Those who'd believed the family's star would fall after the death of the outspoken Koben Yiro had not accounted for his widow riding her husband's martyrdom into public prominence and onto a seat in the Royal Council.

"It's comforting to think that Ayt Mada probably finds Koben Tin Bett as obnoxious as I do," Wen had commented with a surprising amount of acidity when she heard the news of the election victory. It seemed unlikely to Shae that Ayt Mada could feel jealous or threatened by the popularity of the Koben family, none of them with a fraction of her ability or fame as a Green Bone leader. Then again, she surely hadn't forgotten that when the city had thought her dead, the Kobens had rushed to make a statement before her body had been found.

The taxi arrived at the gates of the Kaul estate. When Shae walked into the Weather Man's house, Tia ran into her arms, smearing finger paint all over Shae's blouse and skirt. "Ma, you're home! I'm drawing pictures with Da."

Shae let her daughter lead her into the kitchen, where poster paper had been unrolled and taped down on the kitchen table. Colorful, child-sized handprints and much larger adult ones had been turned into butterflies, birds, and other animals. "These small ones are mine and the big ones are Da's," Tia pronounced.

"I was wondering how your hands got so big," Shae teased.

"Silly, Ma." Tia laughed. "Jaya says you're not funny, but I think you're funny."

Woon came over and shook his head apologetically at the sight of Shae's stained clothes. "It's washable paint," he said. "I figured the piglet would need a bath before dinner anyway."

When Woon had retired last year from his role as the clan's Seal-giver and passed the position onto Terun Bin, Shae had worried her husband was making a mistake. She was skeptical that a man who'd been one of the highest-ranked Green Bones on Ship Street could possibly be happy finger painting with a five-year-old and packing snacks. But Woon had seemed certain in his decision. "I've spent many years being ordered around by a tough little woman and managing thankless details," he reminded her. "I'm well prepared for this job."

"That's unfair of you," Shae protested. "I'm hardly *little*." In truth, she was jealous of all the time her husband and daughter spent together. Woon had waited for children for so long that he relished being a father, and the reality was that he hadn't recovered as well as Hilo had from the Janloon bombing. He was deaf on one side and walked with a slight limp, and Shae knew that as stoic and humble a man as her husband appeared to be, those things hurt his pride and had played some part in his decision to retire from the demands of clan life sooner.

Woon had not, however, stopped paying attention to issues affecting the clan and regularly discussing them with her. "Have you seen the news about the Lybon Act?" Without waiting for her answer, he picked up the remote and turned on the television in the living room. KNB's commentators were discussing the passage of an unprecedented international accord establishing ethical guidelines for military use of bioenergetic jade. Eighty-five nations, led by the Republic of Espenia and including Kekon, had met at a convention in Stepenland to condemn and outlaw breeding programs, child military camps, forced addiction, and ingestion of ground jade.

Shae wetted a kitchen towel and wiped the paint from Tia's hands as she watched the news. The Lybon Accord followed a comprehensive report released last year by the Espenian military on Ygutan's nekolva program, based largely on firsthand accounts provided by Ygutanian defectors, most notably a former nekolva agent referred to only as Agent M. "So the ROE has convinced most of the world to sanction their enemies," Shae said.

Woon carefully removed his daughter's artwork from the kitchen table and set it aside to dry. "Bringing down the nekolva program is a good thing." Stories had circulated in Kekon for years, of women from Abukei tribes and low-income areas being lured or trafficked into forced surrogacy on the Orius continent. "But the Espenians are denying justice to Kekon."

"Something they'll never acknowledge," Shae pointed out bitterly. "And we have no hard evidence to prove them wrong." Although it was widely believed that the Janloon bombing had relied on foreign support, no one from the clans or law enforcement had been able to pin down proof that Ygutan was involved, nor find those who were responsible. Several Clanless Future Movement members had revealed under interrogation that a foreigner named Molovni was a key figure in the CFM, but this Molovni, if he existed, was a ghost.

Shae was certain he hadn't vanished into thin air. The ROE had either captured him or offered him sanctuary in exchange for defecting. Molovni, or "Agent M," as he was now facelessly known to the world, was sitting in Espenian custody and would never face justice for murdering hundreds of Kekonese citizens.

The KNB news desk reported that the Ygutanian Directorate had issued a defiant statement characterizing the Lybon Act as disingenuous Espenian fearmongering. The call for Ygutan to submit to international inspection of its nekolva program was a bald-faced attempt to impinge on its sovereignty, the officials in Dramsk declared. A commercial came on and Woon turned off the television.

Shae rinsed the towel in the sink, staring at the muddy water as it swirled down the drain. "Papi, was I wrong to have ever dealt with the Espenians?" He was the one person to whom she voiced her worst doubts. "I've been attacked for it so often over the years, but I always thought I was doing the right thing for the clan in the long run. I'm not so sure anymore."

She'd tried for so many years to walk No Peak down a tightrope, benefiting from foreigners without falling prey to them. But ever since the bombing, it seemed to Shae the country was spinning in a storm, manipulated and abused by forces within and without.

Woon took the towel from her hands and blotted the biggest stain on her shirt. "Foreigners have always come for Kekon and for our jade," he reminded her solemnly. "They would be here whether you were Weather Man or not. No one else could've done a better job of handling them with No Peak's interests at heart."

"Ma, look, Ma!" Tia interrupted, grabbing Shae's hand and trying to drag her over to the tea party she'd set up for her dolls.

"I'm sorry, I can't play right now, Tia."

"You have to go to work *again*?" Tia complained, sticking out her lips in a pout.

"Only for an hour or so," Shae told her. Despite longing for more time to spend with her family, Shae sometimes wondered if she was even qualified to be Tia's mother. She was confident she could face nearly any situation on Ship Street, but she was hopeless at meeting the little girl's demands for friendship stories about every single one of her dolls. "You and Da are going to come over to the big house later, and we'll all have dinner together with some guests."

"Who're we having dinner with? Will there be any other kids?"

"Just Ru and Jaya," Shae said, although they hardly qualified. Jaya was already sixteen, almost a year-seven at the Academy, Ru was a year older than that, and sometimes Shae wondered if Niko had ever been a child at all. Tia had no siblings or cousins near her own age.

"They're big kids!" Tia objected.

"You're getting to be a big kid too."

Tia shook her head, wide-eyed. "I *never* want to be a big kid."

"You don't?" Shae exclaimed curiously. "Why not?"

The girl hugged Shae's legs anxiously. "Big kids have to learn to fight. When I fell down and got a nosebleed and cried, Jaya said I have to get used to blood. She says big kids don't cry when they get hurt."

Perhaps, Shae thought, it had not been a good idea to ask her niece to babysit. Jaya was utterly without tact. Shae crouched down and pulled her daughter into her arms. "Not all big kids are the same. But if you're worried about it, you can stay a little kid for as long as you like. I won't mind."

Shae changed into clean clothes and walked over to the main house. Ru was doing homework at the dining table, chewing the end of his pencil. Koko lay sprawled under the table at his feet, gnawing a rubber toy. "Hey, Aunt Shae," Ru said, glancing up for a moment before returning his attention to his textbooks. He was in his last year of high school and only a few months away from final exams.

Wen stepped out of the kitchen and pulled the pencil away from his mouth. "Don't do that," she admonished. "It's a bad habit that makes you look weak and nervous." Peering into the kitchen, where her mother and the housekeepers were working, Shae could see some of the dishes being prepared: fish in milk broth, cold sliced pork with pepper sauce, greens with garlic, fried noodles. "Gods forbid our guests think we aren't good enough patrons to feed them well," Wen said. Shae, who hadn't experienced a clean house since Tia was born, noticed jealously that the main residence appeared immaculate. Fresh-cut dancing star lilies, symbolizing friendship, scented the foyer in elegantly tall vases. Wen claimed to have never wanted nor expected the public role of the Pillar's wife, but she'd nonetheless made herself an accomplished hostess.

"The Pillar and the Horn are in the study," she told Shae.

Shae walked in to find Hilo and Juen in serious conversation. "Lott Jin's changed a lot since he was a Finger," the Horn was saying. "He's diligent and fair with everyone, maybe a little too moody at times and soft at others, but no one doubts his greenness. He takes great care of his mother and siblings. My only small concern is that he doesn't have a wife or children, which seems a bit unlucky at his age." Juen blew out a thoughtful breath. "As a First Fist, however, he's been excellent, and when it comes to the job of the Horn, he's the best person for it. It's your decision, Hilo-jen, but he's who I would trust."

Promoting someone into the highest circle of leadership in the clan was tantamount to making them an honorary member of the Kaul family. They would be living on the estate, having dinner in the house, brought into the closest confidence. It was a decision that needed to be made with great consideration, and the person's character was as important as their capability.

"If you decide you're not ready to retire after all, just say so," Hilo said to Juen. "You're only forty-five."

"Forty-five is old for a Horn," Juen said ruefully. "Being on the greener side of the clan is like living in dog years, you know that, Hilo-jen. My wife and I had barely any time to ourselves when we were young, not with four children and the life of a Fist, so I always said I would make it up to her later on."

"Then of course you have to keep your promise," Hilo said with a sympathetic smile. "I've watched Lott Jin for years and I agree with all you've said. I'll name him as the new Horn at your retirement party." The Pillar glanced at Shae as she came in. "What took you so long?"

She hesitated to say she'd been at Nau's memorial service. When Hilo had heard of Nau's death he'd snorted. "Good riddance to that old snake. I never met a Horn I liked less. Not even Gont Asch, and that bastard killed a lot of my Fists and Fingers and nearly sent me to the grave. But at least he was up-front about it all. Nau Suen was creepy as fuck."

Instead of answering, Shae opened her purse and took out a padded square envelope. She handed it to Juen Nu. "The latest gift from our Espenian friends." Juen opened the envelope and took out a floppy disk.

"Espenian friendship," Hilo said with a grimace, "lasts about as long as a cheap hand job. Every time we try bringing up the issue of offshore mining, they tell us to go fuck ourselves. Then they turn around with a smile and say they want to help us."

Two ROE military intelligence officers had walked into the Weather Man's office six months after the Janloon bombing. They'd introduced themselves as agents Berglund and Galo and seated themselves in front of Shae's desk. The pale-haired one named Berglund said, "Ms. Kaul-jen, the Republic of Espenia stands firmly with Kekon in the fight against radical political terrorism."

His Keko-Espenian partner, Galo, removed an envelope from his briefcase and placed it on Shae's desk. "The Green Bone clans have been combating the threat with impressive speed and effectiveness, and we want to help in the effort by sharing our information on the Clanless Future Movement. Our superiors hope this intelligence will help you to dismantle the CFM."

"Why haven't you shared this with the Royal Council or the Kekonese military?" Shae asked the foreigners.

Galo leaned forward. "We have an established relationship with your clan. With Cormorant." She stiffened at the mention of the code name the Espenian military had given to her more than twenty years ago. "We trust *your* clan has no ties to Ygutanian interests." The same could not be said for the Mountain, which possessed both legitimate and illegitimate business interests in that country. The two men stood up to leave.

Shae put her hands on her desk and rose from her seat. "It's a shame," she said, her voice as flat as a sheet of ice, "that we didn't receive this information *before* hundreds of people lost their lives."

The men paused at her office door. Berglund glanced over his shoulder, his washed-out eyes unmoved. "The Janloon bombing was a terrible tragedy. We all wish it could've been prevented, but there's no reason to cast blame. What's important is that we prevent anything like it from happening again, wouldn't you agree?"

After that, information arrived every so often at the Weather Man's office. The floppy disks contained names of Clanless Future Movement members and affiliates, addresses of safe houses or meeting places, and the identity of individuals and criminal groups suspected to have supplied or aided the CFM. However, the Espenians were not entirely up-front. Some parts of the files were redacted, no doubt because they named Espenian agents. There was also never any mention of the Ygutanian nekolva, or a man named Molovni.

She passed the information she received on to Juen Nu, who combined it with knowledge gathered from his own impressive network of spies. When Juen had become the Horn, Shae had not considered him to be a leader with much personal presence compared to Hilo or Kehn. As it turned out, an operational mastermind was the perfect Horn for the times. Over sixteen years in the job—a longer tenure than any other Horn in No Peak history—Juen Nu had made the military side of the clan more nimble and responsive. He'd distributed responsibility, expanded the clan's technical capabilities, and vastly improved its network of informers. He was a key reason efforts to crush the clanless were going well. Prudent and unsentimental, he coordinated operations with the Mountain but never trusted them; he triple-checked everything himself. Aben Soro of the Mountain commanded more people and was a more visible Horn, but No Peak was more tightly run. Lott Jin would have a sizable shadow to fill.

Juen slipped the floppy disk back into the envelope. "The Espenians aren't giving us much of anything we don't already know these days. The early stuff was detailed and useful. It must've come from spies inside the CFM. Now it's mostly conjecture and weak links."

Shae said, "I'm still getting phone calls—from within the clan, from the press, and from our people in the Royal Council—asking about our stance on branding."

Juen snorted. "It's ineffective. More of a hollow publicity stunt than anything else."

Shae personally thought the practice, though popular, was cruel and pointless and usually directed at immigrants, but it was her job as Weather Man to point out the ramifications of every decision. "There are people who say we're not following the Mountain's policy because of pride or softness."

"Those people are shortsighted fools. Branding clanless sympathizers only makes it easier for them to find one another and gives them more reason to feel unified in their enmity toward society. And those who are wrongly branded are going to be driven into the Clanless Future Movement even if they weren't in it to begin with."

Hilo laced his hands behind his head, slouching into his armchair as he considered the issue. "Juen is the Horn. I trust his judgment. People who help the clanless should be punished, but there's no reason our Fists have to follow exactly what the Kobens do in Mountain territory." Juen nodded, satisfied by the verdict.

Shae sat down in the remaining empty armchair. She thought about what she'd seen earlier in the afternoon outside the Temple of Divine Return. "I doubt even Ayt Mada fully believes in the Kobens' methods," she mused. "She's partnered with barukan and Uwiwans and Ygutanians in the past. She's brought outsiders into the Mountain clan. She'll work with foreigners so long as doing so serves her goals, but the Koben family targets and opposes them on principle."

"Ato is a young and popular traditionalist," Juen pointed out. "Ayt Mada will be sixty in another couple of years and people will start wondering when she'll retire. If she's planning to name Ato her successor, she has to let him show some of his own strength." The Horn pursed his lips. "Maybe she's willing to let the Kobens have their way in certain things, even if it antagonizes some parts of her clan, so long as they continue to support her while they wait their turn."

"Even the biggest tigers grow old." Hilo took out his silver cigarette lighter and rolled it absently between his fingers. "But if the Kobens think Ayt Mada is going to hand leadership over to that pretty boy any time soon, they're deluded. The old bitch will be worse than Grandda—let the gods recognize him—hanging on to power until it's pried from their withered claws." He ignored Shae's remonstrative glare for his disrespect toward their grandfather. "Ayt's using the Kobens the way she uses everyone. Wiping out the clanless is the thing we can all agree on right now. But she won't let the Kobens' zeal endanger the Mountain's foreign businesses or barukan alliances. As long as she keeps her nephew waiting, she has them on a leash."

And thank the gods for that. Shae nursed the fear that a day would come when she would deeply regret saving Ayt Mada's life, but for now, she was grudgingly glad their old enemy lived and continued to rule the Mountain. Wiping out the CFM was one thing, but the Kobens epitomized a broader reactionary backlash that, if unchecked, would lead to equally extreme policies—closing trade, expelling foreigners, more draconian measures against anything perceived as anti-clan thinking.

There was a knock on the door of the study. Wen came in with her hair pinned up in an elegant coil and wearing a high-collared forest-green dress that made Shae abruptly self-conscious about not changing into something nicer or refreshing her makeup. "Our guests from Toshon are here," Wen said.

Hilo, Juen, and Shae stood up to greet Icho Dan, the Pillar of the Jo Sun clan, who entered the room with his Weather Man and his Horn. Jo Sun's former Pillar and Weather Man had both been killed in the Janloon bombing. Since then, Icho had valiantly tried to fill his brother-in-law's position as best he could. But even though he was a competent leader, he had health problems that made it difficult for him to wear jade, and no one could run the business side of their clan as well as the former Weather Man. That was the weakness of the minor clans. Many of them did not have a deep pool of talented Green Bones and losing their key leaders was a death sentence. In the years following the Janloon bombing, some of the minor clans had combined with each other or been absorbed by one of the major clans. The Black Tail clan in Gohei had been peacefully annexed by the Mountain last year. Icho Dan had begun discussion with No Peak six months ago. Today, the Jo Sun clan would cease to exist.

The big clans were getting bigger. *We're still two tigers,* Shae thought grimly, *eating all we can before we have to face each other again.*

Icho was dressed in his best suit and tie, and his voice was resolute but sorrowful as he said, "Kaul-jen, I've been dreading this day ever since my brother-in-law's death, but I'm also filled with relief and gratitude that it's finally arrived." He lowered himself to his knees and clasped his hands to his forehead. His Weather Man and Horn knelt behind him on either side, mirroring Shae's and Juen's positions next to Hilo. "The Jo Sun clan belongs to you now, Kaul Hiloshudon. Its jade is your jade. Its businesses will report to your Weather Man, its warriors will die for your Horn. Your enemies are my enemies, your friends are my friends. I surrender the title of Pillar and pledge allegiance solely to No Peak. The clan is my blood, and the Pillar is its master. On my honor, my life, and my jade."

There were tears in Icho's eyes as he touched his head to the carpet of the Kaul study. The other leaders of Jo Sun did the same, with dignity and resignation. When Icho straightened up, Hilo drew the man to his feet and embraced him warmly. "It's a hard thing you've done, maybe the hardest thing a man can do, to sacrifice his own pride, even if it's for all the right reasons, even when there's no other choice. The Green Bones of the Jo Sun clan are now Green Bones of No Peak. I'll treat them no differently than my own warriors. And the city of Toshon is now No Peak territory. We'll make it prosperous and defend it as fiercely as any district here in Janloon."

Shae could see that the poor man did not entirely believe Hilo's words, but he nodded gratefully. "Thank you, Kaul-jen."

"Now that the hard part's over, let's all have a good dinner together," Hilo said, putting a hand on the man's shoulder. "Tomorrow when you wake up, maybe you'll still be sad, but maybe you'll also feel better, knowing you're finally free from a difficult job you never asked for, and proud that you did all that your brother could've expected."

CHAPTER

33

Truthbearers

Art Wyles, CEO of Anorco Global Resources, resided for two weeks of every second month in his house in Kekon. Wyles had six houses around the world. In Port Massy, he had the mansion on Jons Island where his wife and two children lived, and the penthouse apartment in downtown Quince where he kept his mistress. He owned a family cottage on the southern coast of Espenia outside of Resville, as well as a small but luxurious vacation condo in Marcucuo, and a country house and vineyard in the rolling green hills of Karandi. His residence on Euman Island was relatively modest in comparison—a two-story refurbished brick Shotarian colonial on a rocky ridge overlooking the Amaric Ocean—but it was where he preferred to spend his time these days.

There were two reasons for this. The first was his business, which he admired from his sunroom through a pair of binoculars. The sea was a chalky gray this morning and flat as a sheet, with not a cloud or wave in sight. Perfect conditions.

Offshore jade mining was poised to make Wyles a great deal of money, but it was a risky venture. The initial capital investment had been enormous, and the Kekonese—more specifically, the Janloon clans that held real power in the country—were touchy about bioenergetic jade being extracted or used by outsiders. *Touchy* was too mild a word, Wyles admitted. *Murderous* was more accurate.

The clans had repeatedly sabotaged his ships, causing serious delays and millions of thalirs' worth of property damage. The Kekonese were a brutal race; Wyles did not rule out the possibility they might try to assassinate him. He was undeterred. One did not rise from a rough working-class neighborhood in Port Massy to the highest levels of the Espenian plutocracy without a stubborn determination and an unhealthy appetite for risk. He possessed vast wealth, powerful friends, and most importantly, an unwavering faith in God and the Truth. Together, those great weapons would not only protect him, but guarantee his eventual success.

Quality bioenergetic jade was so rare and valuable that even a modest amount could return on the high operating costs. After years of research and development, of failures and refinement, his ships were finally churning and sifting through enough seawater, sand, and gravel to extract a profitable yield. Anorco was the sole legitimate non-Kekonese processor of bioenergetic jade in the world. The thought made Wyles's heart race.

There was another reason Wyles spent so much time in Kekon and it made his heart race in a very different way. Her name was Lula. As Wyles set down his binoculars and stepped away from the window, an even more lovely view came into his vision, drifting into the room in a lavender silk dressing gown tied loosely around her waist, leaving exposed the milky-pale skin of her breasts and stomach. She set a tray of brunch down on the table. A basket of freshly baked yellow buns, soft as pillows, steamed enticingly. The fruit on top of the bowls of egg custard was arranged into the shapes of flowers.

"Come," Lula coaxed him. "Let's eat."

"You spoil me," Wyles told her with a smile. He opened the front of her gown and trailed his hands over her breasts, flicking his thumbs over the nubs of her nipples. Lula was the most exquisite specimen of a Kekonese woman he'd ever laid eyes on, and he considered himself a connoisseur of international beauty. The town center on Euman Island was full of brothels catering to Espenian servicemen, but even though Wyles spent many weeks away from home, he never considered dipping into the common well with the navy boys. He was a wealthy man with refined tastes, fifty-two years old, a global traveler who'd sampled what the world had to offer in food and art and women. His wife was an elegant society woman who had the best of everything. His mistress was a former runway model who'd graced the covers of all the fashion magazines. So it took a special class of woman to catch and hold Art Wyles's attention.

He'd first seen Lula at a private dinner held for the Espenian ambassador. She and four other courtesans had been brought in for the event, but Lula stood out among the other women like a swan among geese. The demure sequined black dress she'd worn showed off every curve of her taut, youthful body. Her face had the radiant glow of a moonlit lake, framed by glossy waterfalls of darkest ink. She sang and danced with unearthly grace and beauty. Wyles knew at once that he had to have her, but he was afraid his expectations could not possibly be met. He needn't have worried. Sex with this island angel was transcendent, pleasure on another dimension.

Wyles quickly arranged to have an exclusive arrangement with Lula. Whenever he came to Kekon, he phoned her three days ahead so she could prepare for his arrival. She lived with him in his house on Euman Island, prepared his meals, and shared his bed every night. When he traveled back to Port Massy, she was free to return to Janloon to visit her family or go shopping with the allowance he gave her. She could speak a bit of Espenian and was quickly picking up more. She was perfectly agreeable, considerate, anticipating his needs, but never demanding. Wyles sighed. You could not find a woman like Lula in Espenia.

They sat down to enjoy their meal, and afterward, Wyles said, "My sweet, I'm expecting a visitor this afternoon, and I'm afraid we'll be talking business for hours. Why don't you go shopping or to the gym?"

Lula stood and leaned over to give him a kiss. "I wait for you, Arto-se." He loved the way she said his name, Kekonese-style; in her delicate mouth it was so arresting. Picking up the empty tray, she slipped out of the room on noiseless, slippered feet.

Wyles went into his library with a fresh cup of coffee and a newspaper while he waited for his guest to arrive. The phone on his desk rang. When he picked it up, Joren Gasson's reedy voice said, "I hear congratulations are in order, Artie."

Wyles shifted uncomfortably, glad the man on the other end of the line couldn't see his expression. "News sure travels fast." Of course Gasson, with all his connections and one ear always to the ground, would be among the first to hear of anything that might affect him, even if it wasn't yet public. Wyles had hoped to at least tell his wife and children before fielding this inevitable call. Jo Boy Gasson was a friend, but the sort of friend Wyles preferred not to speak to very often.

"President-elect of the Munitions Society," Gasson said proudly. "Not a shabby way to make your big entry into politics. Not shabby at all." The Munitions Society was one of the largest and most powerful Trade Societies in Espenia. As its president, Wyles was guaranteed to have access to the premier and influence over politicians in the National Assembly. "We've come a long way, haven't we?"

"We sure have." Wyles looked at his watch; he wanted to get Gasson off the phone.

"We've been friends for—what, now? Twenty-five years? Sometimes, it's a wonder to think I was there at the start, I was the first person to say, 'That Art Wyles is going somewhere.' I've always had a knack for betting money on a sure thing."

"I'll never forget what you've done for me over the years, you know that. Listen, I've got an important meeting in a couple of minutes. It's about the jade business. How about I talk to you later?"

"Sure, Artie," Gasson said. "I only called to say how proud I am."

"Thanks, Jo Boy. That means a lot to me." After he hung up, Wyles let out a sigh of relief. He knew he was only one of many people on the payroll of the Baker Street Crew, just as Joren Gasson, who effortlessly straddled the legitimate and illegitimate spheres of business and politics, was only one of his many stakeholders—both an asset and a liability. Wyles tried to keep Gasson in the background as much as possible. Right now, he had more important things to think about.

With characteristic military precision, Jim Sunto arrived right on time. The armed guards that protected Wyles's house let Sunto pass; they were, after all, employees of Sunto's company. Wyles had made a sizable investment in Ganlu Solutions International during its early days and become its first major client. GSI provided security for all of Anorco's offshore mining operations as well as a personal security detail for Wyles himself.

Wyles stood to meet his guest. "Jim, it's good to see you. Thanks for coming out to my place. I thought it would be best to have this conversation in a private setting where we won't be overheard." He motioned the ex-Angel into a chair. "What'll you have to drink?"

"A spot of whiskey, if you've got any northern brands," Sunto said.

"Of course I do," Wyles said, pulling out a bottle from one of his favorite distilleries in Cape Glosset on the shore of Whitting Bay. "After all this time here, you haven't converted to hoji?"

Sunto took the glass that Wyles offered and sipped appreciatively. "I suppose that makes me a failed repatriate. What's on your mind, Art?" Sunto was that kind of person, always straight to the point. "There hasn't been much trouble lately. Sabotage attempts have fallen off dramatically." Since the Janloon bombing, the Green Bone clans had been too busy suppressing anti-clan elements to keep up their attacks on Anorco assets and facilities.

Wyles waved the issue away as he poured a glass for himself. "Those sword-wielding clan thugs are a local problem." He settled himself into the leather armchair across from his visitor. "The spread of Ygutanian influence and the blasphemy of Deliverantism, on the other hand—that's a global threat."

"Seer forbid the lies of the unTruthful," Sunto said firmly.

"May we all see and bear the Truth," Wyles added. Both men lifted the Dawn of Icana pendants hanging around their necks and touched them to their lips. Devout Truthbearers understood that the Slow War with Ygutan was not only an economic or military conflict, but a spiritual one. The Deliverantists, led by the Ygutanian religious order of the Protecks, sent missionaries all over the world to preach their religion of austerity, claiming that the known Truth was incomplete and would be revealed by Ygut visionaries, among other heretical beliefs.

The missionaries did not travel alone. According to information obtained by ROE military intelligence, nekolva agents advanced their nation's unTruthful agenda far beyond its borders. The specially trained, bioenergetic jade-enhanced agents spied for their masters in Dramsk, carried out assassinations, and supported and supplied pro-Ygutanian uprisings.

Wyles said to Sunto, "I've been having some very interesting discussions with officials in the War Department. What do you know about Operation Firebreak?"

Sunto's eyebrows rose. He sat back and crossed his arms. "Only rumors that I heard on my way out of the Angels," he said slowly. "Supposedly, it was a secret program approved by Premier Galtz during the Oortokon War to combat Ygutanian expansion wherever it occurred in the world."

Wyles chuckled. "At this point, it seems to be the most well-known secret in the military. Operation Firebreak initiated covert operations in places as far apart as north Tun, Krenia, and Sutaq, partnering with local allies to repel Deliverantism and Ygutanian influence."

Sunto nodded, arms still crossed. "What does this have to do with us?"

Wyles smiled. He liked Jim Sunto. He knew some people in the top brass of the ROE Navy and in the halls of the National Assembly who would never fully trust or accept Sunto because of his Kekonese ancestry, but they were racists. Wyles believed that devotion to the Truth superseded everything, including the color of a person's skin and the blood in his veins.

Wyles said, "Premier Roburg is cutting funding and resources for Operation Firebreak."

An immensely disappointing decision for the ROE military and the Church of One Truth, but an unsurprising one. Bad press over the rates of mental illness and drug addiction among Oortokon War veterans had caused the government to scale back its emphasis on equipping soldiers with jade and training them in IBJCS. Given the economic downturn, voters were opposed to the idea of committing to more overseas wars, and the National Assembly was pressuring Roburg's administration to bring troops home. "As you can imagine," Wyles added, swirling the glass of whiskey under his nose and looking none too concerned, "this puts the War Department in a conundrum."

"In other words, they won't be buying as much bioenergetic jade from Anorco as you'd hoped." Sunto gave Wyles a shrewd look. "But if I know you, Art, you've already figured out a way to make the shifting political winds blow a few hundred million thalirs into your pocket."

"And yours as well," Wyles replied. "Operation Firebreak is going to be scaled down, at least officially. But even if the National Assembly and the Espenian public lack the political will to fight the proselytizing of the Ygutanian Protecks, there are devoted Truthbearers in the War Department and in the Munitions Society and, confidentially, in the Premier's Office as well. Men of reason who won't let shortsightedness put the world at risk of being overrun by unTruthful ways."

Wyles handed Sunto an envelope. With curiosity, the former soldier removed the pages inside and began to read. The man's face remained composed as he took in the meaning of the contents, but the rapid rustling of the pages soon betrayed his excitement. "Is this..."

"A confidential memo from the secretary of the War Department, authorizing the engagement of private military contractors in Operation Firebreak." Wyles sipped from his glass tumbler with a smile.

Sunto looked up from the papers, stunned. "Art, this is a huge step. Maybe too huge."

"It's our big break, Jim," Wyles said. "There's only one PMC with jade-equipped, IBJCS-trained personnel capable of fulfilling this government mandate, and that's GSI."

Sunto slowly folded the memo and returned it to the envelope, staring awestruck at it in his hands as if it were the original scripture of the Seer. "I always knew that once I got it off the ground, there would be demand for GSI's services." He stood and paced back and forth in front of Wyles's bookshelves, his brow knitted as he absorbed the implications. "This is what I hoped for all along, but it's happening sooner than I expected. I've been building GSI and taking on clients gradually. I don't have enough qualified people, equipment, or bioenergetic jade for an operation of this scale."

Wyles steepled his fingers. "I'm prepared to put another three hundred million thalirs into GSI."

Sunto broke into a cough. When he recovered, he exclaimed, "That would make..."

"GSI a subsidiary of Anorco Global Resources. I'm offering to buy you out, Jim. You'd remain president and CEO, of course." He gestured out the window toward the Amaric Ocean where his ships were churning the seafloor. "Anorco has the capital and the jade. GSI has the expertise and personnel. Together, we have a vertically integrated private army. One that'll make us rich, but even more importantly, beat back encroaching unTruth around the world."

Jo Boy Gasson was not the only one with a knack for putting money on a sure thing. With the acquisition of GSI, Wyles's conglomerate would own the means of procuring jade as well as soldiers with the ability to use it. And, as president of the Munitions Society, Wyles would possess the political connections and influence in Adamont Capita to make wars happen. "I realize this is a lot to digest," Wyles said. "But my advice is that you start stepping up your recruitment efforts."

"God, Seer, and Truth," Sunto muttered. He held out his whiskey glass. "Let's have another drink."

CHAPTER

34

Unreasonable

the twentieth year, second month

Our college student gets to pick first," Hilo announced, brushing aside Jaya's quick reach toward the plate of sticky fruit cakes that Wen placed in the center of the dining table. "Ru's the one we're celebrating tonight. Go on, son, take the one you want."

Ru elbowed his sister out of the way and chose the peach cake. "Good choice," Hilo said, putting an arm around Ru's shoulders. "Always go for the best." The teenager grinned blearily. His high school graduation ceremony had been yesterday, and he'd woken up around noon after a night of partying with his classmates. Tonight's dinner had been a celebratory meal with all of Ru's favorite foods—short ribs with red pepper sauce, shrimp cake, crispy fried green beans—and now the new graduate was too full to even finish his cake. Koko sat eagerly thumping his tail and eating morsels that Ru snuck him under the table.

After the upcoming New Year's break, Ru would enter Jan Royal University. The campus was less than thirty minutes away by subway, but Ru had decided to live in student housing to get the full college experience. Hilo understood. At eighteen, the young man needed to break away from his parents. He was the only one of his siblings and cousins not to have lived at Kaul Du Academy. Nevertheless, the thought of his son moving out saddened Hilo. Ru was the most agreeable of his children. He didn't have moods like Niko or a temper like Jaya. He got along with everyone and only ever ran into trouble as a result of jumping at ideas without entirely thinking them through, which was natural for a teenage boy. Occasionally he clashed with his mother, but only, Hilo thought, because Wen was too hard on him. Overall, he was a joy to have around; it would be too quiet without him.

"Ma, do you want dessert?" Wen asked her mother-in-law.

"No, give more to the kids. I'm going to watch television and go to bed." Kaul Wan Ria rose creakily from her chair and Sulima helped her out of the room. Hilo's mother was still in good health at age seventy-eight, but her hair was completely white and she seemed to be shrinking and softening, fading even further into the background that she had always occupied. His grandfather had aged into a leathery cobra spitting venom, but his mother was causing no one any trouble.

Wen asked Ru, "Have you thought any more about what you're going to study?"

"Aunt Shae suggested a business degree," Ru said. "She says that'll open up a lot of job options in the Weather Man's office and in our tributary companies."

"Your aunt's very smart and practical," Wen pointed out.

"A lot of the course requirements in business look boring, though," Ru said. "The social sciences seem a lot more interesting to me. Sociology, or public policy, maybe. It's not that I don't want to work in the clan," he added quickly, "but I want to do something that helps people outside of the clan too—like other stone-eyes."

Ru could be a bit too optimistic and unselfish for his own good, but Hilo said encouragingly, "I'm sure you'll do well in politics or law or whatever you put your mind to. You've got time to figure it out, that's what college is for. And your backup plan can be making it big as a movie star like Danny Sinjo, since you've got your mother's good looks."

Jaya burst out laughing, catching a spray of cake crumbs in her hand.

Wen shook her head, smiling. "Everyone knows who Ru looks like."

"Da, come on," Ru said.

"Don't roll your eyes at me," Hilo said, teasing, but with an undercurrent of seriousness. "And don't ever let any superstitious asses stand in your way. You're my son. You're a Kaul. If you're not a Green Bone, it means you're meant to do something else, something great."

"Yeah, okay, Da," Ru said, waving his father off, although everyone could see how much Hilo's words made him glow. He prodded Niko. "Hey, maybe next year, we'll be on campus together."

Niko glanced at his brother, then back down at the napkin he was twisting into a knot. "I think you're the college kid in this family, Ru."

"What do you mean? You're still going to go to Jan Royal after you've spent a year as a Fist, right?"

Jaya tried to catch Ru's eye and cut him off with a warning hand motion, but it was too late. The conversation came to a sudden icy halt. Ru looked around, confused. He wasn't well connected into the military side of the clan, and he'd been so busy with final exams and graduation that he hadn't heard the news that the Horn had given out rank promotions and jade a week ago.

"I'm not going to be a Fist," Niko said. "And I'm not going to college either."

"Of course you are," Hilo snapped. "Lott Jin says you're doing fine, you carry your jade better than anyone else at your rank. You just need to put in the effort. By now, you should be taking more initiative, setting an example for junior Fingers. You can't expect to become a Fist by doing the average amount."

"A college education is important these days, of course," Wen added, "but it can wait another year or two until you've earned more jade. Even if you're a little behind on rank compared to where you expected to be, you can catch up if you put your mind to it."

Niko remained mute, as was his habit when he was upset. When criticized or disciplined, Ru would cajole and argue; Jaya would storm off in tears. Niko would withdraw, as he was doing now, staring sullenly at the table with his jade aura pulled in like a black cloud. Hilo felt his temper rising. "Do you think everything should come easy to you just because you're the Pillar's son? That you don't have to work as hard to prove yourself and can get away with disgraceful stunts, like that thing with the car?" Hilo caught himself; he'd already punished his nephew for that incident and had promised himself he wouldn't continue to bring it up.

Instead, he said, in a calmer voice, "Did you know that when I first met Lott Jin, I wasn't sure about him? It's hard to believe now, but when he was young, he was badly behaved, he sulked and talked back. His father was a top Green Bone and he hated following after him. Fortunately, he found his own footing. He changed his attitude and worked harder than anyone. Now he's the Horn of the clan. My point is that even if you didn't have the best start, even if you made some mistakes, it's not too late to turn things around. You just have to commit to doing it."

Niko looked up. He'd been avoiding meeting his uncle's eyes, but now he said, "I mean it. I'm not going to be a Fist, and I'm not going to college either. I got a job offer outside of the clan and I'm taking it."

Complete silence fell over the dinner table. Even Jaya was too astonished to comment. Hilo blinked as if Niko had spoken in a foreign language. In disbelief, "You made this decision without telling anyone? Without discussing it with your own family? Instead, you spring it on all of us like this?"

"What was there to discuss?" Niko said. "I knew you wouldn't agree."

Hilo wanted to smack his nephew, but Wen put a hand on his arm and he forced himself to take a deep breath. "Despite what you seem to believe," Hilo said slowly, "I'm not unreasonable, Niko. If you really wanted to work outside of No Peak you should've talked to me and your ma about it."

Niko didn't answer, but his jade aura boiled like a storm in a bottle. Niko had once been an easy child—calm and thoughtful, curious and quick to learn, caring for his younger siblings, not the type to act out. Hilo wondered unhappily where he'd gone wrong as a parent, how his capable nephew had turned into such an aimless and uncertain young man. Hilo mustered every remaining fragment of his paternal patience. "Growing up as a Kaul, maybe it's only natural you'd get restless and want to explore and I haven't been sensitive enough to that. A job outside of the clan could be good for you for a couple of years, give you some additional perspective. Your uncle Andy's a doctor, after all. It's not a decision you should make without talking to your parents, though. What's the job, anyway?"

Niko dropped the crumpled napkin on his empty plate and pushed away from the table. "I'm joining Ganlu Solutions International."

Wen drew in a small, sharp intake of breath, the only sound anyone made before Hilo's arm shot out across the dinner table and seized his eldest child by the hair, yanking him bodily out of his chair. A plate crashed to the floor; everyone jumped in their seats. Hilo was on his feet. He shoved Niko away from him into the nearest dining room wall, knocking a framed family photograph to the ground.

"You signed up to work as a *mercenary*?" Hilo let out a guttural noise. "You're going to tromp around in places you don't belong, with thin-blooded, shine-addicted foreigners, whoring your jade abilities to the highest bidder?" He cuffed the side of Niko's head and shoved him again, towering over him even though the young man was as tall as he was. His eyes and aura bulged as he shouted. "What kind of a Green Bone are you? What kind of a *son*?"

Ru jumped to his feet. Koko leapt up with him, barking. "Come on, Da," Ru pleaded, trying to defend his brother. "He made a mistake, it was a whim."

"It wasn't a whim," Niko growled, rubbing the sore patch of his scalp and squaring to face Hilo with his spine straight, shoulders back, and his hands curled into fists at his side. Cold defiance burned in his eyes. "Why do we have to pretend we're different or better than anyone else who wears jade, even if they're foreigners? Just because of race or genetics? I talked to some recruiters at GSI, and the work sounds interesting. They're doing something that hasn't been done before. All I've ever known is the clan, and the only thing I'm qualified to do is be a jade warrior. Why shouldn't I explore what else is possible? I could travel the world while being paid for my jade abilities."

Wen said, with a quaver in her voice, "This is what you do to your family, after your own brother's graduation?"

Niko winced but didn't drop his gaze. "I'm sorry, Ma," he said. "I'm sorry, Ru. I wasn't going to say anything about it tonight."

Wen stood, her mouth in a straight line. "I have nothing to say to you until you come to your senses." She turned her back and walked out of the dining room.

Jaya was the only one still in her chair. She whistled low. "Shit, you really did it this time, keke." None of them wanted to face their father when he was angry, but their mother leaving the room was unheard of.

The tone of Hilo's voice would've cowed any of his men. "Tomorrow morning you're going to call Jim Sunto or whoever you've been talking to, and say that you acted without thinking. You're not going to become a soldier-for-hire and disgrace yourself and all of us. You're going to work directly under the Horn. You're going to go to all of your scheduled training, and you're going to make Fist by next year. *If* you do all that, *then* we'll talk about finding you some new opportunity, inside or outside of the clan, because obviously you aren't going to be Pillar."

Niko's face twitched before stiffening. "I've made up my mind."

"Niko," Ru hissed in distress, looking at him wide-eyed. "Don't you think you're taking this too far? You've made the point that you're not happy. Da is giving you an out. Don't you care what our parents think?"

Niko glanced at his younger brother with a sorrowful expression. "You're eighteen, Ru. You have your own life and you're going to college. You don't need me around." As he turned back to Hilo, his voice dropped and trembled with resentment, but he kept his chin raised and his jade aura smoldered with resolve. "As for what my parents think, I wouldn't know what that is. My father was murdered in a clan war and never even knew I existed. You executed my mother as a traitor, and I have nothing of her, not even photos. What am I supposed to really believe about either of them?" Niko turned away for a second, swiping angrily at his face. "What do *you* think, Uncle? Do you think my parents would want this for me, or would they tell me to walk away while I still can?"

A spasm seized Hilo's heart. He put out a hand; it closed hard on the back of a chair. For one gut-wrenching second, because of some slight thing in Niko's posture or voice, or some subtle aspect of his jade aura, it seemed to Hilo as if the young man he thought of as his eldest son was gone, and his brother, Lan, stood in the dining room in Niko's place. Lan, at his most resolutely principled, at one time the only man Hilo would obey. Then the moment was over, leaving behind only the piercing ache of confusion and regret.

"Your father knew what it meant to be a Green Bone." Hilo's voice was strained beyond his own recognition. "He would never walk away. He gave everything to lead the clan, including his life."

"And because of that, I never met him. Why should I follow his example?" Niko's face was blotchy with emotion. He wheeled away from the dining room and walked toward the front door.

"If you do this," Hilo called to Niko's back, "if you walk through that door and break your mother's heart, don't bother coming back."

Jaya and Ru exchanged openmouthed looks of mounting alarm. "Da..." Jaya began. She fell silent.

For a moment, Niko hesitated, as if restrained by an invisible tether. He took the next step firmly, as if pulling himself out of quicksand. Then the next step, and the next. The door closed behind him, cutting him from sight, but for several drawn-out minutes, Hilo could Perceive the silent pain in his nephew's turbulent aura as it receded from the house.

———

Jim Sunto was in his office, on a morning phone call with two human resources managers from the War Department, when a violent commotion broke out at the gates to GSI's compound. At first he thought the noise was from a training exercise. Then he heard the guards screaming, *"Stop! Stop or we'll open fire!"* and he didn't even need his jade abilities to sense their alarm.

Sunto dropped the phone and raced out of his office, drawing his sidearm. Bursting out the front doors of the building, he took in the scene in an instant. The chain-link fence behind the security guard box was standing open; the rolling gate had been torn off its sliding mechanism and lay askew. Two men in GSI uniforms were lying on the ground—still moving, thank God—and four others were in an armed standoff, shouting, two of them with R5 rifles, the other two aiming Corta 9 mm pistols.

Kaul Hiloshudon, flanked by four of his Green Bone warriors, strode through the breached fence and advanced toward the building with the heedless implacability of a demon. The nearest GSI guard fired twice at Kaul's chest. Sunto could've told the man he wasn't going to hit a skilled Green Bone with a small-caliber weapon from a hundred meters away. With an irritated snarl, Kaul Deflected the rounds, and with a lethal rustle, his Fists drew their own weapons— Ankev 600 handguns and carbon steel moon blades.

"Hold fire!" Sunto roared at his men. He ran ahead of them, waving his arms. "Hold your fucking fire, Seer damnit!" Switching to Kekonese, he shouted at the intruders, "Kaul, for fuck's sake, do you want a bloodbath? Tell your men to stand down!"

Kaul stopped and fixed Sunto with a terrifying glare. Jade gleamed across his collarbone, enough to equip a platoon. "You piss-drinking sack of *shit*. You recruited my own *son*!"

"I did nothing of the sort. He came up to me at one of our information sessions." Moving slowly, Sunto holstered his Corta and held his hands open. "Lower your weapons," he said in Espenian to the GSI guards.

"Sir—" one of them began.

"I said lower them!" Sunto had trained with No Peak's top men and knew what they were capable of. If a gunfight broke out, the Green Bones would throw up a veritable hurricane of combined Deflection and close the gap, cutting down men with blades and knives in seconds. "Think about this," he said to Kaul. "Do you want to be held responsible for an unprovoked deadly attack on an Espenian company and its employees? Call off your men. We'll step into my office and talk about this like civilized human beings."

In all the years that Sunto had known the clan leader, he'd never been sure if the stories he'd heard about Kaul Hilo were true. Now he thought they probably were. He recognized the Fists who accompanied the Pillar—Lott, Vin, Suyo, and Toyi. He'd spent time with all of them, had taught them and learned from them, but they would murder him and all his soldiers at a single word from Kaul. It was no wonder, Sunto thought with resentful abhorrence, that Kekonese people were stereotyped as savage.

Kaul's eyes narrowed to slits. He turned over his shoulder. "Stay here," he said to Lott. Sunto let out a silent breath as the tension eased, weapons reluctantly coming down on both sides. Ever since the two men had ended their friendship, Kaul had not once contacted the ex-Angel or been to the GSI training facilities on Euman Island, but now he strode past Sunto and into the building as if he owned the land it was built on.

Sunto followed. Inside, he pushed open the door to his office. Kaul went in but did not sit down. He gave the utilitarian furniture and boxy institutional surroundings a brief, contemptuous glance, clearly every bit as unimpressed as he expected to be. "I warned you to keep your business out of Kekon," he said, with the cold disappointment of a man about to make good on a threat. "You didn't listen."

Sunto walked behind his desk, putting distance between them. "The only thing I've done is hold information sessions for prospective hires. That's not unusual for any company." He could've guessed even that would raise the ire of the clans, but he couldn't afford to be timid about recruiting. The Operation Firebreak contract depended on GSI being able to field enough soldiers. "We're interested in hiring ex-military personnel, or those with enough private training. We've made no effort to lure Green Bones from the clans, but we'll talk with any interested and qualified applicants."

"Whatever agreement you've made with Niko, break it," Kaul demanded. "He won't be wasting his jade working for your thin-blooded private army."

"Thin-blooded," Sunto intoned. "That's what you've always thought about anyone who doesn't answer to you or the parochial clan system, isn't it? Well, thin-blooded or not, I'm not one of your underlings, Kaul. And GSI isn't one of your tribute companies. Your son is an adult. I asked him several times if he was sure of his decision and he assured me he was. He's already signed the contract and been paid the starting bonus."

Kaul put his hands on Sunto's desk and leaned forward across the space between them, lowering his voice. "Behind that Kekonese face, you have a dirty Espenian soul. You understand money, don't you? I'll pay you ten times whatever you've already paid him if you withdraw the offer."

Sunto scowled. "Bribing a company executive to fire an employee is illegal."

"Years ago, you told me you weren't here to cause trouble, but now your soldiers protect the mining ships that steal Kekonese jade. So don't bullshit me with moral superiority." Kaul's stare was as steady and chilling as his voice. "You knew that by hiring Niko, you would be reaching into No Peak and breaking my family. You did it anyway. Anyone else who tried to do that, I'd kill them. But out of respect for our old friendship, I'm giving you a choice. Take the money or don't, but I'm asking you to solve this, as a personal favor to me. If that doesn't move you at all, at least think selfishly about whether you really want me as an enemy."

Sunto did not. He'd been born in Kekon and had spent the majority of the past fifteen years in the country. He understood how powerful the clans were and how ruthless their leaders could be. He certainly didn't consider himself a prideful or reckless man who blindly tempted danger.

The hard reality, however, was that only three countries possessed jade-equipped and trained military personnel—the Republic of Espenia, Ygutan, and Kekon. Most of GSI's employees were formerly ROE special forces, but he still needed more people. Unfortunately, it hadn't been as easy as he'd hoped to hire current and former soldiers from the Golden Spider Company, some of whom he'd personally trained during his years working with General Ronu to reform the Kekonese military. Green Bones, even those not beholden to the clans, were leery of accepting employment with a foreign company, and strict attitudes about the acceptable jade professions persisted in Kekon.

Kaul Nikoyan coming to work for GSI could be the tipping point that influenced other Green Bones. What candidates like him lacked in institutional military experience, they more than made up for with sheer jade ability, and a surge of such recruits would boost GSI's capabilities within a short time. The No Peak clan could not condemn or punish GSI or those who chose to take a job with the company, not if the Pillar's own son had made the decision to join.

"I'm running an Espenian enterprise." Sunto met Kaul's gaze unflinchingly. "As far as I'm concerned, your son is an employee unless he decides to leave of his own free will."

Kaul's voice held no inflection. "I'm not sure you understand what you're doing."

Sunto did understand. All of GSI's fortunes, his own personal reputation, and perhaps even the fate of the Truthbearing world rested on Operation Firebreak. Art Wyles was an insufferably smug oligarch, widely disliked, but he'd handed Sunto the biggest opportunity of his life and was vouching for him with the War Department, the Munitions Society, and all of Anorco's shareholders, including, if rumors were to be believed, certain people in Port Massy whose disfavor Sunto did not want to court.

Sunto also knew that being an Espenian citizen and a former Navy

Angel war veteran working for the ROE government afforded him a special protection. Kaul might still be reckless enough to try to assassinate him, but he couldn't do so without risking extraordinary scrutiny and sanction, and even that would not bring down GSI. Wyles could hire someone else to run the company. All things considered, Sunto decided he would sooner take his chances against Kaul than disappoint his Espenian stakeholders, against whom he had no such advantages.

"I'd rather not be your enemy, Kaul," he replied, remaining exactly where he was. "But I'm not afraid of you, either."

The Pillar straightened. Sunto remembered the first time he'd met the man in the Seventh Discipline gym. He'd expected to end up in the hospital and been confused to find Kaul amiable, exuding casual arrogance and smiling more than Sunto would've expected from a man with such a reputation. There was none of that now. Sunto thought about the Corta pistol near his right hand.

"Maybe you're right to feel as if you have nothing to fear," Kaul said. "I can't force a foreign company to do what I ask, and I know you're not a man who's easily cowed or killed. So in the short term, this decision may be good for you. But I won't forget that you threw away our friendship and took my own son for your gain." The jade energy coming off the Green Bone seemed too bright to be human, though he'd gone very still. "I promise you that sooner or later, I'll answer that offense."

"You should consider why your son would want to work for GSI instead of staying in your clan in the first place. The Green Bone clans are becoming obsolete. Even your own family can see it." Sunto jerked his chin. "Now take your men and get off my property."

For a frightening moment, the expression on Kaul's face suggested he would resort to the blunt violence with which he'd arrived. Sunto reached in readiness for his own jade energy. Seconds passed, longer and infinitely more tense than the ones that used to stretch between them when they faced each other sparring on the lawn of the Kaul estate.

The fire in the Pillar's eyes shrank behind black coals. "It's obvious you're not a father, Lieutenant." Kaul turned toward the door. "Or you wouldn't feel so invincible."

Sunto followed at a wary distance and watched as the Pillar gathered his Green Bones with a gesture and walked back out through the broken security gate.

CHAPTER
35

Those with a Choice

As the wheels of the plane touched down on the tarmac at Janloon International Airport, Anden rubbed his eyes and peered groggily out the window at a wintry midafternoon sky. His mind was still on the other side of the Amaric Ocean. As one of the directors of the International Bioenergetic Medicine Certification Board, he flew to Espenia at least twice a year to inspect clinics for compliance with standards of practice, which meant he racked up even more air travel miles than the Weather Man. At least there was no smoking on the planes anymore, and Silver status on Kekon Air meant he made the trip in greater comfort than before.

The good news in Espenia was that the medical use of jade was steadily gaining acceptance, helped along by the efforts of WBH Focus and the Kekonese Association of Espenia. The bad news was that for every positive mention of Kekonese jade, there were spectacularly negative ones. Jon Remi, the Bad Keck of Resville, was still growing his power in that city, still eluding death at the hands of rivals and arrest by the police.

"We've tried many times to reason with Remi, to get him to take a lower profile," Migu Sun had explained at the most recent KAE board meeting Anden had attended, "but he won't be reined in."

Cory was beyond frustrated. "The Green Bones of every other city have cut off association with Remi and his Snakeheads gang. We're cooperating with federal agencies, giving them any information that might help the police take him down. Maybe this is an awful thing to say," Cory grumbled darkly, "but if he doesn't get arrested soon, I hope he finally gets popped by one of the Crews."

The problem in Espenia, Anden mused as he collected his baggage, was that there was no loyalty greater than money. In Kekon, there had always been two sources of power: gold and jade. No amount of money could make a man a jade warrior if he didn't have the right blood and training. Even the wealthiest man could be killed. If he did not wear jade himself, he needed the friendship of those who did. So there was always a balancing force.

In the rest of the world, that was not true. The Kekonese Association of Espenia was not a clan with the power to enforce its wishes across the country. Anden had a sinking feeling that Jon Remi was the new template for how to succeed as a Green Bone in Espenia. As he rose in wealth and power, he would gather followers, others who would seek to be like him.

The taxi Anden took from the airport battled holiday season traffic all the way back to his apartment. During the long ride, Anden tried to put pessimistic thoughts out of his mind and return his attention to the present. He'd already done everything he could to help his friends in Port Massy and to advance No Peak's agenda in that country. The rest of it was out of his control.

When he walked through the door of his apartment, he found Jirhuya sitting on the sofa in the living room, reviewing concept art. "Took you long enough," Jirhu sighed, putting down his work and unfolding his graceful body from the cushions. He came to the door and gave Anden a kiss. Jirhu smelled like soap and aftershave—freshly showered and shaved, his coarse, curly hair still damp.

"The flight was late, and traffic was bad," Anden explained.

"Sorry I wasn't a good enough boyfriend to make dinner, miyan." It was his pet name for Anden, an Abukei endearment meaning *mine*. "There wasn't much in your fridge, and I didn't have time to get groceries."

"That's okay. We can go out for dinner." He was not really hungry yet; it was early in the morning Port Massy time. "Or we can order in from the Tuni place."

"Let's stay in." Jirhu put one arm around Anden's waist. With the other he took Anden's hand and moved it to his ass. "It's been a long ten days with you on the other side of the world." He kissed Anden again, more deeply.

Anden felt his shoulders relaxing, the grogginess of travel nudged aside by the stirring between his legs. He dropped the bag he was still carrying and tilted Jirhu's head back to kiss his jaw and neck, inhaling deeply, pressing his lips into the comforting hollow of the other man's throat. Jirhu drew him toward the bedroom and he followed, though he could not help feeling a tiny flutter of reluctance. He was always more than willing to give Jirhu what he wanted, but he was also tired from the flight and tonight he would've preferred to receive rather than have to perform, or simply to enjoy each other's bodies more relaxedly, with mouths and hands.

As if sensing the hint of reticence, Jirhu sat Anden down on the edge of the bed and unbuttoned his shirt, trailing fingertips down his chest and stomach, then crouched between Anden's knees and undid his pants. "Just relax, I'll do the work."

Anden leaned his weight back on his arms and closed his eyes contentedly, feeling the last of the stress in his body melt away into desire as Jirhu skillfully brought him to full arousal. When the heat of his partner's mouth drew away and he heard the snap-top sound of the lube bottle, Anden opened his eyes and climbed onto the bed. Jirhu was already on his hands and knees, ready and breathing hard with eagerness. He was a beautiful sight: his long tawny body and smooth back, the sweep of his shoulders down to his elegant arms, the firm globes of his ass. Long ago, Cory had taught Anden to take his time, to use his fingers and mouth first, to enter slowly and gently, thinking of the way he would want to be treated—but Jirhu was sometimes surprisingly impatient. He pushed back against Anden, engulfing him; he grabbed the headboard of the bed and angled his hips upward, thrusting and clenching rhythmically. Jirhu talked a lot—a shocking amount, in Anden's opinion, though he found it intensely erotic. He ordered Anden to bite his shoulder, to grab his hips, to smack his ass, to stroke his cock. When he climaxed, it was with a string of moaning, ecstatic profanities. By then, Anden felt strapped helplessly into a rollercoaster seat. Jirhu moved against him fiercely and expertly, squeezing him, and Anden careened off the pinnacle, falling onto his boyfriend with a shudder.

They lay together for a while, enjoying the afterglow of their reunion. "I was a bit selfish there," Jirhu admitted sheepishly but without apology.

"I like it when you're insistent," Anden assured him. Perhaps it was because Jirhu had been with more partners, or perhaps, being Abukei, he did not share the same cultural inhibitions, but Jirhu seemed to know what he wanted. He was driven, comfortable in his own skin, and not just in bed—in his work and artistic vision, his opinions.

Anden got up and took a leisurely shower, enjoying the hot water on his back. By the time he got out and dressed, Jirhu had called an order down to the Taste of Tun and takeout containers of lamb and lentil stew, fried potatoes with herbs, and vegetable dumplings arrived a few minutes later. They ate at Anden's kitchen table, knees touching, spooning food from the paper cartons onto each other's plates.

"It'll be nice to have more space soon," Anden said. He'd found a larger apartment three blocks away, in the same Old Town neighborhood, and they were moving in together next month. He and Jirhu had been seeing each other for a year and a half. Jirhu had a key to Anden's place and since it was closer to where he worked, he was at Anden's apartment as often as his own. Still, there had been some disagreement. Anden made a good income as a doctor and was a naturally frugal person, so even with Janloon's steep housing prices, he could've afforded a small house, but Jirhu wouldn't hear of buying a home until he could contribute half of the down payment. His savings as an artist were paltry, but with all the work he was now doing on Cinema Shore's growing slate of movies, it might not be long before they moved again.

"Personally, I'm going to miss this place," Jirhu said with a teasing smile. "It's so much like you." He gestured at the tidy, simply decorated space, the bookcases and shelves Anden had made from plain lumber and painted himself, the heavy punching bag hanging in the living room, small objects and children's artwork from when his nieces and nephews had been much younger. In their new apartment, Anden expected Jirhu and Wen would sweep in and improve everything, bring in more attractive furniture, make the drapes and cushions complement each other.

Anden said, "The clan New Year's party is coming up. It'll be at the General Star Hotel this year, and everyone important in No Peak will be there. Would you like to come? I asked the Pillar if I could bring you and it's fine."

He said this casually, not wanting to make it sound like a big deal. The truth was that he'd asked Hilo some time ago and had been waiting until after his trip to Espenia for the right moment to tell Jirhu. It was one thing for Anden to be sleeping with someone, or even moving in with him. It was quite another to bring him to the biggest No Peak gathering of the year, one hosted by the Pillar himself.

After weeks of delay, Anden had mustered the courage to walk into the Pillar's study. "Hilo-jen," he said, trying not to sound as awkward as he felt, "I've been seeing someone for more than a year now. He's not a Green Bone or a member of the clan, but we get along well and we're planning to move in together. I'd like to bring him to the New Year's party."

"The Abukei fellow," Hilo said. "Bring him if you like."

Anden blinked. He'd expected more questions. "You . . . you're fine with it, then."

Hilo looked up from the towering stack of cards that Wen had left on the coffee table for him to sign. He picked up the remote control and muted the television that had been playing quietly in the background. "Wouldn't I have mentioned it already if I wasn't? Wen told me about him ages ago and asked permission on your behalf. She knew you would take forever to do it yourself." He scrawled his name, stamped a card with the clan's insignia in red ink, and moved on to the next one. "Your personal life's your own business, Andy, unless it affects the clan."

In retrospect, Anden wasn't sure why he was so surprised by his cousin's nonchalance. Societal prejudice against the Abukei had made him anticipate the Pillar's disapproval. But no children would be born into the Kaul family out of the relationship, and an Abukei could never hold any rank or position in a Green Bone clan. They were suspected by everyone, which made them nearly useless as White Rats, or else they were helpless and protected by aisho. No enemy would find it worthwhile to try to turn or harm them. Jirhuya was a safe partner for Anden. The thought was a relief but also made Anden faintly resentful.

Outside, a light rain began to patter against the windows of Anden's apartment—a rare winter shower that would slick the roads but wouldn't last long. Jirhuya pushed the remains of his dinner around the plate. "Please don't be offended, but...I'd rather not go to the party." His eyes met Anden's, then dropped apologetically. "I've worked too hard making a name for myself to start being seen as the Kaul family's charity case."

Anden was taken aback. "What is that supposed to mean?"

"The only other Abukei there will be the janitors and waitstaff. How're you going to introduce me? As your 'friend'? It'll look like I was brought out to show off No Peak's generosity."

"That's not true. I asked the Pillar if I could bring you. It was my idea, not his." He hadn't expected to meet resistance over something he'd thought would be a welcome thing and was offended that Jirhu would ascribe such superficial motives to his family. "You're not the only one who stands out," Anden countered. "I'm a mixed-blood orphan adopted by the Kaul family when I was a child. Does that also make me a *charity case*?"

Jirhu shook his head. "Your mother and uncles were famous jade warriors; you went to the Academy; you were raised by the Kauls. Even though you're a doctor now, you're still a Green Bone of the clan. That makes you more Kekonese than me, because no matter your skin color, *green* is what people see." Jirhu stood from the table, taking his plate and dropping it loudly into the sink. "If you're Abukei you can't be green. So you can never be anything but Abukei."

Anden hadn't until now realized how much he'd been looking forward to showing up with Jirhuya in front of the whole clan, knowing that no one would have the audacity to tug their earlobes at him in the presence of the Pillar and the entire Kaul family. He'd always assumed that a partner who truly cared for him would be happy to be welcomed by his cousins. With a surge of hurt, he blurted, "I thought we were serious. This is a big No Peak event and I'd hoped you'd be there."

Jirhu turned around, his hands clutching the edge of the counter behind him. "I'm sorry. I just don't want to owe anything to your family. Or for anyone to think I do."

"Who *doesn't* owe something to the clans?" Anden exclaimed. "Do you think the movie industry would be what it is, that you'd have the career you do now, if my sister-in-law hadn't invested in Cinema Shore?"

"That's my point. The clans are in everything. They make and break industries and companies and people. I'm already luckier than most Abukei." Jirhuya's father had died while diving for mine run-off, but he'd been raised by his mixed-blood mother and Kekonese grandfather, so he'd been given an education and advantages many Abukei did not have. Jirhu's voice fell and he sounded uncommonly vulnerable. "I don't want people saying it's all because of No Peak, because I'm sleeping with you. Please, miyan, try to understand."

Anden felt that he emphatically did *not* understand, and he opened his mouth to say so, but at that moment, there was a knock on the door. Anden and Jirhu paused their argument and looked at each other in surprise. They weren't expecting anyone. The knock came again, harder this time, sounding desperate.

Anden opened the door and was surprised to see his nephew. The expression on his face was forlorn and distressed, and his hair was wet with rainwater that dripped into his eyes.

"Niko," Anden exclaimed, pulling him inside. "What's wrong? What's happened?"

Niko rubbed the back of his sleeve over his wet face. "Uncle Anden, can I stay with you for a while?"

Anden went to the Kaul house the following afternoon. The first person he saw was Jaya, loitering near the gate with two Academy classmates, skateboards tucked under their arms. "You might not want to talk to him right now," she advised. Jaya normally had some quippy thing to say every time Anden saw her, so he knew it was a sign of how bad the situation was that his niece didn't even crack a smile. "He's in an awful mood."

Anden went inside the house. The thick wooden door to the study was closed and behind it, Anden could hear the Pillar's raised voice, and Lott Jin responding, but he couldn't make out what they were saying. He went into the kitchen and opened the cabinet, taking out a glass and a bottle of hoji and pouring himself a fingerful of drink to strengthen his resolve. Standing at the patio door, he looked out into the courtyard and gardens and saw that on the lawn, a pile of concrete blocks had been smashed into chunks of rubble and left strewn about, some of them lying several feet away, having clearly been flung about in a rage.

The door to the study opened and Lott Jin emerged. The new Horn looked as if he'd been badly taken to task. He wore a tight scowl of chagrin and resentment, mingled with relief that the ordeal was over and he'd gotten away without worse personal consequence. Anden intercepted him. "What's happening?"

"Niko's out," Lott said. "No rank, bank accounts frozen, no help from the clan. The Pillar had half a mind to order him dragged in and stripped of his jade." At Anden's stunned expression, Lott said, "Maybe you'll have better luck talking to him than I did. As far as he's concerned, I fucked up with the kid, didn't give him the right mentoring and opportunities, didn't push him hard enough."

"It has nothing to do with you," Anden said to the Horn.

"You know what he's like," Lott said, and left the house.

Anden walked into the study. Hilo was standing behind the desk, the telephone receiver in his hand and address book open, looking for a number. The knuckles of his hands were untidily wrapped with gauze. At Anden's entrance, he glanced up impatiently and said, "What do you want, Andy?" He found the number he was looking for and began to punch it into the phone.

"Don't do this."

"Do what?" his cousin snapped.

Anden walked up to the desk, forcing the Pillar's attention back to him. "*This*. Raining your anger and guilt down on Niko because he isn't following the plan you had for him. Pushing him away because you feel rejected and offended by the choices he's making in his own life. You've done it before—to me, to Shae, and even to Wen. Gods in Heaven, don't do it to your own son."

Hilo depressed the phone cradle and slammed the phone back down with enough force to make the whole thing jump on the desk. "He's not my son," Hilo snarled. "He was never anything like me, not in the least. He's as melancholy as Lan, and as shallow and disloyal as Eyni."

"Let the gods recognize them," Anden added in a murmur.

"I put up with a lot of bullshit from that boy." Underneath the angry glare, Anden could see his cousin's bewilderment and pain. "I know he's young, he needs some freedom to rebel. I gave him his head as much as I thought was reasonable. But this beats fucking everything. Wasting the jade and training he owes to his family and his clan—to fight for foreigners, for strangers, for nothing but *money*. Even barukan are better than that. You're a doctor, Andy. Don't tell me you agree with what he's doing."

Anden looked at the ground, then back up at the Pillar. "I don't agree with his choice, but I agree less with what you're doing by cutting him off."

"Don't try to talk me down, Andy." There was warning in the Pillar's voice, a layer of menace that would have, at one time, silenced Anden the way it silenced most men.

"I know better than to try reasoning with you when you're this angry."

"At least someone has sense," Hilo said, turning away and opening a desk drawer. "Leave me alone, then. I'm not in the mood to talk." He pulled out an open pack of cigarettes and cursed vociferously to find the carton empty, having forgotten that Wen had thrown them out in an effort to help him quit smoking.

Anden did not move from his spot in front of the Pillar's desk. "Let Niko take the job," he said. "Let him keep his rank, his money, and his jade. Tell him that even though you don't agree with his choice, he's still your son, that he can come home when he's ready."

Hilo barked out a cough, as if he'd choked on his own saliva. "Didn't you just say you weren't going to try this? You go too far, cousin, if you're telling me how to be a parent."

"I don't know anything about parenting," Anden said. "All I know is what I needed from you once, when I was Niko's age. I'm not trying to argue with you. I'm *telling* you what you should do as a father and as Pillar. If you disown Niko, you'll lose your son and No Peak will lose its heir."

"He's not fit to be Pillar," Hilo said.

"People said that about you once," Anden reminded his cousin. "Niko's not like you, just like you weren't like Lan. He's smart, Hilo-jen. Observant. He's always trying to deeply understand things, but he has to do it in his own way, even if it means going all the way over to the opposite side. You say he's cold and selfish, but it's because he keeps what he feels to himself. He does care. He cares what you think of him. And I think he needs to be free of it too."

Hilo's face moved in a brief contortion, but he answered without sympathy. "What message is it going to send to the clan if I let Niko get away with this? A Kaul, joining a foreign private military company? The Mountain will throw a fucking party. They'll go to town poaching our Lantern Men and our politicians and our public support. We'll be eviscerated in the press. Even Shae agrees with me. And other Fingers will think that if the Pillar's son can turn his back on the clan and use his jade to pad his own pocket, then what's to stop them from doing the same?"

"Then do what you have to do publicly. Condemn Niko's decision. Tell everyone that he doesn't represent No Peak with his actions, and he has no clan status or privileges so long as he works for Sunto. Say whatever you have to as Pillar. But at least *talk* to Niko. Don't turn your back on him."

"Why does it matter so much to you?" Hilo retorted, his patience visibly fraying.

"Because it's what Lan would've done!" Anden had not meant to shout. He'd meant to come in and lay down his case with calm and unassailable surety. He closed his shaking hands into fists and leaned them on Hilo's desk, pressing the knuckles against wood. "Lan would never turn his back on any of us. You executed Niko's mother when he was a baby. Everyone in the clan knows it, even if we don't talk about it. He deserves the chance to hate you and leave No Peak, if that's what he needs to do. You owe it to him." Anden drew in a hard breath and let it out again. He straightened. "If you disown Niko, then I'm gone too. I'll leave, Hilo."

Hilo stared at him as if he were holding a match over kerosene. "You wouldn't."

"Am I lying to you?" The Pillar could Perceive Anden's resolve, would know if he was bluffing. Hilo did not say anything.

"From the minute Lan brought me into this house, all I ever wanted was to be a Kaul," Anden said roughly. "I hated my Espenian blood on one side, and I was afraid of being the Mad Witch's boy on the other. But I've learned something over the years. I don't have to be a Kaul if I don't want to be. You and Shae will always be Kauls. Niko, Ru, and Jaya—they don't have a choice either. But I do." His voice landed with certainty, though it seemed a hole opened in the pit of his stomach.

"I've been No Peak's man in Espenia for years, you've said so yourself. I made the alliances we needed in Port Massy and Resville. I'm the one overseeing the clan's stake in healthcare, training Green Bone doctors and certifying clinics. If I leave, you'll lose all of that. Maybe you could replace me, but it won't be the same and you know it."

"Are you *threatening* me, cousin?" Hilo's words were more astonished than angry.

"I'm *asking* you, Hilo-jen," Anden said, "to prove to me that this is the family I still want to be a part of." Anden turned and went to the door. "If you decide you want to speak to your son after all, he's staying in the guest suite in my apartment building. In two weeks, I'm giving him a ride to the airport."

CHAPTER
36

A Fresh Start

Jon Remi took all of his meals at one of three Kekonese restaurants in downtown Resville. His favorite was the Feast of Janloon, not because it had the best food (Kekon Delight, two blocks away, was better), but because it was the most secure. The restaurant took up two floors of a narrow building. Remi always ate at a reserved table near the back of the second floor. Before he arrived, he sent two of his men ahead to make sure no threat was lying in wait for him. Bodyguards kept watch while he ate facing the stairwell, which was the only way up to the second floor. The blinds were always kept shut on the one large window, which led out onto a fire escape that could be used to exit the building in an emergency.

Although the Bad Keck wore enough jade to feel confident he could handle most ordinary threats, he had an uncommonly large number of enemies, and he was not stupid enough to think that just because he had jade abilities he could not be killed by a well-planned ambush.

Every Crew Boss in the country was offended that a Kekonese had risen so meteorically in Resville's underworld and now controlled so much of that lucrative city. A number of them had already made attempts to eliminate Remi and retake the parts of the gambling and prostitution businesses that they saw as belonging rightfully to them. One of Remi's cars had been ruined by a drive-by shooting, and recently two men had gotten close enough to try to murder him at his favorite nightclub, the Blue Olive. He was alive only because years ago, he'd been trained by Green Bones straight from Janloon. The two crewboys who'd taken a run at him were delivered back to their Boss in body bags.

In addition to the Crews, there were the drug lords from Tomascio to think of—vicious wesp bastards. Remi also had to consider that he'd angered many of his fellow Green Bones in Port Massy. They might come after him themselves, though more likely the sanctimonious hypocrites were busy covering their own asses and ratting him out to the police at every turn.

So when rumor reached Jon Remi that a man new to town had been frequenting the local fighting dens and unsubtly asking questions about the Bad Keck, his first suspicion was that the nosy stranger was a police informant. When he had his own people investigate, his suspicions changed and deepened. Then, he became extremely curious.

"Pick this guy up," he ordered. "I want to meet him."

Tonight, the only people on the second floor of the Feast of Janloon were three of Remi's trusted men—Snakeheads who'd all been awarded jade for killing crewboys. One of them peered between the slats of the window blinds at the sound of an arriving vehicle and slamming car doors on the street below. "They're here, boss."

Remi got a good look at the stranger as he was led up the stairwell and across the restaurant floor to Remi's table. The man took off his cap as he approached. He wore plain brown pants and an untucked black shirt under a faded corduroy jacket. Remi had assumed the man would be in his late forties, but he looked older than that, his face hard and lined, his dark hair flecked with gray and receding at the temples. He walked with a certain cautious, unhurried care, but the alertness of his manner, the arrogant predatory quality with which he held himself, indicated that this was a man the Kekonese would call green in the soul.

"Remi-jen," said Maik Tar warily. He touched his forehead and dipped into a shallow salute.

Jon Remi gestured for the older man to sit down at the table. Maik did so, helping himself to a glass of water and leaning back in the chair. He was not at ease—he did not seem to be the sort of person ever fully at ease—but he displayed no anxiety to be sitting in front of one of the city's most notorious crime bosses. Remi studied the man with interest. He gestured to the server. "What'll you drink?"

"Just water," said Maik, speaking in Kekonese.

"Not even hoji?" said Remi. "This place imports the quality stuff from Kekon, none of the cheap shit."

"I don't drink," Maik said. "Not anymore."

Remi shrugged and ordered another beer for himself. The other three Snakeheads at the table squinted at Maik in fascinated disappointment, as if he were a fictional character come to life. "Tell me," Remi said, "what brings a man who used to be a top Green Bone of the No Peak clan here to Resville?"

Maik scowled and shifted in his chair. "If you brought me here to talk about the No Peak clan, you have the wrong person," he said bitterly. "I haven't been a Green Bone for twelve years. I haven't touched jade, I haven't been back to Janloon, I haven't seen my family, not once. I'm no one in Kekon."

The man's words were thick with so much sour resignation that Remi didn't doubt they were true. Besides, he'd already dug into Maik's past. Remi's connections in Port Massy had corroborated the stories: Maik Tar used to be one of the most feared Green Bones on either side of the Amaric Ocean. He'd been Kaul Hiloshudon's right hand. He'd put the notorious Willum "Skinny" Reams at the bottom of Whitting Bay in pieces. Then, a dozen years ago, he'd killed his own fiancée in a blind rage and been exiled from the No Peak clan. Every one of Remi's investigations confirmed that Maik had no contact with Janloon. No visits back to the island, no phone calls, no money sent to him. Maik Tar, people told him, was jadeless and washed up, but not to be fucked with.

"And yet, after all these years, people still know who you are," Remi said, tapping his teeth thoughtfully with the end of a toothpick. "That's one hell of a reputation, old man. So I don't think it should be any surprise that I'd like to know why you've shown up in my city."

Maik's shoulders came down and he blew out a noisy breath. "Port Massy is a big place, big enough even for someone like me to disappear into. But it's getting too expensive to live there. And too many people have ties to No Peak and know who I used to be. I can't ever quite escape it. So it's time for a change. A fresh start. Resville is warmer, and there are Kekonese people here."

Maik tilted his head curiously and gave Remi a straight stare, something that few men dared to do. "Also, I'd heard of this man in Resville they call Bad Keck Remi. And I couldn't help wondering if he might have work for someone like me."

Remi raised his eyebrows, pleased that his own reputation had reached the ears of a man like Maik Tar. "I've always got work that needs to be done," he said nonchalantly. "But why would I trust someone who used to work for the Kauls?"

"You used to work for the Kauls yourself," Maik pointed out. "More recently than me. And now you're your own man." The former Green Bone turned his head, looking around the room at the Snakeheads, but Remi saw that his gaze didn't linger on expensive suits or shoes, or even weapons. He was looking for the glint of green on fingers and wrists. Maik returned his attention to Remi. "I've heard you give jade to those who do a good job for you," he said slowly. "That's something the Kauls will never give back to me."

Remi wasn't highly trained in Perception but he could still tell that Maik wasn't lying. "How do I know you weren't sent here by the people in Port Massy?"

Maik blinked, then smirked. "*Those* pussies? You've got to be joking." Two of Remi's men couldn't help laughing. Maik shook his head. "There used to be thick blood there, back when Rohn Toro and old Dauk were alive, but that was a long time ago."

As soon as Remi had heard that Maik Tar was in town and asking after him, he'd known he would either have to kill the man or bring him onto his side. Now he admitted to himself that having a man of Maik Tar's caliber and aptitude in violence in his employ could be useful indeed. Remi was in need of capable management at the street level. Two of his best lieutenants had been arrested in the past three months, and he was secretly worried about the Crews taking advantage of this weakness.

The Bad Keck wore jade but he was Espenian-born. No matter what sort of reputation he garnered in Resville, it could not compare to the notoriety and mystique associated with the Kekonese Green Bone clans. Keko-Espenians, no matter how they felt about the old country, all understood that the best jade warriors came from the island, that they grew up with jade and began wearing it as children, were trained at grueling martial academies, and wore it openly in a culture that revered greenness. There was simply no way to compete with those advantages. Maik Tar could be an unparalleled asset.

Still, Remi had his doubts. "You haven't been a Fist in a long time."

A shadow of ferocity crossed Maik's face. "I used to be the Pillarman of Kaul Hiloshudon," he said with a note of undiminished pride. "He trusted me with the clan's toughest jobs, where blood had to be spilled, carefully and at the right time and in the right way. I was good at what I did, and it wasn't just because I was young and green. I had the right sort of mind for it." Regret settled over the man's face like a mask. "I made *one mistake*, a terrible mistake, and now I can never go home. I want to do work I'm good at again, that's all. But if you've got too many doubts about me, that's fine, I can understand that." Maik put on his cap and began to stand.

"Hold on, now," Remi said. He chewed the end of the toothpick as he motioned to one of the Snakeheads to bring his briefcase. "A lot of men make themselves out to be bigger than they really are. Now that I've met you for myself, I've got to say—you don't seem like one of those types." Remi opened his briefcase and took out a handgun, a roll of cash, and a set of car keys. He placed them on the table in front of him. "You want work, you've got it. The gun, the money, and the car behind the restaurant are yours. Call it a signing bonus. From now on, you work for me. Talk to Teto after this; he'll get you started."

Maik gave a small, impassive nod of agreement, as if Remi had bought him a meal instead of handing him a new life as the newest member of the Resville Snakehead gang.

"Any questions?" Remi asked.

Maik picked up the cash and pocketed it without counting the amount. Perhaps doing so went against his Kekonese sensibilities. He took the gun and the keys, slipped them into his jacket, and stood. "Just tell me what you want me to do."

CHAPTER

37

Leaving Home

the twentieth year, third month

When the boarding announcement for his flight came over the terminal speaker, Niko thought, *It's not too late.* He could still walk out of the airport and go home, admit he'd made a mistake and ask for his uncle's forgiveness and his place back in the clan. He'd summoned all his angry determination and righteous defiance to face down his parents with his decision. Now, however, an unsettled feeling was rolling around in his stomach, and he was more afraid than excited.

He took out his passport and boarding pass. "I guess this is it," he said.

His uncle Anden walked him to the gate. Neither of them spoke. Anden was the one member of the family with whom Niko could always be comfortably silent. Often throughout his childhood, when his mother had been struggling through her long recovery from brain injury, Niko and his siblings had been cared for by their aunts and uncles. Anden was Niko's favorite relative. Uncle Anden would let him read for hours, take him to the park to feed the ducks, or rent movies they would watch together. He asked only a few questions and listened to the answers without lecturing. Unlike other adults, he didn't ferry Niko around on a schedule, or begin conversations with, "When you grow up and get your jade..." No one else in the clan was like Uncle Anden, so he didn't expect anyone else to be like him.

As they embraced at the gate, Anden said, "Promise me you'll be careful. You're not leaving Kekon as a student, the way I did. You'll be wearing jade into dangerous situations, far from home."

The look of worry on Anden's face made Niko feel more guilty than any amount of shouting or blistering disapproval from his parents. "I promise, Uncle," Niko said. "Thanks for letting me stay at your place. I hope it wasn't too much trouble for you and Jirhuya."

"Of course it wasn't," Anden said, but he was looking around, scanning the passing travelers hopefully. He rubbed his bare wrist, as if wishing for his jade and sense of Perception. Niko knew that Anden had gone to the house and argued with the Pillar. Anden hadn't said anything about it, but Ru had. Ru had come over to the apartment and said a lot of things last night, spilling his feelings out like marbles as he begged Niko to change his mind.

"But *why*, Niko? *Why* would you throw away your position like that?" Ru had been distraught with bewilderment. "I know the pressure must be a lot to handle right now, but *everyone* in the clan is rooting for you to become Pillar." As usual, his brother exaggerated, certain that what was indisputable to him must be the truth.

Niko had turned away from the pleading expression. "I've never been in charge of my own life, Ru. Da tells you to study what you want in college, to become whatever you want to be. He's never once said that to me. What makes anyone think I even *want* to be Pillar?"

Ru grabbed him by the shoulders, turning him back around. When stirred by strong belief, he was easily the more righteously angry one.

"If I hadn't been born a stone-eye, I'd do my best to become the Pillar, no matter how hard it was or even if I thought I might like to do something else." His eyes bored insistently into Niko's. "Think of the difference you could make, of all the good you could do for so many people. The clan affects the lives of millions. It needs a Pillar who's strong and smart. How can you just... *run away* from that kind of responsibility?"

Niko stepped back, pulling roughly out of his brother's grasp. "I'm not running away."

"Then come back home with me right now," Ru exclaimed. "We'll talk to Da together. I'll back you up. So will Jaya, and you know how good she is at getting her way. We'll convince Da to let you go to college part-time while you work toward becoming a Fist. Like what Ayt Ato was doing—if he can do it, you definitely can, you're a lot smarter. You just need a change, and then you'll feel better about everything, I know it. We can go to Jan Royal together, like we planned."

When Niko gazed at him, unmoved, Ru went from cajoling to accusing. "How could you not even tell me what you were thinking? What happened to brothers sticking together?"

Niko shook his head sadly. "We're not kids anymore, Ru."

The disappointment and naked hurt that had swept over his brother's face had curdled Niko with shame, but he wouldn't let it show. Ru was the only one who could've changed his mind, who could've broken his resolve. So he'd had to harden his heart.

Niko picked up his suitcase. He hadn't packed much. Where he was going, he didn't expect he'd have much room for personal belongings anyway. Two weeks of orientation at GSI headquarters in a town called Fort Jonsrock in northeastern Espenia would be followed by three months at one of the company's training compounds. After that, he would be on a two-year work contract and could be sent anywhere in the world.

Anden stopped his fruitless glancing around and turned back to Niko with apology in his eyes. "I tried, Niko." His shoulders sagged under the weight of resignation. "I—"

The unmistakable smooth warmth of the Pillar's jade aura

materialized in Niko's Perception two seconds before Hilo walked up behind them, his hands in the pockets of his jacket. The expression on his face was unreadable, although his eyes were tired.

"Andy," he said, "let me talk to my son alone."

Anden looked between the Pillar and Niko. Wordlessly, he put a hand on his nephew's shoulder and gave it a supportive squeeze. Then he touched his forehead to the Pillar in expressionless acknowledgment and walked away, back through the airport terminal.

"Take a walk with me," Hilo said.

"I'm about to get on a plane."

"It'll only take a minute," his uncle said, with such familiar parental authority that Niko obeyed. They walked farther down the terminal. Niko wanted to act rude and angry. The Pillar knew he'd been staying at Anden's place. If he'd wanted to talk, he could've shown up at any time earlier, instead of at the last minute, with the flight about to depart.

But he'd shown up, in the end.

"Does Ma know you're here?" Niko asked.

"Yes," Hilo said.

So his mother was still furious at him. Otherwise, she would be here as well. Everyone knew the vengeful reputation of Kaul Hilo, but Niko understood that his mother was the one who was less forgiving, who could carry a longer grudge.

"You're not going to change my mind," Niko declared. "It's too late for that."

"It's too late for a lot of things." Hilo stopped and turned to face his nephew. He handed Niko an envelope. "I've given you back access to your bank accounts. There's a calling card in the envelope, and a list of phone numbers—the Weather Man's branch offices in every country where we have them, and contact numbers for Green Bones overseas who are part of the clan or are our allies, who'll help you if you need help. Only if you really need it. Otherwise, you're on your own. "

Several conflicting impulses came into Niko's mind but he couldn't form any of them in words. He wanted to disdainfully reject his uncle's gesture and hang on to the emotional advantage, but that seemed a childish thing to do. He wanted to relent, to say something that would make things right between them before he left, but that felt like admitting defeat. Niko had never been good at responding to his feelings in the moment, so he said nothing.

The final boarding call was announced. He put the envelope in his inside jacket pocket. "I'd better go," he mumbled.

Hilo cupped a hand roughly around the back of Niko's head, pulling his nephew close, and spoke in a low declaration. "I would cut Jim Sunto's throat and burn his company to the ground if I thought that would stop you." His grip tightened fiercely on the back of Niko's neck. "But I know it's not about that. I love you enough to see that you have the right to hate me. Just remember, I only ever made the decisions I thought were best for you."

His uncle let go. His jade aura receded as he walked away through the streams of people.

———

Hilo stepped out of the airport and got into the passenger seat of Lott's Lumezza FT Scorpion as it pulled up to the curb. They drove to an airport hotel and went up to a guest suite on the fifth floor. Vin Solu, the new First Fist of Janloon, was in the room along with Hejo, the First Fist of White Rats, and one of Hejo's tech experts. Three young men were seated around a table covered with small gadgets, listening as Hejo and his technician explained each of the items. At Hilo and Lott's entrance, the men stood hastily and saluted the Pillar. "Kaul-jen," they murmured in unison.

Hilo looked them over. Two of the young men were Golden Spiders from the Kekonese army: a man named Dasho whom Hilo did not know, and Teije Inno, a remote cousin of the Kaul family. The third young man was a junior Finger named Sim. All of them had been quickly but carefully chosen by the Horn. They each wore a little jade, five pieces at the most, and fit the profile of lower-ranked Green Bones looking to better their fortunes. Each had applied separately and been offered employment by GSI. Packed suitcases and bags sat on the floor near their feet.

"Niko's on his flight," Hilo said. "You'll all be leaving on different ones over the next day."

Lott withdrew an envelope from his pocket and handed out airplane tickets to each man, along with credit cards and cash. Hilo surveyed the various items on the table, several of which had been opened up to show their workings: hidden cameras built into travel alarm clocks and pens, audio recorders inside cigarette lighters, bugs that could be planted inside rooms, and most ingeniously of all, recording devices concealed within or behind jade watches, earrings, and pendants. Those had been the most expensive and difficult to create, but were also the most likely to go undetected. GSI recruits could bring their own personal jade and wear it as they liked, and no one would dare to touch or closely examine another man's jade.

"You've learned how to use all this stuff?" Hilo asked.

Hejo's tech expert, one of three that specialized in outfitting the clan's White Rats, said, "They're all pretty straightforward. They can be easily discarded if necessary, and except for the jade, none of it can be traced back to No Peak. Once you get to any new location, use the credit cards we gave you at any bank or ATM, or call one of the contact numbers. We'll know immediately where you are. If you're caught, we have solid cover stories in place to prove that you're being paid to gather information by investigative journalists working for the *Janloon Daily*."

Hilo said to the three men, "Don't worry. You're infiltrating an Espenian company, not the Mountain clan. If you get caught, they won't kill you. They probably won't even cripple you or beat you badly. They'll only fire you and sue you, and that's no problem, we can handle that. You'll be fine so long as you don't act suspicious or tell any outright lies. Sunto's Perception isn't anything like Vin's."

Sim asked uneasily, "Won't he be worried about White Rats?"

The Pillar made a face. "Sunto's convinced that Green Bones are eager to flee the clans to join his company. After the talk we had in his office on Euman Island, he expects me to whisper his name and for any attack from No Peak to come from head-on. After you're gone, you'll all be officially condemned by the clan as shameful traitors.

Remember that your families will know the truth. Send us whatever information you can, but the main thing is that you watch Niko." His nephew was a godsdamned fool, but there was no way under Heaven that Hilo was going to lose him in some stupid foreign war. "So long as my son is alive and well, and you're sending us whatever information you can, the money will keep going to your families." More money than GSI was paying, and more importantly, things that GSI could not provide: loan forgiveness for Dasho's parents, college for Teije's sister, an expedited heart transplant for Sim's niece.

Lott said, "Do you all understand what's being asked of you? If so, kneel and pledge your word to the Pillar."

Together, the three men lowered themselves to the carpet of the hotel room and raised their clasped hands to Hilo in salute.

CHAPTER

38

We've Got to Do Something

Bero snuck back into Janloon like a cat to a dumpster—quietly and hungrily. Nearly six years had passed since the Espenians had yanked him out of the city overnight. Six years! Time that seemed to have magically disappeared. Galo and Berglund had arranged for him to be relocated, not to the ROE, but to Iwansa, an Espenian territory at the southern end of the Uwiwan archipelago. Bero hadn't even known that the Espenians owned a tiny island in the Uwiwas, an unpleasantly dry and mind-deadening place catering to Espenian tourists.

The Espenians had given him a new identity and a one-room apartment. Bero hadn't been stupid and blown all the crisp Espenian thalirs he'd made from his years as an informant by living lavishly and drawing attention to himself in Janloon, so he had enough money to last a long time in the Uwiwas, where everything was cheap.

The main problem was that he hated Iwansa. No one spoke Kekonese. Bero didn't know any Uwiwan so he had to get by with the bits of Espenian he picked up. The local food was all bland mush wrapped in palm leaves, shit like that. He made some money by hanging around the place where the cruise ships docked and finding Kekonese or Espenian tourists who would pay him to drive them around.

There was nothing to do. All he wanted was to go back to Kekon, but the final thing his Espenian military handlers had done was warn him against doing so. He couldn't shake the unsettling memory of the black-clad ROE operatives taking down Molovni and carrying him out of the apartment with a hood over his head. A year after the Janloon bombing, Bero heard the news about an Ygutanian defector named Agent M who gave up all the secrets of the nekolva program to the ROE military. It had to be Molovni, but the Vastik eya Molovni that Bero knew had tried to put a bullet in his own head rather than be captured. Bero could only imagine what the Espenians had done to the man to turn him into their meek tool. What might they do to Bero if they thought he was going to run?

Eventually, however, they stopped paying attention to him. Bero stopped receiving the occasional discomfiting phone calls from ROE government representatives checking up on him. Perhaps with the Slow War moving in some other direction, what Bero did or didn't know was no longer of any interest or concern. Or Galo and Berglund simply forgot about him. Bero still despised Iwansa but he had to admit he'd become accustomed to it. What danger would he be putting himself in if he went back to Kekon?

You're such a fucking pussy now.

The instant he was back in Janloon, however, Bero felt better, as if he'd been slowly turning on a cooking spit for years and finally been plunged into a cool tub of salve. On his first day back, he sat on a park bench in Paw-Paw soaking the city back into his pores—the grease of street food, the sounds of hawkers and cab drivers shouting in Kekonese, the spring damp on his parched skin. Even garbage in Janloon smelled better than it did elsewhere, the rats were sleeker.

Most of the people Bero had known were gone. Out of curiosity, he went back to the Little Persimmon lounge and to his great surprise he found Tadino working behind the bar. The man looked different—his hair was longer and he'd lost his sneering, sharp-tongued bravado. Instead, a hunted look darted in his eyes, and a raised red circular scar on his left cheek distorted the skin of his face.

"Shit, keke, is that you?" Tadino exclaimed. "Where have you been?"

"Nowhere," Bero said. "Staying the fuck away from everyone."

"Left town? Smart move. I thought maybe they picked you up in the raids along with everyone else." Tadino dried his hands on a towel and glanced around nervously before leaning in to speak in a lowered voice. "They had our names on a fucking list, keke. Did you know Molovni disappeared? He must've ratted all of us out. Good thing you got away."

"What happened to your face?" Bero asked.

Tadino winced, involuntarily touching his scarred cheek. "You really have been gone, haven't you? The Mountain clan came in here, saying this was a meeting place for the clanless. I got off easy because they thought I was just the bartender."

Bero said, "It doesn't look that bad."

"It hurt so fucking much I pissed myself." Tadino shuddered at the memory and ran an agitated hand through his disheveled hair. He gave Bero a strangely desperate look. "I've got to say, I'm glad to see you, keke. There aren't many of us left, you know? Why'd you come back here, anyway?"

"I need work."

It was true. He'd used up all his Espenian cash and needed to make money again. The obvious thing to do would be to go back to stealing or drug dealing, but after talking with Tadino, he was forced to conclude that was too risky. The clans had always tolerated some low level of street crime, but these days, anyone caught engaging in anti-clan activities—stealing from or damaging clan businesses, shine dealing, jade trafficking, associating with the Clanless Future Movement or politically radical causes, or simply having too many suspicious foreign connections—would get anything from a face branding up to a gravesite, depending on the severity of the offense. Bero had at different times in his life been guilty of every single one of those things, and now that he was finally back in Janloon, the last thing he wanted was for Green Bones to notice him.

Bero had few legally employable skills, but he could drive and knew the streets well, so he got a job as a package delivery man. The money was shit, though, so after six months, he cooked up a plan with two of Tadino's friends and began using the delivery company's van to move bootlegged video and music tapes to booth vendors who sold them to tourists in the Docks and in the Temple and Monument Districts. As long as they were ripping off foreigners, he figured he was safe, although the money was only so-so. Nothing close to what he'd once made as a jade-wearing rockfish or a shine dealer or an informer. Bero decided he could accept that. Less money, but less danger. So be it. He was thirty-six now, fucking old.

"We've got to do something," Tadino began saying every time Bero showed up at the Little Persimmon to drink. The man's scarred face didn't seem to repel customers. If anything, the sort of people who visited the Little Persimmon seemed to treat it as a badge of honor, or a mark of credibility, like a prison tattoo. "We've got to save the Clanless Future Movement before it's too late. Otherwise the clans win."

"The clans always win," Bero mumbled scornfully. "Guriho and Otonyo blew up a building with all the Green Bone leaders in it and where are they now? Feeding worms."

"'Cause they got it all wrong," Tadino insisted. "I'm telling you, I've thought about this a lot. Trying to take out the clans like that was stupid. All it did was unite them in crushing us under their heels. Now they're hunting us down like dogs." Tadino wiped down the bar counter with violent swipes of the cloth, putting all his hatred into the polished wood. "And what happened to all those foreign 'friends' that bastard Molovni promised us would support the cause? Where are the fuckers now? Left us to be slaughtered, that's what. We've got to save ourselves, 'cause no one else will."

Bero couldn't argue with that, so he said nothing, which only encouraged Tadino. The man leaned an elbow on the bar and jutted his angular face near Bero's. "Don't tell me you're *done*, keke. You're not just going to sit there like a lump and drink, are you? You and me, we're still cut. You still want to stick it to the clans as much as I do."

Bero scowled into his hoji. Just because he still hated Green Bones didn't mean he was going to risk his neck for the sorry remnants of the Clanless Future Movement. Without Molovni bringing in money and weapons from Ygutan, what could they do? Better to move on, forget all that old shit.

See? You really have turned into a fucking pussy.

Bero downed the rest of his drink with a surge of self-loathing. He'd become soft and useless while away in Iwansa. He used to be full of thick blood and daring. He'd done things no one else could've done. Tadino might be talking bitter nonsense, but at least he was still *thinking*, still trying to do what Bero used to do for himself— come up with the plan that could change *everything*. Maybe the rat-faced bastard was right. Maybe there was still more for Bero to do.

He squinted with guarded interest for the first time. "What do you have in mind?"

"Here's the thing." Tadino licked his lips. "The only way to take down a Green Bone clan is with *another* Green Bone clan."

"What're you getting at?"

"When are times best for people like us?" Tadino answered his own question with a glint in his eye. "When there's *war*, keke. The way to bring down the clans is to make them go to war with each other again."

CHAPTER

39

The Stone-Eye Club

On his first day of classes at Jan Royal University, Kaul Rulinshin stood in the main campus plaza, awash in nervous excitement as he watched students strolling across the grounds between the wide lawns and brick buildings. Ru didn't think of himself as a particularly academic person, but having grown up in a ruling clan family where nearly everyone was a jade warrior or a businessman, the sheer wealth of possibilities in college made him giddy.

One dense cloud of sadness marred the clear blue sky of his mood. *Niko should be here.* Niko had always been the smart one, the one who liked reading and was good at school, who would surprise adults with the sorts of things he'd learned and remembered. Now, Ru had no idea where his brother was. He'd received one letter from Niko, saying that he'd finished two weeks of orientation at GSI headquarters in Fort Jonsrock, Espenia. Ru had to look up the place in an encyclopedia to find out where it was. Niko didn't say where he was going now, nor did he mention the painful conversation they'd had before he'd left. In the letter, he didn't even say whether he liked the job so far, whether he was happy. There'd been no return address on the envelope, no way for Ru to write back.

Ru shouldered his backpack and went to his first class, Government and Society 120. It was an entry-level undergraduate course, held in a large lecture hall with hard seats and weak lighting. No one recognized him in that class or the other two he attended that day, which was not surprising. His father saw to it that the media kept away from him, and compared to his siblings, he'd always gone unnoticed within the clan.

When he checked out books from the library the next day, however, the librarian who took his student ID card looked at him curiously, then glanced down at his name. "Oh! Kaul Rulinshin? You're the Pillar's son, the—" She did not finish the sentence with *stone-eye*. Flushing with embarrassment, she touched her forehead in abbreviated salute. "My husband and his parents are Lantern Men of No Peak. They own Wan's Chariot—the chain of autobody shops. All the clan's top Green Bones take their cars there. My husband's worked on the Horn's Lumezza, the Weather Man's Cabriola, and of course your father's Duchesse." She checked his books out with vigor. "We were at the clan New Year's party, the big one at the General Star Hotel last month. I suppose you must've been there? It was huge! I'm sure your father doesn't remember us, since he spoke to so many people that night, but if you get a chance, will you let him know that the Wans from Wan's Chariot send their loyal respects?"

"I'll let him know when I'm home for dinner this Fifthday," Ru promised.

The librarian beamed. "I'm honored to have met you. Come back often. If you ever want to book one of the private study cubicles or the computer stations, just let me know. I'll get you the best one. There's a two-hour limit, but I can override that."

Ru thanked her. The next time he went to the library to check out books, he told Mrs. Wan that his father said he wouldn't trust his Duchesse to any other autobody shop, which delighted her so much she gave him a staff code that he could use on any of the photocopy machines in the library without paying for copies. Ru had a few other encounters with clan members or associates on campus. The teaching assistant of his economics class was the younger brother of a high-rank Fist. One of his classmates in Kekonese Literature 300 was the daughter of a No Peak loyalist in the Royal Council. Occasionally, he was recognized on campus by strangers who stopped him to convey their regards to his family.

This sort of attention would've irritated Niko. He would've started power walking from place to place to avoid being approached by people. Ru didn't mind. He always smiled and replied in a friendly way. With Niko gone, he had to start thinking of himself as the first son of the family. Even though he couldn't be a leader in the clan, that didn't mean he couldn't make a difference. After all, his mother was a stone-eye, too, but she helped his father to be the Pillar. Ru thought he could've been of help to Niko, if only Niko would believe in himself first.

He'll come back, Ru told himself. *He has to.* It had been heartbreaking to see his brother not only condemned by their father, but excoriated by the press, held up as evidence of the declining morals of a younger generation that was less green and no longer respected aisho. Those self-appointed pundits didn't know anything about Niko, and their unflattering characterization certainly didn't apply to Jaya, or Cam, or the Juen twins. It angered Ru to hear people say ignorant and negative things based on shallow impressions or hearsay. So he felt a responsibility to represent his family and No Peak as well as possible. Besides, he liked to meet people and to learn of all the different ways his clan affected the lives of ordinary Kekonese.

Nevertheless, Ru felt lonely on the large campus of Jan Royal University. His family's status had always set him apart from his peers at school and added a layer of difficulty when it came to making and keeping friends. Classmates assumed he wouldn't want to stand in line with them for hours to watch the new Danny Sinjo movie, when his parents could take him to the premiere. They hesitated to invite him to a pool party in Mountain-controlled Summer Park, knowing he would have to come with bodyguards. He was thankful to have had his high school relayball team, and his best friends, Tian and Shin, who treated him no differently than anyone else. But Tian had gone to the Lukang Institute of Technology for college and Shin had joined the Kekonese military. Ru didn't even have Koko to keep him company, as pets were not allowed in student housing.

Ru perused the student center cafeteria's bulletin board with notices advertising different campus clubs and decided to take a chance. On a Fourthday afternoon six weeks into his first semester, he made his way into a classroom in the basement of the Social Sciences building to attend a student chapter meeting of the Charitable Society for Jade Nonreactivity. He knew about the CSJN because his mother had spoken at some of their events and been interviewed for a profile in their magazine. Ru's mouth was dry with nerves when he walked into the room. How would the club members react to the son of a clan Pillar intruding on their meeting? After all, Ru's family sat at the top of the cultural power structure that revered jade abilities and stigmatized stone-eyes and the entire Abukei race.

A few desks pushed together against the wall held an assortment of bottles of soda and a spread of snacks—the expected bowls of nuts and crackers, date cakes, sesame and fruit candies, the usual junk. There were fourteen people in the room—nine Kekonese stone-eyes and five Abukei students. A young Abukei woman greeted Ru cheerfully and directed him to write his name on a name tag. He did so with trepidation, then grabbed a soda and sat down in one of the empty chairs that had been arranged in a circle in the center of the classroom.

One of the Kekonese students stood up and identified himself as Dano, a third-year political science major and the leader of the student chapter of the CSJN. Even though it was the middle of the afternoon, Dano looked as if he'd just woken up. His spiky hair was sticking up in several directions, he hadn't shaved, and he was wearing a rumpled T-shirt and jeans that might've been fished out from the bottom of a laundry basket. Nevertheless, he was bursting with enthusiasm.

"Our club is about supporting each other," he declared to the small group. "I'll bet every one of us in this room has been in a situation where we felt as if we were completely alone. The only unlucky one, someone the gods didn't care about. Well, that's not true. You're not alone. And the more we work together to educate people about non-reactivity and be open about who we are, the less alone we'll be."

Dano went on to explain the meeting schedule, club events, the affiliation with the national CSJN and the campus partnership with the Abukei Student Alliance, and volunteer positions that needed to be filled. "I see we have a few new members," Dano said, "so let's all introduce ourselves." He sat back down in his chair.

Ru did not remember any of the other students' names. When it came time for him to speak, his hands were clammy. He wiped them on his jeans and said, "My name's Kaul Rulinshin. This is my first year at Jan Royal." He cleared his throat. "My family is...well, it's full of Green Bones. I've spent my whole life surrounded by clan culture and jade, so...this is all pretty new to me. I'm glad to have found this club, and I'm looking forward to getting to know everyone."

He couldn't read any of the expressions around him. If only he had a sense of Perception, he would know whether to get up and leave. Of course, if he had a sense of Perception, he wouldn't be here at all.

Dano began stamping his feet on the floor in applause. The rest of the club members followed his example, smiling in welcome, and Ru's shoulders came down in relief.

Dano said, "Welcome to the stone-eye club, keke. By the way, I'm opposed to everything your clan stands for." He grinned so wide his cheeks stretched, then reached over to clap Ru on the shoulder. "We're going to be great friends!"

They did become friends. Dano was a natural social connector who seemed to know people from all walks of life and was always going to or coming from a wild party. Spending a considerable number of his waking hours intoxicated or hungover did not appear to dent his energy. Besides being the leader of the campus CSJN chapter, he was involved in the Independence League, a grassroots organization that advocated for the election of non-clan-affiliated political candidates, the Immigrant Rights Watch, which provided legal and economic assistance to refugees, and the *Royal Creed*, the campus newspaper. At times Ru wondered if Dano even went to class.

They had spirited debates after every stone-eye club meeting. Dano loved to argue almost as much as he loved to drink. After Ru mentioned that he would likely work in the No Peak clan after he graduated, Dano said, "You'll be devoting your career to upholding the very system that stigmatizes nonreactivity. Don't you think that's like a pig building its own roasting pit?"

Ru's mouth fell open. He had never met anyone who would dare to say something like that to him. "You can't blame hundreds of years of superstition on my clan. My da has always supported me and never put me down. He named my ma as his Pillarman. Maybe my ma and me being stone-eyes in the clan is one reason prejudice against nonreactivity is going *down*."

They left the Social Sciences basement and hurried across campus, late for class but still arguing. "Even if your relatives are nice to you personally," Dano conceded, "that doesn't change the fact that the clans exist to protect the interests of Green Bones and keep them in power to the detriment of everyone else."

"Society isn't a contest of Green Bones versus non–Green Bones!" Ru retorted. "Every Green Bone has family members and friends who don't wear jade, and the clans protect all of Kekon. If you studied history"—a shameless dig, because Dano was supposed to be on his way to history class—"you'd know that if it weren't for Green Bones, our country would be a plundered postcolonial mess like the Uwiwas instead of a prosperous modern economy."

Dano shrugged, clearly enjoying getting a rise out of his verbal sparring partner. "I admit the One Mountain Society played a big part in overthrowing the Shotarian occupation, but that was almost fifty years ago. Other countries don't need clans. They're obsolete, parochial institutions."

"Must you talk out of your ass?" Ru almost shouted. "Of course, clannism isn't perfect—no system is. That's why everyone should work together on improving it, not throwing it out altogether like the foreigners and anarchists want us to. Think about international trade, military reform, even the growth of the entertainment industry—the Green Bone clans *led* those changes. My own *relatives* made them happen. You don't know a damn thing!" They reached the Foreign Studies building where Ru's next class was located. "So, see you later on Fifthday?"

"Yeah," said Dano. "Bring cash; I hear there're going to be strippers."

Ru wasn't sure if he actually liked Dano or not. He could be morally pompous, ignorant, and infuriating, but Ru had never had anyone challenge his worldview so regularly. It was invigorating.

He made the mistake of telling Jaya about his new friend. "He sounds like a fat-mouthed little shithead," his sister declared. "Did he really say those things? I'm surprised the Kobens haven't picked him up and burned his face yet." She squinted at her brother with concern.

Jaya always had an insufferable habit of acting like they were the same age, as if her destiny as a Green Bone somehow promoted her up the natural sibling order. When they were in primary school, Jaya had kicked another girl to the ground during recess and dumped all her school books into a muddy puddle for pointing to Ru and tugging her earlobe. "If you do it again, I'll come to your house and kill your pets," Jaya had promised, as if *she* were the older sibling and had to protect Ru from bullies on the playground. The other girl had cried, which had mortified and embarrassed Ru beyond belief. He would've ignored the mild taunting, and he certainly didn't need Jaya to stick up for him.

It was obvious from her expression now that she suspected Ru wasn't keeping good company. "I wonder if any of these people you're meeting in college are on Lott-jen's watch lists. What did you say his name was again?"

"Forget it," Ru said quickly. "He just likes to say provocative things; he's not anyone to worry about." Some of the things Dano said could indeed be interpreted as radical anti-clan sentiment, which might raise suspicion of ties to the Clanless Future Movement. Ru had been twelve years old at the time of the Janloon bombing. He would never forget being pulled out of school and waiting for over a day to find out if his father was still alive. He hated the violent anarchists and understood better than anyone why there was little tolerance for anti-clan attitudes.

Dano, however, was a college student like him, not a CFM terrorist. Ru was starting to think that the threat of clanless extremists unfortunately stifled worthwhile discussions about how the clans could or should change in ways that benefited more Kekonese, including those who could never wear jade or weren't born into clan families. Dano didn't have the insider's view that Ru did. The Mountain and No Peak were vaguely malevolent monolithic entities to him. He couldn't understand that Ru's parents and his aunt Shae and his uncle Anden were real people. Good people. People were what made the clan.

Ru disagreed with his friend on many things, but he didn't want anything bad to happen to him. He resolved to keep his mouth shut around Jaya from now on. His sister was a year-eight at the Academy but sure to take oaths as a Finger when she graduated. If Jaya thought Dano was a threat to society, or at the very least, a bad influence on her brother, who knew what she might do.

CHAPTER

40

⌢

Difficult Daughters

the twenty-first year, first month

Kaul Dushuron Academy had changed in notable ways since Shae had been a student. New buildings and facilities were dedicated to classes in firearms, surveillance, and computer programming, among other subjects. There was now a separate dormitory for adult foreign students, and additional training fields to accommodate trainees in the low-residency program, which had been instituted despite some concern from alumni that it could dilute the school's brand and take away focus from the core full-time curriculum. One thing that had not changed in over twenty-five years, however, was the tradition of Pre-Trials.

Jaya's year-eight Pre-Trials were held on a crisp but sunny late autumn day, and the entire Kaul family turned out for the event to support her. Even Anden and Jirhuya made an appearance, having jointly decided to endure their respective discomforts with attending. For Anden, any visit to the Academy brought up the memory of his humiliating graduation ceremony. Jirhuya might be one of the few Abukei to have ever set foot on Academy grounds.

In a rare show of fraternal support, Ru cheered loudly for his sister, and Hilo glowed with pride when Jaya's name shot to the top of the ranking list after the Deflection event. Her Lightness scores in the afternoon brought her down to sixth, but Hilo said he didn't care if Jaya was First of Class; he only wanted her to be happy with her performance. "This is where all the Green Bones of our family went to school," Hilo told Tia, holding Shae's daughter on his lap while Woon went to buy them all sodas. "You'll come here too when you're older."

At the Massacre of the Mice, Jaya stepped up to her position, cricked her neck back and forth, and slapped hands with the girl next to her. She stuck her tongue out at one of the boys at the end of the row and blew a kiss to one of the watching year-sevens, which made Hilo's eyes narrow with suspicion. The mice in their cages scurried around in circles, their tiny claws scratching against the wire mesh. The bell sounded. Jaya snuffed out two mice in one corner at the same time with her first blast of Channeling. She cursed out loud as she missed the next one, stunning the mouse but not killing it, but finished it off on the next try and killed the last two with successive pops of energy, beating out the next fastest time—the boy at the end of the row—by .85 of a second. The crowd cheered, Hilo loudest of all, and Jaya punched her fists into the air and danced around in victory.

Tia burst into sobs.

Shae and Woon tried to comfort her. "They're only mice," Woon said. "They have to die for people to practice Channeling."

"Why do people cheer when they die?" Tia wept.

"We're not cheering because they died, we're cheering because Jaya won," Shae explained.

"She won by killing them! Does everyone in school have to kill mice? Did you kill them?" When they both admitted they had, Tia cried harder.

Shae and Woon left Pre-Trials before the awards ceremony and stopped Tia's tears by getting fried bread from a Hot Hut drive-thru on the way home. While Woon settled their daughter to bed later that evening, Shae went over to the main house. "She's already six and a half," Shae said worriedly to Hilo. "Is it something I've done wrong? I don't think I've shielded or coddled her."

Today was not the first time Tia had been so easily upset. She refused to watch cockfights. Even sparring matches on the lawn made her anxious. Of course, compassion was one of the Divine Virtues, but violence was also a part of life in a Green Bone family. Where had Tia gotten such softness? "Maybe it's because she doesn't get enough of my time and attention."

She and Hilo were alone in the living room and the rest of the house was quiet. Ru had gone back to campus, Jaya was with her classmates at a Pre-Trials after-party, and Wen, tired from the long day, had already gone up to bed. Jaya had come in third in the final rankings, a great showing.

Hilo pulled out two glasses and a bottle of hoji from the cabinet and poured them each a serving. He picked up his glass and held the other out to her, grinning. "Inside, I'm crowing with laughter that my tough little sister is sitting here moaning and asking me for parenting advice."

"I'm not moaning or asking you for advice," Shae retorted reflexively before admitting to herself that perhaps she was. She snatched the glass of hoji.

"Shae," Hilo said, turning serious, "if there's one thing I've learned in life, it's that you can't make people turn out a certain way no matter how much you try, including your kids. Especially your kids."

She knew he was thinking of Niko, wherever he was. Shae couldn't condemn her nephew for turning his back on the family and the clan, not when she'd done it herself in the past, but now she understood, in a way she hadn't before, what it was like for those left behind to feel the weight of an empty chair at the table. She hoped Niko was doing what he wanted to do, finding whatever it was he wanted to find. All she could do was pray to the gods to keep Lan's son safe.

Hilo gazed morosely for a long moment into his glass of hoji, then swirled it and drank. "Not everyone is suited for this kind of life. And I don't mean wearing jade. I mean all of it."

Shae drew her feet up onto the sofa, tucking her legs under her. She sipped the hoji and leaned her head back against the cushions. "It's not that I want my daughter to follow in my footsteps." She'd made many mistakes in her life, but when she examined her own decisions, she couldn't even say which ones had been right or wrong. "But it hurt a little today, when Tia looked at me with tears in her eyes. I could see her coming to the realization that maybe her mother isn't such a good person."

Hilo's jade aura expanded then contracted in her Perception, a deep mental sigh. "Only children and gods are arrogant enough to judge what they can't understand. There's no point being afraid of their opinions. Don't worry about Tia. She's only six and a half years old, like you said. Still too young for you to worry."

They sat in silence for a few minutes. Outside, Shae could hear workers painting the Horn's house and expanding the garage to suit its new occupant. The Juens had moved off the estate and were spending a year traveling the world. Shae was happy for them. Not everyone at the highest level of the clan had to be like her and Hilo. Not everyone had to be a Kaul.

Shae considered all the motivations that had fueled her efforts as Weather Man over the years—duty, vengeance, rivalry, personal pride and achievement, the hope and belief that she could make No Peak into a stronger, better, more modern clan than the one she'd grown up with and wanted as a young woman to put behind her. Greater than all those desires now was the overwhelming bone-deep need to keep Tia safe, to secure for her sweet-tempered child a future where she would not have to fight the way her mother had.

Shae said, "I want to set up a No Peak office in Shotar."

Hilo said nothing at first, waiting for his Weather Man to continue. "Our growth in Espenia has slowed," Shae explained. "The real estate market there is contracting and the economy's going to be weak for a while. Years of ad campaigns and political lobbying have paid off in some significant ways—we've prevented the Espenian government from criminalizing clan operations and we've gotten existing penalties on civilian ownership of jade reduced. But there's still no sign that jade will be fully legalized."

Hilo drew a hand over his brow and exhaled in resignation. Less, Shae suspected, because of what she'd said than the realization he was not going to be able to enjoy the rest of the evening without discussing clan matters.

Shae went on. "In Kekon, we took over the Jo Sun clan and have Toshon now, but the Mountain added the Black Tail clan so they have Gohei, plus they still have the upper hand in Lukang. There's no room for either of us to pull ahead. We need other markets."

"Hami established an office in Tun," Hilo pointed out. "You can speed up the growth there."

"We've been trying for years, but Tun is a difficult place to do business. It's politically unstable and on the brink of currency collapse. The infrastructure is poor, the language is hard to learn, the laws and financial markets are underdeveloped." She'd already spent countless hours considering all possible avenues. "Ygutan is obviously not an option for us. There's still an active embargo on the Uwiwa Islands. That leaves Shotar."

Hilo drummed his fingers on the arm of the sofa. "Hami thinks it's a bad idea."

Shae had over the years stopped being surprised when Hilo knew something about the business side of the clan that she didn't expect him to. He still couldn't find his way through a financial report without her help, but he knew who he needed to know. He possessed a complete mental map of the clan's Lantern Men by wealth, influence, and loyalty. He knew who among Shae's subordinates in the Weather Man's office held particular expertise or ability, and he would speak directly with them whenever it suited him. Of course, that was his prerogative as Pillar, but sometimes it irked her. It made her suspect that even after all these years, he did not entirely trust her not to act behind his back.

She admitted with a frown, "Hami's convinced the Mountain has an unsurpassable advantage there because of Ayt Mada's alliance with the Matyos. Iyilo was one of the Matyos before he took Ti Pasuiga from Zapunyo, and most of the barukan refugees who Ayt brought over from Oortoko were Matyos. They're the largest of the barukan gangs. They control powerful labor unions and have influence in several industries."

"So going into Shotar would be as hard for us as it was for the Mountain to break into Resville. Your Rainmaker's reasoning seems solid to me," Hilo said, but she could tell from the texture of his jade aura that he was still undecided.

"The big difference is that we have a weapon in Shotar that the Mountain didn't have in Espenia, thanks to your chess master of a former Horn. Juen built a network of White Rats in that country that we can use to pry ourselves an opening."

After she'd laid out her plan, Hilo finished the hoji in his glass. "I'll give my permission to do this if Lott agrees to use his White Rats in the way you suggest, and you can get Hami to come around to your thinking. This will work only if we can protect our assets without sending over many Fists and Fingers. Between Janloon, Lukang, and now Toshon, we're already stretched on the greener side of the clan, and the Mountain still has the advantage of numbers over us." The grudge in Hilo's voice was plain. *Still.* After all these years, they were still locked into the same infuriating stalemate. Every step that No Peak took, the Mountain took another.

"They haven't tried to come at us lately," Shae pointed out. The past six years had been spent in a state of necessary collusion with their rivals, focusing on crushing the Clanless Future Movement and consolidating power among the weakened minor clans and in secondary cities. Both clans were also struggling with internal issues. Shae suspected that Ayt Mada had her hands full holding together the extremes of her clan, from the traditionalist Kobens on one end to the barukan elements on the other. In No Peak, Niko's departure had created a public scandal and thrown the question of succession wide open.

The only upside of all the turmoil was that the Mountain hadn't recently tried to send anyone from the Kaul family to the grave.

Hilo patted his empty pockets, clearly longing for a cigarette. "Ayt's been quiet," he agreed, turning thoughtful eyes on Shae. "Maybe she has some human feeling in her after all." She knew he was thinking that even Ayt Mada must feel some sense of indebtedness, an obligation to stay her hand against the family of the woman who'd saved her life when no one else would.

When Shae had sheathed her talon knife in the sanctum of the Temple of Divine Return, she'd changed something—driven a dam into the blood feud, turned aside the red river of personal vendetta, at least for a while. At times now, it was tempting to forget that Ayt Mada's ultimate goal of one clan over Kekon meant that Shae and Hilo could never rest. The immovable fact remained that even without Ayt whispering their names, they could never stop thinking of the Mountain as an enemy against whom they were racing. As soon as No Peak dropped behind, once it slowed or grew weak, it would fall and be trampled.

Shae looked out the darkening window and sucked the inside of her cheek. "The Mountain isn't sitting back. Iwe Kalundo has been divesting assets and businesses in Ygutan."

Hilo shrugged, unsurprised. "That country's not good for them anymore." The Ygutanian economy had been hit hard by the global downturn, the nekolva program had come under intense international scrutiny and sanction, and the Directorate in Dramsk was going through internal strife of its own. Widespread belief about Ygutanian support of the CFM prior to the Janloon bombing had vaulted them into being the most hated of foreigners, so Ayt Mada's prior investments in that country were surely not sitting well with many in her clan.

"Yes," Shae mused, "but the Mountain wouldn't retreat without a plan. As far as I can tell, they haven't yet reinvested the proceeds elsewhere. They're moving chess pieces but I can't see the shape of it. If Ayt's been quiet, it's because she's planning something."

The phone in the kitchen rang. Hilo got up to answer it. Seconds later, Shae Perceived the explosive flare of his jade aura from all the way across the room. She bolted to her feet in alarm. Hilo was squeezing the phone receiver so hard she thought he might inadvertently crush it with his Strength. "What is it?" she hissed. "What's happened?"

Hilo spoke into the phone through clenched teeth. "I'll be there in a few minutes." He hung up and grabbed his jacket and car keys. "Jaya's been arrested."

———

The chief of police explained to Hilo that Jaya had been involved in a violent altercation at a house party and a young man was in the hospital in serious condition but would fortunately survive. The party had consisted primarily of Kaul Du Academy students, and all the families affected were from No Peak, so it was clearly a clan matter. Jaya was released to her father, who drove her home, ordered her into the study, and shut the door. She dropped into one of the armchairs.

Hilo stood in front of his daughter. "Explain yourself."

Jaya slid down in the chair. She was wearing black jeans and a leather jacket over a bright red top that showed off her navel. She propped her feet on the coffee table and looked up at her father with a shrug. "What do you want me to say? He deserved what he got."

"Were you having sex with him?"

"Da!" Jaya looked mortified at her father's question. "Do you really want to know that about your own daughter?" When Hilo's glower didn't change, she admitted, "We were dating for a little while, but I broke it off last month. He's cute, but he was getting clingy, and also he could be *such* a pompous jerk. Anyway, I didn't want him or his family getting any ideas."

Hilo grimaced at her matter-of-fact assessment. With Niko gone, Jaya had become the focus of clan speculation. Since the Pillar's son was a stone-eye, an accomplished son-in-law might become heir to No Peak, so the thinking went. At least a dozen prominent No Peak families had approached Hilo about introducing their eligible sons—ranging from age fourteen to forty—to his daughter.

He ignored them, or responded, "When she's old enough, I'm going to hold a tournament to the death for Jaya's suitors." Coming from any ordinary protective father, this would've elicited laughter, but as this was Kaul Hiloshudon, the laughter was nervous enough to shut people up.

"If it was over between the two of you, then why this mess?"

"He was following me and Hana around all night," Jaya complained. "Always trying to get Hana's attention. Maybe he *was* really into her, or maybe he was just trying to make me jealous. I don't know and I don't care. Anyway, the two of them went upstairs at some point. I was hanging out downstairs playing pool with everyone else when Hana started freaking out. Seriously, Da! I could Perceive it like—" Jaya made an explosive motion around her own head.

"What were you even doing wearing jade off Academy grounds?" Hilo demanded. Jaya was still three months away from graduation and not allowed to wear jade without adult Green Bone supervision. "And wearing it *hidden*, no less, like some sort of thief," Hilo added, his temper rising. "Hand it over."

Jaya groaned and rolled up the cuff of her jeans, taking off the Academy-issued training bracelet she'd fastened to her ankle. She made a face at the discomfort of coming off jade, then smacked the leather band and its three stones resentfully into her father's outstretched hand. "It's a good thing for Hana that I *was* wearing it," she pointed out. "What if he'd tried that shit with me?"

"He wouldn't have dared," Hilo replied. "Mal Ging is the only son of Councilman Mal Joon. You're lucky he didn't bleed to death. It would've been a lot of trouble to deal with, not to mention you would've gotten yourself expelled."

Jaya rolled her eyes. "Da, no one is going to expel me from the Academy. What are you so upset about? You think this is the first boy I've screwed? Or the first one I've knifed?" She laughed at his staring face.

It occurred to Hilo that his daughter deserved a sound beating, but he'd never been able to find it in his heart to treat Jaya harshly. She was a girl, and his youngest. "She craves your attention and she knows how to get it," Wen had said crossly on more than one occasion.

"What am I supposed to do about you, Jaya-se?" Hilo growled, more to himself than to her. "We have to make some amends to the Mals."

"I'm not giving them my ear," Jaya insisted, crossing her arms and sticking out her lower lip. "They don't deserve it, and also I don't feel sorry for what I did to that asshole. I don't see why we have to do shit for the Mals. If anything, *they* should make amends to Noyu Hana and her family. Would *you* apologize simply for defending a friend? Come on, Da, I've heard all the stories about you."

"At least I never stabbed a classmate in the groin with a talon knife!" Hilo's eyes narrowed. "And what stories are you talking about?"

Jaya looked at her father with the particular cutting exasperation mastered by teenage girls. "You know, stories from when you were a Fist. Like what you did to Tanku Din. Or about you as the Horn. Or the ones about the war with the Mountain."

"Don't throw around examples you know nothing about."

Jaya got to her feet and wandered around the study despondently. "No one will duel me, you know. Even if I offer them a clean blade, they're afraid if they scratch me, you'll tear them limb from limb. That's why Ging didn't try to rape me and went after Hana instead, the coward. How am I supposed to earn *any* jade after I graduate, much less become a Fist? It's hard enough to be a woman who's green, even for someone on the *boring* side of the clan like Aunt Shae."

Hilo was so astonished he forgot his anger over the maiming of the Mal boy. Jaya had always been the child he'd found easiest to understand and love. He recalled that when she was a little girl, she could be exhausting; she rarely napped or stopped moving, wanting him to chase her or push her on the swing set for much longer than either of the boys, until she was near to throwing up. She was always open with her feelings and seemed to live in the moment. Hilo hadn't known such anxious thoughts about being a woman Green Bone were on her mind, even though he realized now that it shouldn't have been a surprise. He sat down, rather hard, in one of the armchairs.

"Jaya-se," he said, "for the rest of the year, you should concentrate on Final Trials and earning your graduation jade without getting into any more trouble. And you're absolutely not allowed to go to any more parties, or to wear your jade off campus, or to get involved with any other boys, or gods help me, I will tear them limb from limb like you said. I'll handle things with the Mal family, but the next time you land yourself in jail—and there better not *be* a next time—I'm not going to pick you up, you can stew in a cell for a week like some common criminal."

Jaya fell into the chair across from her father, pouting.

Hilo went on, "As for after you graduate, we should talk about that with your ma and with your aunt Shae. We shouldn't have left it this long, that's my fault, but it's been busy and there's still plenty of time, so don't worry. There're a lot of things you could do. You could go to college. You could study in Espenia if you want. You could spend a year or two as a Finger. Or there are plenty of tributary companies in the clan where you could intern."

Jaya sat up. "I'm taking oaths to the greener side of the clan, Da. I'm going to become a first-rank Fist. One day I'll be the Horn of No Peak."

Hilo hated to discourage any of his children, but now he said, "The Horn is the greenest, most dangerous position. There's never been a woman Horn."

"There wasn't a woman Pillar before Ayt Mada," Jaya retorted. "Are you saying our enemies can do more than we can? I'm your daughter! Don't you believe in me?" She was suddenly almost distraught.

"Of course I believe in you," Hilo snapped. "But being the Horn... It's not just about being a good fighter or a Kaul or wearing the most jade. It's..." He frowned; he was having a hard time articulating why the idea of his daughter aspiring to the position he'd once held disturbed him so greatly. The Horn needed to be a top warrior, cunning and calculating, a leader of *men*. Even among extremely capable and heavily jaded Green Bones, few were suited for the demands of the role. Most of all, he was fearful of Jaya having such a lofty and perilous ambition, one that might get her killed at a young age, and his instinct as her father was to steer her toward a part of the clan that was less violent. "You're not even eighteen yet," he reminded her reasonably. "You should think about all your options and not set your mind on one thing so soon."

Jaya leapt to her feet, eyes flashing with hurt and indignation. "Don't say that! Don't make me out to be a silly girl with silly ideas. I would've thought my own father of all people would understand!" She began to storm toward the door.

"*Sit down.*" Hilo's tone of command made even his most obstinate child flinch and turn around. Hilo pointed to the chair and Jaya grudgingly obeyed, landing back in the seat with a scowl aimed at the floor.

Hilo rubbed a hand over his face. He could've guessed Jaya would grow up to be hopelessly green, and as he'd told Shae earlier in the evening, it was a mistake to try to push people in directions they weren't meant to go, or to push them away from what they most wanted.

"All right," he said. "If you're serious about being a Fist, I'll talk to Lott Jin. We'll think about who might be good mentors, how you can get the most opportunities to earn jade. Between now and the end of the year, you should be talking to the senior Fists, getting a sense of which ones you respect the most and might like to be placed under. Talk to the woman Fingers, especially, to find out their opinions." He cut off his daughter's growing smile with a growl. "All of this happens *only* if you behave perfectly for the rest of the year and graduate from the Academy with four jade stones and no more problems, or I'll jade-strip you myself and send you to be the lowest-level Luckbringer in the most boring job I can find in some tiny tribute property, I swear to Heaven."

Jaya came over and put her arms around her father's neck and kissed his cheek sweetly, all of her teenage bluster and pique gone. "I promise I won't disappoint you, Da." *I won't be like Niko.* She didn't say the words, but he knew it was what she meant. Despite his apprehension, Hilo hugged her back and said, "It's late. You should go to bed. I'll drive you back to the Academy tomorrow."

One of the Fingers who guarded the estate knocked on the door of the study. "Kaul-jen," he said when Hilo opened the door, "the Noyu family is here to see you."

Hilo went out of the room to find four people waiting anxiously in the entry foyer. A trembling teenage girl of Jaya's age, her parents, and a young Green Bone who was surely her brother. Upon seeing Hilo, they all bent into deep and respectful salutes. The mother's eyes were teary, and the father's face was pale as he stepped forward with his eyes downcast. "Kaul-jen," he said, "we've come here to show our gratitude for what your daughter did, defending Hana from harm, not to mention our family's honor and reputation. We heard that Jaya spent hours in jail, and it surely ruined your evening." He swallowed noisily. "Our family is small, but my son is a Finger in the clan, and our daughter hopes to become a Luckbringer. If there's ever any greater way we can be of service to the No Peak clan and to your family, we would undertake it gladly."

Noyu knelt on the hardwood floor and touched his head to the ground. His entire family followed suit. The girl, Hana, said with a stifled sob, "It was my fault! I led Ging on, because I knew that he and Jaya were broken up, and I thought I could get him to like me instead. We both had too much to drink, and I didn't—"

"Be quiet, girl," Hana's mother hissed at her. "Haven't you caused enough trouble already?"

Jaya went to her friend and pulled her to her feet. "How can you think it was your fault at all?" she exclaimed angrily. "Ging was a worthless little shit. Why do you think I broke up with him in the first place? And even though it's very kind for your whole family to come here to show your thanks, it's hardly needed, because what's the point of friends if we don't defend each other?" She hugged her classmate tightly. "I don't care at all about spending time in jail, I'm only glad you're safe."

Hana began to cry in earnest, and would've stayed there, clinging to Jaya, if her parents and brother didn't pull her away, saying the Pillar's family had given entirely too much time to them already. Hilo was a little bewildered by the feeling that he had absolutely nothing to add to the situation, other than to place a hand on Noyu's shoulder and thank him for coming.

The man's lips trembled with emotion. "Kaul-jen, not only are you the Pillar, but you're managing to raise children who're as green and good-hearted as you are. Looking at you, I feel humbled as a father."

CHAPTER

41

Second Chance

Three men stood in excited expectation in front of Bad Keck Remi and his two bodyguards. It was past midnight and the Feast of Janloon restaurant had closed an hour ago; the six men were the only people remaining on the second floor. The single window was cracked open to dispel Resville's unseasonably warm spring heat, but the blinds were drawn and the lights were dimmed to create an atmosphere of solemnity.

"For centuries, our ancestors claimed the jade off the bodies of their enemies." Jon Remi spoke with an air of ceremony as he unfolded a black cloth on the table. He'd given this speech many times before and was well practiced at the ritual. "Only the strongest could wear jade. Once they had it, they had to fight to keep it. Kill or be killed. It's part of our culture. It's in our blood. Tonight, we continue a tradition handed down to us from generations of jade warriors." Remi laid out three identical gold chains, each with a jade medallion. A reverential hush fell over the Snakeheads.

Jade was hard to obtain—thanks to those greedy fucks in the Kekonese clans—so Remi was extremely discerning about who he elevated as Vipers. The three men in front of him had all been in the gang for a year and proven themselves by carrying out at least two assigned killings. "You've all earned this," Remi said. "As soon as you put it on, there's no going back." Remi raised his tattooed arms. "Who are we?"

"The Snakeheads!" The men forked their fingers in the gang salute.

Remi called forward the first young man from the line, who'd shown his thick blood by executing two members of the Copa cartel. The Snakeheads were currently playing spoiler in the war between the Copas and the allied East Resville and Cranston Crews. Remi hated both sides and had been in violent confrontation with them both before, but enmities and alliances were always shifting in Resville.

Remi placed the chain with the jade medallion over the bowed head of the new-made Viper. A look of awe came into the man's face and his energy changed, rose in pitch as it began to hum with jade power. From now on, he would have to train every day with the other Vipers to control and use his new abilities, and he would need daily injections of SN2. Remi had heard that in Kekon, Green Bones didn't use shine at all because they were exposed to jade as children— another old country privilege. Fortunately, Remi had plenty of shine to go around and the drug was safer than it used to be. There had only been three deaths from overdose among the Snakeheads in the past year, and that was preferable to even one case of the Itches. The one man Remi had seen die of the Itches had gone out in a bad way, killing his own wife and children with a cleaver before turning it on himself.

With a dazed look on his face, the first man stepped back and Remi motioned forward the second Snakehead in line, a half-Kekonese ex-con who'd left Migu Sun's outfit in Adamont Capita and had proven himself by hijacking a Copa drug shipment and killing three dealers. Over the years, the Copas had taken over most of the region's drug trade by bringing narcotics—primarily amphetamines like sweet flour and buzz—across the border from Tomascio. They had a reputation for indiscriminate savagery; in their own country, it was common for the drug lords to leave dismembered bodies nailed to fences as a warning to their enemies.

The Crew Bosses of Resville were not about to be muscled out by the wesps, but they were also afraid of inciting prolonged violence in a major Espenian tourist city, so they had reluctantly hired the Bad Keck to do the difficult work for them. The Snakeheads were not the most populous gang in Resville, but everyone in the Espenian underworld agreed that man for man, you couldn't get more efficient killers than those jade-wearing Kekonese. In exchange for this service, the East Resville and Cranston Crews had agreed to cede all the gambling and prostitution business on the glitzy eastside Laholla Street to the Snakeheads. A worthwhile trade, in Remi's book.

The second man accepted his new jade and stepped back, clutching it in his fist.

Going up against the Copas was no joke, and even though it got the Crews off his back, Remi would've hesitated to take on such a challenge were it not for certain assets that no one else in the city possessed. One was his jade-wearing Vipers. The other was the third and final man standing in front of him now.

Maik Tar was at least twenty-five years older than the other two men who were being promoted today, and he looked every bit of it. But he was the most reliable man among the Snakeheads. At first, as he did with all new members, Remi had given Maik simple tasks—make a delivery, shake someone down, hand out a bribe or a beating, as necessary. Maik did them all to perfection, without batting an eye. Remi sent him to murder a man, a former Snakehead who'd gone to the police. The informer disappeared the following day; the police never found a trace of him.

Remi was delighted and a little shaken. He sent Maik out on other jobs and Maik never failed. The man was a steely killer. A savage genius. Last month, three Copas had robbed one of Remi's bookies, beaten him to death, and escaped town. Remi had given Maik two

men and sent him after the thieves. Maik left the trio of charred bodies burning in a car at a gas station eight kilometers from the Tomascio border.

Unlike some other members of the Snakeheads gang, Maik Tar
didn't drink or do drugs, he didn't start senseless fights, he didn't
have a wife or a mistress, he never talked back or questioned the work
that Remi gave him. He was a league above the others in terms of
his exceptional instinct for street operations and violence. He noticed
and remembered crucial details, he emanated dangerous authority,
and he was always good in a fight. Remi could only imagine what
Maik must've been like as a young man. So *this*, Remi mused with
jealous resentment, was the kind of work ethic and discipline you
could find in the old country clans. These were the sort of people
that the Kauls had. Nothing like some of the slipshod fuckups he had
to deal with.

And Maik had done it all *without jade*. How much more could he
accomplish after tonight? The other two men had never worn jade
before and it would be months before they could do anything useful with it. Maik had worn a great deal of jade for decades before his
exile. Remi lifted the final chain, and with everyone watching, he
undid the clasp and slid two more precious jade medallions next to
the first. It was the most jade he'd ever handed out at once, but Maik
could handle it. Indeed, he would become an unstoppable force.
With Maik at the head of his Vipers, Remi could wreak destruction
on the Copa cartel and anyone else who dared to be his enemy.

Maik's eyes widened. Remi could feel the man's almost unbearable anticipation. "Once again, and from now on, a Green Bone warrior," Remi said with a savage grin. "Maik-jen."

Maik bent his head and Remi placed the chain over his neck. The
man reached up and pressed the green medallions against his bare
skin, shivering as the rush of jade energy hit his brain for the first
time in nearly fourteen years. His roughened face lit with pure joy
and triumph as he raised it toward the ceiling as if in transcendent
communion with the gods. "Thank you," he whispered hoarsely.
"Thank you for this second chance."

With the incredible speed and Strength of an Academy-trained first-rank Fist, Maik Tar drove his Steeled fingers through Remi's throat, crushing his trachea.

Remi's bodyguards and the other Snakeheads in the room were immobile with astonishment for two full seconds before they drew their guns. In that time, Tar seized the closest man and Channeled into his brain, bursting the vessels and killing him instantly. He threw the body into the second guard, bowling him over, and took off running as the remaining Snakeheads opened fire.

The Deflections that Tar hurled behind himself diverted most of the gunshots, but not all of them. He was using his jade abilities for the first time after a long absence and struggling as one might with a numbed limb. He was also much older than he'd been as a Green Bone in Janloon.

A bullet punched through Tar's shoulder and another caught him in the thigh, causing him to stumble and fall. The enraged gang members set upon him with knives. They didn't have any idea how to use their new jade, but it still made them faster and stronger than they otherwise would be. Tar cut open the ex-con's face and dropped him to the floor screaming, but was too slow with his Steel and suffered a bad slash to the ribs himself. He was so vicious and terrifying with the talon knife however, snarling like a rabid animal, that the two remaining men hesitated to be the next to attack. That gave Tar the few seconds he needed to throw himself out of the restaurant's only second-story window, shattering it with his Steeled body.

He crashed into the railing of the fire escape and tumbled over it toward the pavement. Controlling his fall with Lightness, he landed on his feet amid a shower of glass and the screams of bystanders, spraining his ankle in the process. Tar ran limping into the street and covered a block and a half, trailing blood behind him, before two Resville city police cars showed up and he surrendered to them without a fight.

———

In the hospital, under strict police guard, Tar was allowed a private phone call to contact his family. He used it to call Hilo long distance on an unlisted number that had been known only to the immediate members of the Kaul family back when he was Pillarman and that he was relieved to discover still worked.

"Hilo-jen," Tar said, still in a lot of pain from his injuries, "I'm in the hospital, but don't worry, I'll be okay." He stopped, overcome with emotion, and didn't continue. It was the first time the two men had spoken since that terrible night so many years ago.

Hilo said, "Don't say anything to the cops. We're sending a lawyer to you. We'll get you out of there, Tar."

When he'd learned that Jon Remi was dead, and that the assassin had been none other than his former Pillarman, Hilo had been assailed by the surreal sensation of being shocked and entirely not shocked at the same time. Now he felt as if he'd been thrust into the past to that awful moment when he'd stood under the trees at the back of the Kaul property with a talon knife in his hand and Tar kneeling in front of him, and his hands were shaking on the phone receiver as they had been on the knife. "We'll push on the legal side, and if that doesn't work, we'll figure out something else. Remember, don't say anything, and don't worry. Just get better and be patient." He paused to steady himself. "You did good, Tar."

After a long moment, Tar said, "It's good to hear your voice, Hilo-jen."

"You know I've always counted on you more than anyone," Hilo said. "Call me again in a few days, after you've talked to the lawyer. You'll be okay."

Tar did not phone the Kaul house again. While still recovering in the hospital, he was questioned by police detectives, and with an interpreter present to help him answer questions, he explained that he was a member of the Snakeheads gang. He said he'd been summoned to the restaurant to be killed because Jon Remi suspected he was a spy for the Kekonese clans, who were opposed to jade being used by criminal groups. Tar claimed to have killed Remi in self-defense. He cooperated fully with the authorities, naming all the known members of the Snakeheads, providing the locations of their hideouts, and giving detailed evidence of the crimes they had been involved in.

Cory Dauk arrived not long thereafter to visit Maik Tar in jail and provide him legal counsel. The lawyer remembered Maik all the way back from Kaul Hilo's first visit to Espenia. Cory had been only a young law school student back then, and Maik Tar had been the Pillar's aide, a man every bit as intimidating as Rohn Toro had been. Now Maik was grizzled, tired, and pale from his time in the hospital before he'd been transferred to jail. He'd reacquired jade for a few minutes, expended an enormous amount of energy, and then lost it again upon being taken into custody by the police. All that strain on his mind and body showed in the sunken hollows of his eyes. His injuries hadn't been life threatening, but the bullet in his leg had chipped the femur and he was likely to walk with a limp for the rest of his life.

Maik asked if he could have a cigarette, and even though Cory didn't smoke himself, he asked the guards if any of them would spare one for the prisoner. Tar accepted the smoke gratefully, lit up, and sank into the metal chair with a look of contentedness, closing his eyes.

"You shouldn't have spilled everything you know to the cops before I got here," Cory said. "We've lost a lot of leverage that we could've used to bargain."

Maik didn't answer, merely taking another pull on the cigarette, eyes still closed.

"You'll probably get fifteen to twenty years in a maximum-security prison," Cory explained to him, annoyed but remaining professional. "Because of how cooperative you've been with the police, we can get that taken down, maybe to ten years. When you get out, you'll be given a new identity and placed in a witness protection program in another city, where no one can find you and you can start life over again."

"I've done that already before." Tar opened his eyes halfway, supremely unimpressed by the idea. "I'd be nearly sixty by the time I got out. Too old."

Cory looked at Maik for a long moment. "They're trying to get you out, you know. No Peak." The two men were speaking in Kekonese and none of the guards standing nearby could understand them. "Your old boss Kaul Hilo is asking about all the ways to tie up the court process, bribing cops and judges. He wants details about prison security. If you end up behind bars, they'll do whatever they possibly can to free you."

Tar smiled, with satisfaction but also sadness. "They shouldn't do that."

"No," Cory agreed. "It would involve breaking a lot of laws, and it would throw the spotlight onto your past ties with the clan. I've been trying to tell them that, but I'm not sure your Pillar will listen. If you could convince your family that they shouldn't interfere in the legal process, it would be better for everyone in the long run, yourself included."

"Thanks for the advice," Tar said. "I'll try to convince them."

Cory studied Maik with unease. "Why did you do it?"

Tar smirked. "Are you asking as my lawyer?"

Cory shook his head slowly. "Anden came to see you, didn't he? He asked you to deal with Jon Remi."

Tar was amused by the flat tone of the lawyer's voice that suggested the man was quelling a sense of horror. He finished his cigarette and ground it out against the surface of the metal table that separated them. "Remi made the wrong enemy," he said simply. "You don't stand in the way of the No Peak clan."

"You're not a Green Bone of No Peak anymore. You can't ever return to Kekon. So, why? What's in it for you?"

Tar shrugged. "A death of consequence." He could tell that the term was not one Cory Dauk was familiar with. "Never mind. It's a Green Bone thing back in the old country, not something they do over here."

CHAPTER
42

Death of Consequence

Eighteen months earlier, Anden had made a trip to Orslow, a southern suburb of Port Massy with a growing Kekonese population. When he arrived at the brown bungalow on the corner, Anden saw a man mowing the front lawn but didn't recognize him at first. The idea of Maik Tar sweating and pushing a lawn mower in the sun outside his modest home, like an ordinary neighbor on a Seventhday afternoon, was beyond what Anden could've ever imagined. As he got out of the car and crossed the street, Tar squinted in his direction. He turned off the lawn mower and watched, eyes widening in astonishment as Anden approached. Then he broke into a wide grin and came to meet the younger man.

"Hello, Tar," Anden said.

"Godsdamn. It's good to see you, kid." The two men embraced and Tar led the way up the short walk to the house. Inside, Tar turned and put his hands on Anden's shoulders, squeezing, as if to make sure that it was really him, that he was really there. "Godsdamn," he said again. "I wish I'd known you were coming." He spun in sudden agitation, opening his fridge. "You want something to drink? All I've got is soda, but I could run out to get something else." He glanced around the kitchen and a look of embarrassment came into his face as he realized how small and meager his place must appear, for a man who had been one of the most powerful and feared Green Bones in Janloon, the right hand of the Pillar.

"A soda's fine," Anden said. Tar brought back a couple of bottles and they sat down together at the table. "How're you doing here?" Anden asked cautiously. The last time he'd seen Tar had been on that tragic night when he'd treated the Pillarman's injuries and helped to wash the blood off his hands and face. Looking at him now, Anden didn't know how to feel. He'd thought of Maik Tar as a brother-in-law, but he hadn't been close to the man and had never been entirely at ease around him. Tar had always seemed so sharp and dangerous, a wolf that only Hilo and Kehn could control. Still, Anden had known Tar for so long, had eaten dinner with him at the Kaul house so often, it was hard to think of him as the man who'd murdered Iyn Ro. It didn't occur to Anden to consider the other lives Tar had taken. Those had been on the Pillar's orders and done for the good of the clan.

Tar shrugged. "I'm not complaining," he said. "You know, I'm okay. I'm better than I was. It took me years to stop hating everything, including myself. No jade, no clan, no family, *nothing*. The only reason I didn't kill myself was because Hilo-jen had spared my life and I thought maybe, just maybe, there was a tiny chance I could be forgiven and come back one day." Tar's eyes went a little distant, and he shook his head. "I know it's not possible," he said, but the slightest bit of a question lingered in his voice and the quick, sidelong glance at his visitor showed that when he'd seen Anden crossing the street toward his house, he'd still felt a stir of hope.

"It's a good thing you were able to feel at home here, eventually," Anden said. He had to hide the sympathy he felt upon seeing the small spark of possibility go out of Tar's eyes, slackening the muscles around the man's mouth. Tar was the same age as Hilo, but in his exile, he'd aged badly. His fingers and wrists and neck seemed indecently bare, devoid of the jade he'd carried all his adult life in Janloon.

"Yeah." Tar's posture slumped a little. "I lost my jade, but I had enough money to live on when I arrived. There were a couple of guys, Green Bones who answered to the old Dauk, who checked in on me to make sure I was okay, but also told me they'd put me down like a mad dog if they had to." Tar smiled a little.

"When did you move to Orslow?" Anden asked. He wouldn't have thought Tar would ever be in a place like this, quiet and residential. He'd always seemed like a creature of the city, at least back in Janloon.

"A couple of years ago." Tar glanced out the window as if taken aback to realize that he'd indeed been here for that long. "It's... different here. Cheaper, sure, that's good, but also..." He rubbed his jaw, searching for how to explain. "Southtrap's got jade medicine clinics now. And jade schools that fly under the radar. We started sending Fists over to train Dauk's people fifteen years ago, and some of them go to Janloon now and come back. Out here in Orslow, there aren't any Green Bones."

Anden understood. It would be painful for Tar to be around jade and Green Bones, to be constantly reminded of who he used to be. And yet, even now, when he spoke of No Peak sending Fists to Port Massy, he'd said *we*, as if he were still a leader in the clan. Anden asked, "How about work? Do you have a job out here?"

"I started out as a bouncer at a club downtown. Stupid, boring work, but it was easy," Tar told him. "After a while, it occurred to me that what I was doing wasn't all that different from what the lowest-level Fingers do—stand around, look tough, deal with trouble when it happens. I didn't have jade anymore but I knew how to be more than a junior Finger. I'd been Second Fist of the clan, I'd been Pillarman." A flicker of fierce light came into Tar's eyes for a mere second. "So I started doing some work on my own. I'd been avoiding the grudge halls—gods, they're so tacky, you'd never find anything like that in Janloon—but I started going to them and spreading my name a bit. After I did some jobs, I got other people wanting to hire me. It's mostly tracking down guys who owe money or cheaters who ran out on their wives, getting dirt on someone, that sort of thing. Sometimes it's more interesting. The work comes and goes, but it pays the bills."

Tar sat in sheepish silence for a few seconds, then said to Anden in a much more lively voice, "What about you, kid?" as if Anden was still Hilo-jen's teenage cousin and not an accomplished doctor and thirty-eight years old. "You look good. What's going on at home these days? Are you in Espenia on clan business?"

In broad strokes, Anden filled Tar in on happenings in No Peak and with the family. Tar listened avidly, hungrily, asking after each of the kids, especially Cam, who was a year-six at the Academy, one year behind Jaya. At the time, Niko had been a senior Finger and Ru was in his final year of high school. Anden had brought photos, knowing that Tar would be happy to have them. The former Pillarman looked through them all carefully and in silence, except when he gave a snort of laughter at some funny picture or silly expression on one of his nephews' faces.

He paused for a long moment on a candid photograph of Hilo and Wen, sitting together in the stands at one of Ru's high school relayball games. It had been taken by someone sitting next to them, perhaps Shae. They were smiling for the camera and looked happy.

Tar finished going through the photographs, then turned away and rubbed quickly and surreptitiously at his eyes. "Thanks for bringing those."

"They're yours to keep." Anden glanced away, not wanting to injure the man's pride by sounding too concerned. "Have you met people here? Made friends?" The house was obviously a bachelor's residence, with utilitarian furniture, little in the way of interior decor, and one set of used dishes in the sink.

"A few," said Tar. "Started playing cards with some guys I met at the gym. Got into a book group with the Espenian as a Second Language Conversation Club at the library. A few flings here and there, nothing serious. Never got married, though. Couldn't do it, after... you know." He squared the pile of photographs.

Anden was struck by an odd mixture of pity and admiration. He remembered how hard it had been for him, that first year in Port Massy as a student—and he'd had the clan's support, a host family to care for him, and the knowledge that his exile was most likely temporary and he would return home sooner or later. Tar had had none of that. He was older and it was hard for him to learn another language. He'd had to go through jade withdrawal, find work, rebuild his life entirely. That he was not only alive, but had a modest house in the suburbs, work that suited him, and a few social connections— it was nothing short of a miracle. A decade and an ocean away from the Green Bone life that had defined him, Maik Tar was both broken and more whole. "It's good to see you, Tar," Anden said, and he meant it.

Tar cleared his throat and gave the stack of photographs another pat before raising his eyes to Anden with expectant understanding. "And how's clan business?"

Despite his happiness to see a member of the family and the chance to hear about how everyone was doing, Tar surely knew that Anden's visit could not merely be out of kindness and sentiment. Although Hilo had not expressly forbidden communication with Tar, it was understood that he was dead to the clan. The Pillar himself hadn't spoken to his brother-in-law since exiling him. Anden knew this wasn't out of cruelty, but kindness. It would be wrong to give the man any shred of hope. He needed to be cut off in order to accept his situation and make some sort of new life for himself. And Hilo did not trust himself not to soften toward Tar in time and he could not allow himself to do that. But Maik Tar knew enough Green Bones in Espenia to have learned by now that when Emery Anden was in the country, he spoke for the Pillar of No Peak.

Anden said, "Doing business here is more challenging for us now that Dauk Losun is gone—let the gods recognize him." Anden told Tar about No Peak's efforts to change the perception of jade in Espenia and remove legal barriers that stood in the way of the clan's expansion. Some Green Bones, he explained, were defying the urgings of their peers and instead becoming notorious criminals.

"There's one man in particular," Anden said with a grimace. "Remi Jonjunin, or Jon Remi, who's called Bad Keck Remi, just like a Crew Boss. And the worst thing is that he built his success on No Peak." He told Tar about the history of Remi's alliance with No Peak, his rise in Resville and his refusal to change his ways now that he was rich and powerful. "No one can talk any sense into him. Last month, two of his men, one of them wearing jade, were busted running a shine lab. Remi's Snakeheads stand in the way of everything No Peak is trying to accomplish in this country."

Tar asked matter-of-factly, "Has anyone tried to kill him yet?"

"The Crews have tried," Anden said. "But Remi is too careful. He has at least three different apartments and moves between them. He only eats in Kekonese restaurants and wherever he goes, he sends people ahead to scout it out. He has jade-wearing bodyguards with him at all times. No crewboy assassin could get close."

Tar nodded. "And what about other Green Bones?"

"The Green Bones in Port Massy and Adamont Capita have tried to negotiate with Remi and rein him in, but they won't whisper his name. They don't want to create more legal troubles and make everything worse for the community, or turn themselves into targets of vengeance for Remi's followers. So they've been working with the police to shut down his businesses and have him arrested, hoping that'll take care of the problem, or that the Crews will eventually succeed."

Tar shook his head. "This sort of thing would never happen in Janloon."

"They can't help it," Anden said, feeling compelled to defend Cory Dauk and his Keko-Espenian friends. "Without a clan or Pillar, without people like Dauk Losun and Rohn Toro, they don't know how to act like real Green Bones. Even so, they're our allies and business partners. Even after Remi insulted us directly, Hilo-jen gave Dauk's widow his word that he would keep No Peak out of Resville and not do anything to create negative attention." Anden paused and looked at Tar meaningfully. "The Bad Keck is an enemy of the clan, and the Pillar wants him gone. Since I'm the one who's most familiar with the situation in Espenia, it's up to me to figure out the right way to handle this problem, in a way that can't be traced back to No Peak."

Tar said, "Trust me, as someone who's been in your shoes, getting difficult assignments straight from the Pillar, I wouldn't trust a job like this to just anybody."

Anden said, "Hilo doesn't know I'm here."

Tar raised his eyebrows and sat back. Anden could tell the former Pillarman was disappointed. He'd no doubt hoped that Anden's visit had been suggested, or at least condoned, by the Pillar. But Tar was nevertheless flattered Anden had come to him, even after all these years, and that he was willing to risk his own standing with the Pillar by seeking out a clan pariah without Hilo's knowledge and blessing.

Tar got up and brought back a couple more bottles of soda. When he sat back down, it was clear from the furrow in his brow that he was thinking about everything Anden had said. "You promise killing this man will be good for the clan? That it'll be helpful to Hilo-jen?"

"Yes," Anden said. "I wouldn't be here if that wasn't the case."

"This Jon Remi. Does he deserve to die?"

The question caught Anden off guard. It didn't strike him as the sort of thing that Maik Tar would've ever wondered, that he would've ever thought to ask in the past. But Tar was looking at him steadily, expecting an answer, and with an expression on his face that seemed unlike him, the face of a man who had been asking a lot of questions in the past decade of his life and was still hoping for answers.

Anden thought for a minute before replying. "Remi is what he is. In some ways, he's admirable because he wants to live as his own man, and he demands respect for himself even when it seems everything is against him. But he uses jade only to prey on others. He extorts even Kekonese businesses. He's killed many people, but always for money or drugs, never with a clean blade. His Snakeheads are no better than crewboys." Anden paused. "He's not the sort of Green Bone that should be allowed to exist. So he deserves to die as much as anyone in our world does."

Tar was silent for a while. The answer had been more thought out and honest than he'd expected, and he appreciated Anden showing him—a disgraced, exiled clan murderer—enough respect not to lie to him or give him a pat response. Tar stood and they walked together to the door. He said, "I'll always do what Hilo-jen needs done. Don't worry about a thing, kid."

As Anden stepped out the door of the small house, Tar asked, "Will you tell the boys, especially Cam, that their uncle Tar misses them and loves them? I know some mistakes can't ever be fixed, but we've got to go on, don't we, and try to make the most of what's left. Tell them for me, all right?"

The downfall of the Snakeheads was shockingly rapid even by the standards of the Resville underworld. The city police and federal authorities had never before received so much insider information about the country's most notorious Keko-Espenian gang. Within a week of Remi's death, they'd arrested nearly all the Bad Keck's direct subordinates and charged them with a slate of crimes.

The remaining Snakeheads were unable to reorganize quickly enough to survive the onslaught by law enforcement and the opportunistic attacks by the Copa cartel and the local Crews. Those of Remi's followers who managed to evade arrest went into hiding, fled the city, or left behind their activities and associations. Some of them went so far as to stop wearing jade. A few minor splinter gangs emerged, but they stayed strictly small-time and were looked down upon as being simple crooks. They had little or no jade and now none of the Green Bone leaders who sided with the Dauk family in Port Massy would grant jade to anyone with a criminal record.

The Crews moved quickly to take over the void left by the removal of the Snakeheads. Within a short time they brokered a tenuous agreement with the Copas, leaving their rivals most of the drug trade but reasserting control over the gambling, prostitution, and racketeering in most parts of Resville, except in the predominantly Kekonese areas, where they were liable to find themselves quietly and forcefully run out.

Within the Keko-Espenian Green Bone community, the line had been drawn. The message spread: Train in secret, wear your jade, protect your neighborhoods. If you become too greedy and make yourself into a Crew Boss, you'll end up the same as Jon Remi, who paid for his defiance and disrespect to the Kaul family of No Peak.

While awaiting trial two months after his arrest, Maik Tar was found dead in his prison cell, having hanged himself with a torn bed-sheet. Earlier that day, he'd walked around the prison yard in apparently good spirits, having nearly fully recovered from his injuries. He'd eaten dinner and joked with the guards and not been considered a suicide risk. He did not leave any note, although that evening he talked at length about his older brother, who'd been dead for eighteen years, and he said that he hoped there really was life after death, as some people said.

Maik Tar's body was sent back to his family in Janloon and buried next to Kehn in the Kaul family plot in the Heaven Awaiting Cemetery. The funeral was not widely known about even within the No Peak clan; many friends and relatives of Iyn Ro would be angry that the Pillar had ended Tar's exile even in this one final way. Only the immediate members of the Kaul family attended the event. Afterward, Hilo stood for a long time staring at the place where three of his brothers were buried: Lan, Kehn, and now Tar. Wen stood beside him, not making a sound, but tears streamed silently down her face, and it was only because she was weeping that Hilo was unable to. The sense of grief sitting heavy in his chest was not the burning rage that had animated him after Lan's and Kehn's murders. Tar's death felt like the much-delayed end of a tragedy that had happened long ago.

Anden came up on Hilo's other side and looked down at the casket. His face was drawn with regret, his voice muted and uncertain. "I understand if you blame me, Hilo-jen."

Hilo didn't reply at first. Then he said quietly, "Tar was the best, the only one who could've done it. I don't blame you any more than I blame myself." He put a hand on Anden's shoulder and leaned against it heavily, so that he nearly sagged against his cousin. "I was angry at you for a long time after you refused to wear jade. Of course you remember. Now, though . . . I'm thankful you're not a Fist, Andy. I need—" Hilo's voice faltered. "I need one of my brothers to live."

CHAPTER

43

Freedom

Niko lay flat on his stomach in the snow, his R5 rifle trained on the road leading into the town. He'd been lying in concealment in white-and-brown camouflage gear for over three hours. The cold in Udain was assaultively dry; Niko's throat and tongue felt as coarse as sandpaper, no matter how much ice he sucked on while he waited, and as the sun began to set, the temperature dropped even further. The wind picked up, stinging his eyes and chafing his face. He could no longer feel his extremities, which was a problem considering that he was counting on his stiffly curled fingers to pull the trigger when the time came. When he'd been a student at Kaul Du Academy, Niko had gone on training trips into the densely forested mountains of Kekon, where it could get cold at night, but never cold like this.

To take his mind off the discomfort, he imagined what Janloon would be like today. A pleasant day in autumn, the sun warm over bustling streets, the slightly sweet, spicy smell of the city wafting on the cool breeze coming off the harbor. With the nice weather, his grandmother would be outside cleaning up the flower beds. His mother would be redecorating. The Pillar would be holding meetings on the patio or overseeing the training of Fists on the lawn. Ru would be walking across Jan Royal campus to his next class. Jaya would've graduated from the Academy—was she a Finger in the clan now?

You chose this, Niko reminded himself. Most of the time, when he wasn't freezing and homesick, he was pleased with his life-changing decision. He still had to go where he was sent and do what he was told, same as when he'd been a Finger, but no one treated him differently because of his name. No one asked for his family's favor, or expected any greater performance from him than usual. He had the same clothes, the same weapons, the same shitty food as the next guy. Anonymity was something he'd never had before, and it was a glorious freedom that suited him. He was finally his own man.

He'd also seen for himself how much more there was to the world outside of Kekon and the clans. All of Niko's life, the blood feud between the Mountain and No Peak had permeated Kekonese society and every aspect of his existence. Beyond the island, however, few people knew about it or cared. Most foreigners who wore jade never questioned where it came from, just as they never wondered where their food was grown or their clothes were made. The Green Bone clans seemed as irrelevant as Jim Sunto said they were—an isolated cultural anomaly. This was a revelation to Niko, the sort he'd been hoping for when he left Janloon. It confirmed suspicions he'd nursed for some time that the clan had given him only a narrow view of reality.

Next to him, Teije Inno shifted, trying to find a less uncomfortable position. Niko had met Teije and a dozen other Kekonese recruits at GSI's orientation week at the beginning of last year. He'd recognized the man's name, if not his face. Even though the Teijes were relatives of the Kauls and part of the No Peak clan, the families rarely socialized. In Kekon, the status difference between Niko and Teije Inno would've precluded much of a friendship, but out here they were two

Kekonese away from home and surrounded by foreigners, and Niko was grateful for Teije's presence.

Teije nudged him and made a small gesture, tapping his head. *Perceive that?* He jerked his chin toward the left. Niko could not see anything coming down the road. The sky still glowed an indigo blue, but under the cover of the pine trees it was already dark. Niko let his vision slide out of focus and stretched out his Perception, wishing it was stronger. All he could pick out at first were nearby energies—Teije's aura right next to him, tiny flickers of rodent life under the snow and birds in the branches, the other two GSI soldiers across the road. After another two seconds of concentration, however, he made out the faint impression of several people, crammed too close together to distinguish their individual energies, but rapidly approaching his position. A single vehicle.

Niko pushed up on his elbows just enough to flash a hand signal toward where Falston and Hicks were concealed. He hoped the Espenians saw it through the gloom, or at least sensed the alertness in the jade auras of their Kekonese colleagues. Niko wouldn't say he was friends with the two other men, but after three months together in the desolate countryside of Udain, he'd grown accustomed to them. Falston was gruff and cynical, and Hicks was bad-tempered, but they were generally decent and less condescending than other foreigners that Niko had interacted with. Ex-military Espenians were by far the most numerous group in GSI. Although they wore the least jade, they were the most annoyingly dogmatic about their way of doing things. They often lumped the Kekonese, the Keko-Espenians, and the Keko-Shotarians together even though the three groups didn't speak the same language and avoided each other.

The vehicle came into sight: a muddy brown four-door pickup truck with a black tarp over the back, rolling slowly down the single-lane road, its snow tires crunching on the packed ice as it made its way toward the town of Hansill—a nondescript settlement of two hundred thousand people that Espenian intelligence had pinpointed as harboring members of an Ygutanian-supported Deliverantist rebellion against the autocratic Udaini government.

Niko squinted down the barrel of his R5. He remembered that Vin Solunu, one of the most senior Fists in No Peak, had such a precise long-range sense of Perception and extraordinary aim that he could shoot a living creature with his eyes closed from two hundred meters away. Niko had once seen him take out a squirrel in a tree while blindfolded. Niko had no such confidence in his own marksmanship, even with a night scope. Changing his mind, he slung the R5 over his shoulder and brought his knees and feet up into a crouch, motioning his intentions to Teije.

Teije's eyes widened, but he nodded and stowed his own rifle, readying himself beside Niko. They breathed in together, gathering their jade energy. Falston and Hicks would not do it this way, but Niko and Teije were Kekonese Green Bones, and they did things the Kekonese way—close and personal.

Niko burst out of his place of concealment. His stiff muscles screamed in protest at the sudden change from stillness to explosive motion as Strength poured into his limbs, turning him into a blur of speed as he launched himself toward the road, clearing the snow and underbrush in two Light bounds.

His timing was perfect. As the truck clattered past, Niko rammed himself shoulder-first into the passenger side door at full Strength, like a stampeding bull shoving aside an obstacle. No one except a Green Bone with the highest level of Steel would try anything so dangerous. The impact threw Niko clear of the road. He flew several meters and tumbled into the trees. As the world upended in his vision, he glimpsed the truck swerving wildly as the driver hit the brakes—perhaps thinking he'd hit a deer.

Teije landed in the road in front of the truck and unleashed a powerful low Deflection that struck the vehicle's wobbling front wheels, sending it into a dramatic 360-degree spin before it lurched into the nearest snowbank and came to a halt like a stuck cow.

Niko clambered to his feet, his head ringing. His legs went wobbly as he let the massive surge of Steel drop from his body, but nothing was broken. His rifle had been tossed into the snow a short distance away upon his landing. He snatched it and ran toward the truck, grasping for Lightness to keep from sinking into the powder, but sprinting low and hunched over. Alarm from the people inside spiked in his Perception, a sudden eruption of jagged red in his mind. Niko glimpsed the man in the driver's seat raising a shotgun.

Bullets punched through the windshield, flinging the driver's body backward. Falston and Hicks had reached the pickup and were releasing concentrated bursts of automatic fire that sparked in Niko's vision like New Year's firecrackers. The rear door of the truck's cab opened and a man tumbled out, holding a pistol. He took a step and collapsed in the middle of the road, an unmoving lump on the ice.

By the time Niko reached them seconds later, the sharp report of rifle fire was fading through the forest. Spent shell casings littered the ground. "Seer's balls!" Hicks whooped, smacking Niko on the back. "You crazy fucking keck, you *ran into a truck*!"

Niko gasped for breath, his heart still thudding with adrenaline and the elation of his own successful daring. A voice in the back of his brain exclaimed: *If only the Horn had seen that!* When he opened his mouth to speak, a noise emerged from inside the truck: a high-pitched cry of pain.

The men froze at the chilling sound. Niko moved first, pushing past Hicks and approaching the open cab. He saw the middle-aged driver and another, younger man, both dead, sprawled in their winter coats in the front seat. In the back seat was a boy—perhaps twelve, flopped over into the lap of a smaller child, a girl, maybe his sister. Nine or ten years old, covered in blood, but alive and wailing feebly.

"Fuck the gods," Teije breathed behind him.

GSI's intelligence sources in the Udaini government had told them that their target was an insurgent scouting party, that the men in the truck were the leaders of a radical Deliverantist cell. The dead men did not look like trained and hardened soldiers. They looked like ordinary townspeople.

Teije yanked the tarp off the back of the truck. "There's nothing here." No weapons, no explosives—just bundles of firewood, a coil of rope, and a red plastic sled.

Niko could not stop looking at the girl. Her hair was pale beneath a pink wool cap and she had dark freckles. Her mouth opened and closed as she stared back at him in confusion and terror. He reached into the truck and tried to unbuckle her seatbelt, to lift her out.

Falston seized Niko's arm. For a second, the man's Espenian words didn't register with Niko. "We have to get out of here," he said. "Before reinforcements arrive."

Niko jerked his arm out of the man's grip. "There aren't any reinforcements. *We fucked up.*" Then realizing that in his shock and anger, he'd spoken in Kekonese, he said, in rough Espenian, "The girl. We have to help her."

"You can't," Falston said, his voice deadened with certainty. "She's not going to make it." The man was right. Niko could Perceive the life escaping the child like white smoke spilling into darkness. He pushed the girl's dead brother aside and began to Channel into her, but it was like trying to keep water inside a colander. The energy was pouring out in multiple directions and he didn't have the level of Perception and medical training to know where to focus.

If only Uncle Anden were here. He'd know what to do. He could save her. He even brought my ma back from the dead.

The girl's chest stopped moving. Niko knew the moment he was Channeling into a corpse—it felt like trying to push his own energy into a dry sponge. Her eyes were still open, gazing unblinking at nothing.

Niko turned around. Teije was standing behind him, staring over his shoulder. The man's fingers were moving agitatedly over the jade he wore around his neck. He backed away from the expression on Niko's face. "We couldn't have done anything," he said weakly.

Niko launched himself at Falston. "Why did you fire?" he shouted, grabbing the man by his tactical vest. "I stopped the truck. You should've looked inside. You should've—" He could not string the right Espenian words together to express himself coherently, to scream that any moron could fire an assault rifle, but Green Bones trained their jade abilities for a reason. Any Finger careless enough to spray gunfire into innocent people would be jade-stripped by his own clan before being exiled or executed for breaking aisho.

Falston was a large, strong man. He shoved Niko away, hard, sending him stumbling back. Hicks got in between them, and Teije grabbed Niko. Jade auras flared, sharp and white with aggression and panic.

"Get a fucking grip!" Hicks shouted at Niko. "It's no one's fault, we were doing our jobs. There must've been a mix-up, we obviously got some shitty intel, all right?"

Teije glanced back at the truck and blanched. "Should we report this?" According to GSI's policies, all noncombatant casualties were supposed to be escalated to an ethics review committee.

"Fuck, *no*," Hicks exclaimed, aghast at Teije's question. "We're not soldiers in the ROE military! We're contractors; we don't get any government protection. If they decide we used inappropriate force, we're liable."

"There are...*rules*," Niko choked out. "We have jade and these people don't."

"We also have armored tanks and rocket launchers and satellite imagery," Hicks retorted. "What's your point?"

Falston said with brusque reasonableness, "Listen, if the bad guys didn't hide among civilians, this wouldn't happen, but sometimes it does. It happened when I was in Oortoko too, more often than I like to think about. You can't let it eat you up, crumb. This is war. The company has to have written policies and shit, for legal reasons, but trust me, *no one* higher up wants us to report this."

Hicks said, "We eliminated the target, that's what we report. The three men in the truck probably *were* Deliverantist rebels." When Niko opened his mouth again, Hicks put his face right up to him, so close Niko could smell the man's breath and see the hairs in his thin nostrils as they flared. "*Enough*, you thick-headed keck. Some crazy shit happened and we're all rattled, but *I'm* the team leader here, and we're going to do what *I* say. You got a problem with that?"

No one had ever spoken to Niko with such aggressive disrespect before and for several seconds, his brain was as blank as his face must've appeared. Then a number of replies sprang to mind—but he didn't possess a profane enough vocabulary in the Espenian language to express any of them. His inarticulate shame felt as hot as a sudden fever. If it were possible to offer a clean blade, he would've done so on the spot.

He could defy his Espenian teammates and go up the chain of command, all the way to Jim Sunto, or to GSI's parent company, Anorco Global Resources. And then what? His mind veered in help-less directions. Would their superiors believe his word over that of Falston and Hicks? Would the men be disciplined, or would the blame fall harder on him and Teije? Was Falston correct, that any report would be unwelcome and met with recrimination, and in the end, the incident would be deemed unavoidable collateral damage?

Either way, the girl in the truck would not come back to life.

Hicks's eyes were still drilling into his. The jade auras of the other men were blaring shrill in his mind. He glimpsed Falston's grip tight-ening on his R5 as Teije's head swung between Niko and Hicks with skyrocketing anxiety. "Niko-jen..."

Niko stepped back and dropped his gaze. He hated himself for doing it, for deferring to a man he'd just seen unload an assault rifle into a truck with children, a man who would be dead if he'd spoken to Niko in such a way in Kekon.

But they were not not in Kekon. Niko had none of the clan's Fin-gers behind him, none of his family's power, no one else but Teije watching.

"No problem," he muttered.

Hicks grunted an acknowledgment. "Good," he snapped. Then he added, with less force, "I didn't mean to call you a keck. We all got too worked up, is all."

"We should get out of here," Falston urged. He turned around and began to trek purposefully through the woods toward the rendez-vous point two kilometers away, where a GSI armored vehicle would pick them up. Hicks followed. After a moment, Teije did as well. Niko brought up the rear. He did not look back at the road.

Once, when he was a child, Niko had asked his aunt Shae why she believed in the gods. She'd given him a strange but clear-eyed look. "Because I've felt them watching me."

Niko had been disappointed. He'd expected a more rational explanation from the Weather Man. Now, at last, he understood her answer. With each step he took in the snow, Niko sank beneath the feeling of some terrible attention turning toward him, reaching from the other side of the world like a curse.

CHAPTER

44

⌒

This Is Not Kekon

the twenty-second year, fourth month

Ten months after the clan established its branch office in Shotar, Wen accompanied her sister-in-law on a business trip to Leyolo City. She'd never been there before and was keen to see some of the sights, but more importantly, she had business of her own she wished to deal with in person.

Shae's husband and daughter saw them off at the airport on the morning of their departure. "Will you bring something back for me?" Tia asked her mother.

"What would you like?" Shae asked.

The seven-year-old considered her options. "A pretty dress!"

"I'll get you one," Shae promised. "Aunt Wen will help me to pick it out."

"I will." Wen agreed with a smile. She was happy to buy nice clothes for her niece. Her efforts to dress up Jaya had always been rejected, resulting in wasted money or ruined outfits. Tia, in contrast, was a considerate, artistic child who adored animals, sparkly things, dancing, and making up stories. It amused Wen to see that as much as Shae loved her daughter, she also seemed bewildered by her, unsure of how such a dreamy and gentle child had been born into the Kaul family.

Shae hugged Tia and kissed Woon goodbye, issuing half a dozen reminders that her husband accepted with the same discerning patience with which he'd once handled the Weather Man's affairs on Ship Street and in Wisdom Hall. Watching them, Wen was struck with nostalgia and sadness. Her own children were grown; even Jaya had left home. Hilo had reluctantly agreed to send their daughter to Toshon, in the far south of the country, where she could get out from under the spotlight of being the Pillar's daughter and be given room to prove her prowess as a Green Bone. A long time ago, Wen had secretly hoped to one day have the kind of idyllic mother-daughter relationship that included womanly pastimes such as going to brunch and the spa, shopping, talking on the phone every day. Jaya only called when she needed something, usually her father's advice on dealing with some issue. Wen was begrudgingly proud of her daughter, but she regretted not being able to relate to Jaya any more than Shae could fully comprehend Tia.

Although she didn't say it as much as she ought to, Wen was proud of Ru as well, who by all accounts was doing well in college. She'd worried so much about her son when he was young, fearing he would be dismissed and disrespected, saddled by stigma, left with no meaningful prospects—the destiny she surely would've faced were it not for marrying Hilo. But Ru had grown up far differently than she had. He was full of big ideas and confidence, perhaps too much of both. "He talks enough to become the chancellor of the country. Then we'll have gold and jade together in one family," Hilo said jokingly, though sometimes Wen thought he might believe it.

As for Niko...Wen's heart ached every time she thought of him.

With her eldest, she felt she'd failed as a mother. She'd convinced Hilo to bring him back to Janloon as a baby, she'd raised and loved him as her own son, believing with utmost certainty that he was a fated gift, the gods' compensation for Ru inheriting her deficiency. Yet he'd hated the weight of that expectation, had run away from it and taken the family's hopes with him. Now Wen didn't even know where he was. Perhaps Hilo did. She knew her husband had people watching Niko, reporting on his whereabouts, but out of consideration, he didn't volunteer the information to her unless she asked. She did not ask.

During the three-and-a-half-hour flight, Wen and Shae studied a travel magazine and made plans to go to a Shotarian bathhouse and to see a musical at the world famous Leyolo City opera house. It had been some time since the two of them had had the opportunity to spend time together without the immediate demands of family. Wen could see her sister-in-law's excitement growing, and when breakfast was served in the business-class cabin, Shae asked Wen, with an uncharacteristically sly grin, "It's not too early in the morning to have a cocktail, is it?"

"Shae-jen," Wen exclaimed, "I would never gainsay the Weather Man's judgment." The flight attendant mixed them slender glasses of lychee juice and sparkling wine.

"We'll have to make dinner reservations for tonight, like normal people," Shae added with bright anticipation. Even the fact that they could not expect to show up and be given priority was a novelty to look forward to, one that made the trip seem like an adventure.

They were not alone, of course; Wen's two longtime bodyguards, Dudo and Tako, were sitting nearby and would accompany Wen wherever she went. The two former Fists were like extended family members to her. She'd gotten to know them well over the years, had met their spouses and children. The men had become adept at blending into any event that Wen attended, from clan gatherings to public appearances and charitable functions.

At times, Wen's days were as busy as her husband's, although she tried not to overschedule herself. She needed to bear in mind her own physical limitations, and her first responsibility was always to support the Pillar. No other Green Bone leader had ever made the questionable choice to appoint his own wife as Pillarman. Wen knew the clan's lukewarm acceptance of her unusually elevated position depended on her striking the delicate balance of being active without overstepping. She embraced a visible role as wife and hostess, promoted causes such as the arts and the environment, and raised awareness of nonreactivity and disability. She was careful never to speak publicly about clan affairs nor to draw attention to herself in any way that might detract from Hilo's authority.

Only privately within the family did she discuss the important issues facing No Peak. "Has the Leyolo City office had any trouble from the Mountain or their barukan allies?" she asked Shae.

Her sister-in-law closed the window shade as they flew east into the morning sunlight. "Fortunately, only a little, thanks to our relationships with the police."

Shotarian law enforcement agencies had never had much success infiltrating the country's insular ethnic Kekonese criminal groups. No Peak, however, possessed an effective network of White Rats in the Shotarian underworld. During his tenure as Horn, Juen Nu had calculated that the barukan gangs were a weak link in Ayt Mada's power structure. Keko-Shotarians were an underclass in Shotar—generally impoverished, legally persecuted, accustomed to living in fear and treachery. It didn't take much in the form of bribes or threats to induce them to give up information.

Although No Peak's overseas spies yielded little truly useful information about the Mountain itself, since Ayt Mada would not be so careless as to share her plans with outsiders, it often did reveal the movement of money and people, which No Peak used to its advantage to blunt Ayt's superior numbers. In an impressive example of cooperation between the military and business halves of the clan, this capability had become the Weather Man's weapon in Shotar.

Shae was passing on information from the Horn's side of the clan about barukan activities—major drug deals, weapons sales, prostitution rings, and so on—to Shotarian police officials, who were very willing to secretly accept tips from No Peak spies and receive all the

credit from the press, the government, and the public for the resulting busts. Of course, she was not giving them this boon for nothing. Business permits, working visas, and important meetings were
made to happen, and No Peak's offices received special attention and
security from the Leyolo City Police Department. The exchange had
enabled the clan's expansion into Shotar, and even skeptical Hami
Tumashon had come around in support of the plan.

Wen lifted her glass to Shae's. "Who could've imagined the irony
of a Green Bone clan working with the Shotarian government?"

They landed in Leyolo City shortly after noon and parted ways. A
prearranged car and driver were waiting to take Shae directly to the
Weather Man's branch office. Wen waited for their luggage, which
Tako carried out to the parking lot behind her while Dudo inspected
every inch of the rented black SUV. Satisfied with its safety, Wen's
bodyguards drove her to the Oasis Sulliya, which was not a typical
downtown hotel, but a resort slightly south of the city, close to the
Redwater area that was the heart of the Shotarian film industry.

Wen checked into her room, changed, ordered a light lunch from
the room service menu, and called her husband to let him know
she'd arrived. "Leyolo City looks as glamorous as it does in the movies," she told him, reaching him in his study between meetings. On
the drive through the city, Wen had admired the capital's steel spires,
which ranked among the highest in the world, its elevated superhigh-
ways and high-speed trams, the enormous rotating neon billboards
that burned with light even in the middle of the day. So much of
Leyolo City had been destroyed in the Many Nations War fifty years
ago that when it was rebuilt, it had burst from the ashes like a phoe-
nix. "It's colder than I expected, though, for springtime."

"Don't spend too much money, unless you're buying a company,"
Hilo teased.

"And what if I am?" Wen asked, unable to resist prodding him.

"I'll assume Shae put you up to it. The two of you are a bad influence on each other," he said, in a good-natured way that made light
of the past, but was still a stern reminder. *No secrets.* "I have to go," he
said. "Have a good time. I love you."

In the afternoon, Wen's bodyguards drove her to the headquarters of Diamond Light Motion Pictures. A translator, vetted and hired by the Weather Man's office, was waiting for them and accompanied Wen as she was received at the reception desk and shown into a massive corner office. Standing behind the desk was a man wearing tinted, wire-rimmed glasses, a soul patch beard, and an expensive blue shirt with the sleeves rolled halfway up his thick forearms. He was probably only forty, but bald as an egg. Wen couldn't understand the rapid Shotarian he was shouting into a headset, but he was either very excited or verbally tearing apart the person on the other end of the line. Hanging up the call, he tossed his headset down and looked over at Wen.

"Pas Guttano," said Wen, using the respectful honorific and speaking the few formal words she'd carefully rehearsed in Shotarian. "It's my privilege to meet you." She pressed her hands together and touched them to her heart.

Guttano returned the gesture of greeting, though his expression turned guarded. He gave Wen a tight smile as he offered her a seat. "You must be Mrs. Kaul."

Wen sat down in the comfortable armchair in front of the studio executive's wide desk. The translator, a prim young woman with long, thin hands, perched alertly in a seat next to her. Dudo and Tako stood against the wall by the office door. Both Green Bones were wearing their jade concealed, but Guttano studied them with faint unease before turning back to Wen. "I know who you are," he told her, "but I can't think of any reason I should be visited by representatives of a Green Bone clan. Diamond Light doesn't have any projects currently filming in Kekon."

The translator repeated Guttano's words back to Wen in Kekonese. Wen said, "I'm here on behalf of the No Peak clan to ask you for a favor. It's not a small request, and because we don't know each other, I felt it was important that I come to Leyolo City to discuss it with you in person." She waited for the translator to catch up. "The No Peak clan is a major investor in Cinema Shore, a Kekonese film studio that's not very significant in terms of the global movie industry, but is the largest production company we have on our island. It's enjoyed some recent commercial success, most notably a series of action movies starring Danny Sinjo."

"*The Fast Fists*," Guttano said enthusiastically, sitting forward and losing some of his initial reticence. "I've seen all three of them! Great entertainment. Second one's still the best, but I like what they did with Danny's character in the third one."

"I'm partial to the first movie myself," Wen said with a smile. "The Fast Fists series was domestically successful, with steady home video sales in Kekon and abroad. But they were made on a tight budget for the Kekonese audience. Cinema Shore's next project is more ambitious. It's a joint venture with a major Espenian studio, a big-budget action movie, the first Kekonese film poised to do well on both sides of the Amaric. But in order for the project to go ahead, it needs Danny Sinjo."

Guttano was shaking his head before the translator even finished relaying Wen's sentence. "I'm sorry, I've already spoken to Danny's agent two or three times about this. Danny Sinjo is under a multi-year contract with Diamond Light, and it's simply not possible for us to release him from that obligation. I know Sian Kugo from Cinema Shore and I like him, but he'll have to find someone else for his project."

"Danny Sinjo is the only Kekonese movie star with the international recognition to carry this film and the only major actor with the Green Bone training to pull off the stunts. The entire script was written with him in mind as the lead."

Guttano opened his hands regretfully. "Then they'll have to rewrite the script. Diamond Light has a filming schedule that's depending on Sinjo as well."

Wen folded her hands over her knee and gave the Shotarian studio executive her most calmly persuasive smile. "I completely understand that it's not in your interest to release Sinjo from his contract. I'm here to make it in your interest to do so. Whatever you've discussed with Sinjo's agent, set it aside. No Peak will pay twenty million sepas to Diamond Light to release Danny Sinjo from legal obligations to your studio. I understand that is three times what you were planning to pay him to play the underboss in the next *Streets of Blood* movie, which has not yet begun filming. Even accounting for the cost of potential delays and the trouble of finding a new actor to play the villain, you have to admit that is a generous reimbursement for your loss."

Guttano had begun to look supremely uncomfortable. He swiveled back and forth in his chair and crossed his arms, still shaking his head. "I'm afraid that's simply not possible," he insisted again.

Wen felt annoyance rising steadily within her, but she kept speaking in the same convincing tone. She thought of the casual yet intimidating persuasiveness Hilo would have in this situation and tried to project some of her husband's energy into her words. "Before you refuse so hastily, consider that my family would remember this favor. My husband is a powerful man in Kekon and our clan has strength in many other parts of the world as well. I don't know how familiar you are with Kekonese culture, but we take friendship very seriously. Suppose you were to need the support of an influential ally at some point in the future—and who doesn't, especially a man in your position? Think about how much more valuable that would be to you than the casting of a supporting actor in this one movie."

"Mrs. Kaul, I'm afraid you don't understand." Guttano began to move some items around on his desk in agitation, not looking directly at her, but glancing at the translator and Wen's two bodyguards, anywhere except straight at her. "It's not that I'm trying to antagonize you or your husband. If it were entirely up to me, I'd be inclined to negotiate with you. But it's not the money that's the issue. Danny Sinjo made an agreement with Diamond Light before this other film was greenlit. He can't leave *Streets of Blood* to go work for the Kekonese, on a project funded by a Green Bone clan. That would...look very bad. It would be unacceptable, embarrassing to certain stakeholders of the studio."

Wen was nearly fed up with the man's evasiveness. She let a little of the friendliness slide out of her voice and a strong hint of disappointment creep in. "I was under the impression that *you* were the final authority on these matters, Pas Guttano. If I was misinformed, if there's someone else in Diamond Light I should be speaking to, please let me know, and I'll have this discussion with them instead."

Guttano pushed his chair back as if to create space between them. "As I've said, the money isn't the main issue. The friendship of the No Peak clan might be valuable in your home country, but it would make enemies in Shotar." Instead of looking at Wen, he looked at the translator and spoke a phrase in Shotarian.

The young woman hesitated. Wen was surprised. Up until this moment, the translation had been fast and flawless. Wen said, "What did he say?"

The translator said, nervously, "My apologies, Mrs. Kaul, I'm not sure how to translate the meaning into Kekonese. In Shotarian, the words are, 'Marry the devil, get the devil's mother.' It means... It's a saying that's used to describe an agreement or relationship that you can't escape from."

Wen sat with this information. "You're saying he's already married the devil."

"I think that is what he is trying to say, yes."

Wen finally understood Guttano's obstinance. She'd heard that the enormously profitable Shotarian film industry was rife with organized crime involvement. Barukan gangs controlled several labor unions, bankrolled films, and demanded to be consulted on the glorified portrayal of Keko-Shotarian gangsters in pop culture, even going so far as to dictate casting choices. Guttano and Diamond Light Motion Pictures must have ties to people they were unwilling to antagonize.

She couldn't get around this obstacle with money or charm, not if one of the barukan gangs had a hold on Diamond Light. She would have to go to Shae, think about what could be done.

Wen smoothed her skirt and stood up, keeping her face neutral despite how crestfallen she was. "I'm disappointed that we couldn't come to an understanding," she said to Guttano. "Now I'll have to return to Janloon and disappoint my husband as well. That's not something I want to do. He's not a man who's accustomed to being told no, so I don't know how he'll react."

Wen knew exactly how Hilo would react. He would shrug and say it was too bad, but that it didn't really matter—Cinema Shore had already handsomely returned the investment she had convinced him and Shae to put into it, and the movie business was just a little piece of No Peak's vast portfolio of tributaries. He would console her by wrapping his arms around her and saying, that was business, not everything went your way, but had she at least had a nice time in Leyolo City?

The Pillar would not send Fists to Shotar to force Guttano to comply, to kill him, or destroy Diamond Light, especially not if such a drastic reaction jeopardized the Weather Man's expansion plans. Any good Green Bone leader knew the power of violence and used it without hesitation when called for, but it was a potent tool, not to be flung about carelessly over something like a movie star's contract.

Guttano, however, did not know this. Shotarians stereotyped the Kekonese as vicious and lawless, and jade, some of them believed, was a corrupting substance that drained a portion of a person's soul every time they used it. Wen saw fear flicker behind the studio executive's tinted glasses. All he knew about Kaul Hiloshudon was his reputation as a man with a great deal of jade and a greater capacity for bloodshed. That was something Wen could use to her advantage.

Genially, she said, "Think about it some more. I'll be here in Leyolo City for a couple more days. You can reach me at the Oasis Sulliya resort if you decide you gave your answer too hastily."

Wen turned away. Dudo and Tako moved silently to open the office door. She left the Diamond Light building unhappy, but she hoped her words would sit with Guttano and the apprehension she'd left him with would motivate him to reconsider.

———

Shae sighed and kicked off her shoes in the back seat of the SUV as Wen's bodyguards drove them back to the hotel late that evening. "You should come on business trips with me more often," she sighed to Wen. "We could make a habit out of this." After an excellent meal of *oshoys*—small plates served alongside poetry—and a production of *The Lady's Scarf,* a romantic musical Shae had first seen in Espenia as a university student and which was still enjoyable decades later even in Shotarian, she was feeling uncommonly relaxed, clan worries pleasantly pushed from her mind. She doubted she would've been so self-indulgent on her own.

"It's nice to spend time without the men or the children around, isn't it?" Wen agreed. She seemed preoccupied, though, and the smile slid from her face as she picked at a bit of chipped nail polish. "Shae-jen," she said after another moment, "is there anything we can do about the Diamond Light situation? Can we find out who's standing in our way, who Guttano is afraid of?"

Shae rubbed the balls of her feet. "I can try," she answered ambivalently. It would be easy to find out the information Wen wanted; that was not the problem. "I know this film deal is important to you," she said, "but we don't want to show No Peak's hand in Shotar too strongly." The Weather Man's branch office in Shotar was small and Shae was being careful to keep it unobtrusive, but the Mountain was surely aware that No Peak was in Leyolo City, and it would be looking for any misstep. Trying to muscle in on the barukan over the film industry seemed risky, even if Shae agreed with her sister-in-law that they shouldn't underestimate the power of popular culture and entertainment when it came to growing the clan's influence. Applications to martial academies and requests for clan patronage went up every time one of the Fast Fists movies came out.

Wen drew the silk shawl over her shoulders. "You're right," she said with resignation. "I think maybe I've become so invested in this project to prove something to Hilo." The Pillar supported his wife's activities and acknowledged their value to the clan, but they were side projects, peripheral to No Peak's core concerns of territory, jade, money, and warriors. A Kekonese film breaking onto the international scene in a major way might've changed that, and it would've been Wen's victory alone.

Sometimes, when Shae was overwhelmed by the demands of being the clan's Weather Man while also managing life as a wife and mother, she considered every obstacle her sister-in-law had overcome with quiet but immeasurable determination. She was always forced to conclude that in comparison, she had no reason to complain and no excuses for failure. "Wen, you have nothing left to prove to anyone."

Wen gave her a sad smile. "Remember, Shae-jen, most of the clan would say I had only one truly important job." To give the family an heir. It was no wonder that Wen had taken Niko's departure even harder than Hilo had.

Red lights pulsed behind the SUV, causing them both to turn in their seats. Dudo, who'd just taken the freeway exit leading to the hotel, glanced in the rearview mirror at the Leyolo City police car behind them. He cursed incredulously.

"Pull over," Shae said. "It's only a Shotarian cop."

Shae saw his foot hover indecisively between the gas and brake pedals. Then he obeyed her, pulling over to the side of the road and shutting off the engine. The squad car parked behind them. A uniformed officer emerged and walked toward the SUV. Shae's Perception was not as sharp as it had once been when she used to carry more jade, but she could still easily sense the lone policeman's nervous caution as he approached the driver's side of the vehicle. Wen looked to Shae with a question in her eyes.

"There's nothing to worry about," Shae told her. Leyolo City police officers carried only a double-action revolver and a baton. A single policeman would be no threat to one, much less three, trained Green Bones. Nevertheless, Dudo's and Tako's jade auras were humming warily, and Tako, in the passenger side seat, slid his pistol out of his jacket and tucked it out of sight under his leg, within easy reach.

"Calm down and be respectful," Shae ordered. Gods forbid the police officer should be unwise enough to try to detain them, or that either of the Fists would give him reason to draw his weapon. None of them knew how to speak much Shotarian, and the last thing No Peak needed was for a foolish police officer to be accidentally killed by visiting members of the No Peak clan over some misunderstanding.

Dudo rolled down the window. The police officer shone the flashlight into the front seat and asked a question in Shotarian, which Shae assumed to be a demand for identification. She said to Dudo,

"Hand him your driver's license and the car rental paperwork." The policeman swung the flashlight over to Shae's voice coming from the back seat, playing the bright beam over the two women dressed for the theater—Shae in a short white coat and black skirt, Wen in a maroon dress and silk shawl.

"We are visitors. We don't speak Shotarian," Shae said, making use of a few phrases she knew in the language. The officer studied Dudo's Kekonese driver's license and the papers from the car rental company. He returned them and stepped back, giving an order in Shotarian and motioning for Dudo to step out of the car.

"What the fuck," Dudo muttered.

Wen said, worriedly, "Maybe he wants to search the car for drugs."

"Or weapons. Or jade. Both of which we have," Tako said.

In Janloon, a police officer that stopped a car full of Green Bones would apologize and send them on their way. If there was some issue with behavior, he would bring it up with the Horn. Cops didn't police the clans. The clans policed the clans. Dudo had never in his life obeyed a city police officer and didn't move.

Any Green Bone of No Peak who traveled on official business for the clan was required by the Weather Man's office to sit through an information session explaining what to do in case of a run-in with local law enforcement. Don't hurt or kill anyone if you can possibly avoid it, cooperate fully, go to jail if you have to. The clan's lawyers will take care of you and the clan will resupply you with any jade confiscated by foreign police and reward you further for your trouble—*if* you follow the rules. But Wen's bodyguards were not going to adhere to those edicts if it meant being handcuffed or separated from the person they had sworn to the Pillar to protect with their lives. This unfortunate patrolman would be dead before such a thing happened.

Shae Perceived the police officer's escalating apprehension as he put his hand on his belt, near his pistol. "Do as he says," she ordered Dudo. "Get out of the car."

"Kaul-jen—"

The police officer repeated his order in Shotarian, more insistently. His hand moved to the grip of his sidearm, his eyes darting between the occupants of the vehicle. Dudo swore under his breath, opened the door and stepped out. The officer motioned for him to turn around. Dudo did so, placing his hands on the side of the SUV. Cars passing them on the road cast pulses of light across the scene. Briskly, the cop patted Dudo down, finding the handgun in his waistband and the talon knife in his shoulder holster and removing them both with a few declarative words in Shotarian that none of them understood. Dudo didn't move but Shae could Perceive the Fist's jade aura swelling. What if the officer tried to take his jade as well? Shae's mind raced, trying to think of a way to prevent the situation from escalating.

Tako's shoulders jerked in alarm. "Something's not—"

Three black cars roared up and surrounded the SUV. Before the vehicles had even stopped, masked men were spilling out of all the doors. The police officer dropped flat to the ground on his stomach, arms shielding his head, and with a flash of dreadful understanding, Shae understood that it had all been a setup. The sweating cop, if he was a cop at all, had kept them in place, distracted their sense of Perception.

Even taken by surprise, Dudo and Tako reacted with remarkable speed. Dudo hurled a powerful Deflection at the men jumping out of the nearest car, knocking several of them to the asphalt. He dropped and scrabbled for his weapons—the gun and knife the cop had taken from him—but before he could rise, three assailants set upon him with the startling speed and force that came only from having jade Strength. Tako leapt out of the passenger side, firing over the hood of the SUV.

Barukan. Shae flung open the rear door, drawing her talon knife. Wen let out a scream as a man's silhouette filled the frame of the vehicle's opening, reaching toward them. Shae slashed at the masked face. When the man jerked back, she kicked him in the chest with her bare foot and followed it up with a Deflection that sent him stumbling backward.

Tako yanked open the rear door on the other side, pulling Wen out of the vehicle and shielding her with his body as he continued to fire around the SUV at the attackers. One of his shots dropped a man. Another two were Deflected wide, punching into the sides of the black cars. "Kaul-jen," Tako shouted.

Dudo had killed one of his assailants, who lay in the street with his neck obviously broken. Another was rolling on the ground, clutching his leg and moaning in agony. A man with a steel pipe smashed Dudo across his broad shoulders, and then square in the back of the head. The Green Bone's Steel prevented his skull from being split open but he collapsed to the ground, limp.

Adrenaline and rage flooded into Shae's brain. She could not believe this was happening. A part of her mind expected more No Peak Fists to appear at any second, to fly to their protection and slaughter these men. But this was not Janloon. These barukan thugs were crude and clumsy in their attacks. Their jade auras, burning with violent excitement, were as wild and uneven as those of untrained teenagers—but there were over a dozen of them.

Shae launched herself out of the car with a cry and felt a rush of fevered satisfaction when her Strength carried her to the nearest barukan in a second and her talon knife plunged into the side of his neck. The man's eyes were the only part of his face visible; they flew wide with shock. For a second, Shae felt only astonishment. It had been *years*—more than a decade—since she'd drawn her knife to kill an enemy and she was disoriented by the moment, by the blood and the Perception of the man's pain. Then instinct took over; she ripped the talon knife straight across with a surge of Strength, severing the carotid artery. "Get Wen out of here," she shouted at Tako.

Another man grabbed Shae from behind. She twisted and sent a spear of Channeling into his chest. She could tell immediately that the strike was nowhere near strong or precise enough. That one kill had been a lucky thing. Shae was a Green Bone twenty years past her fighting prime. She didn't have enough jade, she was too old and too slow. The Channeling strike meant to burst the man's heart only made him gasp and cough violently.

At least he lost his grip on her. Shae tore away from him, sharp pebbles digging into the soles of her feet as she backed up with her talon knife extended. Other men came toward her, emboldened by her failure.

Tako was still firing his gun and throwing Deflections from behind the cover of the SUV and protecting Wen with his life. Shae thought she heard her sister-in-law screaming her name, but if so, the gunfire and the roaring of blood in her ears drowned it out. She glimpsed Tako's face, twisted with frantic uncertainty. Dudo was unconscious, and Shae was too far away for him to help her without exposing Wen. Abandoning the Weather Man was unthinkable, but his first duty was to protect the Pillar's wife. Snarling, the bodyguard unleashed a final volley of gunshots that sent the barukan diving behind their cars. Lifting Wen, crying and protesting in his arms, he ran.

The SUV was penned in, but a steep ravine dropped off from the side of the road. Even weighed down with Wen clinging to him, Tako cleared the gully in a single Light bound. Half a dozen masked men gave chase, leaping after him and firing at his fleeing figure, gaining quickly as he struggled to keep sprinting with Wen in his arms. Tako set Wen down on her feet and they ran, the Fist urging her along ahead of him.

Shae tried to follow. As if sucking in a breath with her whole body, she gathered her jade energy and leapt Light over those in her way. In three more steps, she reached the edge of the ravine and stumbled to a horrified halt as another gunshot rang out and she saw Tako go down. He scrambled up again, but Wen had spun around and run back toward him. Shae let out a guttural scream of denial as one of the masked men reached and seized Wen, pinning her arms, and from a distance too close to Deflect, another barukan unloaded two bullets into Tako's torso. Even from a distance, Shae Perceived the bodyguard's blinding red agony as he folded at the waist and collapsed into the brittle grass.

Shae turned. Four masked men with guns stood behind her, four across the ravine around Wen and Tako. The man with his arm around Wen's throat walked back toward her, forcing Wen to stumble along in front of him. Shae could see the whites of her sister-in-law's eyes, glistening with tears of fear and rage. The man called out to

Shae, in accented Kekonese, "Kaul Shaelinsan! You think you're one tough Janloon bitch. We'll see how tough. Do you think you can move faster than the bullet of this gun?" He pressed the barrel of his weapon to Wen's temple.

Shae said, "If you pull the trigger, every single one of you will die." She was thankful her voice did not come out trembling, but it seemed to her that the world was tilting under her feet. These men knew who she was. They surely knew who Wen was as well. They'd gone to the effort of setting up the ruse with the police officer and they'd attacked with overwhelming force, clearly prepared to suffer casualties. They already expected death, so her threats were not going to make any difference.

"Drop the knife," the man called. "Then take off your jade."

If it had been only her own safety in question, under no circumstances would Shae allow herself to be disarmed and for her jade to be taken. Even outnumbered, she would've turned and fought until she was killed or subdued—which was sure to happen, seeing as how Dudo and Tako, trained Fists much younger than her, had been overpowered. But that would mean leaving Wen to the mercy of their enemies, which she could not do. The barukan hadn't fired on the women. They wanted them alive.

Which meant they wanted something from No Peak.

Shae let the talon knife slip from her fingers and fall to the ground. She willed her fingers not to shake as she removed her earrings and bracelets. A sick sense of degradation crawled up her throat and made her face burn with shame and disgust. She felt as violated as if she were being forced to strip naked before her assailants. When she'd removed her jade, the man said, "Set it down on the ground and walk backward."

Shae's hands closed tight around her jade. *It won't get you out of this*, she told herself. *It won't help Wen, either.* She bent her knees and dropped the gems on the ground in front of her. The first disorienting jolt of withdrawal hit a couple of seconds later. Shae curled her hands in the folds of her skirt. She swayed, light-headed. A layer of gauze seemed to fall over her eyes and ears and turn the night even more surreal.

Slowly, she stood up and took two steps back. Rough hands came down on her shoulders and forced her down to her knees, scraping her skin against asphalt. Shae caught a glimpse of Wen's terrified face, trying to say something—and then the black hood went over Shae's head, her wrists were bound behind her back, and she was half pushed, half dragged into a car that began to move.

———————

Hilo was in the training hall with his eighteen-year-old nephew, Maik Cam, when the housekeeper, Sulima, ran up from the main house and slid the door open without knocking. "Forgive me, Kaul-jen," she panted, her face pale with alarm, "but someone...On the phone..."

The Pillar strode through the dark courtyard into the main house and picked up the phone in the study, hitting the button for the main line. An accented voice said, "Kaul Hiloshudon. If you wanted to invade Shotar, you should've come yourself instead of sending your bitches. You're used to being in charge, but from this moment on, you're not in charge anymore. If you want your wife and your sister returned alive and intact, you'll do exactly as we say." Silence. "Are you listening carefully, Kaul Hilo?"

"Yes," Hilo said. "Prove they're alive and unharmed."

A rustle of movement in the background as the phone was handed off. There was a considerable amount of static interference, as if the connection was bad. Hilo's heart stuttered as Wen's voice came onto the line, hoarse and frightened. "Hilo?"

He managed to keep his own voice unchanged. "Have they hurt you?"

"No," she said weakly.

"And Shae?"

"They took her jade, but she's not hurt. Dudo and Tako are badly injured."

"Stay calm," Hilo said. "I'll solve this."

"Hilo, I—"

The phone was snatched away and the kidnapper's voice returned.

"You have the proof you asked for. Now this is what you will do. You'll deliver forty kilograms of cut jade and two million Espenian thalirs in cash tomorrow at midnight, at a location of my choosing, in exchange for your wife. If this transaction goes smoothly, you'll have seven days to shut down the operations you set up in Leyolo City, remove every single member of your clan from our country, and publicly announce that No Peak will make no further attempts, now or in the future, to enter Shotar. Then, and only then, will you get your sister back, along with your two men if they are still alive."

"I'll do as you say," Hilo replied. "You'll get the money and the jade you want. I'll pull No Peak out of Shotar. I can overlook losing material things. If you harm the people I care about, however, that is a very different matter." A fever was engulfing his brain. He felt as if the edges of his vision were closing in. All the most terrible possibilities he could imagine were crashing against a bulwark of consuming rage.

What he said next would have to be perfect. He could be neither defiant nor meek. If he was too aggressive, they would abandon their plans and kill their captives. If he sounded desperate, they would not fear him enough to commit to their end of the bargain. This damning calculation happened without conscious thought.

Hilo said, quietly, "You're obviously thick-blooded, whoever you are, since you're willing to do things even my worst enemies would not. I've led dangerous operations before, so let me tell you something: *I'm* not the one you have to worry about now. I'll be as cooperative as a baby goat. Your own men, however . . . I know how dark men can be, how hard it can be to keep them in line. Safe, well-cared-for prisoners are your only leverage right now. If they're mistreated in any way, none of you will get to enjoy the jade or money you've gone to the trouble of getting from me, because you'll all die very badly."

"You're exactly as people say you are, Kaul Hilo," said the amused voice of the man he was going to kill. "You could be burning in hell and have some arrogant thing to say to the devil. Just to be clear: If we see any police, your wife and sister will both die. If we see any reporters, they die. If we see any of your Fists or Fingers, they die. You may rule Kekon, but this is not Kekon." The caller hung up.

CHAPTER

45

Very Bad People

Wen's captors placed her in an empty room by herself and made her sit against the wall with her hands duct-taped together in front of her. They were in a house, but Wen had no idea where. When they'd thrown the hood over her head and pushed her into the car, she'd been hurled back in time to the garage in Port Massy and the agony of suffocating to death. She spent the interminable ride shaking and sweating with panic, certain she would choke or throw up, until at last one of the men noticed her hyperventilating and pulled the bag up so only her eyes were covered and at least she could feel the air on her face and not pass out.

Hours later, she was still seized by intermittent fits of trembling, and her heart would start racing as if it were trying to kill her before anyone else could. She pulled her knees close to her body and tried to take long, deep breaths, picturing herself in the garden back home, sitting by the pond amid blooming magnolia and honeysuckle. She told herself this was not like the situation she'd been through with the Crews. If it was, she would already be raped or dead. These men wanted something from her husband, otherwise they wouldn't have put her on the phone with him for those two seconds. Hilo would move Heaven itself. He would bring down the full might of the clan to find her and get her out safely. In the meantime, she had to stay calm as he'd instructed, to think clearly and not surrender to blind terror.

That was a difficult task when she could hear Tako moaning in pain somewhere down the hall. The Fist had been shot multiple times while trying to defend her. Steel could not stop bullets, but it could slow their passage through the body, which would've only increased Tako's suffering. Wen hated to hear the sounds, but at least she knew he was still alive. She had neither seen nor heard any sign of Shae since the barukan had stripped her of jade and pushed her into one of the other cars.

Wen rested her head against the wall and closed her eyes. She didn't sleep, but she drifted in and out of exhausted semiconsciousness until cracks of light began seeping in from around the black plastic taped over the window. The door opened, and a man came in with a plastic tray of food and paper cup of water. He cut the tape around her wrists with a pocketknife and stood over her as she ate. It was a limp meal of instant rice and reheated frozen vegetables. Wen had no appetite, but she ate the food; she needed to keep up her strength. The irony that she'd been dining with Shae in a five-star restaurant the previous evening almost made her want to laugh.

When she was done, the guard motioned for her to put her wrists together so he could bind her again. Wen said, "I need to go to the bathroom." The man hesitated. He was young, no older than Wen's own sons, with an indecipherable tattoo on the side of his neck and the faintly hostile look of a nervous dog unsure of its place in the pack. Last night, his boss had posted him in the hallway, pointed at Wen, and issued orders in a tone that suggested the young man was responsible for her, and that he would deeply regret it if he failed. "Please," Wen said. "The bathroom."

The young man—she decided to call him Junior—escorted her

to the bathroom at the end of the hall. Along the way, she passed an open doorway and saw Tako lying on top of a plastic sheet in a caked pool of his own blood, curled around his stomach wound. His eyes were closed and his face moved in pain with every shallow breath. As the hours passed, his moans had grown weaker but more continuous. His fingers and neck were bare. Even in his helpless state, the barukan had taken his jade.

Wen tried to go to him, but Junior didn't let her; he prodded her straight toward the bathroom and only allowed her to close the door partway while she relieved herself. Wen's maroon dress, which she had bought only yesterday at one of the trendy shops in the Redwater area, was torn at the shoulder and the hem. At the sink, she splashed cold water on her face, trying to shock herself back into alertness.

On the return trip down the hallway, she stopped in the doorway next to Tako and faced Junior, staring him in the face. "You can't leave him like that," she insisted.

Junior grabbed her arm and began to pull her back toward her room. Wen clung to the door frame, struggling and shouting that she wouldn't go until they treated Tako's wounds. Junior became agitated. "Bitch," he hissed as he pried her fingers loose, breaking two of the nails. Two other barukan showed up to see what the problem was. One of them was the leader who'd made the call to Hilo and put her on the phone last night—a wiry, unexpectedly short man in camouflage cargo pants, a black T-shirt, and a carved skull pendant of bluffer's jade around his neck. Physically, he didn't seem that formidable at first glance, but the jade rings on his fingers were real, and he had a pinched, ferocious face with protruding eyes and a feral stare. Wen thought of him as Big Dog.

"What the fuck is going on here?" Big Dog snapped at Junior, who began to defend himself in Shotarian. The barukan readily mixed the languages when they spoke.

Wen interrupted and addressed the leader directly. "That injured man is a Fist of No Peak," she reminded him. "He's no good to you as ransom if he dies. You have to help him. Call a doctor. My husband will be more forgiving toward you if you do."

Big Dog sneered. "You think you can still order people around like a queen?"

"She's right," said the mixed-blood man with the jade nose ring who seemed to be the second-in-command. "We have to do something about that gods-awful moaning."

Big Dog drew his pistol and before Wen could even scream, he shot Tako in the head, silencing him. "Took care of it," he said. Second Dog let out a startled burst of laughter, but Junior turned pale. Wen's vision blurred. Tako had been her bodyguard for years. He had a wife and two daughters. Her fear of the barukan fell apart beneath rage and disgust. They had never meant to let Tako live. They'd only let him suffer.

"You...you....*dogs*," Wen whispered. "Tako was...was a friend... of m-my family." It had taken years of effort to recover her ability to speak smoothly, but now stress and emotion made words stick in her throat again. She hated the sound of her renewed weakness when she most needed to be strong against these animals. "You're...all...dead men."

Big Dog backed her against the wall, putting his brutal face close to hers. Wen flinched at the menace in his eyes. "Do you think we're afraid of your husband? Just because you're used to everyone bowing and scraping to him, you think it's because of his threats that we're treating you so nicely? He's powerless here. He can't find us and he can't touch us. Think about that before you decide to open your mouth again."

Second Dog and Junior dragged her back into the room and shut the door.

The Kaul house was a war room. Multiple phones and computers were set up in the Pillar's study. Lott and Hejo had the clan's tech wizards trying to trace the location of the ransom call. The perpetrators weren't careless; Hejo's analysts suspected they'd attached a moving cellular phone to a two-way radio, so there was no way to pinpoint where the call had come from. All they could say confidently was that it had originated in Leyolo City, so Wen and Shae had not been transported far.

Federal police might have superior technology to narrow the search further, but Hilo quickly decided against involving either the Kekonese or Shotarian authorities. He could not risk Leyolo City cops getting involved and putting Wen and Shae in greater danger, and he wished to prevent, or at least delay for as long as possible, word getting out that the Pillarman and Weather Man of No Peak were being held hostage by lowly foreign criminals. Already, whispers of concern were circulating in the clan over the Pillar's abruptly canceled appointments.

Hilo wanted to get on a plane with an army of the clan's best Fists and go to Leyolo City himself. He would make it known that he was on the hunt. He would offer a staggering reward for anyone who led them to the kidnappers, and he would spread the word that if Shae and Wen were not returned safely within twenty-four hours, he would tear the city apart, kill every barukan member he could get his hands on until he found the men who'd done this, and they and their families would all die.

He voiced this sentiment to Lott, who said, with some worry, "Kaul-jen, of course, every Fist and Finger is willing to follow you and give our lives if it would bring Shae-jen and Wen back, but I'm not sure that's the best way to—"

"I know that," Hilo snapped. Leyolo City was not Janloon. He couldn't land a plane full of Green Bones there. He didn't control the streets, the police, the government, or the people. Wen and Shae would be dead as soon as the barukan found out he was in the country, and those responsible would flee, knowing he couldn't easily find them.

Although he was too sick with worry to sleep, he was also bored. After issuing orders, there wasn't much he could do while he waited for more information. He'd already instructed Jaya not to come up to Janloon straightaway, but to stay calm and remain at her home in Toshon until they knew more. He was finding it hard to do likewise. Lott told him politely but firmly that his constant pacing and the stress in his jade aura were distracting, so Hilo went out onto the patio and smoked, quitting be damned.

In the morning, word came from one of the clan's secret contacts in the Leyolo City police that the black SUV Tako and Dudo had rented had been found seemingly abandoned on the side of the road five kilometers from the hotel. There were no skid marks, no signs of a car chase or collision, and no signs of mechanical failure. If they'd known they were being followed, Wen's bodyguards would've driven to a safer, more defensible place. The only plausible explanation for them to be calmly stopped in a random location was that they'd been pulled over. If the kidnappers had fake or real Leyolo City police in their employ, they were expert criminals.

"It wasn't the Matyos," Lott reported, getting off the phone. None of the clan's White Rats embedded in the largest of Shotar's barukan gangs had any knowledge of the abduction. If the Matyos were responsible, there would've been some leakage within the gang. People would know something big was going on. Arrangements would've been made, safe houses secured, gunmen organized. Either the Matyos were not involved or it was an outsourced job, known only to the highest-level leaders. Given how quickly the operation had been put together, that seemed unlikely.

If the Matyos weren't behind this, Ayt Mada most likely wasn't either. Hilo was almost disappointed, even though he knew his oldest and greatest rival had no reasonable motive for a crude ransom kidnapping with such high odds of being botched. But if the clan's usual enemies weren't to blame, then who was? The answer came a few hours later. Members of the clan in the Leyolo City branch office had examined all of Shae's and Wen's activities since the instant they arrived in Shotar. After they accounted for everyone Shae had met that day, suspicion fell on Wen's meeting at Diamond Light.

Hami Tumashon, who was on the ground in Shotar, took two of the clan's Fingers from the Leyolo City branch office and drove to Guttano's home. They snatched the studio executive off the driveway of his Redwater area mansion, stuffed him into the trunk of the car, and drove twenty kilometers out of the city to a secure location.

Through a translator, the terrified man confessed. After Wen had come to his office to demand the release of Danny Sinjo from his contract, Guttano feared for his life. He'd phoned a barukan boss named Choyulo to plead for protection, revealing that the wife of Kaul Hiloshudon had visited him and that she was staying at the Oasis Sulliya resort.

Hami explained over the phone that Choyulo was a member of the Faltas barukan. The Faltas were a smaller gang than the Matyos, although the two organizations maintained an arm's-length alliance. The Faltas acted as muscle for the larger gang but were also known for their own activities, primarily extortion and corporate kidnappings. They had tentacles into the sports, music, and film industries, and most of the Shotarian gangster films that glorified the barukan were about the Faltas.

"What should I do with Guttano?" Hami asked. The clan's Rainmaker had been on the business side of the clan for decades, but he had once been a Fist.

Lott depressed the mute button on the phone set and said, "We shouldn't kill this man now, Kaul-jen. A wealthy Shotarian movie executive going missing will bring in the local police. In any case, we may need to ask him other things about the Faltas."

Hilo took the line off mute and gave instructions to Hami. "Put Guttano up in a hotel. Have him phone his wife and tell her that he's been called out of town on urgent business. A problem on a film set, something like that. Post guards to make sure he doesn't talk to anyone else and doesn't leave. If we get Wen and Shae back safely, he goes free. If we don't, he's dead. So if there's anything else he can tell us about the Faltas, he should do it, if he wants to see his family again."

Hilo fell into an armchair and longed for another cigarette. Woon Papidonwa was sitting in the chair across from him with his head in his hands, looking wretched. Hilo wished the man would go back to his own house, as there wasn't anything Woon could do here, but he wasn't cruel enough to send Shae's husband out of the room.

"I should've gone with her," Woon lamented in a whisper.

Hilo berated him more harshly than he deserved. "If you had, Tia would be in danger of losing both parents instead of one. You think you could've changed anything?" Nevertheless, Hilo understood deeply how difficult it was for a jade warrior to accept that there came a time when he couldn't fight his own battles anymore, couldn't with his own strength and abilities protect those he loved. "Shae is smart enough to stay alive until we figure out a way to get her and Wen back, and we're already doing everything we can," he told Woon more gently.

"What can I do to help, Kaul-jen?" his brother-in-law begged.

"You can take care of your daughter," Hilo replied, stalking back out. Tia was clearly aware that something was wrong. As Woon would not leave the war room, Anden had driven the girl to school that morning and picked her up again in the afternoon. Now Tia was worriedly tugging on her father's arm every few minutes to ask when they were going home, and why there were so many people in Uncle Hilo's house.

Woon hugged his daughter but couldn't bring himself to tell her the truth. He said, "Why don't you finish your snack and then go over to your grandma's house."

Tia ran out of the room after her uncle. "Something bad has happened, hasn't it?"

Hilo squatted down next to his niece but hesitated to answer. He didn't believe in lying to children and had never shielded his own from reality. But Tia was different. "Yes," he said. "We're going to fix it, so I don't want you to be frightened."

"Is it about my ma?" When Hilo nodded, Tia's eyes welled with fear. "I want to know."

"Some very bad people took your ma, and your aunt Wen, and two of our Fists while they were on their trip to Leyolo City. They want some things from our clan—jade, money, other important things—before they'll give them back."

Tears spilled down Tia's face as she clutched Hilo's arm. "Uncle Hilo, you have to get my ma back, no matter what. Just give them whatever they want!"

"I'll do everything I can, Tia-se, I swear it," Hilo promised. "But our family has terrible enemies, and sometimes what they want most of all is to hurt us."

"Why would anyone hate us so much?" Tia wept. "None of this makes sense!"

Ru had walked through the door only a few minutes earlier, having skipped the day's classes to rush back home. Everyone could hear Koko leaping about and barking with excitement despite his age. Ru came over and crouched down. "Tia, all the grown-ups are busy right now and we shouldn't distract them. Your ma would want you to be strong and to let everyone work so they can find her and bring her home." As frightened as he was for his own mother, Ru spoke to his little cousin as if everything would be fine. "Why don't the two of us go into the other room and play video games? I'll show you a new one I got last week." He took the girl's hand in his own.

"Thank you, son." Hilo put a hand on Ru's shoulder, grateful to have one of his children near home who he could count on. Since going to college, Ru had become even more expressive and opinionated. He'd dyed copper highlights into his hair and was wearing a T-shirt that read *I'm Nonreactive to Bullshit.* He was often bringing up this or that charity or social cause that he thought No Peak should be supporting, but he was also a great help to his parents.

The afternoon light was starting to wane, and Hilo hadn't slept since the night before last. Wen and Shae had been in barukan hands for eighteen hours. Two million thalirs in cash had been procured from the clan's accounts and forty kilograms of jade taken from its vaults. Locked in four steel briefcases, they were now being loaded onto a chartered plane. In three and a half hours, a small team of the clan's most trusted Fists would arrive in Leyolo City with the money and jade. In eight hours, they would make the planned handover with the Faltas.

Eight hours. They would be the longest of his life. In eight hours, Wen might be safe, or he might be searching for her body.

Hilo did not share Shae's stalwart belief in the gods, but he was not above praying. All his power as Pillar of a great Green Bone clan could not guarantee him anything in this moment other than the promise of vengeance, and that was far less comfort to him than it had once been.

CHAPTER

46

Valuable Things

Wen sat with her ear pressed against the door, listening to the men speaking in the hallway. She could hear Junior's worried voice, although she couldn't make out the words, and then Second Dog's sharp response, "Of course she knows! After tonight, we'll have time. Stick with the plan and we won't have to worry about the Matyos."

Their footsteps approached. Wen scrambled away from the door and slumped back to the floor in the corner, closing her eyes and feigning sleep. The door opened, spilling light from the hall across her face. "Get up," Second Dog ordered.

Wen sat up slowly, not even needing to pretend to be groggy. Junior came toward her with a cloth sack and she shrank back in renewed fear. "I . . . can't . . . breathe in that. Just blindfold me. Please." She hated the way she sounded, but Junior relented. He folded the cloth up and tightened it around her eyes, leaving her nose and mouth uncovered. They pulled her to her feet and told her to walk.

Already weakened and without her sense of sight, her painstakingly reacquired sense of balance failed her. She swayed and stumbled, bumping against the wall. "What's wrong with you?" Second Dog demanded. The two men took her elbows and led her through the house like a hobbled ewe. A door opened. For a blissful few seconds, cool night air slapped against her face. Then she was steered into the back of a car and shut inside.

The vehicle was full. Two men on either side of her penned her into the middle back seat. She heard Second Dog speak from the front passenger seat. "Let's go. We have to get this done." The driver started the car and it began to move.

Wen clenched her trembling hands together and pressed them between her knees. She was afraid but no longer panicked. She had been killed before. By all rights, she ought to have died in Port Massy eighteen years ago. Instead, she'd been given the chance to see her children grow up and to spend more years with Hilo, some of which had been difficult, but many of which had been happy. She'd overcome her injuries to stand in front of crowds of people and dozens of cameras to speak for the clan. She was the only wife of a Pillar to also be Pillarman. So she had no regrets about how she'd spent the gift of extra time in her life, and she promised herself that at least she would not beg, no matter what they did to her. She was, however, desperately worried about Shae and Dudo.

"Where's Kaul Shae?" she asked. "What are you going to do with her?"

They did not answer her. The drive lasted for a long time, perhaps an hour, although Wen couldn't be sure. At last, the car stopped. The men inside conversed in Shotarian. Two of them—Second Dog and the man on her left side—exited the car while the others waited behind. Long minutes passed, during which Wen wondered where they had gone, whether they were digging a shallow grave for her body.

A two-way radio crackled to life from the driver's seat. Another curt conversation was exchanged over the radio, and then the baru-kan on Wen's right side opened the door and exited the car. "Get out," he ordered. She recognized Junior's voice. Wen put her feet down firmly, holding on to the side of the car as she stood. She heard and smelled water, then the blindfold was pulled off her head, and she saw that they were on one end of a fog-obscured bridge spanning the Gondi River. Junior cut the tape around her wrists, then pointed her toward the bridge's pedestrian path. "Walk," he ordered, and prodded her forward.

Wen began to cross the bridge, Junior walking behind her. The cold, damp air filled her needy lungs. The fog thickened as they went farther out onto the water. Wen couldn't see the end of the bridge; its silver girders disappeared into white mist. A few cars passed on the road in either direction, their lights smearing the pavement before disappearing, but the pedestrian walkway seemed entirely deserted. Wen hung on to the railing to steady her steps, but she regretted glancing over the side. It was a long drop to the dark, fast-moving water below.

"Stop," Junior said. "Don't move." Wen heard him draw his pistol and then she felt the cold metal barrel of the weapon touch the back of her head. She remained motionless and kept her eyes open. She knew better than to expect her life to flash before her eyes. That was a myth. When death came, it was with terror and pain and nothing else.

"Is it your job to kill me, to prove yourself to the others?" she asked Junior. When the young man didn't answer, she said, "Do you really want to be a part of such evil?"

"Shut up," Junior whispered, but Wen heard the hint of doubt in his voice. "You don't get to talk about evil. *We're* the ones minding our own business, but the clans have to come in where you're not welcome and fuck over everyone who doesn't bow to you. If it were up to me," Junior hissed fiercely, "I'd kill every last member of your family."

Wen had enough experience with teenage sons to know that young men often didn't know their own feelings, even when they insisted they did. She could feel the gun shaking a little behind her head. "Then what are we waiting for?"

Two figures appeared on the pathway, walking quickly toward them. As they neared, Wen saw that it was Second Dog and the other barukan who'd left the car earlier. They were each carrying two metal cases, their arms tensed with Strength. They strode past Wen and Junior with barely a glance. Wen didn't dare to turn, but she heard the trunk of the car opening behind her and the heavy thud of the suitcases being placed inside. "You're the lucky one tonight, you cunt," Junior said. The gun came away from her head. Wen's heart began to beat again. "Keep walking."

Wen took a step forward and then another. She kept walking, faster and faster when she realized that the barukan were not following. She was stumbling now, using the damp metal railing to pull herself along. At first, there was nothing ahead but fog, then shapes resolved out of the gloom. Two men. Another few steps, and she recognized her nephew, Cam, standing with Hami Tumashon.

With a choked cry, Wen ran toward them. Cam ran to her and caught her up, hugging her tight. "Aunt Wen, thank the gods," he said, his voice catching. Hami threw his jacket over her bare shoulders, and the two of them led her, shaking with relief, to the other side of the bridge, where a car waited. Vin, one the clan's First Fists, was behind the wheel, and as soon as they were all inside, he began to drive. Cam sat in the back with Wen, putting a hot thermos in her hands and warm blankets on her until her violent trembling abated. "We'll be at the airstrip in twenty minutes," Hami assured her.

Wen felt her wits slowly coming back together. "What about Shae?"

She saw the line of Hami's jaw tighten. "They still have her," he said. "They demanded money and jade for your release. They say they'll release the Weather Man once we dismantle No Peak's office and evacuate Shotar completely."

"How much longer will that be?"

"A week," Hami said, glancing over his shoulder at her. "It'll hurt our business badly, to tear up everything we've done here in the past year, but it's what we have to do for now to meet their demands. We've already begun making the arrangements to pull people out.

After we get Kaul Shae-jen back, we'll think of whether there's some way to salvage the situation and strike back at those barukan dogs."

A week. The words that Wen had overheard in the hallway earlier in the night came back to her. She hadn't known what they were talking about. *After tonight, we'll have time.* Wen lurched forward and grabbed Hami's shoulder. "We can't get onto the plane yet," she cried. "We have to stop and phone Hilo."

"Don't worry, I had Fists watching the bridge," Vin told her. "They're phoning the Pillar now to let him know the handoff went smoothly and that you're safe."

Cam said, "Hopefully that means we'll get the others back safely too."

Wen shook her head vigorously. She'd gotten off too easily. Those men—Big Dog, Second Dog, even Junior—she'd seen their reckless hatred. They would've been pleased to send Hilo her violated corpse. Only some truly compelling reason would've motivated them to release her unharmed. They didn't fear No Peak's vengeance, so that wasn't the reason. She hadn't heard them crowing with anticipation over the money or jade.

No, delivering a hostage right away in exchange for ransom was a sign of cooperation. A misdirection, meant to lull the Pillar into withdrawing his people in the belief that the kidnappers were sincere in their demands. "I have to talk to Hilo myself," Wen insisted, growing frantic. "We can't believe them. We shouldn't pull anyone out. We need everyone we have in this country searching for Shae, because they're not going to give her back."

———

Shae had reviewed the possibility of escape and determined it to be minimal. Without any of her jade, she had no hope of overpowering her barukan captors, even if she wasn't tied to a chair, gagged, and suffering from jade withdrawal. She'd been through jade withdrawal twice before in her life, and it had been unpleasant, but she'd been cared for or able to care for herself, not bound and starved by enemies. A relentless headache sat at the front of her skull, hammering into the backs of her eyeballs, and her face and neck were filmed with a layer of sweat that made her shiver with chills. For some reason, she found herself thinking of Yun Dorupon, a man she'd despised and who was long dead, but with whom she felt a sudden miserable kinship, because as Weather Man, he had once been captured by Shotarians, jade-stripped, and tortured.

At some point, she thought she heard Wen shouting and her mind had filled with the worst sort of imaginings. Then there had been footsteps and a gunshot. Now, without any sense of Perception, she had no idea if her sister-in-law was still alive. She'd assumed that the barukan had captured them as leverage against No Peak. She'd counted on the possibility of using her position as Weather Man to negotiate for Wen's life, but no one had come into the bare room to see her in many hours.

She grew heavy-headed and fell unconscious for indeterminable periods of time. After what she guessed to be over a full day, the door opened and two men came into the room: a short, mean-looking man in cargo pants and a skull pendant of bluffer's jade, and a young man with a tattoo on the side of his neck. The short man, who seemed to be the leader, said, mockingly, "You must be getting bored, Kaul Shaelinsan."

The younger man went behind the chair and untied the gag. Shae moved her sore jaw and tried to force saliva into her dry throat. "Did you kill my sister-in-law?"

The barukan leader smirked at the torment he knew she must be feeling. "On the contrary, she's on her way home right now," he said. "Your brother loves his wife very much and paid the full ransom for her safe return."

Shae wished desperately she had her jade and the Perception to discern if the man was lying. She couldn't help but clutch at the hope that he was telling the truth, that Wen was indeed free. She kept her voice carefully neutral. "If that's true, then there's a lot more we could talk about. You know who I am and how much jade and money I control. I'm sure we can come to some sort of deal."

"I'm sure we can," said the barukan leader in his accented

Kekonese, his lips rising in a way that made Shae distinctly uneasy. "After all, the most valuable thing that the Weather Man of a clan possesses isn't jade or money. It's *information*."

He stepped forward directly in front of her, fixing Shae with his bulging eyes. "Your clan came into Shotar by making friends with the police and the government. You give them information from your spies. Two months ago, federal agents busted a shipment of sweet flour worth two and a half million sepas—there's no way they could've known about that deal unless there was a rat in the Matyos."

Shae shook her head slowly. "You're not Matyos." Due to No Peak's spy network in Shotar and its cooperation with Shotarian law enforcement, she was aware of who the main leaders of the Matyos were, and these men were not among them.

"Fuck the Matyos," the man snapped. "They bring the goods through Oortoko, but they lean on *us* to move and guard the product, so it's Faltas who end up dead or in prison and the Matyos blame *us* for the lost dope, when it's No Peak rats who are to blame." He leaned so close she could smell his strangely sweet cologne mingling with his sour breath. "Two weeks after that bust, the No Peak clan received business permits and liquor licenses for four properties it had recently acquired in Leyolo City. Maybe it's a coincidence, but I don't believe in coincidences. Who was your rat?"

Shae said, "I'm the Weather Man. I'm not involved in handling White Rats. The Horn's side of the clan manages informers." Ordinarily, that would be a plausible denial, but Shae had been personally involved in every aspect of the clan's risky expansion into Shotar. She'd worked with Lott and Hejo. She'd seen the names.

"You must think that we don't know how to use our jade, that we can't tell you're lying," said the Faltas captain, sounding insulted. "Perhaps you don't understand: No one is going to rescue you. Your brother has his wife back safe and sound and is pulling your clan's Green Bones out of the country. If you give us what we want, you can have a pleasant stay with us and go home as well. If not, it will be over a week before they start hunting for your body. I don't want to have to do that to a woman."

As the leader spoke, another man came into the room with coils of rope and chains. Shae's mouth went drier than dirt. The men lashed her ankles and wrists, then untied her from the chair and wound rope and chains around her torso and legs, securing them with padlocks, until she was entirely immobilized, like an escape artist about to be lowered into a closed container only to astound everyone with a feat of magic. Except that Shae had no such trick. Her heart was running like a jackhammer.

The younger man lifted her over his shoulder like a heavy sack of rice and carried her into a bathroom with a Shotarian-style soaking tub large enough for three or four people. Dudo was sitting in the dry tub, also securely bound and weighed down with chains. When the barukan placed Shae inside the tub across from him, the Fist raised his bowed head. Dudo's face was badly bruised and his eyes were having difficulty focusing. The blow to the back of his head had given him a concussion. "Kaul-jen," he croaked. "I'm sorry I failed to protect you."

Shae couldn't manage a reply. It was not Dudo's fault, but hers. It had been her decision to expand into Shotar and make enemies of the barukan. She had brought Wen on this trip, and she had ordered Dudo to stop the car for the false police officer. Like so many choices she'd made in her life, they'd seemed reasonable at the time.

"You may be one tough Green Bone bitch," said the barukan leader, "but are you soulless enough to watch another person suffer and die for your stubbornness?"

Shae felt a strange urge to tell him that she was no stranger to seeing others pay for her mistakes. Lan, whom she'd failed as a sister. Maro, dead by her hand. Luto, her chief of staff for only a few months. Wen and Anden, ambushed in Espenia. The unborn child she'd aborted. Woon's first wife, Kiya. Dudo would be the next. Was this what it truly meant to hold power, Shae wondered, almost detached from her own sense of ballooning fear. Passing on the worst consequences of your failure to others, whether you wanted to or not? The chains pressed into the skin of her wrists. The white ceramic was cold against her bare legs.

"Give me names," said the short man. "The names of your rats."

If she surrendered the identities of No Peak's sources, those people would surely die horrible deaths of their own. She would cause death and suffering no matter what.

"No? I'll even give you a choice," the man went on reasonably. "How about the names of the officials in the police and government who are on No Peak's payroll?"

With such a gold mine of information constituting vital importance to the Shotarian underworld, the kidnappers had no need to fear No Peak's retribution. They could count on protection from the Matyos. They could even sell their knowledge to the Mountain clan, to cleanse No Peak from Shotar, regardless of what Hilo decided to do.

Dudo roused enough to slur, "You're all dead men, you barukan dogs."

The leader motioned for two metal briefcases to be brought into the bathroom and set down on the linoleum floor. He unlatched the cases and opened them to reveal piles of cut and polished jade. Gemstones of various sizes and weights, ready to be set and worn, all of it gleaming with deep, translucent brilliance even in the dim yellow of the bathroom's sconce lighting.

Shae sucked in a breath. It was a staggering fortune, a treasure trove of near mythological scale. The barukan in the room stared in rapt admiration. Some of them began fingering their own meager adornments, no doubt imagining themselves as Baijen reborn, wearing more jade than any Green Bone. Their leader whistled low. "Beautiful, isn't it? Beautiful and deadly."

Two men pulled on thick, lead-lined gloves and lifted the first briefcase over the edge of the tub, tipping all of its contents inside. Jade clattered against the inside of the tub like pennies thrown into a pail, spilling over Shae's and Dudo's legs. The barukan hefted the second briefcase as well, piling tens of millions of dien worth of jade into a thick layer that covered the bottom of the tub like green glass pebbles at the bottom of a fish tank. Shae jerked and tried instinctively to pull herself away from the cascade, but it was futile. Thousands of pieces of jade—more jade than any human being without jade immunity should ever be in contact with at one time—tumbled on top of her thighs and calves, were caught between the toes of her bare feet, became trapped under her clothes as she struggled in mounting panic.

Many years ago, Shae had visited a jade mine high up in the

mountainous interior of Kekon. She'd seen boulders of raw jade cut open and lying in the beds of trucks and wondered morbidly what would happen if she placed the flat of her hand against that much seductive green. She'd imagined instant death, and also slow sickness, but what she experienced now was this: A rush of familiar, disorienting power as her jade senses snapped back into awareness—she could Perceive every person in and around the building, she could feel energy streaming through her body with every pulse of her cavernous heart, she sensed time slowing as her mind leapt out of the confines of its flesh. In that instant she grasped for her abilities, tried with a desperate cry to focus every iota of her formidable training into enough Strength to break her chains. The ropes and metal links strained but held—and then the pain began. It escalated quickly, as if she'd thrown herself struggling against a huge metal door, only to discover that it was warming to a red-hot temperature and she was now welded to the surface, unable to tear free as it began to glow crimson and burn her alive.

Shae had all the jade tolerance of a top-rank Green Bone, built up over a lifetime of exposure and training. Her body was intimately familiar with jade. So it was a hideous violent perversion that what had been natural throughout her entire adult life suddenly turned into sheer agony. She tried with mindless desperation to grasp for the control techniques she'd known since she was a child—awareness of her breath, dispelling tension in the body, visualization—all of it was useless. She was drowning in a flaming deluge. Even if she weren't immobilized with restraints, she couldn't summon Strength or Channeling or anything that could help her escape any more than someone could control a kite inside a cyclone. She plummeted back into physical sensation: Her muscles began to shake uncontrollably, sweat broke out all over her body, her heart rate and temperature and blood pressure skyrocketed.

She saw the cords of Dudo's neck stand out as he screamed.

"This jade is from No Peak's own vaults," Shae heard the short barukan leader say thoughtfully as if from a great distance. "Isn't that poetic?"

CHAPTER

47

What Must Be Done

Hilo sat on the edge of the bed, watching the blankets rise and fall gently in time with Wen's breath. After the tearful relief of coming home, there had been utter exhaustion; she'd finally fallen into a deep slumber. He touched the back of his hand to her cheek, reassuring himself that she was truly there, that he was not in a hopeful dream from which he would awaken to the nightmare of her still being lost and in danger. Slowly, he bent and pressed his lips to her brow, careful not to wake her.

He rose, dressed quietly, and went downstairs. Anden was sitting on the bottom step of the staircase, his shoes already on, waiting. "Let's go," Hilo said.

Anden drove the Pillar's new Duchesse Imperia south on Lo Low Street. The sun was not up yet and the streets of Janloon were shambling through the shift change between the city's nighttime denizens and its earliest risers—drunks, prostitutes, and graveyard shift workers stumbling home while street hawkers, newsstand owners, and shopkeepers opened up for business.

Hilo broke the silence. "This reminds me of that time you drove us to the Twice Lucky on New Year's Day."

Anden said, "That was a long time ago."

"A long time ago," Hilo agreed. "You're a much better driver now." When Anden glanced over at him with a furrowed brow, Hilo broke into his famous lopsided grin.

"I'm glad you're not counting on me to kill anyone today," Anden said. On the other side of the Lo Low Street tunnel, he took the interchange onto Patriot Street and turned into High Ground, navigating the large bulk of the Duchesse up hilly residential roads. The corners of Anden's mouth lifted a little. "I didn't think we'd ever joke about that day."

"Let's hope we'll feel the same way about today in another twenty years." Hilo draped an arm out the open window and gazed at the sunrise crawling over the manicured trees. "Gods. We were young men back then, Andy," he said, losing the lightness in his voice. "That day, I was ready to die at the hands of Gont Asch if I had to. Now...I could still do it, but I think it would be harder. You'd think it would be easier to face death as you get older, but it doesn't work that way. You get more attached to life, to people you love and things that are worth living for."

Hilo saw his cousin eyeing him with concern, and he said, "Don't look so worried, Andy. As much as I didn't want to hear it, you were right, what you said last night. We lose no matter what, so this is the only way. You know what to do if you have to."

Anden said, "I know, Hilo-jen."

"When something has to be done, there's always a way to do it," Hilo said quietly. They pulled up outside of the enormous iron gates of the Ayt mansion. The security cameras mounted along the approaching road had already alerted the guards to their arrival. Four Mountain Green Bones armed with moon blades and handguns met the Duchesse in front of the gates. Anden stopped the car and shut off the engine, then lifted his hands off the steering wheel, holding them open for the guards to see.

Hilo opened the door and stepped out. His Perception buzzed with the hostile alertness of the four Green Bones in front of him and two others inside the gate that he couldn't see. He raised his voice to the guards. "I'm here to see your Pillar."

———

One morning when he was twenty-two years old, Hilo met his older brother, Lan, for breakfast at the Twice Lucky restaurant. It was the first time he'd ever eaten there, and he was pleasantly surprised that although it was an older place, loud and a bit stuffy, the food was much better than anything else in the Docks. Lan, however, did not appear to be paying attention to either the meal or their conversation. He seemed troubled and didn't smile at anything Hilo said.

In Hilo's opinion, there was little for Lan to be unhappy about. His brother wore plenty of jade, was recently married, and their grandfather was giving him an increasing amount of responsibility over the day-to-day running of the clan. At last, Hilo threw his napkin down. "What's wrong with you, anyway? You have this look on your face like you've been constipated for days."

Lan's expression twitched with surprise, then annoyance. "I have things on my mind, Hilo," he replied. "I don't happen to share every single issue that's bothering me."

Hilo scratched his jaw and considered this, feeling a little hurt by the dismissal. True, he and Lan were not close in the manner of siblings who were similar in age. They had not grown up as rivals or confidants. Nevertheless, there was an unspoken understanding between them, because one day Lan would be the Pillar and Hilo would be his Horn. He would swear oaths to his older brother, to obey him, to kill and die for him if necessary. So he felt it was only fair that Lan trust him enough to explain why he was ruining a perfectly good breakfast with his melancholy. "Is it something to do with that meeting Grandda had last week?"

Lan's left eye narrowed into a squint. "How do you know about that?"

Hilo shrugged. "Is it or isn't it?"

Lan exhaled through his nose, as if giving in, but he relaxed slightly, apparently relieved to finally talk about what was troubling him. "You know that Grandda and Uncle Doru are worried about who will succeed Ayt Yu as Pillar of the Mountain."

"Ayt's not that old," Hilo said. "He could be Pillar for another ten years."

"The rumor is that he's taken off some of his jade because of high blood pressure. The Spear of Kekon might be a living legend, but if his jade tolerance is starting to go, it won't be long before he has to retire. Maybe five years, maybe less. Ayt Eodo is his son by adoption, not blood, and Eodo's a joke, not respected as a Green Bone."

Hilo broke apart one of the nut pastries. "His daughter is the Weather Man."

"A woman Pillar?" Lan shook his head. "Ayt won't go that far. So the door is open for some other family in the Mountain clan to rise into the leadership."

"Why's any of this our problem?" Hilo asked. "The Mountain can sort out its own shit." As a junior Fist, he had no love for the Mountain clan. He and his peers had skirmished violently with them for territory and business, particularly in disputed districts, and some of those confrontations had left hard feelings on both sides.

"Grandda and Uncle Doru had a meeting last week with Tanku Ushijan," Lan said. "The Horn of the Mountain proposed that we unite our families through marriage."

Hilo stopped in mid-chew. The thought of Wen flashed through his mind. He was not one to keep secrets, but he hadn't yet told his grandfather or his brother that he was in love with a girl in the Maik family, a *stone-eye*. His face or his jade aura must've given away his sudden panic because Lan said, with a dry smile, "I don't think I've ever been able to scare you like that before. Is the idea of settling down really that frightening? Anyway, you're safe. Tanku's son, Din, is a first-rank Fist. People are saying he could follow in his father's footsteps and become Horn. A marriage between Shae and Tanku Din would tie the leadership of both clans together."

Relief washed over Hilo and he began breathing again. He finished chewing and swallowing. "Grandda won't go for it," he said with confidence. "Shae's his favorite."

Lan didn't reply at first, but the texture of his jade aura grew scratchy as he pushed at the food on his plate. "When it comes to decisions about what's best for the clan, sometimes there's no room for personal feelings, not even for the Pillar. Doru thinks it's a good idea, and you know how much sway he has with Grandda."

Hilo grimaced. "Doru should go back to the Three Crowns era where he came from." The creaky old Weather Man would've been one of those scheming palace courtiers.

Lan looked at his younger brother with a resignation that Hilo would not understand for many more years, not until he was Pillar himself. "Grandda and Ayt Yu have had their differences over the years, but now that they're both getting older, they want to ensure there's still respect between the clans after they're gone. That's getting harder to do when we have different businesses, different territories, different schools." Lan tugged absently at the jade-studded cuffs on his forearms, uncertainty written on his face. "The Tanku family says that if we ally with them, Ayt Yu will pass over that playboy Eodo and name Tanku Ushi as the next Pillar of the Mountain. It would prevent infighting over the succession and assure everyone of peaceful relations. Shae would be daughter-in-law to their Pillar, and if the younger Tanku is promoted, we would be brothers-in-law to their Horn."

Hilo was liking this vision of the future less and less the more he heard. He had no personal grudge against the Tankus, but he certainly didn't want them as in-laws. The elder Tanku was in his fifties; his son was two years older than Lan. If the families merged, the Tankus would be dominant. How was Lan supposed to maintain his own standing as Pillar against a man who was essentially his father-in-law? And if Hilo became the Horn of No Peak, he would surely have to face his own brother-in-law as a rival and be forced to back down to protect his sister's marriage. A union might preserve the peace for the foreseeable future, but in the long run, surely No Peak would be diminished. It might even become a tributary of the Mountain.

He was still not worried, though, because he knew his sister. "Shae will never agree," he scoffed.

Lan tapped out a cigarette for himself and offered the pack to his younger brother, who took one, even though it was not his preferred brand. "You and I know that," Lan said. "I don't think Grandda does. He's always doted on Shae, so he believes she'll obey him. If she doesn't, we'll lose face with Ayt Yu and the Tankus. No matter what, the family's not going to be the same after this." At Hilo's silence, Lan grumbled, "So that's why I haven't been so cheerful this morning. And now I can tell I've ruined your morning as well, although it's your own fault for asking."

Hilo lit his cigarette but found he couldn't enjoy the taste. "The old man hasn't given his answer to the Tankus yet, has he? Maybe you can still talk him out of it."

"Maybe," Lan said, not sounding hopeful. "Grandda's getting more stubborn as he gets older. You know the position I'm in. In the end, it's his decision."

The owner of the restaurant came to their table to introduce himself as Mr. Une and to ask if there was anything unsatisfactory with the meal since Lan hadn't eaten much. When they assured him the food was excellent, the restaurateur saluted them deeply, saying he was pleased to serve the Pillar's grandsons, and he hoped they would carry a favorable review of his humble establishment to the Torch himself.

Lan conversed with Mr. Une with all the courteous gravity Hilo had watched him develop over the past few years, but his smile was thin. Grandda was already seventy-six, much older than Ayt Yugontin, yet despite grooming Lan for the leadership, he had not yet announced his own retirement. Lan was in a predicament as the Pillar-in-waiting. No matter how much he disagreed with Kaul Sen, defying or disobeying him might further delay when he would be named Pillar.

When Mr. Une left, Lan said to Hilo, "Not a word of this to Shae, understand? I don't want to start any feud between her and Grandda if we can avoid it."

Two years later, Shae would feud vociferously with their grandfather all on her own, but at the time, neither Lan nor Hilo knew what was to come.

"I'm trusting you, Hilo," Lan said. "Swear you'll keep it quiet."

Hilo widened his eyes innocently and spread his hands with affable nonchalance. "On my jade, brother," he said, though he wondered if Lan had told anyone else. He doubted his brother confided about clan issues with that haughty wife of his. "Anyway, I'm not stupid enough to be the one to deliver the bad news. If Shae found out from me, she'd probably throw me off a roof." They sat together in silence for a few minutes, finishing their cigarettes. Hilo said, "I'm glad I'm just a Fist and don't have to deal with the clan politics bullshit that you do."

But Hilo did not stop thinking about what Lan had told him. Their grandfather was an old fool, Hilo decided, for trying to turn back the clock, on a decision *he* had made, no less. The One Mountain Society had divided a generation ago. Attempting to bring the Mountain and No Peak together made about as much sense as trying to glue a cracked egg. Instead of behaving like an ancient warlord by arranging a political marriage for Shae, Grandda ought to simply *retire*. Once Lan was in charge of the clan, he could name Hilo his Horn and Shae his Weather Man. Together, they would be stronger than the Tankus or any of Ayt Yu's potential successors, instead of yoked to them like some feudal tributary. The sooner Lan took over as Pillar, the better.

The more Hilo thought about it, the angrier he grew toward his elders. He was also selfishly worried about his own prospects. He was too young, in everyone's opinion, to rise to the position of Horn for several more years. When Lan became the Pillar, he would be expected to choose a senior warrior to command the military side of the clan, someone with a great deal of jade and experience.

Hilo couldn't afford to gradually rise up the ranks, awaiting his turn. Even in retirement, their grandfather was sure to have a say in everything. Lan would be surrounded by old cronies. Unless he was the Horn, Hilo couldn't be certain of having influence with his elder brother or authority in the clan, nor would he have enough status in No Peak to make everyone accept his relationship with Wen.

Much to the delight of Mr. Une, Hilo returned to the Twice Lucky two days later to try its dinner menu. This time he had Maik Kehn and Maik Tar with him. Lan had told him not to speak to Shae, but Hilo decided he could safely discuss the situation with his two closest and most trustworthy fellow Fists.

"I have to kill Tanku Din," he told them after the appetizers arrived.

Tar paused with a crispy squid ball halfway toward his mouth. "The son of the Mountain's Horn? Big, mean fellow with the flat nose and a shitload of jade?"

"That's the one," Hilo said. "And it has to be soon, and with a clean blade."

"It's been nice knowing you, keke," Tar quipped. "I'll ask the gods to recognize you." When he saw that Hilo was completely serious, Tar's smirk disappeared and he said, "You're good, Hilo-jen, everyone knows that. But even you're not Baijen reborn. Tanku Din is above our level, at least for now." Tanku Din was a first-rank Fist of the Mountain. Duels between Green Bones were usually fought between those of roughly equal status. It was poor form to fight someone beneath one's own level, and simply unwise to challenge someone far more heavily jaded than oneself. It was possible to win against someone with a significant jade advantage, just as it was possible to prevail against an opponent who was twice one's size. *Possible*, but *unlikely*.

Kehn said, "What sort of grudge do you have against Tanku that it can't wait?"

"Nothing personal. I barely know the man, though I don't especially care to." Tanku Din had a reputation for being an excellent fighter and an organized Fist, but also a petty human being, someone easily angered by criticism, who would punish subordinates or abandon Lantern Men for offending him in minor ways.

Hilo explained the situation to the Maiks and his reasoning behind the need to act urgently. "Grandda can't make Shae marry a dead man."

Even Kehn and Tar looked a little taken aback at this, although they couldn't argue with the logic. Kehn rubbed the back of his neck and blew out a contemplative breath. "One-on-one is too risky. Maybe we could take him together in an ambush."

Hilo shook his head. "We can't have anyone thinking that Lan whispered his name to me. Lan has to stay on Grandda's good side until the old man finally steps down. So it has to seem unplanned." When the Maik brothers looked at each other with undisguised skepticism, Hilo snapped, "Don't ever sit in front of me with a look that says you're giving up right away. Think about the Charge of Twenty. My own father found a way to do the impossible at the cost of his own life because failing wasn't an option. When something has to be done, there's always a way to do it." This was to become something he was known to say to his many Fists in the years to come.

The following Thirdday afternoon, Hilo and the Maik brothers drove into Mountain territory and visited a bar in a neighborhood they knew was controlled by Tanku Din and his Fingers. Hilo strode into the Black Goose, set his sheathed moon blade on a table, and declared to the bartender, "My friends and I aren't here to cause trouble. We're just looking to have a drink or two."

Hilo and the Maiks sat down and each ordered a beer. They drank and talked and ordered more beers, followed by a bottle of hoji. After two hours, the bartender went to the back of the building and phoned Tanku Din, who arrived fifteen minutes later to see what the trouble was with the No Peak Green Bones who weren't leaving a Mountain property. When Tanku arrived, Hilo's face lit up and he motioned the Mountain Fist over to their table. "Tanku-jen, come have a drink with us!"

Tanku looked at the several empty beer and hoji glasses on the table and said, "I think you've had enough, Kaul. You realize you're in the Stump, don't you? It's time for you to go home." He rested a hand casually on the hilt of his moon blade.

"That's not a very hospitable thing to say to family," Hilo replied. "You're going to marry my little sister, aren't you? We're going to be brothers, so my home will be your home, and your home"—he gestured around the bar—"will be my home."

Tanku blinked in surprise, then leaned his hands on the table, glancing at the Maiks before lowering his voice to Hilo. "How do you know that?"

"Tanku-jen, you don't know what you're getting into. My little sister's spoiled. My grandfather told her the good news, and she came to me crying her eyes out, saying that she didn't want to be married off to a pig-faced brute." The thought of Shae coming to him with any of her problems, much less in tears, was so amusing to Hilo that his grin was genuine. If Tanku had an especially good sense of Perception, maybe he could sense that Hilo was spinning a tale, but it didn't really matter.

Tanku's face flushed dark at the insult. Nevertheless, he seemed to reconsider his tone with Hilo. Pushing aside a cluster of empty drink glasses, he made space for himself at the table and sat down. Neither of the Maiks shifted over for him. Kehn scowled at the newcomer blearily. Tar was resting his head on the table, using his arm as a pillow. Tanku wrinkled his nose, and said to Hilo, "Look, Kaul, neither of us has a choice in the matter, so let's not get off on the wrong foot with each other. I'll treat your sister well. She'll have money, a nice house, whatever she wants."

"That's exactly what I told her," Hilo exclaimed with vigor. "And I also reassured her that you're not nearly as stupid or ugly as people say you are. She still wasn't happy, so I promised to talk to you in person to clear a few things up." Hilo tossed back the hoji in his glass, then leaned forward and raised a finger, taking a long time to gather his thoughts. "First of all, I'm frankly relieved that she's going to be your problem and not mine anymore. But if you ever hit her, I will kill you. Second, your pussy-hunting days are over. I don't want my little sister catching some nasty disease from your wandering cock or being treated like another one of your whores. Third..." He squinted blearily at Tanku's face, which was reddening with anger. "I can't remember what the third thing was. Anyway, that's all I have to say. Let's have a toast to our impending brotherhood, you prick." He stole Tar's glass and poured a shot of hoji for Tanku and then himself, spilling half the pour over the rim onto the sticky table.

Tanku stood up. "You're drunk out of your mind," he said with disgust. "Get out, and come back with your ear in a box when you're sober." When no one at the table moved, Tanku seized Hilo by the upper arm and began to pull him out of his chair.

Hilo yanked his arm away. "Don't fucking touch me," he shouted, his bloodshot eyes blazing, spittle flying from his mouth. "You Tankus used to be goatfucking southerners and now you think you're at the level of us Kauls? You think you can push my grandda around and get what you want from us? You don't deserve us."

The roughly dozen other customers in the Black Goose had been eyeing the table with the Green Bones nervously, and now many of them took their drinks and food and moved to tables farther away from the confrontation. The bartender cleared his throat and said, "Tanku-jen, do you want me to call anyone?"

Tanku answered without turning around. "No, don't bother." He was taller and larger than Hilo, and now he loomed over the younger Fist like he was about to wrap his hands around his future brother-in-law's throat. "I'd heard you were a reckless, arrogant bastard, but I didn't expect you'd be so *pathetic*. I thought you'd be more like your brother, but you're an idiot pup, and from what I hear, your little sister's a whore who runs around with foreigners. I bet no other man will have her. It's *your* family that doesn't deserve *ours*. If not for your grandfather, you'd be less than trash."

Hilo staggered to his feet. "Tanku Din, I offer you a clean blade."

The Mountain Fist snorted in derision. "I don't duel drunken boys."

"Coward," Hilo spat. "Piss drinker. Dog fucker. Take my clean blade or I'll trash this building, you pussy." He put his face right up to Tanku. "Knife or blade?"

He saw the inevitable decision being made. Tanku's eyes went black with malice. The man's thick jade aura was shrilling with eagerness to send this offensive young No Peak Fist to the hospital. "Blade," he said. "Right now."

It was not ideal. Hilo had hoped Tanku would issue the challenge to *him*, so he could choose the talon knife. Despite his reputation for being thin-skinned, Tanku had resisted the baiting better than Hilo had anticipated. Hilo grabbed his moon blade and kicked the Maiks' chairs. "Come on," he said. "I'm dueling." He weaved his way out the back door and into the alley behind the Black Goose.

Tanku Din followed, drawing his own weapon. Only now that he was about to face the man in combat did it truly strike Hilo that there was a good chance he could end up dead or maimed, the jade torn from his body. Clean-bladed duels were unpredictable, and even if Tanku Din didn't intend to kill him, he might be angry enough to do so in the heat of the moment. The Mountain Fist wore twice as much jade as Hilo: a row of studs in the cartilage of both ears and stacked bracelets on his wrists. Hilo could tell, simply from the way the man moved and the confident manner with which he held his moon blade, that he was an opponent to be feared.

Hilo had not spoken of his wild plan to anyone other than Kehn and Tar. That could hardly be helped, but now he regretted not having said some small thing to Wen before he left. He wondered, abruptly, if his own father had said anything to him and his siblings before he'd left to fight for the last time. Hilo held his moon blade out to the Maik brothers, who both spat on the metal for luck. "If I die, tell my family I fought well," he declared to Tanku and the more daring bar patrons who were watching from the mouth of the alley.

The combatants touched their blades to their foreheads in salute. Hilo attacked immediately, rushing in Light with a blindingly fast hurricane of slices. Tanku parried the cuts expertly and countered with precise, powerful strokes, shearing Hilo's weapon with steady, battering force. It took Hilo all of three seconds to grudgingly admit that Tanku was more skilled with the moon blade than he was. He wasn't surprised, but that didn't make the fact easier to swallow under the circumstances.

Staggering back from the man's Strength, Hilo repositioned his stance and attempted to create defensive space by throwing up a quick Deflection. Tanku twisted his body and dispelled the energy with a perpendicular cross-Deflection before Hilo's wave could travel even an arm's length from his body. Hilo pulled in his jade energy for another try, but when the tip of his moon blade dipped, Tanku's weapon darted instantly into the momentary opening, slashing him across the top of his sword arm. Hilo Steeled in time to prevent a terrible gash, but it hurt badly.

"Where's your shit-talking now, Kaul?" Tanku asked with a smirk.

With a snarl, Hilo charged Tanku with the fury of a bull, slashing and hacking. Tanku kept his Steel up, flexing and shifting it with each of his opponent's attacks. When Hilo's energy began to wane and his arms started to shake, Tanku exploded forward and broke through his defenses with ease, cutting the younger Fist across the ribs and then nailing him in the face with the pommel of the moon blade.

Hilo swayed and fell against the wall, hanging on to his weapon but clutching his injured side and blinking through tears of pain as blood poured from his nose. He retched and spat. Kehn yelled, convincingly, "Hilo-jen! Concede before he really hurts you."

"Listen to your friend, Kaul," Tanku suggested, lowering his weapon. The fury in the man's jade aura was ebbing with the satisfaction of seeing his arrogant opponent in great pain and so thoroughly outclassed. Tanku's energy hummed confident and steady. He could fight like this forever.

Hilo sucked in a wounded breath along with his jade energy and leapt Light at Tanku, who tossed up a Deflection that threw Hilo against the brick wall. Hilo managed, somehow, to Steel against the impact and still hang on to his weapon as he crashed to the floor of the alley.

"You really want me to kill you?" Tanku asked.

From the corner of his blurry vision, he glimpsed Tar taking an alarmed step forward before Kehn stopped him. Hilo shook his head as if clearing cobwebs from his eyes. He'd told the Maiks that he held no personal grudge against Tanku. Now, Hilo saw the man's scornful thoughts written clearly across his face and in the relaxed set of his shoulders: *You're a stupid kid, a thug, that's all*—and he found it easy to summon a real sense of hatred.

Hilo crawled to his feet and came forward again like a stubborn mule. Tanku sighed. He caught Hilo's sluggish downstroke and they clinched close, blades locked. Hilo spat in Tanku's face. The man flinched and Hilo, who had deliberately not employed Channeling once in the entire fight so far, sent a spear of destructive energy straight toward the man's sternum.

The unexpected suddenness and power of the attack caught Tanku off guard. All his Steel came up into his chest like a door slamming, and with stone-cold sober precision, Hilo went low and slashed open the man's femoral artery.

Tanku's eyes flew open in abject astonishment as blood emptied down his legs upon the asphalt. Without any sluggishness or hesitation, Hilo's left hand seized Tanku by a fistful of his hair, jerking forward with all his Strength to bring the man's throat down onto the edge of his moving moon blade with a horrible sound.

For several seconds after Tanku's body hit the ground, Hilo stood panting in a fog of adrenaline, barely able to believe he'd done it. The small group of spectators from the Black Goose stared at the scene openmouthed. Hilo recovered his wits. Raising his moon blade, he wiped it down the inside of his sleeve. "My blade is clean."

Clean blade or not, he needed to get back to No Peak territory as fast as possible. The bartender had already run back into the building, no doubt to alert other members of the Mountain clan, who would arrive within minutes. Hilo couldn't count on the Maiks for much help. They were both extremely drunk, having surreptitiously consumed Hilo's alcohol for him over the course of hours. A squeeze of lemon juice had made Hilo's eyes bloodshot and a whole spicy pepper had made him sweat and raised his heart rate, so when he confronted Tanku, he would appear to be what the older Fist expected of him—drunken, heedless, unworthy of a real fight.

Later, Hilo would recall, as if in a disjointed dream, the frantic rush to collect Tanku's jade and get all three of them back to the car, followed by the madcap drive with one hand on the wheel and the other staunching his wounds with wads of cloth that Tar tore from his shirt and handed to him from the back seat. The amount of jade Hilo claimed in that one day made him the most heavily jaded junior Fist in all of Janloon.

Kaul Sen was apoplectic. He harangued his youngest grandson for being an impulsive lunatic and had him whipped so severely that Hilo was bedridden for three days. Even lying around in pain, Hilo was rather satisfied with himself. His grandfather could whip him all he liked, but he couldn't put his plans back together, he couldn't bring Tanku Din back to life.

The only problem, as Kehn wisely reminded Hilo, was that he'd now made a mortal enemy of Tanku Ushijan, the slain Fist's father and Horn of the Mountain clan. A clean blade notwithstanding, the man was not going to forgive the disingenuous murder of his only son and would surely find some justification and means to kill Hilo in the future.

Hilo was secretly and profoundly relieved a year and a half later, when Ayt Yugontin died from a stroke and his adopted daughter, Ayt Madashi, shocked everyone by immediately killing Tanku Ushijan and his closest Fists. Hilo didn't know much about Ayt Mada, but she'd inadvertently done him a great favor by eliminating the one man Hilo feared would be his most dedicated enemy.

By that time, Kaul Sen's wife had passed away, and Shae had fallen out with the family and fled to Espenia. A few months later, weary and despondent, the Torch of Kekon retired at last. Within a year, Lan named his younger brother as his Horn. At age twenty-five, Hilo was the youngest Horn anyone could recall.

At times, when faced with difficult decisions, he would think back to the duel that had dramatically earned him his jade and reputation, and he would remind himself that sometimes the most obvious solution required only the willingness to take the most unreasonable of actions.

———

Two Green Bone guards of the Mountain clan escorted Hilo through the front doors of the Ayt mansion. It was not a place Hilo had ever expected to visit, and he couldn't help but look around curiously at the expansive entryway with its inlaid wood flooring, mounted antique weapons, and landscape art. It was precisely the sort of home

Hilo expected from a wealthy, powerful, unmarried and childless tycoon—stately and well-designed, everything in its proper place but lacking any human warmth.

The two Fists motioned Hilo to a stop in the foyer, where he waited, Perceiving the approach of that long-hated dense red aura. Two other men pulled open a pair of wooden sliding doors and Ayt Madashi stepped inside from the garden. The doors shut behind her. Hilo glanced left and right as an additional pair of Green Bones appeared silently from the hallways that stretched to either side, bringing the total number of Ayt's bodyguards in the room to six.

"A little excessive," he commented wryly. He'd come completely unarmed, with no blade or knife or gun.

"It's been my experience," Ayt replied, "that no measures are excessive when it comes to dealing with you, Kaul Hiloshudon." Ayt was more paranoid than she used to be. Hilo recalled that she used to go around without bodyguards at all, as if to make a public statement of confidence in her own jade abilities. She did not do that anymore.

"I'd like to speak alone," Hilo said. "As one Pillar to another." When she regarded him with deep incredulity, he spread his hands. "I didn't come here by myself to commit suicide. And I think you'll prefer that what I say remain private."

Ayt's mouth flattened into a line. "One would think that your arrogance would at some point cease to surprise me." She spoke to her Fists. "All of you, wait outside." Jade auras humming with suspicion, the other Green Bones in the room reluctantly withdrew, although Hilo had no doubt they were lurking just out of sight and would return in less than a second if they so much as Perceived him sneezing aggressively.

The Pillar of the Mountain crossed her arms expectantly. She was wearing a gray woolen dress and a long black scarf that covered the puckered scar on her neck. Ayt never hid the disfigurement of her left ear, which she had sustained in battle with Shae, but ever since the Janloon bombing, she'd concealed the reminder of how one second of carelessness had nearly ended her life.

Hilo came straight to the point. "Shae's a prisoner of the Faltas barukan. They captured her, my wife, and two of my Fists in Leyolo City."

Ayt showed no surprise. The clans had kept a close watch on each other's activities for so long that by now the Mountain surely knew something was amiss in No Peak. "I had nothing to do with it," Ayt replied. "Your Weather Man took a risk by going into Shotar and making enemies of the barukan. What did you expect? Although, I hear your wife is already safely back in Janloon. You must've paid dearly for her return, but surely you have even more jade and money to offer to the Faltas, to secure the release of your Weather Man."

Hilo said, "Their demands are a ploy. They let Wen go to make me believe they're sincere, but they're not. They've already killed one of my Fists. After they get everything they want, they have no reason to return Shae alive."

"Because you will surely slaughter them, regardless of whether they return her or not," Ayt pointed out. "Not that I disagree. I would do the same in your situation."

Hilo paced slowly toward his old enemy. "I have to ask myself," he said thoughtfully, "why would these barukan pig fuckers take such a big risk? Why aren't they afraid of what I'm going to do to them? They must have some reason for believing that they'll be protected. That reason, Ayt-jen, has to be you."

"I've already told you I had nothing to do with it," Ayt said impatiently. Her glare warned Hilo to remain where he was. "You can Perceive I'm not lying to you."

"You may not have planned or ordered it," Hilo said, coming to a halt, "but you're still the reason. The Faltas gang works for your allies, the Matyos, but I'm guessing they're tired of being in second place and want to move up. If they get valuable information out of Shae that benefits all the barukan, they can count on the Matyos to keep them safe." Hilo's back teeth came together, flexing the line of his jaw. "They'll mail you Shae's head in a box, expecting your approval and protection as well. So when I peel back everything, you're still the reason why my sister will be dead in a few days."

Ayt blew out a soft chuckle, as if she'd solved a simple puzzle.

"So you've come here to tell me that if your Weather Man dies at the hands of some opportunistic barukan criminals in Leyolo City, you'll blame me and wage war against the Mountain?"

"No," Hilo said. "I've come to ask for your help."

For the first time in Hilo's memory, Ayt Mada was too surprised to give an immediate reply. She stared at him for some time. "Why on earth and under Heaven," she asked with the slow, deliberate rasp of drawing a rusted blade, "would I help the man who stood by when I had a knife in my neck, happily watching me die?"

"You would've gladly done the same if it were me," Hilo said.

"I should have you killed where you stand right now," Ayt declared. "After you're dead, the barukan will kill your sister, and that will be the end of the Kauls. The end of this long and hateful war between the clans, with the Mountain victorious."

"You could do that," Hilo admitted. "At least, you could try. Let's face it, neither of us is the warrior we used to be, Ayt-jen, but we could still have a good go at it. I'm in your house, unarmed and surrounded by your Fists and Fingers, so it wouldn't be much of a fight, but I like to think I could still do some damage going out."

Hilo's voice did not rise or fall, but it hardened to a sharp point. "After I fail to come out of your house, my cousin Anden, who's sitting outside in the car, will leave here and walk into the offices of the *Janloon Daily* and in front of KNB cameras to explain exactly what happened on the day of the Janloon bombing. The entire country will know that Kaul Shaelinsan saved your life when no one else would—and you repaid her by murdering me and letting her die in a foreign country at the hands of barukan scum."

"Ah yes, I'll be lambasted and condemned in the press," Ayt scoffed. "They'll call me vile names. I'll suffer poor public relations for a while. All things I've endured before, and a small price to pay for the immeasurable satisfaction of your death."

"Even now?" Hilo asked quietly. "When people can look to the Koben family?"

Ayt's expression lost only a touch of its confident scorn, but her jade aura swelled and bristled—evidence enough that what he said had struck a nerve of truth. It had become well known in Green Bone circles that Ayt Mada and her adoptive nephew's family were not always in alignment. Right now, Councilwoman Koben Tin Bett was cosponsoring a bill in the Royal Council that would ban further immigration from Shotar, even though her Pillar had remained silent on the issue, so as not to jeopardize the Mountain's alliance with the Matyos.

Times had changed. Ayt Madashi was in her sixties and no longer viewed as indispensable to the Mountain clan. With a strong, popular thirty-year-old man waiting to succeed her as Pillar, she needed the complete confidence of her clan if she was to remain in power. She would make compromises she might not have considered earlier in her reign in order to uphold her leadership and delay the inevitable rise of her own heir.

Just like Grandda, Hilo thought.

Nevertheless, Hilo could read the black calculation in Ayt's eyes, one that he could entirely understand: Perhaps it would be worth *any* risk, to finally *win*. "After all these years," she intoned with all her usual cold scorn, "is there anything you believe I won't do if I have to?"

"No," Hilo replied. "I half expected you'd kill me as soon as I walked in the door. But you didn't, which means my suspicions were right." His stare was steady and honest. "You're not a machine after all. As much as you'd like to see me feeding worms, you would feel *something* after the Faltas torture Shae to death for information that they'll sell to you. I don't know what kind of a human being can imagine facing the gods with that on their soul—and we're all human, even you."

He saw the nearly imperceptible shift in her posture—a subtle defensive stiffening of the shoulders and neck, a shadow of doubt. Hilo lowered his voice. "You have far more men on the ground in Shotar than I do. You have power over the Matyos. You can intervene. You can condemn the Faltas. If the men who took Shae realize they have no one to defend them, that we'll hunt them like animals, then the situation becomes very different for them."

With long strides, Ayt walked to the window and looked out at her garden with the willow trees drooping over the gazebo. "I don't control the Matyos," she said, her back to him. "I've allied with them when it's been advantageous, but they're not a clan. They're not truly Kekonese. They're barukan. They may decide they don't care whether I approve of their actions or not and choose to side with the Faltas."

Hilo came up behind her, stopping at the point where their jade auras scraped against each other like shelves of granite along a fault line. "The Ayt Madashi that I know doesn't take no for an answer, not from anyone. Those who do stand in her way"—Hilo opened his hands in self-indication as he stood in her foyer—"have to be ready to die. It's why you're the only one in the world who can help me right now. The gods have always had a sick sense of humor."

Ayt let out a soft derisive laugh and touched the scarf around her neck. She turned to face him. "In that regard, Kaul-jen, you and I are in complete agreement."

"After all these years," Hilo said, repeating Ayt's own words, "is there anything you believe I won't do if I have to?" With the grim dignity of a man stepping up to the executioner's blade, Hilo lowered himself to his knees in front of the adversary he'd spent decades of his life trying to destroy. "Help me find my sister and bring her back to Janloon alive. Your debt will be repaid—a life for a life. Whatever happens between you and me in the future, we'll call that fair. Shotar will be yours completely. I'll pull No Peak out of the country and leave it to the Mountain for as long as I am Pillar." Hilo touched his clasped hands to his head in salute. "I swear this to you, Ayt Madashi, Pillar of the Mountain. On my honor, my life, and my jade."

CHAPTER

48

Debts and Losses

Shae's captors dragged her out of the tub full of jade and deposited her onto the linoleum floor of the bathroom. The smooth, cold surface under her cheek was a tiny, tantalizing relief—an ice cube in an inferno. A needle slid into the vein of her arm, and seconds later, blessed cool liquid salvation spread through her body as the SN2 hit her brain. It was never enough, of course—small doses that temporarily abated the worst of the physical agony, keeping her lucid and preventing her from falling headlong into the madness of the Itches. The short barukan leader with the green skull pendant bent over her and removed the gag that kept her screams muffled. She had never hated anyone in the world more than she hated him. Not Ayt Mada, not Zapunyo, not anyone.

"Give me names," he said again. "The names of your White Rats."

"I've already told you what I know," Shae rasped. Even her tongue felt hot and swollen. She wanted to writhe on the floor, to claw at her face—anything to alleviate the feeling of heat bubbling under the surface of her skin. When she was inside the tub, at least there was the almost transcendent delirium of jade energy. Lying on the ground in chains, she didn't even have the strength to lift her head off the floor.

"You've only told us some of the cops and officials we already know are in your pocket. You'll have to do much better than that," her tormentor said regretfully.

When Shae didn't answer, the barukan sighed and motioned for the men wearing the lead gloves to lift her back into the tub. Shae twisted and gasped, "Wait, please! I'll tell you, if you give some of the shine to him." She looked at Dudo. The Fist was dying. Having already suffered a head injury, he was in no way able to bear the lethal level of jade overexposure. When Shae was in the tub, even through her own throes she could Perceive Dudo's heart intermittently racing out of control, then crashing to dangerously low levels. She'd been forced to watch him scream and thrash, vomit and convulse, but after that ceased, he was deathly still, barely breathing.

"The bastard snapped my friend's neck." The barukan leader poked Dudo experimentally. The Fist did not move at all. "If you really want me to use up my expensive shine on him, you'll have to give me something that's actually *valuable*."

They were going to die anyway. She had the blood of so many on her hands already, what were a few more? "The second captain of the Matyos—" she began.

"Hannito?" one of the men in the room exclaimed. "I don't believe it."

"Not him," she said. "His younger brother, the deliveryman."

Someone nearby let out a curse. "That fucker's dead meat."

The barukan leader leaned in eagerly now. "Is that true? Who else?"

"You know I'm not lying," Shae said hoarsely. "Give Dudo the shine."

The man looked over at one of his subordinates and shrugged, as if to say, *Why not? He's going to die anyway.* The thick-lipped second-in-command took out a syringe and emptied the contents into Dudo's arm. Shae had no idea if Dudo was too far beyond help at this point, but she imagined that at least it would ease his suffering. A few seconds after the shine went into his bloodstream, the man jerked and began to breathe more steadily—a sign of life at least.

"Other names," the barukan demanded.

Shae gave up another White Rat—the wife of a gang leader—and couldn't even muster the will to wonder what would happen to the woman. When she didn't cough up any additional names, however, they put her back into the tub. After a while, they took her out again, gave her another dose of SN2, and asked her more questions. The process took on a certain familiar predictability. How slowly could she offer up information in exchange for enough shine to stay sane and alive?

Whenever she was in the tub, she wanted to give up. She was drowning in jade energy the way a person might drown in their own blood. It was impossible to describe the feeling. Every particle of her being was boiling over and the only way her primitive nervous system could interpret the sensation was *itching*. Itching in the soles of her feet and the palms of her hands, itching on the inside of her legs and down her arms and all over her scalp, itching inside her *mouth*, on her *eyeballs*. She understood now why the disease drove people mad, why they mutilated themselves and threw themselves into the sea. Shae forgot who she was and wanted only to die.

But when they gave her shine, she would come back to herself for long enough to think, *I have to give Hilo time.* Hilo would find them. He would not be fooled by the barukan's ploys. If there was anything she had faith in besides the gods, it was her brother's cunning vindictiveness. So every moment she was lucid enough to think, she prayed silently and fervently, *Yatto, Father of All, help me, help my brother.*

She had to live. She would not leave Woon to raise Tia alone. She refused to fail her gentle daughter in the way that Green Bone parents too often failed their children, the way her father had failed her before she was born, the way Lan had failed Niko, and Anden's mother had failed him—by dying. Drowning in blood and jade.

"What is the Euman Deal? Tell us about the Euman Deal."

This was new. She hadn't heard this question before, at least she didn't think she had, although it was getting harder and harder to remember. They'd moved her to the living room at some point and dumped her in an armchair, her limbs still tightly bound. It must be nighttime; no glimmer of light bordered the covered windows. The faces in front of her swam in her warped vision. Moving mouths seemed to stretch in slow motion like those of grinning demons, melting like hot wax, grotesque and abstract. Someone slapped her face. Her head lolled back and her tongue protruded.

"Give her some more," the barukan leader said. More shine. There was no way they could've done this ten years ago without killing her. Thanks to Espenian medical advancements, it was much harder to die from SN2 overdose. Shae thought this was terribly funny and began to laugh uncontrollably.

"Crazy bitch," the barukan growled. They threw water over her, and when she stopped sputtering, the man said again, "The Euman Deal. What is it? What's the Mountain's big plan? We know they're cutting in the Matyos somehow."

"I have no idea what you're talking about," Shae slurred. A small, still functioning part of her brain stirred weakly. What *were* they talking about?

"The Matyos are moving money to the Mountain," the barukan leader said slowly and impatiently, speaking as if she were an imbecile. "What are they getting for it? You're the fucking Weather Man of No Peak, you know what Ayt is up to, don't you?"

Did she? She knew . . . she knew what they were saying must have something to do with . . . with what? With something that had once seemed clear and important but that was now impossibly out of reach. "I don't know." Tears spilled out of her eyes and down her face. She was so tired. "I don't know. I don't know. *I don't fucking know.*"

"Throw her back in the tub," the barukan said with weary anger.

Hands began to lift her yet again and the last of Shae's willpower unspooled as rapidly as a thread on a spindle. "No," she sobbed. "No no no no no no—"

Somewhere in the house, a phone rang.

———————

From the third-floor room of an apartment building down the street, four hundred meters away, Vin Solunu set up his Fullerton TAC-50 sniper rifle well back from the open window and closed his eyes as he adjusted the aim. The windows of the house he was targeting were completely blocked. Every once in a while, someone peeked through the slats of the closed front blinds. All the other windows were covered with black plastic. At this distance, he was at the farthest edge of his range of Perception, which meant he was confident no one inside the house could Perceive him in turn, but he'd also never placed a Perception shot from so far away before, and with the stakes so high.

Lott's voice came to life in his headset. "Vin, what's going on in the house?" The Horn was waiting in a vehicle on the street below with several other Fists, ready to attack under cover of darkness.

"There are six people in there right now," Vin said into the radio mic. "Two of them aren't moving. I think the other four are the barukan piss rats we're looking for, along with the three others who are standing or pacing around outside as lookouts."

Vin heard the Mountain Green Bone behind him in the apartment mutter, "Can he really Perceive that from over here? I can't Perceive shit," and Kenjo replying, "Quiet, let him concentrate." Vin found it a touch unnerving that one of the two men guarding his position was a member of the Mountain clan, whose name he didn't even know, but that was not the most unnerving aspect of this situation by far.

The Pillar had struck a deal with Ayt Mada, who had in turn struck a deal with the Matyos barukan to betray the kidnappers in the Faltas gang. In short order, the Matyos had provided a list of all the known Faltas safe houses in Leyolo City within an hour's drive of the spot Shae and Wen had been taken. When the private plane carrying the Horn and a dozen other carefully chosen No Peak Green Bones landed in Leyolo City, the information was waiting for them, along with a contingent of Mountain Green Bones who'd been tasked to help in the search.

Reconnaissance on all seven of the addresses was conducted via drive-bys at a cautious distance. Vin doubted any Keko-Shotarian barukan would have the training to Perceive farther away than the length of a relayball court, but they would certainly have sentries patrolling around their position. Tato, whose talent in Perception was second only to Vin's, thought she sensed the Weather Man inside one of the houses. Vin confirmed that it did feel like Kaul Shae's aura, although it was flaring erratically and he could not be completely sure it was her. Photographs of the building were taken from a distance and the images faxed back to Janloon. Wen hadn't seen the outside of the house, but she could describe the size and layout of the main floor based on what she was able to remember. It aligned with the shape of the house Vin was now concentrating on.

All evidence told Vin they had the right place. Eyes closed, finger on the trigger, breathing as lightly and steadily as possible, he could sense the different jade auras inside the house vibrating with strong emotion: fear, pain, anger, urgency. From this distance, they were like colored tea lights dancing in his Perception. Fortunately, the walls were merely stucco and insulated drywall, not brick or concrete, but he had no way of knowing how thick the windows were, or if there was furniture in the way that would stop a rifle bullet or change its trajectory. Ideally, his target would be directly in front of a wall or window. And the timing of the whole operation had to be perfect. As soon as the first shot went off, the men inside would know they'd been found. They would kill the prisoners unless Lott and the other Green Bones in the car arrived in seconds.

Vin's hands were steady, but beads of sweat ran down his forehead and over his closed eyelids. He blotted out the energy of every other living thing around him and narrowed his Perception until it seemed he was stretching his senses down a very long tunnel. *Don't fuck this up.*

In his headset, the Horn's voice spoke to everyone. "We move on Vin's signal."

"Something's changed," Vin whispered. At this point, one of the jade auras was so weak he was quite sure it was near death. Another wasn't much better, flickering and blinking in and out like a bad light bulb. The four others, however, which had already been vibrating with unusual stress, now flared with extreme agitation and hostility. People were moving around, slipping in and out of Vin's narrow field of fire. The Fist drew a bead on the strongest, most energetic jade aura he could Perceive. As his finger curled over the trigger, he sensed his target's energy turn murderously dark.

"Go, now!" Vin hissed into the radio. He exhaled, held his breath, and fired.

When the phone rang, the barukan were startled. They looked at each other as if questioning who among them was expecting a call. "Who the fuck—" The man with the jade nose ring stomped into another room and answered the phone. The others waited. They left Shae slumped and gasping in the living room chair where they'd been interrogating her. When the phone clicked off and the man came back, the blood had gone out of his face. "That was Choyulo," he said numbly. "He said the Matyos have turned on us. He said we have to let these Green Bones go and get out of here."

Stunned silence. Then the short leader exploded. "Does he think this is some sort of fucking video game? That we can hit 'erase' and start over? Choyulo said the Matyos would have our back if we got heat from Janloon, and now he's saying they're going to fuck us over? After we lost four guys? What the *fuck*?"

The barukan broke into heated argument punctuated with shouted Shotarian and profanities. Shae struggled feebly to understand what was going on.

"If the Matyos have sold us out to No Peak, we're worse than dead." The young man with the neck tattoo swallowed noisily. "We better do what Choyulo says."

"Fuck Choyulo," the leader shouted, eyes bulging from his head. "And fuck the Matyos! I'm sick of being second to those Oortokon pussies. None of them could've pulled this off. Once they know about the information we've got, they'd be out of their fucking minds not to back us up. Otherwise, we go straight to Ayt Mada and the Mountain."

"What if Ayt's in on it too? What if she turns us over to the Kauls?" the man with the nose ring murmured, his eyes starting to dart back and forth fearfully.

"She wouldn't do that, she *hates* the Kauls." The lead barukan crossed over to the closed window and pushed down on the slats of the aluminum blinds, creating a tiny crack through which he peered out onto the empty, moonlit street with narrowed eyes. Satisfied that all the guards were still in place, he turned back to his men with a fearsome glare. "We're all in this together, so none of you can turn chickenshit now, you hear? Go pack up the money and jade, kill the guy in the tub if he's not already dead. We're going to get out of the city first. Then we'll bargain with the Matyos."

"What about her?" asked the young man with the tattoo, looking at Shae.

The leader stared down at her. Shae saw the heartless calculation made in a few seconds. He couldn't expect mercy even if he let her go. She was more a liability than an asset now and would slow them down. "We didn't get everything we wanted from this bitch, but we got enough," he decided, and drew a knife to slit her throat.

Shae's body seemed to move with a will of its own. In a final instinctive bid for survival, it flung itself forward like a suffocating fish flopping on the deck of a boat toward the water and the tiny chance of living. Shae crashed to the floor, knowing that her final spurt of defiance was useless, simply a trapped animal response. She twisted onto her side, staring up with mute hatred. The man with the knife snorted in amusement at her struggles and took a step toward her—then jerked and stumbled, as if he'd been punched in the back. The knife tumbled from his fingers to the carpet. Shae followed the movement of his empty hand as he raised it in confusion to his chest, and then she saw the two exit wounds that had punched through his body, a pair of darkening flowers in the front of his black T-shirt.

The other Faltas stared in disbelief as their captain's body hit the floor with a thud. Then they broke into a panic, drawing pistols and pointing them at the broken window as they dove behind furniture and flattened themselves against walls. "They shot Batiyo!" someone screamed. "How the fuck did they shoot him?" The blinds and black plastic now worked against them, obscuring their attackers.

"Look outside the window," the man with the nose ring ordered.

"*You* look outside," someone else hissed, but he edged along the wall toward the glass. Two more gunshots punched through the side of the house. Everyone ducked as the man by the wall dropped to the ground shrieking, clutching his shoulder.

The front and back doors of the house burst open with tremendous noise as they were torn out of their frames. The largest windows shattered inward from the force of Steeled bodies. Gunfire erupted as the Faltas unloaded their pistols at the Green Bones crashing into the house without any pretense of restraint. Everything around Shae erupted in deafening violence.

She blinked at the mayhem as if it were happening in a dream. The young gangster with the neck tattoo grabbed for her, trying to use her as a shield to save himself. Seizing the ropes binding her, he began to drag her across the floor with him, pointing his gun and screaming over the tumult, "*Stay away or I'll kill her, I swear I'll—*"

Shae writhed frantically, catching the man in the shin with a flailing kick that made him yelp with pain. He lost his grip for a moment and reached down to seize her again, but the hand with the gun came off his arm and spun end over end. The moon blade that had severed it flashed back around and sank into the space between the young man's neck and shoulder, opening his torso with a meaty diagonal cleaving. Shae made a muffled noise as his blood sprayed across her hair.

A final gunshot reverberated elsewhere in the house and then the fighting was abruptly over. Lott Jin's face appeared over Shae, breathing hard. He was wearing a bulletproof vest and his moon blade was streaked, glistening red. Sweat plastered his wavy hair to his forehead. The Horn dropped down to his knees and broke the padlock on her restraints. "Shae-jen," he said hoarsely as he unwound the chains. "Thank the gods in Heaven."

Tears filled Shae's eyes at the sight of Lott's face. On weakened arms, she tried to push herself up into a sitting position, but couldn't manage it; her entire body was shaking with violent relief. "Are they dead?" she asked. "All of them?" She was thinking of the safety of all the White Rats whose names she'd surrendered.

"All of them, Shae-jen," Lott reassured her. "We'll get everyone responsible."

Two Green Bones that Shae didn't recognize appeared next to Lott and helped him to cut the ropes off her raw, bruised wrists, then her arms and legs. They brought over a stretcher and lifted her carefully onto it. Shae was too weak to protest the gentle treatment as they carried her out of the house that had been her prison for days. She gasped at the shock of cold air and the sight of so many Green Bones moving about under the orange streetlights. Where had all these people come from? She knew some of them, but other faces were unfamiliar.

"Kaul-jen," said one of the strangers, inclining his chin and touching his forehead as he helped her into the back of a car. "Ayt Madashi sends her regards."

A month after the ordeal, Shae was still unable to wear jade. Weeks of being treated with high doses of medical-grade SN2 had cured her of the Itches, but the first time Woon had wrapped his arms around her, she'd cringed merely from the nearness of her own husband's jade. Anden assured her that every examination showed she was physically recovered, but with tears in his eyes he told her that her body might never tolerate wearing green the way it used to. As the one member of the family who knew better than anyone what is was like to be scarred by jade overexposure, he explained that it was not so much a physical issue as a psychological one. Shae knew he was right. She suspected she would have nightmares for years to come.

She reminded herself of how comparatively lucky she was. Tako was buried in Widow's Park. Dudo had survived, miraculously defying all odds, but he was deeply damaged; he would likely need antipsychotic medication and therapy for years if not the rest of his life, and he would never wear jade again. Wen visited the unfortunate man and his family every week.

No Peak's foray into Shotar had been a disaster, a loss of years of work in the course of three days. They did eke out a few final satisfactions. With the Mountain's support, No Peak's Fists remained in Leyolo City for another two weeks, long enough to find and kill another thirty-two members of the Faltas, wiping out the entire upper echelon of the country's second-largest barukan group in a spree of unstinting violence that the police ignored as an outbreak of ethnic gang conflict. Shortly afterward, Wen received word that Diamond Light Motion Pictures had agreed to release Danny Sinjo from his contract so he could star in Cinema Shore's tentpole feature film, *Black & Green.*

One evening, as Shae sat with Hilo in the courtyard of the Kaul estate after the sun had gone down, she asked him, "Have you ever heard of the Euman Deal?"

He shook his head. "What is it?"

Shae frowned. "Something I heard. Maybe nothing. I don't know yet." Without her jade senses, the garden seemed oddly lessened, like a washed-out painting, and being near Hilo without being able to Perceive his aura was strange. She studied his face, wondering if it was even more peculiar for him, to see her once again, after so many years, without any jade at all. For the first time, she noticed flecks of silver in her brother's hair.

"What did Ayt promise the Matyos, to gain their cooperation?" she asked.

"She killed the proposed immigration ban." Hilo put his feet up on an empty chair. "She sent word to the Mountain loyalists in the Royal Council that they were to make sure the bill was voted down."

Shae nodded. The defeat of the legislation ensured the border would remain porous between Kekon and Shotar. The barukan could continue to travel freely between the countries, sending their relatives to Kekon to work legally or illegally. That was something the Matyos would value above any alliance with the Faltas gang.

"The Kobens must've been livid." Councilwoman Koben Tin

Bett was one of the most outspoken proponents of the widely popular view that Oortokon refugees had increased crime in Kekon and
barukan immigrants eroded traditional Green Bone values. Now, her
own Pillar had scuttled the legislation she'd been advancing in the
Royal Council. Shae was pleased the isolationist measure had failed,
but seeing the shrewd old widow being so plainly put in her place, she
couldn't help but feel a bit sorry for her.

"What can the Kobens do?" Hilo said with a shrug. "As long as
their boy is a Pillar-in-waiting, they can't afford to get on Ayt's bad
side too much. It was the same with Lan and Grandda. You didn't
see it up close the way I did." Shae waited for an accusatory glance
to come her way, but it didn't. Hilo was staring off into the distance.
"Ayt can control the Kobens as long as she has other options. I'm sure
the Iwe family hasn't given up hope that she'll pass the leadership on
to her Weather Man."

"Ayt Mada won't be quietly stepping into retirement."

"No," Hilo agreed, turning his eyes slowly toward her. "Overall, I
don't think she's unhappy with how things turned out." The alliance
with the Matyos renewed, the Kobens back under her heel, the Shotarian market under sole Mountain control.

And Ayt's debt to the Kaul family erased. Shae knew what saving
her life had cost Hilo in his soul. She'd never doubted her brother's
ability to take lives or to give his own for the clan. She'd never imagined he would go on his knees to beg his worst enemy for help. In his
mind, it would've been a betrayal of all the Fists and Fingers who'd
fought for him and given their lives under his leadership. She thought
about saying something, voicing an acknowledgment of what he'd
done—but the idea of putting such feelings into words between them
seemed trite, distancing, even insulting. They sat in silence.

After a time, Hilo asked, "What will you do, if you can't wear jade
again?"

Shae touched her bare wrists, unsure how to answer. She thought
of Tia, asleep in her bed, and of the simple, profound joy that existed
in seeing her daughter's face and hugging her tight. Having nearly
been deprived of that, she couldn't muster any great regret over the

loss of her jade. During her life, she'd earned plenty of green, taken it off, reclaimed it, lost much of it in combat. Jade was her armor and her weapon, but it was not a part of her, the way it was with Hilo. She missed her abilities, but she was not empty, not any less of a person than she would've been if she'd lost an arm or a leg or an eye.

It was strange, Shae thought—Green Bones revered jade, but it was not the gems themselves that were worthy of reverence. Jade had meaning because of the type of person one had to become to wear it. Jade was the visible proof that a person had dedicated their life to the discipline of wielding power, to the dangers and costs of being a Green Bone.

She did not require proof anymore. She was past needing to carry her green as a coveted mark of status and credibility, one that declared to everyone that she was equal to her brothers and worthy of being a Kaul. She had two decades on the top floor of Ship Street to do that for her. She had work to do now, to rebuild from their losses, to guide the clan and the country toward growth and progress, to keep it safe from outside threats but also from the perils of its own worst impulses.

"What will I do?" she asked quietly, turning to her brother and touching her hands to her forehead in salute to the Pillar. "My job. As Weather Man of No Peak."

CHAPTER

49

~

The Prince's Stand

the twenty-second year, twelfth month

For Ru's birthday, his friend Dano invited him to a party in the Dog's Head district. "It's at this place called the Little Persimmon, and it's going to be a great crowd," he told Ru as they walked to class. "You should come. These guys I know really want to meet you."

"Really?" Ru wasn't accustomed to getting any attention on his own, but he guessed that with Niko and Jaya gone from Janloon, he was the only one of the younger Kauls to take notice of now.

"Sure!" Dano insisted. "Anyway, keke, you could stand to cut loose a bit."

Ru supposed his friend was right. Midterm exams were around the corner, and Ru had been studying until late into the night for weeks to catch up. His third-year classes were more difficult and there had been a lot of stress in his life over the past year. The terrifying abduction of his mother and his aunt had caused him to miss classes right at the beginning of the school year. That summer, Typhoon Kitt, the worst typhoon in thirty years to hit the East Amaric region, had pelted Janloon for three days, causing enormous damage. Jan Royal campus had been closed for a week, and even after it reopened, Ru had spent all his time outside of classes helping with the No Peak clan's clean-up and relief efforts. The latest problem was that his dog Koko was going deaf and blind in old age, and had several teeth removed last month after difficulties eating. Ru tried to go home every weekend to see him.

On top of everything else, Ru was torn about what to do when he graduated next year. He'd decided to major in public policy. Time spent living on campus away from the clan and getting to know the other students in the Charitable Society for Jade Nonreactivity had cemented a realization that he'd been born as the luckiest stone-eye in the country. Sometimes he felt like a walking paradox, possessing all the privileges of being a son in a ruling Green Bone family despite his deficiency, and suffering few of the indignities that other nonreactive people experienced, especially the Abukei. It seemed only right that he consider how he could use his position to help others.

Ru thought he might like to work for a nonprofit organization, with a goal of getting involved in political advocacy, but he wasn't sure his father would approve. When he was in a good mood, the Pillar was receptive to Ru's ideas, but at other times he would respond impatiently. "You're too idealistic, son. No Peak is a Green Bone clan, not a charity house." After the disastrous loss of the office in Shotar, the most pressing need was on the business side of the clan. The best way for Ru to contribute to the family would be to work for his aunt Shae after graduation. The Weather Man had already suggested she would be pleased to have him on Ship Street, and Ru's mother had reminded him sternly, "You have to put your family first, before you think to help strangers."

Ru decided to take Dano's suggestion and blow off some steam. The Little Persimmon being in Mountain territory gave him a moment's pause, but he was twenty-one years old now and not about to inform his parents of every minor risk he took by crossing clan district boundaries like an ordinary adult. When he arrived at the address Dano had given to him, he went up to the second floor and found the lounge to be a dive, with dim lighting, red benches around a small dance floor, scratched wooden tables, and a black bar with mini-lights strung behind a mirrored backsplash.

Dano excitedly brought him over to meet a lean, sharp-faced man working behind the bar. "Tadino here didn't believe me when I said I knew you." Dano tapped the bar top. "Pay up on that bet, keke!"

The man named Tadino leaned closer. "Are you really Kaul Rulin-shin?" He had an accent—Shotarian?—and to Ru's surprise, a circular burn scar on his left cheek.

Ru dug out his driver's license and showed it to the man, who laughed and said, "I'll be damned. All right, Dano, I'll pay you in free drinks." He poured them each a generous shot of hoji and touched his forehead to Ru in salute. When he grinned, his puckered scar stretched and pulled at the corner of his eye. "I've always wanted to meet one of the Kauls in person. You could even say I'm a bit of a clanmag addict."

The comment made Ru dislike the man. The cheap, trashy magazines that printed clan gossip and photos of Green Bones had been unkind to Niko. Although, to be fair, they were unflattering to everyone, even Ayt Ato. Clanmag photographers had had their camera equipment smashed, vehicles set on fire, and even bones broken by irate Green Bones, but apparently the money was good enough for them to continue their activities. Tadino didn't notice Ru's grimace. He prodded another man sitting at the bar, a pale, sullen fellow with a crooked face who was presumably a regular at the Little Persimmon, as he was alone and studying his half-empty drink. "Hey, you hear that?" Tadino said. "This is the Pillar's son, show some respect."

The unsmiling man glanced at Ru and warily touched his forehead before returning to his beverage. Tadino was not done; he shouted above the music and waved a young woman over to the bar. "Juni, guess who this is," he exclaimed.

The woman's thin, tattooed eyebrows rose under the fringe of her straight bangs and her full red lips parted in appreciation. "Tadino, this shitty bar is more cut than I gave you credit for. I didn't know Kaul Ru came here slumming." She sidled up to Ru and gave him a nudge with her hip, lowering her voice to a sultry, suggestive whisper. "Come find me on the dance floor whenever you're ready to show off your moves." She took her drink and sauntered back into the crowd.

Ru was tempted to follow her, but he drew Dano away from the bar and whispered, "How do you know Tadino?" He was aware that his friend led a freewheeling lifestyle and did not always keep the most reputable company.

"We met through the Immigrant Rights Watch." One of the organizations Dano was involved with. It extended assistance to refugees. "Tadino's from Oortoko. He used to be in a barukan gang and he's been through some rough times in his life."

Ru said, "Do you know why he was branded?"

"Don't tell me you believe in that barbaric policy," Dano exclaimed. "Green Bones have branded thousands of innocent people for having foreign blood, or an accent, or for simply being in the wrong place at the wrong time. It's heinous."

"I'm not saying I agree with it." Ru wanted to point out that Dano was as usual generalizing about Green Bones. The enthusiasm for branding people suspected of anti-clan activities was driven by one large faction in the Mountain clan and not uniformly followed even by all of the Mountain's own Fists. But that wasn't the point. Dano was so outspoken and righteous, so quick to see every branded person as having been wronged that Ru was concerned his friend would one day be caught with actual clanless criminals and, through no fault of his own, end up with a red-hot pipe against his face, or worse. "You have to think of yourself," he insisted. "You could find yourself in the wrong place at the wrong time, too—and with the wrong sort of people." Ru had not forgotten that his own sister had been ready to assume the worst about Dano, even to bring his name up to Lott Jin.

"Don't worry about me, keke. Just have a good time, all right?" Dano pulled out a small plastic bag of black powder. "Hey, you want to do some sand?" When Ru shook his head, Dano shrugged and said, "Let's get you another drink, then."

Reluctantly, Ru dropped the subject, though not before resolving to talk to Dano about it again, some other time. Tonight it would only ruin the mood; they were here to enjoy themselves after all. He asked for another hoji, this time with ice and a splash of anise.

On the dance floor, there were plenty of pretty girls, but Juni was the most striking, in a short black skirt and tall nylon boots. The plunging neckline of her sequined tank top showed off a tattoo on her chest, a black arrow pointed straight down into her cleavage. She smiled at Ru with invitation and danced in front of him, moving to the music in tempting ways. After his second drink, Ru was feeling relaxed and daring. He put his hands on Juni's hips and they danced together, drawing closer with each bass throb from the speakers. She slid her leg in between his, pressing the top of her thigh against his warming crotch as they ground their bodies together in the dark.

Ru was a little embarrassed by how excited he was that this beautiful woman was throwing herself at him. He suspected that Niko and Jaya got laid more often than he did, and while he'd never envied the social climbing advances his siblings had to put up with, he still wondered, sometimes jealously, what it would be like to enjoy *all* the advantages of his family name. To have status as soon as you walked into a room. To have women want you. To carry the greenness of an entire clan and thus always be *more* than yourself. That's what it would be like, he decided, to be a true prince of No Peak.

Niko and Jaya took their place for granted, but Ru didn't. When the perks occasionally did come his way, why shouldn't he enjoy them to the fullest? Juni's breasts pressed against him and the scent of her perfumed sweat filled his nostrils and rose up into his brain. Ru moved his hands down her back, over her waist, onto her buttocks. His rising desire was like a spreading liquid heat suffusing him from groin to fingertips. She was what he needed tonight, to push aside all his worries, to stop thinking so much. Juni wrapped her arms around his neck and the warmth of her cheek tingled against his. Her lips brushed his ear. "Come on, I want to show you something."

Taking him by the hand, she pulled him off the dance floor. Ru looked around for Dano, catching a glimpse of his friend on one of the red benches with two others, snorting sand off a tray. Giggling, Juni led him around the side of the bar, where, to Ru's surprise, behind a purple curtain there was another room with a couple of sofas and mirrors hung all over the walls so that whichever way he turned, he saw flushed, bright-eyed reflections of himself.

"Wow, a secret room," Ru said, grinning. "I wonder why it's here?"

"Who cares?" Juni grabbed him and they kissed, their colliding mouths hot and hungry. She tasted of vanilla lip gloss and lychee rum soda. "No one is going to bother us here."

––––––––––

"Stay here by the bar and make sure they don't leave," Tadino hissed to Bero. "I'm going to run outside and make the phone call. Just keep an eye on things."

"I'm not going to stand here and listen to those kids fucking," Bero said sourly. Most of tonight's young crowd in the Little Persimmon was blissfully drunk or high. A few were passed out on the benches, and others were slipping out of the lounge in pairs. But Tadino had only let Bero have one drink. "We've got to stay cut," he insisted. "Tonight, we're going to start the next clan war and turn everything around."

Tadino rushed out to the pay phone on the street to call Koben Ashi and inform him that his girlfriend was at the Little Persimmon lounge and some stranger was laying his filthy hands all over her. Koben Ashi, a mid-rank Fist in the Mountain clan, son of a prominent councilwoman and a close cousin of Ayt Ato, was a jealous bastard who would beat the shit out of any man who so much as looked at his woman for too long. According to Juni, she and Ashi were broken up at the moment, but apparently Ashi never got these notices. Every man in the Mountain clan knew Juni was a poisonous flower and wouldn't touch her, which was why she sought other places to fool around. She didn't seem to mind that Ashi put her conquests in the hospital, and in fact, she was always back together with him shortly thereafter.

Bero had to hand it to Tadino—it was a wildly unlikely but clever setup, the sort of risky thing that Bero himself might've come up with when he was younger. As a bartender, Tadino met a lot of people and heard a lot of gossip about both clans. He'd seen Juni at the Little Persimmon before, and when he discovered that he knew a college kid who was personal friends with Kaul Ru, he'd come up with a plan to put the pieces together.

"We've been stepped on like shit for long enough," Tadino said. They had to fight back, to do something about the relentless persecution heaped on them by the clans. Starting a wildfire of clan violence would relieve the pressure. It would allow the CFM to regroup and recover.

Bero approved of the scheme, but he still had doubts. Over the years, he'd taken every possible run at the Green Bones. He was a killer and a thief, a grave robber, a smuggler, spy, and terrorist. It was a wonder he was even alive. Did he have anything left in him to try again? He wanted to believe he did, that his smoldering inner fire could be whipped up anew.

On the other hand, it would be a whole lot easier to stay away from it all and drink.

"You don't have to do anything," Tadino pointed out. "You just have to keep those kids here and make sure no one interrupts them. And then stay here as a witness. How about that? You can fuck things up for the clans by barely lifting a finger."

That possibility was appealing enough to Bero that he agreed. Koben Ashi would arrive at the Little Persimmon and unknowingly hand the Pillar's stone-eye son a savage beating. Kaul Hilo was sure to respond with ferocious retaliation, and the fragile cooperation the clans had maintained since the Janloon bombing would shatter.

Since Tadino had closed down the bar and left it unattended, Bero helped himself to another glass of hoji. Through a crack between the purple curtains, he could hear and see Juni and the Pillar's son making out. Juni's skirt was hiked up to her hips, and the buttons of Kaul Ru's shirt were undone. They were all over each other, oblivious to being sorely used by people they didn't even know. Bero was accustomed to feeling sorry for himself, but sitting at the abandoned bar, listening to the wet smacking sounds and moans of desire, he felt a pathetic kinship with the young man in the room next to him, whose uncle he'd opened fire on with a Fullerton machine gun on a dark pier, a lifetime ago.

At the age of forty, Bero had come to the cynical conclusion that he'd always been a piece of detritus tossed about on the tides of fortune. Good luck and bad luck were two sides of the same betting chip, thrown carelessly onto a cosmic games table to prolong the inscrutable amusement of the gods. Yet he was not the only one the gods abused. Even the Pillar's son was a pawn to fate.

"Hey, don't be a pervert," Juni called to Bero. "Close the curtain, will you?"

Juni's short, sexy hair and her heart-shaped face reminded Bero of Ema. Or maybe they seemed alike because she too was leading a clueless man by his cock. Ema was long dead, blown to smithereens, but Bero still resented her. Now he disliked Juni as well, just from looking at her. Ema had been a bitch to Bero, but she'd been nice sometimes, too. She'd let him fuck her, if only because she was planning to die. When Bero was very drunk, he thought maybe he missed her. Maybe he even missed Sampa and Cheeky and Mudt.

When Bero didn't move, Kaul Ru got up, holding the top of his pants closed with one hand, and went to draw the curtain shut himself. Bero said, "She's using you, keke."

The young man had a flushed, stupid grin on his face. "Fine with me."

"You dumb kid, you think you're calling the shots?" Bitter contempt spilled thoughtlessly out of Bero's mouth. Youthful, naive, reckless confidence was something he'd once believed made him special and would get him everything he ever wanted. "She has a boyfriend, that one. Koben Ashi, a Fist of the Mountain."

Kaul Ru paused with the curtain in his hand. He glanced back at Juni, then again at Bero as disbelief and then dawning comprehension slackened his face. Bero sneered with savage delight. "You've been set up, keke."

Footsteps pounded up the stairs and into the lounge. Koben Ashi stormed past the few remaining partygoers, his head swiveling back and forth, his eyes wild with insensible fury. Two of his Fingers were right behind him, as was Tadino, who shouted, "Back there, Koben-jen," and pointed at the curtained room by the bar.

The Fist pushed past Bero, yanked the curtain aside, and saw Ru backing away with his pants undone and Juni sprawled half-naked on the sofa. With a murderous curse, he seized Kaul Ru by the throat and hurled him out of the room against the bar.

Ru crashed into the bar top and fell, hitting his head against a barstool on the way down. Sparks burst in his vision and a ringing sound erupted in his ears. Dazed and crumpled on the sticky floor, his first, ridiculous thought was to fasten his pants before trying to get back up. He fumbled stupidly with the button and managed to do up his fly before Koben Ashi seized him by the back of the collar, pulled him off the ground, and threw him into another wall. Shouts of surprise and alarm broke out. Most of the meager crowd still left in the Little Persimmon grabbed their belongings and ran for the exit stairs. They knew how inadvisable it was to be anywhere near a furious Green Bone.

"Who do you think you are, touching my girl, you little piss rat?" Koben snarled. "After I'm done with your face, you'll never get laid again, fucker."

Juni stumbled out from behind the purple curtain, pulling down her skirt and crying, dry-eyed, "Ashi, he's just a kid, he didn't know any better. Don't kill him!"

Ru staggered to his feet and raised his hands to defend himself, but he couldn't possibly match the jade-fueled speed of a Green Bone. Koben hit him in the stomach, doubling him over, then kicked him to the ground. Ru wheezed with pain, clutching his midsection. From the corner of his eye, he saw Dano shouting and trying to wobble drunkenly to his defense, but the bartender, Tadino, grabbed him by the arm and held him back.

I'm so stupid, Ru thought in agony. *Stupid, stupid, stupid.* Stupid to trust Dano, stupid to come to this party in Mountain territory and let down his guard, stupid to think for one second that just because he was a stone-eye and the least of his father's children that he would be spared the attention of enemies.

Koben grabbed a nearby barstool and snapped off one of the wooden legs to use as a club with which to beat Ru unconscious. Koben's two Fingers watched with slightly anxious but unsurprised expressions. One of them said, "Ashi-jen, this kid isn't even a Green Bone, he's not worth it."

Ru dove frantically out of the way as the chair leg came whistling down. It missed his head and struck his shoulder. His entire arm went numb. *They don't know who I am*, he realized. His family had always kept him out of the spotlight and his face was not in the clan-mags. He was barely known to anyone outside of No Peak circles, much less in the Mountain clan. The man with the crooked face had been right—Ru had been set up. But so had the Koben family.

Ru threw himself behind a table. The enraged Fist kicked it out of the way and raised the chair leg again, but the obstacle had finally given Ru the two seconds he needed to yank out the compact talon knife he carried sheathed inside his rear waistband. Koben's eyes flicked down at the sudden appearance of a weapon, and in that moment of distraction, Ru cried out, "A clean blade!" He scrambled into a fighter's crouch, his talon knife held up in front of him, blood trickling from his nose. "My name is Kaul Rulinshin, son of the Pillar of No Peak, and I offer a clean blade!"

Koben Ashi paused with the chair leg still raised. His eyes flicked from the talon knife to Ru's face. The Fist's cheek twitched as he exchanged glances with his two Fingers, who stared at Ru with dubious astonishment.

Koben swung his head back toward Ru with a growl. "Don't be a fucking clown. The No Peak Pillar's son in a place like this?"

"It's true!" Dano babbled, finally breaking free of Tadino and stumbling forward. "He really is Kaul Ru. We came here to have a good time, that's all! He hasn't done anything wrong, he didn't know who she was. He's just a stone-eye college kid!"

Koben's knuckles whitened around the chair leg. He wheeled on Juni. "You little whore, you found out he was a Kaul and you couldn't keep your legs closed? Are you trying to get me tangled up with No Peak, you bitch?"

The woman's face lost all its color. "No, no, Ashi, I would never..." She fell to her knees, crying for real now. "He came on to me, and I was afraid to say no."

"That's not true." Ru's eyes glittered with outrage. "Koben-jen, I had no idea who she was. I hope you can Perceive that I'm not lying when I say I didn't mean to cause you any offense. But you attacked me without even bothering to find out the facts, so you've caused offense too. The only way to settle this is with a clean blade."

Koben frowned. "Even if you're a Kaul, you're not green. You can't duel me."

Ru shook his head. "Not you. *Him.*" He turned his attention toward Tadino and pointed at him with the tip of his talon knife. "*You* set this up. You asked Dano to bring me here tonight, you introduced me to Koben's girlfriend without telling me who she was, and you called the Mountain here to hand me a beating." Ru's expression was so fearsome that everyone left in the room could now see without a doubt that he was indeed the son of Kaul Hiloshudon. "I've never met you before tonight, so I can't see why you'd hate me. You must've wanted to use me to harm my family. I take that personally. So you can fight me now, or you can answer to my father later."

Tadino bolted for the stairs but didn't get far. Koben's two Fingers moved with the exceptional speed of Green Bones and caught him by the arms, dragging him back into the lounge and forcing him to face Ru. The bartender's lips were pulled back in a frightened grimace; he appeared dumbfounded at the way his plot had so abruptly unspooled and unexpectedly reknit to ensnare him instead. His eyes darted around the room but found no help anywhere. Dano seemed as fearfully bewildered as a hare trapped in a fox den, and the crooked-faced stranger from the bar hung back.

"Choose your weapon," Ru demanded.

According to Dano, Tadino used to be a barukan gang member.

The man didn't look weak or cowardly. In fact, he seemed like someone who'd been in his share of scraps before, not a person that most people would normally want to fight. He was larger than Ru by a comfortable margin. But he hesitated at the sight of the talon knife in Ru's hand, the way the younger man held it with easy confidence, having been trained by his father from a young age.

"N-no weapons," Tadino replied. Bare-handed, he held the physical advantage.

Ru spoke to Koben Ashi. "Koben-jen, if I fight a clean-bladed duel with this man to settle our grievance with him, will you agree that there shouldn't be any offense remaining between the two of us? And that our families don't have to get involved?"

He held his breath for Koben's answer. In the panic of the moment, he'd blurted the challenge of a clean blade because it had been the only way to reclaim control of the situation, to defend his own honor when it seemed he wouldn't be given any chance at all. Now though, he truly wanted to punish Tadino. If Ru was going to face his father after this fiasco, he wanted to say he'd fought a proper duel to preserve his reputation, not that he'd been beaten black and blue for groping the wrong girl in Mountain territory. Niko had already broken their da's heart so badly; what would the Pillar think of him, and what might he do to the Kobens, for such a humiliating incident?

Koben Ashi seemed to be considering the same thing. "Yes," he said. "I agree."

Ru sheathed his talon knife and wiped his bloody nose on his sleeve. Ordinarily, he was inclined to think generously of others, so when he encountered genuinely malicious people, his temper was ferocious. "Offer up any prayers you have to the gods, because a bare-handed duel isn't going to hurt any less, I promise you." Seething, he touched his forehead in salute to his opponent without offering so much as a nod of respect. "Why did you do it?"

Tadino's features contorted as he bared his teeth. He touched the angry circular scar on his cheek. "*Why?* Why does a rat try to bite the dog that's killing it? Do you know how many people I've seen beaten or branded or taken away? Look at my *fucking face.*" He spat on the

ground. "There was supposed to be a revolution. The Janloon bombing was supposed to kill all the clan leaders, and the Clanless Future
Movement was supposed to build a new society." Tadino's words
were thick with venom, but he seemed near tears. "You know why I
read the trashy clanmags? I keep hoping to see you Green Bone dogs
finally kill each other off."

"I'm not a Green Bone," Ru said. He attacked with four strikes to
the head in quick succession—two jabs, a left hook, and right cross
that grazed Tadino's cheek as the man dodged instinctively, protecting his face. Ru dropped a blistering shin kick across his opponent's
thigh.

Tadino hissed with pain and swung for Ru's face, then his body,
hitting him repeatedly before driving his shoulder into Ru's chest and
trying to pin him to the nearest wall. They struggled in a clinch,
both trying to jam each other's limbs. Ru took one of Tadino's sharp
knees to the stomach, and all the breath in his body whooshed out
in a grunt as he folded forward. His eyes watered fiercely. He was
already hurting in a dozen places from being knocked around badly
by Koben, and every blow he took from Tadino made it worse.

But Ru was accustomed to being weak and fighting anyway. He'd
never attended Kaul Du Academy, but the Pillar would not let his son
grow up without a martial education, so Ru had been given plenty of
training by his father, his uncles, his family's stable of private coaches.
He'd done knife fighting drills and shooting practice and sparring
matches with Green Bones whose abilities he could never equal.
Although he was no match for a Fist like Koben Ashi, against another
man without jade, he had every advantage afforded by preparation.
He was also twenty years younger and much fitter than Tadino, who
was gasping after only a couple of minutes and a few hits.

Tangled up close with his opponent, Ru kept his wits; he ducked
his head between his folded arms and used the tip of his elbow to nail
the larger man in the sternum and ribs several times, hard. Tadino's
grip on him slackened. As they broke apart, Ru threw a wicked back-
fist that smacked Tadino in the jaw, sending him staggering back,
holding his face and cursing.

"You clanless dog," Ru said with contempt. "You deserve worse than a branding."

Tadino ran at Ru and tried to take him to the ground with his greater size and weight. Ru leapt backward, sprawling, seizing Tadino around the neck in a headlock. The two men crashed to the floor. Dano made a muffled noise of alarm and the Mountain Green Bones stepped back, pushing chairs out of the way.

Tadino, red-faced, tried to wrap his meaty arms around Ru's waist and flatten him to the floor. Ru moved too fast for the other man; he swung his whole body around and threw a leg across his opponent's back. Riding astride him, with one arm wrapped around the man's neck, he swung furiously, punching Tadino in the ear, and the jaw, dropping the tip of his elbow repeatedly into the back of the man's neck, snarling.

Tadino collapsed to his stomach, putting his hands over his head to protect against the blows. Ru switched to burying punches in the man's kidney. In desperation, Tadino tried to buck Ru off, to roll away. Ru put his feet down and loosened the grip with his legs just enough for the man to turn over, then leapt on him again with the weight of a knee in the man's chest and continued wailing on him, hitting him in the face repeatedly. Tadino sputtered blood and cried out, "Stop, I give up!" Ru did not stop. No one else in the room moved to stop him either. "I concede!" Tadino gurgled. "I said I give up. Stop, stop, *stop*!"

"You thought you could fuck with me because I don't have jade?" Ru punched Tadino again, flaying his knuckles on the man's teeth. "You want to fuck with my family, with the No Peak clan?" He did not really intend to kill Tadino, but he was soaring high on adrenaline and principled wrath, and he was going to make sure the man got every bit of what he deserved, that he served as a message that even the Kobens could not misinterpret. Ru might be a stone-eye, but he would *not* be a weak link in his family. He was his father's son; he would not back down from any fight or be used by anyone. You did not fuck with *any* Kaul.

Bero had seen many terrible things in his life, but what happened next would never leave his memory. Tadino, panicked, believing he would be beaten to death, tried frantically to push Ru off, shoving at his chest and hips. The bartender's hand fell upon the loosened talon knife sheath in Ru's waistband. In a flailing, fateful instant, he seized the hilt of the weapon and slashed wildly at the man on top of him. The talon knife caught Ru across the neck and the fine steel opened the side of his throat.

For a second, no one understood what had happened. Both men stared at each other in shock as blood poured down Ru's shirt and onto the man below him. With astonishment, Ru clutched his neck and toppled over onto his side, his mouth opening and closing. Juni let out a choked scream. Dano collapsed to the ground in shock.

"Shit," Koben Ashi whispered. "*Fucking shit.*" The Mountain Fist dropped to his knees and clamped his hands to Kaul's neck, trying to Channel into the young man, but it was no use. The cut had been too clean and deep, and Koben was no Green Bone doctor. Bero stared into the frightened eyes and saw the life inside them go out.

Tadino scrambled backward on hands and knees, the talon knife still clutched in his hand. His face was a ruined red pulp, his nose crushed and his lips split open, but the whites of his bruised eyes rolled about the room, trying to find safety. They landed on Bero, begging. His mouth opened to plead, but no sound came out.

Koben sat back on his heels, his hands and sleeves sticky and red. His face was draining of blood as quickly as Kaul's body. One of the Mountain Fingers said, in a tremulous voice, "What do we do, Koben-jen? If the Pillar of No Peak blames us..."

"Kaul Hilo will kill everyone in this room," Koben said.

Tadino tried again to escape. He was too injured to get more than a few meters. Koben threw a Deflection that knocked the man over, then he seized Tadino by the throat and held him at arm's length as if taking a goose out to the chopping block. "You chose an empty-handed duel but you drew a talon knife," Koben said. "You dirtied a clean blade. Your life is worth less than nothing."

"He was going to kill me," Tadino sobbed through broken teeth.

"I'm a *Koben*," the Fist breathed. "My cousin is the godsdamn heir to the clan! I'm not taking the fall for this. I *can't*." He glanced down again at Kaul Ru's body and then at his Fingers. Bero had never imagined the faces of powerful Green Bones could look so scared and desperate.

Dano was on the floor, crying and retching. Juni stumbled up to her boyfriend, her makeup smeared with tears, and clutched his arm frantically. "Ashi, I don't want to die. Please, let's run away together, right now. Ashi, I love you—" Koben backhanded her viciously across the face and she fell to the ground, stunned.

"If we run, we're fucked." Koben dug a shaking hand through his hair. "My family will help us. My ma is on the Royal Council. We have to prove to the Kauls that we had nothing to do with this fuckup, you hear? *Nothing.*"

Bero should've left with everyone else in the club when he'd had the chance. He'd never had the good sense or normal human instincts to walk away when he should. Now Koben's Fingers were blocking the only exit, so Bero had no choice but to watch as Koben dropped Tadino to the floor and began to break his arms and legs.

Considering that Tadino was already so badly injured from the duel, one wouldn't think he'd last as long as he did. The man screamed and thrashed and begged for his life, but in the end, he couldn't move at all. He was a sack of cracked bones and twisted limbs, staring at nothing when Koben finally snapped his neck.

Juni cowered in terror when her boyfriend turned away from Tadino's shattered body and came over to her. "Ashi, please, no," she whimpered, tears and streaks of mascara running down her face. "I only wanted to make you jealous because I love you. Don't you still love me too?" Koben wrapped his hands around his girlfriend's throat and squeezed with all his Strength, choking her to death in minutes.

"What do we do about them?" asked one of the Fingers, looking at Dano and Bero.

Dano was curled on the ground, nearly catatonic with fear. He'd pissed himself. Koben nudged him with a foot. "You were Kaul's friend, weren't you? We'll turn you over to No Peak and they can decide what to do with you." He yanked Dano partially upright and leaned over him. "But you have to tell them. You saw everything and you have to tell them what happened here, got it?"

Koben looked over at Bero for the first time. "And who the fuck are you?"

Bero turned his head, taking in the carnage of the Little Persimmon—the blood and bodies, the broken and scattered furniture, the smell of piss and fear. A vast and yawning emptiness swirled through Bero like a dry, howling wind in an empty town. Kaul Ru's youthful, unmoving face seemed to stare at him sadly and with grave accusation. *Bad luck*, it seemed to say. *Always bad luck.*

"I'm just a regular at the bar," Bero said. "I'm nobody."

"Nobody," Koben repeated, then chuckled with an edge of mania in his voice. "All right, Mr. Nobody, here's what you're going to do, if you want to live. Go out there and tell everyone the truth, understand? Every Lantern Man, policeman, news reporter—you tell them what you saw. I never lifted a finger against Kaul Hilo's son after I found out who he was. It was the clanless scum who were responsible. The same sort of people who carried out the Janloon bombing and killed my own da—it was one of *them*. I made him suffer before he died, and I killed my own woman for her part. You tell everyone, you hear me? They'll believe you. They'll believe a nobody."

One last time, Bero thought. *Bad luck to good, one last time.* "Sure," Bero said. "I understand."

And he did understand, with an uncommon clarity that made him want to laugh himself to death and spit in the faces of the gods on his way to hell. It wasn't a purposeful and powerful fortune that had always swept him along in its inexplicable currents, that trapped him in suffering yet in the oddest moments protected him. It was insignificance.

Bero clasped his hands together and touched them to his forehead in salute. "I'll tell them. It was bad luck for everyone. It was fate." He walked, unmolested, out of the Little Persimmon, down the narrow stairs and into the night.

50

Terrible Truths

Hilo woke all at once, with the vague awareness that something—a noise or unusual energy—had tripped his senses while he slept. The feeling of unease thickened as he lay still in the darkness, stretching out his Perception as far as it could reach. It was not his jade abilities that convinced him something was wrong, however, but a flickering gleam of light against the bedroom windows. Headlights of a car, coming through the gates of the estate and up the driveway toward the house.

He got out of bed without waking Wen. Closing the bedroom door quietly behind him, he went down the stairs. By the time he reached the foot of the staircase, the car was arriving in the round-about, and his hyperalert Perception picked out four men in the vehicle. One of them was his cousin Anden. When Hilo opened the front door, he saw two of the clan's Fingers get out of the parked car. They didn't move toward the house, but remained standing by the vehicle, guarding a slumped figure in the back seat, and letting Anden walk up alone to meet the Pillar. This detail told Hilo immediately, even before he saw his cousin's face, that something terrible had happened.

Over the years, it had become common knowledge within the clan and among its observers that Dr. Emery Anden had the Pillar's ear, that Kaul Hilo trusted his cousin perhaps more than anyone. If there was a particularly sensitive or difficult subject to broach with the Pillar, Anden would be the best one to do it. So in the few seconds that it took for Anden's steps to carry him to the house, Hilo had a brief window of time to prepare himself for why the doctor would be arriving in the dead of night. When he saw Anden's harrowing expression illuminated in the yellow light of the house, he said nothing, but stepped aside and let his cousin enter without a word. Hilo closed the door and turned around.

Anden didn't sit down or take off his shoes. He stood in the foyer before the Pillar. His face was haggard and his eyes were swollen, and despite being the one sent to deliver the news, it seemed he couldn't speak. "Hilo-jen," he began, but struggled visibly to go on.

A wave of prescient grief swept over Hilo like a tide coming into shore. "It's okay, Andy. Just say what needs to be said."

The unexpected gentleness of the words affected Anden like a violent physical blow, rocking him back on his heels, but they broke down the dam in his throat. "Ru was killed in a duel tonight."

Hilo blinked. When the terrorists' bomb had gone off and the Kekon Jade Alliance building had collapsed on top of him, the sensation had been unlike anything he'd ever felt before or could even describe. The ground under his feet coming apart. The momentary weightlessness, then instant muffling darkness engulfing him, along with a pressure so intense that he could barely move or breathe or even think.

What he felt now was similar, although it happened invisibly and without a sound—a shattering disintegration that was silent, private, and complete. The one thing that kept him tethered to the awareness of the moment was Anden, standing in front of him. His cousin's sorrow was palpable, but he was doing his best to control and hide it, so as not to make things any worse for his Pillar.

Hilo took three steps into the living room and gripped the back of the sofa, leaning against it until he regained enough control to look up into his cousin's face and speak. "Tell me what happened."

Anden sat down on the edge of an armchair facing Hilo and told him everything he knew. He'd been on call, but napping in his apartment, when his pager went off and he was summoned to the hospital. The shock he experienced after expecting to deal with an ordinary patient emergency only to learn instead that the body of his nephew had been brought in by Fists of the Mountain must've been extreme, yet he'd come prepared to speak as calmly and factually as he could manage. When he was done, he stood and with shaking hands poured himself a shot of the strongest hoji in the cabinet.

The entire time, Hilo had listened and not said a word. The onset of agony was more intense than anything he could've prepared for even after the deaths of his brother and brothers-in-law, yet a small but conscious part of his brain remembered that Wen was still asleep upstairs in their bedroom, and that knowledge alone kept him from waking her by collapsing to the ground and howling like an animal.

He spoke at last. "Do you believe the story?"

Hilo, of all people, knew that with a strong enough motive and planning, a clean-bladed duel could be manipulated, that murder might've been arranged. Yet even as he asked himself feverishly, *Who needs to die?* he could not see the logic of an enemy at work. Ru's death accomplished nothing for the Mountain, even less for the barukan gangs, or the Crews, or anyone else. Ru was not a Green Bone or an heir to the clan's leadership. He was not a threat or an obstacle to anyone. All he had been was Hilo's son.

Anden said, "The man in the car outside is Ru's friend from college. I was wearing my jade when I talked to him and to the Kobens separately, and I didn't Perceive any deceit. I'm not saying there was no ruse, Hilo-jen. Lott Jin's men will do their own interviews and investigation, and if there's anything suspicious, they're sure to find it. All I can say is that from what we know so far, it seems..." Anden swallowed hard before looking into the Pillar's face. "Right now, it seems like an accident. I'll beg for death if I'm wrong."

Outside, it seemed as if the world had ceased moving. Hilo came around the sofa and walked past Anden toward the stairs. The Pillar placed a heavy hand on his cousin's shoulder as he passed. "Thank you, Andy," he managed to say, quietly. Then he went upstairs to wake his wife and to tell her that their son was dead.

––––––––

The city of Janloon waited for the murderous rampage. No one was more reliable than Kaul Hiloshudon when it came to retribution, and for the death of his son, surely, there would be *some* terrible vengeance to be taken *somewhere*. Jaya spoke for many of No Peak's expectant warriors when she arrived home from Toshon with a dozen of her Fingers and threw herself at her father's feet, begging tearfully, "Da, tell me who we should kill, and I'll do it!"

No one had an answer for her. Ru had offered the clean blade. The Horn's men turned up no evidence that the Mountain nor anyone else had plotted Ru's death. The college student who'd been with Ru at the club had been questioned so many times that he was near mental breakdown, and his story was corroborated by another eyewitness who spoke anonymously to the police. At Shae's urging, Hilo spared Dano, whose only crime was that of being a worthless friend. Although they might be tangentially blamed for what had happened at the Little Persimmon, there was no evidence of a wider resurgent scheme by the Clanless Future Movement. After years of relentless persecution and the loss of foreign support, the CFM was already in its dying throes. Tadino's attempt to goad the clans into war had been a desperate last gasp.

The day after the tragedy, the Pillar had gone into his study with his Weather Man, his Horn, and his cousin Anden. Hours later, they emerged, red-eyed and grim-faced, and Hilo had given orders to the clan. Until the circumstances of Ru's death were fully understood, there would be no retaliatory attacks on the Mountain, no whispering of names, no shedding of blood without approval. He made it clear that his orders might yet change, but they were to be obeyed. Everyone in the clan knew it had been the Pillar's advisors, all of them level-headed and prudent even at a time like this, who had together been responsible for his decision.

On the morning of Ru's funeral, councilwoman Koben Tin Bett arrived at the Kaul estate with several members of her family. The heavyset, matronly widow was in her sixties now, still on the upswing of her political career despite recent frictions with her own Pillar. She wore a white shawl and her face was dusted with white mourning powder. With her was Ayt Ato, a college graduate at long last, and recently engaged to a member of the Tem family. Hilo agreed to come out of the house and meet them in the courtyard with his Horn and Weather Man in attendance.

"Kaul-jen," councilwoman Koben said, saluting Hilo deeply and without any of her usual smug maternal manner. The woman seemed truly nervous, wetting her lips and fidgeting with her shawl. "My heart aches for your loss. Our clans and our families have opposed each other in the past, but losing a loved one is a universal suffering. Please accept the deepest condolences of the Koben family."

Ayt Ato followed Koben Bett's lead, saluting Hilo solemnly. He cleared his throat. Without any cameras around, he seemed uncertain of exactly where to stand and which direction to face. Ato glanced warily at all of the No Peak guards nearby before speaking. "Kaul-jen, I wish we were meeting under different circumstances. My aunt, Ayt Mada, has asked me to convey her assurance as Pillar that she's questioned my cousin and his friends and found them innocent of any ill intention in this tragedy."

The three men in question, Koben Ashi and his two Fingers, came forward and lowered themselves to their knees in front of Hilo. Their heads were wrapped with gauze and bandages. With eyes downcast, they each offered up a small black wooden box in their uplifted hands.

"Kaul-jen," said Koben Ashi. "I beg forgiveness for failing to save your son from the scheming of clanless dogs who tried to bring down both our families. I hope it brings you a small measure of comfort that your son's killer suffered greatly before I ended his life. I nevertheless deserve to die, but if, in your great mercy, you spare my life and those of my blameless Fingers, I will be relentless against our mutual enemies." The words came out stiffly and with little inflection, having clearly been rehearsed.

A flicker of familiar emotion crossed Hilo's face—a wrathful light across the eyes, a twitch of the mouth. For a moment, everyone watching on both sides thought he might draw his talon knife and kill all three men where they knelt on the pavers. And why not kill Ayt Ato as well, while he was at it? The courtyard was immobile with held breaths. Koben Ashi paled but kept his eyes on the ground. The black box trembled slightly.

Then the shadow of violence was gone from Hilo's eyes. The Kobens had not come with any protection, but they had counted astutely on the fact that the Pillar of No Peak would not cast any taint of bad luck on his son's funeral. Hilo reached out and took the black box containing Koben Ashi's severed ear. He accepted the ears of the two Fingers as well. He did so without speaking a word.

"May the gods shine favor on you for your mercy, Kaul-jen," murmured Councilwoman Koben. All of the Kobens retreated as hastily as decorum allowed, their relief palpable. It wasn't merely fear of No Peak's retaliation that had caused them to distance themselves from the incident so forcefully and to take the extraordinary step of humbling themselves before the Mountain clan's greatest enemy. Ru had been a jadeless stone-eye, barely out of his teens. The Kobens were a proudly traditional Green Bone family with political clout and their sights set on clan leadership. Any implication or even lingering suspicion that they had broken aisho might severely tarnish their reputation. Kaul Hilo's acceptance of their gesture was an exoneration. A statement to everyone that there would not be war.

Everyone in the Kaul family knew it wasn't the decision Hilo wanted to make. But it was what Ru would've wanted. Ru had always championed compassionate causes, always maintained that No Peak bettered not only its own Green Bones but all of Kekon.

His faith had been absolute. He never doubted that his father could make anything happen. In the wake of his death, Ru would never want his family's actions to harm ordinary people and reflect badly on the clan.

———————

Wen stood silently by her husband's side at the funeral and accepted condolences from the long line of mourners. She leaned heavily on her cane, but she no longer cared whether she appeared weak. She *was* weak. After two days and nights of vigil, she could barely stay upright. But she would do this—she would bear this miserable duty with Hilo.

Ru always knew his father loved him. Hilo has that at least. Wen couldn't say the same for herself. If only she could have one last minute with her son, she would ask him to forgive her for being so hard on him all these years. She would tell him that every time she'd been critical or impatient, it had been her fault, not his. She'd worried for him because he was a stone-eye. She'd seen herself in him, and on some shameful level she'd begrudged him for not being the heir she'd hoped to bear. Now he was gone, and she would never get the chance to tell him that she was proud of him. Ru had always seen himself as whole, even when she could not. He'd been confident and generous and he'd never allowed discontent over his deficiency to define him, the way she had.

Wen hated herself for letting sorrow make her resent even her own husband, especially since she could barely recognize Hilo. The warmth in his eyes, his lopsided boyish grin, his magnetic energy, like that of a star burning in the sky—all of it had been snuffed out like a candle. He seemed as inhuman as a marble statue. He acknowledged the clan loyalists who approached with nods, occasionally a hoarse word, nothing more.

Wen let her gaze drift in slow detachment over the rest of the family, dressed in white clothes and grief, until her eyes fell upon the figure of her eighty-one-year-old mother-in-law, hunched under thick blankets on a plastic folding chair. Kaul Wan Ria seemed completely lost in her own world, mumbling quietly to herself. It was unclear whether she knew what was going on. At the pitiable sight of her, Wen ached with numb, bone-deep kinship. Why not escape reality, when it was so unbearably cruel to wives and sisters and mothers?

At last, all the guests departed and only the Kaul family remained in the Heaven Awaiting Cemetery. The afternoon temperature was dropping. A wintry breeze tugged at hats and scarves as it moaned through the trees of Widow's Park. Wen thought about stepping into the open pit of her son's grave to join him at the bottom.

Shae bent down and chose a few of the flowers that had been left behind. She handed them to Tia, who threw them onto the closed casket. Shae bent her head and whispered, "Lan will be glad to meet his nephew. He'll take care of him."

Hilo's hands closed into trembling fists at his sides. When he spoke, his voice was coarse and disused. "The minute that boy was born, I should've given him away to some other family." Only Wen and Shae, standing beside him, heard his savage whisper. "Some good but jadeless family with an unknown name. What was I thinking, raising a stone-eye into this life?"

She knew Hilo was only trying to wish away his pain, but the words lanced Wen's heart. "You don't mean that," she breathed. She realized she could still feel fear. Fear that she would lose Hilo as well, that he would become unrecognizable to her.

Ru's death had been an avoidable and meaningless accident. That was the terrible truth staring the family down. Green Bone warriors counted on deaths that meant something. They gave their lives for honor, for jade, for the brotherhood of the clan. Ru had been steeped in Green Bone culture from birth. Its values had shaped his entire existence, had made him as green in the soul as anyone. But he was not a Green Bone. Now he was dead because he'd acted like one. Wen of all people understood that folly.

"I did it all wrong," Hilo went on in quiet anguish. "I encouraged him, I gave him as much freedom as I could, I made him believe he could do great things, accomplish anything he wanted to." Hilo closed his eyes. "*Lies.* Whether you wear it or not, there's no freedom when you're surrounded by green. I wish..." The Pillar's voice cracked like a brittle twig. "I wish he hadn't dueled. If only he'd been a coward, just once."

Wen reached for her husband across what felt like a vast and lightless gulf. She put her hand into his. At first it remained limp, then slowly Hilo's fingers closed over hers. Tears stole Wen's vision and painted tracks in her white face powder. Ru had idolized his father. He could never be a coward. He'd fought without Steel or Perception or any abilities that might've saved his life that night. And he'd won. Perhaps that was the great tragedy of jade warriors and their families. *Even when we win, we suffer.*

At last, Woon said gently, "It's getting late. We should go."

As they turned away from the family memorial, a lone figure came up the path toward them. Wen heard Anden suck in a breath. The sun was behind the approaching man's back, and for a few seconds, Wen couldn't see his shadowed face, even though she recognized his silhouette, the way he walked, the set of his shoulders.

Niko was dressed in a black suit and white scarf. His hair was longer than it had been, and his face had changed as well. It was leaner and stubbled, and there was something in his eyes that had not been there before—a slow, haunted softness. He'd been twenty years old when he left Kekon, but he looked as if he'd aged a decade in the nearly three years he'd been away.

Niko walked past all of them and stood at the lip of his brother's grave. Tears welled in his eyes and he let them run down his cheeks without wiping them away. Wen recalled that as a child, Niko rarely cried and would often hide in his room when he did.

"I'm sorry, Ru," he whispered. "I should've been here for you. We should've gone to college together. I was wrong about so many things. I'm just...so damned *sorry.*"

Niko turned around to face his staring, silent family. With slow steps, he went to Hilo and knelt in front of him. "Uncle, I'll never be as good a son as Ru. I've done things...inexcusable things. But I've come home again."

Wen had not seen her eldest child since the family dinner the night after Ru's graduation. The muffling grief that had encased her for the past week split open under a surge of feeling. Without thinking, her feet moved, carrying her to him with quick steps. When he looked up at her with those large, watchful eyes, her heart flew into her throat.

"Ma," he said.

Wen drew her hand back and slapped Niko hard across the face. The sound of it rang out like a gunshot. Niko turned his face but didn't flinch as the red mark of Wen's palm rose on his cheek. Shae stared at Wen in shock and even Jaya made a noise of exclamation.

"Three years," Wen exclaimed. "Three years with no visits, no phone calls or letters, *nothing*." After his initial employment contract with GSI had ended ten months ago, no one in the family had heard from him. Who knew what he'd been doing all this time.

"I deserved that," Niko mumbled. "I was thinking only of myself when I ran away. Ru tried to tell me, but I..." Niko's face buckled with emotion and he didn't finish. Composing himself with effort, he raised his eyes to Hilo, who stared down at his nephew, an unreadable mess of emotions raging across his expression. Niko clasped his hands together and brought them to his forehead in salute. "The clan is my blood, and the Pillar is its master. Will you forgive me and accept me as your son again?"

Without waiting for Hilo's answer, Niko drew a talon knife from the sheath at his waist. Drawing a fortifying breath, he grasped the top of his left ear and sliced downward with the knife, cutting into the groove between his ear and skull.

Hilo's hand shot out and seized Niko's wrist. Their eyes locked over the knife. For a moment, neither man moved. Blood streamed down the side of Niko's face, running down his neck and soaking the collar of his shirt. He was trembling with pain. Slowly, the Pillar loosened his nephew's fingers from the hilt and took away the talon knife.

"You never stopped being my son." Hilo closed a hand fiercely on a fistful of Niko's hair and kissed his brow, then lifted his nephew's scarf and pressed it against the damaged ear, holding it in place as a bloom of red spread across the white fabric. "We all make mistakes. Sometimes terrible mistakes we can barely live with. But we learn from them. And maybe..." His voice collapsed. "Maybe we can forgive each other."

~

The Charge of Twenty

In the final year of the Many Nations War, the Empire of Shotar relied heavily on its control of the East Amaric Ocean, with the occupied island of Kekon being its most significant asset. For this reason, the Charge of Twenty, a famous event in Kekonese history that is rarely studied by outsiders, is considered by some experts to be a far more important turning point in the global conflict than it's given credit for.

The One Mountain Society's attack on the heavily fortified Shotarian military base near present-day Lukang was nearly a complete disaster. Shotarian spies provided early warning of the assault, so the element of surprise was lost. Instead, the advancing Green Bone warriors were met with heavy artillery and twice the number of expected defenders. Leaving a small force inside the base, the Shotarians sallied into the surrounding area with superior numbers, encircling the rebels' position.

When Kaul Dushuron realized that he and his men were trapped and facing slaughter, he gathered together twenty of his strongest Green Bones, himself included, and sixty of his weaker and less experienced followers. "This is the true test of our brotherhood," he said. "Only together, in our most dire moment, can we reach for the power of Heaven and turn the favor of the gods."

The sixty less powerful men willingly gave their jade to their commander and their more skilled peers. Wearing far more jade than their bodies could normally handle was asking for death from the Itches, but health effects were of no concern.

That night, the twenty chosen Green Bones cut their tongues on their knives to seal their commitment. Together, they struck the lightly defended Shotarian base with so much savagery and extraordinary jade ability that surviving eyewitnesses claimed they leapt over walls and moved too fast for their enemies to see, that bullets flew away from them and they killed soldiers with a single touch. Twenty Green Bones brought down the gates and slaughtered nearly three hundred men before they were finally slain. Kaul Dushuron's torn body was hung from the watchtower.

Several contingents of Shotarian soldiers rushed back to help defend the base. When dawn broke, the exhausted troops saw the entire force of the One Mountain Society descending upon them. Believing that every Green Bone would be as terrible and nearly unkillable as the twenty sent in advance, the defenders panicked. Many of the soldiers were not even Shotarians, but Tuni, Uwiwans, and other poorly trained conscripts brought from other parts of the empire. In the first wave of the attack, they fled or surrendered.

The One Mountain Society spread news of the heroic Charge of Twenty across the country through secret radio broadcasts, print, and word carried through the country's network of Lantern Men. Within days, all of Kekon was in open rebellion against the remaining occupation forces. Two weeks later, the beleaguered Shotarian military officially withdrew from Kekon.

At Kaul Du's belated state funeral, his grief-stricken father declined to speak, asking his comrade Ayt Yugontin to do so in his place. "Good men are remembered with love by their friends," declared the Spear of Kekon. "Great warriors are remembered with awe by their enemies."

Ayt brought the hero's two small sons and his pregnant widow onto the stage and declared that Kaul Du's descendants would be forever favored by the gods. A new martial school would be built and named in his honor to train generations of future Green Bones to protect Kekon and carry on his legacy.

CHAPTER
51

~

Enough

Lula kept her eyes lowered as she was ushered into Ayt Madashi's presence. *Please let it be today*, she prayed silently. *I can't do this anymore.* She stepped through the rising midday heat into the shade of the gazebo and sat down in her usual spot, hands folded in her lap. She glanced up briefly. The Pillar of the Mountain was wearing a bright green silk scarf that complemented the jade coiled around her bare arms. For a woman in her midsixties, Ayt was still admirably fit. Her skin was wrinkled but not saggy and the gray in her hair was blended into silver highlights. When the lines around her eyes tightened, however, Lula thought she looked ancient and terrifying.

The Pillar uncrossed her legs and smoothed a crease in her linen pants. She lifted a pitcher and poured cool mint tea into a glass, setting it in front of Lula before pouring one for herself. The gesture of regard for an honored guest made Lula's breath catch with hope. She glanced at the thick stack of paper that the Pillar had been examining and could see that they were transcripts. Pages and pages of dense text with only a few pertinent sections highlighted and marked with red tape flags. They represented hundreds of hours of recorded conversation from the meetings and phone calls of Art Wyles, CEO of Anorco Global Resources, gathered from wiretaps and recording devices that Lula had hidden inside the Espenian executive's houses.

"How's your family, Lula?" asked the Pillar.

"They're very well, Ayt-jen," Lula answered quietly. "My mother's new medications are helping and now that we have the nurse coming in as well, my sister is able to work again. They're happy in the new house." It was appropriate that every time they met, the Pillar reminded her of her family's greatly improved fortune. "As always, they pray for the gods to shine favor on the Mountain, and they thank you for your generosity."

"They ought to thank *you*," Ayt said matter-of-factly, leaning back and sipping from her glass. "It's your work for the clan that has rewarded them." Sharply, "Look at me when I speak to you. You know I hate that demure expression you use."

Lula firmed her lips and forced her eyes up. "I'm sorry, Ayt-jen, it's become a bad habit." She'd learned that the foreigners liked it when she acted awestruck in their presence, but right now, she was not acting. How could she not be nervous when sitting across from the forbidding woman who controlled her life completely?

"What have you learned since we last spoke?"

"Premier Waltor has officially approved the cabinet appointment," Lula said. "Mr. Wyles will take office as secretary of Foreign Trade at the end of the month."

"And he will step down as president and CEO of Anorco?"

"Espenian law requires that he do so to avoid conflicts of interest. But he'll maintain a controlling stake in the conglomerate and remain president emeritus of the Munitions Society. As for Operation Firebreak, he's putting his Keko-Espenian business partner Jim Sunto, the head of GSI, in charge of the contract with the War Department."

The Pillar nodded. "And what of his arrangement with the Crews?"

"He'll continue to launder money for the Baker Street Crew for the usual cut. The Crews will still buy jade from Anorco at a guaranteed set price and move it onto the black market. In addition, Mr. Wyles will receive increased monthly payments for being Joren Gasson's influential friend in Adamont Capita." Wyles had never told her any of this directly, but Lula had pieced it together over time, eavesdropping on phone calls with "Jo Boy," asking about Wyles's childhood friends from Port Massy, noticing that when they traveled to Marcucuo, he had meetings with Espenian men in dark suits who left behind briefcases of bundled thalirs. "Wyles is taking greater precautions now, to keep the association secret. He won't meet or communicate with Gasson directly anymore and won't be seen near him."

The Espenian press portrayed Art Wyles as a devoutly Truthbearing self-made man who had come from a poor family in a tough neighborhood of Port Massy and risen to wealth and power through business acumen and savvy investments. Lula, who had out of necessity done her homework on the man, was surprised that Espenians wished to believe this fairy tale, or at least conveniently ignore whispers and evidence to the contrary.

Kekonese people know that no man rises without patronage and protection. The oligarch Wyles owed his early success to the Baker Street Crew—the largest, wealthiest, most politically well-connected organized crime outfit in the Republic of Espenia. Ayt Mada hadn't known this for certain when she first found Lula and placed her in the foreigner's path—but the courtesan's discoveries had not surprised her. Obtaining enough recorded proof to make this knowledge useful, however, had taken years.

Lula's hand shook, rattling the ice cubes in the glass as she drank down the cool tea, trying to drown the anxiety curled in her stomach. Each time she'd come to Ayt's mansion to make her report, she'd left with the Pillar's words dragging down her steps. "We don't have what we need yet. You'll have to go back and get us more."

So she had. Over and over again, to be the foreigner's mistress. She took his cock into her mouth, her pussy, her ass. She pretended to love it, to love *him*. She learned to lie fluently in Espenian, to whisper that he was the best lover she'd ever had, that she was so lucky and grateful he'd noticed her and made her his woman, given her such nice things and treated her so well. She accompanied a man forty years older than her on business trips and stayed with him in five-star hotels. She planted bugs in his houses in Marcucuo and Karandi— but not Espenia, because he had a wife and family there, and another mistress, so she could not be seen in that country. She pretended to convert to the Church of One Truth and went to services with Wyles, mouthing the foreign words of worship to a foreign God and Seer. She coaxed him into talking about his friends, his businesses, his political ambitions. She pretended to struggle with Espenian, to not understand all the things he spoke of, so he talked about them freely, with the sense of safety a person feels around their cat.

When Wyles was away from Kekon, Lula could pretend she was free. She could take singing lessons and dream about going to college and one day having a real career as a music teacher. She could be with Sumi and imagine a future together. Sumi wept over the trap they were in and vowed she would wait, but Lula knew no one's resolve was infinite. Every time the phone rang and it was the foreigner summoning her back to his house, their fragile illusions of happiness were snuffed out.

She asked the question she'd been dreading. "Do you have enough, Ayt-jen?"

Ayt Mada considered the stack of evidence in front of her, one of the many that Lula had provided for her over the years. "Do I have enough?" The Pillar gazed out across the perfectly still pools and carefully arranged rocks of her garden, her expression thoughtful and distant. "Is it ever enough?" Her eyes drifted back to Lula and lingered on her as if she were a mildly interesting sculpture. "How old are you?"

"Twenty-four, Ayt-jen." She'd been seventeen when Wyles had discovered her.

An expression Lula did not fully understand passed like a shadow across the Pillar's face. Nostalgia? Pity? "You're still a young woman," Ayt said. "Enjoy it while you can."

It was the closest thing to an acknowledgment of her sacrifice the Pillar had ever made. Lula had given up seven years of her youth to be a foreigner's whore, a White Rat for the Mountain clan. She suspected she was the only one of the clan's many rats to report to Ayt directly, a great honor, surely. She was grateful for what the clan had provided to her family. And she hated the Pillar with the quiet and resigned hatred a rabbit has for its captors.

Ayt Mada motioned one of her Green Bone bodyguards over and asked him to bring her a phone. "You've done well, Lula," she said. "I have what I need. Go home to your family. You won't need to worry about the foreigner calling for you again."

Lula dropped from the bench onto her knees and pressed her forehead to the wooden decking of the gazebo. "Thank you, Ayt-jen," she choked out through tears. She sat up and saluted with trembling hands. "May the gods shine favor on you."

The bodyguard returned and passed the handset of a cordless phone to the Pillar. Ayt was no longer looking at the other woman. She was flipping through a small book of notes as she dialed. The weeping courtesan might as well not exist anymore. As Lula rose to her feet and backed out of the gazebo for the last time, she heard Ayt speaking into the receiver. "Iwe-jen," said the Pillar, "it's time we made those arrangements we've been planning."

CHAPTER

52

A Search Ended

the twenty-sixth year, fifth month

Niko entered the slum house in Coinwash and wrinkled his nose at the smell of urine in the stairwell. The poorest parts of Janloon were not as bad as some of the most desperate places he'd seen in his worldly travels, but they were still the sort of place nearly everyone would avoid, including Green Bones. Too dark to see green, as the saying went—literally in this case, as the lights were burned-out in the hallway.

The two Green Bone bodyguards that the Pillar had assigned to him followed close behind Niko up to the second floor, where he found the unit he was looking for and knocked. There was no answer, but he could sense someone inside. He knocked again. "Go away," came a muffled voice from the other side. There was no lock on the door, so Niko pushed open the flimsy barrier and stepped into the room.

A middle-aged man in shorts and a stained T-shirt was slumped on the threadbare carpet in front of a dilapidated sofa, watching a small tube television that rested on top of an upside-down wooden crate. The smell of mold and stale beer pervaded the windowless space. Several empty liquor bottles lay discarded on the floor. The man glanced up at Niko with incurious hostility.

"Are you Betin Rotonodun?" Niko asked.

The drunk grimaced with one-half of his face. The other half remained slack. "No one calls me that," he snorted. He looked away and took a swallow from the bottle of beer in his hand. "Who the fuck are you? Are you from the government?"

"I'm from the No Peak clan," Niko said, "and I have some questions to ask you."

That got the man's attention. He jerked up straight and stared at Niko alertly now, his bloodshot eyes bulging to the size of lychees as they came to rest on the long string of jade beads around the visitor's neck.

"You're..." The man blinked twice and wet his lips. "You're one of the Kauls."

Niko motioned for his bodyguards to remain in the hall. He walked across the tiny room and turned off the television. Noticing a step stool against the wall, he moved it before sitting down on it, facing his interviewee, who remained where he was on the floor, still staring with disbelief. "You weren't an easy person to find, Mr. Betin," Niko said.

"Bero," the man corrected sharply. "I never use that other name, and I don't owe anything to the bastard who gave it to me. How do *you* know it?" His heart rate had shot up, even Niko could Perceive that, though he didn't seem frightened, exactly. Unnerved. Perhaps excited. "Do you *know* who I am?"

Niko nodded. He took a digital voice recorder from his pocket and placed it on the edge of the crate next to the television. "You're Catfish. You were a spy for the Espenian military who fed them information on the Clanless Future Movement for several years up until the Janloon bombing. After that, you disappeared from any records, so I assume you were whisked away with a new identity. But you used your legal name to apply for government assistance, so I knew you were back in Janloon."

Bero gaped at him. Niko couldn't blame him for being astonished. The Janloon bombing had been twelve years ago. The Clanless Future Movement still existed but had been ground down to dregs. The decades-long Slow War had exacted a staggering cost in money and lives in wars all around the world, but if it wasn't quite coming to a decisive resolution, at least it was going into a state of dormancy, with Ygutanian retrenchment and negotiated bilateral withdrawal from overseas conflicts. The former spy probably figured no one would try to find him. Even the Espenian government seemed to tacitly agree with that assessment, since it had declassified most of its documents over ten years old.

The No Peak clan, however, had a long memory and longer grudges. Niko's aunt Shae had given him an unusual assignment: Use newly declassified information that the clan had obtained to track down firsthand accounts of the ROE's secret activities in Kekon prior to and immediately after the Janloon bombing. She'd assigned a couple of people to help him with the project, which they both knew would involve chasing a lot of dead ends. Niko was aware that the Weather Man was testing him, but that didn't bother him. Time-consuming, methodical detective work far out of the spotlight suited him fine.

Unfortunately, after six months, Niko still didn't have enough concrete evidence of the ROE's activities to help the Weather Man substantiate her suspicions. The two retired military intelligence operatives he tracked down refused to talk to the fake reporter he sent their way. The ROE used code names for its informers; sometimes he could determine their identities, but most of them could not be found. The file on Catfish had come with a copy of an arrest record for anti-clan vandalism, which could be cross-referenced with the Janloon police database, but it was sheer luck that Bero's legal name had shown up again recently in the government's system, and only, it appeared, because the man was a destitute alcoholic surviving on social welfare.

"I want to know about your previous work for the Espenians," Niko said. "In as much detail as possible."

Bero was silent for nearly a full minute. Then he laughed out loud, a raspy bark of incredulous delight. "That's it?"

"You'll be paid for it, if that's what you're asking." Niko took an envelope out of his breast pocket and set it down near the recorder. It seemed a waste of clan money; he was confident the man would spend every last dien on liquor.

Bero looked at the envelope and then at Niko. A strange expression suffused his crooked face, a faintly deranged eagerness as he sat forward and let out a foul-smelling sigh of satisfaction. "Sure, keke, sure. I'll tell you everything."

"Good." Niko turned on the recorder. "Did you know a man named Vastik eya Molovni?"

———

Upon his return to Janloon, Niko hadn't expected to be welcomed or forgiven by the clan. Indeed, he hadn't been. Plenty of naysayers, inside and outside of No Peak, speculated unkindly and sometimes outrageously that he'd come back because he'd run out of money, that he was a foreign agent who would betray his family again, that he had a secret lover and couldn't marry until he restored his position in the clan, among other theories.

Niko could do nothing about the harsh gossip except endure it and try not to let it affect him. He performed the most painful penance he could think of, worse than cutting off his ear, as far as he was concerned: He agreed to television, radio, and newspaper interviews where he spoke candidly about his decision to leave and to return. Over and over again, he apologized humbly and publicly for having hurt and disappointed his family and his clan, and promised that he would do his best to prove himself a worthy son and potential heir from now on.

His grieving parents hadn't been of much support at first. The Pillar officially accepted his return to the clan, but was otherwise withdrawn, and Niko didn't expect his mother to ever forgive him, not when he hadn't been there to protect Ru when it mattered.

Niko soldiered on regardless. Over time, the doubters' angry grumblings would fade, so long as he put his head down and proved he could back up his intentions with action. He'd done as Ru had once suggested, attending Jan Royal university part-time and progressing steadily toward a joint degree in economics and organizational management. For two years, he worked evenings on the military side of the clan. Ironically, all the training and experience he'd gained during his employment with GSI had improved his martial confidence, and his motivations were different now. He was promoted to Fist in six months, laying to rest the question of whether his previously unremarkable performance had been an issue of ability.

With his aunt Shae's blessing, he began shadowing Terun Bin, the clan's Master Luckbringer, to learn about the Ship Street side of the clan. Soon after, the Weather Man began to give him work to do on his own time, including this project of chasing down old breadcrumbs. Recently, he'd begun attending and observing his aunt's meetings with Lantern Men and other clan stakeholders.

In the three years that had passed since his return to Janloon, Niko had determinedly done everything that could be expected of him and more.

"You used to be so stuck-up, always wanting to ignore the rules and do your own thing. Now you're a worker ant who doesn't seem to sleep," Jaya said, in an unexpected moment of sisterly concern for him. "What happened to you?"

"I'm not a moody teenager anymore. I grew up and gained perspective, Jaya. That's all."

It was a shallow answer when the truth was more complicated, not something he was sure he could ever explain. He'd left Kekon in search of the indefinable. A sense of who he was, independent of the clan. An answer to the nagging question of who he could've been, if his uncle hadn't taken him from his birth mother and made him the first son of the Kaul family. When he'd joined GSI, he'd imagined that the foreigners were right—the world of Green Bones was brutal and outdated, nothing like the rest of the world.

Now he knew better. There was jade and blood and cruelty everywhere.

After leaving GSI, he'd wandered without any destination in mind, chased wherever he went by guilty memories and the vague dread that he was tainted for breaking aisho and could never return home for fear of bringing disfavor back with him. Instead, he traveled east across the Orius continent and spent two months in Lybon, Stepenland, hoping to awaken some revelatory connection to the city of his birth. It was a pleasant place, utterly foreign, rarely a Kekonese person in sight. He felt nothing there.

He left and crossed the ocean to Karandi, then went on to the Spenius continent, then south to Alusius. Along the way he worked menial jobs for cash, more to do something with himself than any real need for money. He cut wood and stacked boxes, cleaned tables and mopped floors. He wore his jade hidden, like a thief.

He'd been living in a motel room across from a pleasantly quiet beach on the Alusian side of the Mesumian Sea when he received a phone call from Teije Inno, one of the few people he'd kept in touch with after leaving GSI and who knew where he was. Over the phone, Teije apologized. For the whole time they'd known each other and been friends, he'd been a White Rat for the No Peak clan. Now Teije was calling on behalf of the Horn, to give Niko the news that his brother had been killed.

When Bero was done speaking, Niko nodded and turned off the recorder. "You've been very helpful," he said. He took a pen from his pocket and wrote on the envelope that he'd left beside the television. "The money in the envelope is yours, but I'm also giving you a phone number in the Weather Man's office. If you call tomorrow morning, and say who you are, they'll have orders from me to find you a place to live that's better than this dump. Three months of rent will be paid for. You can use that time to get sober and find a job and maybe improve your life. Or you can spend the money to drink yourself to death in slightly nicer surroundings. The offer is there for tomorrow only. It's up to you." He stood to go.

"You're done?" His interviewee sounded disappointed, almost angry. As Niko reached the door, Bero called after him. "Hey, wait! You asked me plenty of questions, so I get to ask you a question too. That's only fair, right?"

Niko turned around. Bero was climbing to his feet, bloodshot eyes fixed in a reckless stare. "That's a really nice necklace you're wearing. Really distinctive looking. Tell me something. How did you get that jade?"

Niko brought a hand up to the string of beads around his neck, each stone identical and flawless, separated with black spacers on a silver chain. "It belonged to my father," Niko said. "I earned it, piece by piece, by proving myself in the clan."

Bero gave a strange giggle. "Your father was Kaul Lan, the Pillar of No Peak. You're his son."

"That's generally how it works, yes," Niko said impatiently.

The man pointed to him. "I'd recognize that jade anywhere, because it used to be on *my* neck." He jabbed a finger proudly toward his own chest. "I was more than just a tool for the foreigners, you know. Before that, I was a smuggler and a thief, a grave robber, and most of all, I was a *killer*. Everyone around me ends up feeding worms. I'm a fucking demigod of death, keke. I've probably killed more people than most Green Bones. More people that you have, I bet."

Bero's grin was the leer of a bleached skull. "Long ago, the Mountain sent me after your da. I did it for the jade. *That* jade. I found him at the Docks and I pulled the trigger. *I* started the clan war all those years ago. *I'm* the reason you're an orphan. And here we are." He laughed like an injured hyena. "Finally, the gods are tying up their sick comedy act."

When Niko had walked into the room, the man on the floor had been a tired, huddled figure wrapped in sour apathy. Now he was standing straight, his thinning hair drooping over dark eyes that shone down into the bottomless well of rage and despair that came from staring too long into an abyss and seeing nothing. His sweating face bore the mad stamp of a man holding a knife to his own throat and shouting, desperate for recognition at the end of it all.

"*Well?*" Bero swayed alarmingly toward Niko as if toward the window ledge of a building. "Don't you have anything to say? Can't you use your Perception to know I'm telling the truth? If you believed everything else I told you before, you have to believe me now. Aren't you going to—"

With a sharp motion of his wrist, Niko flicked out a short, horizonal Deflection that struck Bero in the midsection like the thwack of a pole to the gut. The man grunted out his breath as he was knocked onto his rear. He looked up expectantly for the next blow, but Niko hadn't moved from his spot.

"Do you think any Green Bone can be goaded into killing carelessly at the drop of a pin?" Niko spoke with calm but astonished contempt. "Just because I could break your neck, you expect me to do you the favor? Do you honestly believe it would make your sorry life more dramatic or meaningful, for you to be murdered by the No Peak clan?"

Niko's pity confused and enraged the man. "Don't you get it? I'm *everything* the Green Bones hate and want to crush under their heels," Bero snarled. He picked himself off the floor, breathing hard and holding his stomach. "It's because I won't settle for being a nobody! I'm *somebody*, you hear me? I'm not like all those other pussies out there who settle for scraps. I've *done* things! I go after what I want, and I *get it* no matter what. *That's who the fuck I am!*"

Without warning, he collapsed to his knees and put his face in his hands.

"I'm not giving you what you want," Niko said bluntly. "Move on. Want something different."

"Didn't you hear what I said, you weird fucker? What kind of Green Bone are you, anyway?" Spittle flew from Bero's mouth as his head jerked up. His shoulders were heaving. "I killed your *father*."

"You didn't," Niko told him bluntly. "I never knew my father, but he was a good person, a respected Pillar, and one of the most powerful Green Bones anyone could name. That's what I've been told all my life, and it's what I choose to believe. The Mountain clan murdered him, but the truth of it is that a man like that can only be brought down by his own flaws, in the face of forces beyond anyone's control. Not by someone like you."

The bodyguards out in the hall hadn't moved despite the yelling, since the unarmed jadeless drunkard was of no threat and they Perceived no alarm from their boss.

Niko squinted at Bero coldly as the man stared up at him in mute disbelief. "You're not from a Green Bone clan, so you don't understand," Niko explained, as if to a dim child. "Ending lives out of vengeance is an important decision. I wouldn't disrespect my father's memory by taking what you said seriously. If you want to end your life, do the job yourself, but don't fool yourself into thinking it has meaning."

Niko left the room and walked out of the building with his bodyguards. He was deeply unsettled. Not by what the drunkard had said, but by what he'd seen in those hollow eyes. Even a wretched man like Bero, sunken to the bottom of society, still harbored an intense, maddening desire to be part of the great myth. It was a myth that ruled Kekon and its people down to its bones, that drove society's obsession with the trappings of greenness, that even seduced foreigners who could never truly understand it.

Clans and jade, murder and vengeance, burdens and feuds and failures passed down from father to brother to son—none of it was a myth to Niko at all, but part of his lived experience, inescapable but malleable truths that it had taken him a world of searching to accept.

CHAPTER

53

Old Secrets

Shae had been waiting patiently for the inevitable request that she meet with the Espenian ambassador. She took Niko with her. In the car during the drive from Ship Street into the Monument District, she tested her nephew. "How do you think we should approach this meeting?"

One of Niko's eyes narrowed thoughtfully, an expression that always reminded her of Lan. "The Espenians never ask for a meeting unless they want something, but they're always prepared to give in return. It'll be an offer they feel confident will buy our cooperation. The current ROE government, unlike previous administrations, seems more interested in money than jade, which may be good for us, since it'll be easier to bargain with them. But we're also in a tricky position right now. We can't give in to their demands, but with the jade decriminalization bill finally moving through the National Assembly, we also don't want to do anything to jeopardize the relationship."

Shae nodded, pleased with his astute answer. "I see you've been keeping up with the news." Niko had applied himself to learning the workings of the clan with a dedication that had surprised everyone. She suspected that he grieved for Ru by occupying himself with work during every waking hour. She wasn't sure it was healthy for him, but she also couldn't begrudge his accomplishments.

The Espenian embassy was a modern, gleaming glass cube of a building flying a dozen ROE flags from the top of its steel gate and deliberately overshadowing the other, more modest foreign diplomatic offices in the Monument District. Upon being admitted past security, Shae and Niko were led into the ambassador's private sitting room, a sunny but formal chamber with high-backed cushioned chairs and portraits of famous Espenian premiers on the walls.

Ambassador Lonard greeted them and introduced Colonel Jorgen Basso, the newly installed commanding officer of Euman Naval Base. In the years that Shae had been Weather Man, she'd dealt with seven different ROE ambassadors and three military commanders. She remembered how nervous she'd been the first time she'd sat down with Ambassador Gregor Mendoff and Colonel Leland Deiller in the White Lantern Club, the outright skepticism they'd shown toward her as a young woman and an inexperienced Weather Man. Both men were long gone, retired to their home country.

Lonard and Basso saluted the longtime Weather Man in the proper Kekonese manner, then shook her hand, thanking her for coming to meet with them. Shae did not introduce Niko, as she'd brought him as an observer. He positioned his chair behind and to the left of Shae's seat.

Ambassador Lonard was a long-faced woman with thin lips and straight, dark eyebrows over unsmiling eyes. She was at least a decade younger than Shae but carried herself with the unpretentious confidence of an old political hawk. She perched straight-backed in her chair and folded her hands over her knee. "Ms. Kaul," she said, "I was hoping your Pillar would join us as well."

"My brother is busy today," Shae said. Hilo still hated diplomatic bullshit. "Your predecessor ought to have explained to you that as

Weather Man, I speak on the Pillar's behalf." She gave the foreigners a polite, expectant smile. "What can the No Peak clan do for our Espenian friends?"

The ambassador motioned for an aide to close the door to the sitting room. It swung shut on silent hinges. "I assume you're aware of the situation that's been developing on Euman Island."

"If you're referring to the protest camp, yes, I'm aware of it," Shae said.

Colonel Basso, a large, bald, brown-skinned man with spectacles, perhaps Tomascian in ancestry, said with gruff indignation, "There are over two thousand civilians camped within two kilometers of an ROE military base, with more joining every day for the past month. They pose an unacceptable security risk."

"They're not on your property," Shae replied calmly. "That part of Euman Island is historically an indigenous area. Last year, the Royal Council passed a bill to restore it to Abukei governance. The people who've gathered there are doing so with the permission of tribal leaders, as protest against the offshore jade mining that's continued despite years of national opposition."

Ambassador Lonard's thin lips all but disappeared when she tightened them. "An unruly mob is not the best way to address a complicated issue."

Shae raised her eyebrows. "There's nothing complicated about it. The issue persists because the Espenian government continues to support Anorco's exploitative business operations."

Over the course of a dozen years, neither the diplomatic efforts on the part of the Kekonese government nor repeated attempts by the clans to destroy the mining ships had been successful. The local Abukei tribes, fed up with the ongoing environmental destruction of their fishing grounds, had mounted a protest that had rapidly garnered widespread public support.

Ambassador Lonard adeptly refused to be drawn further into the underlying argument. "My immediate concern is for the safety of the Espenian *and* Kekonese citizens who could be endangered if this intentionally provocative gathering turns violent."

Shae didn't bother to point out that the ambassador was likely more concerned about the ongoing press coverage of the Euman Standoff, as it was being called by the media. The Espenians preferred not to draw public attention to the fact that they still had such a large military presence in the country, despite promises to the Kekonese government that they would reduce their forces as part of the international effort to bring the Slow War to an end.

Shae sat back. "What is it you want the No Peak clan to do?"

Ambassador Lonard and Colonel Basso exchanged glances, as if the answer was self-evident and Shae was being obdurate, which she was. She already knew what the foreigners were asking for, but she wanted them to have to say it out loud.

The colonel was the one to be blunt. "Break up the encampment and persuade the protestors to leave."

"By force, if necessary," Shae added for them.

"Green Bones are more than capable of force," Lonard pointed out. "Although I would hope that a strong show of intent would be enough to control the situation."

Even though the request was exactly what Shae had expected, she was nonetheless deeply offended and filled with a cold anger that she controlled and folded carefully into her answer. "Over the twenty-six years that I've been Weather Man of No Peak," she said, "I've seen the relationship between our countries go through many phases. In some ways, we're friends who're closer than ever before. But friendship is something that can be abused. When that happens, it can lead to hard feelings and even enmity. Espenia has asked Kekon for jade, soldiers, land, military support, and political concessions. And now, you're suggesting that Green Bones turn against the people we protect. Most of the protestors encamped on Euman Island are jadeless civilians. You're asking us to break aisho."

Colonel Basso glanced down uncomfortably at Shae's frankness, but Ambassador Lonard did not. "Ms. Kaul, I have a doctorate in East Amaric Studies. I've lived in Kekon for years, and I've learned enough about the country and its Green Bone clans to say with confidence that aisho is an ideal that's . . . not always feasible or strictly followed."

The Espenian inclined her head as she held Shae's gaze. "Can you honestly claim that Green Bones—including you and your family— have never bent moral principles for your own self-interest? Haven't you brutally punished anti-clan dissidents, unsanctioned jade wearers, and foreign competitors without any moral compunction?" Lonard spoke, unexpectedly, in accented but fluent Kekonese. "Gold and jade, never together. Has that ever *really* been true?"

The Weather Man's silence was enough of an answer for Lonard. Switching back to Espenian, she said, "Your clan and its supporters in the ROE have been trying for a very long time to repeal the ban on civilian possession of bioenergetic jade in Espenia. A decade ago, I would've said that was impossible. But admittedly, public perception and attitudes have shifted over the years."

Growing mainstream acceptance of Kekonese healing practices, the long-standing and consistent marketing strategy of WBH Focus, worldwide pay-per-view broadcasts of jadesports events in Marcucuo, advances in the safety and effectiveness of SN2, and now, Green Bone abilities being displayed in dramatic fashion on movie theater screens to rapt audiences—all those forces together had transformed jade in the eyes of Espenians, a majority of whom now believed it should be regulated instead of outlawed.

Ambassador Lonard tapped her fingers lightly against her knee. "The decriminalization bill will be voted on in the National Assembly next month. If it passes, it still has to be signed into law by Premier Waltor. He could choose to oppose it by exercising an executive veto. On the other hand, if he were to publicly support the bill before the vote happens, its approval would be almost guaranteed."

The cleverest Espenians were like Fists in their own way, Shae thought—wielding words and money like moon blades and talon knives. Lonard smiled with cool persuasiveness. "If you were to assist us with the problem on Euman Island for the sake of everyone's safety, I'm confident the premier would ensure the smooth passage of legislation that's certain to benefit your business interests."

Shae did not return the smile. A few fortunate bright spots in No Peak's business—the rebounding real estate market, growth in the city of Toshon, and successes in the film industry—had made up for some of the damage incurred as a result of the clan losing all its prospects in Shotar. But there was no question that the long-term legal security of the clan's Espenian holdings was needed more than ever. She'd underestimated Lonard's understanding. The ambassador was not making an ignorant request, but a fully knowledgeable one. Colonel Basso grunted in smug agreement and crossed his arms.

Shae let a pause hang in the air before responding. She'd waited more than a decade for what she was about to say. She wasn't going to rush. "Since we're discussing Kekonese interests in Espenia, it's only fair that I also say a few things about Espenian interests in Kekon." She leaned forward. "Twenty years ago, an Ygutanian spy plane was shot down over Euman Island, raising fears of Ygutanian aggression. In response, Espenia expanded its naval base despite widespread public opposition, and it also increased its intelligence assets in Kekon. At the height of the Slow War, you had more spies here than our government ever suspected. ROE military intelligence learned of a planned terrorist attack that would kill the leaders of all the Green Bone clans and incite a foreign-backed uprising that would destabilize the nation."

Shae remembered as if it were yesterday the moment she'd seen the collapsed building and the sight of so many dead bodies, knowing her husband and her brother were under the rubble. Her voice was entirely calm, a mask over her rage. "Instead of sharing this information, the Espenian military allowed the Janloon bombing to occur and for hundreds of people to die. If the attack had succeeded in destroying the clans, the ROE was prepared to step into the power vacuum and exert proxy control over Kekon. By not tipping its hand, ROE agents were able to capture an enemy operative named Vastik eya Molovni, who yielded a trove of information about Ygutan's nekolva program."

Ambassador Lonard's reply was bluntly dismissive. "I've heard all this unsubstantiated conjecture before."

"It's not unsubstantiated," Shae said. "It's taken years, but my people have gathered enough firsthand accounts to paint a full picture of what actually happened—including evidence that places Vastik eya Molovni in Janloon on the day of the bombing and an eyewitness report of him being captured by the ROE." She gazed steadily at the two Espenian officials. "How many *more* protestors would be on Euman Island right now, if they knew the Espenian government allowed, even hoped for, the Janloon bombing? That our supposed allies seized the man who was responsible for the attack and secretly used him for their own purposes, denying justice to the Kekonese people?"

Colonel Basso sputtered for a second before leveling an affronted glare. "The Espenian military has protected your country for decades. The number of lives tragically lost in the bombing was small compared to the many that were saved by intelligence gathered on the Ygutanian threat."

"Of course, Espenian lives have always been worth far more to you than Kekonese ones," Shae said. "But as the ambassador pointed out, attitudes have shifted over the years. Premier Waltor's political rivals have been questioning his track record during the Slow War. He was deputy premier at the time of the Janloon bombing, and he later played a key role in the creation of the Lybon Act. He might not want to be associated with so many dead civilians while campaigning during this election year. Nor would he appreciate scrutiny into Agent M not being a defector at all. Torture and pharmaceutical interrogation of captured prisoners of war are both outlawed by international conventions signed by the ROE."

The polished pleasantry had left Ambassador Lonard's manner. Her thin nostrils flared with vexation, and there was doubt and rapid calculation in her eyes. Nevertheless, she responded with a defiant lack of concern. "All of your accusations are related to events that happened over a decade ago. Yes, if you were determined to create a public stink about them, you could do so. It would damage relations between our countries' governments, but the Espenian voter is not going to care about—"

"Operation Firebreak," said Niko.

Shae swung a look over her shoulder at her nephew's unexpected lapse in decorum. Throughout the meeting thus far, he'd been a proper silent observer, but his outburst caused both of the Espenians to snap their gazes over to him in surprise.

"This is my nephew, Kaul Nikoyan." Shae offered a belated introduction even as she hid her displeasure at his bewildering interruption and tried to make it seem deliberate. "He has something to add to the conversation."

"Operation Firebreak," Niko repeated, speaking in uneven but passable Espenian. "That's not old news. Maybe it could cause a public stink, as you say, that would be more interesting to Espenians."

Colonel Basso nearly rose from his chair. "What do *you* know about—"

Niko stared back at the large Espenian military officer with an expression that Shae found disquieting. Niko's face resembled Lan's, but his stare was like Hilo's.

"Kekonese Green Bones were hired as contractors to help fight in Espenia's wars. I was one of them. And I know others."

After four years, Shae still regularly wished for her jade. She felt strange whenever someone mistakenly addressed her as "Kaul-jen," but even stranger when they said, "Ms. Kaul." She often woke up with the vaguely panicked feeling that she was missing something vital, and sometimes she still reached for her jade abilities instinctively only to grasp at nothing, like trying to move a phantom limb. Most of all, at moments like these, she wished she still possessed the advantage of Perception. The foreigners were making no further pretense at this being a friendly conversation. Their expressions were uneasy and deeply guarded. Niko gazed back at them without saying anything more.

Shae no longer had her jade senses, but she did have instincts honed from decades of reading the clouds. "Ambassador. Colonel. It seems our countries are closer than ever, since our relationship is based on so many old secrets." Shae stood. Niko stood with her. "The No Peak clan won't send Fists to break up the Euman Standoff," she told the foreigners. "It's true what you said earlier. Green Bones aren't paragons of the Divine Virtues. For all our abilities, we're only human, and often fail to live up to our own ideals. But we aren't vassals who would break aisho for Espenian convenience.

"I propose a different bargain. We'll let go of our old grievances over your treatment of Kekon during the Slow War. We'll keep your secrets about the Janloon bombing, and Molovni, and Operation Firebreak—so long as you don't hinder the jade decriminalization bill in the National Assembly. Consider it an alliance of inaction."

Colonel Basso glowered without answering, but Ambassador Lonard rose stiffly. "I had hoped," she said, "that given No Peak's economic ties to Espenia, you would be more cooperative than your rivals or the Kekonese government. If the Green Bone clans won't intervene on Euman Island to control the populace, then my government won't be held responsible if Kekonese lives are lost."

Shae turned to leave. "Ambassador, when it comes to Kekon and its jade, responsibility is the last thing I expect from your people."

―――――――

When they were back in the car, Shae instructed the driver to take them to Tia's school. There was still half an hour before classes were done for the day, so they sat in the car under the shade of a tree, windows rolled down to let in a breeze.

Niko broke the awkward silence. "I'm sorry for my rudeness during the meeting, Aunt Shae. I thought it was important that I speak up in that moment, but I should've told you everything I knew beforehand."

"Yes, you should have," Shae rebuked him. "If your knowledge of Operation Firebreak might've been important in any way during the discussion, then you were wrong not to bring it up with your Weather Man well in advance."

"I understand my mistake." Niko hunched forward. After a minute of castigated silence, he explained, "Operation Firebreak is what I was sent to carry out when I worked for GSI. Years ago, the Espenian government began reducing its military use of jade and drawing down its involvement in overseas conflicts. Secretly, though, it hired Jim Sunto's company to fight wars against Deliverantism and Ygutanian influence around the world."

"Sunto told you this?" Shae asked.

Niko shook his head. "Not directly. We had to sign a lot of non-disclosure forms and we weren't allowed to talk about assignments to anyone outside of GSI, but many of us figured it out piecemeal from things we heard. I spent some time digging into it afterward." Niko avoided meeting her gaze. "I'm not proud of what I was involved in."

"That's no excuse," Shae replied, although her annoyance was already fading. Seeing the guilt in her nephew's curled shoulders, she wanted to reach across the seat, to hug him tightly the way she used to when he was a little boy and would come to her for comfort. She wanted to tell him that she understood what it took to leave, and to come back. There was pride and shame in both of those decisions. Niko's reasons and experiences had been different from hers, and so were his regrets, but she wished she could offer him something that would smooth the premature lines on his young face.

"Niko-se," she said, "there're a lot of things I've done in my life that I don't want to talk about. Every week, I ask the gods for their understanding and forgiveness. And yet, when I walk out of the temple, I still have to make decisions that might stack up even more against me. I'm not sure there's any other way to be a leader in a Green Bone clan."

Niko looked out the window toward the school building. Two years ago, Shae and Woon had come to the obvious but nonetheless difficult conclusion that Tia would not do well in Kaul Du Academy, that they should honor their daughter's wishes and allow her to continue on a scholastic track instead of training her to become a Green Bone. It had been the right choice, Shae told herself. Tia loved Janloon North Hills Primary, the school Ru had also attended.

A shadow passed over Niko's face as he gazed across the parking lot to the entrance. Shae wondered if he was thinking of Ru, imagining him coming out of the front doors so the brothers could bike home together. She could see the white scar down the front of Niko's left ear, where the cartilage had been stitched back into place.

When Shae had come back to Kekon from her years abroad, she'd done so reluctantly, doubtfully, still trying to avoid being drawn into the clan business. Niko demonstrated no such uncertainty. From the moment he'd set the talon knife to his own flesh, he hadn't wavered from his decision to rise within the clan. Anden seemed to be the only one capable of getting him to relax on occasion, but Shae's cousin had confided to her, with worry, "Sometimes, I'm not sure Niko thinks of himself anymore. That's why no amount of work or humiliation bothers him."

Studying the young man's troubled expression, Shae's heart ached. She wished Lan could see his son. She knew he would be proud, but perhaps sad as well. He would ask what Shae asked now. "Is this really what you want, Niko? Do you want to become the Pillar?"

Niko didn't answer right away. "Aunt Shae," he said at last, with quiet conviction, "while I was away from Kekon, I realized there are only two types of people in the world. It's not Green Bones and non–Green Bones. It's those who have power and those who don't."

Her nephew turned toward her with a distant gaze that made him seem as if he were standing on the other side of a wide valley. "Even with jade, we're not guaranteed a place in that first group. If the clans stop defining the meaning of jade, then others will take that power from us. They'll amplify all the worst parts and preserve none of the good."

Shae gave a nod of silent understanding. Niko had put into words something she'd felt for a long time—a sense that she struggled not only against the Mountain and all the other enemies of the clan, but against something even larger and more inexorable.

Niko lowered his gaze to his hands. "I thought I could escape and find some other meaning in my life. But if the clan crumbles, either quickly or slowly, if it becomes as obsolete and irrelevant as people like Jim Sunto believe, then everything that *made* me, including my father's murder and my mother's execution, would be meaningless. Every drop of blood spilled, every sacrifice made, every child ever trained to wear jade as a Green Bone warrior of Kekon over centuries of history . . . *That's* what the Pillar carries. That's our power, and ours alone." He looked back toward the school with a small, sad smile. "Ru tried so hard to tell me that I was a selfish fool to run away from it. He was right."

Shae was filled with a nameless, foreboding fearfulness for her nephew. Niko was still young—too young, she thought, to be so clear-eyed and grim of character. Yet he'd already contemplated the legacy of the clan and the weight of leadership far more than Lan or Hilo or herself at his age. Shae and her brothers had grown up with the sentimental expectations that came from being the grandchildren of the Torch of Kekon, heirs to the clan following a generation of victory, peace, and national reconstruction. They had each, in their own way, been forced into their positions and done the best they could.

Niko had grown up with his eyes open to war and cruelty. He'd stepped away from everything he'd known to find an even more dark and tangled wilderness beyond, and his return was an unflinching choice, made without the sentimentality of love or honor. Shae thought, *He is more like Ayt Mada than any of us.*

At least Niko has us. People who loved him, who reminded him to be human.

The school bell rang and excited children began to pour out of the front doors. Shae got out of the car and stood by the bike racks. She waved when she saw Tia. Her daughter said goodbye to two of her friends and came jogging up, her backpack bouncing on her shoulders, the ears of her puppy-shaped knit hat swinging from side to side. Tia's twelfth birthday was approaching and she'd been begging for a pet, a dog to finally replace poor old Koko, who'd died a few months after his master, too heartbroken to live.

"Ma," Tia exclaimed. "Guess what? I got a part in the school play!" She looked over Shae's shoulder and said, more shyly, "Hi, Niko." Tia was always a bit reticent around her eldest cousin, who was fifteen years older than her.

"Hey, little cousin," Niko said brightly. "I like your hat." Tia smiled and relaxed, and they walked to the car, chatting, leaving Shae to follow a few paces behind, watching them.

CHAPTER

54

~

Master Plans

the twenty-sixth year, seventh month

Anden watched the news on television alongside Shae and most of the staff from the Weather Man's office, all crowded into the main boardroom on the top floor of the clan's Ship Street building. Even Woon Papidonwa and Hami Tumashon, who were both retired but who'd dedicated so many years of their lives to the clan, were in the room, chatting amicably in a way they never had when they'd been the Weather Man's Shadow and the Master Luckbringer.

It was late in the evening Janloon time, midmorning in Adamont Capita, when NA3882, a repeal on the twenty-four-year-long ban on civilian possession of bioenergetic jade, passed in the National Assembly by a narrow margin. When KNB's foreign correspondent reported the results on-screen, cheers broke out and celebratory bottles of hoji were opened. Starting tomorrow, the No Peak clan could expect to save millions of dien in legal fees alone. The use of jade in healthcare, martial practice, and entertainment was sure to grow, along with the clan's investment interests in all of those areas. Dozens of additional visas would be filed for Green Bones to work or study in Espenia. Meanwhile, the Horn would quietly begin to move additional jade into Espenia to bolster the clan's military strength and allies.

Anden used the phone in the conference room to call Cory Dauk, the president of the Kekonese Association of Espenia, to congratulate him on the victory they'd been working toward for over a decade. Up until the day of the vote, the KAE had been lobbying politicians and running ads produced by WBH Focus in all major media outlets. The outcome had been far from assured. Several Crews, wanting neither to lose the black market in jade and shine, nor see the Kekonese grow any stronger, had mounted their own secret campaign to defeat the legislation by bribing and threatening policymakers, ad executives, KAE members, and anyone else who spoke out in support of the bill. Lott Jin's small but effective squads of Fists and Fingers in Espenia, in partnership with local Green Bones from Port Massy, had been kept busy for months neutralizing the effort by providing security, counterbribes, and the occasional judicious whispering of crewboy names.

"I'm expecting this means less business for my law practice," Cory said cheerfully over the phone. "Maybe I'll become an entertainment lawyer. Work in movies or jadesports. That's where all the money is now anyway, right?"

Anden said, "If you find the next Danny Sinjo, let my sister-in-law know."

"My son loves that movie!" Cory exclaimed. "We've seen it three times."

The box office success of *Black & Green* on both sides of the Amaric last year had been an unexpected tipping point in the long public relations battle, catapulting Danny Sinjo to international stardom and creating a wave of favorable mainstream interest in Green

Bone culture. Much attention was paid to Sinjo's thrilling action sequences, which were done entirely without visual effects, stunt doubles, or wires. The movie was a crowd-pleasing buddy cop story in which a rakish Fist from the fictional One Sky clan, paired with a fish-out-of-water IBJCS-trained Espenian secret service agent, fought their way through Ygutanian ex-military underbosses on the way to capturing a notorious drug kingpin.

Cinema Shore, and thusly No Peak, was raking in money from what was now a planned franchise. As Jon Remi had once predicted, Anden could boast that he'd met Danny Sinjo long before he was famous—although it had been his sister-in-law who'd made the Bad Keck's words come true. Wen was missing from the gathering on Ship Street tonight because she was presenting the top award at the Janloon Film Festival, which had grown considerably since its inception and was now an event that the Pillarman attended with a clan budget.

"I hope your son knows that *2 Black 2 Green* comes out this summer," Anden said to Cory. "I might be able to lay my hands on a signed poster and send it to him."

"That would be mass toppers, crumb." Cory stopped. It seemed he'd been about to say something else about his son, or to ask after Anden's family, but he held back. Ever since he'd learned of Anden's role in the murder of Jon Remi, there'd been another wall between them, one that Cory kept in place by always ending the conversation before it became too personal and turned to his own wife and children. Anden was disappointed but not surprised; Cory was Espenian after all. It was just like him to wish for a difficult thing but maintain a distance from the way it was accomplished.

Anden rescued him. "Please give my respect and congratulations to your mother."

"Thanks, Anden. I will." A pause. "May the gods shine favor on No Peak."

After Anden hung up with Cory, Terun Bin thrust a plastic cup of hoji into his hands. "This all started with you, Dr. Emery," Terun said. "You were No Peak's man in Espenia before there was even an office there." They drank to the clan's victory.

Anden did not know the Master Luckbringer well, but in all their interactions, he'd been struck by how quickly and energetically the man spoke, and how much more quickly his mind worked. Terun was a career Luckbringer, starting on the business side of the clan right out of college. Now, he was one of the highest-ranked members of No Peak despite not coming from a strong Green Bone family and having never worn more than a single jade stone in his life. This would've been an insurmountable disadvantage in Janloon twenty years ago, but the Weather Man had wisely sent Terun on a long-term assignment to Espenia before bringing him back to Kekon and rotating him through several Ship Street positions, including making him the Sealgiver for several years, so by now he knew every part of the clan's business.

"I'll need to talk to you about how the jade medicine clinics were expanded," Terun said. "They're the best precedent to help us determine how to handle overseas martial education. Can you believe I already have six requests sitting on my desk from teachers and private trainers anticipating the passage of the bill? They're requesting No Peak patronage to open schools in Espenia to teach the jade disciplines to Keko-Espenians and even to foreigners."

Anden wasn't surprised to hear this. The market for martial gyms and coaching was crowded in Janloon. Even in smaller cities like Lukang and Toshon, a trainer needed top credentials from Wie Lon Temple School or Kaul Dushuron Academy, along with years of experience as a Fist and connections within the major clans. However, in Espenia, even a relatively average senior Fist could open a school and take on students. Some had already done so years ago, albeit covertly.

Anden began to tell Terun that he would be happy to offer whatever knowledge he could, when a shout rose up from the hallway. "The Pillar! The Pillar is here!" When Hilo walked into the boardroom half a minute later, the jovial noise cut out in a ripple of clasped hands and tilted salutes. Hilo's visits to Ship Street were uncommon. "Kaul-jen," several Luckbringers murmured. "Our blood for the Pillar."

Hilo's gaze traveled through the crowded space. A slow smile curved the side of his mouth. "Don't stop the fun for my sake," he said. "I just couldn't stand to think my sister was staying up partying while I went to bed." He quieted the burble of laughter by raising his hands. "The truth is that of course I came to congratulate all of you. I don't come here very often, but that's because I have such a strong Weather Man. Even when we don't agree, she does what's right for the clan."

Hilo went up to Shae and saluted her. "Far do your enemies flee, Kaul-jen," he declared, uttering the traditional Green Bone congratulations to a victorious warrior, before putting an arm over Shae's shoulder and kissing her brow. Even though the Weather Man could no longer wear jade and her triumph had been a distant political one decades in the making, echoes broke out at once, and people stomped their feet and raised their cups of hoji in jubilant agreement. The Weather Man looked deeply embarrassed. As people returned to their own conversations, Anden saw Shae muttering to her brother, "You always did have to upstage me at parties."

He's like himself again, Anden thought, turning away to hide his heavy-hearted relief.

Ru's death had devastated all of them, but it had nearly ruined Hilo. He'd withdrawn and lost interest in life. The Pillar who used to want to personally handle every important issue in the clan no longer cared about anything. For nearly a year, Hilo left the running of No Peak to his Weather Man and Horn, who had to guiltily hound him for even simple things. He wouldn't leave the house for days, or would spend hours driving aimlessly around the city, sometimes picking a direction and ending up in the countryside and sleeping in the car. A few times he parked the Duchesse in Mountain territory, baiting someone to attack him for being there. To Aben Soro's credit, no one did, although on several occasions Lott Jin had to frantically scramble to find out where the Pillar had gone. Anden was not the only one worried that his cousin, only in his fifties, was already going the way of Grandda, sinking irretrievably into loss and regret.

Slowly, however, he'd reemerged. Perhaps it was because he and Wen leaned on each other so much in their mutual grief. The rest of the family would see them walking around the estate, or eating at the patio table in uncharacteristic silence, or going to Widow's Park together to visit the family memorial. Or perhaps Niko's return to the family drew Hilo back to life; instructing his nephew in the skills of clan leadership forced the Pillar to return to his responsibilities in a way that felt personal and necessary. Over time, he began to smile again, to train, to attend to clan affairs.

And he took a gradual interest in things that hadn't interested him before. Without any prompting, he gave a large endowment to the Charitable Society for Jade Nonreactivity. He donated to the Janloon public school board and paid for a new auditorium at Jan Royal University. Although he was well known for avoiding politicians, he unexpectedly appeared before them, sometimes with Wen by his side, to voice his support for legislative proposals that he'd never previously deemed to be important: A bill to prevent employment and pay discrimination against stone-eyes and those with mixed blood. A return of thousands of hectares of traditional tribal land to Abukei control. A limited allowance for the Kekonese military to use medical-grade SN2 in conjunction with its training programs, and to lower the threshold of martial education required of adult recruits into the Golden Spider Company—measures proposed by Jim Sunto fifteen years ago that Hilo and nearly everyone else had opposed at the time, but were now being reconsidered given the gradual destigmatizing of shine.

Some observers, particularly those aligned with the Mountain, muttered that the Pillar of No Peak was growing soft, pandering to the sentiment of jadeless reformists because he kept too many close advisors who were not typical Green Bones, or not Green Bones at all. Others praised the clan for being in touch with current social concerns and setting an example of philanthropic leadership.

Anden knew the truth. His cousin did all these things for Ru. All of Ru's social causes, the arguments he used to make to his father about the good the clan could do, the things he'd wanted Hilo to care about that his father had humored or ignored—they had taken on a different meaning. Now they were deeds Hilo could do for Ru that he had not done during Ru's short life, that would've made Ru proud of his clan and happy to be a Kaul—the only way left for Hilo to prove he still loved his son.

"Uncle Anden." Maik Cam came up to Anden, perhaps noticing him mulling his plastic cup of hoji too seriously. Kehn's son was proudly sporting a new jade ring and three new beads on a platinum chain—understated and professional, a good look for a young lawyer. He'd won his latest spoils in a recent duel against a disgruntled member of the Mountain clan who'd not taken well to the filing of a trademark infringement case. Cam had all the famous greenness of his father's family but his scholastic leanings came from his mother, Lina, a teacher. He touched his forehead in casual salute and said, "Thanks again for overseeing my duel. I really appreciate it."

"You're fast with the blade," Anden complimented him. "I'm glad you won. I'd much rather be patching up your opponent than you."

Under new laws, clean-bladed duels required the presence of at least two witnesses, one from each side, along with someone with emergency medical training. As the most prominent Green Bone physician in the No Peak clan, Anden's schedule was peppered with requests to attend contests. That was not the only change to dueling custom. A twenty-four-hour waiting period was now required between the issuing of the challenge and the fight itself. Only Green Bones were allowed to duel using moon blades or talon knives, and there were limits as to how much jade a combatant could take from an opponent who conceded defeat.

Previous attempts to place restrictions on the tradition of clean-bladed dueling had always failed. The shocking difference this time was that Kaul Hilo had publicly supported reform. He even went so far as to admit that some of the many duels he'd fought in his life had not been strictly necessary. Green Bones, he said, could gain combat experience and earn jade with less injury and death, and jadeless citizens should be encouraged to try to solve disputes in other ways. His own son, Hilo declared, might be alive today if he'd not felt the need to duel, or if the duel had been delayed or better controlled.

The Pillar's astonishing shift in position had caused fierce debate in the Green Bone community, but even the traditionalist Koben family couldn't argue against it without seeming ridiculous, as Hilo had fought more duels and won more jade in his life than any of them. The Pillar wielded his will toward the issue with the same amiable, dangerous persuasiveness with which he ran the clan, so what he wished for happened quickly.

Cam grinned. "The other fellow could've beaten me if he wasn't so exhausted from dealing with our lawsuit," he said, managing to be both polite and cleverly self-aggrandizing at the same time. Cam was burly and broad-shouldered, as tall as his father had been, but unlike Kehn, he had a quick smile and sense of humor. "Where's Jirhu?" he asked Anden. "Is he not here tonight?"

"No," Anden said. "This is…" He glanced around at the gathering. "A bit too much of a clan occasion for his liking." He and Jirhuya had come to a long-standing compromise. Anden's boyfriend came to Kaul family gatherings, where he got along with everyone despite being a little more reserved than usual, but he avoided large No Peak clan functions. Jirhu faithfully wore a ring of bluffer's jade on his right thumb and did not hide their relationship, and he was accepted by the Kauls because of his importance to Anden, but he was not associated with No Peak in any other way.

Over time, Anden had come to appreciate what had initially seemed to him to be Jirhu's unreasonable concerns about the optics of patronage. In fact, he was thankful his boyfriend's career and daily concerns had nothing to do with the world of Green Bones. Jirhu was a refuge from the clan. He listened to Anden's troubles and encouraged him but never pressed for details or demanded explanations about clan affairs. In return, Anden didn't pressure Jirhuya to interact with No Peak beyond what he was comfortable with, not even picking up the phone to solve a simple problem through a Kaul family contact rather than accomplishing it some harder way on his own.

"Niko," Cam called out, and motioned his cousin over to join them. Seeing Cam, Niko's face relaxed into a smile. He came over and embraced both Anden and Cam warmly and let Cam refill his cup. Despite his size and tough looks, Cam was naturally gifted at putting people at ease. Whenever the cousins were together, he seemed to bring out a different side of Niko. "Where've you been hiding, keke? The Juens want to know when we're all going to train together again."

"We're a couple of suits now, Cam," Niko said. "The Juens will destroy us." The twins, Ritto and Din, were both first-rank Fists.

"That's what they think too," Cam said, glowing with eagerness to put his newly acquired jade to use. "We should do our part to keep our clan's Fists from getting too cocky."

Anden left his nephews to continue their conversation and went over to Hilo and Shae. "Where did all these young people come from, Andy?" Hilo wondered. "It's barely past midnight and I'm tired as fuck. Let's sneak out together so it looks like we're talking about important clan issues." He put a hand on his cousin's shoulder and they made their way toward the elevators. Anden smiled, and when Hilo said, "What is it?" he shook his head and said, "Nothing, Hilo-jen. It was a good evening."

———

The world came crashing down in the form of a simple newspaper clipping that Shae read while waiting for her daughter's dance practice to finish. Behind the studio's soundproof windows, the girls leapt and twirled in flowing silks to music she couldn't hear, but Shae sat immobilized, a deafening roar building in her ears.

The Euman Deal.

Shae's ordeal with the Faltas had given her lasting emotional scars and ruined her jade tolerance, but it had also left her with a burning question, the only one the barukan captors had asked her that she had not been able to answer: *What is the Euman Deal? Tell us about the Euman Deal.* She shuddered and felt tendrils of panic crawl over her every time she thought about it, yet the demanding questions came back to her, swimming into her waking nightmares, taunting her years later.

What's the Mountain's big plan? You're the fucking Weather Man of No Peak, you know what Ayt is up to, don't you?

She'd investigated all the Mountain's tributary businesses and assets connected to Euman Island. There was not much: a few properties in the town center, an upscale escort service catering to foreigners, a shipyard. She could find no evidence that any of them might be part of a major deal with the barukan.

Euman Island was best known for the Espenian naval base. Had the Mountain struck a secret alliance with the ROE military? Ayt Mada's relationship with the Espenians was hostile to nonexistent, so it seemed unlikely—though not impossible. But Shae could not find any sign that Ayt Mada was in contact with the ROE government. If she was, Ambassador Lonard and Colonel Basso would've gone to the Mountain instead of No Peak to ask that the protestors be run off.

We know they're cutting in the Matyos somehow. That was what the Faltas had said. *The Matyos are moving money to the Mountain. What are they getting for it?*

That part, at least, No Peak's spies had been able to verify. The Matyos barukan were moving millions of Shotarian sepas into overseas bank accounts. Shae's informers had long ago told her that Iwe Kalundo, Weather Man of the Mountain, was divesting the clan's businesses in Ygutan. Perhaps that was simply because he didn't want Mountain capital tied up in a country that was losing the Slow War and sliding into political instability, but it seemed the clan was still sitting on the proceeds and not reinvesting them elsewhere. It was not like Ayt to be passive. The Mountain and the Matyos were building up a joint hoard of cash and liquid assets. For what purpose?

Niko had told her that both Jim Sunto and the CEO of Anorco, Art Wyles, had part-time homes near GSI's training compound on Euman Island. Perhaps the Euman Deal had something to do with those foreigners. Hilo and Lott Jin already had No Peak spies planted in Sunto's organization, but they hadn't investigated Wyles directly. Shae had dug up every bit of information she could about the man. She had the clan's branch office in Port Massy keep an open file on him, informing her every time he appeared in the news. Now Shae was looking at an article from yesterday's *Port Massy Post*, the story clipped, photocopied, and faxed along with other memos and reports.

The article was short. It announced that Art Wyles, newly appointed secretary of Foreign Trade, had tendered his resignation as president and CEO of Anorco Global Resources. Although he was not required by law to do so, he would be selling his controlling share to an unnamed private Kekonese investment firm. The article ended with a statement that Anorco was valued at sixteen billion thalirs and the conglomerate's assets included proprietary offshore bioenergetic jade mining technology and Ganlu Solutions International, a private military company. The deal would close in ninety days.

The Euman Deal.

In the dance studio, the class ended. The girls saluted their teacher and began to mill about, chatting as they gathered their bags and shoes. Tia stayed behind with another student to practice a section of their routine, leaping with such height and elegance that she seemed on the verge of Lightness. She had all the natural athleticism of a Green Bone's daughter, channeled toward warmth and imagination.

Normally, Shae would get up and gather Tia's belongings, waving from the window to remind her that they had to get home for dinner, but she remained on the bench, a slow panic beginning to crawl over her as all the pieces fell into place.

The "private Kekonese investment firm" cited in the article was the Mountain clan. The proceeds from the sale of Ygutanian assets, combined with money from the Matyos, would be used to conduct the Mountain's largest-ever acquisition. Ayt Mada would take over Anorco and become the owner of her own jade mining company, with technology and assets completely separate from the Kekon Jade Alliance and beholden to no one. She could supply jade to military forces and other organizations around the world with no oversight from other clans. She would also gain control of GSI, which had jade-wearing soldiers, training campuses, helicopters, weapons, and gods knew what other military assets. Anorco and GSI had offices, personnel, and assets in Espenia, so in one swoop, the Mountain would leapfrog No Peak's presence in the ROE. The passage of the bill repealing the ban on jade, which Shae had pursued doggedly for so many years, would now, ironically, benefit the Mountain clan more than anyone else.

In exchange for their financial partnership in the Euman Deal, Ayt Mada would give the Matyos enough jade and military power to assert complete dominance over the Shotarian underworld, especially in East Oortoko, which was rife with organized crime in the wake of Ygutan's diminishing control. She would not only make peace but cement the loyalty of the barukan factions in her clan alienated by the Kobens.

Tia came out of the studio. "I'm starved," she exclaimed as she put on her shoes. "What's Da going to make for dinner?" When Shae stood without answering, her daughter looked up at her. "What's wrong?"

"Nothing, Tia-se," Shae murmured. "Just...thinking about work."

They walked out to the car, one of Shae's bodyguards following and opening the door for them. Ever since she'd stopped wearing jade, she had to put up with having personal security at all times. On the drive home, Tia talked about rehearsals for the school play, her upcoming math test, brand-name jeans she wanted to buy. Shae wasn't able to hear any of it. She was thinking that Ayt's acquisition of Anorco would be lauded as a great national victory, a repatriation of Kekonese resources from the hated foreign offshore mining company that thousands of people were protesting against at this very moment.

Public support for the Mountain clan would surge during a year of Royal Council elections. Assuming that all the newly districted seats in Lukang went to politicians loyal to the tributary Six Hands Unity clan, the Mountain was poised to control a commanding majority of the Royal Council, something neither clan had been able to accomplish for years. With so much power—military, financial, political— Ayt would install the successor she preferred. She would no longer need the Koben family's numbers or popularity. Iwe Kalundo's grand accomplishment as Weather Man would provide ample justification for her to bypass her nephew and name her loyal second-in-command the next Pillar of the Mountain, ensuring her will continued to prevail.

How had she done it? Shae wanted to scream the question. How had Ayt coerced the Espenian business tycoon Art Wyles to sell his multibillion-thalir conglomerate? What leverage did she have that would force Wyles to surrender his business empire, his claim to Kekonese jade, his Truthbearer's commitment to Operation Fire-break? It could not be anything so simple as the threat of death. She had clearly been planning this for years.

Shae was rendered speechless with awe. She should've read the clouds. Ayt Mada was simply a better Weather Man than she was, a master strategist on a level she couldn't hope to match. Where others sought honor or vengeance, Ayt sought only *control*.

"Ma? Ma, are you listening? Are you sure you're okay? You look like something's bothering you." Tia was looking at her with pouting concern.

Shae felt an ache in her chest, the opening of a chasm. This was what it meant, to not send her daughter to the Academy, to not raise her as a Green Bone. Tia lived in a bubble of ordinary preteen concerns. Even when she was older, she would never fully understand her own parents, or the rest of her family.

"I'm sorry, it's...clan things. Nothing for you to worry about," Shae said as the car pulled up in front of the Weather Man's house. "Go wash up for dinner."

Tia ran inside, dropping her bag by the door and shouting hello to her father as she went up the stairs. Shae followed slowly. The house smelled of garlic and spices and cooking meat. Woon came out of the kitchen, wiping his hands on a towel. "I didn't oversmoke the duck this time," he said proudly. Woon had barely cooked anything before the age of fifty but was now far more skilled at it than her. Seeing her expression or Perceiving her churning emotions, he stopped, the smile sliding off his face. Shae went to her husband and put her arms around him, laying her head against his broad chest without a word.

It didn't matter how quickly No Peak grew or how strong its warriors and businesses were. It could not compete against such over-whelming weapons. Ayt Mada would finally destroy the Kaul family and take the No Peak clan. It might be quickly orchestrated, or it might simply be a slow, inexorable defeat. Either way, the outcome was not in question.

It's over, Shae thought. *Ayt's won. We're finished.*

"We're not finished until we're all dead," Hilo said.

Shae had called an immediate meeting. The leadership of the No Peak clan was gathered in the Pillar's study in the Kaul house. When Shae had been a child, this room had seemed huge and intimidating. Her grandfather, his Weather Man, and his Horn would sit in leather armchairs, smoking and discussing clan affairs, sometimes late into the night.

Now, the study seemed intimate and conspiratorial. Hilo sat slouched in the largest armchair, tapping the edge of a playing card against his thigh. He had them lying around all over the place to keep his hands busy whenever he felt the craving for a cigarette. Lott was standing next to the flat-screen television. Wen and Shae shared the sofa, and Anden occupied the remaining armchair. Shae had explained all of her conclusions to them, laying out every aspect of Ayt Mada's master stroke. "It's a brilliant and elegant plan," she admitted.

Hilo flipped the playing card between his fingers and looked around the room at his family, his closest advisors. "We always knew we'd have to face Ayt directly again, to finish what was started so long ago," he said. "All these years of slow war between the clans have been about making ourselves strong enough. We became too big to swallow, too big to kill, so now Ayt has to gamble with everything she has. The thing about brilliant, elegant plans is that it doesn't take much to fuck them up."

Shae said, "The Euman Deal closes in less than ninety days."

"Then we don't have a lot of time, obviously," Hilo said, a bit impatiently. "When something has to be done, there's always a way to do it. So let's decide what that is."

Hours of discussion ensued on that night and the following nights. Phone calls were made, flights were booked, meetings were arranged.

The No Peak clan was a beast with arms that reached across the world, and it would need to move several of them quickly and quietly and at the right time, brandishing weapons that it had cultivated and kept hidden until now. Ninety days. Boat Day was approaching. By the time of the Autumn Festival, either the Mountain clan would be in de facto control of the country, or Ayt Mada's reign would be over. There was no middle ground. This was the last great gamble either clan could make.

To Shae's surprise, her brother didn't seem to share her dread, at least not outwardly. Hilo gave the orders and made the arrangements that would doom them or save them, but he also talked about plans for the summer, possibly taking Wen, Niko, and Jaya on vacation for a week before everything became too busy. "I've heard good things about the Bittari Valley in Tomascio," he said. "You and Woon and Tia could rent the villa next door." He commissioned renovation plans for the estate, saying that the courtyard looked dated and they needed a bigger home theater and a nicer training hall. He spent many hours with Niko, in conversations that Shae was not privy to.

"What else is there to be worried about?" he asked her, when she expressed incredulity at his lack of concern as they sat on the patio together one night after the heat had burned off the last of the drizzly Northern Sweat. "Don't you remember we once sat out here all night before New Year's Day, thinking we might both soon be dead? And here we are. So many good things have happened since then, and also so many terrible things that it's hard to be afraid of anything anymore. Whatever's going to happen will happen, so the most important thing is that we appreciate what we have and the people we care about." He drew a single stowed cigarette and lighter from the breast pocket of his shirt and said, as he lit up, "I'm going to have a smoke, though, just in case it's my last one. Don't tell Wen."

Shae looked up at the sky that stretched over the lights of the city. She couldn't share her brother's apparent equanimity. No Peak was everything she'd once hoped it would become—a powerful, modern, international entity, green at its core but far more than the sum of its jade or warriors. It was too difficult to wrap her mind around the possibility that after a lifetime of striving, after everything they had accomplished and sacrificed, they might still lose to an enemy they'd held at bay for decades, like an ancient city buried at the pinnacle of its glory by the volcano whose shadow had loomed threateningly over it for so long.

Tia is still too young. She still needs me.

"How do you do it, Hilo?" she wondered out loud. "How do you handle this world when you don't believe in the gods?"

Hilo exhaled twin streams of smoke and leaned back contentedly, his vision sliding out of focus. She knew he was stretching out his Perception, perhaps sensing where everyone was as he made a circuit of the Kaul estate in his mind—Wen upstairs in the main house, Woon and Tia across the courtyard, their mother doing slow stretching exercises in the garden, Lott and Niko engaged in evening training with a small group of Fists in the field behind the Horn's residence. Or perhaps Hilo was casting his jade senses even farther out, letting the surrounding energetic burble of the city wash over him, surveying it from a distance like a lion on a rock.

"How do we do it?" Hilo sighed deeply. "You of all people already know the answer to that, Shae. We don't handle this world. We make it handle us."

55

The Little Knives

Kaul Jaya chose several of her best Green Bones and traveled from her peninsula base in Toshon to the city of Lukang. Before she left, she spoke to her father over the phone. The Pillar told her, "Lott Jin is going to send the Juen twins down there with another twenty of our warriors. They'll get there tomorrow evening."

"I'll have it taken care of by then," Jaya assured him. "They can help clean up."

"Don't be so cocky," Hilo said. "Cleaning up is the hardest part."

"I'm joking, Da," Jaya said. She was only half joking. She wanted to accomplish her task quickly and independently, to prove to her father that she and her people could be trusted with difficult missions and didn't need help from Janloon. She suspected Lott Jin had persuaded the Pillar to give her this important responsibility. If it were up to her father, Jaya thought, he would have her back in Janloon, living at home and patrolling some safe and boring district like

Green Plain where he could keep an eye on her. After Ru's death, he'd wanted her to move back right away. She'd had to argue and beg to be allowed to stay in Toshon.

"Jio Somu is an old wolf by now," Hilo reminded her. "He betrayed his own uncle, and he's hung on as Pillar of Six Hands Unity ever since. His Fists and Fingers are trained by the Mountain. You shouldn't underestimate him."

"Don't worry, I know what's at stake."

Her father said, "How often have you been training? When was the last time you dueled?"

"Every day, Da. And I dueled last month—followed all the new rules and everything. A former Fist from the old Jo Sun clan, she was pretty good, wicked fast, and I got two new studs out of it." Her father was silent, and Jaya said, "Don't worry so much, Da." He didn't use to be like this.

"After this, we should talk about when you'll move back to Janloon. I miss you, Jaya-se."

"I miss you too, Da. I love you." She flipped her phone closed and went out to the parked Brock Compass. Eiten Asha and Noyu Kain were packing the last of their luggage, weapons, and gear into the ample trunk. "Leave the cooler in the back seat," Icho Tenn called from inside the SUV. "It has all the drinks and snacks."

The drive to Lukang took most of the day. The train could've gotten them there faster, and in another two years, when construction of the national high-speed rail line was complete, the trip would take under two hours. But considering everything they needed to bring, driving was the only option. It was slow going at times—many of the roads in the peninsula were single lane, and not always well maintained. But the Brock handled the occasional potholes with ease and they were in no rush.

They stopped along the way to take photos of the coastal scenery and have lunch in the small town of Yanshu. Tenn drove, with Jaya sitting in the front passenger seat, and Asha and Kain in the back. The summer heat grew thick by midafternoon, when the roads widened into Kekon's flatter central countryside. The four young Green

Bones blasted Shotopop music from the open windows and talked about fights they'd been in, movies they'd recently seen, the best and worst sex they'd had, and whether summer and low-residency students at Kaul Du Academy could be considered real graduates or not. All four of them came from traditional Green Bone families and scorned those who were "light green," but as Tenn said, "Not everyone can be cut." They all agreed that Danny Sinjo was cut, but the other actor, the Espenian, was obviously using stunt doubles and wires. Asha scoffed, "That scene on the rooftop. Have you *ever* seen a foreigner use Lightness like that? No way."

Jaya rested an arm outside the open window, drumming the beat of the music on the side of the Brock, laughing and joking in high spirits despite the fact that she was driving toward certain danger. Or perhaps because of that, the joy of life was greater. She was proud of what she'd accomplished over the past four years. Toshon was not nearly as big and important a city as Janloon, but it had grown and contributed to the clan at an important time, and it was where she'd risen into being a Fist on her own merits. People in the far south cared little about the clan dynamics in the capital. Even though the rivalry between the Mountain and No Peak affected the entire country, southerners had their own concerns.

The biggest problems were unemployment and drugs. Jaya spent more time than she liked on the phone with her aunt Shae and the people in the Weather Man's office, advocating for patronage for new Lantern Men in the area. She coordinated with the municipal government and the police to crack down on crime and lure more businesses and visitors from up north down to the peninsula. And she went after the drug trade—sweet flour, sand, buzz, and of course, shine—with the brutal efficiency of not just a Janlooner, but a Kaul. This was one area where Jaya did not at all mind leaning on her father's reputation. Drug dealers had one thumb cut off for a first offense, the other thumb removed for a second transgression, and their throat opened for a third.

She assembled a core group of up-and-coming Fists loyal to her, young Green Bones who were known for working hard and partying harder. Gray-eyed Eiten Asha, the only other woman on the original team sent from Janloon, was two years Jaya's senior and acknowledged as such a tough and capable Green Bone that it would surprise most people to learn she was also heiress to the famous Cursed Beauty hoji company. Noyu Kain, the elder brother of Jaya's Academy classmate Noyu Hana, had transferred south to Toshon to work for Jaya specifically. Icho Tenn was a member of the previous ruling family of the Jo Sun clan; he was the only Toshon-born member of their group, but he got along well with everyone and was also deeply loyal to his city. Together, they had roughly sixty Fingers who reported to them.

As a woman Fist, Jaya could not expect to be automatically obeyed, not even with the amount of jade she wore. She didn't see herself being able to pull off Ayt Mada's authoritative poise, or her aunt Shae's cool competence. Besides, those aloof old women sat in boardrooms. She would have to find her own style.

Many of her Fingers initially followed her because she was known for being fun and generous, for holding movie nights and group training, for making decisions as a team when it was feasible to do so, which was something that could be accomplished in a smaller territory. Using confiscated drug money, Jaya purchased two large houses that were social gathering places for her Green Bones and often the site of much raucous behavior, drinking, and promiscuity. Shine and other drugs were strictly forbidden, however.

The first Finger she caught defying her rules, she packed him back to Janloon. The second one, she tied into a chair and cut off the jade studs in his ears and nose, leaving him permanently disfigured before kicking him out. She never used her family name as a weapon but she did not need to; everyone murmured that she was her father's daughter. Her team was known as the Little Knives, and word of their tight-knit culture had reached even Janloon.

Jaya and her friends arrived at the outskirts of Lukang before dinner and spent the night at a motel outside the city, so their arrival was unlikely to be noticed and reported to any of the local Green Bones. The following morning, they had brunch at a roadside noodle shop, then drove to meet up with six more of the Little Knives who'd driven up the previous day in two other vehicles. Together, they went to the Big Triple club, where Jio Somu could regularly be found on Fifthdays.

The sign on the outside of the building read in big white letters: COCKFIGHTS. ARCADE. INTERNET. Tenn circled the block and dropped Jaya, Asha, and Kain off on the street corner before driving away. The three Green Bones walked inside. The Big Triple was a musty old establishment valiantly trying to freshen itself up with modern attractions and amenities. To the left was a small cockfight pit with electronic betting terminals. This early in the day it was empty except for a couple of bored trainers sitting on benches, talking about their birds and waiting for more people to show up. To the right was a room with several computer stations behind a counter selling snacks and a poster with the sign displaying the prices in fifteen-minute increments.

Jaya strode farther into the room and found Jio Somu, Pillar of the Six Hands Unity clan, sitting at a circular table in a booth at the back of the club, having lunch with two of his Green Bones. Three bodyguards stood near them, their hands already on the grips of their pistols and the hilts of their knives, jade auras humming. They'd Perceived the No Peak Fists as soon as they'd walked in the door.

"Jio-jen," Jaya said, walking up to the table with a smile and saluting respectfully. "My name is Kaul Jayalun, and I've been sent on behalf of my father, the Pillar of No Peak, with an important proposal for the Six Hands Unity clan. May I join you?"

Jaya could see that Jio Somu had been handsome in his youth. Now in his midforties, the color in his hair was fading, but he still possessed a strong jaw and taut skin around shrewd eyes shielded by amber-tinted glasses. Plenty of people had tried to kill Jio over the years, and the paranoia he'd developed had paid off. As one of the only Pillars not in the KJA meeting on the day of the Janloon bombing, he'd been in a position to strengthen Six Hands Unity in Lukang while other minor clans had struggled and collapsed.

Jio pulled his glasses down and regarded Jaya and her two associates with a mixture of suspicion and amusement. "Since when does No Peak send its children to make business proposals?"

His eyes moved up and down, taking her in from head to toe. Jaya was wearing fashionable sneakers, a patterned summer skirt, and a red top with flared sleeves and a scooped neckline under a custom-fitted leather vest that suggested a modern, feminine twist on the traditional Green Bone fighting attire. Artfully arranged jade pieces gleamed from her gold torque necklace and armlets.

"Jio-jen, my words are for your ears only." Jaya glanced meaningfully at the other people in the club—the gamecock trainers, the waiters, the few other patrons.

Jio raised his eyebrows with curiosity and distrust. Then he spoke to his two Green Bone subordinates. "Get those people to clear out and then wait by the door and stop anyone else from coming in." Jio considered the two young Fists standing to either side of Jaya. He did not feel especially threatened—he was more heavily jaded than either of them, but he said to Jaya, "If your bodyguards stay, then so do mine."

"Whatever you like," Jaya said without concern. As the Pillar's lunch companions reluctantly departed, she slid onto the cushioned bench next to Jio. The man's bodyguards shifted closer, but he waved them back to their spots. Kaul Hiloshudon would not sacrifice his own beloved daughter in an assassination attempt. "May I have some of that cool tea?" Jaya asked him. "It's terribly hot in your city today."

Jio poured Jaya a glass of the citrus-infused tea and slid it toward her, watching her pale throat bob as she drank. When she was done, she wiped the half circle of lipstick from the rim of the glass with a finger. "Jio-jen," she said earnestly, looking the man in the eyes, "Six Hands Unity has been a faithful tributary of the Mountain clan for many years. But you're obviously a practical man who puts his own interests first. After all, you betrayed your uncle and watched him murdered in front of you, so you're willing to be flexible with your loyalties."

The bemused, tolerant expression on Jio's face vanished. "Is Kaul Hilo so deluded that after all these years, he thinks he can *bribe* me for my allegiance?"

Jaya's eyes widened and she said vehemently, "I swear on my jade that my father wouldn't insult you by offering any sort of bribe! He understands that you're genuinely loyal to Ayt Mada. Some would say you're an even better ally to her than the Kobens. He's simply, out of courtesy from one Pillar to another, offering you the opportunity to switch allegiance now and save yourself from sharing the same fate as the Mountain." Jaya gave him a winning smile. "He's sent me to tell you that old hag Ayt Mada will soon be on her way out, and he would be pleased to put any enmity with Six Hands Unity in the past and to accept your oath as a tributary of No Peak."

Jio blinked at Jaya before letting out a rich, throaty laugh. The smile returned to his face. "Jaya-jen," he said, using her personal name as if they were friends, "your family's been trying to take down the Mountain for decades. You'll forgive me if I'm quite confident Ayt-jen will be Pillar for many years to come."

"I'm sorry I can't give you the details of how exactly No Peak is going to bring Ayt down, only my father's assurance that it'll happen soon," Jaya said. "Ayt will be succeeded by the Koben family, and from what I understand, they don't like you all that much. You're southerners and they're northerners, and also they look down on the barukan immigrants in your clan. So you can't expect to get the same sort of favored tributary status under Ayt Atosho that you enjoy now." She called out to Asha and Kain standing a short distance away. "Is there anything else I'm forgetting?"

"There's the issue of the embargo, Jaya-jen," said Asha helpfully.

"Ah, yes." Jaya smacked her own forehead and turned back to Jio. "Since it seems likely the Royal Council is going to normalize relations between Kekon and the Uwiwa Islands, shipping traffic will be restored to Lukang, and No Peak still controls the docks here. So it would be better for you to ally your clan with ours. The alternative, of course, is to go down with Ayt. But why would you want to do that?"

She could Perceive Jio Somu's jade aura glowing with smug scorn. He saw her as a spoiled princess, twenty-three years old, playing at being a Fist and getting away with it because of her father's indulgence. It was hardly the first time Jaya had encountered this reaction—indeed, today she was counting on it—but it never ceased to gall her. "You certainly are confident, aren't you?" Jio said. "To come all the way to Lukang in person to suggest I betray my oldest ally on the word of a pretty girl."

Jaya kept her smile in place but averted her eyes. "That's kind of you to say, but I'm actually quite nervous, to be given so much trust by my father that he'd ask me to make such an important alliance." She fiddled with one of her jade earrings. "Do you really think I'm pretty, though?"

Jio chuckled and moved closer to her on the seat. "I'm not blind. Why did your father *really* send you to Lukang?" When Jaya gave him a confused look, he lowered his voice and whispered, "I know how these games are played. You're one of the best cards in your father's deck, aren't you? One that he's been keeping in reserve for some time."

Jaya was well aware of the suitors and families who'd approached her father, as if she were a prize for him to grant. She was selfishly relieved that Niko's return meant she had to put up with less bullshit clan speculation about her own personal life. Nevertheless, she wasn't surprised that even Jio Somu, a man known for being extremely cautious, responded presumptively to even the tiniest encouragement. Underneath the table, Jio's knee touched hers and stayed there. "It's Lukang's seats in the Royal Council, isn't it? Kaul Hilo doesn't want them going to the Mountain."

Jaya took a chance by reaching over and placing a hand on Jio's knee, the one pressing against her own. She lowered her own voice and her gaze. "My father could've sent a platoon of Fists to lay down an ultimatum, but he didn't. He sent me, his only daughter, to speak with you so that you would take his proposal seriously, and so that you'd see we want this to be a friendly conversation, not a threatening one."

"That's surprisingly politically savvy of Kaul Hiloshudon," Jio said. "Your father's not known for subtlety. Perhaps he's gained some wisdom over the years."

"I'm told that's what happens sometimes," Jaya said. "So are *you* wise enough, Jio-jen, to take this offer my family is extending? What should I tell my father?"

Jio ran his tongue over his bottom lip. His eyes traveled slowly over her face and body. "I would need more information to decide how worthwhile a change in allegiance would be." He glanced at the two other No Peak Green Bones, who were watching him carefully. "You could come to dinner with me tonight. Send your bodyguards away so that we can discuss the potential alliance in more...depth." He placed his hand on top of hers under the table.

Jaya drew back her hand and her head, her lips parting in a small intake of breath. "Jio-jen," she exclaimed with feigned disbelief. "Are you suggesting...you might betray the Mountain clan and side with my family if you could fuck me?"

"Of course not," said Jio. "It would have to be a lot more than one fuck."

Jaya stood. "I came here to discuss a serious alliance. You're insinuating that I'm a whore, and that my father would expect me to seduce you for political gain."

"I can't see what else No Peak has to offer," Jio said with a smirk.

Jaya's eyes flashed fire. It didn't matter that Jio could Perceive her true anger and malice. "I can overlook an insult, but not when it's against my parents. Jio Somusen, Pillar of Six Hands Unity, I offer you a clean blade."

Jio's mouth fell open. Then he laughed uproariously. His bodyguards bit their lips and fought not to join in. They didn't even notice that Jaya's coy manner and her show of ire were both gone. She stood expressionless as she waited.

Jio stopped, dabbing tears of mirth from the corners of his eyes with a napkin. "Go home, princess." He waved her toward the door of the club. "I would've shown you a good time, you know. I wouldn't have turned to No Peak, but it was entertaining to see you try to win me over, especially when you're so naive. Go back to your father and tell him that he'll have to do better than that."

"So you refuse my clean blade?" Jaya asked.

Jio shook his head, grinning. "You really are something. No

self-respecting man in the world will duel a girl. Let me give you some advice. If you want to be of worth to your clan, stop playing at being a Fist and use the assets you do have."

"I didn't ask for your advice," Jaya replied. "No man has agreed to duel me yet, but that doesn't mean I'll stop offering a clean blade when I've been insulted. And now I'll have to disappoint my father by telling him that you refuse our friendship."

"Do that," Jio said. "Tell him I look forward to finally seeing Ayt Mada crush No Peak like a snail."

"Let's go," Jaya called to her Fists. The three of them departed the Big Triple to the snickers of the Six Hands Unity men. One of Jio's bodyguards followed them and opened the front doors, waving Jaya through with exaggerated courteousness. She could hear their laughter as the doors closed behind them.

Jaya flipped open her phone and hit the speed dial. "Now," she said to Tenn.

In seconds, three Brock Compasses full of the Little Knives roared in from different directions and surrounded the building. Young No Peak Green Bones piled out of the vehicles with Fullerton machine guns and blew the windows of the club apart with bursts of automatic fire. Roaring with Strength, Tenn hurled two incendiary hand grenades. The old wooden structure went up in crimson flames.

From across the street, Jaya could feel the intense heat attacking her skin. She Steeled herself and wrapped a handkerchief over her nose and mouth as she stood near enough to Perceive the pain and terror of the men inside. Some of them never made it out of the building, but Jio Somu and two of his bodyguards were strong enough in jade ability to escape the inferno. Deflecting their way through the fire and Steeling against burns, they managed to plunge out of one of the broken windows in a blur of Strength and Lightness, their hair and clothes alight, screaming like elemental ghosts. The Little Knives mowed them down with volleys of machine gun fire. Jio Deflected the first burst, but not the second or the third. Not even the best Steel stood a chance against such a close-range onslaught of lead. The

Pillar of Six Hands Unity, who'd held Lukang for twenty years, collapsed on the sidewalk in a mangled mess.

Jaya spat on the ground. "How's that for using my assets?"

She had to thank Jio Somu. If he hadn't felt so secure after surviving so many previous attempts on his life, then he might not have underestimated her. When Jaya had become a Fist, her father had advised her, "In my experience, as long as your friends have a high opinion of you, it doesn't hurt when your enemies have a low opinion, the lower the better."

Noyu Kain phoned the fire department and the police. By the time they arrived, the Little Knives had put out most of the fire already. Asha and two others had opened up the nearest fire hydrant and several Green Bones were Deflecting the spray toward the flames. The buildings next door suffered damage but there had been no one inside. While Jaya was in the Big Triple speaking to Jio, phone calls had been placed to the neighboring businesses to quietly clear out everyone on the block.

Later, it would be determined that there was one civilian casualty— the kitchen manager of the Big Triple, a friend of Jio's cousin, had not left with everyone else and had been caught in the fire and killed. It was unfortunate, but Jaya could explain to everyone that she'd observed aisho to the greatest extent that could be reasonably expected. She didn't feel any guilt over the death of one bystander who didn't know what was good for him.

News trucks arrived minutes after the emergency services. Jaya checked herself in the Brock's side mirror. Ash dusted her face, but her makeup was holding up remarkably well and she made a mental note to get more of this brand of waterproof eyeliner. She buckled her moon blade onto her waist. "How do I look?" she asked Eiten Asha. Her friend pursed her lips critically, made a small adjustment to straighten Jaya's jade-encrusted torque necklace, and gave her an enthusiastic thumbs-up.

"I take full responsibility for what happened here," Jaya solemnly told the cameramen who surrounded her. "My father sent me to Lukang to discuss improving the relationship with the Six Hands

Unity clan. No Peak has opposed Jio Somu for twenty years, ever since he betrayed his uncle, the rightful Pillar of the clan, and my aunt was nearly killed in the crossfire. But we were prepared to finally turn over a new leaf in this city."

Jaya glanced back regretfully at the burned-out shell of the Big Triple. "Instead, Jio Somu made threatening sexual advances toward me. For the insult against my family's honor, I offered him a clean blade, which he refused. My Fists witnessed this and any Green Bone is welcome to Perceive what we say is true."

Jaya lowered her eyes for a moment, leaving the obvious unsaid. To offend a family like the Kauls and neither apologize nor settle the matter with a clean-bladed duel left no choice but unavoidable retribution.

"To the rest of the Six Hands Unity clan," Jaya said, "No Peak seeks no quarrel with you. My family would be happy to sit down to talk with you about how we'll coexist in Lukang." Niko might be terrible in front of the media, stiff and unlikable to any casual viewer, but Ayt Ato wasn't the only Green Bone who could look good on camera.

A reporter shouted, "Do you expect the Mountain clan to retaliate?"

Jaya had asked the same question when the Pillar and the Horn had given her this assignment. "Aben Soro has never liked Jio Somu, so he won't care to lose his own people to avenge him," Lott had answered, "but the Mountain will have to send down Green Bones from Janloon to prevent us from taking all of Lukang."

"Which is what Aben will be expecting us to try to do, as soon as he hears the news," Hilo agreed. The element of surprise was why they were relying on Jaya's Little Knives. Any large movement of No Peak warriors from Janloon down to Lukang would've alerted the Mountain, who in turn would've warned Six Hands Unity. But the Mountain would not be paying any attention to Toshon. Jaya's father had said, "Ayt Mada and Aben Soro can send all the Green Bones they want. We don't need to take Lukang. We only have to confuse the shit out of the situation down there."

Jio Somu had children, but both of them were too young to succeed him. His Horn might assume leadership, but he was not popular within the clan. Most of the other members of the Jio family who'd been loyal to the old Pillar had joined the No Peak clan already, and with Jio's death, there would likely be more defections. Some segment of Six Hands Unity would remain faithful to the Mountain, but they would require increased support from Janloon. Lukang would become a patchwork quilt of confused loyalties, and no one clan would command unified allegiance of the city's Royal Council representatives.

No Peak did not need to control all of Lukang. Over the years, that goal had proved difficult if not impossible. It only needed to finally kill the longtime Ayt loyalist Jio Somu and remove Six Hands Unity as an entity that the Mountain could count on for political and military support. That was what Jaya had accomplished.

Jaya said humbly into the cameras, "I'm only a Fist, so I can't speak on larger matters. I only hope that Ayt Mada allows the rest of Six Hands Unity to make their own decisions. Nevertheless, we all know how senselessly violent the Pillar of the Mountain has been in the past. I'm sure my father will send additional Green Bones from Janloon to make sure there are no further attempts on my life or honor."

A few reporters began to shout additional questions: Why had she brought warriors, machine guns, and grenades for a supposedly peaceful discussion? Did she have anything to say about the reputation of the Little Knives? Was she romantically involved with anyone at this time? Jaya waved away the questions without answering any more of them and walked back toward the Brock Compass. While she'd been talking to the reporters, her people had efficiently stripped Jio of his jade, then picked through the smoking remains of the building to claim the green from the charred corpses. They looked like coal mine workers now, all grimy, covered in dust and soot.

"Don't you still look nice," Asha exclaimed, sticking her tongue out at Jaya.

Kain offered up Jio Somu's jade-hilted talon knife, his rings, bracelets, and the studs that had been in his ears. "Jade for the biggest of the Little Knives," he said.

"I didn't kill Jio," Jaya reminded him. "I only set him up so that he practically killed himself. Even though I led the mission, it's not right that I claim so much of the prize." Jaya took the talon knife, which was of excellent quality, but told Kain and Tenn to see to it that the rings, bracelets, studs, and remaining jade from all the bodies of the Six Hands Unity men were equitably split between the rest of the team.

As they drove back to the motel, Jaya tried to call Janloon, but couldn't get any cell phone reception. She finally managed to get two bars on the screen by standing in front of the lobby while the rest of the Little Knives put away weapons, set up sentries, and went for a beer run to the nearest convenience store. She called the number that went straight to the Pillar's study. Her father picked up on the first ring.

Jaya said, "Hi, Da, did you see me on television?"

"I swear to the gods," Hilo shouted at her, "you're trying to kill me from stress. Why didn't you phone right away? The first thing I saw on the news was the building on fire, without any other information. I called twice and you didn't pick up."

"I was busy, Da! My phone was on silent. We had to talk to reporters, put out the fire, tromp around in a building about to fall down to collect all the jade and split it up, and that always takes time, deciding who gets what so no one leaves unhappy, all those little things. You know how it is! Just trust me a little, why don't you?"

Hilo let out a breath of relieved laughter. "You're right, I do know how it is."

"How did I look on TV?" Jaya pressed. "Okay?"

"You looked great," her father said. "No wild parties tonight, understand? Jio might be dead, but he'll have friends who will take some time to get rid of. Don't let down your guard or get on anyone else's bad side in that city. The Juen twins will be there soon with more people, and you and your Little Knives are to obey your seniors. I know you're used to having the run of Toshon, but this isn't Toshon."

"I'm a senior Fist now, you don't have to remind me of every little thing, or lecture me about how to keep people in line," Jaya groaned, rummaging hungrily in the cooler as she held the phone against her ear with one shoulder. "Anything else?"

"Only that I'm proud of you."

Jaya grinned with pleasure.

CHAPTER
56

Life and Death

Anden looked around with great curiosity when the plane landed in Tialuhiya. He'd never been to the Uwiwa Islands. In his imagining, it was a sun-bleached tropical island full of palm trees and dirty, desperately poor people, a haven for illegal drugs and smuggled jade. So he was surprised that the new airport was modern and air-conditioned, and the professional driver who picked him up in a black town car spoke passable Kekonese. As they drove through the main town of Walai, Anden saw evidence of ruin and reconstruction everywhere—crumbling and abandoned buildings covered in graffiti, building cranes over high-rise projects, policemen directing traffic around road closures, a military truck flying an Espenian flag.

Typhoon Kitt, which had caused considerable damage in Kekon four years ago, had laid waste to the Uwiwa Islands, killing two hundred thousand people and destroying the country's neglected infrastructure. The Republic of Espenia, which controlled the tiny island of Iwansa for their own military and recreational use, had provided humanitarian aid and sent their military to help in the extensive rebuilding efforts. Of course, the Espenians did not do anything without exacting a price. In this case, it was a price that benefited Kekon as well. The Uwiwan government had been forced to clean house. A new Espenian-approved president and new head of national security had fired hundreds of state and law enforcement officials on charges of corruption. Jade smuggling, the drug trade, sex tourism, and political graft were all being rooted out in favor of luring foreign companies to build electronics manufacturing facilities.

Travel restrictions between Kekon and the Uwiwa Islands had been partially lifted. Technically, Green Bones were still banned, but Anden had been able to enter because he was a doctor, officially visiting for humanitarian purposes. It was far from the first time his unique situation and his credentials outside the clan had proven useful to No Peak in some unexpected way.

Anden felt he was at a crossroads. He was unsure what his future held even if No Peak was able to survive Ayt's machinations. He'd done all he could to promote jade medicine and the clan's interests in Espenia; that work was being continued by others now. He was lending his experience to the Weather Man's office as schools of the jade disciplines began to open up overseas, but Terun Bin would soon have that process well in hand. Of course, he could continue to work as a physician, but he was troubled by a feeling that that was not enough.

Sometimes he thought of how Lott Jin had determinedly climbed straight through the ranks of No Peak step by step into clan leadership. Anden's own path had been filled with twists and detours. Now both men frequently sat at the same dining table in the Kaul house, discussing clan affairs late into the night with the Pillar and the rest of his inner circle.

Despite their regular interactions and respect for each other's abilities, Anden couldn't say if he and Lott were friends. It seemed a faint yet inescapable discomfort persisted between them, an inexplicable resentment from having known each other as confused teenagers.

Years ago, at Juen's retirement party, when Anden had congratulated Lott on being named the new Horn, his old classmate had replied, "Maybe I should be the one congratulating you, Emery, for avoiding the job, so I could be the one to take it." His sulky mouth had curved in a good-natured but sardonic smile. "I suppose neither of us is who we once thought we'd be."

Anden had given the other man a searching look. "Was it worth it?" he asked. "Giving up whatever else you might've been, to take the path you didn't think you would?"

Lott had shrugged. "Who can ever know? Was it worth it for you?"

When Anden had mentioned his recent musings about the future to Jirhuya, his boyfriend had listened and said, with sympathy, "I think it's natural in our forties to start wondering if we're past the main events of our lives, or if there are still other mountains to climb. Your position in the clan is an incredible accomplishment in itself, miyan. Maybe you're wondering what else you could do with it."

Jirhu was no doubt speaking from his own heart; his accelerating career in the Kekonese film industry wasn't the only thing on his mind these days. Typhoon Kitt had damaged impoverished Abukei villages far more severely than the rest of Kekon. Jirhu had become increasingly involved in advocating for aboriginal communities and was now taking part in the ongoing protest on Euman Island, sometimes staying out for days at a time.

Anden worried for Jirhu's safety, but he was hardly in a position to demand he stay away from possible violence when, as his boyfriend pointed out firmly, "If I can put up with even half of what you do for the clan, you can accept me doing something important for my own people."

The town car took Anden beyond the city limits of Walai proper, onto a wide, freshly paved road reeking of asphalt fumes in the summer heat. Anden saw the tall barbed-wire walls and blocky watchtowers of the maximum-security penitentiary long before they arrived. At the security fence, Anden presented his paperwork to the sentry in the box, and then again at the office, where he was issued a visitor badge. After additional check-in procedures and thirty minutes of waiting in a small, yellow reception area, a guard escorted him into a room with a metal table and two chairs.

Anden sat down in one of the chairs. A door on the other side of the room opened and another guard brought the prisoner into the room, handcuffed and dressed in a gray jumpsuit. Anden had never met the man in person before, but looking at him, it was hard to believe he'd once been a formidable enemy of the Kaul family. Iyilo had been the right hand of the notorious jade smuggler Zapunyo, before he'd betrayed his boss, struck an alliance with the Mountain clan, and taken over the Ti Pasuiga crime ring. Now the barukan gangster was fat and middle-aged, his hair long and thinning away from his shiny forehead. All of his jade had been taken from him upon his arrest six months ago.

Iyilo sank ponderously into the seat opposite from Anden and squinted at him with disdain. "Who the fuck are you and what do you want?" he asked in accented Espenian.

Anden answered in Kekonese. "I'm Emery Anden from the No Peak clan."

Iyilo sat forward slowly. "You're one of the Kauls. The mixed-blood cousin."

"You knew me for a short while as the journalist Ray Caido."

The smuggler thought about this, then barked out a gruff laugh. "So I have you to thank for killing Zapunyo all those years ago. Or maybe you should thank me for helping your family to get its revenge." He rested his hands on his belly. "That's one thing I can say I have over Zapunyo. I went down, but none of my enemies took me out."

Iyilo had run Ti Pasuiga well enough at first. He had come from the Matyos gang in Shotar, and he'd learned from Zapunyo, so he did not lack for any ruthlessness. His partnership with Ayt Mada had allowed him to continue to dominate the lucrative black market jade triangle between Kekon, the Uwiwa Islands, and the Orius continent.

Unfortunately for Iyilo, he lacked Zapunyo's skills in management.

As a Keko-Shotarian foreigner, he held the Uwiwans in contempt. He viciously punished betrayals but did not spend money to cultivate loyalty by building village schools and hospitals as Zapunyo used to do. Over time, he failed to keep up relationships and pay off the right people, so he lost the iron control over the politicians and police that Zapunyo had wielded. In the years after Typhoon Kitt, when the Espenians demanded evidence from the Uwiwan government that they were taking steps to combat crime and corruption, the axe had finally fallen on Ti Pasuiga.

Even so, Iyilo could hardly be blamed for believing himself safe. He wore jade and lived in a fortified compound defended by dozens of guards who also wore jade. The understaffed, undertrained federal police force could not hope to go up against him. Instead, the Uwiwan government hired GSI to do the job.

A squad of well-equipped, jade-wearing private soldiers monitored Iyilo's habits for weeks, then ambushed him on the way to a sporting event. They killed four of his bodyguards but took Iyilo alive, in accordance with the terms of their contract. The Uwiwan government made a victorious announcement and showed news footage of Iyilo in handcuffs, with credit for his arrest given to the national chief of security.

Neither the Mountain clan nor the Matyos gang had made a noise of protest or come to Iyilo's aid. With the dissolution of the nekolva program and the decline in Slow War tensions, along with the decriminalization of jade in the ROE, jade smuggling was not a growing business. Ti Pasuiga was past its usefulness, no longer of vital importance to its old allies.

"Did Kaul Hilo send you to gloat?" Iyilo asked Anden. "Seems like something he would want to do in person, the arrogant bastard. I met him once, you know."

"The Pillar sent me, yes," Anden said. "To offer you our help."

"Your help," Iyilo repeated with manifest contempt. "Kaul Hiloshudon tortured my cousin Soradiyo and slit his throat. I'd sooner shake hands with the devil."

Anden took off his glasses and wiped the dust from them,

reminding himself that he was here for a purpose and ought not to be provoked by this man who was so low and helpless but still potentially useful. "Soradiyo tried to assassinate the Pillar with a car bomb but killed his brother-in-law instead. Even Ayt Mada wasn't going to protect him after that. Just as she's not protecting you now. You're hardly in a position to be choosy about the help that comes your way."

The smuggler's upper lip curled. "Yes," he said bitterly, "all of you Green Bones are the same in the end, aren't you? You protect yourselves, and you use the rest of us."

"Has your lawyer explained that you'll be sent to Kekon?"

Iyilo shrugged fatalistically. "Kekon is only a name to me. I was a baby when my family was shipped to Shotar as laborers during the Many Nations War. Kekon is only the wrapping around my life—where I was born and where I'll die."

Anden felt a scrap of pity for the man. Iyilo had become the center of a three-way legal tug-of-war between the Uwiwa Islands, Kekon, and Shotar. Both Kekon and Shotar wanted the barukan leader extradited to face trial for crimes committed in their own nations. Iyilo was not a citizen of the Uwiwa Islands, despite having run a massive criminal enterprise there for decades. He was not a citizen of Shotar either, as he could not claim at least seventy-five percent Shotarian ancestry. His official nationality was Kekonese, even though he'd only lived there for a year of his life. Now, however, the Kekonese government wanted to make a public example of Iyilo, to march him off the plane in handcuffs, demonstrating the disgraceful end of Ti Pasuiga and all those who dared to steal jade. The Royal Council had made the extradition of Iyilo a prerequisite for the lifting of the embargo and normalization of relations between Kekon and the UI, and after much hassling, the Uwiwan government had agreed.

Anden said, "You'll likely be dead within hours of setting foot in the country."

Iyilo did not answer, but his dulled expression showed that he understood reality perfectly well. The former leader of Ti Pasuiga was a loose end for Ayt Mada. There's no sort of person the Kekonese hold in lower regard than a jade thief. Any number of fellow inmates or prison guards would be more than happy to do the Mountain a favor and ensure Iyilo never spoke in front of a judge.

"What do you want?" Iyilo's anger sounded weary.

Anden glanced at the guards by the door. They were out of earshot and almost certainly could not understand Kekonese, but nevertheless Anden lowered his voice. "You still have a card to play. You know too much damaging information about the Mountain: the deals Ayt struck with Zapunyo, her alliance with you and the Matyos, her profit from the black market. It's why she's sure to have you killed."

Anden took a cell phone out of his briefcase and placed it on the table. "There's a private aircraft waiting in Janloon, ready to bring KNB news anchor Toh Kita over here to Tialuhiya. All I have to do is make a phone call to get you a national interview."

Iyilo's smile was slow and very cold. "Do you know what I hate more than anything else in the world? *Rats.* When Zapunyo and I found rats in Ti Pasuiga, we made sure they *begged* for death. I'll take my secrets to the grave."

"You're in a prison while Ayt Mada sits in her mansion in Janloon."

"As does your cousin Kaul Hilo. What do I have to gain from being a pawn of No Peak instead of the Mountain? I'm not stupid enough to think it'll save me."

Anden was not a Fist accustomed to inspiring fear, but he knew his family's fate might hinge on his ability to do so at this moment. At other times in the past, he'd been the one to speak or act for the clan when no one else could. In his youth, Anden had felt acutely his difference, his separateness from the rest of the Kaul family. Only over many years had he come to understand this as an advantage. Since he held no official role in the strict hierarchy of the clan, he'd been many things—a healer, a killer, an emissary, an advisor. Today, he was a hammer.

"You're beyond saving," Anden agreed. "But what about your family? The one that you've gone to such great lengths to keep secret?"

He reached back into his briefcase and pulled out an envelope. He opened it and laid three color photographs on the table in front of

Iyilo. In the first photo, a pretty, thirty-something Uwiwan woman sat on a beach. She wore a pastel sundress, her long hair pulled into a messy bun. Her face was turned to the side, speaking to another woman while two children, perhaps ten and eight years old, played in the sand nearby. The second photo showed the same woman and children getting out of a car. In the third photo they were in the front yard of a nice house.

Iyilo's darkly tanned face lost much of its color.

"I'm sure you've made private arrangements for your wife and children to be cared for after your death, but how can you protect them after you're gone? How can you be sure that the men in Ti Pasuiga that you hired to guard them will have any reason to remain loyal to your memory? The Uwiwa Islands is a dangerous place."

"How did..." Iyilo croaked without finishing.

"It doesn't matter how we found them," Anden said calmly. "If we could do it, others can. You're not a Green Bone of Kekon, so you can't count on aisho to protect your jadeless relatives. You're only a barukan smuggler, and your family is only Uwiwan. Who is going to notice or care if something happens to them? Can Ayt Mada be absolutely certain you haven't told your wife anything inconvenient that she might share with Uwiwan authorities?"

A subtle tremor went through Iyilo's body and rattled his shackles against the metal table.

"Here is my Pillar's offer." Anden reached back into his briefcase and took out another envelope. He extracted three airplane tickets and spread them out next to the photos. "We can put your family on this flight which leaves tomorrow for Port Massy. They would be escorted to the airport under guard, and once they reach Espenia, they'll be under the protection of the No Peak clan. We have many people and resources in that country. We can set them up with housing and new identities. Your children would live safe, ordinary lives. They would go to school there. Maybe they could even train in the jade disciplines. They'll have the money you leave for them. And most importantly, they'll have a future far from the sort of life you've led."

He could sense the man's will crumbling, but Iyilo still needed that final, gentle push toward the inevitable decision. Anden gathered the plane tickets and placed them back into the briefcase. He saw the smuggler's eyes twitch as the papers disappeared out of sight, leaving the vulnerable photographs alone on the table.

"The Kaul family always keeps its word, even to enemies. Especially to enemies. This is my Pillar's promise, which he's entrusted me to convey to you. Share Ayt's secrets, and we'll keep yours. Speak against the Mountain, and we'll protect your sons as if they were members of our own clan. However, if you refuse, I can't tell you what my cousin will do with these photographs and whether he'll feel any obligation toward your wife and children."

Iyilo's throat bobbed. "You're a doctor. You can't put them in danger."

"You'd be surprised by the things I've done," Anden told him. "I've taken lives and saved others. I've felt equal doubts about both." He'd killed Gont Asch and saved Ayt Mada. He'd ordered the death of Jon Remi, and in so doing he'd cost Maik Tar his life. He'd healed innumerable strangers, yet he was haunted every day by Ru's death and the possibility that if he'd been there, he could've saved his nephew. All those doubts had over time folded themselves into Anden's duality—of being a Kaul and not a Kaul. It was a contradiction he'd long ago struggled to reconcile but that now simply was.

"In my family, one gets used to making decisions about life and death. But I know which type I prefer to make, when I can," Anden said to the condemned man. "We can't save you, Iyilo, but we can offer your family a life where not even the Mountain can reach them."

He picked up the cell phone. "I told the Pillar I would phone him right away to tell him your decision. What's it going to be?"

CHAPTER
57

Standoff

The wheels of the Duchesse Imperia rolled over unevenly packed dirt. Mud streaked the massive luxury sedan's gleaming chrome grill and white doors. Hilo rolled down the window. He'd seen images of the Euman Standoff printed in the newspapers and shown on television, but they couldn't convey the restless energy or the *smell*. The site seemed like a refugee camp crossed with an open-air music festival. Canvas and nylon tents were set up wherever their owners could find space. The smell of cooking food came off portable gas stoves on makeshift wooden-plank tables. A group of Abukei women danced and played traditional music for a circle of onlookers. Rows of bright yellow portable toilet stalls stood in a row along one side of the camp. Dogs rested in whatever shade they could find, often beneath cars draped with Kekonese flags and hand-painted banners. ANORCO: STEALING OUR JADE AND RAPING OUR LAND. ABUKEI RIGHTS! SPENNY SOLDIERS OUT.

The encampment had swollen to over eight thousand strong, with still more arriving. The small towns on Euman Island were deluged. Hilo had heard that hotels were fully occupied and stores were running out of basic necessities such as toilet paper, bottled water, and rain ponchos.

Lott stopped the car when it was obvious they couldn't go any farther. The arrival of the Duchesse was causing an enormous stir. People were running over and jostling each other to get closer, shouting that the Pillar of No Peak was here. Hilo got out of the car along with his Horn and two other Green Bones—Vin Solu, the First Fist of Janloon, and Hami Yasu, son of the clan's former Rainmaker.

"Kaul-jen! Pillar!" Shouts came from the crowd. Others started to chant, "No Peak! No Peak!" Many of the people here were not clan members, and some were surely loyal to the Mountain, but there were enough voices that the noise grew and followed the Green Bones as they made their way through the encampment.

Lott and his well-trained Fists ignored the attention, their jade auras humming with alertness, their formidable demeanors serving to keep anyone from approaching too closely. Hilo envied them. *It's been a while.* A long while since he'd stepped out of the Duchesse with a pack of his warriors, laden with jade and weaponry, prepared to face any enemy. As a young man, he'd lived for the proud adrenaline of those moments. The feeling was still sharp, but bittersweet nostalgia tinted its edges.

One figure broke out from the rest of the crowd and approached the Pillar directly. Jirhuya looked less well put together than he normally did. Instead of his usual custom-fitted shirt and pressed slacks, he was in jeans, boots, and a black track jacket. He wore a colorfully woven traditional Abukei sash around his waist and several days' worth of stubble on his jaw. He saluted Hilo respectfully. "Kaul-jen."

Hilo said, "You've had dinner in my house, don't act as if you barely know me."

Jirhu's tawny skin flushed to a russet color. "Sorry, Hilo-jen, it's only that we don't usually see each other in public and without... more of the family around." *Without Anden around.*

Hilo put a hand on Jirhu's shoulder and smiled to show that he was not really annoyed. The man's awkward reticence was understandable, since the social division between him and his partner's family could not be helped. To be honest, Hilo was surprised Anden and Jirhuya's relationship had lasted for so long, although he supposed they were a good match in other ways. "Show us what's happening here," Hilo said.

Jirhuya led the Pillar and his men up a gradual slope at the farthest edge of the encampment. Roughly six hundred meters away stood a tall chain-link fence topped with razor wire, surrounding a compound of three buildings and a helicopter landing pad. Armed men in fatigues guarded the gates and were spaced at regular intervals all around the fence, holding rifles and eyeing the protestors suspiciously. "GSI soldiers," Lott said.

"Yesterday, there were ten of them. This morning that number doubled," Jirhuya explained. "If anyone gets within a couple hundred meters of the fence, they fire at our feet. We're pretty sure it's because there's a shipment coming in this afternoon."

Several people who'd followed behind the Green Bones muttered angrily and spat on the ground. Anorco's specialized mining vessels collected jade off the seafloor, then sorted the gems on board before transporting them by helicopter to the processing center where they were packed for distribution. One of those final destinations was less than two kilometers away. Shielding his eyes with his hand, Hilo could make out the outline of Euman Naval Base in the distance, its flags flapping in the stiff wind.

Over the course of the standoff, protestors had thrown bricks, paint, and cheap homemade explosives onto Anorco's property, hurled verbal abuse at the guards, and tried to disrupt deliveries of jade into and out of the facility. The company had responded by increasing security, so GSI soldiers now stood watch day and night.

The occasionally violent demonstrations were not openly condoned by either the Kekonese government or the Green Bone clans, but they weren't being reined in either. Several members of the Royal Council had expressed sympathy and solidarity with the protestors, and more than a few Green Bones from multiple clans had joined in the demonstration with the tacit permission of their Pillars. Kaul Hiloshudon showing up on Euman Island in person, however— that was new. It was the most dramatic sign of clan support for the standoff to date. A wave of shifting, murmuring, restless energy was sweeping over the crowd. Thousands of people were gathering on the ridge where Hilo and his men stood. News reporters emerged from trucks along the camp's sidelines, cameras ready, eagerly waiting for something to happen.

"What can you tell us, Vin?" Hilo asked.

"Some of those GSI mercenaries are definitely wearing jade, but I'd need to get closer to tell you more, Hilo-jen." The First Fist's long-range Perception was legendary by now, but even Vin the Sniper couldn't be precise at this distance.

"Let's get closer, then," Hilo suggested.

They began to walk down the other side of the slope toward the fence. Before they could get far, half a dozen Green Bones pushed through the crowd, running up to the Pillar and dropping to their knees in the dirt before him. Not one of them appeared to be over the age of twenty-five. "Kaul-jen," gasped a young woman with dyed orange hair and a jade nose ring, "we're all fairly worthless members of the clan—my friend and I are junior Fingers who used our vacation days to join the protest, my other friend here is a Luckbringer, and I don't know about these other two—but we're all ready to obey you."

"No Green Bone of No Peak is worthless," Hilo said, smiling at their youthful enthusiasm.

Four additional strangers stepped forward together out of the crowd and saluted warily. "Kaul-jen," said one of the men. "We're Green Bones of the Mountain, but we're all Kekonese first and foremost. We'll stand with you against the foreigners, if you'll allow us. Our Pillar hasn't ordered us to do otherwise."

Hilo nodded. He wasn't surprised that Ayt Mada remained silent on the Euman Standoff, since she was secretly in the process of buying Anorco outright. "Bring any weapons you have," he commanded the gathered Green Bones. "Your most important task is to protect the people here from harm. Otherwise, obey whatever my Horn and Fists tell you to do. Understand?" They all saluted Hilo and assured him that they did.

Hilo and his warriors approached the fence surrounding the Anorco facility, trailed by the additional Green Bones and an enormous crowd of excited people, including many driving slowly in vehicles, waving signs and flags. Summer rain began to fall. The warm, heavy drops struck uncovered heads and splattered the hoods of the cars.

Vin's stride slowed, his gaze unfocused. "There are at least thirty-two people in that facility, Kaul-jen," he said. "I can't Perceive all the way to the other side of the property, so I might have missed a few. I think most of them are security personnel, but not all of them are wearing jade. I've picked out eighteen jade auras in total."

"Eighteen's not too bad," Hilo said. "But not too good either, when they all have rifles and body armor and are already upset."

Although his own Perception was not as superb as Vin's from this distance, he could sense the crackling apprehension emanating from the GSI soldiers guarding the fence, and he could see them with their R5 rifles held at the ready as the wave of vehicles and bodies flowed toward them.

One of the guards shouted at them through a bullhorn, first in Espenian, then in barely understandable Kekonese. "Stop! You're approaching private property. Stay where you are or we will open fire. You've been warned!"

Lott said to the Pillar, with a hint of apprehension, "We don't have enough Green Bones with us to take out all those guards, much less capture the facility."

"We don't need to do either of those things." Hilo stopped at the point where he could Perceive the anxiety of the guards starting to crest, their fingers sliding toward the triggers of their raised rifles as he came near two hundred meters of the fence. The Pillar turned to face the line of protestors who'd followed him like an army. He spread his arms, throwing a slow, shallow Deflection that rippled outward, nudging those in the front row with a firm but gentle pressure. They came to a halt.

"What do we do now, Kaul-jen?" asked Hami Yasu.

"We wait. Shouldn't be long." Hilo lifted his gaze to the sky. The wind was picking up. It lashed his face with rain, forcing him to squint as he stared into the clouds. The gathered mass of protestors milled about impatiently, talking among themselves, but they didn't venture past the point where the Pillar stood.

The sound of a helicopter rose in the distance, then grew louder as it approached. *Right on time.* The clan's White Rats embedded inside GSI had been earning their keep.

Hilo motioned Lott and his Fists over and explained what he wanted them to do. They nodded, none of them showing any surprise or uncertainty. When Hilo said, "Hami-jen, your father tells me that your Lightness is excellent," the Fist looked abashed and humbly promised he would do his best.

Hilo leapt Light to the top of a nearby van, landing in a crouch. When he stood and raised his arms, the large crowd fell silent and everyone turned toward him, pressing forward expectantly.

"Can you hear me?" Hilo bellowed. "*Can you hear me?*"

An answering tumult rose from the throng. Among the sea of upturned faces, Hilo saw Jirhuya, looking up at him with an uncertain expression but listening to every word along with the others.

"No matter which part of the country you're from, which clan you swear allegiance to, whether you wear jade or not, we are all Kekonese. We defend and avenge our own. You wrong any of us, you wrong us all. You seek war with us, and we will return it a hundredfold." Hilo was not one for speeches—that had always been Ayt's strength—but the words that came to him now sprang to mind fully formed. He couldn't place where they'd come from, yet they felt strong and correct. The Pillar tilted his head back and roared even above the growing noise of the arriving helicopter. "*No one will take from us what is ours!*"

The helicopter came out of the sky, thundering toward the landing pad in the fenced compound. As the pilot slowed to a controlled hover, Hilo shouted a signal to his Fists. Gathering all of his jade energy like a tide sucking in the ocean, he bent his knees and launched himself Light into the air.

Gravity seemed to slip its hold on him as he hurled himself away from the ground and the people below. Lott, Vin, and Hami leapt Light alongside him, driving themselves upward by bounding off cars or springing from a Strength-fueled running start. They couldn't reach the helicopter—it was too far away and they were only men after all, not birds. But they could get closer, close enough.

At the apex of his leap, for a dramatic heartbeat of time, Hilo hung in the air at the height of a second-story window. He could feel his momentum reversing. He needed to hold on to enough Lightness to control his descent or he would plummet to a bone-shattering landing. The pilot's surprise sparked in his Perception like a pulse of light in the corner of his brain before he glimpsed the man's face, leaning over, mouth open at the remarkable sight of four men leaping up as if to grab on to the helicopter's landing skids.

Hilo maintained his grip on one discipline while reaching for another. His mind and body strained in painful protest as he flung his arm toward the cockpit of the helicopter with a snarl of exertion and a violent heaving of nearly all the remaining jade energy he possessed.

Four shafts of Channeling hit the pilot almost simultaneously. These were not the precise close-quarters strikes that would deliver a fatal blow to the heart or lungs of a combatant. From such an unwieldly distance away and in midair, the force of Channeling was blunt and badly dissipated. Any Green Bone could've easily Steeled against the ridiculous, unorthodox attack.

But the man in the helicopter was not a Green Bone. The combined buffeting of jade energy from all four assailants did not kill him, but the disruptive shock to his organs and nervous system knocked him unconscious. His body fell back against the seat, then slumped over the controls.

Hilo landed harder than he would've liked. After such a powerful burst of Channeling, he had barely enough jade energy left to let himself down Lightly and to Steel against the impact. Pain radiated up his shins and thighs into his hips as he hit the ground and tumbled forward onto hands and knees, all the breath knocked out of his lungs. Hami Yasu dropped down Lightly next to him, breathing only slightly harder than normal. "Kaul-jen, are you all right?"

Damn the young. Hilo nodded that he was fine as he got to his feet, wiping the sweat off his brow and brushing the dirt from his hands and knees. He looked up at the helicopter. Everyone else was staring at it transfixed as well, including the security guards surrounding the landing site, as if watching a train crash in slow motion. The uncontrolled machine listed in the air, still on course for a landing, but coming down far too fast now. It tilted and began to spin laterally, churning rotors kicking up a tremendous wind that tore at the clumps of grass and sent many people in the crowd running for the cover of their vehicles. Hilo heard the Finger, the young woman with orange hair, let out a shout of astonishment and elation. *"Holy fucking sh—"*

The pilot regained consciousness at the last minute, realized what was happening, and tried valiantly to right the helicopter. He was too late. With the horrifying sound of rending metal, the aircraft missed the landing pad and hit the ground barely inside the perimeter of the fence, bouncing sideways and back into the air off one landing skid and its tail rotor. Guards ran from the out-of-control machine as it spun in a circle, hitting the top of the chain-link barrier and ripping an entire section of the fence apart as it careened back into the ground with a concussive boom and explosive cloud of dirt. The helicopter's rotor blades were torn apart by the impact and went flying in all directions.

"Deflect that shit, *now*," Lott bellowed, raising his arms. Vin, Hami, and half a dozen of the younger Green Bones hastily threw up a patchy but adequately effective wall of Deflection that veered the shrapnel away from the crowd.

When the dust cleared, the helicopter with its cargo of jade was lying on its side a hundred meters outside of the ruptured fence, twisted and smoking, the Anorco logo clearly visible on its upward-facing surface. For a prolonged moment, no one made a sound. Then a victorious roar exploded from the crowd. For months, they'd been watching the fenced compound hatefully, seeing deliveries of jade enter and leave the processing facility, unable to do anything besides exact minor sabotages and make their unhappiness known. The sight of the crashed helicopter—brought down by only four of No Peak's top Green Bones!—seemed to light the protestors on fire. Like a flood wave through a broken dam, they ran shouting toward the wreckage and the open fence.

GSI soldiers were also sprinting toward the helicopter, on a collision course with the crowd. Other security guards ran to defend the gap in the destroyed fence, rifles raised.

"Get in front of those people before they get themselves killed," Lott shouted to the Green Bones. He was barely heard over the collective clamor. The Horn took off running, Vin right behind him. Hami, the youngest, quickly caught up and passed them. With their Strength, they outpaced the rest of the crowd, but they couldn't catch up with the bouncing off-road vehicles some people were driving toward the Anorco soldiers like charging cavalry troops.

The orange-haired Finger and her companions reached the helicopter first and tore into it triumphantly like wolves on a carcass, pulling out the dead pilot and dumping him in the dirt, then pooling their Strength to yank open the damaged doors, hauling out the cargo of sealed metal containers.

"Get away from there!" hollered a running GSI soldier. He skidded to a halt, aimed, and fired his R5. The sound of bullets zinged off the helicopter's metal body. A few people dove for cover behind the machine. Green Bones threw up Deflections. One of the men from the Mountain clan hurled a powerful wave that knocked the soldier to the ground and sent his rifle flying out of his hands. Shouting curses in Espenian, other GSI mercenaries opened fire into the rampaging crowd.

Hami, Lott, and the other Green Bones closest to the soldiers tried to Deflect the gunfire away from the civilians, but Hilo saw two people—an Abukei man and a woman holding a placard—both go down. The man screamed and clutched his leg. The woman didn't move. Green Bones drew handguns and returned fire. Maddened protestors grabbed any weapon they had on hand—knives, sticks, rocks. They continued running heedlessly and throwing abuse and objects at the soldiers, who balked and retreated toward the fence, responding with rifle bursts that sailed into the crowd or struck approaching vehicles, puncturing tires and breaking windshields.

Hilo jogged up to the scene as it turned into a pitched battle. Deflections, bullets, rocks, and profanities were being thrown every which way. Some protestors were charging ahead to fight; others pushed frantically in the other direction, trying to flee the gunfire. It was a noisy, disordered frenzy, like a fighting pit packed full of game-cocks. The GSI soldiers were panicking in the face of the enraged mob. Gunfire hit one of the young No Peak Green Bones and three additional civilians. Lott hurtled forward in a blur of Strength and Lightness; two throwing knives left his hand and sank up to their hilts in the neck of the soldier who'd fired, right above the collar of his bulletproof vest. His companions dragged the body backward, screaming for assistance and still firing.

Talon knife in hand, Hilo pushed and Deflected his way through the melee. He called out to Vin and pointed back at the helicopter. "Don't let any jade from there go missing in this shitstorm!" Spotting Jirhuya, rumpled and muddy, eyes wide with adrenaline and fear, he seized the artist by the arm and ordered harshly, "Don't you fuck-ing break my little cousin's heart. Get behind something, now. That truck."

Jirhuya gaped at the Pillar, who'd always seemed tolerant and friendly with him, as if seeing him for the first time. Hilo gave the man a shove toward safety, then continued in the direction of the fighting. "Stop firing!" he demanded, spreading his arms. His Per-ception was jangling discordantly from all the frenetic energy and emotions swirling around him, but he still sensed the nearby mur-derous intent of the GSI soldier aiming for his head. With a snarl of angry impatience, he shoved the man's aim upward with a snap of Deflection and was upon him in an instant, wrenching the handgun away with a surge of Strength that unpleasantly tweaked something in his shoulder joint. Hilo smashed the soldier across the temple with the butt of the Corta 9 mm and kicked him in the side of the head as he went down into the wet dirt.

"I *said* stop fucking firing!" he roared.

Hilo had come to Euman Island intending to create a dramatic public statement, but perhaps it had worked too well. He'd underestimated the demonstrators' pent-up frustration. They'd certainly been galvanized, but many might soon be dead. In hindsight, Hilo wished he'd brought along more of his warriors, but none could be spared given that the Juen twins and their teams were busy in Lukang. There weren't enough Green Bones here to fight the soldiers and protect so many jadeless civilians.

The GSI soldiers were falling back to Anorco's main building, pulling slain or wounded comrades, still pointing their rifles into the threatening mob. "Let them go!" Hilo ordered. When his words didn't reach far enough, he hurled powerful Deflections in both directions, knocking people staggering and forcing the mercenaries and the protestors apart. Lott and Hami followed the Pillar's lead and did the same, up and down the line as the GSI men continued backing away. One foreign soldier shouted frantically into a radio handset, too quickly for Hilo to make out all the words in Espenian, although it was clear he was calling for reinforcements, most likely from the GSI training compound eight kilometers away.

Hilo grinned savagely as he pointed at the man. "Call your boss," the Pillar shouted in Espenian. "Call Jim Sunto and tell him to come."

He had no idea if the mercenary with the handset heard him or if he relayed the message, but the cameramen from the news trucks did. They crouched on the sidelines like war zone correspondents, creeping closer to get a better shot of Hilo and his men standing in front of the crowd as the military contractors retreated. The space where the fence had stood became, by unspoken agreement, a line in the battlefield that neither side crossed.

Vin approached, trailed by the young, orange-haired Finger and her friends, who staggered under the weight of the metal containers they'd confiscated from the ruins of the helicopter. They dropped them at Hilo's feet and saluted him.

"Jade for our Pillar," the woman exclaimed, her face flushed, her eyes bright with the high of battle. "Far do your enemies flee, Kaul-jen."

Hilo looked past the fence. Summer rain continued to fall, dripping off his hair into his eyes, turning the trampled dirt and grass to mud. Shouting continued on both sides. Some people had climbed on top of the helicopter and were waving Kekonese flags. The Euman Standoff had turned into a siege.

"Not yet, they haven't," he said. "But they will."

CHAPTER

58

A Promise Kept

Eighteen hours later, Jim Sunto arrived in an armored vehicle outside of the Tranquil Suites Hotel. The CEO of Ganlu Solutions International had been at his home near the company's headquarters in Fort Jonsrock when he'd been woken in the predawn hours by a phone call informing him that following a violent clash on Euman Island, two of his employees were dead and another three were in the hospital. A helicopter pilot employed by Anorco was also dead. Nine Kekonese civilians had been killed by gunfire and thirty others had suffered injuries.

Sunto had gotten onto the earliest possible flight to Kekon. Two No Peak clan Fingers intercepted him when he walked into the hotel lobby. They took his sidearm and escorted him into the elevator and up to the top floor, which had been entirely taken over by the Pillar and his men. Sunto was boiling over with fury when he walked into the suite.

"What the fuck have you done, Kaul?"

Hilo was sitting on the sofa, finishing breakfast and watching the news, an ice pack wrapped around his shoulder. Lott Jin was standing by the window, talking into a cell phone, pacing around trying to find better reception. Additional Green Bones of both clans had arrived on Euman Island along with the army, state police, and more reporters. The protestors had withdrawn to the ridge beside the original encampment while GSI contractors salvaged the helicopter and repaired the fence around the Anorco property. Lott had left a dozen No Peak Green Bones at the site of the standoff and was coordinating with Aben Soro in the Mountain clan to establish rotating patrols to maintain peace in the area. The Horn hung up the phone when Sunto came in. He exchanged a glance with the Pillar, then went through a door into an adjoining hotel room.

Hilo took a final bite of a meat bun, chewing and swallowing as he picked up the remote control and hit mute to silence the television, which was replaying dramatic images from yesterday—Hilo on top of the van, the smoking ruins of the crashed Anorco helicopter, GSI soldiers firing into the crowd, people being carried away on stretchers. Hilo wiped his mouth with a napkin and looked up at Sunto calmly. "Do you remember the promise I made to you, Lieutenant?"

The man's aura, normally so subdued and unreadable, was vibrating like a tuning fork. "This is your twisted idea of vengeance against me? You destroyed a helicopter, killed its pilot, and incited a violent mob to charge Anorco's company property and attack my employees. You're a psychopath. You have the innocent blood of a dozen dead people on your hands."

"Spoken with the true hypocrisy of an Espenian," Hilo said with a slow sneer, "by a man who created a company of mercenaries to fight for the highest bidder in wars around the world. What blood do you have on your hands, Sunto?"

Sunto bristled. "Only the unavoidable losses that any commander has to accept."

"Unavoidable because they didn't follow your religion? Or because the Espenian government was paying you millions of thalirs to carry out Operation Firebreak?"

Sunto's jaw tightened. He didn't ask how the Pillar knew about Operation Firebreak; the answer was obvious now that Niko had returned to No Peak. But he wasn't about to be put on the defensive when it was Hilo's actions he had come halfway around the world to confront.

"Don't change the subject to equivocate on morals with me," Sunto growled. "You've set off a diplomatic shitstorm that will backfire on you. I'll see to it that you're charged for the deaths of Anorco and GSI employees as well as provoking public violence and destroying private property. You'll never travel to the ROE again without being arrested."

At Hilo's expression of utter nonchalance toward these statements, Sunto's voice rose and gained vehemence. "The founder of Anorco, Art Wyles, is the incoming secretary of Foreign Trade. You might believe you're untouchable in your own country, but do you think your supporters in the Kekonese government will continue standing behind you when they realize how badly you've jeopardized the relationship with the ROE?"

Hilo took the ice pack off his shoulder. He stood, rolling out the offending joint and stretching his neck from side to side. "You say I've risked Kekon's relationship with the ROE. What have you done to Espenia's standing in Kekon?" The Pillar's voice was low and calm, a sure sign of danger. "For years, your jade-wearing private military contractors have been protecting Anorco's ships as they stripped Kekon's seafloor. Yesterday, your men opened fire on civilians. They could've defended themselves with Deflection or Steel, but they used their rifles. It's all been captured on video and played on every news channel. GSI soldiers shot first, before a single Green Bone or protestor even drew a weapon."

The glower on Sunto's face didn't change, but the cords in his neck tightened and his jade aura swelled. Hilo stalked toward him, head tilted. "Espenian soldiers don't know how to use jade abilities in a crowded city street, surrounded by ordinary people. IBJCS doesn't teach aisho."

Sunto seethed, "Those soldiers wouldn't have fired if their lives hadn't been threatened. No matter how you spin the story in the Kekonese media, the fact is that there wouldn't have been *any* deaths yesterday if you hadn't gone there to make a spectacle of yourself. *You started this, Kaul.*"

Hilo shook his head, his lips parted with scorn. "Do you know much Kekonese history? Green Bones alone didn't defeat the Shotarian army in the Many Nations War. They had the support of the people. In Kekon, it's *always* been Green Bones who inspire the people to fight for themselves." Lott Jin walked back into the room with a large cardboard box, which he set on the coffee table in front of the sofa. Hilo walked over to it, speaking to Sunto over his shoulder. "No matter what happens now, you and your company are done in Kekon."

For all his anger and threats, Sunto had lived in the country long enough to know that Hilo was correct. The importance the Kekonese placed on aisho meant that the public outcry over foreign soldiers wearing Kekonese jade while gunning down unarmed Kekonese citizens was already building into a tsunami in the media, in the streets, in the Royal Council. Wen's rapidly deployed campaign with a roster of top movie stars raising money for the families of the slain and injured protestors was only three hours old but had already amassed hundreds of thousands of dien. More people were heading to Euman Island to shore up the protest, but also gathering in outrage in front of Wisdom Hall. By the end of the week, the Kekonese government would ban GSI and any other foreign private military contractors from ever operating in Kekon again.

Sunto's large hands closed into fists and the veins on his forearms stood out. "I'll see you in court, you smug asshole. I'm going to make sure the Anorco corporation and the Espenian government use every tool in the book to bring you and the No Peak clan down." The CEO of GSI turned on his heel and stalked toward the door. "There are unavoidable casualties in war, but this isn't a war between our countries, as much as you want to make it seem that way. This is your own personal grudge."

"Why can't those two things be the same?" Hilo opened the cardboard box and took out a videocassette. He slid it into the player attached to the room's television, then hit the button on the remote control to unmute the set. Sunto reached the door of the hotel room, but stopped as the voice on the videocassette began speaking.

"GSI's company people didn't say the name 'Operation Firebreak,' but we knew that was what it was. It's what the senior guys all called it. We were ordered not to discuss any of our assignments. The ROE wasn't officially supposed to be in any of those places. Eighty percent of the contractors were ex-Espenian military, though. The Kekonese recruits, we got spread around because we had more jade and were better at certain things, like Deflection and Perception."

Sunto turned around. The person speaking on the recording was backlit and darkened so his face was not visible, and his voice had been electronically altered, but Hilo knew it was Teije Inno. He wondered with idle curiosity if Sunto could recognize the man, whether he knew his soldiers personally the way a good Horn would know his Fists and Fingers, whether beneath the corporate pragmatism he felt any sense of personal betrayal.

On the screen, Teije continued to speak. *"In Udain, our objective was to suppress the Deliverantist rebellion. We trained the Udaini government's soldiers and secret police, and we helped them to track down and round up suspected rebel leaders. The rebels were mostly farmers, townspeople..."* Teije's voice trailed off. When he spoke again, it was more slowly and with a thickness in his voice that could be heard even through the electronic distortion. *"This one time, we were sent to ambush a rebel scouting party, but the intelligence turned out to be wrong. The people we shot weren't soldiers. Two of them were children. And to make it all worse, we were wearing jade and should've Perceived they weren't a threat. It all happened too quickly."* A long pause on the tape. *"I heard about another incident where—"*

Sunto strode over to the television and jabbed the power button, turning off the video playback. He spun toward Hilo and Lott with naked disgust. "Is that your own son, on the video? Did you write a script and force him to recite it into a camera?"

Hilo's face changed with frightening suddenness. "I ought to kill you where you stand," he whispered. "No, that's not Niko."

"So you've found a former GSI employee, a Kekonese man you could threaten or bribe to slander the company without providing any context," Sunto inferred. "Without Operation Firebreak, pro-Ygutanian forces would've spread Deliverantism around the world. Yes, there were occasionally civilian casualties, but they were isolated incidents, a necessary cost in the fight for Truth." Sunto reflexively touched the triangular pendant around his neck, then seemed to remember he was around unTruthful nonbelievers and turned the gesture into a dismissive wave at the television. "Do you think this trash journalism-style tell-all is going to give you some sort of leverage over me? That it'll be newsworthy anywhere outside of Kekon?"

"Not by itself, no," Hilo admitted, as Lott reached back into the box and pulled out more videocassettes, audiotapes, sheafs of paper, and photographs in file folders, all of which he stacked on the coffee table in an impressive pile. "All of it taken together, though? It'll be interesting to some journalists and politicians in Espenia, I would think."

Sunto stared at the accumulating damning evidence. "How did you—"

"You arrogant fuck," Hilo said quietly. "You were so certain the clans were headed to the trash pile of history, as if we haven't been fighting wars ourselves this whole time, on every level and around the world. When I said I'd bring you down, you only ever assumed I'd have you killed."

Sunto's face did not betray him, but his aura did. It bulged and churned.

"It's an election year in your country, isn't it?" Hilo asked. "Operation Firebreak was a trillion-thalir, decade-long initiative that the Espenian government hid inside the War Department budget while supposedly pulling ROE troops out of foreign proxy wars. I'm sure your superiors must have political enemies who would be happy to turn this information into a major scandal." Hilo smiled, not in amusement, but in appreciation of Shae's unfailingly detailed and persistent briefings. "When that happens, someone will have to take the fall. You've worn an Espenian uniform, and you pray to their God and Seer, but your face and blood are Kekonese. They'll turn on you, Sunto."

Sunto was quiet for an entire minute. Then he nodded. "All right, Kaul." His jaw was clenched. "I see how it is. How much am I going to have to pay you?"

"You spenny piece of shit, do you think I want your dirty money?" Hilo exclaimed with so much violence in his expression that even the ex–Navy Angel took an involuntary step backward. Lott and his Fingers near the door tensed, their auras humming. "I'd like to see your company burned to the fucking ground and you thrown into an Espenian prison by the same politicians who paid you so handsomely," the Pillar snarled. "Instead, I'm doing what I *don't* want to do. I'm offering to save you, Sunto."

Hilo pointed to the cassettes and papers on the coffee table, representing countless hours of effort on the part of the clan's White Rats. "I'll lock all of this into a vault where it'll never be seen by anyone. All you have to do in exchange is work for No Peak one last time."

"Work for *you*?" Sunto exclaimed in bewildered suspicion. "To do *what*?"

"Bring down your boss," Hilo said. "Wyles."

"Art Wyles?" Sunto repeated uncomprehendingly.

"You heard me," Hilo said. "I want Anorco destroyed."

Sunto breathed through his teeth. "GSI is part of the Anorco Global Resources conglomerate. Art Wyles invested in my company from the beginning. He's the reason we landed the War Department contract. I won't turn on a friend and fellow Truthbearer."

Hilo was tempted to remind the man that they had been friends at one time as well. *Espenian friendship*, Hilo thought, *is worth exactly what you can pay for it.*

Instead he said, "Wyles is selling his share of Anorco to a private investor. That private investor is the Mountain clan. Unless you find a way to extricate GSI from its parent corporation, you'll soon be answering to Ayt Madashi." As Sunto's face slackened with disbelief, Hilo could not help but smile at the irony that one of his detested enemies should end up eaten by the other. "The company you founded based on supposedly modern, Truthbearing, Espenian ideals will be used to protect Mountain clan assets and advance Mountain clan interests."

"That's not…" Sunto shook his head. "Art's stepping down from Anorco, but he never…" Hilo could see that the man wanted to accuse him of lying, but behind the stare of blistering animosity, confusion was spinning quickly into doubt and grim understanding.

Sunto broke eye contact first. He went over to the sofa Hilo had vacated and sat down hard. Hilo stood in front of the man and leaned down to peer into his face. "Wyles betrayed you. He's selling his company to protect himself. I know this because I know Ayt Madashi. *You* know Art Wyles. What does the Mountain clan have that could bring him down?"

Sunto's jaw worked back and forth. "Proof," he said reluctantly, but with certainty. Even with Hilo watching him, he touched the Dawn of Icana pendant to his lips and whispered a prayer in Espenian, perhaps for strength or forgiveness—Hilo could not tell. "Proof of Art's criminal connections to the Crews. Plenty of Port Massy tabloids have brought it up before—old photos of him with Joren Gasson and other members of the Baker Street Crew—but it was always just gossip and rumors. Anything concrete could sink his political career or land him in prison. That's the one and only thing I can think of that could make him sell Anorco."

Bitter silence stretched between the two men as they stewed in hatred and grudging regard for each other and their mutual enemies. Hilo nodded and straightened. "The sale of Anorco will close in six weeks. My Weather Man tells me it can't proceed if Wyles is charged with financial crimes and his assets are frozen. She's also told me that if Anorco is broken up, you'll be able to regain control of GSI in a management buyout."

Hilo studied Sunto's wretched expression as if unsure whether he wanted to put a comforting hand on the man's shoulder or snap his neck. "You and your mercenaries will never set foot in Kekon again. You'll never recruit another member of No Peak." He looked at the stacks of tapes on the table in unspoken reminder that he could still bring GSI crumbling down. "But you can save yourself and your company, if you tell me right now that you'll do as I ask. You'll help me to bring down Anorco and the Mountain clan."

From the moment he'd met Jim Sunto, Hilo had judged him to be refreshingly pragmatic, a man with no allegiance to anyone except himself and his foreign God. Sunto put a hand over his eyes for a second. When he looked up at Hilo again, his futile anger had solidified into dignified resignation—the expression of a captive bear coming to the realization that it must debase itself to eat. "What do you want me to do?"

Lott brought over a phone and set it down on the coffee table.

"You can start," Hilo said, "by talking to a woman named Kelly Dauk."

the upcoming investigation linked the company's assets to organized crime syndicates, the conglomerate would likely be broken up.

According to Hilo, it was the first time Kelly Dauk had ever accepted, even grudgingly, any outreach on the part of the No Peak clan. The woman had an entire case file on Art Wyles and had been trying, along with federal prosecutors, to gather concrete evidence of his crimes for years. The one thing they needed was for Wyles's trusted business partner, Jim Sunto, to meet with the suspect and elicit a confession while wearing a wire.

Sunto had confronted Wyles to demand an explanation for the unexpected sale of Anorco, and thus GSI—to a Kekonese entity, no less. After attempts to convince Wyles to halt the sale, threats to tell his wife about his mistresses, and reminders of their joint involvement in Operation Firebreak, Sunto had prevailed on Wyles as a fellow Truthbearer. He'd walked out of the room with a recording of Wyles admitting to his past dealings with the Baker Street Crew but assuring Sunto that once he was installed as secretary of Foreign Trade, Joren Gasson would help them take care of the Kekonese problem. "Men of Truth pay their debts," he'd promised. Art Wyles, Shae suspected, would be paying his debt in prison for a while.

The Cabriola was finally forced to a stop by the thick throng of people standing in front of the iron gates of the Ayt mansion. The driver said, over his shoulder, "This is as far as we can go."

Shae opened the door and got out of the car. Her two bodyguards got out with her. "Are you sure this is a good idea, Kaul-jen?" one of them asked in an undertone. She hadn't told Hilo, or even Woon, where she was going this afternoon.

"I know what I'm doing." Shae approached the mansion's gates. Her bodyguards flanked her but there was no trouble. People stared and murmured but stepped aside, and even the news reporters that ran up to try and take photos kept a respectful distance. It seemed everyone present was aware that an event like this had never happened before. Certainly, the gathering in front of the Ayt mansion was something Shae could never have imagined. Over a thousand members of the Mountain clan—Fists and Fingers, Lantern Men,

CHAPTER
59

❧

End of a Long Judgment

the twenty-sixth year, tenth month

The driver of Shae's Cabriola Sentry inched past rows of cars parked haphazardly all along the shoulder of the winding hilly roads of High Ground. The motion of the car became too uncomfortable for Shae to continue reading. She put away her papers as soon as she'd finished perusing the scanned news articles from the *Adamont Capita Tribute* that the clan's satellite office in AC had faxed to her that morning.

Business tycoon and politician Art Wyles had been indicted on charges of corruption and money laundering in connection to the infamous Baker Street Crew criminal empire. Kelly Dauk, chair of the National Assembly's Anti-Corruption Panel, was convening a special government hearing on the matter. The pending sale of Wyles's company Anorco to foreign investors had been blocked. If

Luckbringers—standing in silent but public condemnation of their own Pillar. As Shae reached the front of the crowd, she was forced to duck under a huge, hand-painted white cloth banner that half a dozen Mountain Green Bones were holding up on wooden poles. It unfurled in long lines of writing:

The Pillar is the master of the clan, the spine of the body. The Pillar must uphold aisho and never break it. The Pillar should not consort with foreign criminals. The Pillar knows when it is time for another to lead.

To someone who was not Kekonese, the demonstration would seem tame, even oddly respectful. There was no shouting or chanting, nothing like the mob of protestors Hilo had so easily roused to violence on Euman Island last month. For a Green Bone clan, however, the situation was shocking and unprecedented. Green Bones kept clan issues within the clan. Openly demonstrating disapproval and opposition to the Pillar, in sight of enemies, civilians, and the media... It was outright rebellion. It was national news that eclipsed even the deaths on Euman Island and certainly the downfall of some politician in Espenia.

A thick wall of tension stood between the Green Bones holding the white banner and the dozen of Ayt's loyal Fists who guarded the gates of the estate, hands resting on the hilts of their moon blades, watching their fellow clan members with wary venom. Shae could feel the animosity as tangibly as if she could Perceive it. Civil war was coming.

She walked straight up to the most senior of the Fists in sight. "Tell your Pillar that the Weather Man of No Peak is here to speak with her."

The guard spat at Shae's feet. "You Kauls are scheming, opportunistic dogs. None of you are half as green as Ayt-jen. She should've cut off your heads years ago."

Shae said, "If you're truly loyal and obedient to your Pillar, you'll carry my message to her. Tell her I'm here on my own and not as an emissary of my brother."

Still glaring hatefully at Shae, the Fist barked an order to one of his Fingers, who turned and hurried into the mansion. Shae waited patiently. The crowd waited with her in the sweltering, late summer heat. Sweat shone on their faces. People fanned themselves and sipped water and shifted their weight, but still they remained. After several minutes, the Finger reemerged, and with great reluctance, the Fist ordered that the gate be opened and Shae be allowed inside.

She was escorted up the paved path to the stately front double doors, into a spacious wood-floored foyer, and down a hall to a thick, closed door. "Wait outside," she instructed her bodyguards, then pushed open the door to Ayt Madashi's office.

Shae had never before been in Ayt Mada's presence without wearing jade. Seeing Ayt without being able to Perceive her unmistakably dense, powerful aura was like seeing a photograph of the Pillar instead of the real woman. Ayt was standing at one of the large windows that spilled sunlight across her overflowing office. She was wearing tan slacks and a draped burgundy tank top, her arms bare as usual and densely encircled with jade. Even in the heat, she had a white silk scarf snugly wrapped around her neck. She did not turn at Shae's entrance. From her office window, Ayt couldn't see past her front gates, but she was no doubt Perceiving all the members of the clan gathered in rebellion outside the walls of her estate. It was a sight Shae would always remember: the Pillar of the Mountain in profile, standing straight-backed and silent in the sunlight, arms crossed, her gaze unmoving and slightly off-center. A statue of an old warlord before her final battle.

A heavy apprehension gathered and settled in the pit of Shae's stomach. Every time she'd confronted Ayt Mada in the past, the consequences had been dramatic and irrevocable, affecting both of their clans and their lives for years afterward. She'd come here counting on a pattern that seemed set by the gods.

"It was cleverly done, Kaul-jen," Ayt said at last.

Shae stepped farther into the room. "I've learned from a clever enemy."

Ten days ago, Iyilo's interview with KNB news anchor Toh Kita had aired on national television. In thorough testimony, the imprisoned barukan smuggler detailed over two decades of Ti Pasuiga's collaboration with the Mountain clan. Iyilo explained that during his employment as Zapunyo's closest aide and bodyguard, he and his cousin Soradiyo had acted as messengers between the Uwiwan kingpin and the Mountain's Pillar. The conspiracy to assassinate Kaul Hilo with a car bomb, which had instead killed Maik Kehn and injured several civilians, had been suggested and encouraged by Ayt Mada in exchange for promised lenience over jade smuggling.

Afterward, Iyilo had cleverly cut his boss out of the conversation and conspired directly with the Mountain to take over Zapunyo's business and kill his sons. With undisguised self-satisfaction, he told viewers that he agreed to partner with Ayt Mada in exchange for the promise that the Oortokon Conflict Refugee Act would be passed in the Royal Council—which it had, due to the sudden death of former Chancellor Son Tomarho.

Iyilo gave further detailed information about the ensuing triangle of trade established between Ti Pasuiga, the Matyos, and the Mountain clan, to move smuggled jade and shine from Kekon to the Uwiwa Islands to the Orius continent. Ayt Mada, Iyilo explained, controlled the price on the black market by buying back jade for her own clan and bringing it into the country covertly through Lukang, a scheme that had provoked a civil war within the Six Hands Unity clan. She thereafter allowed and even helped Ti Pasuiga and the Matyos barukan to move jade unmolested into Ygutan and East Oortoko to supply the nekolva program and other Slow War proxy conflicts in exchange for a cut of the profits, which she funneled back into growing the Mountain's legitimate businesses. At times during the leisurely interview, Iyilo spoke of Ayt Mada with admiration and cautious respect as a business partner, at other times he expressed sneering disdain for all Green Bones, and at others still, such as when he lamented the way Ayt had abandoned his cousin Soradiyo to No Peak's vengeance, he was openly bitter and full of resentment.

When asked if he feared Ayt would kill him for speaking, the fallen kingpin of Ti Pasuiga chuckled. "Of course she will kill me," he said, with a dismissive wave at the camera. "There's a saying in Shotarian: 'Marry the devil, get the devil's mother.' It's the deal you can't escape. The jade business is the devil and Ayt Mada is its mother."

Iyilo's television interview had been immediately amplified by newspaper and radio, and excerpts were being rebroadcast despite outrage from Ayt's supporters, who insisted the interview was fiction, a ploy by the No Peak clan to bring down the Mountain by bribing a condemned criminal to lie for their benefit.

Nevertheless, the damage that Shae and Anden had hoped for was done. Iyilo's testimony was too believable. It did not possess any of the rehearsed quality of a canned speech, but instead had the defiant, nostalgic, rambling quality of a man with nothing left to lose, taking the opportunity to get all his thoughts off his chest. At the request of Kekon National Broadcasting, two capable Green Bones of the famously neutral Haedo Shield clan had accompanied Toh Kita, and they swore on their jade and their clan's honor that they did not Perceive any deception in the prisoner's statements.

Iyilo's stories validated whispered rumors that had circulated for years within Mountain circles. A few days after the news broke, the clan fractures became impossible to hide. Ayt Atosho, thirty-five years old and long the successor-in-waiting, remained silent, but his relatives spoke for him. Councilwoman Koben Tin Bett was the first to sound the call for Ayt Mada to step down as Pillar. Six high-profile Lantern Men defected from the Mountain clan en masse; two of them went so far as to switch allegiance to No Peak. Four other members of the Royal Council declared they were ending their affiliation with the Mountain and were joining the ranks of independent councilmen; they would not accept patronage from the clan until Ayt Mada was out of power.

And now this: Ayt's own warriors standing outside her gate.

"Did you have Iyilo killed?" Shae asked.

"No," Ayt answered bluntly. "Perhaps it was done by someone acting out of service to the Mountain, but I didn't whisper his name. Why would I? All the damage he could do was already done. I've told you before, Kaul Shae-jen, I don't kill out of spite." It was a remarkable admission—Ayt confessing that she no longer possessed an iron grip on the clan, that she was losing control of the people under her.

Iyilo had been scheduled to be extradited to Kekon, but security in Uwiwan prisons was notoriously poor. Within forty-eight hours of the interview being aired, Iyilo was found dead in his cell, his throat slit by one of the guards, who was himself nowhere to be found. Most people assumed the Mountain had done it. Some believed that No Peak had killed the man now that they had no use for him. Yet others said it had been one of Iyilo's enemies in the Uwiwa Islands, of which he had many. Shae supposed it didn't matter what the truth was. If Hilo had given the order, he had not informed her. He had, however, kept his word to the man, as he always did. On the afternoon before his death, Iyilo had spoken for two hours on a long-distance phone call with his wife and children, all of them safely in Port Massy with new identities.

Ayt turned to face Shae at last. The past several years had not been kind to the Pillar. Her spine was unbowed, but gray the color of steel wool showed at the roots of her coarse, chin-length dyed hair and there were deep grooves between her nose and lips from a lifetime of holding her mouth straight and steady. The two women regarded each other across a gulf of long understanding and enmity. Shae wondered if Ayt was noticing her decline as well, pitying her jadelessness.

When did we get old? Shae wondered. Some believed, with little scientific substantiation, that jade slowed aging, at least for a while, although no one would suggest the lifestyle of a Green Bone was conducive to longevity. There was even a saying among Green Bones: *Jade warriors are young, and then they are ancient.* It had been true of her grandfather, Shae admitted, and it seemed true of Ayt Mada as well.

"Would you like some tea?" Ayt asked unexpectedly. "I have a fresh pot steeping." She crossed to one of the leather armchairs and sat down.

"I would like that." Shae seated herself on the sofa across from Ayt.

Ayt took out two cups and poured for her guest first. It occurred to Shae that without any sense of Perception, she would have no warning if Ayt decided to kill her, nor would she have any chance of defending herself. Ayt could snap her neck as easily as pour her tea.

Shae took the proffered cup and sipped. Her hands did not shake.

I don't kill out of spite, Ayt had said, and she'd never, in all the years their clans had warred, given Shae reason to believe that was untrue. Despite all the cold-blooded things she had done, all the times she'd broken aisho for her own aims, Ayt Mada followed her own rules.

"I'm impressed you moved so many pieces so quickly." Ayt poured her own tea and wrapped her long fingers around the cup. "The Six Hands Unity clan is ruined, and their hold over Lukang broken. Whatever powerful threat or bribe you worked on Iyilo, it made him sing beautifully for the press. I'm still working out how you made Sunto into your tool after that ridiculous spectacle on Euman Island, but I'm well aware that Kaul Hilo has a gift for turning even his bitterest enemies to his own purpose. The foreigner Wyles has been brought down and the sale of Anorco, which I spent years orchestrating, has been forced to a halt." Ayt tapped the edge of her ceramic teacup and lifted it to her lips. She sipped and leaned back in her seat with a slow exhalation. "Any one of these, I could've anticipated and overcome, but all together, they were too destructive. I couldn't have pulled it off better myself."

"You give me too much credit," Shae said. "It was a full family effort."

Months ago, Shae had been the one most demoralized by Ayt's master plan, convinced that the Pillar of the Mountain had finally solved the long riddle of how to destroy No Peak. The rest of the family had simply gone to work. None of it could've been accomplished if the clan did not have its unique advantages—if Jaya was not a powerful force in Toshon with her Little Knives, if Anden could not travel covertly to the Uwiwa Islands, if successive Horns of No Peak had not embedded White Rats everywhere the clan needed them, if the Weather Man's office in Espenia had not detected the Mountain's scheme in the first place and connected it with the right lawyers and politicians, if Hilo had not already spent years determined to ruin GSI.

Shae had spent decades admiring Ayt Mada as a master strategist. Perhaps Ayt, for the sake of her own pride, would prefer to attribute her defeat to the cunning and ability of a younger woman. Shae knew the truth. She was not smarter than Ayt Mada; she never had been. The way to defeat a chess master was not with greater genius, but by forcing her to play a different game.

The No Peak clan had grown many limbs across the country and around the world to defend itself from attacks by a larger foe. It had raced to become modern and responsive in order to survive. If anyone had tried to win against Ayt on her terms, they would've been destroyed. But from the beginning Hilo had surrounded himself with the people he most needed, and so No Peak was propelled by many strong personalities pushing and pulling against each other but somehow together carrying the clan. The family had suffered terrible strife and losses that had at times torn them apart, but they were also bound tightly in a way that Ayt and the Kobens could never be.

"I imagine you think of yourselves as heroes." Ayt's voice was sharp with sudden scorn. "You've roused the common people in a show of strength, brought down the foreign companies, kicked out the mercenaries, and turned my own clan against me in disgrace." The familiar fire in Ayt's eyes flared and her voice was its old steel. "Yet all you've done is delay the inevitable. There will be others— other foreign powers, other mercenaries, others grasping for our jade and for the soul of our country." Ayt spoke in a hiss. "The struggle between our clans will continue, for what purpose? I would've built an unassailable bulwark. I would've put Kekon firmly in control of its own destiny."

"You would've put *yourself* in control of Kekon's destiny," Shae replied. "That's not the same thing. You're one woman, Ayt-jen—not a god, no matter how brilliant you are, no matter how much jade you wear." She looked Ayt squarely in the face without uncertainty, without fear or doubt. "Green Bones weren't *meant* to be gods, not until the day of the Return, and so long as we try, that day will never come."

"The gods don't care about people or nations." The sudden roughness in Ayt's voice hinted at a depth of pain she never let show. "We're all the same to them. They don't care who lives or dies, who wins or loses, who should lead and who should suffer. *I do.*"

Shae swallowed her sympathy. "It's over, Ayt-jen," she said. "You've lost your final, masterful gamble, but most importantly, you've lost control of your clan. Your own warriors stand outside of your gates demanding that you step aside. To remain the Pillar, you would have to slaughter all of them." A cloud passed over the sun and Ayt's spacious office dimmed. Neither of the women moved. "I don't believe you will do that. Even you will not shed the blood of so many of your own Green Bones."

Quietly, Ayt said, "Even now, you don't know what I'm capable of, Kaul-jen."

Shae felt a shiver travel down her spine, but she replied calmly. "I'm perfectly aware that you've always done what you deem necessary, no matter how terrible. But I also believe you when you say you did them not for your own satisfaction, but for the good of your clan and country. What would be good for them now, Ayt-jen? For you to resign willingly, to transition power to your nephew—even if you judge him and his family to be lacking—or to unleash bloodshed that'll tear your clan apart and set it back for years to come?"

When Ayt did not answer, Shae once again wished intensely that she still possessed her sense of Perception. The Pillar's face was suddenly as unreadable as blank marble.

She touched her bare throat, where her jade had once rested. *We've lost so much, all of us.* She and Ayt Mada could never escape the rivalry of their clans, but they understood each other, as women who were green in a man's world.

"Do you remember the story from history about King Eon II?" she asked the Pillar. "He gave up his throne in disgrace. His supporters wanted him to continue to fight, but he laid down his crown to spare the country from further destruction and suffering. Even though the people couldn't understand or appreciate his sacrifice, he ensured the nation could rise in the future without him. Only he, the gods, and those in later generations whom he would never meet, would know he did the right thing.

"Do the right thing now, Ayt-jen. Step down peacefully, and I promise you that I'll prevail upon my brother to forge a lasting truce between the clans. We'll renounce the blood feud that's existed between us ever since Lan died." Speaking Lan's name seemed to stir something in the room, and inside Shae's chest. "No Peak will pledge friendship and brotherhood to your nephew Ayt Ato. Together, we'll lay out a plan that will bring the clans together, gradually and equitably."

The corners of Ayt's mouth lifted in humorless irony. "So now, after years of war, when you finally hold the advantage, you'd have me believe you're in favor of bringing the clans together? Do you expect me not to see that you mean the No Peak clan will conquer the Mountain?"

Shae shook her head. "The time for conquest is past us. Our clans are too large to merge unwillingly. The younger Green Bones on both sides have fought alongside each other against clanless and foreigners more often than they've fought each other, and the older ones have seen enough war. If you pass the position of Pillar down to your nephew, Hilo and I will retire within five years, and all the old grudges can finally leave with us."

Ayt was silent for a long minute. She did not look at Shae but instead stared out the large windows. A slight curve to her shoulders suggested a dragging, unseen weight. At last she asked, "Your Pillar will agree to this?"

"He will." As it had become apparent No Peak would not only survive Ayt's scheming but emerge ahead of its rivals in the public eye, the conversations she'd had with Hilo on the patio had turned toward talk of the future, and how to secure the clan's strength. "I can't swear on my jade anymore, but I would."

Ayt closed her eyes, then opened them again. They glittered from within a nest of hard wrinkles. "Many years ago, Kaul Shae-jen, I sought you out. I wished to persuade you to join me, to chart a stronger course for our clans and the country. You refused. Ever since then, I have hated and admired you for that choice. Surely, you see the irony of this moment, as you sit here, trying to convince me to accept your vision instead of mine."

"Look at us, Ayt-jen." Shae sighed, from deep within her core.

"We're old women now. We've tried to kill each other for so long and instead by some cruel luck we owe each other our lives. Maybe it's time we stepped away and let the next generation try to do better than we did."

Ayt finished her tea and stood. Without looking at Shae again, she crossed to the window and became an outward gazing statue once more, but now the reddening light struck her differently, turning her from the still figure of a waiting general to that of a lone survivor on the empty battlefield.

"Perhaps you were right, Kaul-jen, on that day in the Temple of Divine Return. The cruelest thing you ever did to me was not slit my throat." The Pillar said, "Leave me. You've said and done enough."

———

Shae sat in the Cabriola. The sun was slowly descending behind the trees. She had been in the car for over an hour. One of her bodyguards stayed in the car with her, and the other stood around nearby, but they did not interrupt her thoughts.

Her phone rang. "Hi, Ma," Tia said when Shae picked up. "I know you said not to call your cell phone unless it's really important, but your secretary said you left the office hours ago, and Da wants to know if you're planning to be home for dinner."

Shae looked at the Mountain Green Bones still standing at the gates of the Ayt mansion. Some had left and others had arrived, but many had been there the entire time, standing from dawn to dusk and perhaps through the night as well. As stoic as students in a martial school training in the sun and the rain, hardening themselves to the physical and mental hardship that went along with becoming Green Bone warriors.

"I don't think so, Tia-se," Shae told her daughter. "Don't wait for me."

"Can you take me to the mall on Sixthday?" Tia asked.

"Maybe. Finish your homework before I get home and we'll talk about it." Shae hung up and stared at the phone in her hand. *Let her stay this way for as long as possible, just an ordinary soon-to-be teenage girl*, Shae prayed to no one god in particular, simply offering up a wish to the universe. She knew it could not last forever. Tia already struggled with the cruelty of her mother's world. As she grew older and understood even more, it would drive her apart from the family.

Unless, starting today, that world could be different than the one Shae had known. *Let it be possible. Let this be a world where I can keep her.*

Something about the crowd changed. Shae's bodyguards Perceived it and turned alertly toward the gates. Shae got out of the Cabriola and stood in front of the car. She could not see anything different at first, but then a faint ripple of backward movement opened a gap in the crowd. Ayt Mada came down the path from the front of her mansion, her loyal Fists and Fingers flanking her on all sides. The great iron gates opened with smooth electronic silence unbroken by any other sound. The Pillar walked out among the dissidents, and even the ones holding the white banner condemning their leader murmured warily and touched their foreheads. *Even the biggest tigers grow old*, Hilo had once said. But even the oldest tiger was still a tiger.

Ayt's gaze did not seek out her longtime enemy standing across the street, but Shae knew the Pillar of the Mountain could Perceive her, waiting and watching with everyone else. Ayt Mada adjusted the coils of jade on her arms. She raised her chin and spoke in the firm, clear voice she'd become known for over the years, the one that Shae had heard in person and on television and that needed no amplification because it silenced those around it.

"The Pillar is the master of the clan, the spine of the body," Ayt declared. "But the clan is more than the Pillar, and a body cannot be at war with itself. I will not justify all the actions I've taken for the ultimate benefit of my clan and my country. However, it's clear that too much doubt has been cast on my past decisions for the Mountain clan to remain strong and united under my leadership.

"I hereby step down immediately as Pillar of the Mountain. I name my nephew, Ayt Atosho, as my successor. I give him my blessing. I ask all the members of the clan—Green Bones and non–Green Bones alike, Fists and Fingers, Luckbringers and Lantern Men—to pledge their allegiance to him as you've done for me. Under Heaven and on jade."

The momentous announcement was met with powerful silence. Then voices rose, reporters shouted questions, and Ayt Madashi turned and walked back into the house.

CHAPTER

60

~

Final Debts

Ayt Atosho's first act as Pillar of the Mountain clan was to throw the city of Janloon an enormous Autumn Festival celebration. The Koben family, eager to rehabilitate the clan's damaged image, spared no effort connecting the clan's change in leadership to the public's good feelings about the popular holiday. Streets in Mountain districts were lined with glowing lanterns in alternating colors—the traditional festive autumn red and the pale green of the Mountain clan. Vans full of Fingers and Wie Lon Temple students drove around town handing out yellow cakes decorated with the clan's insignia. Ayt Ato's handsome face was seen all over town as well as on television talk shows and in full-page newspaper announcements.

The No Peak clan held more subdued holiday celebrations in which members whispered cautious optimism and wide-ranging speculation about the future. The clan's oldest and most formidable enemy was out of power. It seemed impossible to believe. An entire generation of No Peak Green Bones had grown up thinking of Ayt Mada and the Mountain clan in the same breath—as one constant, hateful threat. No one yet knew what to think of her replacement, or what to expect from the Kobens.

Hilo called the entire family and its closest friends together for dinner. After a leisurely meal consisting of all the traditional seasonal favorites—gingery seafood soup, thrice-glazed smoked pork, spicy pickled vegetables, and sticky fruit paste cakes—the Pillar said, "It's a nice evening, still warm outside. You should all stay as long as you want." A gentle signal to those not in the inner circle of the clan's leadership to take their leave. They did so promptly, knowing the Pillar and his advisors would be talking for hours to come.

Sulima helped Hilo's mother back to her room. Kaul Wan Ria was eighty-five years old now, the longest-lived member of the family, though mentally and physically feeble. Woon Papi, Juen Nu, Juen's grown sons, and Maik Cam went out into the courtyard with a bottle of hoji, decks of cards, and a relayball. Kehn's widow, Lina, and Juen's wife, Imrie, took their conversation into the garden. Tia wanted to play a movie in the home theater. When Jirhuya offered to join her, Anden looked relieved and a little surprised. Ever since the violence on Euman Island, Jirhu had behaved more nervously around the family than usual. Hilo suspected it had caused some friction between him and Anden, but what did they expect? If they intended to stay together, Jirhu would eventually see his partner's relatives for the Green Bones they were, no matter how much distance he tried to maintain from the clan.

Hilo looked around at those who remained at the dinner table: Shae and Wen together on one side, Lott and Niko on the other, Anden at the far end. He wrapped a hand tightly around the armrest of his chair, warding against the familiar but undiminished pain that closed over his heart every time he felt Ru's absence. One peach cake remained on the plate in the middle of the table, and Hilo imagined, as clearly as if it were really happening, his son jumping up out of his chair to claim it. The only other person missing was Jaya, who'd returned to Toshon. Everyone else was gazing at him expectantly. For a few seconds, he didn't speak, overcome by a sense of poignant pride.

Then he said, "Ayt Atosho has asked for a meeting between our clans."

He let Shae explain further. "The Mountain wants to discuss a pledge of friendship," the Weather Man said. "They made the request properly and with all the expected assurances, although they want it to happen soon, and privately, with only the Pillar and two attendants from each side. We would choose the time and place."

No one was entirely surprised by the news, although Lott noted, "That happened quickly." Ayt Mada had resigned only three weeks ago. For her successor to so quickly reach out to his aunt's enemies might be regarded as hasty and weak, signaling a lack of savvy on the part of the new Pillar. If Hilo were to offer counsel to the Kobens, which he assuredly would not, he would say it was a bad idea to meet with one's enemies before being sure of one's friends—something he doubted the Kobens could claim with confidence.

Wen poured tea for everyone out of a fresh pot. "They must feel they don't have a choice. Stepping into the shadow of Ayt Mada, the Kobens have to move as quickly as possible to prove they're in charge." Many in the Mountain were still loyal to Ayt Mada and considered the Kobens to be a second-rate Green Bone family undeservedly rising to the top because of their size, traditionalist zeal, and media darling scion as opposed to any real merit.

Ayt Ato, no doubt aware of his detractors, had already cleaned house. Aben Soro and Iwe Kalundo, Ayt Mada's Horn and Weather Man, had both been asked to follow their Pillar's lead and resign from their positions, which they had done immediately. Aben had been Horn for so long that retirement was no surprise. Iwe was also an old-timer, too closely connected to Ayt Mada and too deeply embroiled in the years of activities that Iyilo had detailed in his interview.

Shae accepted the cup of tea her sister-in-law placed in front of her and eyed the remaining cakes but resisted taking one. "Right now, the only people Ayt Ato can trust are the members of the Koben family." The new Pillar had named his second cousin Sando Kin as his Horn, and one of his uncles, an experienced but relatively unknown Lantern Man named Koben Opon, as Weather Man. "Everyone knows Ayt Mada passed the leadership onto her nephew reluctantly and doesn't truly support him, so that might leave the door open for potential challengers."

"He's afraid we'll take advantage of his inexperience as Pillar and the disunity in his clan," Lott reasoned. "We have the public on our side right now, and the Kobens are afraid more of the Mountain's Lantern Men will defect to No Peak."

Wen said, "Ayt Ato's the pretty face of his family, but I think he understands his position and is more shrewd than most people give him credit for. If he's learned from his aunt Koben Bett, he'll try diplomacy before blades. He married a woman in the Tem family to cement their support. Now he wants to secure a peace agreement with us so he has time to sort out his own house."

Hilo's mouth tilted ironically. "An alliance with the Koben family is what that old snake Yun Dorupon pushed for decades ago."

"Back then, Ayt Mada was determined to annex No Peak and send us all to our graves," Shae said. "Any alliance would've been on unequal footing with the threat of destruction hanging over us. The Kobens have grown in power since then, but we've grown more. They can't conquer us."

Anden nodded from the other end of the table. "We've changed a lot as a clan. Now, maybe for the first time, we're in a stronger position than the Mountain. The question is whether friendship with the Kobens will keep it that way."

Hilo could feel Shae's eyes drilling into him. She was the one who'd gone to Ayt Mada's mansion to convince their old enemy to yield. "I swore on behalf of the family that the grudges would end, Hilo," she'd told him when she returned. "I promised we'd begin to bring the clans together, without bloodshed."

Hilo cut one of the remaining sticky cakes in half. "Where's Ayt Mada now?"

"She's left the Ayt estate and moved into another of the Mountain's properties, a townhouse in the Commons," Lott said. "She hasn't gone out or spoken to the media, but it seems she's been cooperative in peacefully transitioning power to her nephew."

"How many people does she have with her?" Hilo asked.

"A handful of Fists are guarding her. All of them are her own loyalists." Lott paused, looking straight at the Pillar before answering the question that was truly being asked. "It wouldn't be easy to get to her, but it can be done. The townhouse is far less secure than the Ayt estate."

"Hilo," Shae objected, "the Mountain is reaching out to make peace."

"Ayt Mada is no longer the Pillar of the Mountain," Hilo reminded her tersely. "Any peace we make with the Koben family doesn't extend to that old bitch. As long as Ayt Mada breathes, she's a threat to us. She'll find a way to control the Mountain without being Pillar. We haven't fought her for thirty years only to buy some act of her stepping down. She has to die, sooner or later. Better sooner."

Wen agreed, "As long as Ayt Mada lives, we can't trust in any alliance with the Mountain."

A cheer and laughter broke out from somewhere outside. Hilo could hear raised voices and something that sounded like a relayball hitting the side of the house.

"Now isn't the time," Shae argued. "Ayt's been judged in the court of public opinion and lost the support of her own clan. I agree with you that it would be just like her to try to come back, to exert power from behind the scenes, but she won't be able to do that right away. She'll let her nephew have his moment in the spotlight and allow everyone to believe she's out of the picture. We should do the same. If we kill Ayt Mada now, the new Pillar will be honor bound to respond to us as enemies. It'll sabotage all chance of a lasting peace."

"Sparing Ayt Mada's life has become a bad habit of yours, Shae."

His sister gave him a scathing look. "Once Ayt Ato's position as Pillar is secure and peace has been established between the clans, public attention will fade from Ayt Mada. Then, we can find a way to whisper her name quietly. But first, we have to get to that point."

"The Weather Man's made her opinion clear," Hilo said, taking half of the divided fruit paste cake and putting the other half on Wen's plate. "What about the rest of you?"

Lott looked down, his bow-shaped mouth curved into a pensive frown. "I've hated the Mountain clan for a long time, but in the years I've been First Fist and then Horn, we've had to work alongside them as much as we have against them. Even if we don't see eye to eye with the new leaders, they're not the same as Ayt Mada. They haven't done anything that makes them our blood enemies. I don't believe anyone—not even our foes—should be condemned because of their relatives, or forced down a path they had no say in."

The rest of the table was silent. Lott Jin was the only one in the room who was not a Kaul, but no one could deny he'd been devoted to the clan for decades, overcoming a lot of struggle and doubt in his own life to become a capable Horn for the past seven years. "Sometimes, it seems like violence is a destiny that's impossible to deny," Lott added, "but once in a while, there are small windows of time when that can change. I agree with the Weather Man. With Ayt Mada gone, we should set aside our feud."

Hilo looked to Anden, who glanced at Lott with a curious expression of muted admiration before taking off his glasses and wiping them on the hem of his shirt as he thought about his reply. "The Koben family is large, but they're nowhere near as green or cunning as Ayt Mada or the people around this table. They're outspoken and capable in the moment, but they aren't clever enough to seek out new opportunities to really gain advantage." Anden put his glasses back on and said to the table, "I think we should agree to friendship with the Kobens and do our best to keep them in the leadership of the Mountain clan. That way, over time our clan will do better than theirs. If and when the clans do come together, No Peak will be dominant, with the Kaul family and not the Kobens leading the country and all Green Bones."

Hilo smiled at his cousin's cold and farsighted assessment. He recalled that when they were young, he used to tease Anden for his careful and polite demeanor, trying to get him to lighten up. Now he could not imagine wanting Anden to be any other way, as it only made the green in his soul more apparent at times like this.

"What do you say, Niko?" Hilo asked his nephew, who had been quiet so far. "You should have a say in this decision as well, since you and Jaya and your Green Bones will be living with it more than us. Could you work with Ayt Ato? Would you trust the Koben family's pledge of friendship?"

Niko looked up at his uncle. "I wouldn't trust anyone," he said. "But I'd still work with them. I don't have to like or agree with the Koben family, but I've met Ayt Ato and watched him over the years, and I think I understand him in some ways. He needs something from us, and I agree with Uncle Anden that it'll be to our advantage in the long run to give it to him."

"It's decided, then. As Pillar, I've relied on all of you for so many years and won't stop now." Hilo turned to his Weather Man. "You're right, Shae. The next generation shouldn't be burdened by our vendettas. Tell the Mountain we agree to meet." He glanced back at his nephew. "I want you at this meeting, Niko. You'll come in place of the Horn."

Lott's head jerked backward in surprise. "The Horn should be in the room," he protested. "I'm not saying this in disrespect. Any discussion of an alliance has to include the greener side of the clan."

Hilo said, "It's more important that Niko be there. When I retire as Pillar, Niko will be the one to deal with Ayt Ato, so really, this alliance will impact him more than me. He should be involved in whatever agreement we come to. I'll discuss all the issues on the military side with you beforehand and bring them to the meeting."

"Kaul-jen," Lott objected once more, but Hilo's stern look silenced him.

Hilo spoke again to Niko. "You'll be sitting at the table."

Everyone looked surprised at this, even Wen. For four years, Niko had been learning every aspect of the clan's operations under the tutelage of the Horn and the Weather Man and other leaders on both sides of the clan. By all accounts, he was contributing in useful ways. He'd proposed a new IT system on the military side of the clan that would better optimize deployment of Fingers across multiple regions. He resolved a dispute between two Lantern Men by having one man's son work for the other as restitution. And he'd done sensitive work for Shae, gathering evidence against the Espenians.

Yet, so far, Hilo had given no indication as to if and when he expected his nephew to start taking on any responsibilities from him directly. After all, Niko was still young, only twenty-seven. And many in the clan wondered if the Pillar harbored anger or doubts over his nephew's years away from the family.

Now, however, he was saying that Niko would have the authority to speak for the clan in an important meeting with their former enemies. It was the first time he'd made it unequivocal, even around the privacy of the family dinner table, that Niko was his intended heir.

If Niko was surprised, he didn't show it. "I understand, Uncle," he said solemnly, but everyone saw the cautious way he glanced at Wen for her reaction.

"You'll do fine," Wen said. "Your uncle and aunt will be with you, after all." She said it more matter-of-factly than kindly, but Hilo was glad she'd voiced some encouragement, even if her smile seemed reserved.

"I'll be ready," Niko promised.

"Good." Hilo turned to Anden. "What's going on, Andy? You've gone quiet and you have that expression on your face that you get when something's on your mind."

Anden's head came up and he looked around the table at the sudden attention of his family members. He said with a touch of chagrin, "I'm sorry I seem distracted, Hilo-jen. I've been meaning to ask you something, but it can wait until some other time."

Hilo said, "Just say it. There's no better time, and we're all family here, except for Lott Jin, but it's impossible to be Horn of No Peak and not be an honorary Kaul."

Anden hesitated, then cleared his throat and sat up straight in his chair. "I want to run for political office, to become a member of the Royal Council." Everyone stared at him, until Anden fidgeted and said, "I know it would mean giving up my jade. But I've thought long and hard about it, and I'm prepared to do that. Treating people in the clan one at a time is worthwhile work, but as an elected official I could affect many people at once. I ask for your blessing, Hilo-jen, and for the patronage of the clan."

No one said anything for a moment. Then Niko said, "Uncle Anden, I'd say you're too honest to be a politician, but come to think about it, you've already been a statesman for the clan for so many years, so there's no one who'd be better suited to the job."

Wen smiled knowingly at Anden from across the table. "In this family, you can be honest and still shrewd. Jadeless and still a warrior."

Anden said, "Most members of the Royal Council who're affiliated with the major clans have never worn jade themselves, so they don't always understand how to do things the Green Bone way. The rest are independents, who have no allegiance to the Green Bone way of life at all. As for our influence there, even after Jaya broke the hold that Six Hands Unity has on Lukang, the election is going to be close, and the Mountain might even get a boost from the Kobens ascending to power.

"There are things that need to be done—standing up to the Espenians and demanding the withdrawal of troops, combating harmful superstitions, military reform—that need someone who can speak as a Green Bone without being green. Look at how the widow Koben Tin Bett has risen in government, coming from a Green Bone family and advocating their views in national politics even though she's never been a Green Bone herself. I think I could do that for us. I could represent the clan but also sit apart from it and think of the greater good."

Wen said, still smiling, "Did Jirhuya give you this idea?"

Anden's face reddened a little. "No, but he encouraged me. I don't think I would've hung on to the idea if he hadn't kept pushing me to take it seriously." He averted his gaze self-consciously but there was a slight smile on his face. "I used to worry that maybe we couldn't stay together, because he's so far outside of the clan, but now I think it's a good thing that he always gives me a different perspective."

Hilo spoke and everyone else became quiet. "No member of the Kaul family has ever held political office. We've always been jade warriors who've never given up our green for anything, not even the right to rule." The side of the Pillar's mouth rose in a lopsided grin.

"One thing I can say about my little cousin is that he always does things his own way, even if it's never been done before. Of course you have my blessing, Andy, and the support of the clan."

Anden rose from his seat and touched his clasped hands to his forehead in deep salute. "Thank you, Hilo-jen. I'll do my best to win and not let everyone down."

Hilo stood as well and the cousins embraced. Hilo said, "Let's all go to bed on this good news. Shae will set up the meeting with the Kobens, and then we'll talk more. There's still a lot to do—there always is—but I'm sure you're all tired."

———————

After everyone else had departed and the house was quiet, Hilo went upstairs. Wen was already in bed and waiting up for him. When he got under the covers, she set aside the book she was reading and came into his arms. He kissed her brow and stroked her hair. They lay together in silence for a few minutes.

"When will you do it?" Wen asked.

"During the meeting," Hilo said. "Bringing Niko in gave me the excuse to keep Lott out. Not because I want to exclude him, but so he can be doing other things."

Wen nodded. "It'll take a few weeks for the Weather Men to negotiate all the details of the meeting—the location, the penitents, the security and so on. Hopefully by then, Ayt Mada will have faded from everyone's attention. Most of her small group of loyal guards are older Green Bones, no match for our best Fists."

"I'll give Lott instructions tomorrow, when no one else is around." He cupped Wen's chin and tilted it up toward him. Sternly, "You have to be careful not to let it slip to Shae. You might forget. I know how you two talk when I'm not around. Shae and Niko can't know anything until it's done. They can swear truthfully for everyone to Perceive that they had nothing to do with killing Ayt Mada, that I whispered her name to Lott alone."

Wen pulled away in indignation. "I wouldn't forget something so important," she said. "Didn't I agree with you at the table tonight?

Shae says it's risky to act right now, but it's even more risky not to act. We can never be careless when it comes to Ayt Mada. She and her supporters have to die."

Hilo nodded. "It'll be a tricky thing, talking the new Pillar into friendship while sending his aunt to finally feed the worms."

Wen leaned her cheek against her husband's shoulder and traced the jade studs on his collarbone and chest with the tenderness of long familiarity. "Ayt Ato will have to make a fuss over it for the sake of appearances, but he won't go to war over it," she said. "Like I said, I think he's smarter than people assume, and he has that cunning old widow Koben Tin Bett advising him. He knows Ayt Mada will be trouble to him so long as she remains in the wings of the clan. He'll never have the full support of the Mountain if she's still alive and pulling strings. She never favored him as the heir, and her terrible shadow will loom over him as long as she lives. The Kobens will be secretly grateful when we take the old Pillar out of their way."

"Especially if I give them an easy way out of having to pretend to be angry," Hilo said. "Which I will. As soon as this is over, I'll step down as Pillar."

Wen's fingers stopped moving. She breathed out, her long exhalation warm against his skin. "Niko's not ready."

"It would be better if he had a few more years, that's true, but this has to be the way it's done. He's about the same age I was when I became Pillar," Hilo said. "And no one thought much of my chances, not even you, my kitten, if we're going to be honest here."

Wen said, "You were the Horn. You had the loyalty of the clan's Fists and Fingers in a time of war. You knew how to lead people in a crisis because you care about them. Niko's not like you."

Hilo wrapped one of her hands in his own and sighed. "I know how hard it is to forgive someone when they don't turn out the way you expect. I'm not very good at it myself. But you can see how Niko's changed and how hard he's been working. You should be nicer to him and show him some affection even when he doesn't ask for it or seem to want it."

Wen was quiet for a moment. "Of course I love him, but he's like a closed book, even more so than when he was a boy. Can someone with a personality like that ever inspire others as a leader? I think he needs a girlfriend, but he doesn't seem to want any of my suggestions."

Hilo laughed. "Young people put romance off these days, you shouldn't worry too much about that. And remember that I was different from Lan, and all the men who've been the Horn were different from me and from each other. As long as Niko knows himself, he'll learn to be his own sort of Pillar. Also, these are better times, and he'll have all of us standing behind him. I didn't have any advantage like that, so I know how important it is. I won't be like Grandda, dragging other people down because of his own regrets. I have you, and I'll be glad that we can finally relax a little after all these years, won't you?"

"Yes." Wen turned his face toward her and kissed him.

"Whatever agreement we come to with the Mountain will be between Niko and the Kobens. I'll abide by it happily, so long as I've avenged Lan and Kehn and all our Fists and Fingers that Ayt Mada put in the ground." Hilo reached over to turn off the bedside lamp before settling down and pulling Wen close. "Shae's right; our clans should put the blood feud in the past. The younger generation should start fresh with a real chance at peace. But *our* generation— we still have our debts to pay."

The phone rang in the home of Iwe Kalundo, where the former Weather Man of the Mountain had isolated himself ever since his disgraceful forced resignation. Iwe answered the call and listened in silence to the informer on the other end of the line. Then he hung up and placed a phone call of his own.

"Ayt-jen," he said, "I have the information we need. Everything will be arranged as we discussed."

CHAPTER

61

~

Old Tigers

the twenty-sixth year, twelfth month

The secret meeting between the leaders of the No Peak and Mountain clans, the first such occurrence in twenty-five years, was held on a Seventhday morning in the headquarters of the Kekon Jade Alliance, in the perennially neutral Temple District.

The original KJA building had been a square, squat, utilitarian government building. Its replacement, built with national and joint clan funds after the Janloon bombing, was a far grander structure—ten defiant stories of steel and green marble, overshadowing even the ancient stone pillars and clay roof of the nearby Temple of Divine Return. An enduring *fuck you* to anyone who might imagine that the clans had been destroyed or diminished by the attacks against them.

When Hilo, Shae, and Niko arrived at the appointed time, Ayt

Ato and his retinue were already in the room, as were four penitents from the Temple of Divine Return, standing against the back wall with their hands folded inside their long green robes.

The Mountain Green Bones stood, and Ayt Ato touched his forehead in wary salute. "Kaul-jen."

"Ato-jen," Hilo said, returning the informal gesture. "I hope you won't take offense if I call you by your personal name. Ayt isn't a name I'm able to say in a friendly way, so I'd prefer not to use it for you if we're to start off on good terms."

Ato said, "I don't mind. It's what most people call me anyway."

Hilo had seen Ayt Ato's image many times but had never directly faced the man in person before. Ato was indeed as handsome as he appeared on television, nearly as camera-worthy as the movie star Danny Sinjo. The distinctive rows of tiny jade studs in his eyebrows accentuated his large eyes, although a rigidity in his face spoke to the enormous pressure that the young Pillar had been under for the past two months. His jade aura felt closely held and tightly stretched, frayed at the edges.

Ato introduced a stout, bearded man as his Weather Man, Koben Opon, and a muscular Green Bone with a flat nose as his cousin and Horn, Sando Kin. "I was raised to fear and hate you, Kaul Hiloshudon," Ato admitted. "And now I'm speaking to you as one Pillar to another. You've harmed the Mountain in so many ways over the years. You've also stood with us at times and fought fiercely against criminals and clanless and greedy foreigners. You brought down my aunt Mada as Pillar, but now you're here, willing to discuss friendship. So in truth, I don't know what to think of you, whether you're an enemy or an ally."

"I hope to be neither, Ato-jen." Hilo was honestly not sure what to make of Ayt Ato either. It seemed incredible that a man could be in the public eye for so much of his life and still be so unknown when it came to whether he had any true capability. Hilo said, "You asked me here to discuss the future between our clans. I'm not the future of my clan. I've been Pillar of No Peak for twenty-seven years, and I intend to step down soon and hand the position to my nephew. I've asked him to sit at the table and lead this meeting for our side. That way, any agreement today will be made looking forward and not behind."

Ato was surprised by this unexpected announcement, but he turned toward Niko with a cautious, pleased expression. "It's been a long time since we last crossed paths, Kaul Niko-jen. We've both been through a lot since then, I think. I'm sorry if I came across as an insufferably arrogant buffoon in the past. But I did say I hoped we could work together and not have to follow the examples of our elders. I hope that's still true."

For the past several evenings, Niko had been sitting in long consultation with his aunts and uncles, preparing for what would be expected of him, being briefed on everything that might come up in the discussion with the Mountain. Now, he stepped forward next to Hilo and said, humbly but with assurance, "I'm not the Pillar yet, Ato-jen, and I still have to prove that I'm worthy of my family's confidence. So my aunt and uncle will sit at the table with me and the final decisions are theirs. But I want to say that I don't hold any grudge against you or the Koben family, not even over the death of my brother. I truly hope we can end this long war."

Niko's mention of Ru caught Hilo off guard. It caught Ayt Ato off guard as well; Hilo Perceived the beat of startled uncertainty in the other man's jade aura. Shae darted a glance at both of them. Niko's aura didn't change. Hilo couldn't tell if his inscrutable nephew had spoken sincerely about his hopes, or if he'd invoked Ru's death as a way to gain the subtle mental advantage over Ato and the Kobens, as if to say: *I could hate you. But I choose not to.*

"Since before I was born, my whole life has been defined by the clan war that killed my father," Niko said. "That's one thing we have in common, Ato-jen—our lives were shaped by the deaths of men we never knew. Maybe we can break that legacy."

Ayt Ato studied Niko with guarded, optimistic respect. "I hope so, Kaul-jen."

The six Green Bones sat down together at the table. As they did so, Sando Kin noticed something amiss. He leaned over to Ato. "Where is the Horn of No Peak?"

"I asked Lott Jin not to come, so Niko could attend without making our sides unequal," Hilo answered. "As a former Horn myself, I'll speak for the military side of the clan." None of that was a lie. Even Green Bones with better Perception than these men would not Perceive it as such.

Hilo waited until their attention was elsewhere before putting his hand into his pocket and depressing the button to send the preloaded message on his phone.

Lott Jin sat in the front passenger seat of a black ZT Bravo in the Commons district, watching the townhouse at the end of the street through a pair of high-powered binoculars. Two Green Bone guards walked circuits around the building, but they looked bored. Lott had the townhouse under constant surveillance, keeping his own Green Bones well out of Perception range and relying on jadeless White Rats to pass by and get closer looks. Ayt Mada had met her former Weather Man, Iwe Kalundo, for dinner at a nearby Mountain-owned restaurant the previous evening. She had returned to the townhouse afterward and no one had seen her emerge so far today. Lott estimated there were two other bodyguards inside, but that was all. This was Mountain territory after all; Ayt's people were not overly concerned. Lott and Vin were alone in the inconspicuous ZT Bravo (Lott's red Lumezza FT Scorpion would be far too recognizable) and Vin could reliably Perceive patrols before the patrols could Perceive them.

Lott's pager buzzed and he looked down at it. It was the signal he'd been waiting for: a short numeric code that he and the Pillar had agreed would mean Hilo, Shae, and Niko were in the KJA building with Ayt Ato and his people, and Lott was to proceed.

He made a cell phone call. Hami Yasu picked up at once. "It's time," Lott said.

"We'll be there in five minutes," said the Fist. Two cars full of No Peak's best Green Bone warriors were waiting in a parking lot across the district border in Old Town. As soon as they arrived, they would storm the townhouse from all sides, kill Ayt Mada and her bodyguards, and steal back across into No Peak territory. If all went according to plan, they would catch Ayt unawares and it would take no more than a few minutes.

Lott fingered the sheathed moon blade lying across his lap. On the surface, the task should not be difficult. Four Mountain bodyguards plus Ayt Mada, against ten of No Peak's greenest fighters. Ayt Mada was still the most heavily jaded woman in Kekon, but she was in her midsixties. Jade did not stop a person from getting old, and it didn't matter how much green someone wore if they didn't have the physical stamina and reflexes to employ it, particularly against men forty years younger. Nevertheless, Lott was worried. Ayt had survived assassination attempts before. She'd won a duel against Kaul Shae. She'd had a knife plunged into her neck and fallen out a window. She seemed legendary, unkillable.

It was possible that other Mountain Green Bones would be alerted and rush to her aid. Bystanders might get in the way. There might be other guards inside that they didn't know about, as they were parked too far away for even Vin to Perceive how many people were inside. Lott sent up a silent prayer to the gods. By nature, he was a risk-averse person. He knew he was not unusually talented, but he'd reached the position of Horn as a result of being lucky, hardworking, and dependable, giving others no reason to doubt him or his ability to deliver on his responsibilities. Now the Pillar was counting on him, had left this final mission in his hands.

Vin started the car engine. A minute later, two Victor STX SUVs roared past them up the street. "That's them, let's go," Lott said. Vin hit the gas, and they tore down the length of the block to the townhouse, squealing to a stop behind the other vehicles. Lott threw open the door and dove out.

The two guards patrolling the building Perceived the murderous rush and raced to defend the entrance. They drew Ankev pistols, but they were badly outgunned. Shotgun muzzles aimed out the open windows of the lead SUV sprayed them with ammunition. The Mountain Green Bones threw up a surge of Deflection that sent the pellets flying into the townhouse's windows, peppering the siding and shattering windows. One man's Steel was not quick or strong enough; he took lead to the knees and went down screaming and clutching his legs.

In the brief pause after the first volley of gunfire, No Peak Green Bones exploded out of the cars with guns and blades and were upon the sentries in an instant. Suyo and Hami shot the man on the ground several times at close range, his body jumping on the lawn as if from hammer blows as his Steel collapsed under the barrage. Juen Din flew Light at the other guard, moon blade descending in a lethal overhead chop. When the guard raised his own blade to meet the high attack, Juen Ritto rushed into the opening in a blur of Strength and disemboweled the man in the time it took to blink.

Lott and Vin were already flying past the fighting on the lawn. Wary of traps, Vin blew the lock out on the front door with a shotgun blast, and Lott Deflected the door inward. They braced to Steel themselves, but the door slammed open on its hinges, revealing an empty hall. No trip wires were snagged, nothing exploded. Lott was about to rush inside when Vin shouted, "Wait!"

Lott turned to his First Fist with alarm. Vin tapped the side of his head and pointed to the house. "Can you Perceive that? *Nothing*. There's no one inside."

The Horn took a wary step closer, throwing knives in hand, stretching out his Perception to take in as much of the building as he could. Vin was right. He couldn't sense a single jade aura in the house.

"That's impossible," he exclaimed. "We saw Ayt go inside the house yesterday and we've had eyes on the building all night and this morning. No one came in or out."

No one doubted Vin's Perception, but they searched the house anyway. It was empty. There were signs that Ayt Mada had been here recently: dishes in the kitchen, food in the fridge, clothes in the bedroom—but no one in the house. The back door was still locked. No Peak Green Bones had surrounded the townhouse and they were certain no one had left through the windows. Ayt and her bodyguards had vanished.

Vibrating with furious disbelief, Lott walked back out to the front lawn and crouched beside the guard lying on the ground with his entrails spilled out, still alive but only for a short while longer. "Ayt was here," he said. "How did she leave?"

The guard didn't answer. His face was waxen and sweaty and he was gazing far away. Lott stood and ground a foot on the man's open abdomen, eliciting a scream. The sound made Lott wince, but there were times cruelty couldn't be avoided. He waited until the dying man's eyes focused on him. "Suyo here is excellent at Channeling," Lott said, motioning the Fist over. "Tell me how Ayt Mada got away and where she went, and I'll have him end your pain in an instant. Otherwise, I'll throw you in one of our cars and ask him to stop the bleeding enough to keep you alive and suffering for hours."

"Tunnel," the man moaned. "I don't know where she went, but this building...used to be a safe house for the Clanless Future Movement. There's a tunnel...under the laundry room."

"Godsdamnit," Lott breathed. He pointed to the guard. "Save him if you can, kill him if you can't," he told Suyo. He gave instructions to Vin and half the other Green Bones to find and follow Ayt's escape route. He ordered the other half to get in one of the cars and follow him. "We need to get to the Kekon Jade Alliance building."

––––––––––

Ayt Ato leaned over to consult quietly with his Weather Man before turning back to the table. "We're amenable to the idea of Euman Island being officially declared clan neutral territory, and we agree that there should be no more jade mining there, offshore or otherwise. A national park ought to be established to protect that area from further exploitation. But how do you propose to deal with the foreigners?"

Niko took a moment to confer with Shae before answering. "From what we know about how the criminal investigation into the company's CEO is unfolding, it seems likely that Anorco will be broken up and sold. Its assets include a sizable amount of jade inventory. I'm sure we can all agree that we want that jade back in Kekon and not in the hands of other foreign companies or criminal organizations." When Ato and his people nodded, Niko said, "The Weather Man has a proposal."

Hilo had told his nephew, *When in doubt, get your aunt to do some talking. She'll say something smart, and meanwhile you can watch them and have time to think ahead.*

Shae leaned forward. "If the Mountain and No Peak both try to acquire Anorco's jade, we'll end up in a bidding contest, one that could turn violent and have us at each other's throats again. We propose that our clans form a joint venture company under the auspices of the Kekon Jade Alliance, to acquire Anorco's reserves and allocate them in the same way as jade produced from the mines—equitably between the Green Bone clans, as well as to schools, temples, doctors, and the national treasury."

Hilo was finding it difficult to pay attention to what was arguably the most significant and far-ranging negotiation that had ever happened between the Mountain and No Peak. He glanced surreptitiously at his watch. At this moment, the Horn was leading a team of the clan's strongest Fists in an attack on Ayt Mada's residence.

"That seems reasonable," Ato replied. "But can we expect any trouble from the Espenian government, after what happened this summer with the GSI soldiers?" Ato glanced at Hilo. "To be clear, I admire what you did, Kaul-jen. Making a public statement like that. It played so well on television. I wish I'd thought of it myself, honestly. Although, of course, I wasn't in a position to say so at the time."

Hilo brought his attention back to the conversation. "Don't worry about GSI," he said. "As for the Espenian government, they'll gladly pretend it didn't happen."

Shae said, "The ROE is already lagging in its diplomatic commitments to reduce its military presence, and the protests and deaths of unarmed civilians hardly plays to their advantage. If the clans stand together, we can put even greater pressure on them."

Ayt Ato said, "We have a common interest in cooperating against overreaching foreigners, but we also need to discuss how we'll treat our clans' overseas markets."

Hilo's phone vibrated. He waited until he had an opportunity to discreetly take it out of his pocket, flip it open, and sneak a glance at the small green screen, which displayed two lines of text from Lott Jin: *Escaped. Before we arrived.*

Hilo closed the phone and slid it back into his pocket. Slowly, he leaned back in the chair and breathed in and out, calming himself, not wanting to betray his fury and agitation. Niko was focused on the conversation with the Kobens, as he should be, and didn't notice any change in his uncle's aura. His nephew's Perception had never been any better than average. Shae, however, was glancing at Hilo suspiciously, questioningly. Even without any jade senses, his sister could tell something was amiss.

A dull roar began to fill Hilo's head. *Fuck the gods.* Ayt Mada, always one step ahead, even now—publicly disgraced, unpopular, old and ousted from power—she was not yet defeated, not yet *dead*. Which meant that the bitch was still going to make a play, still going to find some way to get what she wanted, to bring down everyone who stood in her way. Wherever she was now, she was still a threat to No Peak, to the family.

Niko and Ato, in consultation with their respective Weather Men, had agreed that the clans would no longer block each other's expansion overseas. No Peak would allow the Mountain to enter Espenia and set up businesses there without attacking their operations or their people, directly or through allies. In exchange, the Mountain would extend the same courtesy to No Peak, allowing it to expand into Shotar, Ygutan, and the Uwiwa Islands, where the Mountain had been dominant for decades.

At last, they turned to the heart of the negotiation, the decision that would seal peace between the clans: a pledge of friendship between the Koben and Kaul families. As the petitioners of the meeting, the Kobens were expected to make the overture. Hilo could tell, however, that Ato was still uncertain. He wanted greater assurance from the Kauls, whom he had no reason to trust.

Ato cleared his throat. "You don't have a girlfriend you're planning to marry, do you, Kaul Niko-jen?"

The question surprised Hilo, but Niko answered without so much as blinking. "No," he said. "Not yet."

Ato said, "Since our families hope to be friends, I hope you won't consider it too forward that I offer to introduce you to some of my younger cousins who are about your age." He glanced cautiously at Hilo. "With your uncle's permission, of course."

Hilo's eyes narrowed. "I know the Kobens are an admirably traditional family, but a man's heart is his own."

"Nevertheless, I would be happy to meet your cousins," Niko said to Ato without smiling or hesitating. "My uncle is concerned for my happiness, but my heart's more sensible and less picky than a lot of other men."

"I'm glad you're willing to consider it," Ato said. "After all, words, money, and even jade—they don't bind people together the same way family does. That's something that hasn't changed even in modern times, wouldn't you agree?" Ato stood and his Horn and Weather Man stood with him. With ceremonial deliberation, the young Pillar placed his moon blade on the table in front of Niko. The weapon was a fine thirty-three inches in a beautifully carved scabbard and with small inset jade stones running down the length of its black hilt.

"Kaul-jens," Ato said, speaking formally to all of them, "as Pillar of the Mountain, I pledge to you my friendship, the honor of my family, and the strength of my clan. I give my blade to you in service."

Niko, Hilo, and Shae stood as well. The sheathed thirty-four-inch Da Tanori moon blade that Niko set on the table in front of Ayt Ato was made of twenty-two inches of tempered white carbon steel, with five jade stones in the hilt. It had once belonged to his father.

Lan, are you watching? Hilo wondered, with a tight feeling in his chest. This was what his brother had wanted, so many years ago. No Peak strong enough to stand against any foe. True peace between the clans, as equals.

Bullshit. Something was wrong. Hilo could sense it like a ghostly flickering in the periphery of his Perception, or perhaps it was simply the terrible knowledge of being outmaneuvered by Ayt Mada yet again, even after everything he'd done, every sacrifice his family had made, every last drop of his clan's strength, cunning, and resolve given over the years. Shae was glancing at him frequently now. Despite his efforts to appear unperturbed, the other Green Bones in the room could not fail to Perceive the disquiet in Hilo's jade aura. Niko looked over at him. "Uncle?"

Hilo forced a smile. "This is a difficult and emotional moment for me. I hope you all understand. I've fought the Mountain clan all my life, so it's hard for me to accept this is happening, even if I agree. I'm glad I made the decision to have Niko speak."

His sincere explanation satisfied everyone, except for Shae, whose gaze lingered on him another moment before turning back to the matter at hand. Hilo stretched his Perception out through the building and onto the street. Both clans had Green Bones standing guard outside, but nothing was out of the ordinary. Hilo brought his focus back, rested his Perception carefully on every person in the room in turn.

Niko echoed Ato's words. "As the Pillar's son, I pledge to you my friendship, the honor of my family, and the strength of my clan. I give my blade to you in service."

A pledge of friendship, sealed with a personal exchange of moon blades, was not made lightly between Green Bones. It meant they could not go to war with each other, at least not before failing at other means of resolution and formally breaking the friendship by symbolically returning the other's blade, since it was unthinkable to take a warrior's weapon and use his own jade to strike him down— tantamount to theft. From now on, anyone who attacked the Kobens would be an enemy of the Kauls, and vice versa. Each would come to the aid of the other if asked.

The practical implication of this promise in the short term was that No Peak would help the Kobens to put down any mutinous challenge, by Ayt Mada loyalists or anyone else, and to support them as the rightful ruling family of the Mountain clan. It was what Ato needed more than anything at the moment, even if it meant appearing to lower himself to the Kauls.

Ato smiled a movie-star bright smile that did not quite reach his eyes. "I'm not like my aunt," he said. "I'm not ashamed to admit that. I don't believe that one clan has to prevail over the other, and I promise I'll do everything I can to put the long grudges behind us. Under Heaven and on jade."

Niko inclined his head. "When I was a boy, I felt a lot of pressure to one day match you, Ato-jen," he said. "Now I welcome you giving me a good reason to feel that way. I'm still a Pillar-in-training, so I can speak for my clan only with the final blessing of my uncle." He turned to Hilo.

Hilo's eyes focused on Ato and he nodded. "Under Heaven and on jade," he declared, then drew his pistol and fired twice.

The shots went over Ayt Ato's shoulder and hit the penitent behind him. Shae saw the man's brains spray out across the wall. The Fullerton carbine he'd begun to raise to waist height beneath his voluminous green robes fell from his hands and clattered to the floor. As everyone else in the room spun in alarm, Shae glimpsed the baleful, fiery vindication in her brother's eyes, his expression twisted with savage understanding.

The other penitents opened fire.

Sando Kin threw himself onto his cousin, pushing Ato under the table. The bullets meant for the young Pillar tore through Sando's back. Hilo fired again and hit another penitent in the chest, then began to raise a Deflection as the remaining two guns turned on him. A split-second realization as his jade energy swelled: In the tight quarters of the meeting room, the Deflected bullets would swerve into Niko and Shae.

Hilo twisted and sent the Deflection straight into his nephew's chest. The force of it knocked Niko to the ground. Bullets chopped through the air above him and stitched into Hilo's side.

Shae saw her brother fall as if in slow motion. Later, she wouldn't remember anything else. She wouldn't recall throwing herself to the ground under the desk. She would have no memory of the Green Bone guards outside charging into the room with drawn weapons,

Koben Opon shouting for them to cut down the remaining two penitents, who were not penitents at all. She would remember only the jerk of Hilo's body and the pistol falling from his hands, the way her brother's shoulders struck the wall before he slid to the floor.

The next sound to break into Shae's awareness was a ragged cry next to her underneath the desk. Ato had pushed himself out from underneath Sando Kin and was holding his cousin's limp body, clutching his face and keening. *"No no no no..."*

Shae scrambled over to Hilo on hands and knees. He was slumped against the wall, his legs straight out in front of him as if he were slouched lazily after a hard workout. His face was contorted with pain. Shae watched in horror as blood spread across his shirt and pants, pooled around her knees on the hardwood floor.

"Hilo." She could not say anything else.

Niko crawled over to them. He stared down at his uncle and went completely, terrifyingly still. In that moment, Shae saw another face emerge beneath that of the coolly determined young man her nephew had become. She saw unmistakably the face of the frightened toddler in the airport, the one who would follow her around the house and clutch her legs, full of confusion and loss.

"Niko." When he didn't answer, she shouted, "Niko!" He looked at her, eyes blank with fear. She seized his hands and pressed them over Hilo's wounds. "Do you remember emergency medical Channeling? Try to stop the bleeding. I'll call an ambulance." She grabbed her bag and fumbled for her cell phone with shaking hands. Where was it? *Gods, please please please.* Her thoughts turned into an unthinking litany of pleading. She found it, began to punch in the emergency number.

Hilo shook his head vehemently and grabbed her by the front of her shirt, his hands twisted in the fabric. "Get me home, Shae," he said, his voice strained.

"We need to get you to a hospital."

Hilo shook his head again. "I'm not dying in a fucking hospital."

"You're not going to die," she told him.

"Shae," Hilo said gently, "I can't feel my legs. I want to go home. I want to see Wen. Please, Shae."

She began to cry. There was no warning—only the abrupt, hot blurring of vision, the strangling pressure in her chest. Hilo gripped her tighter, more impatiently. "Are you my Weather Man or not?"

All of a sudden, they were surrounded by No Peak Green Bones. Lott Jin was there—*When had he arrived? How had he gotten here?* Shae did not know. The Horn stared down at them, ashen-faced. Then he shoved Niko aside roughly and shouted, "Suyo!" One of his senior Fists rushed over, dropped to his knees and began Channeling while Lott and several others applied pressure to the wounds.

Hilo screamed in pain and frustration. "Get me home, gods-damnit, *that is a fucking order from your fucking Pillar!*"

"Do as he says," Shae whispered. Then she shouted. *"Do as he says!"*

Several Fists together lifted Hilo and took him outside. He sagged between them, his legs limp, trailing blood as they carried him to the ZT Bravo parked beside the building. They placed him across the back seat, where he lay breathing raggedly, eyes closed. Niko got in with him, cradling Hilo's head and shoulders in his lap. Shae got into the front passenger seat and hung on to the door of the car, her head pressed against the window glass as if the vehicle were a life raft.

Lott rushed them home. The only thing Shae remembered from the journey was Niko's voice, almost too quiet to be heard. "Da," he begged, "don't leave me."

Hilo did not answer.

When the car stopped and the doors opened in front of the main house, Anden was there. Someone must've called him, to tell him what happened and warn him to be prepared. Even so, when he saw his cousin, Anden swayed violently, as if he'd been struck across the face. He put a hand against the ZT's door frame to steady himself. Then he went to work. Before they even had Hilo out of the vehicle, Anden was Channeling for all he was worth, forcing blood to clot, raising the Pillar's body temperature, forcing energy into his heart and lungs. By now, Hilo was barely conscious; his eyes were closed and his face waxen.

Wen ran to the front door, saw her husband, and collapsed to the ground with a wail of pure animal pain.

"I'm not a godsdamned surgeon," Anden cried at Shae.

"Would it make a difference?" she asked numbly. "Just do what he wants."

Hilo was laid out on his bed and Anden worked feverishly to keep him alive and dull the pain. At times, he barked orders and others ran to help him or bring him supplies. During that time, word of what happened spread through No Peak and members of the clan began to gather silently in front of the Kaul estate. Fists and Fingers, Luckbringers, Lantern Men. Cars began to arrive, packing the road around the house. Makeshift Deitist shrines went up along the gate, dozens of cups of incense trailing smoke.

Lott Jin went out and came back again to report that the entire city was in shock. The Mountain clan was in turmoil. Ayt Ato was alive, but his Horn was dead, and his Weather Man was in critical condition from a gunshot wound to the chest. Four penitents from the Temple of Divine Return had been found tied and gagged, locked inside the stairwell of a parking garage near the Kekon Jade Alliance building. The four gunmen who'd taken their robes and their place inside the meeting were former employees of GSI, all recently out of work. One of the four mercenaries had survived long enough to confess that they'd been hired by Iwe Kalundo and promised an enormous sum of money by Ayt Madashi for the murder of everyone in the room.

"They were told to wait until the pledge of friendship had been made and moon blades exchanged," Lott said. "Then they were supposed to kill Ayt Ato first."

Shae sat in the kitchen, hugging her arms, folded in on herself and staring at nothing. Ayt Mada had whispered the name of her own nephew. She'd never intended to pass the leadership of the clan to Ato, only to lure them all into the belief that she had. That afternoon, after she'd sat across from Shae, serving her tea, after they'd talked of sacrifice and vision, of ending feuds and doing the right thing for the country, Ayt had resigned her position in anticipation of one final opportunity—the Kauls and the Kobens in the same room, discussing what the future would be without her. When they were all dead, she'd claim that the Kobens had betrayed the clan by pledging friendship to the Kauls. She would install her preferred successor, Iwe Kalundo, and rule from behind him.

The phone in the study rang and Lott answered it. After he hung up, he said, "They have her." Vin and his men had followed the tunnel under Ayt's townhouse into Janloon's subway system. By then, the Koben family was on the hunt as well. Every Green Bone in the city was looking for Ayt Mada, but within an hour, she showed up back on the Ayt estate. She walked onto the grounds and into her office as if it were an ordinary day. That was where the Mountain's people had found her.

"They say she didn't try to run, or fight," Lott said.

"No," Shae said. Ayt Mada would never flee Janloon like a criminal, nor waste energy toward no purpose. As soon as she'd learned her nephew and the Kauls were still alive, she'd surrendered, knowing her final, murderous gambit was over.

Because of Hilo, Shae thought. Because old tigers understand each other.

Anden came down the stairs. His eyes were ringed with exhaustion and he looked pale and aged. "I've done all I can. I stopped the bleeding, put him on an IV line, stabilized his temperature and blood pressure for now. He's loaded with painkillers." Anden rubbed a hand over his face, then looked up at the family, tearful. "All it buys him is a few more hours, maybe the rest of night. A bullet went through his spine, and the others tore up his insides. He's conscious right now, but it might not be for long."

Anden sat down next to Jirhuya on the sofa and put his face in his hands.

Shae went up to see her brother. Wen and Niko were on either side of his bed. Gauze and sheets covered Hilo's torso. The jade studs across his bare collarbone stood out stark against unnaturally pale skin. When Shae touched Hilo's shoulder, she nearly drew back at the shocking change in his jade aura—the smooth, bright river was a dim trickle. His eyes were open and focused, however, and he said to his wife and nephew, "Let me talk to my Weather Man, alone, just for a minute."

After Wen and Niko had stepped out of the room, Shae crouched down near the head of the bed. A thousand things came into her throat and closed it completely.

The Pillar asked, "Is Ato alive?"

Shae nodded and told him everything she knew. "Ayt whispered all of our names. She only resigned and handed power to the Kobens to mislead them. To mislead *me*."

A weak smile crawled up Hilo's face. "But she failed. She's done. This was her last shot, and she got me, in the end. But she didn't get *us*. That's what's important." He licked his lips. His eyes were glassy but bright, and he turned them on her with insistence. "Shae, you have to help Niko. You have to make him better. A better Pillar, a better person. Help him, the way you helped me."

"You know that I will," Shae said.

Hilo closed his eyes. Shae pressed her hand over his heart and listened to his labored breathing. He asked her, "Is there anything you want me to say to Lan?"

Shae bowed her head over him. "Please, don't talk like this Hilo," she whispered. "I can't handle it. I can't stand to think I'll be the last one left."

"You're not."

A noise rose from outside. Shae did not at first recognize it as the rumble of a huge crowd. She went to the window and drew back the curtain. Lott Jin had opened the gates of the Kaul estate and let in the clan's Green Bones—hundreds of them were standing in the driveway. Shae saw the entire Juen family, Hami Tuma and his son Yasu, and Maik Cam. She saw Terun Bin and Luckbringers from her office standing alongside Vin the Sniper and Hejo, the First Fist of White Rats. She saw her own husband and daughter, Woon's arm around Tia's shoulders, both of them looking up at Lott Jin, who stood on top of the Duchesse Imperia in front of the house. When the Horn raised his arm, all the clan's warriors shouted, and the sound of their combined voices thundered. *"The clan is our blood, and the Pillar is its master!"*

The crowd stayed for the rest of the night. Every once in a while, their voices rose up in spontaneous chorus, proclaiming their allegiance. Wen and Niko and Anden came back into the room, and Hilo said, "Stop looking so godsdamned glum, everyone. Andy did a great job, it doesn't even hurt anymore." He talked with them for a while, and he dictated a letter to Shae for their mother, insisting that they shouldn't wake the frail old woman only to put her through more pain. He joked that it was true the closer you got to the afterlife, the more you believed in it, and personally he couldn't wait to see Ru again. He reminded them of all the times they'd persevered despite the odds, and all the things they'd done. "I'm lucky, really."

He said he would try to hang on until Jaya got home, but at some point he slipped into unconsciousness with Wen holding his hand. The rest of the family left the two of them together in the end. Shae sat with Anden, her head on his shoulder, gripping his left hand and wrist in her own, both of them using his jade, Shae unflinchingly for the first time in years, to keep Hilo in their Perception as long as they could. In the early hours of the morning, as dawn broke over the skyline of Janloon, Shae felt her brother's irrepressible jade aura fade out of her mind.

Hours later, Wen emerged from the bedroom, dressed in white from head to toe. She said nothing, but went out into the garden where she had been married and sat under the cherry tree in the courtyard to mourn from the bottom of her soul.

CHAPTER

62

Pillar of Kekon

the first weeks

When word reached Jaya in Toshon that her father had been shot and would not survive for long, she got onto a motorcycle and drove through the night up the KI-1 freeway at top speed for ten straight hours. She arrived too late. Her cousin Cam and her uncle Anden met her at the gates of the estate and told her that her father had died from his injuries two hours ago.

Jaya stormed into the house, shrieking with grief and rage. She found Niko sitting in the living room, his head bowed in solemn conference with the Horn and Weather Man. "Why haven't you done anything?" she demanded. "I'm going to call twenty of my Little Knives up here and go after Ayt and Iwe myself. I'll cut them into pieces!"

"You won't do anything," Niko said to his younger sister. "The Mountain is already in an uproar. We'll wait to see how the Kobens handle it first."

Jaya said to Lott, "So we're going to sit back and leave it to those fools?"

"Niko-jen is the Pillar now," the Horn reminded her. "It's his call."

Shae said, "Niko exchanged a pledge of friendship with Ato, so we won't act until we've heard from the leaders of the Mountain. Ayt Mada intended to murder all of us, but her most serious offense is betraying her own nephew after naming him her successor. If there's anything we need you to do, you'll get your orders from the Horn." When Jaya opened her mouth to argue again, Shae said sternly, "You're a first-rank Fist; show respect."

Jaya wheeled on her aunt with tears spilling from her eyes. "My da is *dead*, and it's your fault! You convinced him to go to that meeting. You could've killed Ayt years ago when you had the chance. You always had a soft spot for that evil hag, but you never showed love to your own brother, you coldhearted bitch."

Shae slapped her niece hard in the face, twice, across one cheek and then the other. Jaya ran from the house and was not seen for days. The Horn sent two of his Green Bones to follow her and make sure she didn't do anything rash, but he needn't have worried. Jaya's base of command was in the south and without her own people in the city, she could not do much.

Nevertheless, in a haze of vengeful anguish, Jaya made her way to Iwe Kalundo's residence in Cherry Grove, only to find it already surrounded by Mountain clan members calling for the former Weather Man's execution. As Shae predicted, the consequences of the assassination plot were rapidly unspooling. The backlash against Ayt and Iwe was surprisingly swift and strong. Public tolerance for Green Bone leaders murdering their way into power was lower than it had been thirty years ago. Ayt's violent choices had once been accepted as those of a legitimate ruler defeating less worthy rivals. Now they were viewed as the treachery of an old tyrant desperate to hold on to power. Many in the Mountain clan had continued to regard Ayt

Mada favorably even after her resignation, but for the crime of gro-
tesquely violating the sacred peace-keeping role of Deitist penitents,
everyone except her most committed followers denounced her.

No one, it seemed, could find out where Ayt Mada was now being
held by the Kobens, but outside Iwe Kalundo's house, Jaya watched
along with dozens of spectators as Fists of the Mountain arrived to
demand the traitor surrender himself.

Iwe asked for three hours to prepare himself for death. The former Weather Man composed a letter explaining that he'd only ever
wanted to prevent the clan he loved from falling to incompetent
leadership and eventual destruction by its enemies. He thanked
his former Pillar, Ayt Madashi, apologized to his family, and gave
instructions as to the distribution of his jade upon his death. Then he
dressed in his best suit, walked into the courtyard of his house, and
shot himself in the head.

All over Janloon and across Kekon, spirit guiding lamps went up
to recognize the passing of Kaul Hiloshudon, a man as dramatic in
death as he had been in life, let the gods recognize him. The televised
public vigil and funeral were enormous. It seemed every Green Bone
in the country, whether they were grieving friends or celebratory enemies, had a story to tell about their personal encounters with Kaul
Hilo—his exploits as a young man, his cunning as a Horn and his
determination as a Pillar, his famous generosity and fearsomeness.

The Kaul house was draped in white. A steady stream of clan
faithful left incense, fruit, and flowers at the gate. On the day of the
funeral, Anden walked near the front of the massive, snaking proces-
sion to Widow's Park as if he were drifting through a waking dream,
swept up like a single fish in a swift river of collective sorrow. The day
was dry but overcast, the sky streaked with purple clouds. The gongs
and funeral drums seemed to reverberate through the streets of a city
leached of color.

All these people around him, Anden thought, felt as if they knew
Hilo in some way, no matter how small. When Anden looked out

at the sea of faces, he felt strangely, ungenerously resentful of all of them, savagely jealous of their sadness, as if there was only so much of it for him and they were not entitled to it. They were not Hilo's brothers. They did not truly know him. They had not Channeled their own energy into his body in his final hours.

Anden left the funeral reception early and found Niko alone in the study—the room that had belonged to Lan and then to Hilo and that now belonged to him.

"Niko-s—" Anden began, then caught himself. His little nephew, who he'd pushed on the swing set and taken to relayball games, who used to curl up quietly next to him on the sofa, holding out story-book after storybook asking to be read to, was now the Pillar of the clan. Anden touched clasped hands to his forehead and bent into a properly respectful salute. "You wanted to talk to me, Kaul-jen?"

Niko looked up from the armchair where he'd been sitting with his elbows on his knees, as if studying the carpet. "Don't do that," he pleaded, his face stricken. "When we're around other people, it's okay, but when it's just the two of us, don't treat me any differently. Please, Uncle Anden. It's hard enough being in this room." The young man's voice was calm yet unspeakably desolate, full of a quiet, private panic.

"I'm sorry, Niko, that was thoughtless of me." Anden took the seat next to his nephew and looked around the study, taking in the clut-tered desk, flat-screen television, family photographs, wall-mounted moon blades, mini-fridge, children's artwork from decades ago that Hilo had put up and never taken down.

"I miss him," Niko whispered. "I loved him, and sometimes I think I hated him. I'm nothing like him and don't want to be. Yet somehow all I want is to live up to him."

Anden understood how Niko felt, although he also knew his own grief had not yet fully arrived. Rather than shut down entirely, he'd thrown himself headlong into the things he could do: helping Shae to make the funeral arrangements, working on his election campaign, handling questions from the media and condolences from all parts of the clan including tributaries and overseas offices. On some level, he did not yet believe that Hilo was gone and expected his cousin to walk through the door at any minute. The mind cannot adjust quickly to a fundamental change in reality without breaking. If the moon vanished from the sky, people would not believe it; they would think it was a trick of light or clouds. Anden felt it would be a long time before he accepted the truth.

Niko turned to him. "Is there any way, any chance at all, that I can persuade you not to run for the Royal Council? If there is . . . I would ask you to be my Pillarman." His expression was almost childlike in its hopefulness. "I trust you more than anyone, Uncle Anden. You've always been a Green Bone in your own way. You've never held any official position or lost yourself to the clan, yet everyone knows you're a man of No Peak. You're always honest with me. I'm going to need your advice now, more than ever."

Anden looked down at his hands. In the silence, he could hear the mingled strains of harp music and the muted noise of people from the enormous gathering outside, too large to fit in the courtyard and spilling all over the estate grounds. "I've thought about suspending my campaign," he admitted. "I'm not sure I can handle it right now, and it seems selfish. But then Jirhu asked me what I thought Hilo-jen would want me to do, and of course, I know the answer to that." He raised his eyes back to his nephew. "I'm sorry, Niko-se. As you said, I've always made my own way in the clan without any official position. It's been the right thing for everyone, I think. It should stay that way."

Niko's face fell, but he nodded as if it was the answer he'd been expecting. Anden added firmly, "You can always come to me, no matter what. I don't have to be your Pillarman for that. And I'm not the only one, of course. Your aunt Shae says she'll remain Weather Man for another year, and Terun Bin will be a worthy successor. Lott is a strong and prudent Horn, and there are the Juens, and your sister is the sort of Green Bone every clan needs. And your ma—she knows the clan best."

"She hasn't spoken to me." Niko's voice was quiet. "I think she blames me, again."

Anden shook his head. Wen had not spoken to anyone as she kept vigil day and night for her husband's spirit. If his presence were to appear to anyone, it would be to her. "It's only because she loved Hilo so much that it seems that way to you. She's too green in the soul to leave us for very long." Anden stood. "If you're willing to take my advice right now, I'd say you should choose Maik Cam to be your Pillarman. Your cousin has a lot of common sense and is an old friend that you can count on to care about you and always tell the truth."

Niko was silent for a time. "Thank you, Uncle Anden," he said at last, and stood as well. "If there's anything else you need from the clan that would help your campaign—money, volunteers, anything at all—you only have to ask and it's yours."

The tentativeness and vulnerability slid away and he spoke like a Pillar. The sense of grave burden was still there, but there was also, Anden saw with relief, composure and acceptance. Anden felt a heavy weight lift off his chest, one that he hadn't known had been sitting there until now. *He'll be okay.*

As Anden left the study, he saw Wen come silently into the hall, walking slowly and with care, a white-clad vision of sorrow and dignity. She seemed unspeakably delicate yet enduring, like a finely wrought vessel, broken and hollowed out, but too strongly tempered to crumble off its pedestal.

Anden stepped aside as the widow and matriarch of No Peak walked past him toward Niko, her immaculately powdered face held as still as a ceramic mask. She stopped in front of her son. The Pillar's fragile new confidence wavered and slipped off his shoulders. Anden saw his throat bob, twice, and his mouth trembled as he looked into her eyes. "Ma," he said.

Wen did not speak, but her quiet strength seemed to fold in on itself like the petals of a flower in the cold. She stepped forward and wrapped her arms tightly around Niko with a whisper that Anden couldn't hear. Like a child, Niko buried his face in her shoulder, and Anden, heart aching, quietly shut the door of the study.

———

A steady stream of people—Lantern Men, politicians, emissaries from tributary clans and No Peak's overseas offices—arrived over the following weeks to pay respect and allegiance to Kaul Nikoyan. Some in the clan didn't take well to the pledge of friendship with their old enemies, or were skeptical of Niko's youth, inexperience, personal demeanor, and past failings—but the sentiments never rose to anything above grumbling. No one could dispute that Kaul Hilo had chosen his nephew as his successor, and with Hilo's longtime Weather Man and Horn both standing behind the new Pillar, the clan soon fell into line.

Ten days after the funeral, Ayt Ato appeared at the Kaul estate accompanied only by a pair of bodyguards and asked to speak with the Pillar of No Peak. This was a remarkable occurrence. Ordinarily, a meeting between two Pillars of comparable status would be formally arranged on neutral ground by the clans' Weather Men. For one Pillar to present himself at another's home and request an audience like any ordinary petitioner was a sign of debasement.

Shae watched her nephew greet the other Pillar in the foyer. "Ayt Ato-jen."

"Kaul-jen." Ato's handsome face was worn down. The tiny jade studs over his eyebrows accentuated not his eyes but the dark hollows underneath them. He cleared his throat uncomfortably. "I've decided to reclaim my maternal family name of Koben. It's the name I grew up with. When I was positioned as the future leader of the clan, I was never consulted on the choice to go by the name of Ayt. In truth, I've never felt any personal connection to that name."

Niko nodded. He glanced toward the study, but Shae could see his reluctance to go into that room. Hilo had been the same way at first, when it had still felt wrong to sit in Lan's space. "Would you like to walk outside, Koben-jen?"

Out in the garden, the damp chill of approaching winter was in the air, and the late season chrysanthemums were in full bloom. Slim, wind-plucked petals of white, red, and gold floated atop the still pond. Niko glanced at Shae, wordlessly asking his Weather Man to accompany him as they took Koben Ato along the pebbled path around the grounds. She did so at a slight distance, close enough to hear the conversation, but not so close as to join it. She didn't feel capable of talking to anyone, not yet. At times, she felt Niko was doing a better job of shouldering his new role as Pillar than she was in occupying her old one as Weather Man.

"I must be the first person in the Mountain clan to receive a personal tour of the Kaul estate," Ato said. "It's as nice as I imagined."

"I haven't been to the Ayt residence myself," Niko said, "but I've heard it's equally impressive." It was a strange sight, the two young Pillars strolling through the garden together, Niko casually pointing out this and that about the houses and the landscaping as Ato nodded in appreciation. It was nothing like a proper meeting of clan leaders, but perhaps it was what was needed in the moment. Their first attempt had ended in unfathomable tragedy; this was something else.

At last, they circled back to where they had begun, in the courtyard of the main house. Ato turned to face the other Pillar. "Kaul-jen," he said, "I'm sincerely sorry for your loss. Your uncle was always a ruthless enemy of my clan, but no one can dispute that he was a great Green Bone warrior. That day, he saved my life and lost his own."

"I'm sorry for the losses on your side as well." Niko didn't say more. Shae thought perhaps he should've, but either he couldn't make himself talk about that day more than necessary, or he was deliberately holding back, waiting to hear what the other man had to say. Perhaps both. His expression gave nothing away, and Shae suspected that his jade aura didn't either.

Ato said, "I'm sure you already know that Iwe Kalundo took his own life. Ayt Mada has been stripped of jade and confined in a secret location, under guard by Green Bones loyal to my family, for her protection as well as ours." Ato's face moved in a brief, involuntary contortion. "The Mountain is in a state of shock and disarray. I'm afraid it's broken somewhere deep inside. At this point, I'm not sure what will become of the clan and whether it's even worth saving."

It was an astonishing statement to make. Who could ever recall any Pillar uttering such a thing? What Green Bone leader would admit he'd lost control of his own warriors, failed to maintain authority over his clan?

Perhaps, however, Koben Ato was simply tired of denying what was becoming increasingly obvious to everyone. The Mountain clan was riven. Although most of its members condemned Ayt Mada's shocking attempted coup, they did not necessarily flock enthusiastically to support the Kobens, who were seen by some as imprudent and divisive. Ato, for all his years in the public eye, had not been given much latitude by his Pillar, and thus did not have many personal accomplishments to suggest he was a strong and visionary enough leader to command widespread loyalty and rebuild the clan's tarnished image in the wake of so much accumulated shame and carnage.

Many of the Mountain's Lantern Men and tributary minor clans, disenchanted by the constant infighting and no longer fearful of Ayt Mada or the Kobens, were continuing to steadily defect to No Peak. A few families in the Mountain were breaking off entirely and forming their own independent minor clans. Local offshoots of the barukan gangs were recruiting the Mountain's Keko-Shotarian members. A faction of Ayt Mada's most die-hard loyalists had left Janloon and regrouped in Gohei, where they were reportedly forming their own small clan, the Spear Carrier clan, claiming spiritual lineage to Ayt Yu and his daughter Mada.

Koben Ato's face tightened in a weary grimace. "Ever since I was a boy, I've been used like a chess piece. My relatives expected me to be the shining heir to Ayt Yugontin, to lift up the whole family. My aunt Mada named me her ward to secure their support and to keep her detractors in line, but she never showed me love or considered me worthy. The media and the public were always watching. I was told what to say, how to dress, who to marry, who to be friends and enemies with, and sometimes even those demands were conflicting."

Ato made no attempt to hide his envy as he looked into Niko's face. "I know you felt the pressure of a similar position, and I was jealous when you rebelled and left the country. But I'm not sure you saw what seemed apparent to me—for all his faults, your uncle did his best to surround you with his strength, rather than pushing you out front like a sacrifice. All of my greatest suffering has come from within my own clan."

Ato turned his face away and silence stretched between the two men. They carried a long and terrible legacy between them, but they were young and trying to change things. Ato said, "I can't execute my own aunt. She whispered my name, and she deserves to die, but she sponsored and trained me. If I have her killed, I'll be continuing the cycle she began when she murdered her brother—my father, who I barely remember. She sent a message to the entire clan that personal ties mean nothing. Strength is all that matters and any action can be justified. Under her rule, the Mountain grew ever larger and more powerful, but vicious and dysfunctional."

Niko said, "Maybe you can take what's left and build something better."

"Maybe," Ato conceded. "It'll take time, but I'll try."

Seeing the two Pillars standing together, lines already stamped across their young features, Shae tilted her face toward the sun, closing her eyes for a moment against the burning tightness in her chest—sadness and pity jumbled with pride and hope. She wasn't done yet; she had to help Niko as she'd promised she would—but with that final step, she could lay down the burden she and her brothers had carried across a canyon that had so often seemed impassable.

Hilo. Lan, Shae whispered in her mind, *can you see this, from wherever you are? We did it at last. We kept our clan. We made it stronger and passed it on.*

I miss you both.

Ato turned back to Niko, but his eyes settled upon Shae. "Your family has suffered more from Ayt Mada than mine. Whatever justice she gets should come from you, not from me. Kaul Hiloshudon was my enemy, but I owe him my life, so it's only right that I repay that debt. I'm handing Ayt Mada over to the Kaul family. I beg that you accept this as a gesture of repentance and goodwill."

Niko did not respond at first. Then he nodded slowly.

Ato said, "In return, I ask that No Peak consider its blood debt paid and that you not take any additional vengeance on the Mountain clan. It seems clear by now that Ayt and Iwe acted alone in their scheme. Reigniting hostilities between our clans would empower the small faction of Ayt's old guard that remains."

Niko exchanged a mute glance with Shae. Then he turned back to Ato. "You have my word as Pillar, under Heaven and on jade. The old hatreds—they're over with."

Koben Ato nodded in gratitude. "My aunt was right all along. I'm not a strong Pillar and could never be her heir. But maybe we've had enough of those types of people. Whatever happens after this—whether the Mountain survives, whether I remain Pillar—No Peak will be the largest and most powerful Green Bone clan in the country. It will be up to you, to be a Pillar for all of Kekon. I know I should feel defeated, but mostly, I feel relieved."

He touched his clasped hands to his forehead and tilted forward in salute. "Far do your enemies flee, Kaul-jen, and may the gods shine favor on No Peak."

CHAPTER
63

Remembrance

the third month

Dr. Emery Anden won the seat in the Royal Council for Janloon Central—including Sogen, Old Town, Sotto Village, and North Sotto—by a comfortable margin. Much commentary was made of the fact that he was the first known queer candidate elected to national government, only the third councilman of mixed race, and the first member of the Kaul family to ever serve in public office. Although the victory was celebrated, it was not surprising given his advantages. He had the sponsorship of the No Peak clan, credentials as an accomplished doctor with international experience, and a reputation as a clan loyalist and a man who was green in the soul.

Anden found it ironic that what had once been a disgraceful blemish on his past—refusing jade at his graduation from Kaul

Dushuron Academy and leaving the country in exile for some time as a consequence—was now cited as evidence of his upstanding moral character at a young age. Voters apparently admired the way that, given his mother's tragic death from the Itches, he'd turned away from violence and shine use despite prodigious jade abilities and severe pressure from family and society. Anden sometimes wished he could travel back in time to reassure his eighteen-year-old self that he would find his own way after all—but then again, it would've been cruel, at that age, to learn of all the other struggles and sorrows that were still to come.

Early on a cool but sunny Seventhday morning, the day before he was to be sworn into office, Anden walked into a small, second-story apartment in an unremarkable building in Little Hammer. He passed three guards along the way, Mountain Green Bones loyal to the Koben family—one posted at the building's entrance, one outside the door to the apartment, one inside the small unit itself. They recognized Anden of course—who else could he be?—and when he produced the letter from Kaul Nikoyan, Pillar of No Peak, bearing the insignia of the clan, the guard at the door grumbled, "About time," and let him enter.

Ayt Madashi sat cross-legged on the only sofa in the apartment, watching the news on a small television. Anden was shocked by her appearance. Ayt's undyed hair was coarse and gray and she was hunched, as if she were very cold, inside a baggy turtleneck sweater with long sleeves that drooped all the way to her fingers. Anden had never seen Ayt with her arms covered. He knew that beneath the bulky fabric, they were bare. The silver coils of mounted jade that Ayt had worn and proudly displayed for so many years were gone. After surrendering herself to Koben's people and ordering her loyalists not to fight, she'd been stripped of her jade and confined under house arrest in this unknown safe house. Although she'd made it through the ordeal of jade withdrawal, Anden could not help but marvel at how much *less* she seemed to be. One of the most formidable Green Bones of her generation—now a weary, thin, jadeless, sixty-six-year-old woman.

Ayt switched off the television and turned her head toward Anden.

Seeing the pity in his expression, her mouth flattened into a line and some of the old fire flared in her eyes, a flash of the ruthless iron will that had been the bane of the No Peak clan for decades.

"Are you surprised to find me still here, Emery Anden?" Ayt asked, a touch sardonically. "Perhaps you thought I'd follow Iwe's example?"

"The thought occurred to me," Anden admitted.

"As it did to me." Ayt's shoulders slackened. "But I seem incapable of taking the easy route in anything. Survival is a habit, it seems, one that's hard to break."

"So is jade," Anden said, looking steadily at her. "So is power."

Ayt uncrossed her legs and set her feet down but didn't rise from her seat. "Koben Ato hasn't come. Not that I expected him to. He always was a coward who shrank from tough decisions, letting others make choices for him. Even knowing that I whispered his name, he would rather avoid the distasteful problem of executing his own aunt by foisting the task onto No Peak." She sounded disappointed and regretful, as if she wished she'd been proven wrong in her assessment of the young man who she'd attempted to have killed. Ayt narrowed her eyes at Anden. "However, I'm surprised *your* nephew waited so long. It's been three very dull months. I would've thought the new Pillar of No Peak was greener than that."

"If it were up to some members of the clan, you would've already been publicly executed, beheaded, and buried without a grave," Anden said. "But Kaul Niko wanted to wait until after the dust settled, after the elections and the holiday season, when people would've stopped thinking about you."

Ayt looked past Anden, as if expecting to see other people behind him, but there was no one else. "And then he sends you alone. He won't even face me."

Anden said, "You're nothing to him, just a defeated enemy. He's not like other Green Bones in that way. You're responsible for the death of his father—*fathers*, the one by blood, and the one who raised him—but he doesn't care for personal vengeance and won't let it determine his decisions. He doesn't want to see you or speak to you. He only wants you gone."

"So you're here," Ayt said. "Dr. Emery. I should say, Councilman Emery. To speak for the No Peak clan and deliver the justice of the Kaul family."

"I am," Anden said.

Ayt's face twitched. "What about Kaul Shaelinsan? After all her efforts, I deceived her. I put both of her brothers in the ground. Why isn't she here?"

"She told me she has nothing else to say to you," Anden answered. "She spared your life once, and she says that's all the gods can ask of her in this lifetime."

Anden handed Ayt the letter he had brought with him, written in Niko's hand. Having read it, he knew it was short and impersonal, explaining the details of the decision without any personal comment. A copy of it had been sent to Koben Ato.

"You're to be exiled from Kekon," Anden explained to Ayt. "You'll live out the rest of your days in Ygutan. Arrangements have been made to transport you to a small oil town in the north that's supposed to be quite dull. Jade is still illegal in that country, and there's none of it within hundreds of kilometers of that place."

Color rose slowly in Ayt's face and the pages of the letter trembled in her tightening grip. "Why?" she demanded. "Why the pointless mercy? Why not execute me properly?"

"There's no gain in it," Anden explained. "You're a jadeless old woman now. Killing you would look bad, no matter how much you deserve it. You were a powerful leader not only of the Mountain clan, but the country. Surely, there are people out there who are still sympathetic toward you. Why make you into a martyr, why give you that last satisfaction and risk more strife when we're turning over a new leaf with the Kobens and taking the remnants of the Mountain as tributaries?" Anden opened his hands. "At least, that's what the Pillar thinks."

It was the first real decision that Kaul Nikoyan had made as Pillar, after talking to Anden, Shae, and Lott, then quietly considering the issue himself for several weeks. If the careful, dispassionate way he had come to his conclusion was indicative of the type of Pillar he would be, Anden was certain his nephew would turn out to be a formidable Green Bone leader in his own way.

Ayt's sneer pulled back the corners of her eyes and seemed almost physically painful. She looked as if she wanted to laugh or kill someone, and for a moment, she was frightening again. "I can't believe I would ever miss Kaul Hiloshudon."

Anden said, "You'll have two more days in Janloon to pack the personal belongings you need, and to visit your family's grave, if you wish. Should you change your mind during that time and decide to follow Iwe's path after all, none of the guards will stand in your way. If you accept your exile and never make another attempt to gain jade, return to Janloon, or affect the course of Green Bone matters, after your death you'll be brought back to Kekon and buried in the Ayt family plot. If you break the terms, your name will be quietly whispered by every clan, and your bones will never touch Kekonese soil."

Ayt's proud bearing crumpled bit by bit as Anden spoke. The indignant scorn she'd mustered for a few minutes dissolved into exhaustion, as if a mask she'd worn for her entire life was slipping off, revealing a person underneath that Anden had never seen before, not even when she'd lain near death in his apartment. Ayt looked sad, more deeply sad than Anden could've imagined.

"Tell your Pillar that he has nothing more to worry about from me," she said, when he was done. There was no more anger or vindictiveness in her voice, only a factual defeat. Dignity if not grace. "I've given everything I have, and I have nothing left. I know my time has passed."

Ayt turned to gaze out the narrow window of the tiny apartment, over the bit of the city she could see. The sunlight slanting into the room cut a line across the carpet and lit dancing motes of dust in the air. Noises from the street below—the rumble of a bus, a bicycle horn, something heavy being tossed into a garbage bin—intruded faintly. None of the people going about their day outside had any idea that the woman who'd been Pillar of the Mountain sat in a small room above them, listening.

"Many years ago, when I saw what was happening around us, I

imagined a bold and necessary future," Ayt said. "Green Bones united into a single powerful clan, wielding control over our jade and standing strong over Kekon, preserving our traditions and protecting us from enemies across the ocean as well as those here at home. It was up to us, as jade warriors, to meet all the threats and opportunities that time would inevitably bring to our door."

Ayt pulled her sweater close but lifted her chin, as if facing a crowd waiting for her to speak. "Everything I've done, every great and terrible choice I've made over many years, every bit of normal human happiness I sacrificed from my own life, I did willingly and purpose-fully, to see this future. And I can see it now, finally—only not in the way I imagined, not with my clan, and not with me. Yet maybe by some terrible irony only the gods can understand, *because* of me." She placed her hands inside her sleeves, holding her bare arms. "That's the one satisfaction I will take with me to my death."

They remained in silence for what seemed like a very long time. "I've heard a saying before," Anden said, "that great warriors are remembered with awe by their enemies."

Ayt stood, in one slow but smooth motion that hinted at her once peerless poise and strength. "Then I ask you to remember me, Kaul-jen."

Kaul-jen. At his Academy graduation ceremony, the crowd had shouted the name at him. How astonished and mortified he'd been back then, to be hailed as someone he was not.

Anden touched his clasped hands to his head and bent into a salute. "Goodbye, Ayt-jen." He turned away, walked out of the room, and left the building.

Outside, Anden buttoned up his coat and walked, letting the brisk air fill his lungs and clear his head. People were sweeping the burnt remnants of firecrackers off the streets and standing on ladders, tak-ing down New Year's decorations. Some businesses in Little Hammer still had pale green lanterns in their front windows, but others had changed over to white, and a few windows were empty, their owners undecided, waiting to see how territorial jurisdictions would shake out. When he crossed into the Armpit, two of the clan's Fingers posted along the district border touched their foreheads and dipped into shallow salutes of recognition as he passed.

Anden stopped on the street corner and raised his face to the sky. He felt heavy and light at the same time, and the world seemed sharp and beautiful even in a way that jade senses could not improve. There was an ache in his chest—some of the grief that had been arriving in pieces—but also relief, and love. Love for the life pumping through his heart and veins, love for those dear to him—the ones who were gone and the ones who remained, and love also for his city, for Janloon—a place as fierce and honest, as messy and proud and enduring as its Green Bone warriors.

Anden hailed a taxi. When it pulled up to the curb, he got into the back seat and said, "The Twice Lucky restaurant."

The driver looked at Anden in the rearview mirror. He was a sallow, unsmiling man with a crooked face that made the skin around one of his eyes sag. "That old place in the Docks?"

"That's the one," Anden said.

The driver hesitated. He looked as if he wanted to say something, then he pulled the cab away from the sidewalk and into traffic. "I can't believe that place is still around," he grumbled, flicking another glance back at Anden. "There are better spots, you know."

"It's an old favorite," Anden said.

"The only reason it's still there is because it's been around so long," sniffed the cab driver. "I heard it was headed downhill, but then the Une family hired some young, internationally renowned chef up from Lukang to change things, so it's got a new look. It's survived enough wars by now that I guess nothing can take it down."

The light turned red. The driver stopped the cab and turned over his shoulder. "I used to work there once, you know. As a dishwasher. A long time ago. I was just a kid back then. A dumb kid with big dreams."

Anden said, "We were all like that once."

"Yeah, well, my life could've been different. Real different." The light turned green and the driver turned back around and took his foot off the brake. "Of course, I could be dead, so there's that." He laughed. It was an unpleasant sound.

They pulled up in front of the Twice Lucky and the man hit the meter. "Did you know that the Twice Lucky is a spot for No Peak clan Green Bones? The Kauls come here. Even the Pillar himself. The old one, that is. Who knows about the new one." He took Anden's money and Anden motioned for him to keep the change. "The shit I've seen, keke. I sure could tell you some stories," the driver said. "Stories about the clan."

"I'm sure you could," Anden said. "There are a lot of them." He got out of the taxi and walked through the double doors of the restaurant to have brunch with his family.

Acknowledgments

When I first began writing the Green Bone Saga, it would've been difficult to imagine this moment: the end of a journey much longer and greater than I anticipated, one that pushed me to my creative limits and occupied a majority of my waking hours for six years. Honestly, I'm a little dazed. It's with deep pride, relief, and sadness that I imagine you, reader, turning the final page on the Kaul family and seeing these words.

My gratitude extends first and foremost to the many enthusiastic readers and reviewers who spread the word about this epic urban fantasy gangster family saga of my heart. Whenever the writing was difficult (and there were many such times), an email or tweet or piece of fan art would appear to remind me that there were clan loyalists who wanted to see this story through as much as I did. These books wouldn't have found their audience without you.

Thank you to all the folks at Orbit: my first editor there, Sarah Guan, who brought the series in and gave it a running start, and my new editor, Nivia Evans, who came in to push it over the finish line. My thanks to marketing and publicity gurus Ellen Wright, Paola Crespo, Angela Man, and Stephanie Hess, the UK team including Jenni Hill and Nazia Khatun, production editor Rachel Goldstein, cover designer Lisa Marie Pompilio, copyeditor extraordinaire Kelley Frodel, and everyone else who helped to shepherd this book into the world in fine form.

I'm deeply fortunate that my stalwart agent, Jim McCarthy, has believed in my work and had my back since the start of my career. I'm sure he would like me to write shorter books from now on. (Don't worry, Jim, I will, I promise! At least sometimes.)

Beta readers Curtis Chen, Vanessa MacLellan, Carolyn O'Doherty, and Sonja Thomas came through once again even when I asked them to do early reads on a 250,000-word novel. I owe them for staying with me on this long road.

Andrew Kishino narrated the audiobooks and I can't say enough about his talents in bringing this story to life in audio form.

Writing may be a solitary profession, but for me it has never been a lonely one, because of the friendship and support of fellow authors— here in the Pacific Northwest, at conventions across the country and the world, and online at all hours. The word trenches may be long and dark, but they are warm with camaraderie.

Finally, my unending appreciation to my husband and children, for their continued and necessary patience with me while I spent so much of my time with another, fictional family.

I wrote much of *Jade Legacy* during the global COVID-19 pandemic and the tumultuous events of 2020. In addition to all the considerable but expected challenges of writing a climactic series-ending novel, I frequently struggled, as many writers did, to maintain a sense of community, hope, and joy in the creative process. I was reminded daily that life is fragile and uncertain, that there's triumph in endurance, and that it's not only Green Bone warriors but all of us who depend on the strength of our clans.